Buffalo Afternoon

Buffalo Afternoon

Susan Fromberg Schaeffer

ALFRED A. KNOPF · NEW YORK 1989

THIS IS A BORZOI BOOK
PUBLISHED BY ALFRED A. KNOPF, INC.

Library of Congress Cataloging-in-Publication Data
Schaeffer, Susan Fromberg.
Buffalo afternoon / Susan Fromberg Schaeffer. — 1st ed.
p.   cm.
ISBN 0-394-57178-9
1. Vietnamese Conflict, 1961–1975 — Fiction.   I. Title.
PS3569.C35B84   1989
813'.54 — dc19   88-45820   CIP

This is a work of fiction. The characters in this novel are
not intended to refer to or portray any actual living persons.

Manufactured in the United States of America

FIRST EDITION

For all these, with love, respect, and admiration:

John Anderson, Anthony Bianco, John Breeden, Arthur Cohen,
James Daino, Lawrence Davis, Nurit Davis, Danny Friedman,
Jim from Nebraska, Michael Lichtenstein, Judith A. McCombs,
Wenny Pas, Frank Puleo, Joseph Reiter, Ngog Von Trong

With thanks to Virginia Barber and Sonny Mehta, and:

For Neil.

I mean the truth untold,
The pity of war, the pity war distilled.
— WILFRED OWEN

Contents

ONE

 HERE IS so much I would like to tell you, for example about the rice paddies and how beautiful they are under the wide sky, and how different they look depending on where you are standing when you look at them. For instance, if you have climbed a slight hill and are looking down and the sun is out, but behind a cloud, the paddies look like huge panes of glass. And if you are just high enough, the paddies are mirrors for the sky, and in them float white clouds tangling with the new shoots of rice. If you are higher up, and the day is greyer, the paddies gleam like sheets of gunmetal laid down upon the fields. At other times, before they are flooded and before they are planted with rice, they are ugly, tumbled fields of mud. But I liked them best when they were filled with water, when the sun shone on them turning them to sheets of silver, and when the newly planted rice grew straight up from the surface of the water like spiky hairs on the head of a newborn child. And yet there were times they were still more beautiful, when I looked at them as the sun went down, and almost all the color had drained from them, and in back of them, the layered hills rose up, not bluing in the twilight, but charcoal hills against deeper charcoal, against black.

At other times, if I looked over the fields before the sun came up, there was only the silhouette of a lone buffalo with the little bird who is always his companion, standing straight up, perched on the buffalo's shoulder like a sentry, waiting for the buffalo to wallow in the mud so that he can eat the insects that creep onto the buffalo's skin. The bird is so small, so purposeful, and looks so aware—as indeed he is, because if you catch one, you can teach him to speak as other people teach parrots. And I can see the blue canals and rivers winding through the rice fields, and the flat-bottomed boats bringing the bright green bamboo to market, or the newly cut sugarcane, or the palm sugar that is so delicious when it is boiled until it hardens into a kind of candy. I can see the elephants as they come down the road, driven by the loggers toward the teak forests. I see the betel plant flickering in the sun outside the window of my house, and I see the black teeth of my grandmother, and I again watch her roll her betel in a palm leaf and spread it with lime as the tea plants in the garden move lazily in the breeze. I can see the light dying away and inking in the black outline of a lone palm tree against a lavender sky. And I can see lavender islands rising up out of the purple and blue mists the river becomes when the sun drops below the earth's rim.

There is so much about my country that I would like to tell you, and I have all the time in the world, far more time than you can possibly have, because for you the clock still ticks, while for me it does not. But then I do not have to tell you everything at once. I can tell you some of it now and some of it later. Later I can tell you more about how we caught the small frogs in the rice paddies, frogs smaller than the smallest joint of the hand's little finger, and how we put them in a plastic bag and hung the bag from a nail on a tree, and ate them with pepper sauce for lunch. I can tell you about setting snares for the wild ducks, and about how we cooked and roasted grasshoppers, and how the elders preferred eel and crab to pork and chicken. I can tell you about the spirits we feared and what we did to calm them. But even as I think of telling you these things, my spirit sinks. Frogs, eel, crabs! Roasted grasshoppers! So much that meant so much to me, that holds the flavor of my life, will disgust you. So much of it will. I know. I have seen it happen before.

Yet, my life was, for a long time, wonderful beyond description, and even today I say that anyone who lived even one week of it would never give it up for the most elaborate city in the world. None of us in my village would.

When I was nine years old, my favorite aunt was expecting her first child. Before she had the child, according to custom, in order to assure the safe carriage and delivery of her child, she walked back and forth beneath the belly of an elephant. When she had the baby, a little boy, the joy and excitement knew no limits. And then I, who had four younger brothers, saw what I had never before seen for myself. I saw how the woman who produced her first child was really queen of the world.

According to custom, my aunt lay in her bed, draped with mosquito netting, for almost three months. Her husband was forbidden to her. The other women of the village, my mother and grandmother among them, painted her face, hands, and legs with a yellow powder. My mother was from Siam, and so it was her custom to place hot coals in an iron pot beneath my aunt's bed, and for five days and five nights, its heat warmed her, keeping illness and evil spirits from her. All day and all night my aunt had to wear special white stockings so that she could not catch cold. She dared not to read because, after giving birth to a first child, a woman's eyes are weak. I remember following my mother and the other women of the house outside, where they buried the afterbirth under the banyan tree.

To me, these things were marvels I never saw the like of afterwards. Because of the heat, my aunt's skin, under the yellow powder guarding her from evil spirits and disease, shone like hot gold. Her movements were soft and languorous, like the movements of a carp through reeds in water. She beaded and shone like a solid gold idol. Behind her mosquito net, she seemed to float on the other side of this world — of this world, but for the time, beyond its reach. There were days when I thought I could see the evil spirits reaching for her, when I thought them visible in the folds of the mosquito netting, but they could not reach her and nothing could disturb the serenity, the pure beauty of her smile. When my mother was in the fields helping my father, and when my grandmother stirred the pot for the morning meal, an older cousin came to give my aunt her medicine to drink, and this, too, was mysterious, because even the medicine was golden. And then I discovered what it was. My grandmother ground ginger in a stone bowl with her wooden pestle, and then it was slowly mixed with the urine of a sixteen-year-old boy. The urine of a sixteen-year-old boy! How my body cringed at that knowledge!

When I was not in the hut, watching my aunt, or out in the field gathering grass for the water buffalo, I would look at the sixteen-year-old boys of our village, and wonder: Is it this one? Is it that one? I considered the boys and their bodies, the strength of them, the rippling of their muscles across their bellies and backs as they bent and stretched, tilling the fields or planting the rice, while the first wind of the day blew in gusts and the tips of the seedlings fluttered and waved back and forth in rhythm, graceful as dancers welcoming the sun, and a fine shower fell, silvering everything, and the wind stirred the fat yellow leaves of the banana trees, and I thought then, Whoever has seen this, how can they ever leave this village? How can they think there is a better place on the face of the earth? And although I was only nine, inside me gusts of wind blew in the rice fields beneath my belly and one boy's body seemed stronger and longer and more beautiful than the others, and I thought, surely his is the urine that my aunt drinks, and I shuddered a shudder that was half disgust and half thrill, and after that, whenever I had to go gather grass for the water buffalo, whom I called by my own name, Li (although he was a male and I a female, I saw nothing odd about it), he was always in sight. I wonder if he noticed my presence, if he thought to himself, In all these acres and acres of grass, why does this child gather only the grass that grows about my ankles? I wonder this now, but at the time I thought I was clever, and so young I was not worth noticing — almost, perhaps, invisible.

During those long days when my aunt lay, gold and beaded, behind her netting, and the wind blew the young rice this way and that, and the little silver showers played over the wide sweep of paddy and grass, banana tree and palm, and my mother and grandmother and women from the village came and told my aunt stories because she was not permitted to read, but also because they did not want her resting mind to fill with evil thoughts which might bring harm to herself and her new child, I would stand in the entrance to our house, my hand resting against the cool wall beneath its roof of dried banana trees, which would rot by the end of the year and be replaced by new ones, and think there was nothing so beautiful as my aunt.

Even the sun, necessary for life, capable of turning the rice and the grass, the palms and the bananas to gold, was not as beautiful as my aunt. My aunt behind her mosquito netting was more beautiful than the sun behind its long trailing veil of cloud! And as I stood there with my hand on the wall of my house, the wall I had helped build, helping to smear the clay mixed with buffalo dung over the woven bamboo mats beneath, the wall which still retained the print of my small hand, I thought, There is no place else on earth but this. All other places revolve around this place. Truly my aunt is the center of the earth and those of us who are here with her will be at the center of the earth forever. Everything else—the people in other towns, the cities I had heard spoken of—all these floated like leaves caught in the whirlpool whose center was my aunt. And there were hours—no, days—when I believed that I had already reached the place in the center that does not move, that it was not possible to be more happy than I was, and I was ready for my life to end, and to come back to earth, or not to come back, as the lord of the earth intended.

But of course what I really wanted was to become my aunt and I looked hopelessly at my poor, forked twig of a body with its sheer cliff of a chest, my body as flat as any boy's in the fields, and the hairless triangle between my legs and despaired. In those days, my mother used to stare at me and then grin. Of course she must have known what I was thinking, although at the time I believed my face was a flat sheet of water the breeze did not wrinkle in its passing.

And then they removed the charcoal fire from beneath my aunt's bed, and all the women in the village laughed and smiled and joked about how much stronger she was than the men believed, and what a good joke it was, lying there for three months, listening to stories while the other women bent over stoves and worked in the fields along with the men, and the baby was carried back and forth to her like a treasure from another world, and I envied my aunt. They say women who have just produced their first child are especially vulnerable to evil influences, and perhaps it is true, because the very next day, the day after the charcoal fire was removed, my aunt began to cough. All day long, the women of the village hovered over her, propping her up in bed. The midwife from the next village came and instructed my aunt in how to breathe, and when her breathing did not improve, the doctor was sent for, and he had my aunt lie on her stomach, and with his strong fingers, he pressed here and there on her back, leaving purple welts. I, who had envied my aunt, believed nothing would help her, and when the women murmured among themselves, saying there was no spirit more dangerous and evil than the spirit of a woman who had died in childbirth, I began to weep. I wept in a corner of the house until my mother sent me outside. Then

I wept in the fields. I rode my water buffalo far from the town and wept on his wide, patient back. I looped my arms through his horns which curved back over his wide grey forehead toward me, and fell asleep, weeping. I awoke feeling cold and wet and realized that the water buffalo, still bearing me on his back, had settled into the shallow water of an unplanted field. I wept and told him I had heard that some spirits of women who died in childbirth were so evil they bored through the anus and chewed on the living entrails, and it was I and my envy that had brought such evil spirits to the village. The buffalo rose slowly from the mud, snorted, and began walking back to the village. I watched his right shoulder rise, then his left, and I saw him turn to look at me, and when I saw the wisdom and patience in his eye, I was comforted. Surely if I were evil he would not so patiently carry me homeward.

Even before I reached home, even as I was still on the outskirts of the village, I knew events had taken a turn for the better. The voices of singing women floated toward me like a breeze of golden pollen, and by the time I had slid down from the water buffalo's back and walked toward my house, I knew all was well. The porch of the little spirit house my mother had brought with her from Siam was heaped with flowers and sweetened rice. These were not the offerings to implore the help of the spirits: these were the rewards to the spirits whose help had already arrived. And inside the house, my aunt once more lay on her back, her breathing smooth as the little winds that do not make themselves heard but move the leaves, and as I came in, she rose, propped herself on one elbow, and my grandmother drew the mosquito netting aside to give her the cup filled with the golden liquid. The welts on her back left by the doctor from the next village were purple and violent but they would soon fade. My mother, who might well have chased me out into the field to collect straw for the water buffalo, said nothing to me. I sat in the corner and watched my aunt and was once more completely happy.

It may seem odd that I have not yet mentioned that at this time my mother was also expecting a child. In four weeks, or perhaps six, she too would be producing another infant. But since I had been her first, and since after me she had produced four boys, my four brothers, not much fuss would be made over her. She would have three or four days of rest, and then she would be back in the fields. It was only for the first child that a woman lay in bed for three months, behind the ghostly mosquito netting. Like everyone else in the village, I mistook the moon for the sun, kept my eyes on it, and in the dark walked into deep water.

I have not mentioned that everyone in the village believed that my entire family had been singled out by fate for particularly good fortune. You who did not live in the village may wonder why the other villagers thought of us in this way, since we had no more than anyone else, and we worked our rice fields as everyone else, getting up at four thirty in the morning to till the fields and plant or reap the rice before the sun climbed to the top step of the sky, where, angry at the length of the climb, it became evil and burned everyone up. Like everyone else, we rested until the sun, who had also rested and found his way now led downhill, set forth through the sky as we again went into the fields.

My mother was the source of our good fortune. She had not done well by bearing a firstborn girl, but she had redeemed herself by producing one boy and then another and then another. When my third brother was born the village began buzzing. "What if Mai produces a fourth son?" was the question on everyone's lips. Because, as everyone knows, if a woman bears four sons in a row, the fourth son will bring great fortune to the house. He is the sign and signal of great things to come. And this my mother did. During the time my mother carried her sixth child, I had no sense of coming danger, no feeling that she was about to change our fate, and so when she gave birth to her fifth son in a row, I was puzzled by the sound of lamentation that went up in our house. And it was only then I remembered the prophecy entire: four sons in a row bring wealth and joy to a house; five sons in a row ruin and destroy. Special offerings were made to the spirits. The women of my family wove extra cloth to leave in the forests for the monks who would wear them as robes. But my grandmother was still not contented, and against the advice of the other women, she took my newest brother, laid him in a small coffin my father built for her, and all of us walked past my tiny brother, pouring perfume over the little child's wrist. This was the ritual bathing, the bathing of the dead, and my grandmother believed that the spirits, seeing this, would believe the child was no longer alive and so would give up their plans to harm us. Nothing could dissuade her. To be sure my small brother did not stir or cry and so alert the spirits to the deception, a drink was given him which drugged him so that throughout the bathing, he lay in his coffin as if dead.

After that, the days followed one another. The rice crop was good. The priests were pleased with all of us and said soon some of us might leave the village and go to a school in the city, but none of us wanted to go. We were happy where we were; we were the master of our own days: except for the weather, and occasionally the insects, we had no enemies. I remember one summer the locusts came, but that summer they were not plentiful and did not eat up everything, and we gathered their bodies together, pressed them into bars, and fed them to the livestock. Time drifted by lazily and as I helped reap the rice, I listened to the boys singing courting songs to the girls in the patchwork fields and I knew I had to let time drift by me a little longer and soon someone would throw the leaf of a betel plant at me to show me I had caught his eye, and soon he would be singing those songs to me, and at night, as I lay on my pallet, before sleep settled on me, I thought of the sharp-tongued retorts I would sing in response to the boy's song. *Today when I came to your house, I forgot my heart,* the boy would sing, and I would reply, *Your head and your heart have grown too far apart.* But there must be a better reply, and as the small warm breeze blew through our house, I would fall asleep trying to think of it.

Surely it is the same everywhere. Surely the earth curves so slowly that truths do not have to bend to stay on the surface of the earth as the wind blows them. Things go on as they do and no change is expected. The way things are today is the way they will be forever. I grow into my long body and it is only a matter of time until I move into the body of my aunt and take her place behind the mosquito netting. Is it any wonder I woke up every morning to greet the new day with joy? Under the fish-scale clouds, under the high, thin white flags of clouds, under the black solid cloud of the coming monsoon, every day bears out the promise that things will go on. Deaths occur, but they are expected. New lives unfurl like banners and they are welcomed. The water buffalo plow, and five hours after noon they are turned loose. This is the time we call buffalo afternoon, when the work is done and the buffalo head straight for their wallows and soak themselves happily in the water or the mud, for they have spent the day beneath the hot, hot sun. When they are finished wallowing, they eat the grass, eating and walking as they gradually make their way along. When evening arrives, they turn homewards, and no matter how far they have gone, they know their way home, and when they arrive, they enter their pens of their own accord; it is not necessary to herd them in. So it was with the water buffalo and so it was with us. Days would pass and pass and we would grow older and for us, it would be buffalo afternoon. And so we came to believe that the curse of the fifth son in a row had been lifted from our shoulders.

In my twelfth year, we had begun hearing stories that disturbed us, stories of war coming to our part of the country, and for a time, we awoke every day scanning the country as best we could, our eyes straining to the very edge of the blue mountains on the horizon, listening for any strange sound. But nothing happened and life continued, and soon another August arrived, and as we harvested in the fields, the older boys sang to the girls who were old enough to hear such songs. After the harvest, I would spend buffalo afternoon riding the back of my family's water buffalo. When he lay in the mud of a paddy, I slept beneath a tree. I wanted someone to sing for me, but I was too young, and that knowledge filled the air around me with a mournful sound. And then one day, I was riding the buffalo's back when there was a strange sound in the sky, and I saw it before I heard it, but as soon as I saw it, I knew what it was. It was a plane. It made a wide circle over our paddies, seemed to fly away, and then returned again. It appeared to be leaving, and as it pulled higher into the sky, the whole earth shook beneath me; earth and stones rained up into the sky and then fell back again and I remember thinking the world was ending and the four spirits guarding the four corners of the world had fallen asleep. And then the water buffalo began running as if he would outrun the noise and the flying earth and the shaking of the ground and I could feel the fear in his muscles and I could see it in the way he lowered his head and galloped blindly across the ground.

And then he stopped and stood still, his head lowered. I looked over his head between his horns and I saw men of a kind I had not seen before and my water buffalo was snorting, and I smelled what he smelled, the men my kinsmen had warned us of, men with skin whiter than lime dust who smelled like corpses. And I said to the water buffalo, Run! Run! But even as I said it one of the men in the bushes stood up and I saw his white-moon face, and I heard a sharp cracking noise, and I felt the buffalo jerk backwards, and I saw one flash of fire after another. And I knew then that these men had guns and that they were firing at us. Run! Run! I said again to the buffalo, but he turned his head to me and in his eyes was a sadness deeper than humans can feel, and he did not run. And I know today, as I knew then, that the men were not shooting at me. They were shooting at him, and the buffalo knew it. They fired into him many times, perhaps twenty or thirty times, and each time I felt him jerk beneath me, but not for a long time did he fold his legs beneath me, and I, what could I do? I was crying and shouting at the white-faced men, I was standing up on the buffalo's back saying, Shoot me, too! Shoot me, too! Because I did not want to stay and watch my buffalo die. But they did not shoot me, and when they saw the buffalo was dead, they began laughing and they went away, although they were mistaken and he was not yet dead, for when I got down from his back and looked into his eye, his eye opened wide as he watched me for one last time, and then his eye closed and did not open again. Then I sat by the buffalo's nose and stroked his muzzle and wept. The only sounds now were the sounds of the wind in the palms, the chirping of birds, and the strange, sawing noise of a locust. A brilliant green dragonfly flew straight above me and I knew that was the soul of the water buffalo, rising up. I cannot tell how long I stayed with the animal, but it must have been a long while, because when I returned to the village, my family was running from house to house and through the fields, looking for me. The bombs had not fallen in the village, but in the fields, and everyone was sure I had been killed.

That night, no one slept. Everyone gathered at the pagoda in the center of the town, exchanging what bits of information they had gathered about the war over the past years. The village elder was asked if the people should move into the forest until we knew what would happen next, and when he hesitated, others suggested that we stay and wait. Perhaps it had been a mistake and no more trouble would come. After that, my mother and father sat up with me because I would not stop weeping. Toward morning, my father fell asleep on his mat, but my mother was awake, watching me. I asked her then about the souls of animals; I told her I believed the buffalo had not run because he did not want harm to come to me, and although she would not agree with me at once, after a while she said such a thing was possible. After all, the buffalo might once have been a human who lived in this very village. Who knew what knowledge or passions he had? Then what is the difference between a human and a buffalo, I asked, if the human will shoot and kill for no reason and the animal will stand and let himself be killed? And my mother said that the only difference between the soul of an animal and a human lay in the burden each one carried. An animal soul could be better than a human soul, but an animal soul was not obliged to understand the meaning of its actions, or the actions of others, while a human had to find the meaning in events. But, I protested, an animal could have a conscience! Our buffalo had a conscience! He had sacrificed himself to save me. And my mother said that it was not a question of conscience. An animal could have a conscience and could be compelled to act in one way rather than another because of his conscience, but he did not have to understand the meaning of his actions any more than he had to understand the meaning of the actions of humans. Only when his soul left his body and entered the body of a human would he have such a responsibility. This is what she said she believed. "Then I hope his soul will never enter the body of a human," I cried, "because there is no understanding them! I do not want to understand them!" And my mother cradled me in her arms and scolded me gently and said I would have to try and understand because I was a human, and as long as I lived, I would have to try to find meaning because that is why I had been put upon the earth. And I asked her if everyone in my country believed this, or if this was a belief that came from Siam, her country, and she said she didn't know. It was what she believed.

The next day we went out into the field, and we gathered straw, and my father took his machete and took off the buffalo's head, and we burned his body because we did not want anyone, human or feathered or four-legged, to eat his flesh. We kept his skull, because the spirit of the creature resided in the skull, and perhaps some of it still lingered there. The skull was fastened to the wall above my pallet.

And so the war began for me. The next day, a tall man who was a soldier came with one of our countrymen to see the village elder. Speaking through our countryman, he explained that the plane and the bomb had been sent in error and I was brought before the soldier and I would have told him what happened to the buffalo, but I could not stop weeping, and instead my father told him. The soldier said the murder of the water buffalo had been a mistake.

When he left, everyone was silent. Then the elders began whispering among themselves, and I knew they were trading stories from other villages about the war which had only yesterday reached us. By afternoon, the women who told fortunes were busy reading palms. The woman who looked at my hand said I would live among the white people (this was true) and said I would live to cross the ocean and find another country (this was not). As she held my hand in hers, as I felt the cold touch of her fine, wrinkled skin on mine, as I looked at the brown toad-spots of age mottling her skin, I saw my aunt as she had been, beaded and golden, half hidden by gauze, half in this world and half beyond it, and in that moment I knew that I would never reach the fate of which I had so dreamed. A coldness settled on my heart, and I saw myself with the white men. I saw myself describing to them things they could themselves see, things which were before their eyes, but which they did not see, although they looked. And although I did not know it then as I know it now, I guessed: my life had ended on the day the plane flew over the village, and although I was alive and would remain alive for some time, I was no longer among the living.

This was the first knowledge I kept to myself. This was knowledge I could not share, because if I shared it, I would frighten others, and everyone was already frightened. But I know now what I did not know then. The most terrible spirits are not the spirits of women who died in childbirth. There are more terrible spirits, and for a long time, I was one of them. And while I was one of them I learned many things. For example, I saw the dead need the living to remember them, but I learned that the living need the dead, because it is only the dead who have long memories, far longer than the memories of the living, and without memory there can be no meaning, and without meaning there can be nothing human. And this is why it is necessary to remember the dead and to honor them. You, who walk among them every day unaware of their presence, be careful of your souls! Worlds can end in the blink of an eye. Greed can eat up human souls that were once strong and good. I saw this once, in the city, in a noodle shop, in the eye of the shop owner bent over the piasters he had taken in that day. Whoever has seen such a look can never forget it. Have you seen it? Can you forget it? So many things can destroy a human soul. The passions are like sharp-toothed moths eating away at it. The soul is like a cocoon and the silk-worm's strong teeth and jaws will devour it when it wakes and eats its way out. The soul can rise up like a mist and the wind can scatter it and when, like rain, it gathers itself together again, it may find it has become nothing but rock.

 'VE BEEN nightmaring it pretty good for three weeks straight now, not the usual two weeks off, one night on, two weeks off, three nights on. No, three straight weeks, and today was Saturday. On Saturdays, I do the laundry. It gives me something to look forward to. I look forward to it all week, sitting there in front of the washing machine like a normal person, or at least that's what I think other people think when they look at me sitting there: Hey, look at him sitting there watching the laundry go around and around, just like me, a regular guy, a normal person. I also like my job; it's a good job and regular, it took me long enough to get it, and I like it. It's boring as hell but I love it. You want to know the truth? I love it *because* it's boring, boring and predictable, not like the weekend, two empty days when anything could happen, when I could be out walking or not out walking and something comes up behind me. You know what I mean? Hey, why should you know? It's bad enough that I know.

Anyway, I wake up mornings and I know I've been moaning, I don't know about what; usually I can't remember, but my throat's sore as hell. That's a giveaway, and then the way people look at me in the building, I know I've been making noise. So today I took off the sheet because it's Saturday and what's nicer than clean things, what's nicer than your arms up to your elbows in soapy water, hot water with bleach in it? When I first came back, I soaked my arms so long in water laced with Clorox I swear the hairs on my arms were lighter. Man, they were bronze. For some reason this morning I took a good look at the mattress and there it was, the yellow shape, the fear, yellow, printed all over the striped mattress cover so I had to see it.

I had to think about how long I'd been traveling that same road. The whole outline of my body, piss yellow, a body without a head, and the smell of sweat—you can't get rid of it. You wash the sheets, you wash them in some pretty strong stuff, but nothing kills the smell. I mean nothing. So I looked down at the shape on the mattress and I said, Fuck it, it's time to buy another mattress, and then I sat down on the edge of the bed and figured, I've been in this apartment six years and this is going to be my fourth mattress. So I sat there, tracing the yellow outline with my trigger finger, looking at how the shape in the center was dark, and then around it, like an outline, a halo or something, a wide yellow border, and another border around that, still lighter, and I thought, Hey, man, that's the outline of your body. It looks like a fucking target, and I was so pissed off, I dragged the mattress over to the other wall and I sat on the floor against the wall and I aimed my hand at the target, you know, like a kid does, just like my hand was a gun. Bang, bang. I got myself each time. After a while I got into it. I was only sorry it wasn't a real gun. I was sorry it was a target, not the real thing. I mean, I was going out later to buy a *fourth* mattress in six years for my single bed, and can you tell me what I need a new mattress for?

The last woman who slept all night in my bed was my ex-wife and she swears to the world that I tried to kill her whenever she pulled on the blankets, and then afterwards she says, Oh, he didn't know what he was doing, as if she had some sympathy and wasn't trying to persuade anyone who'd listen, *He's a monster! He's a monster!*

I'm never going to get married again. Why should I? So another one can attach my checks and go up and down the block singing my praises? No one sleeps in the bed here but me and half the time I'm up walking the floor and watching the light come up and it comes up real slow, like someone's out there with a big gas jet, turning the flame up a little at a time, a real magic act, so slow you can't say for sure when you first see the light in back of those houses.

After a while I got tired of firing at that mattress. It wouldn't stand up straight against the wall; the top drooped over so the outline on the mattress looked doubled up, wounded or something. The thick yellow shape in the center, the two wider shapes around it, I looked at it and thought, If I could stand the smell, if I kept sleeping on that mattress, the yellow man would cover the whole thing, from one side to the other, yellow, getting bigger and bigger. I could put a sheet over it so I wouldn't see it, but I'd know. I'd know there was nowhere I could lie on that mattress where I wasn't resting on top of that yellow thing.

I don't have a weak stomach. I've stood still and looked while other men heaved their guts out, but sleeping on top of that: I can't do it. It's worse than sleeping on a grave. I've slept on graves and it's not bad; in fact, sleeping on a grave's pretty good, especially if it's raining heavy-duty raindrops and the burial mound's raised up. Then the drops hit you and run downhill. We used to like sleeping on graves. But that's another story. This one's about having to drag this mattress downstairs, out to the garbage pails, and leaving it there, while everyone in the building walks past it and looks at it, and sees the stain, and shakes his head, and then having to drag a new mattress upstairs, and everyone in the building starts to whisper: What's this? The third? The fourth? The way he carries on at night, it's no wonder. You saw how stained it was? He must have some dreams! I don't like to think about it, what he did over there.

I'm going to take this mattress outside, and I'm going to get pity or sympathy, and you know what? I don't want any of it. They don't understand and they don't want to understand. I've been sleeping on that yellow man for years. The story of this yellow guy is *over fifteen years old.* It's a story that never ends. Never. I never tell it to anyone. Who am I going to tell it to? You? Yeah, sure, in the beginning, I wanted to tell people what it was all about, the moaning at night, the waking up at four in the morning, working the night shift because I couldn't sleep at night anyway, and for a while I thought they were interested, but they have ideas. They know how long something should bother you. O.K., it's been a year, or two years, or three, now forget it. Fine, it's done, the story's over. Go on to the next thing. What's all the fuss about? This story of yours is *more than fifteen* years old. This is old news. The world's full of stories. We all have them. You want to hear mine? Of course you don't want to hear mine. Mine's about the landing at Iwo Jima. I put my story away over thirty-five years ago. I couldn't remember if I tried. Get on with life! It's water under the bridge. Forget it. You've got your future ahead of you.

What can you say to that? That you tried forgetting? That you tried getting on with it? They'll call you a crybaby. I remember standing on the corner of Eighth Avenue and Fourteenth Street and telling my father, "We've got to get them out of there! They're dying over there for no reason!" and he said, "Crybaby! You guys lost your war!" He said that and he turned his back on me. He crossed the street and he was fucking gone. I didn't speak to him for ten years. That's a father? You lost your war? All by myself? The government didn't have anything to do with it? *I* lost it? That's all I was to him, something that made him ashamed in front of the neighbors? Because I lost my war?

Fifteen years later, he had a stroke or something and my stepmother called me and I went out. He was back from the hospital. When I was leaving, going out to my van, he came along with me, and one of the neighbors saw my army jacket, and my father saw him looking at it, and he said, "Yeah, my son was in Vietnam. He's a hero." I could feel the veins in my neck popping. "Don't brag to him!" I shouted. "You tell *me!* You're gonna brag to him that your son's a Vietnam vet and all this time you haven't mentioned it to me? First talk to *me!*"

He got scared. I got scared. I was right, but I was sick of scaring people. There were even times I wondered about my wife, what she would have been like if she hadn't married me or if I'd been different, but I still didn't know what was wrong with me. O.K., so I had a temper. A lot of guys have tempers who didn't go over there and they don't drive everyone crazy. Women can live with men who have tempers. Look at my mother. So it must have been something else. Something more.

You know, when you're a kid you get into a temper tantrum and a few hours later you calm down and people forgive you. But if you get into a tantrum and it lasts for fifteen years? It can last a lifetime. Sometimes, after I fell asleep at night, I'd see things, you know, better things, like my grandmother opening the refrigerator door to look at the pizza dough, or my brother saluting with the wrong hand, or my kids asleep, or divvying up the spaghetti and sausage my mother sent me for Christmas, and if I fell asleep, if I didn't pass out, I'd always see the same thing, a silver light, like light on water, widening and widening.

So to make a long story short, I didn't get a chance to talk. In the beginning I tried. My father walked away. And you don't want to hear what they have to say anyway. It's so much spaghetti. It means what spaghetti means. And you can't say, if you really forgot what happened to you thirty years ago when you went marching off, if you really don't remember, if it didn't make any difference, I feel sorry for you, man. What's life for if you're not supposed to learn something from it? What are you, a stick, a stone? You say that, they'll *know* you're crazy. They know you're supposed to forget what hurts you. It hurts you? Take it out in the yard and bury it. If it hurts you, it's bad.

But they don't know what's bad. They don't know what's good. They don't care to know. If you have a parrot, and you put a towel over his cage, the parrot thinks it's night and he goes to sleep. A person can do the same thing. Forget it! Get on with life! What's he saying? He's saying, Throw a towel over your cage, you turkey! Pretend it's dark and time to sleep and forget what you saw.

You know what? It's a sin to do that! How are people supposed to remember war if they never went to war? The only people who can remember war are the ones who went. They have to remember. Because if they don't, if they don't tell other people what they know, there's going to be another stupid war. Someone's going to come along and say to the people sleeping in their cages like goddamned parrots: Come on. Get your gun. Lock and load, buddy. This time it's a good idea. What does the parrot know? What *should* he know? The parrot's going to say, Sure, why not? He's not going to ask any questions. He's not going to say, Wait a minute. I remember what happened last time and I don't know if I want it to happen again. For Christ's sake, he's only a parrot.

Anyway, who are you to criticize anybody? *You* didn't finish high school. You're an ignoramus (excuse me for using such a big word), a moron who knows how to fix a truck or a door or a telephone line or an electric cable, or bring you the mail, or take the dry cleaning in over the counter and have it ready on the proper day, while they can shuffle their diplomas at you like a deck of cards, and if you don't have any diplomas of your own, you're going to cringe, they're going to turn around and look for you in the mirror behind them and *you're not going to be there!* You're fucking gone! You're going to try and persuade them you know how to read? You're going to persuade them you know how to think? They're surprised you have a forehead. They're surprised your hair doesn't grow right down to the top of your eyebrows. And even if you try, even if you think you're getting somewhere, they can always fix you. They can look at you and say, "You're lucky to be alive."

O.K., now they've got you. You *are* lucky to be alive. You shouldn't be alive but you are. There's no reason for you to be alive. What do you say now? *Some of my best friends are dead.* You can't say how much you envy the dead. No one wants to hear that. It all stopped for the dead. You want to know who put it behind them? The dead put it behind them. O.K., so their spark of life went out and they never knew what that spark was worth, not like you, walking the city streets like an old Asian farmer, guarding your one spark of fire in the husk of a coconut shell, and you can't let it go out because it's all you've got, like the African tribes who beat on their drums every morning to make the sun come up, never skipping a morning because they believe their drums send the sun up the sky. Let me tell you something. No one cries for the dead. It's impossible. Because if you started, you'd never stop.

After a while, you don't trust anyone who wasn't there. If they were there, they know. If they weren't they don't want to know. Time passes and *it's yours.* You lived with it for seventeen years and now it's all yours. It's no one else's. Now you don't want to talk about it anymore. Once you did, but now you don't. You're going to talk to other vets? Where do you find them? On line at the pharmacy at the VA? On the violent ward? They don't want to be found.

You know what a vet's doing when he puts his hand through the bedroom wall? He's trying to show you, or show himself, what's behind that wall. He saw it during the war. It's the place where he found truth. You know what truth is? It's a chopper coming in to medevac out a seventeen-year-old who had his leg blown off by a claymore, and he knows his leg was blown off, or he says he does, and he tells the guys who carried him out to the chopper, "Don't sweat it, guys, I'll be fine," and the company medic comes running up, saying, "I've got it! I've got the leg!" and the medic on the chopper says, "Hey, great!" because when they get back to base, they're going to try sewing it back on, and they put the leg on the guy's chest (his name? I can't remember his name. Maybe it was Smith. I can't remember most of their names) and the chopper takes off, and you watch him, and he's watching the leg on his chest, and after a minute, he moves his arm and cradles the leg, just like it was a baby, and then you see the expression on his face, puzzled, like he's wondering what the leg's doing up there, right under his chin, and the medic's wrapping the end of the leg in some kind of paper, and he starts playing with the laces on his jungle boot and he looks up at the medic, and he's joking, and he says, "That's a great ankle. I always had great legs," and he hugs the leg again, he holds it like it's a goddamned stuffed animal, a fucking toy, and the chopper starts bumping up and down, there's ground fire, and it's peeling off to the left, and he's holding the leg tighter and tighter, every now and then talking to it, as if it had a life of its own, and you know, you know when they get there someone's going to pick up that leg and throw it on the heap and he's never going to see that leg again. He looks down at his good leg and then he looks at the leg he's holding, and he looks confused and maybe he's panicking, but it doesn't matter because now he's passed out.

The army says it's going to make a man of you. When you come back, you'll know what your limit is. How important is it to know your limits? It's not important. It's not normal to watch a man lying there, hugging his leg and smiling at it. It's not normal to see a little child lying in a pool of blood and you go to get him and your CO touches your arm and says, "Don't touch him until they get a pole to roll him over. He's probably booby-trapped." And then you think, No, he's not, and further down the trail, someone turns a woman over and he's blown to hell, and the woman, too. Go look for them in the trees. You know where they are? Where the insects are thickest. That's where they are.

You need to find out how easily you can snap someone's neck so every time you get angry you have to be afraid you'll do it again? You want to live with that? You want to find out your limits so much?

You're in such a hurry to join the dead? Listen, the dead outnumber us already and they are hungry, man. They want our voices. They can't speak for themselves, and they've got plenty to say. It's cold out and misty, and you can feel their hands on your shoulders, and you think you've been reading too many ghost stories, but it's not a story. These ghosts are *real.* They were stopped so suddenly, man, especially the ones who died young. They're not finished yet. Man, they're mean and bitter. You're alive and they're not. They're going to forgive that? They're not going to forgive so fast.

The day they gave the deserters amnesty, I picked up the paper at the Sheepshead Bay station and I saw the headline and I just stopped in the middle of the street. I stopped traffic. Cars were honking at me and I didn't know they were there. When I looked up, a cop was poking me and a bus was bearing down on me and I was thinking, What about us? What about the guys who died there? What about them? What is truth in this country? What they told us we were going to Vietnam for was a lie. That was the biggest lie. What do you get out of lying today? You deceive yourself. I've got to tell the truth to myself because I'm going to die with myself. I'm not going to die with anyone else.

A friend of mine's a lawyer. He's got a phrase: *judicial economy.* Meaning: cut the bullshit. Get to it. Man, get serious. O.K., so I'm taking the mattress down the steps, dragging it over to the tree. Its bark has the same pattern as camouflage cloth. See, even the trees know there's no safe place. I'm leaving it there. Good-bye, headless yellow body. O.K., I'm ashamed of it, dragging it down late at night, looking both ways, hoping no one sees me, like a kid who wet his bed. And it was hard to get down the steps, and heavy—the dead, fucking weight of it, just like a body you're trying to drag back, the arm or the leg grabbing on to a branch or the root of a vine, the whole damn body twisting this way or that like it had its own ideas, like it didn't know it was dead, wouldn't admit it was dead. It looks to you like I'm dragging down a mattress? It's not just a mattress. When you go over there, no one tells you: you're going to live with these memories the rest of your life. This is one blackboard, man, that doesn't erase.

Everyone wants to know: what started it? How did the war begin? Let's find out so we don't do it again. But it began with the explosion that started the solar system. It began with violence and it will end in violence. Because even if I'm not sure where it began, I know where it will end. After the last bomb goes off, after the earth's surface is a crust of ash, after the only living things are the cockroaches and the leeches, after the oily black wind stops circling the ash-covered earth, after all that's left of the earth's surface is sand and black earth and giant anthills and giant ants, somewhere, some-how, a human being is going to crawl out of his hole, and in his hand, he's going to be carrying a gun. He's going to be carrying a gun and it's going to be loaded and he's going to know how to use it and the whole thing will start all over again. It's going to start all over again and this time I'm not going to be there. Thank God I'm not going to be there. I mean, what the fuck? Who wants to live forever? Once is enough.

3 HEN PIETRO BRAVADO came to this country as a young boy, he was sent by a family anxious for him to have a better life. His family had all the usual notions about America, and his mother, who had lost four children—one to scarletina, one to pneumonia, one to a case of measles which turned into a sore throat, then to madness, then to blindness and finally to death, and one to a mysterious fever that seemed to afflict children of her town and about which the parents and townspeople could do nothing but pray—believed there was no illness in America that doctors could not cure. Indeed, if she had been carefully questioned, she might have admitted her ill-formed belief that death did not exist there. Pietro's father was willing to send away his eldest son because he believed America was so big and so far away that the wars forever sweeping back and forth across the continent of Europe could not touch it.

When the family finally saved enough money to pay Pietro's fare, on a steamer, steerage, and when the son was persuaded to go, and agreed to shovel coal to help pay for the cost of the voyage, the father's throat choked with sobs and swelled shut so that he could say nothing, but his wife wept enough for two people, and his son repeated the same thing again and again as if he had forgotten all the other words and sentences he had ever known: "As soon as I have money, I'll send for you."

Pietro's mother held her newborn girl in her arms and wept. Behind her, his two younger brothers wept. And his mother thought, He may mean well. He's a fine boy, but he'll send for no one. By the time he fills his pockets, here there will be only corpses. She looked at her infant daughter and realized that she had come to look at her children as she looked at flowers in her garden, pretty things which brightened a day or a week, even a whole season, but which did not come back the next year. She did not know why, but other people's children were like weeds, hardy and tough and ugly and hard to get rid of, while her children would burn or melt under a hot summer sun, and in a drought they would blacken and blow off.

And now her son was saying that he would send for her, and she thought, What will there be to send for? A shriveled thing dried up with the having of babies, whose breasts, when empty of milk, are long and folded, marked with long creases like silk that had dried without feeling the touch of the iron. But her son was leaving, and he was frail, and he was the one to worry about, not herself, and so she nodded and smiled and clasped her hands and pressed them to her bosom as if to say, Send for me and I'll come! I'll come if I have to swim! But her throat, too, had swollen shut with pain, and for some time she could not speak. Was it her imagination or did she see the same deathly pallor in her son's skin that she had seen in her last child's before his death? Her children ran about in the sun, under the fat green leaves of the olive trees, chasing the chickens until they caught them, throwing them into the air, forcing them into flight. They ran after the donkeys and brought them back. They collected little bundles of twigs and branches for the fire when the nights were cold. In short, they did what all the other children did, but they did not do it long. The first chill wind, the first flush of fever, and they were gone. The sheep clung to the almost vertical green slopes of the mountains and did not fall off. The pigs wallowed in the mud and fattened until it was their turn to be slaughtered; but her children were like the piglets whose own mother, that vicious old sow, killed and ate them.

In her heart, Mrs. Bravado believed that Italy was a bad mother for her family, that for them, the country's breasts had run dry. She had tried the priest's faith and her own with her endless lamenting. She had attended extra masses. She had lit banks and banks of candles, and still, one after another of her children died. There were four small crosses to visit in the graveyard. She had tried the local fortune-teller, whom the priest had forbidden to her, saying the woman was no better than a witch, a dealer in the black arts, and the woman had looked at her hand, and at her son Pietro's hand, and had said, Look! See how your lifeline and your son's are interrupted here and here? Each of these breaks foretells a time of danger.

"Silly old woman!" cried Mrs. Bravado. "I too have the broken line and here I stand with the patience of a tree that not even the lightning will strike down!" But the fortune-teller was not offended.

"Human beings," she said, "will always seek the truth, but they do not always want what they find. Your hand is like your son's. Diagonally across its palm runs the long unbroken line of travel. If a plant will not grow in the shade, will you uproot the plant and throw it on the compost heap?"

"No," said Mrs. Bravado. "I would take my trowel and carefully dig it up and set it in a sunnier place."

"And where is that sunnier place?" asked the fortune-teller.

"It is not heaven!" cried Mrs. Bravado.

"I didn't say that word," said the fortune-teller. "Did I say it?"

"Perhaps," said Mrs. Bravado dreamily, after some thought, "that place is America. I see it as so wide and so large you can see both the day and the night at once. There, the moon and the sun hang at the same time in the same sky. The land is so big you can outrun anything that chases you.

The mountains are so tall you can outclimb anything that flies. In that country, there is so much to look at, you are not aware of your shadow. Here, your shadow is as sharp as a razor, and in the brilliant sunlight, it lies black on the ground, or crooked and black on the whitewashed walls."

"America," said the fortune-teller.

"America," said Mrs. Bravado.

"America," said her husband.

"America," sighed the priest, thinking how even a sick animal ran from the place of its misery, thinking how many of his parishioners would not eat olives because on the day they had last eaten an olive, they had come down with the pox, thinking how none of the villagers would sit under a certain tree when there were clouds in the sky because once it had been struck by lightning. Yet he knew that belief, even ignorant, blind belief, often moved mountains. Where the cross failed, those with weak vision must seize its poor black shadow. Even a shadow could pull them toward God. Even a shadow could keep them from sinking beneath the rippling crust of the earth.

And so Pietro Bravado was sent to America. His was the usual story, but then again, it was not. He did not expect to find streets of gold. He expected a hard, stony place where he would work until his hands bled, but with his blood, he would buy money and he would send for his family and together they would build a nest in the wilderness.

He arrived in America with a small suitcase and a scrap of paper carefully folded and placed beneath his heel. He walked on that paper and its address for two days before he found the place that had been written of, and when he found it, he was happy for the work he found there. A stable filled with horses! This was work he knew! He cleaned the stalls. He carted out the manure. When the stalls were clean, he led the horses in. He carried in their hay. He stroked the horses' long muzzles, and with a sharp tool, he cleaned the mud and the pebbles from their hooves. He slept in the empty stalls at night, and gradually the teamsters, who owned the stables and the horses, began to give him a quarter at the end of the week.

Weeks passed quickly and soon he had many quarters, so many that they became an affliction. Where was he to leave them while he worked? He could no longer hang the heavy bag of quarters around his neck. There was no jacket on earth with a pocket big enough to hold them, and even if he were to find one, the bulge in the pocket would be unmistakable. For many weeks, he suffered in this way, like a cat torn between her desire to remain with her kittens and her need to hunt for food for them. And then one of the teamsters gave him a quarter, saw the odd way he moved across the stall with it, first this way, then that, and guessed at the trouble.

A bank!

But when could he go to a bank? He had to be in the stables from five in the morning until nine at night. The man said he would take the quarters to the bank for him and bring him back a book and the book would tell him how much money he had and whenever he needed the money, all he had to do was take the book with him, go to the bank, and ask for the money. But if he lost the book? "They give you another book!" cried the man.

But handing over the quarters! This was not something to be done lightly. He would need the night to think it over. That night, he decided he must trust someone and he would trust this man. He gave him his quarters, tied in two pieces of cloth cut from ripped feed bags, and said good-bye to his fortune.

That very night, the man returned, a beautiful shiny new book in his hand, its cover embossed with a golden globe encircled by stars. Pietro had never seen such a beautiful book. Not even the priest's white leather Bible embossed in gold was as beautiful as this book, and for a long time he could not open it, but then he heard the man laughing at him. "Look inside!" said the man.

Inside, he saw little black typewritten letters, and in the column headed AMOUNT, he saw this figure: $75.00! "Now you are rich," said the man, still laughing at him.

"How much does one passage on a ship cost?" Pietro asked the man.

"Not so fast," the man told him, becoming serious. "First buy yourself a warm coat. The winters here are cold and dead men buy no tickets." But by spring, he had enough money for two tickets, and by the end of his third winter, he had enough money for five tickets, and he sent for his mother, father, sister, and two brothers.

His younger brothers and his sister loved to hold the bankbook and listen to how it had brought them to this country. His mother, who often cried at night when everyone else was asleep because she missed the old country where it was always warm and where everyone in the village could visit everyone else almost every day, would nevertheless take the bankbook and stroke it as if she were stroking her son's hand.

As time passed and good health settled on her family, as Pietro married and had children, she herself wrinkled yet stayed strong, she missed less what she had left behind, and then one day she deliberately turned her head away. "This is where I live now," she told herself. "This is my family. These are my friends. There is a new church down the street, and even though the street is stony, we will not be here forever."

Sooner than she expected, she saw where the stones ended. Her son Pietro rented a team of horses and they drove across Brooklyn, past the farms and their sleeping vegetables and their cackling chickens, to the cattails and the sea. At night, her son would often hand her the bankbook, and she would take it, and they would look at each other as if there were a secret about it they both shared.

There *was* a secret about the bankbook, but it was not one Pietro could share with his family. When he saw the bankbook, he fell immediately and hopelessly in love with books. Before he saw the bankbook, he feared books. He saw them as dusty, fly-specked things, filled with the words of dead men, long-dead men, square and black, like coffins. Now he saw that books could be beautiful. His own book said so little—$75.00!—but how much those few marks meant! What a story there was behind them!

After that, he could not get enough books. When he left the stables and set up as a carpenter, he went to school at night. He said he wanted to learn English and begin to speak as an American, but he wanted books. He wanted books and more books. Even after he married and had his first sons, he wanted more and more books. His wife, stirring the pot with her long wooden spoon, shrugged her shoulders and was happy. She was not interested in books. But, thought Pietro, when my sons are older, *they* will be interested in books! I will be able to talk to them about books!

During the day, he worked as a carpenter, and sometimes as a plumber. At night he went to school, and on weekends he built his own house, in Brooklyn, in sight of the farms, and when the wind blew, it carried the salt smell of the sea and of the fish secretly swimming in its depths. And his boys grew. But they showed no interest in books. They didn't understand why he kept the old things, like the phonograph with the morning glory horn. They were impatient when they came home and saw him carefully sanding the open mouths of the lions on the oak china cabinet, bending over the face of the lion with a thin chisel, scraping out the last bit of old varnish from between the lion's whiskers. "You should see the *new* one Mrs. Ruggiero has!" they said. "You should see the new refrigerator, the new car, the new house."

He tried to tell his children why he was freeing the lions from the thick, stiff layers of time. He tried to explain to them how he saw the lions sinking deeper and deeper every day until finally one day they would be so dark and ugly and murky no one would care for them and out they would go, onto the fire. "Sometimes," he said, "old things are better than new things." They looked at him, frankly disbelieving, and it seemed to him odd that no matter how many books he read, he could never find words of his own when he wanted them. "Sometimes old things are better because they've been *newer* a lot longer than these new things you're talking about." The children nodded politely, but without understanding. His wife, too, saw their children's uncomprehending look more and more frequently. When one of his sons laughed at a man who'd been caught stealing a cabbage, his wife said, "Most people have to work to eat, but some people have to eat to work." They nodded politely. They had no idea of what she meant. Was it impossible to pass on knowledge?

People listened to Pietro. Everyone listened to him, and he listened to everyone, and Pietro's mother said that was why he prospered. When he first began doing carpentry, he would stop and listen if the woman of the house wanted to talk to him. He would put down his hammer and listen, and the woman would believe that no one on earth listened as this man did. While his black eyes were on you, every word flew straight from your mouth to God's ear. Nothing, not a sigh, not a cough, not a catch in the throat was lost. And so he was always called back. If he had come to fix a basement door, he would be called back when the roof leaked. His wife laughed at him happily. She poked him with the handle of the wooden spoon, and said he would listen to a dog or a cat if it would speak to him. He listened to the wind in the trees! The wind in the trees listened to him!

But if the wind in the trees listened to him, why not his own children? His sons would not pick up a book. The day came when his oldest son, George, was ready to marry and still George had not read a book, had listened to nothing. He was happy to walk in the dark world and pretend it was light. His daughter Theresa was like him. When she was a child, she wanted books and she read them. She watched him sand the wooden lions, and with her little hand she stroked their muzzles, but soon she was married, and then she was pregnant, and then she had no time. She was happy; she said she was, but often enough he saw a little frown, a crinkling of the skin between her eyebrows as if something puzzled her, and he knew what it was: she felt the puzzling tug of something forgotten, the thing that was lost. But then the baby cried and she forgot it even more completely than she had the first time.

As he grew older, his first son, George, grew stranger and stranger to him. George not only had no use for books; he turned against them. "You," he told his father, "did not make your way with books. You made your way with a hammer and nails." This struck his father dumb. Pietro did not argue with his son until George said that books were not for men. Only women sat in chairs, rocking and reading books. At this, something came over Pietro. A red stocking was pulled down over his eyes, and when it was pulled up, his wife was beating him on the back with the dustpan, trying to pull him off their son. After that, the question of books was not raised between Pietro and his son George again.

"Are books so important," asked his wife, "that over them you will have to take down your sign that says BRAVADO AND SONS? Are they so important that you will have to paint a new sign that says BRAVADO alone?"

Pietro and George were working in the Catskills, shingling the roof of a hotel, when a waitress brought their lunch out to them. At first, she lingered, talking to the father, who asked her questions about her own family, and she talked to Pietro so long the owner had to call her back. But as his father talked to the girl, George watched her, and that night he persuaded his father to eat dinner in the dining room, and on their way out, George asked the girl if she would meet him when she finished working. "If your father comes along," she said. Her name was Angelina. And from their meeting it was not long until their marriage, and to Pietro, it seemed no time at all before she made him a grandfather, and then a second time, and by the time his fifth grandchild, Pete, was born, it seemed no time at all.

"Time passes so fast," Pietro said to his wife.

"Yes," said his wife.

"This child," he said, pointing to Pete Bravado, "will grow up thinking the earth is made only of stone. He will ignore the green grass growing up between the cracks in the cement because there will not be enough grass to get his attention. He will think the sky is a small thing that exists in puzzle pieces between tall buildings. He will have no knowledge of animals, except perhaps an alley cat or a dog, and he will not even know those well. He will see rats and think all animals should be hunted down. He will not know that olive oil comes from olives that grow on trees and he will probably never see an olive tree in the sunlight. He will not speak Italian. In a few short years, the world we lived in has vanished forever. Our grandchildren cannot reach it."

"He will be healthy and he will have a good house with a good roof to keep the rain off and a way to earn a living and he will be happy," said his wife comfortably.

"He will not know anything but his block, and the people on his block. He will live and die thinking the world is made out of stone. He will live and die thinking the world should be as he sees it now."

"He resembles you," said his wife. And her husband, Pietro, bent over his grandchild, Pete, named for him, and smiled.

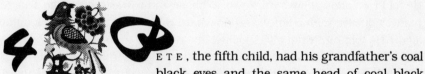 E T E , the fifth child, had his grandfather's coal black eyes and the same head of coal black hair. Third children and fourth children and fifth children sometimes have difficulty making a place for themselves in a family, but from the first, Pete Bravado seemed to take up more space than anyone else his size. Like his grandfather, he listened. Even as a tiny infant, well before he could speak, he seemed to hang upon the word of every adult who bent over his cradle, and the result was that everyone hung over his crib more and more often.

Never in the history of the Bravado family had so many toys been dangled over the cradle of one child. Red-flocked apples, left over from Christmas, were fastened to ribbons and dangled just out of reach of the little child's hands. Pocket watches were removed from vests and swung hypnotically over the child's head. Whatever object manifested itself in the little sky above the child's cradle was instantly the sole object of the infant's attention. His eyes followed the path of the swinging gold watch on its chain as if it were the sun on its heavenly rounds, and his fists waved in the air trying to catch it. People who sat next to the cradle and talked to the child, as people often do, saying what's on their minds, happy to have an audience, especially one that didn't understand them, would often find themselves disconcerted by the intelligent look, the rapt, understanding look the child fastened on them. "Well, then, if you don't agree with that, how about this," George heard his wife, Angelina, saying to their son. "If you don't think Theresa should move away, maybe she should live with us. You don't think that's a good idea?" The baby gurgled and stared intently at his mother. George looked at his wife, shook his head, and went out into the yard to build the older children a new playhouse.

"And what do you think about the new playhouse?" Angelina asked her six-month-old son. "Do children need a playhouse with a turret? Do they need a playhouse with two porches? Even the house on the corner doesn't have a wraparound porch. Does a playhouse need parquet floors? They're children. They're muddy. They're dirty. They ruin everything. He builds and builds because he's unhappy. He builds because he doesn't want to talk. What do you think?" Angelina Bravado bent over her son. "I think so, too," she said with a sigh.

By the time he was two, Pete Bravado had become his grandfather's steady companion. If his grandfather went out for a walk, he walked with his grandson. While they walked, he would tell the child stories. He told Pete about what life had been like on the vertical slopes of his mountain village. He told him about how hard it was to chase and corner a goat who'd eaten his way out through a fence, and how hard it was to bring him back home again. He told him what olives looked like ripening in the sun, and how the leaves of the olive trees shone in the first spring rains, and the child listened to everything and asked to hear the same stories again and again.

When Pete Bravado was not quite three, his grandfather developed a cough, and the family doctor advised him to spend more time outdoors, and, since they lived near the sea, to walk on the beach or near the water. Every day, no matter what the weather, old Mr. Bravado would pick up his grandson and the two of them would walk to Sheepshead Bay. They would walk from Lundy's, the seafood restaurant, across the little bridge, and keep going until they came to Manhattan Beach. There, they would stop at a candy store, buy an egg cream and a hot dog, and then begin the long, slow walk back, and while they walked, old Mr. Bravado would tell his grandson about how he had worked for the teamsters, and slept in the stables, and saved his quarters until he brought over all his family, the child's great-uncles and great-aunt, and how he came to build the house on Neptune Avenue, right under the ramp that now rose up and became the Coney Island boardwalk.

When he came to the end of the story, he would hide a shell in his hand and throw it, and Pete would run to the shell-strewn, ash-grey margin of the sand where the wave had just retreated, hesitate, look carefully at the bed of shells, some broken, some not, some black and tarry, some white and fluted, his hand hesitating over them, finally picking one up and bringing it back, and his grandfather would exclaim in delight because, among all the shells on the beach, the boy had found the very one he threw. Each time his grandfather would say the same thing: What magic, eh? Out of all the shells on the beach, you find the shell from my hand. Then the old man would hold his closed fist up to the light, pretending to try and see through the skin and the bones to the stone he held inside. He would shake his head in puzzlement and pretend to look with suspicion upon the boy, insisting he knew the truth. The boy could see right through his fist! As if it were made of air! Come on, admit it! And the child would laugh in delight, cover his eyes when his grandfather picked up the next shell, and still, whatever shell he brought back was always the correct one!

When they tired of the game, the old man would select one shell and the child another. Pietro would carefully polish each shell with his large white linen handkerchief and slide each one carefully into his vest pocket. These are magic shells, he told his grandson. Tell no one about them. They're our secret. If anyone knows how you found them, they'll vanish. One morning, you will wake up and find them gone. They will lie deep beneath the waves of the ocean.

At home, the child played with the shells, smiling to himself, and while he played with them, he swelled with importance. He looked at his mother and father, his aunt and his uncle, and they seemed far away and tiny. He wanted to tell them about the shells and how he found them, but he didn't dare. Sometimes, when he awakened, some of the shells had disappeared from his dresser. Had he hinted too broadly? Did his parents suspect? Later, he would ask his grandfather: Where were the shells? And Pietro would sigh and shake his head and ask the child, Did you tell anyone? and he would say no, his eyes filling with tears.

Well, then, said his grandfather, if you told no one, you'll surely find this shell, and he'd throw the one he clenched in his fist. And there on the foam-lined black border of the beach, resting on top of the crab-chewed black and green seaweed, would be a perfect white shell, so white it was blinding, impossible to miss, his shell, a shell that must have come from the water simply to seek him!

When he grew tired, old Mr. Bravado would sit the child on his lap and play a game with him he had played as a child. He remembered sitting on the side of the hill in Italy, the light so bright everything began to bleach and fade, and his father would ask him: What is a goat for? He would squint, and look at the goats down in the valley, and say, A goat is there to press down the fields; a goat keeps the fields from flying into the sky, and his father would laugh with delight. Old Mr. Bravado had tried this game with his own children, but he soon abandoned it. What is a cow for? he asked his son, George, and his son said, A cow is for giving milk. The sun is for making things warm. Very true, very true, said old Mr. Bravado, but he was disappointed. There was more to the universe than the obvious. A cow, he once told his son, would not think it existed solely to give milk, and his son looked puzzled and said, But Poppa! Cows don't think.

Now old Mr. Bravado played this game with his grandson. What is a bird for? he would ask the boy, and Pete would look at the sea gulls swooping down over the water and then flying back up, shrieking, or coasting, floating on unseen pillows of air. Sometimes when they called, they sounded like cats. Perhaps they were flying cats. Perhaps they had swallowed kittens. Birds are for making you look at the sky, the child said.

What are shells for? asked the old man. Shells are pages of books from under the sea, said the child.

What are shoes for? asked the old man. Shoes are houses for the ten animals at the end of your feet.

What are clocks for?

Clocks make time, said the boy.

I don't understand, said his grandfather.

They tick and tick, said the boy. The ticks are pieces of time. They come out of the clocks like bugs come out of the bushes at night. Clocks are very busy and watches are very busy and they don't like to stop. Grandfather clocks are the best clocks because when you open their doors, hours and hours fly out and fill up the house with more time. No one dies in houses with clocks.

Did I read you a story about clocks? asked his grandfather, frowning. Did I read you a story about clocks from *The Book of Knowledge?* The child thought and shook his head. Old Mr. Bravado looked at his grandson and shook his head. He patted his watch in his vest pocket. Lately, his watch stopped without warning and he would hit it sharply to start it up again. He would like a clock such as the one his grandson had just described.

The child drew his grandfather's watch gently out of its small pocket and looked at it. He smiled up at his grandfather. Old Mr. Bravado felt a chill. There were times when it seemed to him as if the child could read minds. The boy would often go up to someone—his mother, his aunt—and kiss her as she sat silent in a chair, and minutes later, she would be weeping. If the boy avoided his father, there was a reason. Minutes later came the rage, the tantrum, the smashed glass, the fist on the table. Like the lightning that preceded the thunder, the child seemed to know in advance. Life, thought old Mr. Bravado, would not be easy for this one. The boy was like him.

His own life had been happy, but the truth was, things had been easy for him. He remembered his mother saying that he and his father were like two peas in a pod. Wherever he went, he found people who liked him. But when he was a young man, he asked himself why he met no one who was really *like* him, not as he had been like his father, and at such times it seemed to him as if a voice were telling him to wait. He had waited and now he had this grandchild who was like him, and because of that, he feared for the boy, he didn't know why.

On days when the sun shone and the wind was not too strong, old Mr. Bravado would read to the boy in heavily accented English. He read him *Aesop's Fables;* he read *A Thousand and One Nights;* and then, because the child seemed interested in everything, he began reading some of his favorites. And so, at five and six, Pete Bravado sat on his navy blue pea coat in the sand and listened to his grandfather reading *The Inferno,* Petrarch's *Sonnets to Laura,* stories about lovers doomed to whirl about the world endlessly, never touching, about people waking up as insects in their beds, their feet waggling helplessly in the air, stories about the world ending and beginning again, stories about children who slew giants with nothing more than their own cunning, stories old Mr. Bravado knew his grandson would forget as he grew older, but which now gave him such pleasure to tell the child, who listened to him as if there were nothing else in the world but his grandfather's voice.

And while the child listened, he would look out over the water, which on cloudy days gleamed quicksilver, and, when the sun came out, was sometimes blinding; and at night, when he fell asleep, the darkness in the child's room would give way to that silvery light that seemed to spread out until it filled the room, dissolving everything in the world, until that light became the world. Years later, long after his grandfather was dead and buried, long after his grandson could no longer recall his features ("You want to know what he looked like, look in the mirror," said his mother), Pete would think of his grandfather and what he would see was the room, or the scene from his window (the snow falling, people with their kerchiefed heads down, trudging home carrying brown paper bags, the trolley passing, the room vibrating with the feel of the elevated train), and these things would dissolve in a quicksilver light until there was nothing left but waves of that greyish-silver light pulsing at the edges of everything.

It was the silver-grey color that brought it all back, the color that made sickness so pleasant, because when he was ill, the thermometer with its silver band was brought out, and after it was taken from his mouth, he would stare at the mercury band and he would be perfectly happy. "What are you staring at?" his mother would ask him, or his brother, and he'd shake his head and smile. He was happy.

This child is special, thought his mother.

This child is no different from anyone else, thought George, his father. The sooner he stops dreaming and learns a trade, the better for him.

According to George Bravado, dreaming stopped when the fifth grade began. A fifth grader was ten years old and strong enough to begin helping with the work after he was finished with school.

After old Mr. Bravado's death, it was impossible for George Bravado to keep his own business running well. He never seemed to make enough money to make ends meet. Some weeks he had no jobs at all and other weeks he had offers of three when he could take only one, and it seemed to him he spent most of his time looking for work rather than working. He would agree to take on a small plumbing job, give the customer an estimate, and then the job would turn into a nightmare. The beautifully kept house would have old pipes that had rusted out, and to fix one leaking pipe, half the wall would have to be torn away and lengths of pipe would have to be replaced. The customer would complain about the additional cost while George Bravado complained about the extra time; now he would have to put off the next family whose bathroom he was supposed to repair. It seemed to him that no matter what he did, everyone was angry.

One of George Bravado's brothers was not doing well either, and his sister Theresa's husband had opened a restaurant that finally closed when the health department paid a third surprise visit and this time found a large rat trying to push the lid from a pot of sauce, and George, his brother, and brother-in-law were soon working for someone else.

They lived in the same house. George lived with his children, his wife, and his mother on the first floor of the Neptune Avenue house. His brother rented the apartment upstairs and his sister's family lived in the basement apartment. At night, after the children had eaten and were either in bed or were doing their homework, George and his brother would talk about old Mr. Bravado and how well he had done when he was in business for himself. "Maybe it's the times. Maybe people don't have money," George said.

"That's not it," said their sister, Theresa. She was small and round and resembled her mother, old Mrs. Bravado, but she was somehow paler, more indefinite, as if she had been traced by a faint pencil from an old picture of her mother. She tended to sound like whomever she'd been speaking to, and old Mr. and Mrs. Bravado had joked about her to themselves, nick-naming Theresa the Echo. She loved her mother, and was even fonder of George's wife, Angelina, and followed both of them like a puppy. For her brother, George, she had less affection. When they were children, and when he was asked to watch her, he would slap her, and, when he became truly annoyed, he had locked her in the bathroom.

"It was Pop and the way he smiled," Theresa said. "Everyone he ever smiled at offered him a job."

"It's the times," George said. But when he closed his eyes, he could see his father, who had finished building the foundation for a back porch, and was now beginning to mix the cement, while above him, Mrs. Cohen or Mrs. DeMarino waved her wooden spoon, varnished with red spaghetti sauce, telling him about her recent encounters with squirrels in the attic, or worms in the apples she'd bought for applesauce. He could see all those earnest, stout women, their hair pinned up against the heat, in their shiny, flowered chintz dresses, talking and talking to his father, who never hurried them and who always listened as if he had lived all his life for this moment, for this particular story. "All those women," George said aloud. "Those women with the windup jaws. Did he ever get a job from one who didn't chew his ear off?"

"See?" said his sister, Theresa. "It isn't the times."

"It's the times," said George.

"You're better looking than Pop," said his sister. "If you could be more pleasant."

"Are they hiring me to be pleasant or to put in a toilet?" George asked. "What's there to smile about, putting in a toilet?"

"Case closed," said his sister.

So the sign BRAVADO AND SONS was taken down, and George Bravado got a job with another, larger outfit, and eventually his brother and his

brother-in-law got jobs with the same company. But George had five children, and would soon have six, so he began taking side jobs. During the
week, he would come home, eat, and take his oldest son with him on night
jobs. On weekends, his two eldest boys went with him. And then the boys,
who were in high school, began to get smarter. They knew their father left for
night jobs at six thirty and they wouldn't come home until after eight. "Well,"
said George Bravado, "it's Pete's turn. He's in the fifth grade. That's how old
the others were when they started out."

"Have a heart," said Theresa. "He's a skinny little kid."

"And he likes to study," said Angelina, his mother.

"You take all the books in the library, and that and a nickel won't get
you anywhere," said his father.

"That shows what you know," said Theresa.

"Where did it get Pop? Where did it get him?" George asked, sarcastically.
"His *smile* got him somewhere. Not books. Not *books.*"

"Ignorant as the day he was born," said his mother, rocking silently in a
dark corner of the room. The glare from the lamps hurt her eyes and every
day she retreated further into the shadows. On Friday nights, she still made
pizza dough, rolled it out, covered it with a wet towel, let it rise, and then set
it on the bottom shelf of the refrigerator. In the morning, the children
would come down, look at it, see how it had swelled up, bubbled up under
its towel.

"Is it ready?" one would ask.

"It's ready," said the other.

"It's ready when it's ready!" their grandmother would shout, throwing
open the door and chasing them off, a wooden spoon already in her hand.
Pete Bravado, for whom his grandmother had a weak spot, believed that
this miracle worker, this maker of bread that grew beneath towels, had
somehow cooked herself up from a batch of her own dough. She was white
and soft like the dough, and after a bath or a shower, she was damp and
cool to the touch. Even in the hottest weather she was cool, dusted with
scented talc, as the pizza dough was dusted with flour.

"I'm not too ignorant to make the money around here," said George.

"Your father did it better," said his mother.

"Ma," said his sister.

"His father didn't make him come home from school and go straight to
work," said their mother. "His father didn't interrupt him when he was
studying."

"He didn't have to interrupt me," said her son. "I wanted to go with
him." It was true. He wanted to succeed and success meant money. In time,
he'd have all the money he wanted and he would be happy. He would go back
to Italy and visit the village where his father was born. He'd stand on the
mountain slope looking down at the houses and he'd say, *Look how far I've*

come. His father read books because he hadn't succeeded. He hid from his failure in books. Yet money never seemed to mean anything to him. What he had, he gave away. "Food, clothes, a place to eat, and books," he used to say. "What more could a man want?" It was whistling in the dark, that's all it was.

"It broke his heart," said his mother. "None of you ever picked up a book."

"Tomorrow, after school, right after school, don't even let him come home!" George shouted. "I'll pick him up at the door to the school! He's coming with me!"

"Shame on you!" said his mother. "Shame! This week buy pizza from the store! You don't deserve to eat!"

"Ma!" said his sister, pleading.

"She's right," said his wife. "She's right. She is."

"In the kitchen!" George roared at his wife.

When she came back, the red print of five fingers was visible on her cheek.

"So that's how it is," said old Mrs. Bravado. "I'm glad your father didn't live to see this day."

"If you miss my father so much," roared George, "go dig him up!" The back door slammed after him, then the screen door.

"Go after him," Theresa whispered, but Angelina shook her head no. They turned to look at old Mrs. Bravado, who, under their eyes, was crossing herself. The two younger women did the same and fell silent.

"You know how it is," Angelina said to the room at large, her voice barely audible. "You have five children and for one of them you have special hopes. You know you shouldn't, but you do. For one of them you have special hopes."

"A special place in your heart, right here," said old Mrs. Bravado, thumping her breast. "You're not supposed to have it, but you do."

"It's like a flower in the garden," said Theresa. "Everything else in the garden can die but not that flower."

"Not that flower," said Angelina.

"You'd kill the person who pulled it up," said Theresa.

"Maybe not kill them," said Angelina.

"Killing is too good for them," said old Mrs. Bravado. "Even if he's my own son I say it."

"What should I do?" Angelina asked the air.

Old Mrs. Bravado's rocker creaked rhythmically in the room's dark corner. "Let's play cards," she said.

"Canasta?" asked Theresa.

"Gin," said old Mrs. Bravado.

"Things work themselves out," Angelina said weakly.

"If not in this life, then in the next one," said old Mrs. Bravado, her voice

unnaturally sharp. She looked around the living room. Every piece of furniture was new. The china cabinet was blond wood. Gone was the china
cabinet with the lions' heads. Gone was the old oak table that could stretch,
with its extra leaves, from one end of the room to the other. Everything in
this room is new, she thought. Where do the living go, who now are not the
living, but the dead? Where are the fingerprints of their lives? Why should
she cry? Before he died, her husband told her how it would be. "Take joy
where you find it," he said. What she wouldn't give to hear that voice again!
In the next world, she'd hear it. In this world, she had a hand to play. A hand
to play and a secret bank account she'd started keeping for her grandson.
She didn't want to die and see the money get lost. Someday she'd have to tell
Angelina about it. Someday, but not now. She and George were starting to
fight, and in a fight, all the truth came out. Tomorrow, she thought, I'll look
at the boy's palm.

F PETE BRAVADO had been asked to describe his house, he would have described two houses. There was the light, bright house he loved when the women were home during the day, but when his father came home, it became the dark place, its rooms cold and unfurnished. This seemed natural to him. Like the day itself, the house had its day and its night. If, at times, his family seemed strange to him, other families seemed stranger. Next door, Eddie Lugano, who was two years older, had decided he was part Indian, and he now slept on the narrow wooden ledge outside his third-floor bedroom. Every morning, Pete would hear Mrs. Lugano outside, shouting, "Come in! Come in! What, are you crazy? It's a thirty-foot drop! What if you roll over? What are you doing out there, sleeping with a broom?"

"What's he doing out there?" Pete asked his mother, but Angelina shrugged.

"If he rolled off, he'd be dead," he said, and his mother said life wasn't exciting enough for some people. "Stay away from him," she said. "He's a bad influence."

After school and on weekends, Pete played with the other children on the block. They rode their bikes up and down the neighborhood, carried them up the steps to the boardwalk, and rode down to Coney Island and the parachute jump, where they watched people sway in small, swinglike seats up to the top, where they would hesitate a second, jerk sharply, and then descend beneath a blossom of white silk. When they had enough money, one would stay behind to watch the bikes and the others would dare each other to go up.

"What's a parachute for?" Pete would ask whomever he sat next to.

"So we don't fall down and splatter ourselves over the boardwalk, dope," said his friend.

No, Pete thought. That's not it. That's not the answer.

When the boys went to the community center to play pool, he went with them. He watched the older boys while they repaired their cars. He handed them the tools they asked for and asked them what they were doing. After a while they let him attach wires to batteries. They showed him how to start a car without a key. When his own bike broke down, he'd take it out in front of the house and after a while, the others on the block would come out and join him. When his bike was fixed, they rode off together.

On weekends and after school, Angelina worked in the kitchen and listened for the voices outside calling, "Mrs. Bravado! Mrs. Bravado! Can Pete come out to play?" What an old song that was! She could still hear it. "Mrs. Luisi! Mrs. Luisi! Can Angelina come out to play?" And then one day, she looked up, listened, and realized how long it had been since anyone had called for Pete. Everyone knew he was never home. He was always out, working with his father. She hung the strips of pasta to dry over the back of the kitchen chairs and stood still, listening for the voices from the street, but it was quiet. Pete was still a boy. Why did he have to work? She looked at the noodles hanging from the curtain rod in front of the kitchen window; the light shone through them and turned them gold. Her mother used to hang the strips of pasta from the curtain rod when she knew the whole family was coming. She was older now than her mother was then. Her son's friends were gone. They were tired of looking for him, tired of waiting for him. What should she do? She sat down on the edge of a chair, leaning forward so the pressure of her back wouldn't crack the noodles. She'd wanted a good man, and she'd married a good man, but when it came to the children, you couldn't talk to him. What could she talk to him about? Not much. The clock on the wall struck three. She went to the window and looked out. No Pete. Maybe George had picked him up at school.

In the mornings, Pete got up early, went into the dining room, and looked up at the third floor of the Lugano house. From the dining room window, he sometimes caught a glimpse of Eddie's shoes. Occasionally his arm dangled over the ledge.

When he got dressed, he'd go out and wait behind the oak tree in front of the Lugano house, and when Eddie came out on his way to school, he'd walk along with him.

"Hey," Eddie said, "you having trouble on your way to school?" Pete said no, he wasn't. "Yeah, well, it's your first week, and if you do, you tell me," Eddie said. "Me and my brothers, we'll take care of it. You're from the block. You have trouble at school?" Pete said sometimes he did. He was so much smaller than the others. "You know what you have to do?" Eddie asked him. "This is what you have to do. The first day of school, you pick out the biggest guy. The biggest, the meanest, the heaviest. You pick him out. You can see him? O.K., you walk up to him and you say, 'You wanna fight?' If he says yes, you hit him. If he says no, you hit him. You don't give him no choice. You hit him. After that, you won't have no trouble."

Pete asked him if that's what he did.

"Yeah, I did. You don't have to do it too many times. Once, maybe twice. You won't have no more problems."

"You always won?" Pete asked him.

"Nah, sometimes I lost. I came home once with a broken arm. My father, he said, 'You started it, you finish it.' So I went to the Emergency Room. They put a cast on my arm and I went out looking for the guy and I hit him with the cast. I broke the cast but I cracked his shoulder. My father said, 'Good. You finish it or I'll finish you.' You win, you lose, it doesn't matter. You show them you're not afraid, they won't bother you."

"They'll kill me," Pete said.

"They hurt you too bad, I'll go after them. But you don't tell them that. They won't hurt you too bad. Everyone knows the rules."

"I don't know," Pete said.

"It's not like you're from *Queens*," Eddie said. "You're from the neighborhood. You wanna walk with me? Then fight."

Two weeks later, Pete was waiting in front of Eddie's house. Both his eyes were black, and over his right eye was a cut.

"You needed stitches?" Eddie asked him. "How many?"

"Two," Pete said.

"Not bad," Eddie said. "Any more damage?"

"A broken rib."

"They leaving you alone?"

"Yeah," said Pete. "They are."

"You need any more advice," Eddie said, "you come to me."

"FIGHTING?" his mother shouted. "Now you're fighting?"

"Only once," he said. "I only have to do it once a year."

"What are you talking about?" Angelina asked, grabbing him. "You don't have to do it at all!"

His grandmother said she saw him talking to the Lugano boy. "Stay away from him!" she said. "He's trouble!"

"He's got money," said her grandson.

"Yeah?" said old Mrs. Bravado. "You know where he gets it? He *shoplifts*. The whole family shoplifts. I talked to his brother. They have nothing to do, they go to Woolworth's. They take things they don't need. Whenever someone's got a birthday here, they bring things over? You know how they get them? They *shoplift*. You know what I see when I look at them? I see black and white stripes and a number across the chest. That's what I see."

He and Eddie were standing on the sidewalk outside of Woolworth's. "What've you got?" Eddie asked him.

"I don't know," Pete said.

They went around the corner and Pete pulled the pink garment out from beneath his jacket.

"A negligee," Eddie said. "Hey, terrific, a negligee!"

"What's a negligee?"

"Women sleep in them," Eddie said. "Stay here. I'll get a box. You give it to your mother." He went back into Woolworth's and came out with a gift box.

"How'd you get it?" Pete asked. "You bought it?"

"I didn't buy it," Eddie said. "I didn't buy anything. Give it to your mother. You're always in trouble for something, right? Next time you're in trouble, give it to her."

" W H E R E ' D you get this?" his mother asked. "Where'd you get the money for this?"

"I saved it, Ma," he said. "I got bottles from the neighbors and took them to the store."

"He's lying like a snake," said old Mrs. Bravado.

"This time I'll believe you," said his mother. "This time."

" S O ? " asked Eddie. Pete told him what happened. "That's women," Eddie said. "Don't give them anything. A good smack in the teeth."

"She wears it," Pete said.

"Yeah?" said Eddie. "I knew she would. If it's pink, they like it." Pete asked him when he was going again, and he said he went almost every weekend, and before holidays, when the stores were open at night, he went after dinner. "So you wanna come?" he asked, and Pete said he did, but not too often, because his mother was already suspicious. "So?" said Eddie. "Wait until they cool off. You get something, you give it to me. I get something you want, I'll give it to you."

"So," Pete asked, "why do you sleep out on the ledge?"

"I'm in training," Eddie said. "I'm part Indian. I'm silent and deadly. You know my dog? I'm training him to be an attack dog. I chain him to the landing. You know what happened last week? He was chained up there on his choke collar and he went over the bannister and he was choking and I heard him and I had my knife. I always have my knife, and I cut through his collar and he was fine." Pete said the dog must hate him, but Eddie said, "Hate me? He *loves* me. I have to step on his toes so he won't lick my face off. I tell him one word and he'll rip your throat out. Even if he knows you, he'll do it. That's how he listens to me."

"What's the word?" Pete asked.

"I'm not telling you," Eddie said. "He's *my* dog. He scares the *shit* out of my father. You want a dog like him?"

"My father, he'd poison him," Pete said.

"Yeah?" Eddie said. "Not my father. He'd eat his spaghetti and it wouldn't be Parmesan. It'd be arsenic."

"You're talking big," Pete said nervously.

"Yeah?" Eddie said. "You think so? Hey, you want to walk the dog?"

" STAY away from him," said his mother. "He's doing you a favor, letting you walk his dog?"

"He helps me with my homework," said Pete.

"What?" said old Mrs. Bravado.

"He gave me books on Indians for my last book report."

"He probably stole them from the library," said old Mrs. Bravado.

"He's going to help me with my next one. It's title is 'The Purpose of Man.'"

"He's not a man!" shouted his grandmother. "He's a gorilla!"

"Ma!" said Theresa. "The windows are open! They can hear you!"

"So?" said old Mrs. Bravado. "They're going to kill me? I have something to live for?"

"Oh, Ma," said Theresa.

"In Italy, they didn't have Italians like him!" said old Mrs. Bravado.

"Ma!" said Theresa.

6 ETER BRAVADO, known to the world as Pete, got up in the morning knowing that that afternoon his father would pick him up in his grey, rusting van and take him off somewhere into Queens where together they would replace an ancient bathtub with a modern one. He liked the idea of helping his father. It made him feel important and useful, a man at last, like his older brothers, a person with a reason for being in the world. He'd heard his family fighting the night before, but he had been deep in *The Three Musketeers,* and the argument was only so much noise coming up through the floorboards of his room, suspended, for the time, somewhere between the United States and nineteenth-century France.

As usual, he awakened expecting the new day to take him with it into some new adventure, however small. "Small things grow into big things," his grandmother always said when she first fondled the little envelopes of seeds she bought every spring.

"Every day's something new," said his aunt Theresa. "Every day's like a box of Cracker Jacks, always a different prize in it."

"Is that a saying, or did you make that up?" Pete asked her. He always wanted to know if someone had just that instant invented something new. Someone who could invent new things, now that was a person worth listening to!

"It must be a saying," said his uncle. "Theresa never made up anything in her life."

"It must be a saying," Theresa agreed. "Anyway, Poppa always used to say there's nothing new under the sun."

"He didn't mean it," said old Mrs. Bravado.

"He meant it and he didn't," said Angelina.

"And that's the truth," said old Mrs. Bravado, pausing with her spoon poised above the oatmeal pot. "Oatmeal," she said, looking into the pot. "When I was a girl in Italy, we ate goat stew on winter mornings."

"You never!" exclaimed Angelina. "You were poor!"

"No one was too poor to have goats," said old Mrs. Bravado. "Goat milk! It was good for you. It made such good cheese. Don't make faces, Angelina! Don't make faces at things you don't know about! Very good for you, was goat milk."

"Enough about goats," said George, shrugging on his coat as he crossed the room on his way out to the van. "Enough about the old country."

"Enough about everything, eh?" asked old Mrs. Bravado.

"Where's Pete?" George asked. Everyone else was sitting at the table.

"Upstairs, looking in the mirror," said Pete's older brother.

"Get downstairs!" roared his father.

"Looking in the mirror?" said Angelina. "Since when does he look in the mirror?"

"He's at that age," said his aunt.

"Is there some reason he shouldn't look in a mirror?" asked old Mrs. Bravado.

"Enough, Ma," said George.

"Enough, *everybody*," said Theresa's husband, walking in and sitting down. He had a day job and a night job and was rarely home, but was he imagining it, or was it harder every day to get through a meal without an argument?

"Where is he?" shouted George, slamming the door as he went out of the house. The women looked at one other and shook their heads.

In the mirror of his tall oak dresser (one of the remaining old things not yet replaced, although it was on the list), Pete inspected himself. What was so remarkable about the bones in his face? They weren't sticking out through his skin. When he looked in the mirror, he saw a face like anyone's face. "You have the most *remarkable* bone structure," Judith Mary always said. At first he thought that meant the outline of his skull was somehow visible through the shielding flesh of his face. Then Judith Mary, who lived two blocks away, and who sometimes walked home with him, looked at his face, seemed about to say the same incomprehensible thing, and instead reached up and touched his cheekbone. In the dead of winter, a lead-grey wind blowing, he felt a burning circle of heat where the tips of her fingers had touched his face. "I wish I had bones like that," said Judith Mary.

"Everyone has bones," he said.

"Not like yours. I've got a moon face because I don't have any bones. Your face is all planes and angles. Sister Mary Catherine who teaches sketching? She says anyone who wanted to draw my face, they could put a pot down on the paper and trace around it, and they'd have the very same shape. It's one big curve from under my eyes to my chin. But from under your eyes to your chin, there are sharp places. Like cliffs. Like rock ledges."

"It doesn't sound good," Pete said.

"Oh, it is! You're so . . . "

"So what?" he asked. Why was she blushing?

"Um, you're so . . . "

"So *what*?"

"Interesting to look at," Judith Mary said, speaking quickly. "Handsome."

"Handsome?" he asked. Bones? When he thought of bones, he thought about his grandfather, and the other people his grandfather now slept with in the churchyard, the bone people, growing white and chalky, whiter and whiter, crumbling into dust, and when they had whitened and turned into dust, God came for them and whirled them up into the sky where, turned into the long thin clouds that trailed through the afternoon skies, they wrote out God's incomprehensible messages. He often saw Father D'Angelo looking up at the sky, unmoving, and he imagined that the priest could read what was written and moving fast high over his head.

"Handsome," said the girl, looking for a rock to kick, but finding none above the snow, she kicked instead at a loose bit of ice in her path. And because she was embarrassed, she asked, "Why don't you have a book bag? The nuns get mad if our books get wet."

"This is good enough," he said, looking down at his books placed neatly on a raw rectangle of plywood, held neatly in place by his father's old cracked black leather belt. It had never occurred to him before: why didn't he have a book bag?

"Are you taking the test for the special program classes?" she asked him. "My parents want me to take it. Without an education, you can't get anywhere in this country."

"My father says just the opposite," he said.

"But that's so, so... ignorant!" she blurted out. "Everyone knows you need an education. It's the most important thing."

"No, no, it's not," he said, after some thought. "The most important thing is to have a good heart."

"Oh, well, a good heart," said Judith Mary. "Of course that's the most important thing. But after that comes education."

"My father doesn't think so," said Pete.

"Oh, well, your father," said Judith Mary in the stuffy, smug tones he heard only from the adults, usually from his father, when he displayed his latest purchase, a pink marbled Formica table with chrome legs, replacing the old oak one.

"Do you like Formica tables?" he asked her.

"What?"

"Formica tables," he said impatiently.

"My mother says they're for people who have no taste. My mother says they're for the same people who put pink plastic flamingos in their gardens."

"We have pink plastic flamingos."

"Well," sighed the girl, "no one's perfect. Anyway, your family doesn't fight as much as my family."

"My family fights all the time," he said, astonished.

"Not like my family. In the summer, when the windows are open? The neighbors stand outside pretending to water the lawn. They're listening to the fights. In the summer, I want to die."

"You shouldn't stay there when they fight," he said. When he heard raised voices in the kitchen, he went up to his room, lay on his bed, and looked at the picture on the opposite wall. In the picture, embroidered out of shiny thread, a small boat made its way through rough water toward a small, peaceful town on a green hill. Below the town, goats and cattle grazed in the field. In the picture, nothing ever changed, not the weather, not the town, not the animals grazing in the field. Beneath the glass, he could hear the silence and the peace and the faint sound of the wind blowing through the branches of the olive trees, whipping up the waves of the sea. When his family fought, he looked at the picture. When he'd looked at it long enough, he was inside the frame, behind the glass, in front of the pink house at the top of the hill, looking down at the water.

When he caught cold and was kept home from school, he lay on the living room couch and watched his mother, his aunt, and his grandmother in the kitchen. When they were finished, or when they were tired, they came and sat in the living room, knitting, looking up at him and smiling. At such times, they grew smaller, moved farther away, and, like beings behind glass, promised to last forever. But when his father came home, tired and complaining, the glass over the picture shattered. His mother was not his mother, his aunt not his aunt. The women seemed to run about like bugs while his father pursued them like a giant with a giant's fist.

"Where am I supposed to go when they fight?" asked Judith Mary. "It's cold out in the winter." She looked at him curiously. "What do you do when they fight?"

He thought about the picture. He wanted to tell her, but he'd learned long ago it was best not to say too much. If you kept quiet, no one could run into the kitchen and make fun of what you'd just said. According to his father, everything he said was stupid or crazy.

Now Pete vainly searched the mirror for signs of his remarkable bones, the only thing Judith Mary would find remarkable in a Formica house where books were read, if they were read at all, under the covers with a flashlight. Now, when he went to Woolworth's with Eddie, he'd trade whatever he got for flashlight batteries.

"Time wasters," said his father, picking up one of his books and dropping it, not on the table, but on the floor. "I just came from a house where the whole third floor fell in under the weight of books. Can you imagine it? People crazy enough to live in a house with so many books? Dust collectors! Bug collectors! The house was *filthy* with books!"

"Ignorance speaks with a loud voice," said old Mrs. Bravado.

"Don't call me ignorant," said George.

"And the voice of jealousy is even louder," old Mrs. Bravado said.

"Jealous!" shouted George. "What am I jealous of? Tell me that, Ma! Tell me that!"

"Don't ask me again or I will," said his mother, puffing out her chest, swelling up like a hen out for a walk in the sun. George fled into the yard. Old Mrs. Bravado raised her knitting needle in the air. "Now," she said. "Bang." As she spoke, the sound of a hammer hitting a nail echoed through the house. "When I'm right, I'm right," the old woman said. "Bang, and bang again. If he lives to be a hundred, he won't get the better of his mother. Because his father was a better man than he is and I listened to his father."

"Oh, Ma," said Theresa. "Angelina doesn't like to hear that."

"I don't mind," said Angelina.

"You need more than two legs to run from the truth," said old Mrs. Bravado.

Pete didn't know what to make of his family or anyone else in the world. Insofar as he had an opinion about his place in the scheme of things, he believed he was there to observe what happened, and at some future date, he would make sense of it, not because he wanted to, but because that was what men did when they were older. His uncle had one explanation of why things happened as they did, his father another, and the priest, yet another. Even if there was no sense to be made of things, everyone pretended there was and insisted everyone else see what they saw. He imagined that one day he would grow as tall and heavy as his father, and when that happened, he would know at once how things ought to be, and why they should be that way, and he too would begin shouting down the walls of the house.

Women, he saw, were not like that. They could imagine two or three right ways for things to be done. When he thought of his mother and grandmother and aunt talking in the kitchen, he thought women believed there were as many right ways to do things as there were people. He tended to believe the same thing, but he suspected such beliefs were womanly and it was best not to encourage them.

Outside his window, two squirrels chased one another up the cardboard-grey wisteria vine climbing up toward the roof of the house. He watched the squirrels, one pursuing the other, both twitching their tails. Their muscles were strong and smooth under their fur. The animals were full of purpose. Their purpose was to live and to enjoy their lives. How was man different? What was the purpose of a man? The purpose of a man was to use his mind so that he became, eventually, as happy and full of purpose as a squirrel. No one he knew was as happy as a squirrel or a cat or a rat or a dog. He looked at the squirrels and envied them. They were born making sense of things. If it was too hot, they didn't ask why. They found ways to keep cool. If it was too cold, they tunneled under leaves or lined their nests and slept in heaps.

He'd met Father D'Angelo after school and told him what he'd concluded

about the purpose of man, and Father D'Angelo said that was heresy, and
when Pete asked why, the priest told him to come and see him and they'd
talk about it, but lately, he hadn't gone. The truth was he believed what he
believed. He didn't want anyone, not even the priest, explaining to him that
what he believed was not only wrong, but possibly sinful.

"You have an old head on your shoulders," Father D'Angelo told him last
week when he saw him coming home from school. "I've got a new book for
you. You're still reading books about the Second World War?" Pete said he
was. "I've got a good one," said the priest. "*Submarine.*"

He wanted the book. Late at night, he'd read under the covers, the
flashlight powered by the stolen batteries. He loved the stories of the men
who went off to war, marching through the streets while the families slept
quietly in the houses, walking quickly through the blue dusk, toward the
waiting trucks that would take them to the docks and the huge boats, the
wide water whose other side was adventure and heroism and glorious
death. Before he started working with his father, he sat on the window seat
in his parents' room, and read, and looked up, and when he did, he could
see the shadowy grey armies moving through the purplish-blue streets. In
his imagination, they never marched during the day, only at dawn or dusk
when they were slightly more tangible than the light itself. No one, he
thought, made fun of heroes. Heroes had a right to their words.

He told his mother about Judith Mary, the smart girl from school,
always praised by the nuns, and his mother said there was nothing like a
smart woman. His father, who was passing through the kitchen on his way
to the shed, said there was nothing worse. Her head was filled with ideas
about how wonderful she was and she never wanted to wash dishes or learn
how to cook. She read every book under the sun but she couldn't understand a recipe.

"There goes the voice of experience," said old Mrs. Bravado.

"She doesn't like pink flamingos," Pete said. "For some reason."

"Who does?" asked old Mrs. Bravado.

"*I* like pink flamingos," said his father, recrossing the kitchen.

"You like pink Formica," observed his wife.

"Still, the man can make a living," said old Mrs. Bravado. She could
attack her son and defend him at the same time. Women, thought Pete,
were more complicated than men.

Later, Pete asked old Mrs. Bravado what she thought about smart
women. "Anything that can think is better than something that can't
think," said the old woman. "Who wants to live with a rock? It may be a
nice rock, but it doesn't answer you when you want to talk to it."

"Judith Mary thinks," he said, turning it over.

"Good for her," said his grandmother, whose mind had already settled
on another subject. "Good for her."

He thought about all these things as he stood on the windy corner, snow slanting down, fat, wet flakes settling on his cheeks, waiting for his father to pick him up. In back of him, the cement-block school hummed like a hive. Someone from the block called out to him, waved, and he waved back. He had his work clothes in a brown paper bag and he would change into them in the rear of the van. For the first time, it occurred to him that he would probably get home late, not until nine or ten, and he wouldn't have much time to do his homework unless he stayed up after everyone else was asleep, listening to the secret creaks and sighs a house makes when it thinks it's alone. He would be the only one awake, the only one who would know if something went wrong, the silent watchman over the sleeping people. If a fire broke out, he would wake his parents, and while he stood on the sidewalk watching the fire trucks, his father would thank him again and again. Alone and watching, he would be almost like God. He crossed himself, in the event that that thought had been sinful.

"Get in," said his father, pulling up in the van. His father had little to say to him and few answers for his questions. The boy wanted to know what they would be doing. "*I'm* replacing a toilet and a bathtub," said his father. The boy took out his history book, but his father glared so at him that he put it back. It was a long drive to the house in Queens, a mother-daughter row house whose bricks had long ago blackened with soot.

"First," his father told the woman of the house, "I tear out the old tub, see what the pan is like and if it's rusted, and if the floor's rotted, we have to replace the floor, and *then* we can see about replacing the tub." From the set of his father's shoulders, Pete could see how much his father disliked explaining himself, how much, in fact, he disliked talking to anyone. "You take one end, I'll take the other," he said to the boy an hour later, and together they lifted the cast-iron bathtub from its position against the wall and moved it near the door.

"The thing weighs a ton," said the woman from the doorway. "The little boy, he's strong enough to carry something so heavy?"

"He's ten years old," said his father.

"He doesn't look ten," said the woman. "He's a little kid."

"Stay here," his father said to him, ignoring the woman. "I need something from the toolbox."

"This all happened because of my grandson," the woman said to Pete. "He gets in the tub and splashes until the whole floor's dripping and then it starts leaking in the dining room downstairs and everyone comes running up here screaming, 'Fix the tub! Fix the tub!' "

"Is the trouble," asked the boy, "the tub or your grandson?"

"Both, don't you think so? You splash enough water, you rot the wood beneath. My figure isn't what it used to be, but even if it was, I wouldn't want to land in the middle of the downstairs dining room dressed up in some soap bubbles."

Mr. Bravado came back and found his son sitting on the edge of the tub, raptly listening to the woman, who was, apparently, telling him the story of her life.

"Help me carry the tub downstairs," he said impatiently. "I'll go first." The boy picked up his end of the tub and staggered after his father.

"That thing's heavy," said the woman. "Give the boy a break. I'll call one of the fellows from downstairs."

"Do you want me to do the job or don't you?" asked his father.

The woman pulled down the corners of her mouth. "Don't yell at me! I'm not your wife," she said, retreating to the kitchen.

"You don't have to talk to them," said his father, as they set the tub down on the sidewalk. "We're here to do a job. We're not entertainers." The boy said nothing. "They think if they're friendly, you'll charge less. They give you a glass of tea the first night, a cup of soup the second night, and the third night it's pasta and they want the family price. Don't get too friendly. Wait till she hears the pan's rusted, the floor's rotted, and when we pull up the planks, there's going to be a hole in the downstairs ceiling. You'll see how friendly she is then."

"You want a cookie?" the woman asked Pete as they went back into the house.

"See?" said his father.

"Can I have the cookie?"

"It's up to you."

"No, thanks," said the boy.

When his father told her about the pan, the floor, and the ceiling, the woman sat down at her kitchen table, covered with red and white checked oilcloth, and cried. His father nodded at him as if to say: you see? The cookie didn't work. Now she's asking for sympathy.

It was nine thirty when they pulled into the driveway. Some cold black trees shook their thin arms over the roof and some white clouds unraveled into threads and blew down the ink-blue sky. "No homework tonight," said his father. "Get your rest. We're going back to that house all this week and part of next week too. Your brothers were bigger than you when they were ten. You're the runt. Sleep."

He heard his father waiting in the hall until he turned out his light. He took his flashlight and turned it on under the covers, but before he'd finished a page, his eyes began closing, and by the time he'd reached the middle of the page, he was sound asleep. He woke up the next morning with the blanket pulled over his head, the book under his ribs, and the flashlight dead.

VERY CHILD," said old Mrs. Bravado, holding her grandson's palm, "has a black year. This year is your black year. Here it is," she said, pointing to a small, lightning-shaped mark branching out not far from the base of his lifeline. "The bad thing about every black year is that it is twelve months long. The good thing is that it has an ending."

"That's garbage," said her grandson.

"What?" said his grandmother.

"It's garbage," the boy repeated.

"You say that to me?" asked his grandmother. "To me, you say it's garbage?"

"It is," said the sullen boy.

"You've turned into your father!" his grandmother shouted at him. "I used to beat your father! I can beat you, too!"

The boy started to cry, jumped up, and ran out of the room.

"What did he do?" asked his father, coming in from the backyard.

"What did he do?" old Mrs. Bravado shouted at her son. "You ask me what he did? You who take him to work every night! You who make him go to school in his work clothes covered with mud and grease so all the others laugh at him? You who bring him home in the middle of the night and make him so tired he doesn't eat and you can look through his bones? You ask me what he did? Who are you to ask me?"

"Did he say the others make fun of him?" asked George.

"Does he have to say it?" screamed old Mrs. Bravado. "There's no snake meaner than a child! He walks around looking like a thundercloud! When he thinks you don't watch him, he puts his hand to his head because his head hurts! His report card! Is *D* the only letter in the alphabet? Look what you are making out of him! Once he was a happy child and now people turn their eyes away from him. Good for you! Good for you! I'm glad your father isn't alive to see it! I'm glad," said the old woman, and she burst into tears, loud, choking, gurgling tears. Old Mrs. Bravado never cried. Not even at her husband's funeral had she cried.

A hot flush began in George's stomach and rose to the top of his head. "Ma!" he said. "What's so bad? I did the same thing with the other boys. They're doing fine."

"He is not the other boys," sobbed old Mrs. Bravado.

"How is he different, Ma? He's got two legs and a head just like the rest of them."

His mother started to say something, but was cut off by her own strangled breathing. "He *is* different," she said at last.

"What did I do wrong?" her son asked after a while. "I did the same thing with the others. What did I do wrong?"

"He's not the same and you know he's not the same!" said his mother, who had stopped crying. "He's a dreamer! It's because of the new baby you don't want to see it."

"Don't talk to me about the baby," he said.

"Just because he doesn't have a big brain doesn't mean you send him away," said his mother. "Even wolves keep cubs born with three legs."

The new baby slept in a cradle near her chair. His mouth was unnaturally large and his eyes slanted as if they were Oriental eyes. He would probably never learn to read and write, the doctor told them, but with luck, he could grow up to be a good citizen. Of course, he should never marry and have children. And the priest, who came later, said it was hard to understand God's ways, but he never gave you a burden you couldn't bear, and maybe when the other children had grown up and married, this one would be the company of their old age.

"He won't, because he'll be in a home," said George. Angelina said it was a sin to talk that way and began weeping. "Is it a sin to talk that way?" George asked the priest.

"Do unto others," said Father D'Angelo. "Christ said, 'Suffer the little children to come unto me.' He didn't say some of the children. He said all of the children."

"I'm not Christ," said Mr. Bravado.

"IT'S BECAUSE of the baby," said old Mrs. Bravado. "Who told you the baby disgraces you in the family? These things happen. While I'm alive, he doesn't leave the house."

"This is my house," said her son.

"Isn't anything in here ours?" Pete asked. "Doesn't anything belong to us?"

"He leaves over my dead body," said old Mrs. Bravado, and once again George saw her, the mother of his youth, standing in the doorway waiting for him, holding the electric train he had stolen from the department store. "Where did you get it?" she asked him, and before he could answer, she had him by the collar. She, who was five feet tall, dragged her six-foot son into the kitchen, threw him against the whitewashed wall, pulled a chair out from the table, and threw him down on it as if he were a piece of cloth, and advanced on him with the broom. But this time when she beat him, she beat him with the handle. He could feel the purple welts rising as the red wood handle was brought down against his back. Don't cry, he told himself again and again. Don't give her the satisfaction of seeing you cry, but finally the pain became too much for him and he gave in. He could remember it now, looking up from the chair, and seeing, not his mother, but her gigantic black shadow on the whitewashed wall.

"Disgrace to the family!" she shouted at him, out of breath. "No son of mine is a thief!" And when his father came home, it was worse. He said that tomorrow George would stay home from school and would go with him to the store and George would return the train to the store owner with his own hand. And it was worse yet: after he returned the train, his father paid the protesting store owner for it and came home with the train. His father, under his mother's approving eye, set it in the middle of his dresser.

"You wanted it enough to steal it," said his father.

"If anything happens to that train," said his mother, "if it gets lost, if someone breaks in the window and steals it, you're not my son anymore."

"But Ma!" he said.

"Don't talk to me," said his mother.

Later, in his room, he heard his father asking his mother, "Why did he do it?" Why had he done it? Every day, he looked around him and saw a world full of things, long cars with silver birds swooping from the hoods, houses with gardeners who came and put down squares of green grass as if they were cloth, women who stepped out of front doors wearing long fur coats, got into taxis, and waved to someone watching from the front window. He had a friend whose entire basement was filled with Lionel trains and painted mountains and trestle bridges and covered bridges, and the trains chugged past fields of cows and horses, across the room to the skyscrapers on the other side. The world was full of things, but his father cared nothing for him. What did his father see when he looked into space and smiled? What did he see when he looked at the women in their sauce-spotted housedresses? What was so wonderful about the beach and its ragged, dirty seaweed, its broken shells? If things weren't important, why did other people value them? What did his father see, so that to him things were worth looking at, but not worth possessing? If his father would come into his room, pick up the train from the dresser, and explain it to him! *I don't see it! I don't see what you see!* But he was ashamed and angry. His father always knew what other people thought. His father read other people's minds, but he didn't know his own son and he didn't care. He said nothing and his father said nothing.

And then one day, his father took the train from the top of his dresser and no one ever mentioned it again.

Now his mother was an old woman with pink cheeks and white hair who sat in his house and ate his food and knitted with his wool and rocked in his chair.

"Everyone loves this child you won't even look at!" said his mother. "Over my dead body he leaves this house!"

"You won't live forever," said her son.

"You say that to your mother? You say that to me?" She pushed down on the arms of her chair until the blue, ropy veins stood out on her lower arms, and in front of him, she struggled to her feet. Automatically, he stretched his arm out to help her. "Don't touch me!" she said. Standing, she barely came up to the top button of his shirt. Her black eyes glittered like small, hard stones. "I cannot live here," she said. "No more."

Her son was silent. This had gone further than he intended. "Theresa!" his mother shouted. Who would have thought the old lady's lungs were so strong? Her daughter ran in through the kitchen, asking, "What's the matter? What's the matter?" But when she saw her mother standing, facing her brother, she asked him, "What happened here? What's the matter?"

"Don't speak to him about me," said her mother. "I'm living with you now. Help me pack."

"I own the whole house," said her son.

"Tell him I'll live on the street," old Mrs. Bravado told Theresa. "I'll go to the priest and tell him I have no home. There are families with little children and no old lady to rock the cradle. I don't have to live here! No one lives where she's not wanted! No one is so poor as that."

"Ma!" said Theresa.

"You're not going anywhere," said her son.

"On my own two feet or in a coffin," said his mother.

"Ma!" Theresa said again.

"Angelina can bring down the baby. When the boy isn't working, he can come down to me."

"Ma!" said Theresa. "It's dark down there. Damp! We've been talking of moving!"

"I won't notice," said old Mrs. Bravado. "I'll be figuring it out."

"Figuring out what?" asked Theresa.

"How much he owes me," said the old woman. "For a son, you cook and bake and sew and feed babies. For a son you do that for nothing. For a stranger, you get paid."

"Over my dead body," said George.

"Let's hope so!" shrieked Theresa, beside herself.

"And the most terrible part," the old lady said loudly, as her daughter helped her down the stairs to the basement apartment, "the most terrible part is that he's like all men. They can only be happy when they do as everyone else does. Your father said it: they're only happy in crowds. They're happy in uniforms, like crows, so you can't tell one from another. They're happiest during war. That's all they know. Destroy, destroy."

"Oh, Ma," said her daughter.

"Is it true or isn't it true?" her mother asked. "Tell me, true or not true?"

"Who can answer these riddles?" asked her daughter.

"Where's Pete?" asked the old lady.

"Going to work," said Theresa.

"When he comes home, send him downstairs."

"Ma, it's *damp* down here."

"Not another word," said her mother. "Another word and I go to the priest. In the church it is damp, too."

A F T E R old Mrs. Bravado moved into her daughter's apartment, there was, for some time, no more talk of sending Paul, the baby, away. Angelina began to talk of keeping the child until they were too old to care for him, and although her husband's face darkened, he did not contradict her. His mother always meant what she said. She said she was going to live in the basement. Now she lived there. She would not speak to her son, much less break bread with him. She said the baby would leave the house over her dead body; he didn't want that on his conscience. Still, messages from the basement kept him informed of her dissatisfactions. "The boy was working too hard." He meant to kill "the boy." Only God could create someone in his own image. If he was disappointed in his sixth son, was that a reason for making his fifth over into a copy of himself? God saw everything. His father, God rest his soul, saw everything. His spirit was not quiet. Her son was full of sin and would die full of sin, and the torment of her eternal soul would be laid at her son's door.

"Don't mention her to me again!" George roared when his sister came up with the latest of his mother's pronouncements. "It won't work! This nagging from the basement won't work! My conscience is clear! It doesn't bother me!"

"Don't tell me it doesn't work," said old Mrs. Bravado to her daughter. "The boy isn't working on Saturdays. Now Vinnie works for him on Saturdays and he has to pay Vinnie."

"Yeah, but Ma," said Theresa, "what good is it doing? The kid doesn't have friends anymore. He walks around all day like a thundercloud. He doesn't talk. He doesn't joke. He doesn't *say* things. Remember how he used to make things up? 'I like to see the water swifting over the rocks.' Remember when he said that? *Swifting?*"

"I remember," said old Mrs. Bravado.

"He's not the same, Ma," said Theresa. "He's always angry. He doesn't look you in the eye. Now he doesn't work, he doesn't get an allowance either. What's he supposed to do without money?"

"He'll be the same again," said old Mrs. Bravado. "You'll see. After a month or two months, he'll look you in the eye. Is he working Saturdays? Tell me that."

"No, Ma, he's not."

It was true. Now on Saturdays, Pete would get up early and, instead of going to work, would begin making the rounds. "Hey, Mrs. Lugano, you need anything at the store?" And if Mrs. Lugano needed a bottle of milk, she gave him the money and an empty soda bottle to take back for the nickel deposit. "Hey, Mrs. Luisi, you need anything at the store?" And if Mrs. Luisi didn't need anything, she would give him two soda bottles to return for their deposit. When he had at least seven bottles, he went to the store, bought what people asked him for, collected thirty-five cents in nickels, and went back along the same route. "Here's the money for the bottles," he would say to Mrs. Lugano, and every week, she'd say, "You a good boy. Keep the money." Sometimes she'd ask him to come in and have a cookie and some soda. "When Eddie was a boy," she said, "you know what he used to do? He used to push a doll carriage with a doll in it. Now he sleeps on a ledge."

"Is he really part Indian?" Pete asked.

"I'm pure Italian and so's his father," said Mrs. Lugano. "Who knows where he gets such ideas?" She shook her head, remembering Eddie and the baby carriage.

"Keep the money," said Mrs. Montalte a few minutes later. "For going to the store."

One dollar was more than enough to get him to the Avenue U Cinema, buy him a ticket, a soda, and a box of candy or a red and white cardboard carton of buttered popcorn. He went to the movies alone because he had few friends. How could he have friends when he had to leave school every day and go straight to work and everyone made fun of him for coming to school in his work clothes, and by the weekend, he was tired as much older men who have worked all week are tired, and all he wanted was time to himself, peace and quiet, chewing his candy, enjoying the sensation of chewing, of feeling his jaw work, of sitting in the cool dark and watching a movie he pretended no one else in the world had seen—certainly no one in his family had seen it—feeling his own dreams stir and float up into the beam of white, misty light that ended on the screen, weaving themselves into the images he saw there. And when it was over, he would take the bus back home, go into the house through the basement entrance, and talk to his grandmother.

"So are things better now?" the old lady asked.

"Sure," he said.

I could live forever, thought the old woman. I could live forever to watch over this child.

"What's wrong?" she asked him. He shrugged. "Try," she said. "God gave people mouths to talk with." He shook his head hopelessly. When people spoke the right words, he knew them. But to think of the words on his own, lately that was impossible.

"With so many in a house," began his grandmother, "you can get lost. If the people in here were trees, we'd be in a deep dark wood. It's a crowd here, like a sale at Klein's."

"No," he said. "To me it's not a crowd. There are a lot of people but they're all separate. A lot of separate people. It isn't the same thing as a crowd."

"There's no difference," said Theresa, passing through with the laundry. "A lot of separate people make a crowd. That's what a crowd is. A lot of separate people."

When her daughter went into the kitchen, old Mrs. Bravado said, "She's wrong. She's always wrong. If you're right, you don't care how many people say you're wrong."

"How can I be the only one who's right?" Pete asked her. "Everyone else can't be wrong."

"Everyone else doesn't live under this roof. There's more to the world than Bravados." Until this grandson came along, she'd lain awake at night wondering what they'd done to produce creatures who resembled them not at all. Her children, and then her grandchildren, they might as well have been onions and cabbages. But not this one. Even under his sullenness and his silences, this one was special.

"I'm dumb," he said at last. "That's why I don't think like other people."

"Spaghetti!" said his grandmother, striking the arm of her chair with her fist. "Spaghetti! Your father tells you that. You're the only one in this family with a brain."

"No," he said, hopelessly. "I saw my last report card. I'm dumb."

"Don't say that to me!" said the old lady. "Your father, he's the one who says that. Your father's a crooked picture hanging on the wall. Everyone knows it's crooked. But the person in the picture doesn't know it's crooked." Her grandson smiled. "You like that?" she asked. "You like to hear me talk like that? You're wicked! I'll chase you!" She shook her fist at him and laughed. She rocked, smiled to herself, and looked closer at the boy. "How is the baby?" she asked him. A light went on behind his eyes. "He's wonderful, isn't he?" she asked, bending forward. "He's a secret. Your secret and my secret."

"Pop will get rid of him," the boy said. "You'll see."

"You may see it. I'll never see it," the old woman said. "What are you doing now? You can read down here with me."

"I don't read anymore," the boy said. "I can't finish a sentence." His grandmother looked at him and made the sign of the cross.

LD MRS. BRAVADO had never thought much about Brooklyn and how she came to live there. According to her, people were like seeds, and seeds came to rest whenever the wind that had lifted them died down again. Since people were so much larger than seeds, she assumed it took a larger wind to lift and scatter them. When a seed landed, it didn't ask why it was there: it put down roots. That was its business. When her children asked her about her life before she came to this country, she waved them off with a spoon. All those things were over. What did they have to do with what was cooking in the pot on her kitchen stove?

Now, in her old age, she had little to do but think. Years passed faster than days, than hours, and her youngest grandson was more than three years old. Late in the afternoon, after the children had come back in and gone into their rooms to do their homework, or were dressing to go out, before it was dark, when a silence fell across the house saying another day had ended, old Mrs. Bravado could hear the tolling of the bells in the little village church. And then she found she could float right out of herself, right out through the windows of her eyes, and from there out through the windows of the house, even if they were shut, and once out, she could float up or down, any way she liked. She would float up, at first no higher than the grey slate steeple of her church, and from there, circling the steeple as if it were a spindle, she would look down on Brooklyn.

From there, she saw that Brooklyn was like a vast anthill with only the sky for a cover. People scurried this way and that on errands, their heads lowered into the cold wind. Here and there, one recognized another, shouted and waved, and scurried on. At street corners, lights flickered and large numbers of the dark, bundled creatures stopped and then started up again, heavy with intention, walking until they reached their own dwellings in the earth into which they disappeared. And how peaceful all of those dwellings looked from above. How naturally the doors opened and took in the people who rang the bells or knocked with their gloved fists. How complete the people seemed, their breaths visible in the cold air, testifying to their existence and the existence of their spirits, which they seemed to breathe out and back in again as if rehearsing for the last time, when the spirit would leave and would not return. How peaceful the houses seemed when the doors opened and closed and the lights of the houses went on and the streets darkened and the house glowed with golden squares, and, seen from outside, the inhabitants seemed to move mazily, as if dancing, mysterious with purpose. From the steeple, they were beautiful. From up there, it was impossible to imagine them anything but happy. From up there they were the very definitions of harmony. Only when someone suddenly advanced to the window and jerkily pulled down a shade did a shadow cross this vision of perfection. All this old Mrs. Bravado saw but could not tell anyone because she did not have the words.

And then she would go up higher, somewhere between the steeple and the moon, or so it seemed to her, and from that height she could see the old cemetery where she and her husband had spent much of their courtship, the beautiful old cemetery, with its small ponds reflecting the moonlight like quicksilver, the hills rolling in small, petrified waves like a tiny sea beneath the moon, the asphalt paths winding moth-colored through them like ribbons, the rabbits running across the fields, then stopping to listen, still as monuments of stone, then running on again, the pheasants calling out, or jerkily walking across the crest of a hill, the chipmunks leaping after one another from branch to branch, the squirrels chittering, and now the ducks were swimming, disturbing the silver surface of the ponds while the dry cattails waved in the night winds and the great old trees held on as the winds rocked them, their roots gripped down deeper, the elephant-skinned trees, the elms and the oaks, surely they had long memories!

Not like her memory, a sieve through which years and countries and hopes and children had fallen, fallen without notice or regret, and even now would only slowly come back to her. And then the light shifted slightly, and as if it had passed through a prism and been divided, she saw only the cemetery's many vines as they would look in summer. She saw the small green vines climbing the tombstones, holding on tight with their strong, frog-shaped hands. She saw the huge, heavy vines swaying from the dead trees, fleshing them out once more, dripping from their dead branches, using the dead tree skeletons to form fantastic designs of their own. She saw the vines climbing living trees and covering their branches and their leaves and finally smothering them, and she saw how it was the will of all living things to pull down all other things, living and dead, to sink them back into the cauldron that was the earth, to sink them back again so that they could be used again, and that life itself had only one purpose, and that was to continue. And it could continue in any shape, human or animal or plant, or in some shape not yet created. The cauldron bubbled and new things thrust upwards and those fought to make a place for themselves in the world, and some of them succeeded. And when she saw this, old Mrs. Bravado floated down, back to the steeple, and thought what a mistake it was to have lived in Brooklyn, what a mistake Brooklyn itself was, a place where you could forget what it meant to be alive or even human. She envied the dead in their coffins, the wood slats of their last houses fighting against the iron hands of the vines trying to get in to seize the old bones and put them to one more use. Whether the dead slept or whether they dreamed, whether they lay senseless as any rock or log, they were still part of the struggle. And then she would feel cold and she would wake in her rocker, a purple and rose knitted afghan tucked under her chin.

She supposed she would die soon. She supposed that was the meaning of her trips in and out through the windows of her basement apartment. She would die without again speaking to her son, and when she was dead, her son would try to put Paul, the retarded child, not even four, into a home. So she talked to her daughter, Theresa, and asked her to try and prevent it. "Ma!" Theresa said. "You're not dying! You're healthy as a horse. The doctor says so. And who can do anything about George? I can't do anything about him."

"Try," she said and turned her attention to Pete. "He's pale, he's skinny, and he doesn't grow. He's not happy. He storms through the house and he bangs doors. Yesterday, he cut his hand and he said a window broke when he closed it. He wasn't closing a window. He put his hand through it. But," she said, striking her chest, "he's going to be fine. I know it *here.*"

About Pete, Theresa kept her own counsel. She knew that after work he would sometimes leave the house silently. He didn't wear a jacket and he slipped a piece of wood between the door and the lock so he could get back in without a key. She suspected he did more than walk when he went out at night, but she said nothing to anyone. The boy's anger was alive. It had an existence almost independent of him. At times she thought she could reach out and touch it. So much anger: surely not even her brother had created so much anger.

"Have a heart!" she'd hear Pete say. "One lousy night off! One night to go bowling with my friends!!"

"You don't need friends," said his father.

"He can learn a trade next year!" said Angelina. "He's not even eleven!"

"Get ready," George told his son.

"What about Ma's black eye? What about the marks on her arm? Don't touch my mother!"

"Look who's threatening me," said his father, pretending to laugh, but when the boy threatened him, Theresa could see fear in George's eyes.

"You tell him," old Mrs. Bravado told Theresa, "you tell him I said he's a good boy and in the end he'll be happy. Not like that sourpuss of a son! Not like that ingrate upstairs!"

"Ma," said Theresa, "no more talk about dying. Why do you want to aggravate me? What did I do?"

"You didn't do anything. You're a good girl," the old woman said, picturing herself between the moon and the steeple, watching the thick limb of the elm tree crack and fall beneath the weight of the black vine. "But you tell him. I can see it. I can see him happy. What you see before you close your eyes for the last time is always true."

"Ma!" said her daughter.

Because she died believing that her grandson would someday grow up and be happy, Pete Bravado believed that, too. If, from time to time, sometimes for as long as years, he forgot he believed it, that belief would someday flicker deep within him, joined, finally, with the flame that created life and kept it going. Many years later, when it seemed to him that all the lights in the world had gone out, he would sense that spark and he would not lie down in the cold and fall asleep. When she died, old Mrs. Bravado believed she would never really cease to live until her grandson had also ceased living, and because she saw him as the living tree on whose frame she could entwine her spirit without doing harm to either of them, she died happy.

For a time, it seemed as if she had taken the family happiness with her, and the family priest, Father D'Angelo, said later that he had never seen a more miserable gathering. He didn't mean unhappy. He meant *miserable*. "A gang of people in black under a grey sky and a black rain crying down and all of them turning their faces away from one another. I never saw anything like it." His mother, whom he was visiting for lunch, said it was not his fault and there was nothing he could do about it. "And the last dirt hadn't hit the grave, the light was still shining in on her roof, when that blasted ox of a son asked me for advice about where to send his son." His mother shook her head and heaped his plate with sausages. "These things can kill you," he said to his mother, who shook her head, as if to say, time or sausages, what difference does it make? "She said he'd go to a home over her dead body and that's how he's going to go," said the priest.

"God made him an ass," said his mother, "so don't be surprised if he acts like one."

"He made himself, Mother, he made himself. He doesn't have ears and a tail. He can choose to be some other way."

"If that's what they teach you," said his mother.

"That's what the Church teaches," said her son, dropping his fork. "The Church teaches the Lord gave us free will. He can choose to love God and his fellow man."

"That's all very well," said his mother, "but if they're asses as children, they're asses as young men, and when they die, they're old asses."

"And will God love an ass in the shape of a man?" asked her son.

"God will do what He pleases because He is God."

"There's more to it than that," said the priest. "There's a mystery in character. Some will grow away from the sun and others will be in the dark and grow straight up toward it."

"You see more people than I do," said his mother.

"Fighting over the grave! The wife telling her husband he'd killed his own mother! The daughter saying she was glad the mother wasn't alive to see this! The poor little slant-eyed boy, not much past three, smiling at everyone, not knowing he was the cause of the trouble. That little Pete glaring at his father. And then one of the nuns coming into my office later and telling me someone's been breaking windows in the school at night and from her window she saw someone who looked like Pete Bravado. The family's going to hell in a barrel."

"Watch your language," his mother said automatically. "I don't know," she said at last. "I don't. But she was a fine old woman. You can't tell where the glue that holds the legs onto the table comes from until it's gone."

"She was a fine old woman, but I don't know if she took her faith with her to the grave. Some of the things she would tell me the weeks before she died! She thought she could fly up and see everywhere and she didn't see that human beings were better than anything else on the face of the earth."

"God created everything on earth and found it good," said his mother.

"But He created man *in His own image!*" thundered the priest. "'*In His own image*'! Can't anyone understand the meaning of those words?"

"You'll choke," said his mother, who had her own views on this subject. God may have created man in His own image, but man was not God. Man was not perfect. And so, on the whole, she tended to agree with old Mrs. Bravado, and she couldn't see why humans were superior to any other living things either. "*Mange!*" she told her son. "God likes a fat priest!" Her son shook his head and swallowed. She watched him eat. To her, why people had any character at all was a mystery. But he would be back in that cold stone church soon enough, everyone talking to him through a little door in the wall. Why should she bother him with her silly opinions?

Two weeks later, on one of the first fine days of spring, Father D'Angelo and two policemen, one elderly, one young, stood outside the Bravado house.

"It's a pity to go inside," said the priest.

"Let's get it over with," said the elder policeman.

"*My* son?" Angelina asked, when she heard the news. "My son?"

"We have to take him in," said the elder policeman. "He did thousands of dollars' worth of damage."

"He beat up a *school?*" Theresa asked incredulously.

"Vandalized, ma'am," the policeman said politely.

"Not my son," said Angelina.

"Don't cry," Theresa said.

"If you'd get him," said the older policeman. The younger one shifted from foot to foot.

"He's still in school," said Angelina.

"He's not in school, and one of the neighbors saw him come in through the back door," said the priest.

"I'll look in his room," said Angelina, who left and came back with Pete.

"He did a lot of damage for his size," the young policeman said.

"They don't stay small," the old policeman said. He handed Angelina a large, official-looking document. "He's got to come with us now, but you've got to bring him in tomorrow morning. Juvenile court."

Angelina's white face flushed suddenly and she shook her fist at her son. "Court!" she shouted. "Who can help you now?"

"I'll go with him," said Father D'Angelo. "When he's done, I'll bring him back. Talk to his father. If we're lucky, the judge will send him upstate to the Catholic School for Delinquent Boys."

"Delinquent boys!" his mother shouted at her son, her face still red.

"Let's go," said the old policeman.

ON THEIR WAY to the police station, Father D'Angelo asked Pete if he was sorry. The child thought for some time and then said he was sorry the church would have to spend money for new windows and he was sorry he'd broken so many desks. Would his father have to pay for the damage? No? That was good, because otherwise his mother would suffer.

Why did he do it? the priest asked him. Didn't he like the school? Pete said he liked the school. It didn't have anything to do with liking or not liking the school, but sometimes, when he was walking at night, he'd pass the school and he'd look in a window and there were the desks, lined up in rows, the chairs upended on top of them, their legs sticking up in the air, and he had to get inside, and the doors were locked, and the only way in was through a window, so he'd break one and then he'd be in, and for a long time, that was all he did, go in and sit at a desk in the dark until he got sleepy and then he'd go home and go to bed.

He didn't know why he'd started smashing windows and breaking up the desks. He didn't know he was strong enough to break a desk. The first time he did it, it surprised him, how strong he was, and then he wanted to see what his strength would do, and while he was breaking desks, he saw Paul's face as his mother dressed him in his snowsuit while his father waited outside in the car, waiting to take him to the home on Staten Island, and before the car pulled away from the curb, he'd vaulted over the windowsill in the kitchen and run toward the school. The school was closed and he broke a window and climbed into the classroom. He picked up an upended chair, placed it upright in front of a desk, and sat down, his head on the desk, sobbing.

Did he feel glad he'd broken the desks? asked the priest. No, he didn't feel glad; he felt peaceful. He would sit in the middle of the shattered wood and chrome and feel peaceful and quiet and for once the school belonged to him and he belonged to the school and of course he would cry and then he would get up and go home before anyone could find him. He was surprised someone recognized him. The priest asked him if he would do it again, and the boy thought, and said he didn't know if he would because he didn't know why he'd done it at all, so it was possible he could do it again. He would try not to do it again, but he couldn't promise.

And if they send you to reform school? asked the priest. What then? Won't you miss your family? He said he'd miss his mother and maybe his aunt, but he missed his brother Paul and his grandmother even when he was home, and his other brothers were much older and weren't home much anyhow. And your father? asked the priest.

"I won't miss my father and he won't miss me. It'll be easier for him when I'm out of the house. Now he'll have to pay Vinnie to help on the weekend *and* during the week." He said this with satisfaction.

"Your grandmother had a high opinion of you," the priest said, and before his eyes, the boy's face changed. Under the dirt and grime, there was a handsome young man with intelligent eyes, even a great sense of fun.

"Well, she wouldn't now," the boy said, his face darkening. "Anyway, she doesn't care. She's dead."

"She said you were the family's special child," said the priest.

"She was old," said the boy.

"But was she right?"

"Look where I'm sitting," said the boy.

"You can be on the gallows and still be special. You can be nailed to wood and still be special," said Father D'Angelo.

"I'm not that ambitious," said the boy, and in spite of himself, the priest laughed.

The next day, the judge, considering the child's age, sentenced him to nine months in the Catholic School for Delinquent Boys.

"You're lucky," said his mother.

"You don't know how lucky you are," said his father.

"How lucky am I?" he asked the priest, who was driving him up to the school.

"You're very lucky. You're in the country. They have an indoor pool, tennis courts, basketball, you name it. You get up early, go to classes, eat supper, write letters to your parents, and study until nine o'clock when they shut out the lights." The boy nodded as if to say that was all right with him. "And if you get out of hand, you bend over the pool table with your pants down and they lay into you with the pool cue."

"Pool cue?" asked the boy.

"They'll break you if they have to," said the priest. "They'll break you a lot faster than you'd break a desk."

9 **N**OW, WHEN George Bravado came home at night, the house was quiet. As he sat in the kitchen, eating his dinner, his wife sitting across from him, watching him, he remembered his mother telling him that he'd die alone. That would be his punishment for his sins. His sister brought up a bankbook she found in their mother's top drawer and gave it to him. The old lady had saved two thousand dollars. "I don't know what she wanted it for," Theresa said, handing it to him, "but it was important. Every penny, every nickel she put into that account."

"You take the money," he said.

"No," his sister said. "She lived in your house. She ate your food."

"She doesn't have to pay me back," George said.

"Take it," Theresa said. "I don't want it. Keep it for Pete."

"What's he need money for?" asked his father. "If he needs anything at the school, they buy it for him."

"Generous as ever," said his sister, handing the book to him.

He had the book, he filed the papers, and eventually, the bank gave him the money. He didn't know why, but when the money was handed over to him, he felt guilty about taking it. Who deserved it more? As long as his mother lived, he'd supported her. He deposited the money in his own account, and from the instant the teller came back with his bankbook and its new total, he began thinking about his father. He saw him sawing two-by-fours in a neighborhood backyard, ready to replace the supports for a grey, shingled back porch. He saw him talking to the women in the house. He saw him sitting in the living room, reading a book. And whenever his father looked up and saw him, he shook his head as if in disapproval. He knew he had to spend the money or he'd soon look up and see his mother and his father scowling at him from the corner of his bedroom. But what was he going to do with it? Lately, he had more money than he needed. He could buy some land in the country and start to build a house, and he'd still have more money than he needed.

"We ought to go to Italy," he told Angelina. "You know, visit the old village. Honor the memory of the old folks."

"Why Italy?" Angelina asked suspiciously. "You never wanted to go before."

"Well, I do now," he said. "I remembered the name of the town Pop came from. I found it on the map."

"How long do you want to go for?" Angelina asked. "Not for more than a week. Not while Pete's in that school."

"Sure, no more than a week," her husband said.

"And when we come back, I want a dog," Angelina said. "Someone broke into Mrs. Lugano's."

"Yeah? When?"

"Last week or the week before," Angelina said, waving her hand.

"You walk it, you can have it," her husband said.

"You won't touch it. You won't beat it. It's mine," Angelina said.

"It's yours," agreed her husband. "You walk it. You take care of it."

"We have an agreement?" asked his wife. "I go to Italy, I get the dog?"

"You get the dog," he said.

"Swear," she said.

"All right, Angelina," he said. "Enough!"

"All of a sudden he wants to go to Italy," Angelina said, thinking, Now when Pete comes back, I'll have a puppy. The dog will belong to him. He'll have something of his own.

"So?" shouted her husband. "I'm Italian! Where should I want to go? Germany?"

THE PLANE took off and headed into clouds. From the plane window, they could see nothing. The plane's engines hummed steadily, and Angelina peered out the window, trying to see something, anything, clutching the arms of her chair until her knuckles were white. Her husband stared straight ahead, saying nothing.

"We should have stayed home," he said after a while.

"Oh, yeah?" said Angelina. "Why?"

"Even if we get there, who's going to believe it?" George said. "In here, it sounds like a car going through the Battery Tunnel. How do we know we're going anyplace? We could be standing still and we'd never know it."

"That's because you can't see out the window," said Angelina.

"No," said her husband. "Even if I could, how'd I know it wasn't a fake? It could be painted on paper. How do you know any of it's real?"

"Who asks questions like that?" Angelina asked.

"And even if we get there, and they're poor and sick and dirty, how do we know they're in Italy? It could be Brooklyn."

"Not if there are mountains," Angelina said.

"We could be flying around and around the neighborhood. We could land in the Catskills."

"The government wouldn't allow it," his wife said. "If there weren't other countries, there wouldn't be a United Nations."

"So that's how you know the rest of the world exists? It's no use talking to you."

"And you're making sense?" asked his wife.

T H E Catholic School for Delinquent Boys was a large grey stone building in the mountains of upstate New York. The younger boys lived together in a large stone building. On the first floor were their classrooms. On the second were the dormitories, large, high-ceilinged rooms whose great windows were fly-specked, uncurtained, and secured by metal gratings so that, in certain lights, the windows resembled huge waffle irons. There were three rows of narrow iron cots, one against each wall, and one down the middle of the room.

Father D'Angelo took Pete in to see the head of the school, an old friend of his from the seminary, whom the boys called Father Gabriel. "When you're finished here, you'll have paid your debt to society," Father Gabriel told Pete, and Pete answered that he was ready to do his time. The two men looked at one another and raised their eyebrows. "And don't worry about being lonely," said Father Gabriel. "You'll be too busy."

The first night, Pete, sitting on the edge of his cot, looked around him and saw nothing familiar. He looked at the boys undressing on their cots and saw he was the smallest boy there. Would he be beaten up? What would the brothers who ran the school do to him if he didn't pass his courses? It had been a long time since he'd gotten passing grades. Who could he tell here about his brother, who now lived in a home, too small to understand why he was no longer in his own house? Who would tell him if anything happened to the child? How would he know if something happened to his parents? He looked at his watch. Nine o'clock. His father was pulling into the driveway, and his mother was sighing, getting up from the couch, turning off the television, rubbing her eyes, and taking his dinner from the oven to heat it up on top of the stove. He missed all of them. He wanted to be back there. He wanted to see his brother when his mother brought him home for weekends. He wanted to go with her when she visited him in the home on Staten Island, and instead he was locked up here.

He was in a room full of people, none of whom he knew. He was here because he'd broken windows, but who knew what they'd done. They could be murderers. Someone might get up in the middle of the night while he was sleeping, jump on him, and begin to strangle him. He'd keep his eyes open. He'd stay up all night. He turned on his side and looked down the aisles of beds, watching. Eventually, his eyes began closing and he knew he'd have to sleep. He conjured up the picture on his wall at home, the little boat making its way through the waves, the little village looking down over

the fields out to the sea. He closed his eyes and thought about the picture
until he could see it, and then he imagined himself safe under the glass,
climbing toward the whitewashed house at the top of the mountain slope.
He was still climbing when he fell asleep.

A siren woke them at five the next morning, and after they were herded
in and out of the showers, they were told to sit down and write to their
parents. Then they were marched off to the dining hall where they stood on
line waiting for cold scrambled eggs, cold, greasy bacon, unbuttered rolls,
and jugs of milk. He sat down at a table, and a fat boy sat down next to him.
Pete took a few bites of the eggs and slipped the roll in his pocket. The fat
boy pulled Pete's tray over toward him and shoveled the food from Pete's
onto his own. "You mind?" he asked Pete, grinning meanly. Pete looked at
him and said nothing. On the way back to the dormitory, the boy in front of
him slowed down suddenly and Pete bumped into him. "You hit me," he
whispered. "Wait until we get back there. Then you're in for it," and without
thinking, Pete threw himself at him, and it took two of the brothers to
separate them. The two of them spent the rest of the day in the school's
large barn, shoveling it out.

"You're not bad," the other boy told him. "What are you in for?"

"Attacking a school," Pete said.

"Yeah?" said the boy. "I'm in for hitting a nun. Sister Angela, she hauled
off and hit me for no reason so I hauled off and hit her back. I knocked her
right down."

"You hit a nun?" Pete asked.

"Well, that's not all I did," the boy said. "So what's your name? My
name's Bruno."

By the time they got back to the dormitory, they were on good terms. By
the end of the week, Bruno, by arranging several fights and making several
threats, had the bunk next to Pete. He'd sit on the edge of Pete's bed while
Pete did his homework and when he had a problem, he handed his book
over and Pete would finish for him. After a month, Father Gabriel called
Pete into the office and said he was surprised, everyone was surprised, by
how well he was doing.

"Hey, I'm surprised," Pete said.

Pete was spending a lot of time at the pool and had a talent for diving.
"You're so small," said the coach, "you go into the water like a knife."

"You know, if you win the meet," Bruno told him, "the whole school gets
ice cream. Whenever the school wins in a competition, we get ice cream and
a movie."

"Yeah?" Pete asked. "Then I'm gonna win."

"You don't get lonely?" Bruno asked him. "You're supposed to get lonely.
We're here to suffer. That's what they told me. *This time you're going
to suffer, not us.*"

"I'm not suffering," Pete said. And he wasn't. During study hall, when he finished his work, he looked across the cold grey room at the other boys, most of whom were doodling, or whispering to one another. A bed was empty. Someone said a boy was in the infirmary because his hair started falling out, and the doctors said it was nerves. The boy missed his family.

Pete, however, was happy. In the morning, he wrote letters to his family. He did his homework. He went to swim practice. When his grades were good, the brothers congratulated him. If he was late for practice, they cracked him across the palm of his hand with a ruler. Everything was predictable. Everything made sense. Then he won his first diving competition and after dinner, the brothers came through the dining room. Everyone got a Melloroll for desert. Here, they made good on their promises.

They made good the next day, too, when Pete, puffed up by his victories, decided to sleep late, and he and Bruno, who had once again not done his homework, found themselves in the stable, cleaning out the stalls.

"Hell, I'm sick of this," Bruno said.

"Why?" Pete asked. "It's good, honest work."

"What are you so happy about? You're not supposed to be happy here."

"Yeah, well, here I feel good," Pete said.

"*Here* you feel good?"

"Yeah. At home, I didn't do anything, and my father, he looked at me like a criminal. I must have done something. You get punished, you've done something."

"So what did you do?"

"I don't know," Pete said. "Maybe I don't remember." At night, when he said his prayers, he asked to be forgiven for what he had done and whatever else he might have done that he didn't remember. When he made his confession, he asked to be forgiven for all the sins he knew he'd committed and any he might have committed. Father D'Angelo, hearing this for the third, and then the fourth time, said, "God expects you to be responsible for what you've done, not for the whole world."

"So what did your father do to you?" Bruno asked.

"He hates me, that's all," Pete said.

"He hits you, what?" Bruno asked.

"No, he doesn't hit me."

"And you're complaining?" Bruno asked, astonished. "See this?" He rolled up his sleeves. Right below his right elbow was a two-inch, jagged angry red scar. "He pushed me down on top of the stove and held me there. I smelled like a pork chop. I was *cooking*. So if he doesn't hit you, what does he do?"

"He looks at me like I'm a bug," Pete said. I'm afraid of him, Pete thought. I've always been afraid of him. He couldn't remember a time when he hadn't been afraid.

"So? Looks don't kill," Bruno said.

"Yeah, but I always feel bad. Like I did something."

"So? When you go home, you'll be clean. You paid your time. He looks at you, look at him. Start over. That's what's good about this place. You go home, they think you're a new man. Well, for about a week, they think that."

"Yeah?"

"Sure. You'll see," Bruno said. Pete nodded. Maybe he was right. He'd broken the windows and the desks at school. That was something to feel guilty about. That was something to be punished for, and he was being punished, because even though he liked it here, he wanted to be home. Finally, everything made sense. He'd done something wrong. That was why he felt guilty. That was why he was here. When he'd finished his nine months, he'd go home and his father would no longer look at him as if to say, You may be pulling the wool over everyone else's eyes but *I* know who you are. From now on, he and his father would get along. From now on, his father would like him. From now on, when he looked at his father he would not feel sickened by fear. Tears filled his eyes when he thought about coming home, seeing his father, standing in the doorway, smiling to see him. He would come home *cleansed.*

One afternoon, Father Gabriel called him into the office and asked him if he was sorry now that he'd vandalized the school.

"No," he said. "I was full of sin before and I didn't know why. Now I can confess and do penance."

"I don't understand," said the priest.

"I can't explain it," said Pete.

"Sometimes," the priest said, "we believe that if we're being punished, we must have done something wrong. Sometimes, if we're accused of stealing, we think we might as well steal. We think if we're being punished, we might as well have the fun of committing the crime. Is that why you broke the windows?"

"I guess so," said Pete.

"If someone accuses you of committing a crime, and you've done nothing, the fault is his, not yours," said the priest.

"I guess so," said Pete.

"You have to believe in yourself," said the priest.

"That's a good idea," said Pete. When he got home, his father would listen to him. He'd talk to his father about his brother and his father might let Paul come home.

"You're a good boy," the priest told him. He watched him leave, went to the window, and watched the boy cross the snowy field to the dormitory. How much could you do? Some of them came here, began to work, became decent people, and you knew when you sent them back to their families, it had all been useless. Sometimes, however, you beat the odds. You never knew.

In the dormitory, Pete worked on a story for his English class, a story about people who lived in a small town on the side of a mountain, looking out to sea, waiting for the small boat that would bring them what it was they had always wanted. He didn't know yet what it was they did want, but he was sure he would by the time he got to the end of the story. First he had to figure out how he was going to free the little ship from the spell it was under, the spell that nailed it to the water and prevented it from moving. When he was finished, he went to the printing shop and watched Bruno work.

"This here's a California box," Bruno said, "and this stuff, it's the font."

He watched Bruno set the type, lock it in place, ink the galley, and press the paper against the type surface with a roller. "Hey, you finish your story, I'll print it," Bruno said.

"Let me see that," Pete said, taking the page and staring at it.

"Not bad, huh?" Bruno asked. "O.K., give it back." He looked up and saw Pete still staring at the sheet of paper. "O.K., so keep it. I'll do another," he said.

Pete breathed in the smell of oil and printer's ink. The room was long and narrow and high, and under the rough wood rafters, two or three pigeons cooed. In the school, people treated him well. Everyone was pleased with his progress. But he wanted to go home. He closed his eyes and saw the pattern of cabbage roses on the living room wall. In the kitchen, his mother was slicing the noodle dough and hanging the noodles from the curtain rods. His father was holding his report card up to the light, frowning. He put the report card down on the table, looked at it again, and tore it up. Pete fought down the rage that rose in his stomach. He looked around the room, listened to the presses clatter. He was here to fix things. Sometimes you had to go far away to fix things. When he got home, everything would be changed.

But that night, when the fat boy who sat next to him pulled his tray away, Pete said something to him, he didn't know what, the boy said something to him, and the next thing he knew, he was hitting the boy over the head with a tray. He spent the next two weeks working in the stables or sitting in Father Gabriel's office when the rest of the school went sledding on the grounds.

"What happened?" Father Gabriel asked him. "You want to tell me what happened?"

"I don't know," Pete said. What was he supposed to say? That in the middle of the cabbage roses his father was ripping up the report card?

· · ·

A F T E R   A   L O N G , hot ride in an old car, George and Angelina found themselves looking down a narrow mountain road at old Mr. Bravado's village.
The driver said he'd wait for them until they were finished visiting. It was
unbearably hot and the road, a narrow ribbon, shimmered in the high heat.
George and Angelina climbed down toward the village. They spoke only
household Italian and didn't expect to stay long.

It was almost four in the afternoon when they reached the town. The
sunlight stunned the whitewashed walls. Their shadows were long and
thin before them. From the small houses, people began coming out, some of
them rubbing their eyes as if they'd just awakened. People saw them, smiled
and nodded. "America?" asked one woman, and when they nodded, she
clapped her hands happily, pointed at herself, said her name and pointed
at them.

"Bravado," said Angelina.

"Oh, Bravado!" cried the old woman, and caught hold of Angelina's
wrist.

They followed the woman to a large whitewashed building and went
inside. Inside the thick walls, it was cool and dark, and a mule walked
around and around a huge vat, causing the stone wheel inside the vat to
rotate and press down on the vat's contents.

"Wine," said George.

"No, no vino," said the woman, pointing to a large basket filled with
huge green olives.

"Olives!" said Angelina. "They're making olive oil. Your poppa used to
talk about it. They put it in big urns. Look, there they are! Now you believe
you're here?"

But he didn't. He expected to see misery and sickness, poverty and dirt,
but the people here seemed happy and healthy. They left the buildings and,
as they walked through the village, the women in long dark skirts and
shawls waved and smiled happily at them. When they stopped in front of a
small house, a woman came out and offered them bread dipped in olive oil
and a cup of cold water. "Don't drink it," he told Angelina. "Who knows what
the sanitation's like here?" But she drank the water happily. Bread and
olive oil. She'd forgotten how good it was.

The white goats, some fastened to trees, some free, shone like angels in
the sun. Black and white dogs chased one another and lay down in the
shade. Roosters, their heads bronze and red, clucked back and forth beneath
the overhanging roofs. Here and there, a rooster copulated with a hen.
Overhead, a bird circled lazily in the air.

Eventually, they came to the church, and the priest, his long black
robes flowing, the silver crucifix on his chest sun-struck and blinding,

came toward them, welcoming. "Bravado?" he said, and he led them to the cemetery and pointed at the stones bearing George's last name. "I remember your father and grandfather," he said in halting English. "Very well." They bent over the pitted stones and read the names: Pietro Bravado, Salvatore, Rosario, Mario. So it was true. Once the Bravado family had lived here.

They went back into the church with the priest and Angelina lit two candles, one for old Mr. Bravado and one for old Mrs. Bravado. She knelt down and prayed while her husband watched her. Finally, he knelt down also. It was cool in the church, and peaceful, as if the peace in the village had its source here.

Outside, the women were visiting from house to house, talking loudly, throwing back their heads and laughing. One of them held an olive up for inspection and the women looked at it and roared with laughter.

"You know what?" said Angelina. "I think it's better here. Look how happy everyone is."

"We look happy to them," George said. "Here there are droughts. They have famines. It's a hard life."

"They look happy to me," Angelina said stubbornly.

To George, they looked happy, too. How was this possible? He'd expected to come here and find the reason he worked day and night in Brooklyn. He'd expected to come here and find out why he was lucky to live in America, not in a backward, dirty village. If they were so happy, why had his father left? Here, there were no traffic lights, no cars, no parking spaces, no televisions. How did they know what went on in the rest of the world? For all they knew, this could be the thirteenth century. They would live and die here, just as he would live and die in Brooklyn. What was the difference? Their world was complete. They had everything they needed in it. This was what he got for using his mother's money. This was how she got her revenge. Even from her grave, she confused him, made him think he could do nothing right.

"What are we doing here?" he asked his wife. "You want heat? It's hot in Brooklyn. You want flies? There are flies in Brooklyn. We had to cross an ocean to fry ourselves to death? There are chickens and goats home, too. There are cans of olive oil in the store."

Angelina said nothing. When they went to Cape Cod, he said the same thing. A beach was a beach. They had to drive all the way to Massachusetts to see sand and water when they could walk five blocks and see the same thing and be home in time for dinner? She would have liked to take some pictures to bring back to the family. She could make copies and send some to Pete, away at school, but she knew better than to ask her husband to take out the camera and show her how to use it. "So," said Angelina, "you want to go home?" She was ready to leave. She missed her sons. Who knew what was happening to them, the one in the home, the one in reform school?

"Yeah," George said. "This place doesn't mean anything to me."

The flight home was longer and more silent than the flight over. Angelina looked at George, who stared straight ahead and said nothing, but it seemed to her that he was a sadder man than the one who had come, sadder and more confused.

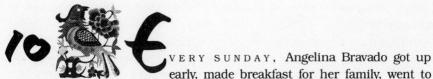

10 EVERY SUNDAY, Angelina Bravado got up early, made breakfast for her family, went to early mass, and took three buses and a ferry to visit her youngest son, Paul. As the ferry crossed the bay and she felt it begin to move with the rhythm of the waves, as the skyline of the city she left began to fade behind her, she found herself thinking of older times. She remembered the Lower East Side and waiting alone in her room until her parents returned from work, and when they called to her from downstairs, she would wrap the key in a rag and throw it down to them.

When the city was eaten entirely by the mists rising from the bay, she would find herself thinking of her father-in-law, and she would remember how he and her son Pete, now in a reform school upstate, would set out in the mornings for Sheepshead Bay. Parts of stories would come back to her, stories she was unaware of being told, of men whose friendship was so great it could surmount anything, even kings and death, of lovers circling the earth in mists like the one which hid the buildings of New York from her.

Her grey wool coat was warm, and the red woolen scarf and gloves Theresa had knitted for her were warmer, but she shivered in her clothes. She remembered her friend coming unexpectedly to the house one morning, asking her to go with her to work as a waitress at a hotel in the mountains, and on impulse, saying she would go. She remembered going to ask her mother for permission (she had forgotten that at her age she still needed permission), and how her mother looked her up and down, shook her head, and said, "So fast, out of the hot pot into the fire?"

"You want to go?" her father asked her. "You're bored?"

She blushed, and her father saw it was true, and they drove her to the hotel, helped her unpack her bags in the big barrackslike room where the female help stayed, while her father pointed out the scorch marks on the ceiling and said, "There was a fire here. You take a bed near the window or the door."

"There was no fire!" she said, eager to be rid of them, but after they were gone, she heard terrible stories of the fire that had, that winter, killed two waitresses and one of their children. "The flames leaped so high you could see them over the mountain," the groundskeeper told her. "The fire engines were here before we knew there was anything doing. In the winter, people sleep the sleep of the dead." He walked off singing, "I'll buy for you a paper of pins, a paper of pins, I'll buy for you a paper of pins, if you will marry me." She had always intended to ask her mother what the verses of that song meant. What was a paper of pins? Why would someone want it enough to get married?

That morning, as she got ready to visit her son, Angelina looked in the mirror and had a common enough experience. Instead of her own face, she saw the older face of another woman, but she didn't see the face of her own mother. No, she saw the face of old Mrs. Bravado. As she grew older, she was coming to look more and more like her husband's mother! Her face was round and doughy and her glittering black stones of eyes were sinking deeper into her puffy white flesh. The cheerfulness which once struck everyone, the senseless good humor, that was going too. Like old Mrs. Bravado's in the last years of her life, her face was shadowed. Hugging herself against the chill mist, Angelina was saddened by the feel of her thickened, fleshy body beneath its stiff corset, almost the same corset her mother-in-law used to wear; her breasts sloped down at a gentle angle, stopped abruptly where they met what was left of her waist, and her stomach was a flat, stony place, and when she sat down wearing her corset, she had no lap, nothing soft but her thighs, and it was across them her nieces and nephews lay. She thought she could see her womb shrinking. She thought she knew what it looked like, grey and hard, like a tiny brain turned to stone, and she remembered how she used to think of it, a blood-red sun that grew inside her, pushing at the lining of her stomach, filling her with light, at times convincing her that her body glowed in the dark, and on cold nights, she pulled back the sheets to see if it was true.

No more of that now. Her last son, her last *child,* was in a home on Staten Island and she had begun her long fight to bring him home for the holidays. She would win this fight, she thought, walking from the side of the ferry facing the city to the side facing the island, which had not yet come into view. The child would come home for Thanksgiving. All right, so he was not so intelligent as other children, but soon she would be able to give him a dollar and send him to the store for bread and milk. In the beginning, she used to send Pete to stand outside the store and watch him. You never knew what people would do to someone who didn't know any better, and later she would let the boy go alone, and when he came back with the long loaf of bread sticking out of the brown bag, the bottle of milk clasped tightly in his arms, she'd take the bag from him and shout, "Where's the change? Give me the change!" And he'd take the change from his pocket and hold it out in the palm of his hand, and she'd count it as it lay in his hand: twenty-five cents, thirty cents, forty, fifty, fifty-five! Very good!

And he had such a smile, he would be so proud of having done it right, had anyone ever seen a more wonderful smile, a more pure smile? It shone right into all the dark places. It lit them up. And behind her son Paul, her short and fat son, Paul, whose eyes slanted so oddly, her son Pete stood, smiling his heart out. She knew Pete would never leave, never get in trouble, not with his brother Paul to care for, but now Pete was gone, too, not forever, but for nine months in a reform school in upstate New York, and every day, or every other day, she got a letter from him saying how hard he was studying, and how the fathers were teaching him to swim, and how good he was at it, and how he was learning to dive, and he was even better at that because he was so small, he cut like a knife into the water, and his grades were so good everyone was surprised. And every letter closed the same way. "Don't worry, Ma. I like it here." The last note from the school priest said this: "Your son's grades are excellent. He is very cooperative and no longer gets into fights." Fights? Had he ever gotten into fights? What did he have to fight about?

If he fought, he could ruin that face. "That face is too beautiful for a boy!" old Mrs. Bravado used to shout at him. "You devil! You think you can look at me with those eyes and I'll give you anything! Eyebrows like that belong on a girl, don't they, Angelina? Even my son doesn't have eyebrows like that. And that straight nose! Put down that cookie! It's not baked! Devil! Devil!" And the old lady, rolling pin held high, would chase her grandson around the kitchen and out of the room. But he'd sneak back in as soon as he thought the women weren't watching. "Tell me, what's so good about unbaked cookie dough?" old Mrs. Bravado asked, and Angelina, who could hear her voice as if she were standing on the ferry with her, laughed.

If the old woman were alive, she'd tell her what she saw when she tried to summon up a picture of Pete. It wasn't like summoning up a picture of Paul: she saw him in the great barracks they called his room, sitting on his little cot near the end of a long line of cots going down one side of an aisle, overweight, smiling to himself, looking at the brightly colored book he'd been given, or the envelope full of pictures he'd brought from home. She saw him as he was. But when she thought of Pete, a picture jumped into her mind: she saw a black silhouette of a child against the ragged edge of a piney wood and as she watched, the silhouette grew smaller and she knew it was because the child was moving closer and closer to the wood line and soon he would disappear into the trees and then she would be left staring at the jagged outline of trees, black against the indigo sky, while overhead stars like rock salt glittered with an inhuman light. Who else could she tell what she saw but old Mrs. Bravado? And now old Mrs. Bravado was gone too.

They were getting ready to dock. The engines strained and reversed. The boat began to heave in the water. Dark thoughts, Angelina knew, were not in her nature. Pete would be home in January, in time to start the second semester at the Catholic school. Paul would come home for Labor Day and Christmas and Thanksgiving and on all other holidays because she had decided he would. If her husband didn't agree, she'd move downstairs with Theresa. What worked once would work twice. For her husband, she had put Paul in the home. But she would not leave him there, forgotten, as if he'd never had a mother or a father. On the ward, her son would be waiting for her, and she would take him for a walk around the island, up and down the steeply sloping streets, out to the water to watch the boats, and she would buy him as many ice cream cones as he wanted. So what if he was fat? No one was taking pictures of him for the Sunday papers.

The puppy she'd bought when they came home from Italy was housebroken. Both boys would love to play with him. So far the puppy had no name. She was waiting for Pete to come home. He'd name the dog and the dog would belong to him.

How quickly Sundays passed and how she cried as the ferry made its slow way through the water, reddening her eyes and swelling her lids, but by the time she took the three buses home, she was smiling as if nothing had happened. Her husband had sent her son away. Now he belonged only to her. Now her sorrow belonged only to her. For the first time, she thought bitterly, she had something of her own.

Three nights before Labor Day, she and Theresa went to the home and brought Paul back with them. After they put the boy to bed, they went into the kitchen and began cooking spaghetti and sweet sausages and Italian cheesecake and hard cookies studded with hazelnuts and packed the food into special plastic containers they'd borrowed from the next-door neighbor ("Airtight. It never spoils," said Helena Ruggiero. "This is how you burp the lids to keep the air out."). In the morning, Angelina was waiting for the post office to open, several dollar bills folded and folded again, until they were tiny, fat green squares. She was the first one in, the first one in front of the unopened grille at the parcel post window. "I want to send these to my son," she said when the window opened and a man's face appeared. "Special delivery!"

"We all thought the food was very good," Pete wrote. "Don't worry, Ma. I'm happy here."

Did he get to eat any of it himself, Angelina wondered, or did the older, bigger boys take it away from him? Was he getting into more fights? The last letter from the priest didn't say he wasn't. Was he forgetting them at school? Thanksgiving wasn't so far away, and after Thanksgiving, it wouldn't be long before he was home. She wasn't sorry Pete wouldn't be there for Thanksgiving. Christmas would be soon enough for him to hear his father shout, "Don't give Paul so much! He's too fat! Don't make him fatter!" Christmas would be soon enough for him to see his brother pick up his fork, look at his father like a frightened dog, move the fork closer to the pork chops, look again at his father, and, encouraged by the nods of everyone else at the table, finally start to eat while her husband glared and they all tried to swallow, their stomachs knotted, their chests tight.

Pete came home taller, with a report card that should have been, according to the priest, framed. His mother looked at it, smiled to herself, and sat down in old Mrs. Bravado's rocker, still looking at it, saying nothing. His father came home, picked up the card from the kitchen counter where Angelina had just put it down, looked at it, dropped it again, and told the boy to change into his work clothes.

Pete awakened the next morning and found he had slipped into the old ways as easily as a stone slips into water. His father still looked at him as if to say, You may fool the others but you won't pull the wool over my eyes. Pete wanted to say, I've been to that school! I paid my debt to society! They said I was smart! I can dive like a champion! I won prizes! The whole school got ice cream because of me! But he looked at his father and knew it was hopeless. From now on, he would keep as quiet as possible. He would notice as little as possible. He would keep himself to himself. The puppy, whom he had named Bruno, slept at the foot of his bed. At night when the house was quiet, he would get up, bury his face in the dog's soft stomach, and fall asleep, his head at the foot of the bed. He thought often of what his grandmother had told him: that if his tenth year was a dark year, still it would end, and his eleventh would be better, and when it was not, he concluded that the kindness of women was great and that they would say anything to keep someone happy or hopeful. Maybe his grandmother thought it was more important to be hopeful than happy. "How many people are happy?" she used to ask, brandishing her spoon. "Name me one?"

Still, he had Saturdays off. He was training his dog, who, when he clicked his fingers twice, would stand up on his hind legs, and there were girls at school who seemed to take an interest in him ("Because you're you!" said his mother. "Because you're you!"), and he became interested enough in Lorraine, a girl from the next block, to overhear his mother and aunt discussing her.

"She seems nice," said his aunt.

"Is she Italian?" asked his mother.

"If she goes to the school, she's Catholic," said Theresa.

At night, after everyone was asleep, he would sometimes put his coat on over his pajamas and walk the silent streets wondering, if you could fly high enough, would there be a meaning or a pattern you could see, a letter or a word formed by all the streets and all the rivers and all the mountain ridges. He doubted it, however, and always seemed to wind up near the church before making his way home. He took his bicycle everywhere, fixed it with a friend's help when it broke, played Ping-Pong and went bowling at the community center, went to school, and worked with his father. His dog followed him wherever he went. His mother bought Pete a basket for his bicycle, and on Saturdays he carried the empty bottles in it when he went to the store.

In February there was a snowstorm that brought down power lines and stopped all traffic in the borough. When the roads were again clear, he took his bike to the store to buy his mother some spices. The roads were still icy and his mother warned him to be careful. When a half hour passed, and then an hour, his mother began looking out the window for him, and when she didn't see him coming down the street, and saw it was getting dark, she put on her coat and went outside. There was a small crowd gathering on the sidewalk in front of her friend Helena's house, and as she started to call out, she saw one of the men lift someone up and carry him down the steps into Helena's basement apartment. She started to run. When the neighbors saw her coming, they rushed over to her, saying they had just been coming to get her. He had a bad fall, but he was all right. He was sitting up inside.

"What happened?" she asked her son, who was sitting on a folding card-table chair in the middle of Helena's living room.

"I don't know," the boy said. The dog sat at his feet.

"Take off your coat," Helena told Angelina, who didn't hear her.

"Did you fall, did a car hit you?"

"I don't know. I was turning into our driveway and Bruno was right behind me. He was barking at something. I don't know how I got here."

"Someone carried him here?" Angelina asked Helena.

"No, no," Helena said. "I went to the window to see if my husband was coming, and there he was, lying on the sidewalk right at the top of my steps. You don't remember how you got here?" she asked the boy.

"Maybe a car dragged me?" He wanted to be helpful, but he didn't understand it: What had happened to the time between his turning into his own driveway and finding himself propped up on a chair in Helena's house?

"Did you go to the store?" his mother asked him. "Were you coming back from the store?"

"I don't remember."

"You didn't go near the school?" asked his mother. "You didn't touch anything there?"

"What do you mean?" the boy asked.

"You did!" cried Angelina. "You went near the school!"

He shook his head. He didn't know what she was talking about. "Angelina!" said Helena. "He doesn't look right. The way he keeps shaking his head. Maybe he hit it. Look how frightened he looks."

"What about the school, Ma?" he asked.

"Don't be smart with me!" shouted his mother. Puzzled, he looked at Helena.

"You know, the windows you broke, the desks."

"I don't know," he said.

"Reform school!" shouted his mother. "You don't remember reform school either?"

"What's she talking about?" he asked, starting to cry.

"Angelina, I tell you he hit his head," said Helena. "Call a doctor," she told her son.

"I'm not sick! I want to go home! Paul waits for me! He won't eat without me!"

His mother burst into tears.

"That's not nice," Helena said to him. "Don't do that to your mother."

"What?" he asked. "What?" His head hurt and he put his hand to the back of his neck and rubbed it. "What am I doing here?"

"You know Paul's not home," Helena said. "You know that."

"He's home," said the boy. "He's always home."

"We have trouble here," said Helena. "He hit his head, he shook his brains up."

"Grandma, you remember what happened to her?" Angelina was frantic.

"She's home," Pete said. "With Paul."

"Angelina, stop crying," said Helena. She told her son to get Mr. Bravado. "He's got to go to a hospital," she told Angelina.

"You remember the spaghetti I sent you? The sausages? Labor Day? You don't remember? No? *Dio mio!* Is this a joke? Tell me it's a joke!"

"I remember who I am," the boy said slowly. "My name is Pete. It's still Pete. He's my father," he said, pointing to the man who had just come into the room. "I know who everyone is. See? There's nothing the matter with me."

"What were you supposed to get at the store?" asked his mother.

"Store?" he asked.

His father picked him up, carried him to the car, and drove him to the hospital. The admitting doctor ordered a brain scan and an EEG and when he had the results he took the parents aside. The child had a concussion and severe memory loss. He knew who he was and who everyone else was but he couldn't remember anything that had happened before. "Nothing?" said his mother. "Not even birthday parties?"

"Unless he's lying," said the doctor. "He doesn't remember. It happens. His memory may come back. Then again, it may not. If it comes back, well and good. Don't pressure him. You'll only frighten him."

Pete himself took calmly the vanishing of much of his memory, but within a month, he began remembering more and more: a trip to the country, his grandmother's funeral, his brother, waving from the car as his father drove him off to the home, and he was sorry to remember. "I don't see what all the fuss was about," he said to the doctor when he went for a checkup. "Before I went to reform school, I came home and worked for my father. He glares at me. I act like I don't notice. It's the same thing day after day, year in, year out. So if I'd lost my memory, what difference would it make? If I lost my memory, you think I'd have lost something? I didn't *have* anything to lose. I don't have anything to lose."

Now he worked for his father less frequently because both the doctor and his mother forbade it. His mother said the child needed his rest and the doctor wanted to watch him to be sure he didn't have epilepsy. "Fits! Fits!" said his mother, who at once had something to worry about and the ammunition she needed. "If he should drop a bathtub on you or on someone else! We don't have the insurance! We'd be in the poorhouse forever!"

He and Eddie fixed their bikes in the family garages, and sometime while they were fixing them, the doctor decided he didn't have epilepsy after all (but his mother never told this to his father), and while they worked, he listened to Eddie telling him about his gang, the Black Eagles, and about the fight they intended to have with another gang the next week, about how much he liked gangs, how much fun they had: he belonged to three gangs now, but Pete didn't have time for gangs. His father still insisted he work for him. On most nights, he was too busy carrying down huge cast-iron bathtubs with wood rims and claw feet.

"It's too bad you're missing out on it," Eddie said. "It keeps you in great shape." He flexed his muscles. "It's not all from fighting. I work out. I lift weights at the center. But it comes in handy when you have to fight. I can lift the front of this car! Watch me! And I don't weigh more than you do."

When Pete was fourteen, he suddenly remembered that one Christmas long ago, Santa Claus rang the front-door bell, and he watched him from behind the living room door. Suddenly, Santa Claus lifted up his beard and there underneath was Helena laughing until she was bent double. "I'm fat enough!" she said, hitting her stomach. "I'm fat enough!" He remembered his mother calling the other children down and he remembered calling out, "It's not Santa Claus! It's Helena!" He wondered what else he'd forgotten. Could he have forgotten important things? Good things? He looked around him. In his opinion, his life had always been as it was now. Nothing had been added or subtracted.

Spring came and it began to rain daily. Baseball managers were on the air complaining about muddy fields and the difficulty of scheduling practice. Radio and television compared this year's record rainfall to previous years. Soap operas were interrupted with storm warnings and notices of floods in outlying areas. Housewives called the station to protest the interruption of their programs. Carts selling umbrellas sprang up on all the street corners and even candy store owners had them for sale next to the newspapers. A novelty company selling a hat with an umbrella sitting on top of it began doing unexpectedly well. There were jokes on the radio about building an ark, news items on television about pleasure boats swamped at their moorings. Finally it seemed as if the whole world were underwater. At night, the streets of Brooklyn gleamed silver and black and when the rain stopped, the fresh smell of the flowering shrubs on either side of most front doors in the neighborhood wafted by in the dampness.

"I've never seen Brooklyn so clean," said Theresa.

"I'm sick of this rain," said Angelina.

"The rain's good for business," George said. "Now if anything's leaking, no one can miss it. Everyone's calling me. I've got more than I can do with my own two hands."

"He's not going with you," said Angelina, scratching Bruno between the ears. "No more. Hire another kid."

"So where does he go at night when he doesn't come with me?" her husband asked. "Tell me where he goes."

"He's old enough for girls," said Theresa. "Leave him alone."

"He goes out alone and he comes back alone," said his father. "He comes back in soaking wet."

"So he likes water," said his mother. "So what?"

When George bent his head to eat, the two women exchanged looks. When he left, Theresa kneaded the pizza dough and Angelina cut up mushrooms for the sauce. She looked at the white-stuccoed walls of the kitchen and decided she'd never liked stucco, especially in a kitchen. The walls were too hard to keep clean and how many times could you repaint them before the paint got so thick it fell off in chunks the way it was falling off now behind the stove? Old Mrs. Bravado used to tell him that. "Put up tile!" she said. "Put up tile!" But this was cheaper and he thought it looked more modern. It was modern and it needed painting. The pink marble Formica tabletop was crisscrossed with little black scars from all the knives everyone had used on its surface. "Use the cutting board, that's what it's there for!" No one listened to her. *She* never listened. She'd liked the old wooden table.

Something was wrong with her son, but she didn't know what to do. The old lady had had long fingers that could reach deep into other people's thoughts, whereas she didn't understand half of what her son told her. Maybe what her husband said was true, and she didn't really listen. What was she supposed to make of his having told her he liked reform school, because there he didn't feel guilty? Sometimes, he'd said, you do something wrong because you know you're already wrong and you want to know why you're wrong. What did that mean? Was that some kind of riddle? He'd said he was never afraid there, not in the school. Did that mean he was afraid here? What was he afraid of? The dark? His father? People dying? What was he talking about? She'd told Theresa what he said, repeated it as best she could, and Theresa'd said, "Maybe he means original sin." Maybe he did, but how did she know? When the Dodgers left Brooklyn, her eldest son had said he'd kill himself. Suppose she'd listened to that? So all in all, it's true to say that she wasn't surprised to find a policeman at her door asking for her son.

"What is it this time?" she asked. "Fighting or windows?"

"Windows," said the policeman.

"I guess the boy likes fresh air," Theresa said behind her.

"They'll put him away for good," Angelina said, tears running down her cheeks.

"He's still underage, ma'am," said the policeman.

"What does that mean?" shouted Angelina. "If he's lucky, he'll go back to that school?"

"That's what it means," said the policeman. "If he's lucky." These Italian women unnerved him. They went from weeping to screaming without missing a beat.

This time, when she packed her son's things, the activity was already familiar, a routine she knew by heart, requiring little thought. How little time it takes to get used to something, she thought, folding and packing the sweater she'd intended to save for his birthday. "Why do you do these things?" she had asked him. "What makes you do it? What are you thinking about? Answer me!"

He said he got angry, but he didn't know about what. He didn't *think* he thought about anything. If anyone had told him you could walk around with your mind blank, he wouldn't have believed it, but his mind was like that, blank. He didn't read because when he read, he began to think. His mind began to wander and then he didn't like the way he felt. Sometimes he tried to fill himself up by listening to other people talk. About what? About anything. About street fairs, calamari, about the big statue of the saint they carried down the street in Greenpoint, about pinning dollars on the wall near the church in the neighborhood, about what Coney Island was like when he was a child, about how he used to roller-skate up and down the block, about how Eddie used to push a doll carriage around until he was four and now look how tough he was, about how the neighborhood was German before it was Italian, and how it was changing again, about anything. He was happy with other people's thoughts. They blotted out his own.

Sometimes at night when he fell asleep he saw a silvery light that grew and grew until he couldn't see anything through it, and then he knew he was almost asleep. Sometimes he heard a voice that wasn't his mother's shouting "You devil!" and he thought that was his grandmother, but he didn't know.

He didn't read because he couldn't concentrate. Whatever was on the page made him think of something else, and whatever it was, he didn't want to think about it. Most of the time, he stared into space and wondered what everything would look like if the house he was looking at, or the street, suddenly disappeared. He believed that hundreds of streets and hundreds of houses could disappear and no one would really know they were missing, and if enough of them disappeared, you might be able to see the ocean and the waves: things like that. He didn't think about anything.

His mother said that when he'd been sent to reform school the first time, he didn't have trouble reading. The priests there had said he was very bright. They'd said he never caused any trouble and that they'd never worried about his breaking anything. And the boy asked her how that could be? How could he have done well? How could they have trusted him? And then he said he didn't mind going back. His mother said he'd have plenty of time to enjoy it because the judge was putting him away until his sixteenth birthday, and when he came out, he'd only have part of a term before he was finished with high school, and then he'd get a job, and soon he'd be a man, and what did he think about that?

T HE HILLS behind the Catholic School for
Delinquent Boys looked steeper, colder, flintier,
and more forbidding, and the school itself looked smaller, as if, during the
time he had been home, it had sunk into the earth. But nothing about the
school had changed. Father Gabriel was still there, and when Pete went into
the cafeteria, the first person he saw was Bruno. Soon the two of them were
working together in the print shop.

"They sent you back?" Pete asked him, and Bruno said, Hell, no, he'd
been here all along. Pete asked him why he'd been sent away, and he
hesitated, looked around at the others, put his mouth to Pete's ear, and
whispered, "Arson."

"What?" Pete asked.

"Arson!" he shouted into Pete's ear, just as the presses stopped. "Oh, for
Christ's sake!" he said looking around. "Don't fucking talk to me!" After
a few minutes, he again put his mouth to Pete's ear and shouted, "What
about you? What brings *you* here?" Pete said it was the same old thing. He
broke some windows and they knew who to come for. "Man!" Bruno said.
"Can't you use some imagination? Do something else!"

"Like what?" Pete asked.

"Like setting fire to a mattress, throwing paint at the front door. It
doesn't have to be windows. How's your brother? The retarded one?" Pete
said he was in a home on Staten Island. When he was older, when he made
enough money, when he was strong enough, he'd take his brother out of the
home and take care of him himself. "You still work for your father?" Bruno
asked him, and when Pete shook his head, Bruno said that even Lincoln
freed the slaves.

"Yeah, well, I'm happy to be back here," Pete said.

"You're nuts," Bruno said. "You've got toys in the attic. No one's happy
to be here."

"I'm happy. I know what's coming. The sun comes up, the sun goes
down. Maybe I'll be a printer. This is O.K."

But Bruno said he'd only been back a few days. The second time around
was worse than the first. He'd see. And it was. This time, Pete knew that
when he went home, nothing would have changed there. His father would
be uninterested in his report card, no matter what it said. If he'd won diving

awards, his father would look at him and say, "Where's that going to get you? It's freezing cold here nine months of the year. Change your clothes and get going." No matter what he accomplished, his father would pay no attention to what he had to say. He'd come home and find Paul's room empty, his mother in the kitchen, cooking and baking for her weekend visits to the home on Staten Island.

One afternoon he sat still, reading *A Tale of Two Cities,* and for no reason at all, he picked up the bottle of ink from the inkwell and spilled it into the pencil tray. He pictured his father's face drawn in the center of the desk and he watched the black ink overflow the tray and begin to wash down the desk, meeting the book. The book soaked it up. He felt the brother's hand on the back of his neck. He was hauled out of his seat, bent over his desk, and, his pants down, struck ten times with the blackboard pointer.

"Why did you do it?" Father Gabriel asked him afterwards. "You were doing so well. Things were going too well for you?"

The boy didn't answer him, but his eyes filled with tears.

"You sin, not against books and desks and windows," said the priest, "but against yourself." The boy said nothing. "And your parents, what of them?"

What of them? thought Pete. They were far away. They lived lives that meant nothing to him. He had a sudden vision of the ghostly, dusky armies marching through the streets of Brooklyn while everyone else slept, keeping everyone else safe, and he smiled.

"Why are you smiling?" the priest asked him, and Pete said he'd thought of *A Tale of Two Cities.* "It's a wonderful book, isn't it?" the priest asked him. " 'It's a far, far better thing I do,' " he recited. The boy was smiling back at him. "Don't take it too seriously," said the priest nervously. "You can do good deeds without giving up your life." The boy nodded, looked at him, looked away, and, when he looked up again, was gone. He was standing there, but he was elsewhere. "A week in the stables, and you're out of the competitions," said the priest. The boy nodded as if relieved to be punished.

"So? Happy now?" Bruno asked him.

"I'm O.K.," Pete said.

"Still so happy to be here?"

"No."

Now he waited anxiously for the packages from home, for the spaghetti and sausages, for the cookies wrapped in pink paper his mother coaxed from the baker. There was nothing new here, nothing new or different at home. The same thing, day after day, and nothing to hope for. What was the word for that? *Damnation.* Why did it take him so long to think of it? He heard that word every Sunday. It was one of Father Gabriel's favorite words.

Near the end of his fifteenth year, Pete Bravado wrote his father, saying he'd had enough of school, but he'd still be on probation when he was sixteen, and the judge wouldn't let him quit school unless he had a job. If his father had any friends who knew of something he could do, would he ask? Two weeks later, his father wrote back saying Mr. Orsini needed an assistant in the butcher shop, and he could have that job if he wanted it, but it was heavy work, carrying sides of beef from the truck, and he'd have to do the deliveries if the regular boy didn't show up. "Tell Mr. Orsini fine," Pete wrote on a postcard.

When he came home, he looked older. He was taller than his mother, whom he took to calling Shorty, and he stood differently, always seeming slightly turned from the person to whom he spoke. He went to work without complaining, turned most of the money he earned over to his mother, and took Lorraine to the movies on Saturday night. She was a nice girl, small and blond, who played the piano, gave concerts in the auditorium, did well in school, and never mentioned his brother in the home on Staten Island or asked him about what it was like upstate. After work, he still fixed his bike in Eddie's garage, or played stoopball with the children on the block, and on weekends they played pool, played handball, or went swimming at the community center, but by now Eddie had a red convertible and was working for Mr. Orsini's brother, a man who was in the "business." Pete's father couldn't pass his son without telling him how much more he'd make working for him. He'd learned a trade from *him*, and now he was wasting his time in a butcher shop, and when he wasn't wasting his time there, he wasted it with that no-good Eddie and that crazy Lorraine, who painted her fingernails black and played the piano and lived in a crazy house. Every square inch of her house was covered with linoleum, all different patterns. So what if her father had laid linoleum for Johnny Carson? Did he have to make his own house a fun house? He went in there and came out so dizzy he thought he was having a stroke. Everyone in the neighborhood knew what Lorraine was.

Pete would leave the house to get away from his father and he'd sit in the red convertible with Eddie, and one day, Eddie told him he was enlisting in the army, and when he asked what for, Eddie said he was tired of sitting in a red convertible with his girlfriend listening to Cousin Brucie on the radio dedicating songs to those brave boys in Vietnam. And *his* uncle Eddie had been killed in the Philippines, *and* he was named after him. He'd be the one who went and came back. Besides, he said, he was part Indian. Indians liked war.

"How do you know you're part Indian?" Pete asked him.

"I know, man," Eddie said.

Pete said he didn't even know where Vietnam was. Did Eddie know where it was? "It's not here, man," said Eddie, waving his hand so that it included all of Brooklyn, all of the flat concrete streets, all the honking cars, all the police and the juvenile courts and the claw-footed bathtubs and the brothers in homes on Staten Island. "It's not *here.* "

Pete looked around him. When he got out of school upstate, the priest had told him he had a chance to start again. His life was one perpetual Easter, full of resurrections, once after the accident on the bike, twice after getting out of reform school. The only trouble was he kept picking up where he left off. The story never changed. *It's not here.* Join the army and see the world. People respected soldiers. The army taught you how to take care of yourself. The army could teach him a trade. Maybe Vietnam was the change he needed. He couldn't stay home with his father. He knew his father raised more than his voice to his mother when he argued with her. He didn't want to be around if his mother ever showed up with a black eye.

"Once I get there, it's going to be all over," Eddie said. "Once I get there."

"You can't sign up until you're eighteen," he said. "I'm sixteen."

"Your mother can sign for you," Eddie said. "As soon as you're seventeen, she can sign, and she won't be able to wait for the ink to dry."

LATELY, Angelina was in the habit of rubbing her forehead above her left eye. Often, when he came into the kitchen, her son found her staring at a picture in the family album. Occasionally, she took out her wedding album and slowly went through its pages. Her concentration was absolute, so intense she began to burn dinners, and Theresa often came running up the stairs with a box of baking soda to throw on the flaming stove, shouting, "Angelina! Wake up! Angelina!" Then she would sit down with her sister-in-law and the two women would look at the pictures. Angelina didn't seem unhappy, only preoccupied.

"Look how the colored pictures fade, when the black and white ones stay just the same," Angelina said, absentmindedly stroking the dog who lay at her feet.

"Mama used to say the same thing," Theresa said, turning a page. "Look at the whole gang in the kitchen. Someone's always taking pictures in the kitchen. Only on holidays are there pictures of us in the living room. Why is that? Remember when the bedroom was painted dark green? Whose idea was that?"

"What color is it now?" Angelina asked absently. "Oh, yellow. I forgot. It's yellow. You know, this is really a happy house. We have a lot of fun here. We always did. But if I get in a bad mood, I remember the bad things. Why?"

"So many questions!" Theresa said gloomily.

"Bad times are black and white pictures. They don't fade," Angelina said.

"Did Pete do anything?" Theresa asked. "Is that the matter?"

Angelina shook her head and turned a page. "Look, you can see the living room from this picture. You can see the lights from the tree." No, Pete had never been happier. He came in whistling and he went out humming. He ate as if he were sorry for the refrigerator which had to hold up so much food. He joked with Angelina when she tried to scold him about his room or his work in the yard. "Don't think you can get away with it because you're taller!" she shouted at him. "With this broom I'm taller than you!"

"Shorty!" he said. "Shorty!" And he ran away from her.

"What are you so happy about?" she asked him, watching him steal an unbaked cookie. "What's making you so happy?"

"*It's not here!*" he'd say laughing. When she saw him like that, he reminded her of his grandfather. "*It's not here!*"

"Tell me what that means!" his mother shouted at him. "Tell me what that means!" And he'd say, "Come on, Shorty, make me!" and with the broom she'd chase him around the kitchen until he escaped through the back door and then he'd jump up and down outside the kitchen window until she went over to it, and he'd mouth the words, *It's not here.* "Devil!" shouted his mother.

"That's grown-up?" asked his father. "That's a child."

"You know what?" said his sister. "You're going to be a grouchy, sour old man."

Pete called out from his room. "*He's not here.*"

"Again?" said his mother, running into his room with the broom. They heard the door slam. His father had gone to work. "He doesn't like to see people happy," said his son. His mother didn't contradict him.

On his seventeenth birthday, Pete came home from work, opened his presents, cut the cake his mother and aunt had baked, waited until his aunt had gone back downstairs, and said, "Ma, I can't stay here anymore." He expected questions, floods of tears, shouting, but his mother only rubbed her forehead and stared at him. *I knew it,* her eyes said. "I can enlist if you sign for me. They'll teach me a trade. I'll be home on leaves. I'll write. Pop always said the army was good for him."

"What does he know about armies?" his mother asked. "During the war he watched ships in the Brooklyn navy yard. He came home at night and slept in his own bed. His feet were flat and he had a collapsed lung. The army's not a school! You can get killed!"

"You can get killed crossing the street," Pete said.

"Who got killed crossing the street?" Angelina asked. "Name one person you know who got killed that way!"

"It happens every day, Ma!"

"It's not the same!"

"Ma," he said, "we can take the bus to the recruiting station on Kings Highway."

"I know where it is!" shouted his mother. "I don't want to go!"

"Tomorrow?" asked her son. "You're not doing anything special?"

"When am I ever doing anything special? I don't want to go."

"I'll pay someone to sign for me," Pete said. "You can pay someone to pretend she's your mother."

"I'm still alive," his mother said. "Why should someone sign for me?"

T H E   N E X T   D A Y, she dressed in her best blue wool suit, put on her grey coat with the fox fur collar, and took her grey fox hat from its striped box and pinned it to her hair. They found the silver trailer on Kings Highway, and she stood near the door watching her son sign the recruitment papers, and she heard the lieutenant telling him to report to Fort Hamilton that afternoon. From the way he chatted with the lieutenant, she saw that he had been here before. From the festive flourish with which he signed his papers, she saw that he had been waiting a long time to do this. When he turned to her, his eyes were bright and distant. He had already gone.

What had she done? But if she hadn't signed, he'd have done what all the other boys did: he'd have paid a woman on the street to say she was his mother, and by the time she knew what he'd done, it would be too late. She wouldn't even get to say good-bye. Maybe he would learn a trade. Maybe he needed to get away. And then he was gone. Her husband didn't seem unhappy to hear it. He said things about the army making a man of him, what he needed was discipline, you couldn't fool *men.* There'd be no breaking windows there! It was all, thought his mother, spaghetti.

That night, after her husband had fallen asleep, she got up and quietly opened the door to her closet. Her dresses hung on their wire hangers, and beneath them, her one pair of good shoes. Her house shoes, her bedroom slippers, and her winter boots stood in a neat row. She looked at them and began naming all the parts of Brooklyn she could think of: Bensonhurst, Brighton Beach, Sheepshead Bay, Prospect Park, Coney Island, Bay Ridge, Bedford-Stuyvesant, Canarsie, Brownsville, Red Hook, Flatbush, Gravesend. The names of the neighborhoods were ugly. Flatbush, Gravesend. Brooklyn was all she knew and she didn't know Brooklyn well. She knew her neighborhood and she knew her house.

Really, she hardly knew her neighborhood anymore. She knew her block and her friends on the block. She touched the dresses hanging in the closet. Under her fingers, they were cool, and she smelled her perfume mixing with the smell of cedar chips. Was this all there was to a woman's life? First you were a girl and had short dresses, and then you were a woman, and your dresses were longer. *First I was young, and now I am not.* That sentence kept floating back and forth through her thoughts. Where had she heard it before?

When she was younger and argued with her husband, her mother used to say, "Wait until the children grow up. Children cause all the trouble. When you're alone in the house together, then you'll have time for each other." Once, being alone with her husband seemed the most wonderful thing in the world. Not now. Now she dreaded the time when the children would be gone and they would be in the empty house together. That time had arrived. And if Theresa and her husband moved away and left them completely alone? She didn't think she could stand it. She would claw at the windows until they broke. She would climb over the windowsill and out into the yard and never come back.

And then she told herself these were mad thoughts. She was only thinking them because she was up in the middle of the night and one of her children had just enlisted in the army. She didn't know how the army took a boy and made him into a soldier. He would come home in a uniform knowing things she'd never dreamed of. He could be killed. People were getting killed every day. The radio said so. But here her mind veered away. Her son would not be killed. Her son would be protected.

If she died now, what would she miss? From now on, one day would repeat another. There would be nothing new under the sun. She looked at her dresses, silent and lifeless in the dark closet. If she died tomorrow, there wouldn't be much to pack up. Her husband would replace her. Already the block was thick with widows in their black dresses. As if she had walked over her own grave, she shivered. Still, she had two sons who had to have some place to come back to, and a house was nothing. A house was just a shell. Still, there should be more, Gravesend, Sheepshead Bay, places beyond the water. But they were not for her. She would live and die on this block.

When she got back in bed that night, she and her husband took up their usual positions. They slept back to back, each looking out his own window, each window giving out onto not only a different scene, but a different world.

TWO

Carthage

12 VERY TIME he wrote a letter, or tried to write one, as he was doing now, with the plane headed for Vietnam, Pete Bravado would ask himself (not in words, not in formed sentences, because he had forgotten he had the words, forgotten he could think, paid so little attention to his thoughts) if it was possible for someone to know something, to see it in all its aspects, to understand it and how it fit in with everything else in the world, and still not be able to express it, and he always concluded that, yes, it was possible, because when he looked into his brother Paul's eyes, he saw all the possible wisdom in the world reflected there, all the sorrow, all the happiness, all the deep, black knowledge of the works of a fate that could commit him for all the days of his life to an enormous building in which children rocked against rails or beat their heads against rails until one day the bruised blood vessels burst and they went home at last. He saw all that and more when he looked into Paul's eyes. He saw the brilliant love Paul had for his mother, and even his father, who deserved none of it, and for him and his older brothers, whom Paul never forgot even if he didn't see them for years. For him, memory was always new, never tarnished by more recent experience. Paul thought, Pete concluded, with his heart, and no one knew what he thought, or even that he thought because he had no words.

He looked down at the sheet of paper on which he had written, "Dear Ma, you should see this plane! Don't worry about me," and he had the premonition that he, like his brother, did not have the words, might never have the words, and if that were so, the less he saw now, the less he understood, the better off he would be, because to understand a world and to carry it around alone, never finding anyone who knew how to look into it, someone who could say, *Oh, yes I remember that,* or, *Things looked like that to me once, too,* to have the world alone, that was worse than not having it at all.

As he looked out the window, he tried to understand his disappointment and his sense of grief, and that sense had nothing to do with knowing he was flying to Vietnam where he could be killed. It came from knowing he was still alone as he'd always been, that his dreams of becoming part of something bigger and better than he was had been fulfilled, but the hole in his heart through which the cold wind blew was still there, and even though he was proud of his uniform (Hadn't his country said, We need your help, and hadn't he answered, saying, All right, I love this country, I was born in this country and I don't know any other country. My country's been good for me, so O.K., what do you want? I'll do it.), he didn't feel part of anything. He knew who he was in his green uniform, identical to everyone else's. He was flying high over the ocean in a fancy jet, but the plane's movements altered nothing that had happened or would happen to the people he cared about. His brother would still wake in the morning to the sound of heads hitting metal cribs. His mother would continue to make trips to Staten Island to see him, and once there, she would inspect her son's body for marks and she would find them. She would want Paul to come home, and now she would want him to come home, and she would be helpless. He didn't like the feel of the seat belt fastened over his lap. He didn't like any restraints, and yet he'd joined up.

Already he sensed the lies beneath the surface. He'd seen it at the end of Basic. In Basic, everything they did was wrong. They couldn't do anything right. They were clumsy. They were in lousy shape, too fat, too slow. The punishment was constant: *Get up! Get down! Give me ten! Give me twenty!* And then, toward the end, everything they did was suddenly right. They had to crawl on their hands and knees in under forty seconds, and they crawled in sand. They never achieved their goal, but when they took their final test, there were canvas mats down. It was ten times easier, and suddenly they were in perfect shape. They were the fastest things in the world. When they swung from rings, the rings would turn on them. Their hands would blister and slip, but when they took the test, the rings didn't turn and they didn't slip. Everything was perfect. They were the cream of the crop, the perfect soldiers, the finest killing machines, and they loved being perfect. *He* loved being perfect. He'd never been perfect before in his life, not even *good.* And that was the lie and they loved that lie.

They'd do anything to keep believing in it, and that's when they got them. That's when they got him. They could always push that switch, call you an asshole, an imbecile, and he'd do anything to get back to that other state. He'd kill for them. He'd do it without question, anything to be once again completely and absolutely good. They all would. That was how they got you and kept you. It didn't make any difference how they did it, and it wasn't anything to worry about as long as he agreed with what they were doing, but what happened if the day came when he didn't? Already he knew things that were worth telling others, and already he knew he'd never be able to. What he knew right now he'd forget ten minutes from now; he was too excitable. He knew things until he became angry or frightened and then he forgot them, and he was angry and frightened most of the time. He couldn't remember a time when the world hadn't frightened him.

He looked around the cabin of the plane and saw people he knew, people with names like Mill Cross Cobb and Geronimo P. Davis, and George Liebowitz, whom some people called Jew, Vinnie Delgado and Ten White Feathers Watson, whom everyone, following the drill instructor's lead, called Chief, and Rosario Paganini, whom some people called Pig, and he saw that, according to their natures, they thought about different things. Some were on a plane for the first time. Most of them, like him, had never been on a commercial jet before, and at least one of them had never seen a plane fly overhead before he was drafted. A few sat stunned by the opulence of the pink and grey interior, and most of them wished their parents or girlfriends could see them now.

For the first four hours, they buzzed the stewardesses incessantly, not that they wanted anything, but it was an unimaginable novelty, pressing the button and listening for the chime that summoned the stewardess. Most of the stewardesses, who had been through this innumerable times before, were good-humored, although some were annoyed or bored, but the good-natured ones would smile while they watched the young soldiers try to think of something to ask for. After the fourth hour, the soldiers would press the button less and less frequently, and when the stewardess came, the soldiers would try to draw her into conversation. Some of the stewardesses, young women, no older than the soldiers, would talk and joke until another button, another chime, called them away. By the fifth hour, some of the soldiers would sleep or pretend to sleep and the cabin grew quiet. Even if two who knew one another were seated together, they tended to keep silent. They had their own thoughts and those thoughts were so palpable that it sometimes seemed to Pete as if the stewardesses were pushing their way through them as they carried trays up and down the aisle.

By the eighth hour, the plane filled with a hospital-room silence. Everyone had asked for and received their grey blankets, and as the stewardesses went up and down the aisles between the apparently sleeping passengers covered by their ash-grey blankets, they would sometimes startle when someone's head tilted back and a pair of half-sleeping eyes fastened on them. Here and there, a still, grey form sat upright, holding a book, but rarely looked at its pages. To Pete, looking around, the plane's cabin seemed a world in which life had stopped, or not yet begun, and he saw, not soldiers, but green-suited mummies in their long grey cocoons.

You could explain the silence. If you thought long enough, you could explain anything. They were on their way out of Fort Benning, Georgia, and that morning, the drill instructor had all those with orders cut for Vietnam fall out and stand in front of the rest of the troops. "Take a good look," he shouted. "These men are going to Vietnam and most of them aren't coming back. You might as well say good-bye to them because you're never going to see them again."

Throughout Advanced Individual Training, they'd heard it again and again. "You're going to Vietnam and you're not coming back." At night, the DI would say, "You made it alive through another day, but you're dying tonight," and in the morning, as they brushed their teeth triple-time, he'd march through the barracks shouting, "Good morning, ladies. You made it through the night, but you're going to die today." What was the purpose of it? Some of them, like him, were determined to become the best possible soldier, to come back alive if only to get that sadistic son-of-a-bitch, while others, also like him, were already confused about the boundary between the living and the dead. Was it really only a matter of time, a matter of miles they had to walk or ride in an armored personnel carrier before they found their land mine or sniper and became, officially, dead? Were some of their deaths so close that they were already dead but didn't know it?

Some were simply afraid, and others shrugged it off, saying nothing would happen to them. Not everyone in Vietnam died. But when meals were served, or snacks, some of them would look at one another: was there a mark, some kind of clue, in the eyes, in the set of the jaw, something that would tell you who would make it back and who wouldn't? Still, as the plane flew on, they learned to think about other things. They knew better than to think too long about whether or not they had the mark on them. They were superstitious. Some had decided not to keep a short-timer's calendar, not to mark off the 365 days they had to serve in Vietnam before coming home, because that might bring bad luck, draw the attention of whatever it was that guided the bullets, set off the land mines, aimed the shrapnel.

When they awakened under their grey blankets and looked out at the sky which never seemed to darken, as they flew into what seemed an endless day, they would either fill their minds or empty them. Some had become good at thinking of nothing and they would become better at it. Some had become so good at it that whole weeks, whole months, would disappear behind the blankness they were now summoning up.

Others, like Pete, went back to the beginning, the swearing in, the trip to the airport, the flight to Fort Jackson, the bus pulling into the fort, the drill instructors getting on, the shouting, *"You've got ten seconds to get out of the bus and you've already used up five!"* the second drill instructor shouting, "Let me tell you about you personnel! Fifty percent of you person-nel are assholes, fifty percent of you are idiots, and fifty percent of you are imbeciles!" and the third one telling them they weren't home anymore, he was their mother and their father and their sister and their brother. He was their God. And Pete thought, Jesus Christ! Is he really my God?

They arrived in the middle of the night, stood on the yellow footprints in size order, listened to the screaming, marched, or tried to march, to the barracks where they had their heads shaved, then lined up to be issued their fatigues and their bed linen, and then they were in the barracks for the night, heads shaved, no longer recognizable to themselves, lying awake in the dark on the linen they'd just been issued, on the cot's thin mattresses, on the sheets they'd just been given, trying to make sense out of the day's jumble, all of them feeling they'd never been so alone, nobody daring to talk because the drill instructor told them there'd be no talking, becoming more and more frightened listening to the beats of their hearts measuring out the time, and Pete lay there, asking himself over and over, *What did I do? What did I do?* until somewhere in the middle of the long, dark barracks someone with a thick southern accent said, "What the fuck am I doing here?" and that broke the ice. Everyone began talking and laughing and the drill instructor was back in, shouting for quiet, but after he left, the whispering went on. They were already learning that the world they knew was gone, vanished, erased. Now they had no one else, only one another. The men in the lower bunks looked gratefully at the curve of the mattress above them, pushing the springs down toward them. There was someone else in the world.

Pete looked at George Liebowitz, sitting next to him, and thought he knew what he was thinking. For as long as he could remember, he'd seemed to know what people were thinking—his brother Paul, when he went to visit him in the home, his mother after she had a fight with his father, his grandfather as he squatted in the yard and studied the tulip leaves cracking the hard, cold earth as if he were trying to see down to the bulb and ask it how it knew when to send the leaves up—but you couldn't let them know. If they knew, you frightened them. People were frightened of everything. He'd known that forever. He'd been born knowing that.

He knew about George Liebowitz, who had kissed his parents good-bye and looked hard at them, memorizing their faces, convinced he would never see them or Brooklyn again. "My father, he remembers everything bad that ever happened to him," Liebowitz said. "You have to remember the bad things? You can remember the good things. There are always good things. Just decide, man."

"There are always good things?" Pete asked him.

"Yeah," Liebowitz said, looking at him. "There are."

"So what are you doing here?" Pete asked.

Liebowitz shrugged. "It's my turn," he said. "That's all."

Pete liked him. Liebowitz had a round, fleshy face and when he wore his glasses, he looked like a bewildered owl. He was always reading something, always laughing to himself about something, and by the time the plane took off, he knew that Liebowitz's parents had cried at the airport before he left for Advanced Individual Training, that Liebowitz's mother had decided to pretend he wasn't going to Vietnam at all but was instead spending the time attending college in North Carolina, that Liebowitz had always wanted to be tall and once put himself in the hospital after he stole and swallowed some of his fat cousin's thyroid extract, almost stopping his heart, but didn't you know, it didn't do enough damage to keep him out of the army.

He knew that Liebowitz had, in the weeks before he enlisted, tried to talk to his father about his time in the army, and, like almost everyone else he'd met, Liebowitz hadn't gotten very far. "You couldn't stay home from that one and live with yourself," his father said. "Of course, afterwards, you *definitely* couldn't live with yourself." When Liebowitz was younger and asked his father what the war was like, his father would laugh it off and tell him to go to the movies, *bang, bang, blood, all that stuff, believe me, it's nothing to write home about. You don't have to go. I read the papers and I don't see any reason to go.* But over the years, he'd managed to piece together what had happened to his father.

In the attic, under a thick pile of magazines, Liebowitz found a crumpled grey envelope filled with articles clipped from the newspaper: his father in full costume, singing Rigoletto. "Sure," his aunt said, "he was a big star before. When he came back he didn't want to sing anymore. You know why he said he stopped? He said he was too short! He had to stand on chairs for some big scenes. Believe me, that's not why he stopped. You want to know what he saw? Go into the garage and look at the painting under the towels. Ask your uncle. Your uncle was in the navy. They used to talk."

His uncle said that except for the day the hospital ship with the big red cross painted on its deck went down in flames in plain sight of them, he hadn't seen anything, but his father, he'd seen plenty. He used to talk about walking into cities and looking at street after street of buildings sliced open like melons, floor after floor of pink enameled walls and bathroom sinks hanging into space attached by wires, living rooms sheared off at the midpoint, grand pianos, two legs on the floor, one dangling in space, rugs flapping over the edge of serrated planks like flags, and the streets themselves jagged piles of rubble; and underneath the blocks of cement, lying there like pieces of a puzzle, the voices beneath crying out, and there was no stopping. They had to keep going.

But the bombed-out building was a beautiful thing. The bomb sheared off a wall and left a pattern of colored rectangles and squares. From the one flat wall that was left, it was apparent what the room had been: a living room, a kitchen, a library. During those days, the streets were like museums, each exposed wall a painting, but the bomb had chased the inhabitants from the frames. It didn't pay to think about where they'd gone. Eventually, the war would end, the buildings would be restored. The people would come back. There was always someone standing in front of the buildings who looked up, crying, someone who'd lived there.

"What do you want to know for?" his uncle asked him. Liebowitz said he wanted to know. "Yeah, well, that's all I know," said his uncle. But over the years, he told Liebowitz more and more: why his father wouldn't go into churches, why he crossed the street so he wouldn't have to walk in front of one. He'd stood in too many ruined cathedrals without roofs or windows or walls but you know what? Every cathedral he stood in, every church, always had its Christ on the cross intact. He sneezed when the wind stirred up the dust, but Christ didn't sneeze. Christ looked down from the wall. If someone from the town came along, they looked up at the Christ on the wall and said the same thing: a miracle. If the Germans had left anyone alive in the camp they liberated, that would have been a miracle. First, the inmates dug their own graves, and when they weren't fast enough, they were taken to a barn, locked in, and the barn was fired. That's what his father saw when they broke open the doors and all the bodies were there, some half-burned, some completely burned, bodies beneath bodies. The ones beneath weren't burned at all. And some of the dead bodies were beautiful, the most beautiful things he'd ever seen, and all of a sudden he could understand the fascination with death, the dedication to producing more dead things; some of the bodies were white and beautiful like sculpture, cool, like marble. For that instant, he saw it: the dead were what art aspired to. They were works of art, corruptible, ephemeral, apparently immortal, purchased at the expense of souls, perishing as he looked at them. And then out of the back doors of the barn, the huge back doors, large enough for a train to come through, were the hills and the fields and the cows grazing and the spires of two white churches and the sky was as blue and clear as it ever gets. Nature was absolutely beautiful and pure through that door. It was beautiful and it had nothing to say. The earth wasn't shocked. The eye moved from the charred bodies and the white, still, perfect bodies, to the hills, the apple trees, and the cows, and the eye wasn't shocked. Time didn't stop. The church steeple pointed up toward the sky as if it still believed there was a heaven. Nothing stopped.

"So why won't he talk to me about it?" Liebowitz asked him.

"He used to chew *my* ear off," said his uncle. "It's a long time ago. You're his kid. He fought a war so you wouldn't have to see things like that. That's what we all fought for. He's not going to the next cousins' club meeting. You know why? They still ask him why he stopped singing. To this day, they ask it. After that day, he didn't want to anymore. He's got a painting under a sheet. It's a painting of that barn, but he doesn't want to see it. He says people shouldn't forget, but should innocent people wake up in the middle of the night because he wanted to paint a picture? You're going to be an artist and ask yourself questions like that? If you ask me, he hates art.

"He's happy you don't do so well in school. He likes it that you're on the football team. He likes it that your mother won't go to parent-teacher's night. He's happy you almost got suspended. He doesn't want you thinking too much."

"He wants me to go to school," Liebowitz said.

"Yeah, but he likes it that you have a thick skin. So why couldn't you go to graduation?"

"Oh, I don't know," Liebowitz said. "We won a game, and we were feeling good, and we bought a chocolate pie, well, four pies, actually, and we threw them up on the ceiling to see if they'd stick. They stuck. We were sitting there laughing, waiting for them to fall, and the principal came in and he looked up and he said, 'That's it. No graduation for you guys.' Listen, we were lucky. I thought we weren't *graduating* at all. *He* meant we weren't going to the ceremonies because we were *disruptive.*"

"You've got to give your mother something to cry about?" his uncle asked.

"Well, that's not what I did it for," Liebowitz protested.

Pete looked at Liebowitz, who occasionally would grin to himself and suppress a laugh. Liebowitz was intent on remembering everything funny about Basic Training and he'd begun by remembering Vince Capilio, who was five feet and three inches tall and who weighed two hundred and fifty pounds, and how he'd helped him onto the back of the truck that drove them from Fort Hamilton to the airport. From there, he'd go on to Loftus P. Cooke, a hillbilly from North Carolina, who'd sat on his bunk watching him, and, unable to account for his looks or his accent, finally asked, "Are you a Polack?"

"No, Loftus," he said. "I'm not a Polack."

"Then what are you?" asked Loftus.

"A Jew," said Liebowitz.

"I never seen one of them before," said Loftus. "What is a Jew exactly?" Liebowitz tried to explain that there were Catholics (Loftus nodded) and Baptists (Loftus nodded again) and Buddhists (Loftus nodded but looked puzzled) and Jews (Loftus looked alarmed). How was he supposed to explain a Jew to him? And then it occurred to Liebowitz: maybe Loftus was like him, a big sports fan.

"You know what Sandy Kofax is?" Liebowitz asked him. Loftus, who was tall and thin, and whose head wobbled on his neck like a baby bird's, tilted that head grotesquely far, thought, and said, "A Polack?"

"No, Loftus, he's not a Polack," Liebowitz said. "What is a Polack?"

"I don't exactly know," said Loftus.

"You think he's going to make it?" someone asked Liebowitz as he passed by. Liebowitz looked up and saw an American Indian opening his footlocker.

"What's he?" George asked Loftus, pointing to the Indian.

"A Polack?" asked Loftus.

When Basic Training ended, Liebowitz was told to take his rifle, load it, go to the stockade, pick Loftus up and escort him back to the Inspector

General's Office. "Don't lose him," the sergeant said, "or you serve his sentence." He asked around, trying to find out what Loftus had done. The scuttlebutt was that he'd gone down on one of the guys and was getting out on a dishonorable discharge.

When he got to the stockade, Loftus was pathetically grateful to see him, so grateful that Liebowitz took the clip out of his rifle. He wasn't going to shoot the bastard even if he had to serve his sentence, and as they were walking back, the rifle strap slipped from his shoulder and his weapon hit the ground, and Loftus went for it, and he saw his career abruptly ending in disgrace. He saw himself going back to Brooklyn (or not going back, a dishonorable discharge would be such a blow to his family), and Loftus handed him the rifle and said, "You better not do that again, Liebowitz. If they see you doing that, they'll put *you* in the stockade," and Loftus was out on bad paper.

That story wasn't so funny, not really, so he thought about Vince Capilio out in the rain, doing push-ups in the mud, shouting to him, "Hey, Liebowitz, you have the name of a smart Jewish lawyer? I'm suing these bastards!" And meeting Capilio in Manhattan on leave, trying to pick up girls, and there he was on Broadway and 42nd, and no Capilio in sight, and suddenly this guy, this display, this spectacle, walked down the street, the chest of his dress greens covered with medals, medals for the air force, medals for the marines, an Italian fruit salad, and they passed two soldiers in uniform, two even younger than they were, and Capilio stopped them and said, "What's the matter with you soldiers? Don't you salute when you see an officer? Where are you boys from?" and the two were from the same base, not the same outfit, but the same base, and Capilio wanted to get away fast, and they spent the night trying and failing to pick up girls, and when he got back to base, no Capilio, and everyone was asking, "Where's Capilio?" And two days later, he heard Capilio was in the stockade.

What was he doing in the stockade? He flew into the Atlanta airport in the uniform with the fruit salad on his chest, and a Vietnamese general was coming in the other direction, wearing his white uniform, and the Vietnamese general saluted him, but Capilio refused to return the salute. He wasn't saluting no monkey general in a white uniform, and the military police arrested him, and the Indian two bunks down said he guessed Capilio didn't study the section on military courtesy, and a couple of guys got nervous and dragged out their footlockers and out came medals they'd bought at the souvenir shop off the base, and then the question was how to get rid of them before the DI got back because if he found them they'd be in the stockade with Capilio, and if not the stockade, they'd be doing push-ups for the rest of their lives.

And when Capilio got out, he broke down and cried, and when Liebowitz walked by, he said, "I want the name of one of those smart Jewish lawyers.

I'm going to *sue* these boys," and Liebowitz said, "It doesn't work that way here, Capilio. Here we have the uniform code of military justice."

"Fuck the uniform code of military justice!" shouted Capilio, where-upon the drill instructor appeared out of nowhere, saying, "Did I hear *fuck the uniform code of military justice?*" and told Capilio to get up, and Capilio got up smiling and kept smiling until he heard he was going to be running around the grinder for the next two hours carrying his footlocker. Ah, thought Liebowitz, Capilio was funny, and he took out his book, but he couldn't read and he couldn't think of anything else to laugh about. He looked over at Pete and saw his eyes on him.

He'd told Pete more than he'd intended to tell him, about Capilio, about his father. Liebowitz called Pete Clark, short for Clark Kent, the man with X-ray vision, and usually he liked it when Pete looked at him, or through him, but he didn't like it now, so he closed his eyes and tried to sleep.

"You can't feel lonely with Pete around," he'd said to the Chief, and the Chief nodded and said, "Yeah, man, he has golden ears. 'Ears like a bat, eyes like a hawk.' I like talking to him, man. Man, he *listens.*" He looked over at Pete, who was staring straight ahead, closed his eyes, and felt himself drifting, floating, as if he were in the water.

The Chief, whose full name was Ten White Feathers Watson, looked out and down at the clouds, spread beneath them like a new, mountainous country, and thought that if his great-grandfather could have seen this, been transported bodily from the ground to the air, and looked down, he would have been certain this was the original world, the world from which his own had been created. He thought back to his childhood, when his father became too sick to polish the turquoise jewelry he made and he and his father used to ride out into the desert where his father would sit still for hours, watching the sheep, and the clouds as they moved toward him over the horizon, moving in from two hundred and fifty miles away. "Now it's a snake," his father would say. "Now it's a thread. Now it's unraveled. Now it's gone." When the Chief came back from hunting snakes, his father would look up and say, "Look at the clouds. What do you see there?" At first, he'd shrug and say he saw nothing, but his father would point out the storm clouds puffing up hundreds of miles away, and occasionally the greyish-beige cone of a tornado. "See that? That's the weather coming closer. That's the future coming closer. It's right there. Clouds tell their stories to anyone who listens."

After his father's death, he would ride out alone into the desert and watch the clouds. One day in school, he picked up a magazine article about Indians who worked the high steel beams in Manhattan. In it was a picture of an Indian on a high beam. The picture must have been taken from below, because in it the Indian appeared to be twelve feet tall, and the sun streamed out as if he carried it on his back, and in his hair the clouds tangled. The top of his head seemed to rest against the perfect blue of the sky. "That's what I'm going to do, that's where I'm going to go," he said to himself, and, when the nuns weren't looking, he carefully ripped the picture from the magazine, tucked it in his geography book, and took it home, where it was tacked over his bed. Eventually, he made a frame for it.

Every morning, he and his uncle Willie went out to the blue wood crosses on the hill, and the hill was full of weeds, and he'd go home, sometimes with Uncle Willie, and occasionally, if Uncle Willie had started drinking early, without him. At noon, he'd go back to the hill, wake up his uncle, and lead him back home. At night, his uncle fell asleep early and he did his homework, went out, listened to the owls, and went to bed himself.

He did well at school. He studied the customs of Indians, and the nuns chose him to take part in an anthropological study, visiting other reservations and recording the customs of the other tribes. He studied the Plains Indians and took part in their ceremonies, and the nuns began to talk of his becoming an anthropologist, and one night two of the teachers from the school came to the house and talked to his uncle. Why shouldn't his nephew be the first in his family to go to college? They brought him brochures and catalogs and he looked at all of them and began to fill out applications. And then one night, he didn't know why, he began to drink with his uncle Willie, and one day he found himself in Albuquerque. He had no idea how he'd gotten there, but he was blind drunk in a strange woman's house. He didn't know her; he didn't know how he'd gotten in, but her door must have been open, and when she saw him, she said, "It isn't the Navajo way to walk into a person's house in the middle of the night," and he knew she was right, so he sat down on a kitchen chair and watched her make some coffee. Somehow he knew her daughter was upstairs calling the police. He got up and walked outside, climbed the garden fence, and from the next street over, saw police cars converging on the house from both ends of the street.

"So," he'd told Pete when Pete asked why he'd joined up, "I figured I just missed out on some big trouble. You can walk the steel beams, but you can't walk them drunk, so I thought, I'll join the army and I'll come home sober and I'll walk right under the sky. The clouds will catch in my hair."

"Yeah," Pete said. "You stay outside long enough and the birds curl up in your hands singing."

"Yeah," the Chief said, smiling at him.

Now the Chief thought about his father and his uncle Willie, who, in the Second World War, joined the army and went into communications at a time when all the country's codes were being broken. The two of them went to Germany, his father to one command post, his uncle to another. His father was behind the lines; his uncle wasn't. They spoke Navajo and no one was going to break *that* code. They were sent all over Europe and they came back with medals and citations; they were in all the papers, and on the reservation, they were still heroes—although he remembered his mother saying she didn't see why her husband was a hero for speaking Navajo when he did that every day at home.

But here he was, flying over the clouds, because he'd been taught Indians were meant to be warriors and he wanted to see it for himself. And when he came back, he'd walk the high beams eighty stories up, the way other people walked on sidewalks. It was all a question of balance.

Before he enlisted, he went to Denver and a building was going up, and he talked someone into letting him go up there. He walked from one end of a beam to another and turned around and walked back. When the war was over, he'd make a lot of money. He had it all figured out. Get this over with, see the world, go home, and walk those steel beams. His feet wouldn't touch the earth.

The Chief was asleep, Liebowitz was asleep. Others were trying to think ahead. They wondered if the heat could be as bad as people said it was. They wondered if maybe it was better to die over there or come back paralyzed, and if it was true you should always save one round for yourself in case you knew you'd lose your legs or be captured. Some people said being captured was the worst thing. Still others composed letters to their girlfriends in which they described the interior of the plane, how it wasn't getting dark even though they'd been flying for over fifteen hours, thinking how proud their girlfriends, or their mothers or their fathers or their sisters or brothers, would be if they could see them now in their uniforms, ready to risk their lives for their country, no longer the kids they were when they left for basic, but men. "Mom wrote last week and asked how are you boys doing?" one of them wrote to his girlfriend, "and I told her, *There aren't any boys here.*" And then he tried to figure out how many days it would take a letter to reach the States, and how long it would take his girlfriend to answer his letter, and how many days it would take her letter to get to Vietnam, and then to find him wherever he was stationed, and when he got past fifteen days, his eyes began closing. A letter could take forever to find him. How long was forever in Vietnam? He didn't want to die in Vietnam. *"You assholes made it through the night but you're going to die today,"* the drill instructor had said.

The plane made its stopovers, took off again and then the plane was landing, dropping straight down, leaving stomachs hanging up in the air, and the stewardesses were saying, "See you boys in twelve months," and they walked out into the heat, an enormous heat, a heat that had weight and pressed down on their chests with a heavy paw and the hot breath of an animal, a heat that made the tarmac waver so that they walked on black water.

"I think I made a mistake," Liebowitz said to the Chief. "I want to play football and run around with topless go-go dancers." Pete, who was walking behind George, smiled.

"Not me," the Chief said. "*This* is the center of the earth. Wherever I put this stick, this is the center of the earth."

"You can be just as dead at the center of the earth as anywhere else," Liebowitz said.

"No way," said the Indian.

"They let you keep that stick? How come they let you keep it?" Liebowitz asked. The stick was long and stout, and carved from top to bottom. The handle was the head of a hawk, its beak forming a handhold. Below the hawk was something that looked like a rodent, and below that, other animals, none of them familiar. Each bird and beast had been carefully painted; the colors were dull, not bright, dull oranges, mustard yellows, muddy browns.

The Indian shrugged and said something about sacred ceremonies. This stick could bless a house or a town and make it the center of the earth. As long as he carried it, he was at the center, no matter how far he went.

It's nice to be crazy, thought Liebowitz.

"You can learn a lot from Indians," Pete said. "They're the only sensible people."

"Yeah? How do you know that?" Liebowitz asked him. "You write a book report on them?" Pete flushed. Liebowitz and the Chief looked at him. They listened to see what he would say next, but he was looking at the wire mesh over the windows of the olive drab school bus waiting for them, and he didn't say anything.

"Why the wire over the windows?" Liebowitz asked a Lieutenant on the bus.

"Going through the villes they have a tendency to lob grenades at us," the Lieutenant said.

"They want us to help them, don't they? What's the matter with them?" Liebowitz asked. The Lieutenant didn't answer.

"Holy shit!" said the Chief, staring at the wire mesh. "Something's wrong here!"

"Something's wrong at the center of the earth?" Liebowitz asked.

Pete touched the wire. It was cold, the only cold thing in the heat, and he sat back in the bus, saying nothing.

HEY DROVE for a while over the bumpy road, raising a red cloud of dust, and someone said, "It's fucking boring," and someone else said, "Where's the fucking war?" and someone else said some people were too thickheaded stupid to thank God for a little peace and quiet, and the Sergeant, who was sitting in the back, turned around and told someone that even when nothing was going on, something was going on.

"They're out there. They're everywhere," the bus driver said without turning his head, his voice a monotone out of which all feeling and color had been drained. Listening to him was listening to a machine, useful and soulless. His voice made your skin crawl.

Once out of sight of the air base, he speeded up. He was driving like a maniac, and they looked nervously at one another. Who wanted to die in a fucking bus crash his first day in Vietnam? What a ridiculous way to die, and then the bus swerved slightly and hit a motorcycle and sent the rider, a thin boy wearing a straw hat, flying off the road and into the ditch at the side, and the driver said, "Sorry," and then he said, "One less zip to worry about," and he drove even faster, and they looked at one another and began to wonder what this was all about. Wasn't anyone going to stop and see if the guy on the motorcycle was still alive, and why the hell were they driving so fast?

The Sergeant said the faster they went, the better, because if they took a hit from a land mine, they'd most likely take it in the rear, and there'd be less of an explosion because the gas tanks were up front. Everyone drove like this in this frying shit hole of a country. Wait until they got to their armored cavalry units. Everyone sitting in the bus looked at one another and then looked down the road. Was anything suspicious there? But they couldn't see anything. Everything was covered in the cloud of red dust that rose up as they drove. When they wiped their faces, the thin layer of red mud streaked their faces. And then they couldn't stand the fear, so they sat back and took their chances because what choice did they have?

The road sped through an enormous basin of land, a gigantic plate, filled with fields divided by rows of mud and stones, some fields flooded with water. The whole place looked as if it were underwater, the bottom of the sea, and on the horizon were rows of palm trees, their fronds motionless in the still, hot air, and behind them, the thin ridges of mountains, grey in the heat and the haze. "Look at the scenery," said the Sergeant. "They don't have banana trees like that back home."

"They do where I come from," someone said, and everyone turned to look at him. He was Hawaiian.

"A smart-ass," said the Sergeant, who pointed out the coconut palms. "Don't tell me. You've got those too."

The Hawaiian smiled. "Those trees can save your lives," he said. "Trees from the land of milk and honey."

"Wait until you come to one with a sniper," said the Sergeant, and then he regretted saying it. He'd been trying to get their minds off the motorcycle and the war and that Hawaiian had stolen his thunder and now he was frightening them himself. "Don't hit anything else!" he called out to the driver. The driver looked at him as if to say, "We all know you're in charge here. You don't have to prove it," and then the Sergeant was ashamed again. Still, they were relaxing. He could tell from the way they talked. He could tell because now they were talking.

"It's *green* out there, man," Liebowitz said.

Pete leaned forward and looked out the window. He'd never seen so many greens, dark greens, electric greens, greens that were almost yellow, little chartreuse shoots waving from sheets of silvery water. It's so green the grass comes out and tells you, *I'm green,* he thought. "It's too green out there to be anything else," Pete said. "It's green and that's all it cares about, being green."

"Never heard it put that way before," the driver said without turning his head. "Whatever it means, I choose to agree."

The bus was slowing down again. "Why are we stopping?" the Sergeant asked, and the driver said the bus in front of them was stopping. There were marines all over the place. The bus radio began chattering. The driver listened to his headset.

"Watch this," said the driver. "The village chief is talking to a marine interpreter and General Walt is down here watching."

The bus inched forward and on the right-hand side of the bus was the village square, red dirt surrounded by mud huts with thatched roofs, and in the middle of the square were two marine helicopters, and down the road, in front of the first bus, was a tank. "Goddamn marines," said the driver. "What a perfect place for an ambush. We're fucking sitting ducks here."

"The General knows what he's doing," said the Sergeant.

"Yeah, sure," said the driver.

The village chief gesticulated, pointed to the sky, and then to the roofs of the huts. The interpreter turned to the General and said something, and the General sketched broadly in the air, smiling happily. The radio chattered. "Winning more fucking hearts and minds," said the driver, listening to his headset. "This is one for the books."

"What's going on?" the Sergeant said again. "Grimsby! What's going on?"

"The interpreter says the village chief's unhappy because the illumination rounds keep falling on his village and setting the thatched roofs on fire. The General's telling the interpreter to explain that they need the illumination rounds so they don't get overrun in the dark, and the interpreter's saying he's only been in country three days, he hardly knows the language. He'll do the best he can, give him a break, a fucking general! He doesn't know what the hell the chief's talking about."

"He said that? To the General?"

"Not to the General, to the guy standing next to him."

"Keep listening to that radio," said the Sergeant, and the driver regarded him with outright dislike. He was sitting here, cooking in a hot metal bus, bored, worried about ambushes, and this was coming over the radio, it was better than a TV program, and the Sergeant had to tell him to keep listening?

Now the Sergeant wanted to know what the General was saying, and Grimsby said the General was promising them many bags of cement in exchange for the damage to their roofs, and the Sergeant wanted to know what the hell they were going to do out here with cement, and Grimsby said they probably thought cement was something to plant, but now the village chief was waving his hands even more violently, pointing at this roof and that, and when the soldiers in the bus followed his outstretched fingers, they saw the charred roofs of the huts.

"He doesn't know why they can't fix it so the illumination rounds don't fall on the village, and the General told the interpreter to explain about wind currents and marking rounds and all that horseshit and that poor bastard's trying to explain it, but the village chief's telling him three huts were burned up last week and a little child crawled under something and burned to death before they could find him. How long is this going to go on?" He was bored and nervous. The men behind him were bored and nervous, dazed and sleepy in the pulsing heat, almost nodding off, jerked awake when they remembered the danger of an ambush, but otherwise bored, bored as they would be back home caught in a traffic jam whose origin was unclear to them.

"Until the war ends," the Sergeant said. "Until hell freezes over and fucking heaven fucking begins."

"I mean how long are we going to wait here?" asked Grimsby.

But apparently the conference was over. The village chief was still apoplectic and gesturing, first pointing to the village and then to the General. The General was smiling as if he'd just seen the promised land, backing away quickly, moving toward the waiting helicopter, and the rotor wash of the helicopter was rocking the bus and bending the grass down and kicking up dirt and pebbles and dust, and the General was standing in the doorway to the helicopter, smiling and waving, and the chopper rose from the ground, rippling in the heat waves, and Grimsby said, "Watch this, folks, watch this!" and as the helicopter lifted over the village, the rotor wash lifted two of the thatched roofs right off the houses and they fell into the grass, exploding in a cloud of twigs and dust, and the second helicopter lifted off a metal roof on one of the larger huts, and it fell with an awful clatter, and Grimsby said, "I bet that's the village chief's," and everyone in the bus nodded his head.

And the village chief was dancing up and down as if the earth was burning the soles of his feet, and the translator finally gave it up and walked away. "We're moving out," said Grimsby, and the bus jolted forward and took off, presumably choking the villagers with its red wake of dust.

"How'd you like those fucking roofs?" asked a soldier in front of them.

"Man, that's not funny," said the Chief. "It's not funny at all."

"You better think that's funny," said the soldier. "If you think that's serious, wait until you see what comes next."

"Don't tell 'em, Sonny, you perverted son of a chicken's gizzard," said Grimsby. "Don't spoil the movie for them. Let them wait."

It was getting dark, the palm trees and the banana trees were turning black against the indigo blue sky, and the men, or the boys (*There are no boys here*) leaned back against their seats and tried to sleep. "What day is it?" someone asked, but either no one knew, or everyone was too tired to answer, and inside, everyone jolted along in silence. The heat pressed on their chests and stole their breath. They concentrated on breathing in and out. They sweated until their clothes were stained and wet and they repeatedly raised their hands to their eyes to wipe away the sweat that dripped like rain from their foreheads.

When they got to base camp, nicknamed Big Red, they were assigned bunks and sent to bed. Almost everyone fell asleep immediately and in the morning awakened cold in their still-damp uniforms, not knowing where they were.

After reveille but before chow, someone tapped Pete on the shoulder, and he saw Eddie, his hair cut so short it seemed a shadow on his head, Eddie from the block, Eddie who told him how to take care of himself the first day at the new school.

"Hey, Eddie!" Pete said. "Hey!" Suddenly, his throat tightened and he couldn't talk. Someone he knew, someone who could tell him what was what; it was more good fortune than he could believe, and immediately, everything around him became less menacing, somehow more familiar, even manageable. He hugged Eddie, and Eddie hugged him, and they pounded one another on the back.

"Come with me when we fall out for chow," said Eddie, "or we're going to be burning shit or doing KP all day." Pete nodded and followed Eddie. They hid out in a ditch until everyone was in the tents, eating, and then they walked through the gate. No one stopped them. "Things are pretty loose here. This is the rear, man," Eddie said. "No one's going to miss us." He asked Pete if he had his PX card, and when he said he did, he told him to hold it out and use it to flag down the right kind of taxi.

"What's the right kind of taxi?" Pete asked him and Eddie said it was the kind that stopped when it saw a PX card, and it wouldn't charge them anything. They were going to do a little black market work. "We'll buy some things at the PX. Don't worry about money," and sure enough, a beat-up Mercedes picked them up, and the driver asked, "You want to make money?" and Eddie nodded, and they got in, and before he started up again, the driver took their PX cards, smeared them with some kind of grease, handed them back, drove them toward town, telling them what he wanted to buy.

They went into the PX, bought radios and cigarettes, electric fans and watches, and the clerk in the PX stamped their PX cards, and when they got out to the taxi, the driver took a cloth and wiped off the stamps so that the cards were once again blank and Pete got nervous. He didn't have a cent left. "Don't worry," Eddie said. "He's going to give the money back. He's going to give us *one and a half times* the money back." And the driver did. They had pocketfuls of money, and the driver asked them where they wanted to go now, to visit the ladies at a car wash or a restaurant, and Eddie said, "A French restaurant!" and the Mercedes threaded its way through the crowded streets and left them in front of a blue and white striped awning.

"What are you doing here?" Pete asked over and over while Eddie wolfed down beef in some kind of pastry covered with brown sauce and mushrooms. "I thought you were in Korea. Your mother told my mother you were in Korea. Yeah, man, when I went home on leave, I called your mother, and then after I went back to base, my mother called your mother. They call each other now. You know mothers."

"I was there," Eddie said, his mouth full. "Then my unit came back, and everyone who had more than ninety days got sent over here. Then my pop died, so they sent me home on emergency leave, and now I'm back here and my unit's out in the fucking field somewhere. They're not holding their breaths waiting for me. They've got better things to think about. Man, it's *cold* in Korea. We stood in front of the tank exhaust breathing in that good old CO_2. Staying warm. That's the name of the game in Korea. I got here and someone told me they had no right sending me. You're supposed to get nine months in the States after a tour in a combat zone, but they don't cut you any slack anywhere. I went to the I.G. here and you know what he said? He said it was true, the nine-month thing, but for an individual, not a unit, and my whole unit came over and it was staying and so was I."

"Join the army and see the world," said Pete.

"Yeah, but once they've got you, it's *Screw you and you're going.*" He sat back and looked at Pete. "So how do you like it here? Hey, man, it's good. It's more fun than Fort Knox, Kentucky. I'm not reporting for *days*. To go from the kind of cold back home to this kind of heat, hell, man, this body's in shock. Let's go to the car wash."

"Car wash?" asked Pete.

"A haircut, a shower and shave, a steam bath, and whatever else you want from the ladies, and all off limits, but don't worry. If they catch you, all they can do is Article Fifteen you. What are they going to do, send you to Vietnam? Yeah, say good-bye to these little red tablecloths. We're going."

"What's it like in the field?" Pete asked. Eddie looked at him. Why hadn't he noticed the difference in his face? An old man was looking at him out of his friend's eyes.

"Watch your ass, man," he said. He's changed, Pete thought. He's *changed.*

At nightfall, they walked back in through the main gate. No one checked. No one showed any interest. "See you in the morning," Eddie said. "Meet me at the ditch." He disappeared into the darkness as if he'd never existed.

"Where were you?" Liebowitz asked, coming up behind him. "Let's see what's going on at the gate." An armored personnel carrier from another platoon had hit a land mine and it was being towed in. They went over to look. The walls of the track had caved in, and the roof of the track had lifted partway off as if it were the lid of a sardine can. "Wow! Look at this!" Liebowitz said. "This isn't boring anymore!"

He took out his camera and began taking pictures of the misshapen APC, and when the soldiers began carrying out bodies wrapped in bags, he took pictures of them, too. One of the soldiers carrying a body saw him, and when he set the body down, he came over to Liebowitz, punched him in the shoulder, and asked him what the fuck he thought he was doing. These guys were their *friends.* This was *sacred* stuff. Man, get out of here while you can still walk!

"What's the fuss about?" Liebowitz asked Pete. "I mean, they're already dead! They don't care who takes their picture."

"The other guys know them," Pete said uneasily.

"What's all the fuss?" Liebowitz asked again. "I don't fucking under-stand it."

"Go get your jungle fatigues," said the Sergeant, and when they got to supply, one of the men looked Liebowitz up and down and said, "Well, I have these. They're your size, but they belong to one of the guys that were killed. Do you want them?" And Liebowitz said, No way. He didn't want any more trouble. These guys were *sensitive.*

"If they're long, roll them up," the man said, handing Liebowitz a bundle of clothes. "Next," he said, looking at Pete, and then called out,

"What's the shortest we've got?" and handed them over, telling Pete, "Roll the suckers up, roll them up."

At night, it was silent in the tent, but after a while Pete thought he could hear a metallic voice, almost ghostly, singing, "I Want to Hold Your Hand," and when he pushed himself up on his elbow, he saw the man in the next bunk had a small radio and earphones. After a while, he heard a click and the silence was absolute.

He thought about the streets of the city, solid with people, all of them pressing different things upon him. Had he seen these things during the day, because now it seemed to him as if he were dreaming them for the first time, now it seemed true that, if you were frightened enough, you began to think, or at least you began to know what you were thinking, and he saw again one man without teeth saying, A watch for the gentleman? A hat for the gentleman? A woman with black teeth, offering a fish, newly roasted? A silver ring with a turquoise stone? Until you expected them to offer you a skull, the hind leg of the dog you'd had when you were twelve, spare parts for lost souls, wandering souls trapped and held for you until this moment when you finally came up and claimed them. They came up to you, slyly offering you anything they had. *Only five dollars MPC for my sister.* Nothing in the world had value there. Everything was for sale. Nothing was tied to anything else by affection or sentiment.

When you tried to walk, they held on to you. They had more than two hands: they had the kind of hands vines must have. Their mouths were open, asking for everything you had, a cigarette, a penny, a piece of chocolate, a dime, a ride in a car, anything, need and greed made visible. He hadn't known there were people who had so little and needed so much, and in the taxi coming back to the base, they passed the garbage dump, the mountains of garbage grey and black against the sharp blue sky, and Eddie said, "Look at this," and tapped the driver on the shoulder. The driver stopped and they watched men and women and children climbing over the mound of garbage, pawing through it, holding up a green frankfurter roll, scavenging frantically for the frankfurter, and if they found it, feeding it right there to the babies on their backs, and while they watched, a truck full of garbage drove up with four GIs guarding it, their guns out, ordering the people off, but the people only moved to the side until the truck had dumped its load and then they were back, clawing through the remains. The smell coated your throat and the roof of your mouth. It stuck to your clothes, but they didn't notice it. A piece of bread, a bone with meat on it, lumps of scrambled eggs, a half-eaten potato black with mold, all popped into the finder's mouth, or the baby on the back of the finder. Why weren't all these people poisoned and dying?

"Watch," said Eddie. "Sometimes the guys get so wired looking at this, they start firing their weapons. I think that one's going to do it." He pointed to one of the young soldiers watching the people pick through the garbage, meditatively fiddling with the safety of his M-16, but the soldier turned away from them. He didn't do anything.

In the car wash, a two-story shack of rough, unfinished brown boards, the walls stained inside and outside by rain until they were streaked black as if by tar or coffee, women cleaned them and shaved them and offered them their bodies, but he'd never had a woman before, and he remembered Liebowitz saying no more hookers for him. The last one cost him fifty dollars, and his pay for the month was seventy-eight dollars, and when it was over, she said, "You're finished, buddy. Roll off." If that was sex, you could have it. He'd save himself up until he got home.

He thought about the misshapen track and the dead soldiers and the soldiers to whom the body bags were more than things to carry, and he touched his own wrist and felt his pulse and tried to imagine what it would be like to be dead. Was it really possible he could become dead? And he tried to remember the inside of the car wash, a building of unpainted wood with a sheet-metal roof, knocked together, probably, in a few hours, and he thought about the cabdriver and the PX cards, and he went through the day, but it didn't seem like a single day. It seemed like many days, even years, and now it seemed more a problem to be alive than to be dead, because if so much could happen in one day, where were you supposed to put all you saw? How were you supposed to make sense of any of it? You took it all in, and it pushed at you. It pushed out your sides the way the mine pushed out the sides of the APC. He could already feel it happening.

And somewhere back down the road, illumination rounds were falling on that village, and the village chief couldn't do anything about it, and soon trucks full of bags of cement would pull up and the village chief wouldn't know what to do with them, and what happened to the man on the motorcycle the bus driver hit? Still, he knew he was a kid from Brooklyn. He knew that much, and so he could fall asleep. He could hear his mother saying, *Tomorrow is another day,* but now that wasn't comforting. These words were a threat, not a promise. He didn't remember falling asleep, and then reveille woke him up and the day was upon him and there was nothing he could do to stop it.

**14** **乙** HE VILLAGERS and a monk known for his power over spirits came to our dwelling and advised my mother to instantly call back my *kwan.* She was to take a brass bowl, a ladle, and a piece of cloth and go out into the fields where the water buffalo, with me on its back, had been shot. Then she was to take the ladle from the bowl, scoop up the *kwan,* put it in the bowl and cover the bowl with the cloth, and return home. This my mother did, and when she returned home, I lay on my bed, and she passed the bowl over and over my body, and the monk said my *kwan* would sense my presence, recognizing me, perhaps by my odor, and would enter my body and I would once more be well.

When this was done, the monk took unspun cotton threads and tied them with a tight knot around my wrists, and then the monk blessed me. Relatives came to bless me and to wish for my good fortune and offered me presents and greeted my *kwan,* addressing it and flattering it in every way. In time, said the monk, my *kwan* would strengthen and I would once more be the person I was before the plane flew over the field and the troubles began.

But I was not the same. I was afraid to be alone in the house, and when the baby grew hot, I wept, believing it was soon to die, so that my mother quickly had two children to care for. If I was sent into the fields with the other children to watch the rice and frighten off the animals who might enter the paddies and eat the new plants, I could not sleep and was frightened by every noise. My mother despaired, and my parents began to quarrel. Our house, like all houses in the village, was made of wood, and my grandmother fell to blaming my father for cutting wood posts from trees in different forests because, as everyone knew, female spirits reside in trees, and females from different forests would naturally quarrel among themselves and there would be no peace for those who dwelt in the house. "Pull the house down," she said, "and start over!" Naturally my father said he would do no such thing, even when I became wild in my behavior and extravagant in my demands.

Because I would not eat, the best foods were saved for me, but I was not easily tempted. Sticky rice boiled in sugar and rolled into balls and steamed in banana leaves was offered to me but I would not touch it, or worse, I would nibble at it like a rat, and put the rest of it down. I grew so thin that my bones showed through my body and were so sharp they hurt the thin skin stretched over them. My mother became angry with me, saying the villagers believed she was beating me or scolding me and had begun to talk, saying it was not my own misfortune that was making me ill, but some ill-doing of my mother's was taking its toll upon me. After many weeks of hearing this, my mother began to have an ill will toward me, and I saw that if this course of events did not change, she would eventually become bitter and I would be sent to the house of a relative. It was then I decided to use my own mind to find the source of the trouble.

After much thinking, I concluded that my *kwan* was not at peace because it had become entwined with the water buffalo's and had taken flight with the water buffalo's, and there would be no peace for me until the buffalo found rest. It was his hooves I heard when I walked alone in the forest and his restless soul that troubled my dreams at night. I dreamed constantly of something wailing in a dark place where there was no food or light or a place to set one's foot and I knew this was the lost soul of the water buffalo tangled with my lost soul waiting for me to help both of us find rest. After I knew this, I waited in the forest for the monk who came in the morning with his begging bowl and I bowed before him and explained to him what I believed to be true and begged him to perform the mourning service for the water buffalo.

The monk was old and powerful among spirits and promised he would meditate on my request and in three days inform me of his decision. Three days later, I waited for him in the forest and he said he would honor my request, unheard of as it was, because many things were possible on this earth, and perhaps the water buffalo had been killed just before he was to come back as a human being. There were many reasons a soul, even a soul of a tree, could not find rest, but most important, he said, was that the dead should not pull down the living, and so, if my family agreed, he would perform the ceremonies for those who had survived the water buffalo, just as if the animal were a family member. But there was an obstacle. To perform the ceremonies correctly, it was first necessary to cremate the water buffalo, and his body had already been buried. "His head and his horns hang over my pallet," I said, and the monk nodded as if that were of great significance.

My mother was not pleased when she heard what I had proposed to do, but neither she nor anyone else would oppose the wishes of a monk, and so, one week later, we cremated the head and horns of the water buffalo and returned to our home. There, all the necessary items were placed in a lacquer bowl: a ball of unspun cotton, one mouthful of betel nut and leaf, one cigarette, two balls of glutinous rice, a boiled hen's egg, and other articles I've now forgotten. The monk tied the mourners' wrists with unspun cotton threads and recited the words to call back the buffalo's *kwan*, and as soon as I heard them, my heart settled, and I felt a desire to eat. To this day, I say these words when the world seems to darken around me and all that is familiar in existence turns strange and steps back into the shadow. Each word from the monk's lips dropped like water onto the parched earth of my soul: "Oh, *kwan,* do return. Do not stay with the dead in the dead land. In that land, there is no food, no clothing, and no place to live. There are only ills and unhappiness. Do stay in the land of the living where there is joy and happiness. Oh, *kwan!* Do return."

After the ceremonies, I began to fatten. I once more slept with the other children in the shelters built at the edge of the rice fields, and during the day, we watched the buffaloes, climbed trees, and pitched pennies using the flat lids of the large snails, fought with one another, and roasted and ate large snails, and when the day was over, we rode the buffaloes' backs, singing and playing the flute as we went through the fields that stretched to the horizon where the half-sunken sun rested like the red-gold arch of a door, and I thought again, There is no such happiness as this elsewhere on earth. I never want to be anywhere else than here, and I entered my thirteenth year happy.

But this happiness did not last long. My *kwan,* if it was back, had learned bitter things in its nightly travels, and I began to look at people, the hills around me, the ripening rice waving in the fields, even the mountains encircling our village as insubstantial things painted on paper. When they wavered in the heat, I waited for the fire that would set them burning, and when I closed my eyes, I could see the world around me in flames that leaped up to the sky, dark smoke roiling, then parting to reveal the red leaping flames, billowing outward, then becoming denser, finally dying down, leaving nothing but an expanse of grey ash, in the middle of which I stood alone. My world, that I had thought so strong, almost immortal, could blow off like a dry leaf in a strong wind, and the rest of the world—there was a world beyond the limits of my village!—was like a hawk, swooping down on my village. I had lost belief in the world.

In front of me the white face of the soldier who shot my water buffalo hung like a moon. If I could find him, he could explain what had happened and what was going to happen. Oh, *kwan,* I said to my soul, if you voyage at night, find that soldier for me. I will follow him and he will explain the ways of the world to me. I waited in the forest and told the monk what I asked for, but he discouraged me, saying that the knowledge I sought could be found only inside myself and if I came to the temple, he would explain all to me. But I did not come.

In our house, my aunt's second child wore a white bracelet of unwoven cotton around its wrist. Its forehead was marked with an X, and the soles of its feet also, and everyone marveled at how it grew, but when I looked at the child, I saw it was already dead. When I looked at my own hand, I marveled at how young and unwrinkled it was, and how alive my pulse seemed, jumping beneath my fingers like a frog, and I thought how different appearances were from the truth, because inside I was already dead. And I asked myself if this had come about because of the plane and its bomb, and the soldiers that shot my water buffalo, and I answered myself saying that the plane was like the first bird of spring, its arrival signaling the arrival of the entire flock, only the bird that had come with its bomb signaled a flock that would fly over bringing destruction and death, and there is nowhere to hide from such birds, because they can climb the heights of the sky, and only those who are already under the ground are safe from them.

And now I was happy only when the boys sang to me in the fields, or walked me home through the forest, or bent over me and kissed me. Much later, my mother would ask me if I knew what I was doing was wrong, but at the time I was beyond right and wrong, as the dead are. And so, one very hot day, after one of the boys and I had strayed deep into the forest looking for a young buffalo, and after we found him, and tied him to the trunk of a palm tree, we lay down in the grass together, looking up at the blue sky, and over us, cockatoos called to one another, and somewhere up above, monkeys chattered to one another. We heard the call of wild ducks near the river, and in the heat we moved slowly and lazily, and when he touched my breast, I did not mind.

It was as if all the noises in the jungle stopped and the only sound was the sound of our breathing. I felt like a seed coming alive in the hot sun, and I did not mind his hand on my belly, which before had felt like a place of death, a graveyard beneath the smooth flesh, but now it pulsed, and when we performed the forbidden act, I saw it all. I foresaw my mother sending me from the village: I foresaw living among the strangers with white faces whom the villagers said looked like corpses. I foresaw the deaths and the world ending again and again in village after village, because each village was its own world, as, in the end, each person is his own world. I foresaw my own exile and eventual death, and I said good-bye to the village square, and the village elder, to the great pan of peanuts roasting over the fire in the center of the village, to my brothers and sisters, and to my new niece with her white bracelet, even to the look of the sun in the heavens, and to the rice that grew in the fields and nourished us all, to the earth and all its creatures, its frogs and its crabs, its pond herons, the paddy birds and the wooden rattles used to scare them off the pregnant rice, the locusts, the needle leeches and the buffalo leeches, and when I had said good-bye to the rain of fishes, the time when the wind blew hard against the water and lifted the little fish from the water's surface and dropped them back down, when I had said good-bye to the fish in the rice paddies that burrowed into the mud in the dry season and came up in the rain and swam in the deep footprints of the water buffalo when their prints filled with water, when I had said good-bye to the whole world and was alone in emptiness, I did not mind.

 *15* **T**HE TRUCKS brought them into the base at night, and when the sun came up, they got their first look at it. Fire Base Pluto, set in a valley, surrounded by mountains, was nothing more than a scar in the red earth surrounded by concertina wire. Olive drab tents rose up in back of packed sandbags. Trucks came in and were unloaded and wooden crates piled up everywhere: crates of hand grenades, ammunition, C-rations, freeze-dried rations for the long-range reconnaissance patrols – the LRRPs – cans of food for their dogs.

A helicopter landed, blew up a storm of dust, discharged an officer returning from battalion headquarters, and took off again. Another helicopter landed, brought back three men who'd been medevaced out some weeks before, and left immediately. Every step they took stirred up small clouds of dust, and the dust tinted the rising mist red. Dogs, kept as pets by men on the base, chased one another and copulated, rolled on their backs in the dust and got up sneezing. A large white rabbit on a white chain, a red ribbon around his neck, protected by a wire fence, had turned reddish in the dust. A few chickens, captured when one of the platoons went into a suspected Viet Cong village, walked aimlessly, occasionally pursued by the dogs, and when this happened, one of the soldiers stopped and chased the dogs off.

"So what do you think of this?" Liebowitz asked. "It looks like a warehouse without walls."

"Yeah, but look at the mountains," Pete said. "I never saw mountains like that. Range after range after range. Blue ones, purple ones, and those clouds. Look at the gold rim around those clouds."

"Pet rabbits, pet dogs, chickens," the Chief said. "This isn't what I expected."

"Most of the dogs spend the night outside the wire," someone said. "Early warning systems with tails. And the chickens, they're good, too. We keep them in the tents. They see a snake, they make a racket."

They were given their platoon numbers, and since their platoons were out in the field, they spent most of the day hanging around the base.

"Liebowitz, Bravado, Ten White Feathers Watson, you three are with Krebbs's track. They'll be back in later. Krebbs, he's a good man. And Big Sal, he takes some getting used to. He's from the Bronx. In New York."

"Big Sal?" asked Liebowitz. "Is there a little Sal?"

"There was," the Captain said. "So, look around, clean your weapons, get used to it. You'll be out on listening post tonight. We're shorthanded. We're never at full strength here. Later on, the Colonel wants to talk to you. He talks to all the new men."

They were dismissed and sat in front of the tent, talking.

"So," Liebowitz asked the Chief, "you volunteered or what?"

"I volunteered," the Chief said. "It's a tradition in my family."

"Yeah?" said Liebowitz. "I never heard of Indians in the army."

"I never heard of Jews in the army," the Chief said.

"You ever hear of Italians in the army?" Pete asked. "We're here. End of story."

"I figure it won't be so different here," the Chief said. "I'm used to snakes and prairie dogs. I used to hunt them. I was always looking for grey owls. I can ride anything bareback. My uncle Willie, he taught me to sit so still animals would come right up to me. I'll show you. I can sit so still you'll think I'm dead."

"Yeah, do it," Liebowitz said.

The Chief sat on the ground, his back to the tent pole, folded his legs beneath him, clasped his hands over his stomach, took a deep breath, lowered his eyelids, and in front of their eyes, became inanimate.

"Is he breathing?" asked Geronimo Davis, coming over from his bunk. "Man, he looks *dead.*"

"Sure, he's breathing," Pete said nervously. "You're breathing, aren't you, Chief?" The Chief didn't answer. Geronimo Davis reached over and pushed hard against the Chief's shoulder. The Chief rolled onto his side and lay there on his arm, his legs still folded. "Hey, I don't like this," Pete said. "Chief! Cut it out, Chief!"

"He do that on purpose?" asked Geronimo Davis. "I never seen anything like it."

"Wake up, Chief," Pete said. The Indian didn't move.

"Oh, man," said Liebowitz.

"I bet if you lit a cigarette and burned his arm, he wouldn't move," Pete said.

"Don't do it," said the Chief, uncrossing his legs and sitting up.

"Hey, that's something!" Davis said. "You want to be with my track? I'm the new TC on 3-5."

"You're a track commander? How come you're a track commander?" Liebowitz asked.

"Because I'm black?" asked Davis.

"No, man," Liebowitz said. "What'd you have to do?"

"I don't know," Davis said. "I didn't ask for it. They asked me if I wanted to go to Officer Candidate School and I said yes, and they made me a sergeant. My folks is real proud of me. It's a lot better than running around the projects trying to find my little sister."

"I never had a sister," Pete said absently.

"Yeah? They're cute. Until they're about ten. Then all they think about is when they's going to get their periods."

"They talk about those things?" Pete asked. His face was hot. He was blushing.

"When they's eleven, that's *all* they talks about," said Davis. "Not to me, you understand. I listened to them through the wall. Man, we had *thin* walls. The day I heard she got hers, that was a bad day for me, man. My ma set me on her like a watchdog. Old watermelon belly! That's what I called my cousin and she was only thirteen!"

"Girls," Pete said.

"You didn't see much of them?" asked Davis. "Keep it that way. Boy, life is simpler without them. Join the army and forget them women." He was thin, wiry, his black hair tight and curly against his head, and over his left ear was a patch of tight grey hair. "See this hair?" he said, pointing to the grey patch. "My sister, she began it and the heat over here, it *encouraged* it. Anyone here play Frisbee? I play Frisbee. They say, Big Sal, he like the yo-yo."

"Yo-yo?" asked Pete. "He still plays with yo-yos?"

"You, Liebowitz," Davis said, "you a Jew?"

"Yeah, I'm a Jew," Liebowitz said.

"Jews don't go into the army," Davis said.

"You wanna see my horns?" Liebowitz asked, flushing, starting to stand up.

"Sit down, man," said Davis. "I thought Jews were too smart for this."

"Yeah, well, no one's too happy about it in my family," Liebowitz said. "My mother's probably still crying. You know what she said before I came over here? She said she's pretending I'm not here. She's pretending I'm in school in North Carolina. On a football scholarship. If anyone asks her, that's what she's going to tell them. I said, 'Ma, why do you want to pretend I'm in college? All I want to do is play football and run around with Jewish go-go dancers.' My father said, "Don't worry your mother. Write to me at work. I'll take the letters home.' He'll take them out of the envelopes and she'll read them and she'll pretend I'm in North Carolina."

"She crazy?" asked Geronimo Davis.

"Oh, man, she *loves* me," said Liebowitz.

"Yeah? Well, I wouldn't want to write letters from North Carolina while I'm frying my ass here," Rosario Paganini said from his bunk. He'd been listening. "You know who you look like?" Paganini asked. "You look like Jackie Gleason."

"I'm not fat!" Liebowitz protested.

"Doesn't he look like him?" Paganini demanded.

"He sure does," said Davis.

"Why shouldn't she think what she wants?" Liebowitz asked.

"Everyone's different, man," the Chief said.

"Yeah, Pig, everyone's different," said Geronimo Davis.

"They call you Pig?" asked Pete.

"Yeah, so what? They call him Geronimo and I never heard of any black Indians," Paganini said.

"It is the name I was born with," said Geronimo Davis.

"Yeah, well, they're sending us out tonight," Paganini said, and they fell silent.

"Jews don't fight," Paganini said at last.

"Again?" said Pete.

"Yeah?" asked Liebowitz. "Tell that to Israel."

"Hey, those Israelis, man," Paganini said. "I forgot about them."

"Yeah, well, my mother, she wanted me to run. She knew a woman in Canada, but I told her I couldn't do it. I couldn't run."

"You should've run," said Paganini.

"To the moon, Alice!" said Liebowitz.

"See, see?" Paganini asked. "He even sounds like Jackie Gleason."

Liebowitz grinned and drew circles in the red dust. "You're a smart boy," his mother had said. "You think that'll help you out there?"

"Come on, Ma," he'd said. "Stop crying."

"This will kill your father," she said.

"This will kill your mother," said his father.

This was his second day and he missed them already. But he could fight as well as anyone else. He'd show them.

"I'm a married man," Paganini said. "The last thing my mother-in-law said to me? She said, 'I hope you got enough insurance.' You know what I told her? I told her, 'I'm coming home to break your balls, bitch.' Well, that's not the only reason I'm coming back. In six months, I'll have a kid. I wasn't going to get married, but when I finished Basic, this funny thing happened. I thought, what if I don't come back? Who'll carry on the name? So I got married. But I'm coming back."

"We're all coming back," Pete said.

"Yeah, it don't pay to think no other way," said Geronimo Davis. "I figure I'm as safe here as anywhere. One winter in Detroit? We had no place to live and all winter it was fires in old oil drums and my mama and my sisters, they went back down south and stayed with my grandma. She wouldn't take me. Down home, you stop at a gas station and the man makes remarks about your mother and your sister and they are waiting to rile you. My mother, she stops for gas, she puts me out on the road and when she gets the gas, she comes back for me. And when she comes back, sure as hell if someone in the car ain't crying. So she left me in Detroit. She says, 'You are one smart nigger, and they find that out, they'll kill you just for the hell of it.' One whole winter out there behind those gas drums in the *cold.* Every morning you wake up blacker than you went to sleep the night before. Soot, ash, cinders, burning newspapers. The man, he wants to keep alive, he doesn't bother you out there. But a few weeks of it? Man, you don't *want* to be alive. So here I am. I freeze there or I cook here, I get paid for it. Look at this," he said, throwing a book over to Liebowitz. "You know what that is? That is *The Uniform Code of Military Justice.* I'm studying it. I could be a *lawyer* when I get out of here, man."

"I wouldn't let them see you studying this," Liebowitz said.

"I don't mean no harm," said Davis.

"Keep it under wraps," Liebowitz said.

"Sure, man," Davis said. "You think so?"

"Yeah, I do," said Liebowitz.

"I told you so," Paganini said.

"You know?" Liebowitz said. "I keep hearing this is a black man's war. You're the only black man on the base."

"You should see an air force base," Paganini said. "If you think this is white."

"Most of the troop's in the field. There be brothers out there, man," Davis said.

"Not too many," Paganini said. "A couple of wetbacks, but not too many blacks."

"Why?" Liebowitz asked.

"The luck of the draw," said the Chief. "You've got me. I should count for at least ten blacks."

"Yeah? Why you so important?" asked Davis, laughing.

"I'm at the center of the world," said the Chief, pounding his stick against the baked red earth. "And if you're with me, you are, too."

"Terrific," Liebowitz said.

"We're going out tonight?" Paganini asked.

"Yeah, and we're all coming back," Liebowitz said.

"We sure is," said Geronimo Davis.

16 T H E Y   W E R E out in the field, a firebase, they had no idea where. They were on Hill 405, whatever that meant, and the sun had disappeared, the moon was full, they could hear the wind in the distant palm trees, and far away, the cries of animals, calling one to another, and birds with voices like humans, echoing back and forth, and the steel pot passed from one man to another, and everyone put in a few Military Payment Certificates, and when the pot got to Pete, he looked at it and asked one of the men near him what the collection was for.

"For whoever kills the Second Lieutenant."

"I don't even know the Second Lieutenant," Pete said.

"It doesn't matter," said the voice in the dark. "Tomorrow someone will point him out. Whoever gets him first, gets the money."

The Chief reached over and tapped Pete on the knee with his center-of-the-earth stick. "Give me the pot," he said, taking the helmet and dropping in two MPCs. "We're out here in the middle of nowhere, we don't know what we're doing, we've got to depend on these guys."

Pete nodded and contributed. Liebowitz contributed and the three of them sat there thinking how matter-of-fact it was: whoever killed the Second Lieutenant got the money, and from the number of men contributing, they'd get a lot of it, about two hundred and fifty dollars.

"What's wrong with the Second Lieutenant?" Pete asked.

"He's not into survival, man," said a voice in the darkness.

"This morning after we dug in?" said another voice. "He had us fucking *police the area,* pick up every damn fucking twig and branch between us and the field of fire. We spent two hours removing a natural layer of defense. Now anything can walk in here without making a fucking sound. The man's bad news. He's been here three days and he hasn't done one thing right yet. Midnight humping? He's all for midnight humping, right, Shorty?"

"Last night, we were going up the hill?" said Shorty. "It was so dark you couldn't see your hand in front of you. We were going up the fucking hill holding hands so we wouldn't get separated, and what happens? My helmet falls off my ruck and I automatically reach for it and I let go of the hand I was holding, and now I'm going down the hill, and half of the company's going back down the hill with me, and all of a sudden Alpha company gets hit on the other hill, and we stood there and watched them and there wasn't a damn thing we could do about it. I mean, you could hear us coming for fucking *miles*. We walked into *trees*. We fell into holes. It was a fucking nightmare. Sam there broke his damn nose."

"I did," said another voice. "In two places. A double deviated septum, that's what I've got now."

"How long's the Second Lieutenant been here?" Liebowitz asked.

"Three days," said the nasal voice.

"Maybe he'll learn," said the Chief.

"He'll never learn," said the nasal voice. "He's from West Point. He knows everything. Two nights ago we were out on a listening post and all of a sudden the sky lights up. Something set off a trip flare, so we let loose with everything we had, and artillery let loose with everything they had, and in the morning, what happened? The Second Lieutenant had set up the wire over a goddamned gopher hole and the creature came out and tripped it and the thing blew the animal all over the place. He scared everyone to death, man. We gave away our positions. Every gook for miles knew where we were. Who sets up a trip flare over a fucking gopher hole? Would you do it? Would I do it? Would Krebbs do it? *He* does it. And he's the one in command here? Fuck that."

"I stay out of politics," said the Chief.

"Sure," said the nasal voice. "You're new. You don't know what it's about. You're here. We're dug in. There's the perimeter. There are the tracks. Wait until he gets you way out in the field. Wait until he gets you so far out what other people call the front we call the rear. You'll get into politics."

"We make a mistake, you're going to take up a collection for us?" asked Pete.

"You're new," the nasal voice said. "We tell *you* what to do. You know how much time you've got to learn? You just used it up."

"We're willing to learn," Liebowitz said.

"Here he comes," said the nasal voice. "That's him. The red-headed sucker. If you get him, you get the pot."

"Liebowitz, Watson, Bravado, Paganini," said the Second Lieutenant. "The battalion commander wants to see you."

"What did I do?" asked Liebowitz. "I just got here."

"The crap lecture," said the nasal voice. "Everyone gets it."

"Shut up, Sam," said the Second Lieutenant. "They just got here. They're not warped yet."

"*You* just got here," someone said.

"The crap lecture," Sam said. "You'll see."

"Where's our Sergeant?" someone asked. "How far can you go with a case of immersion foot? Where is Krebbs?"

"Where he's supposed to be," said the Second Lieutenant, and they got up and followed him. Beyond the perimeter, it was now pitch-dark. The moon had gone behind a cloud. Anything could be out there. "Shouldn't there be illumination flares?" Liebowitz asked. "I mean, how do you know where they are?"

"We don't," said the Second Lieutenant. "That's why we send men out on listening posts. You'll go out after you talk to the Colonel."

"We just got here," Liebowitz said.

"Yeah, well, the other men are tired from midnight humping," said the Second Lieutenant. He opened the flap of the big tent in front of them. "Here they are, sir," he said, saluting.

"No saluting anywhere in the field, Lieutenant," said the Colonel, who got up, returned the salute of the four young men, shook their hands, and sat down on the edge of his desk. "I'm Colonel Johansen," he said, "and I know you're new here and you don't know what's going on, but I want to make you a promise I make all the new men." He paused and looked into each set of eyes as if he were memorizing their faces.

In fact, he was studying them ever since he'd made a bet with the General, who'd been active in the Second World War and Korea, and who swore he could look into a man's eyes and give an eighty-percent-accurate prediction of the man's chances of survival. He looked first at the Chief and thought, if he stood still, if you covered him with oil, he'd look just like a goddamn cigar store Indian, damn, what a target he was, and Paganini, olive-skinned, short and muscular like a fireplug of a person, the bluish-black stubble of what would be a beard and mustache in a couple of weeks if he didn't shave, while the other two were pink-cheeked and smooth, like babies, and Bravado, a kid, a baby. He looked like a movie star, Spanish, not Italian, those big sleepy eyes, would he bet on him? He didn't think so. He already looked wounded, and Liebowitz, short, round spectacles magnifying his huge brown eyes, a surprised, intelligent owl, that one looked mischievous, but the mischief-makers had a way of settling down when things got hot. So who did he bet on? Not the Bravado kid, who looked young and frightened, and looked down at his feet, and stood, half-turned away from him, as if, because he represented the army, he represented menace, looked away from him the way people with sensitive eyes looked away from the sun. He bet the kid didn't see him at all, wouldn't recognize him ten minutes after he left his tent, not even if he tapped him on the shoulder and said, "Remember me?" No, he didn't bet on Bravado. The kid wasn't really *here*. That kid was already in a state of shock. And thin. Out here, the thin ones got thinner.

Liebowitz, maybe. Things struck him funny. You needed a sense of humor out here and he looked intelligent and he had a little extra flesh. He'd be the one to finish up the leftover C-rations the others complained about. They wouldn't be medevacing him out with malnutrition or rickets.

The Indian? He'd bet on the Indian. Something about the way he stood, as if he could walk a rainbow and walk right out of the field without losing his balance, without once looking back. And he was an Indian. Maybe he'd watched too many movies, but they had a jungle here, trails to follow. You needed more than a sixth sense; you needed a seventh and an eighth. Let's face it: he'd bet on the Indian because there was something about him he liked. He didn't want to see anything happen to him.

And Paganini? Your all-purpose soldier. Fifty-fifty.

In a few months, three or four months, he'd call them in again. He liked to see how they'd changed, and they did; they all changed. In three or four months, if they were still here, he'd go over it again and he wouldn't come to the same conclusions. Out here, even the dogs changed. He'd brought out a vicious Doberman pinscher. Now it cowered under the wooden platform of the tent.

The men were shifting from foot to foot, and the Colonel sat on the edge of his desk and looked from face to face. "In this outfit," he said, "we don't leave anyone behind. No matter what happens, *we don't leave anyone behind.* I can't promise you won't be wounded or you won't be killed, but I can promise you you won't be left behind. No one in this outfit will be lost forever. If I have to use up all the battalion's resources and all the resources I can beg, borrow, or steal, and call in all the favors people owe me, we'll come for you. You have my personal word on it. Your family's never going to wonder what happened to you. No one in this company's left out for the buzzards. Once you're part of this company, you're part of it forever. Any questions?"

The four of them looked down at their boots and shook their heads.

"No questions?" asked the Colonel. "I'll be here if you have any later. Dismissed."

"What do you make of that?" Liebowitz asked.

"He's a poet," said the Chief. "No one in this outfit will be lost forever."

"He just told us he expects us to get killed," Pete said.

"I don't know about you," said Liebowitz, "but I'd be very surprised if I found myself killed."

"I wouldn't," Pete said. "Not after the way they took up that collection. Like they were betting on a baseball game."

"New ball game, new rules," said the Chief.

"Yeah, but what's the game?" asked Liebowitz.

"No one said you had to like it, my man," said the Chief. "Is this our tent?"

"You must be used to tents," said Paganini.

"Tents went the way of the buffalo a long time ago," the Chief said.

"This is your tent," said the Lieutenant, coming up behind them. "No LPs tonight. Pick out a rack and get some sleep."

. . .

THE GROUND beneath them rocked. The noise was almost solid, over-
powering, and the sky outside the tent was so bright the inside of the tent
was illuminated. "Get your helmets, get your weapons!" someone was
screaming, and they grabbed their weapons, slammed their helmets on their
heads, and ran out of the tent after the others. While he ran, Pete settled his
helmet firmly on his head. He'd never liked it in Basic, it was so heavy, but
now, with the earth rising up around him and falling back down like a crazy
rain, it felt like a roof, not a hat, and he loved it.

"Go around the corner and get some ammo," someone told them, and
the four of them ran around the corner, and each one was given two bandoliers of ammo for the .50, and they were told to get on a truck with the rest
of the platoon. They were going further up the mountain.

"Who the fucking hell puts a base in a *valley?*" a voice kept asking.
"Everyone and his uncle can shoot down at you. We're perfect targets. Come
and get us, man."

Up front, the radio chattered. "So what happened here?" asked the man
who had passed the helmet.

"What happened is," said the man on the radio, "we have some men in
an outpost up the mountain and some snipers up there shot the CO's jeep
and they got a staff sergeant and a platoon leader. The jeep's turned over on
the road. The two men are in the jeep. No one knows if they're alive and we're
going up to the outpost and we're going to get off and sweep up to the jeep
and see what we can find. Then we'll relieve some of the men up there and
we're up there for the night."

The truck slowed down and everyone got off, got on line, and began
climbing the ridge. It was pitch-dark, but every now and then a pebble would
glow silver. What if I turned and ran? Liebowitz thought. What would happen?
I can feel their eyes, thought Pete. They feel like nails. I feel them. So this is
what it is to be a warrior, thought the Chief. The Lieutenant walked carefully,
his skin tightening, his eyes on the new men. They inched forward, listening
for every rolling pebble, for anything, a sneeze, a sharp intake of breath, but
they heard nothing, and then they were upon the jeep, and in it, the two men
were dead, dead and alone.

The Lieutenant motioned them forward. They climbed until they reached
the outpost up on the mountain.

"This is the outpost?" asked Liebowitz. He saw a string of concertina
wire, a track, a .60 mortar, and eight guys, four of whom didn't know a
goddamned thing about what was going on. All they knew was that they
were on an outpost with mountains rising up all around them. The men up
here had heard shots but they always heard shots; they knew they wouldn't
know what the shots meant until someone came and told them.

"If anyone's up there," said Liebowitz, looking up at the surrounding mountain, "they can throw in whatever they want."

"Wait until you've got something to complain about," Sam said.

"*This* is something to complain about," Liebowitz said. "Didn't anyone study tactics?"

"Now aren't you happy you contributed to the collection?" asked Sam. The men they'd relieved went back down the mountain, and got in the truck that had brought them up. The engine coughed and the truck's lights swerved over the outpost, were extinguished, and in the dark the driver made his way back down the mountain, leaving them there. An owl hooted and was answered by another. A big cat's roar was answered by another, deeper roar. The palm trees rustled and the moon came out from behind a cloud and they got their first good look at Sam, a tall, thin man with a huge swollen nose, thin lips, and a mat of straw-colored hair.

"Put your helmet on," said the Second Lieutenant, passing by.

"It gives me a headache," Sam said.

"Put it on," the Lieutenant said.

"What's your last name?" Liebowitz asked Sam.

"You don't want to know my last name. It don't do to get too friendly up here. Didn't they teach you that in Basic?"

"Yeah, they taught us," Paganini said. "But we're buddies."

"Then you already made a mistake," Sam said. "You call me, I answer. You come to my bunker, and you want to talk and I want to talk, fine. If I don't want, I say, 'Yeah, I'm going to go up on the hill now and smoke a joint and blow a little bubble around myself,' and I'll just sit there and take care of business and not be bothered by anybody, and if you want to talk to me and I want to talk to you, I'll just open my little window and say, 'How are you? Is everything O.K. with you? Everything's O.K. in here. O.K., that's it,' and I'll close my little window again. That's how it is, man."

"Sam, shut up," said the Lieutenant. "You four, over by the sandbags. They ambushed the jeep. Maybe they're coming for us. Get down there and listen. If you hear anything, one click on the handset and start firing."

"Where's everyone else?" asked Paganini.

"In the track sleeping," said the Lieutenant. "It's going to be a quiet night—unless some gooks spring our ambush up the mountain."

"Three hundred and sixty-three days left and already I don't like it here," Liebowitz said.

"And keep *quiet*," said the Lieutenant. "You want to hear them before they hear you. It's cat and mouse out here and there are more of them than us. Listen and keep your mouths shut. Take turns on watch. Two hours each. When you're finished, hand the watch on to the next guy. If you're not on watch, sleep. It's simple, so do it."

The four of them stood in silence, watching the Lieutenant walk off toward the track and disappear into the darkness. They looked around them and saw the faint outline of the sandbags. Around them, the mountains were a darker line against the dark night sky and no stars shone. The longer Pete looked at the mountain, the more clearly he could see that it was covered with tiny figures, all fully armed, all with grenades in their hands, so many of them they had to hold on to one another and to the trunks of trees to keep from falling off the mountain slopes. Once, on the dead body of a dog, he'd seen tiny brown bugs swarm like that.

The Chief asked who wanted the first watch and Pete said he did. The Chief started to put his center-of-the-earth pole up between two sandbags, but Liebowitz said, What, are you crazy? Someone fires off an illumination round or the moon comes out from behind a cloud and we're a perfect target. Man, we're *history,* so the Chief loosened the two brackets on the center-of-the-earth pole, and it folded where it was cut and hinged in the center, and he lay down with his arm over it and rested his head on his arm. "Two hours, brothers," he said. "Two hours. Nice, comfortable ground," and he thumped it with the heel of his hand.

"Hell," said Liebowitz, "I better try it too," and he lay down next to Paganini and the Chief, and then Pete was the only one awake behind the five sandbags. They smelled to high heaven and they were leaking sand through little holes. He thought rats must have chewed on them, but no, the cloth was rotted because it was so old. It wasn't even army issue: probably it was here from the time of the French. He got up and crept over to the other side of the sleeping bodies. Now his hand was on his weapon and his other hand was a few inches from Liebowitz's shoulder. If anything happened, he could start firing with one hand and begin shaking Liebowitz with the other.

He had good eyes and he began to strain them, looking at the concertina wire until he could see the little spikes, remembering someone telling him if he ever needed nails, a pliers would take those spikes off and you'd have all the nails you wanted. Who told him that? Probably the same person who told him that if he had to use his bayonet, not to waste time trying to pull it out of the body, but to pull the trigger and the recoil would free the rifle. But who told him? It wasn't that long ago, and he remembered how good they said his night vision was, and he strained to see anything, a shadow, a tree beyond the wire. He was hearing things. He thought he'd heard a twig snap, and now he knew he'd heard the roar of an animal. Should he wake anyone up? Was it a good enough excuse? He knew it wasn't.

He watched the field beyond the concertina wire, but nothing was moving, and without realizing it, he began leaning over farther and farther until he had to put his hand out to steady himself and keep himself from falling, and he said to himself, *This is the first night.* There are 363 more, and he wondered if Eddie had reported to his unit yet, and now he saw why Eddie hadn't wanted to, and time crawled. It was like a spider or a bee, whatever you were most afraid of, going slowly over your skin. Every minute took an hour, and there was no one left in the world but you, and now he was sure he could feel each and every hair of his head. He could feel the little holes in his scalp through which they sprouted, and his eyes were getting heavy, but now he could also feel each blood cell as it moved through his veins, and to keep from falling asleep, to keep from waking Liebowitz, or Paganini or the Chief, saying he thought he'd heard something or seen something, he began tracing one blood cell as it moved from his toe up the inside of his calf, through his groin, into his chest, up to the top of his head, down through his arm, back up his arm, and around again. He wished he'd paid more attention when he'd been in biology class. Maybe he was following two different blood cells, not one. If he got to know the medic, he'd ask to see a picture of the blood vessels in the body. If he was going to be up night after night following blood cells, he might as well do it right. Now one blood cell was going down through his nose into the roof of his mouth, down his throat, and when he looked at his watch again, the two hours were up, and he shook Liebowitz. He didn't want to deal with the Chief and his center-of-the-earth stick, and as soon as Liebowitz was sitting up and rubbing his eyes, he lay down and was sound asleep.

Something exploded, a car was backfiring, hundreds of cars were back-firing, what was going on on the street? It wasn't the Fourth of July. Maybe a gas main leaked and the pipe blew, but no, these were explosions. He wasn't shaking. It was the ground under him shaking, and lights turned into clouds of smoke, purple lights, rolling in smoke clouds down the mountain, beginning to drift together, now white lights behind them, brightening up the purples and greens, and someone shaking his shoulder, and the radio squawking like crazy, and where the hell was he and what was going on?

"Wake up, man, it's Christmas," the Chief said, still shaking him, and Pete tried to shake him off, saying, "I'm up. I'm up," but the Chief kept shaking him, and they looked for Paganini and Liebowitz, who was getting up on the frequencies and talking back to the radio, and the two of them flattened out on their bellies behind the sandbags, locked and loaded, their rifle muzzles resting on top of the sandbags. They were a flimsy enough barrier before, but now they were almost nonexistent, a joke, and Pete's finger was on the trigger, squeezing it. He was sure he saw something, a little figure, a clot of darkness. How many times could you think you saw something and not fire, and he remembered what his DI taught him: *fire control,* don't fire until you're sure what it is. Suppose it's one of your own people out there? How are you going to feel? If you're in the field, it's fire control and noise control. Control is the name of the game. But still he wanted to fire. The smoke was thinning out. The noise was dying down. Maybe something was over. How did you know if it was over or just beginning?

"So this is what happened," Liebowitz said, putting down the phones, wiping his brow, and sitting back against the sandbags. "The ambush was up on the hill, and the ambush sprung, the guys made contact, and they're coming back down. They've got two guys wounded, four of them all together. They should be down here in an hour, maybe two, and when they come in, two of us stay here, and two of us give them a hand."

"We just sit here and fucking wait?" Paganini asked. "That's it?"

"That's it, pal," said Liebowitz.

"They all look alike in the dark," said the Chief.

"Women?" asked Liebowitz.

"Victory and defeat," said the Chief.

"Shut the fuck up," said Paganini.

"You're the only one who can talk?" Pete asked. "Go ahead. Say it. You're dying to say it."

"I don't like it here," Paganini said. They looked at each other and laughed and George said he'd finish out his watch, but Pete said, no, he couldn't sleep. He'd take over. Nothing more was happening tonight anyway.

He sat there following the course of a drop of sweat beginning behind his ear, curving forward onto the side of his neck, down over his collarbone, and then he lost it somewhere in his shirt, wondering how he could be sweating when it was so cold, and then he heard a low whistle right on the other side of the sandbags, right on the other side of the concertina wire, and he thought, Oh, it's the ambush coming back in, and he whistled back to them, meaning to tell them, *It's fine. Come back in.* He shook Liebowitz and told him to get on the radio to the track and tell them the guys were coming in, and Liebowitz asked him when he was going to learn to use the radio, and the Lieutenant on the track was saying, "Listen, the ambush didn't move. There's too much activity up there. The gooks have them surrounded. The guys are still up there."

"Who the hell did I whistle to?" Pete asked, his skin going cold, looking at Liebowitz, and Liebowitz looked at him, and by this time, Paganini and the Chief were awake and the four of them opened up with their rifles, and Pete's rifle jammed, and he got behind the other three men, and tried freeing up the round, but it was useless, and he was getting hit with the hot, spent shells the others were firing, and he reached back for the ammo can so that he could keep the others supplied. But they weren't ammo cans. They were grenades. He loved grenades. He lined them up between his left arm and his body, and he pulled the pins, one, two, three, and he threw one this way and one that way until it looked and sounded and smelled like holy hell, and finally the guys in the track opened up with the .60s and their mortars and hell was loose on the earth, and Pete was convinced there was nothing living on or below the surface of the earth within range of their weapons, and this continued on and off for five hours, until the sun came up.

The sun was purplish-rose and it tinted the mists they stood knee-deep in, and on the mountains around them the mists were lifting, and the mountain slopes were shades of lavender and purple and blue, and Pete looked around him and thought, I didn't know there was so much to look at on earth, and Liebowitz and Paganini and the Chief were looking at the mountains when the men came up from the tank and the Sergeant said, "Never mind the scenery. What about the fucking blood trails? If we spent another million dollars blowing up a groundhog, I'll court-martial someone's ass!" Sergeant Krebbs was short and round and wore round, wire-framed eyeglasses, and when he spoke, his handlebar mustache contracted and expanded like a small animal.

"What the hell are we doing up here, Sarge?" asked a big guy behind him. "We're *tankers*, man. What the hell are we doing up here on the side of a mountain?"

"First of all, we're not on the side of a mountain. The infantry's on the side of the mountain," said the Sergeant, "and second, they *sent* us here and that's what we're doing here, supporting the infantry, and third, *you* get your ass out there and look for blood trails."

"I'll go with him, sir," Liebowitz said.

"Don't call me sir. Don't salute in the field," the Sergeant said. "You salute in the field, and Charlie sees you, they take the officer out and the officer here happens to be me. Just don't salute and we'll get along fine."

"Where should I look, Sarge?" asked the big guy.

"Sal, look out beyond the wire! No one's hurt *inside* the wire."

Sal, also known as Big Sal, and sometimes only as Big, was six feet five, an Italian from the Bronx with hands powerful as shovels. He punched the open palm of one hand with the fist of the other.

"Beyond the wire?" Sal asked. "There are gooks beyond the wire. Give me a break."

"There ain't nothing outside the wire we didn't put there ourselves," said the Sergeant. "You going?" he asked Liebowitz. "Go. Don't blow yourself up. The wire's booby-trapped."

"You go first," Sal told Liebowitz, who went up to the wire and inspected it.

"We should have been *killed*," Liebowitz said. "We should have been overrun. Who booby-trapped this wire? A drunken three-year-old could get through. Nothing's connected to nothing. These grenades should be daisy-chained. The trip flares should be daisy-chained. Where are the dummies? While they're taking apart the dummies, they set off the traps in the ground. Anything in the ground? Don't tell me there's nothing in the ground!"

"What's your MOS?" Sal asked him.

"Demolitions, small weapons," Liebowitz said.

"Hey, Sarge, we got a demolitions expert here," Sal bellowed. "I feel safer already!"

"Get out beyond that fucking wire!" the Sergeant yelled back.

"I'll dismantle this," Liebowitz said, bending over, "and put the pin back in this, and out we go." He stepped through the wire with Sal behind him. "What's a blood trail, big guy? Hey," he called to the others, "you stand in his shadow you can keep out of the sun."

"*That's* a blood trail," Sal said, pointing to what looked like a flat path in the grass. "That's where they dragged off a body and that red stuff or brown stuff, that's blood. There's another one and another one and another one. And another. Hey, Sarge, there must be seven or eight fucking trails out here. This wasn't no goddamn groundhog."

"Get back in here!" the Sergeant said.

"Why did the son-of-a-bitch whistle?" asked Pete. "If he didn't whistle, we wouldn't have known he was there. He could have walked right in."

"See, Lieutenant," said the Sergeant. "These new ones don't curse so much. The LT doesn't like cursing, do you, Lieutenant? He's a God-fearing man. He spoke to the chaplain about our swearing. We explained to him. We told him 'fuck' was just a word, hell, not even a word, and we use it like filler."

"Yeah," Paganini said. "At home we even use it in the middle of other words. Like *fan-fucking-tastic,* right, Lieutenant?"

"Yeah," said Krebbs. "Like cock-fucking-sucker. But he holds it against us. He does. Every time we get a new guy, he gets his hopes up, right, Lieutenant? Where you guys from?"

"Brooklyn," said Liebowitz and Pete.

"The Bronx," said Paganini.

"Hopeless," said Krebbs. "And you?" he asked the Chief. "You from New York?"

"Out west," said the Chief.

"The air clean out west?" asked the Sergeant, spitting out something brown that looked like tobacco juice. "You don't write anything your mother can't read? You have real *clean* smoke signals?"

"No, sir," said the Chief.

"Don't call me sir," said the Sergeant. "Call me Sarge or call me Krebbs."

"I'm an Indian," said the Chief. "So what?"

"So nothing," said the Sergeant. "I'm a redneck from the South. You like southerners?"

"I don't care one way or another," said the Chief.

"Yeah? Well, I hate southerners and *I'm* a southerner," Krebbs said. "You walk around barefoot and you live on pecans. That's a life?"

"Is he supposed to answer that, Sarge?" asked Paganini.

"You want to answer for him?" asked Krebbs.

"Yeah," said Paganini. "I like pecans."

"You shell them all day and your hands bleed," said Krebbs. "You ever try picking pecan shells out from under your fingernails?"

"Yeah, but you'd like some pecans right now, wouldn't you, Sarge?" asked Paganini.

"Sure I would," Krebbs said. "What do they call you?"

"Pig," said Paganini.

"Yeah, a pig's a good animal," Krebbs said. "I gotta get me another pig. Sal wants a pig, don't you, Sal? He wants a baby pig to lick his feet. A pig's tongue? The best cure for immersion foot there is. So we move out as soon as the ambush comes down off the mountain. You," he said to Pete, "you get acquainted with Sal. You're in my track. So's the Chief, so's Liebowitz. You're all in the command track. What's your Military Occupational Specialty?"

"I'm a mechanic," Pete said.

"Fine, now you're the driver when Sam's off."

"He can't be the driver. He's too young," Liebowitz said.

"Don't give me any trouble," said the Sergeant, who went on to say that just because there were four of them from New York, they weren't part of a street gang here. Here they didn't cause trouble and they obeyed orders just like everyone else.

"Don't you like guys from Brooklyn, Sarge?" asked Sal. "They're real sweet guys."

"Why should I like guys from Brooklyn? They like themselves enough for everyone else."

And Sal wanted to know what was the order of the day, and the Sarge said, how many times did he have to say the same thing? After the ambush came down, they'd regroup back at the fire base and they'd take the infantry out about ten miles, and they'd get out and check both sides of some abandoned railway tracks, and they'd go back to the fire base for the night, and they'd get up the next morning, and they'd start all over again. "What do you want, Sal? A blueprint? You wait and see what goes down. They say it's cold where we're going, no activity for weeks. That's what they *say*. You're a demo expert?" he asked Liebowitz. "Well, so am I. We'll go out together and see who does a better job. Last week someone blew himself up pulling in the claymores. It came in over the radio. 'Sarge, Ah blew mahself up.' Seventy-nine little shrapnel wounds and they medevaced him out and he was back the next day. Stupid! You look the word up in the dictionary and you find his name. You guys from New York stupid?"

"No, we ain't, Sarge," said Liebowitz, and the Sergeant said, "Who'd ever guess it from the way you talk?"

"Your accent don't seem real bright to us," said Liebowitz.

"No?" said the Sarge. "And I thought I sounded like a goddamned professor. What you make of the Colonel?"

Liebowitz said he seemed like a good man, and the Chief, Paganini, and Pete nodded, and the Sergeant said he hoped to God no one ever got stuck up on a hill or in a bunker because the whole damn battalion would be in there after them and he didn't want to die for a dead body. God knew, there were a million senseless ways to die over here, but dying for a dead body, that was the most senseless, and Pete said he wouldn't want his body left behind, and the Sergeant said, "Hell, man, once you're dead, you're dead. That body isn't you."

"Let's just drop that subject," said the Lieutenant. "The Colonel gives the orders," and Liebowitz asked the Sergeant if the Lieutenant was the one they took up the collection for, and Krebbs said, "He's the two-hundred-and-fifty-dollar Lieutenant. He's the one who supervised the booby-trapping of the wire," and Liebowitz looked after him as if turning something over, and Pete looked at Liebowitz and said, "Forget it, man."

Later in the day, they were walking two abreast down the abandoned railway tracks. The rails had been taken away. By now they were already pins in grenades or parts of booby traps made from abandoned mess kits, and all that was left were the rotting wood ties, soft wood splinters like cloth under their boots, and the hunter-killer team had flown over and seen nothing. After a few hours, they began to relax and look around, and Liebowitz suddenly bent over and picked up a purple orchid and turned around to show it to Pete, who was walking with Sal.

"Did you ever see anything like that?" Liebowitz asked. "It's an orchid! Growing wild! In the middle of nowhere. You know how much that'd cost in Brooklyn?" Pete turned the orchid over and over, held it up to the sun, and looked at the trees growing on one side of the ravine, their jade-green leaves and their brilliant orange blossoms, and beyond them, the hills, layer after layer, grey on charcoal on black, and he thought, I didn't know there were so many things, you could love all these things, when Sal asked him if he remembered the hamburgers at Nathan's in Coney Island, and he said he liked the frankfurters better. There was no place on earth you could get a better frankfurter, and the Lieutenant came up behind them and said, "No talking!"

When he passed them, Sal said, "See that? Everyone else is talking. He's not telling them to be quiet. It's because we're New Yorkers. You'll see. When he sends out patrols, it's going to be you, me, and Liebowitz, and maybe Paganini. And he's not supposed to fucking send us. We're fucking mechanics. We're supposed to stay behind with the tracks. Who fixes them if anything happens to us? That asshole can't even light his own fucking matches. He's always borrowing someone else's. You don't believe it? Wait. You know how you keep your matches dry? You write home to Mommy and ask for a box of plastic Baggies and you keep your matches inside. Here," he said, pulling out a Baggie and giving it to Pete. "You want to light one up? See?" he said, watching the match flare up. "It works every time. You'd think they'd get damp in there, but they don't, not if you dry them out in the sun first. That s.o.b. can't figure it out."

They spent three hours walking along the railroad tracks, seeing noth-ing but the mountains and the trees, and in the distance there were sheets of metal gleaming silver in the light, and Sal said that wasn't metal. Those were rice paddies. He didn't want to be anywhere near rice paddies. Where there was a paddy, there was a village, and where there was a village, there was a sniper, and then they stopped to eat their C-rations, and Sal said, "You want to see how to cook C-rations?" and he took the claymore from his rucksack. He peeled off a piece of C-4, a plastic explosive that looked like Turkish taffy, and put it in an empty C-ration can, and lit it, and over that he placed a smaller, also empty C-ration can, upside down, with holes bored in it, and he said, "Now we have a nice stove," and he put his can of ham and lima beans on it, hocks and roids, and in three seconds, it was boiling, really boiling, and Sal started to eat, patting his ruck affectionately, saying, "I've got a can of peaches and a can of pound cake in there, and man, I'm saving them for a celebration. They're *treasures.* You'd have to kill me to get those peaches and pound cake."

"You're cooking with high explosives?" Liebowitz asked. "What's wrong with the heat tabs?"

"First of all," Sal said, "you've never got enough, and second of all, the fumes make your eyes water. You gotta remember, though, you can't get into cooking so much you run out of explosives. That's the trick."

"Yeah, I guess," said Liebowitz.

Sal asked Pete what he'd gotten at the PX. Maybe he'd like to trade something. Pete said he'd gotten a watch and Liebowitz said he did, too, and Sal said, "How fucking dumb can you be? You mean you were in the city and you didn't get any Heinz 57 sauce? No red pepper? No A.1 sauce?" What was worse than a new guy? Hell, *malaria* wasn't worse than a new guy. And then they got up and started back, because the night belonged to the VC, and Liebowitz wanted to know why everyone always said that, and Sal asked him who could find his way better around Brooklyn at night, him or a guy from Nebraska, and who would he let in at night, someone with a Brooklyn accent, or a Chink who didn't speak the language? We don't fucking belong here and if you don't know it during the day, you fucking know it at night.

Liebowitz said he knew what he meant, and Sal said, "Case closed."

"A nice peaceful day," Liebowitz said. "The country's beautiful. It would be a great place for tourists if there were no war," and the Chief said not to praise the day until it was over, and Sal said, "Amen to that," and the Lieutenant came by and said, "No talking! I told you before! No talking!"

They tramped along in silence, trying to remember the look of the mountains, the different shades of green, which trees had the bananas and which had the coconuts, pointing out to one another the huge fan-shaped palms, when at the edge of the horizon, they spotted a Cobra gunship and everyone stopped to watch it. It came closer and everyone began smiling and waving. You always felt safe when that thing was around. What firepower it had! In one minute it could fire one bullet into every inch of a football field. It fired so fast, all you saw was a solid red line of fire. When it was finished, nothing was left alive.

Suddenly, the Cobra tilted its nose down and everyone froze and then they dived into the ditch on the side of the tracks, expecting to die, because when a Cobra dropped its nose it was ready to fire, and the Lieutenant was on the radio screaming, "What the hell's going on here?"

It turned out that someone near the head of the column had a camera and had signaled the Cobra to come down so he could take a picture, and when they heard that, they were laughing, even the guy whose pants were wet, and the LT was screaming that this was an *operation,* not a goddamn boy scout outing, and he didn't want to see that goddamn camera again.

"When's this day over?" Pete asked. "Is it over yet? I mean, *when* is it over?" and Sal slapped him on the shoulder and said he wasn't a bad kid. When they got back to the fire base, he'd show him a cooler they could get at a five-finger discount. "The first rule of the armored cavalry," he said, "is, *Never run out of beer.* " Pete said he'd heard that the personnel at the fire base didn't like cavalry, and Sal said hot food was a problem there, a real serious problem.

"What kind of problem?" Pete asked.

"They have it and we don't," Sal said.

The tracks were waiting for them, boxy green metal creatures with pointed noses, a .50 caliber mounted in the center of the track, a curved metal shield in front of it, and an M-60 on each side of the track, the driver's head sticking out of his hatch like a turtle on the left-hand side, the TC standing up in the cupola, and they got in through the ramp in the back because it was faster to go up the ramp than to go in and out the back hatch.

"Move, move," said the Sergeant. "Before someone gets a haircut. Paganini, you're in Geronimo Davis's track. Up there. Move."

They got into their track, its name painted on its left haunch, BIG ANNIE FANNIE, cartons of C-rations suspended from the hooks on the side of the track, where picks and shovels were also fastened. They always sat on top, not on the long benches that the tracks came fitted out with, because the men ripped those out immediately and sandbagged the floors to protect themselves against land mines.

"In all the time I've been here," Krebbs said, "in all the time, I've never once seen a track painted camouflage. Not since Basic." Then the radio chattered, and Krebbs was saying, "Yes, sir. We do, sir," and when the radio was once again silent, he leaned over and told something to the driver, and then he came back into the cab of the track and said, "Bravado, Liebowitz, Chief, what the hell are you sitting down for? If we hit a mine and you're blown out, you'll have compound fractures in both legs and maybe you'll break your spine or crack your skull. Sit up on top. Bravado, you're not tall enough. Stand on the cans."

"These crates?" Pete asked, looking down at them. They were ammo crates. He climbed from them to the top of the track.

"If you're trapped inside, it won't make no difference what you're standing on, and if we hit something, you'll be thrown out of here before they go off. Stand on the cans." Pete climbed on one of the wooden crates. "Live ammunition," said Krebbs. "Ain't it a wonderful feeling?"

"If it's good enough for the priest, it's good enough for you," said Sam, the driver, whose blond, straw-colored hair now looked red.

"What's he mean?" Liebowitz asked. "What priest?"

"Sam, you're always talking about shutting your window," Krebbs said. "Why's it open today?"

"That priest. The one who stood on ammo crates when he gave the funeral sermon," Sam said. "We were up in the highlands, and he was saying how God picked this time to call them home, and all the time he was standing on ammo crates. Holding a Bible and standing on some ammo crates."

"It don't mean nothing," said someone in the track.

"No, it don't mean nothing," said Sam.

"Anyone want to know why we're not going back to the fire base?" asked Krebbs.

"Aw, shucks, I want to turn on the radio and hear the lady say, 'Good morning to the guys who aren't short but are next in line.' I want to hear her say, 'Here goes the Orient Express,'" Sam said.

"We're going ten klicks down the road and setting up for the night," Krebbs said. "Tomorrow morning, we're going into a ville where they've got some snipers. They're taking too many hits from that village. And, folks, we're going in with the One Hundred and First ARVNs, the great Army of the Republic of Vietnam, our allies, our very own ARVNs. There's nothing I can do about it so don't bitch at me. The choppers are bringing them into the area tonight so they'll be scouting it out and going in with us."

"Yeah, scouting it out," Sal said. "You mean warning everyone to get lost."

"Why would they do that, Sal?" asked Krebbs.

"So no one shoots them, man," Sal said.

"Give us a break," said Sam. "ARVNs!"

"That's it, guys. The driver takes the first watch. After that, you can work it however you like it."

"Corner Z. Krebbs has spoken," Sam said. "Wearing his first pair of shoes."

They turned off the road. It wasn't much of a road, red clay and dusty, forest on one side and a deep ditch and then rice paddies on the other, the mountains lavender and blue in the distance, the perfect place for an ambush, Sam told them, because if they were hit where they were, there was no place they could go.

Then they got their first dose of busting jungle, but Krebbs said this was nothing. It wasn't triple canopy. This was a piece of cake. Still, while they were going through, they should keep their heads down, because last week, the column had been going through jungle, and there were two tracks in front, and the tracks had their guns herringboned, and one of the gunners swung his barrel around, and the barrel pulled up a tree by its trunk and swung it around, just swung it like a sword, and when the column halted, it came over the radio. "We've got a decapitated man here." Krebbs didn't want to hear it again. "Keep your head down," he said.

When they got where they were going, and they never knew where they were going, their destinations had numbers; they were on Hill 44 or 444, the column of eight tanks fanned out and they lowered the ramps and got out and cleared an area so they had a good field of fire around them. They cleared a space in the center of the circle formed by their tracks, lined up Indian-style, and watched it get dark.

"This looks like a good place for us," said Krebbs, the tank commander. "Doesn't this look just like home?" He upended a carton of C-rations and said, "All right, everyone. Eyes closed, pick your box," and Pete got a B-1 meal, sliced beef and fruitcake, and someone asked him if he wanted to trade, but Sam said, "Man, save that fruitcake for the night you want to blow yourself away. That fruitcake means the difference between going on and calling a big halt to all of it, one great big stop. Fruitcake and pound cake, yeah, man, they keep you alive."

"Shut your fucking window and shut the fuck up," Sal said. "They just got here. They're not blowing anyone away, leastways themselves," and Sam said, "You know what, Sal? You're starting to sound like me. *Leastways.* You never said leastways before in your life."

Some of them decided to sleep on the ground outside the track, but Sam said he wouldn't sleep outside unless he made a hammock out of his poncho and tied one end to the track. He wouldn't chance their pulling out without him, and Pete decided to stay up with him for the first watch because he wasn't tired, and Krebbs said, "*Try.* This is no war to be tired in," and Sam told Krebbs to leave Bravado alone.

"Well, Superman, I need to sleep," Krebbs said, and he went out the back hatch with his poncho and his rubber lady.

"You still carrying that thing?" Sam asked him. "You still won't sleep on the ground? The goddamn thing leaks. You're going to be on the ground when you wake up."

"It leaks?" asked Liebowitz. "You got some det cord? I'll show you how to fix it."

"Yeah?" said the TC. "See that? This guy knows something."

"You and that rubber bear," said Sam. "Give me a good rock for a pillow and my poncho liner over me, and I'm home."

Pete watched the right of the track and Sam watched the left, although Bravado suspected Sam was watching everything, just telling him to look left to make him feel better, to make him feel as if he were doing something, and as it got darker, he leaned farther and farther to the side, his weapon in one hand, his other hand holding on to a grip on the track. He heard every blade of grass move. He heard the feet of animals on the grass, the wind picking up and dropping the palm fronds, the hooting owls, the big cats crying to one another, and he thought, the night doesn't fall. Why do people say the night falls? The night rises. Look over there. The darkness was coming up from the ground. Now it was a thick black ribbon around the horizon, and now it had climbed halfway up the sky, and now it had gone almost all the way up and was like a black sheet of paper behind the crescent moon, and now it was all the way up, and the last of the day was gone.

"What's your story?" Sam whispered. "How come you're here?"

"I didn't know what else to do," Pete said. "My father was a washout, so I thought I'd try Uncle Sam. God and country. All that stuff." He thought of the trouble at home, his brother on Staten Island, working in the butcher shop, and that world was far away. It was as if he'd never lived in it, and this world, this wasn't real, either, so he wasn't anywhere. Where was he? It was dark and he was frightened and he didn't believe he was here. It wasn't *serious*. "You?" he asked Sam.

"I was eighteen when I enlisted," Sam said. "You have a story when you're eighteen?"

"You could've waited to be drafted," Pete said.

"Maybe," Sam said. "My father, he worked in the mines in Pennsylvania and at night he had another job. He sells Lionel trains, and all day, it was, 'What are you going to make of yourself?' Every couple of weeks, he came in with something new he just bought. We've got this tiny house. It's *filled* with appliances. We've got a stereo, man, it would be too good for Beethoven. Only dogs can hear all the notes that thing plays. Console TVs. As soon as there's a new model, he's got to get it and go up and down the block bragging about what he's got. I wasn't interested. I got married at sixteen. I had two kids and I didn't have anything. If I forgot I didn't have anything, my father, he'd remind me. I wanted to teach gym in school. So that's no job for a man. I thought, well, I'll enlist and I'll get combat pay and my wife and kids can live on it, and when I go back, I'll go back to school and I'll be a gym teacher. So that's the story. Every time I go down a trail, I think about my legs getting blown off. You can't teach gym in a wheelchair. I'm a tight kind of guy. Sal says I'm wound too tight. I am. One day he came to the bunker to ask me something and I pointed a gun at his head and asked him what he wanted. Now I just close my window. I don't point any guns."

"You got pictures?" Pete asked him. "Of your kids?"

"Sure I've got pictures," Sam said. "But I don't take them out in the field. I leave them back at the fire base. Out here, you don't want to think about what's going on at home. It's too much, man."

"Your father?" Pete asked. "He's glad you enlisted?"

"Yeah, he thinks I'm in the big one," Sam said. "He hasn't figured it out yet. He's too busy selling little signal lights for his little toy trains. Around and around the same tracks in the basement. What a life."

"Night," said Pete, "doesn't fall. It rises."

"Sure," said Sam, smiling. "Sure, kid," and he reached over and squeezed Pete's shoulder, and for a moment, Pete felt real, felt as if he had weight, felt as if everything around him were real and not part of some giant stage set. Before he hadn't realized how canceled he felt, as if he were part of a dream, but the dreamer was gone. He hadn't realized how important touch was. "Night rises," said Sam. "It sure does. I'm going to remember that. *Night rises.*"

**17**

IN THE MORNING, a thick white fog covered everything, the top of the wall of fog beginning to rise in little spires, like the whipped meringue on pies, and out of the mists, the cupolas of the tracks rose with their gun barrels, and one by one, people began waking up, barely able to see their toes through the fog, and then in the distance, a black, shiny palm frond began waving up and down, and soon more and more of the tree freed itself from the fog, and when they touched their fatigues, they were cold and wet, and they realized they were shivering and that even their poncho liners were wet, but it paid to enjoy the cool air however you found it, and then they heard someone singing out in a high falsetto, "Good morning to those creatures and ladies who are not short but are next in line. Here goes the Orient Express ... " and they began to gather in the clearing surrounded by the tracks, leaving the last man on watch, taking out their C-rations, heating them up over their handmade stoves with C-4.

"Don't even *try* the ham and eggs," someone was telling Liebowitz. "Save them for trading with the villagers. They're inedible. Even hot, they're inedible. What am I eating? Ham and lima beans. Hocks and roids."

More trees were stepping out of the mists, their trunks and lower branches coming clear.

"Sure, we can talk here," Sal said. "You'd have to be crazy to attack us, we've got so much firepower," and Sam said, "But they *are* crazy, Sal, they are crazy," and Krebbs was there, eating sliced beef out of his can, saying, "Pick up these goddamn cans. Don't leave anything for them to booby-trap. What are you doing, Sal? You're brushing your teeth in beer?" and Sal said if you could drink beer all day, and no water at all, you'd never get malaria, and for a few minutes it was quiet.

Krebbs disappeared and when he came back, he said, "Ladies and birds, it's S and D today, the big search and destroy. Everyone clean your weapons. Check your ammo. Everyone ready? The ARVNs are ready. We're moving out in twenty. Bravado, what are you looking at? It's a coconut tree, that's all it is. Everyone in, boys," and under his arm was his rubber lady, still inflated. "You should have seen Liebowitz fix it with that det cord," Krebbs said. "From now on we don't leave base without plenty of det cord. He just lights it and drips it like a candle on the rip and it seals up real good. Best night's sleep I ever had. Liebowitz, he's my man. I advise all you fellas to get yourself one of these things," and Sal called out, "Where, Sarge? Where are we supposed to get one of those things out here?" and Krebbs said, "Well, then I guess you'll just have to envy mine," and then they were all in their tracks, going back out to the road, not over the same trail they'd busted on the way in because the VC might have mined it overnight, and roaring down the road, going faster than anything that weighed as much as a track had a right to do, and Sal was saying he was glad he wasn't in the LT's track.

Right now, the LT would be yelling at the driver, saying, "Slow down! This isn't the Indy Five Hundred!" and the driver would be saying, "Lieutenant, one of these days you're going to get someone killed and I hope it's not going to be you." The LT couldn't get it through his thick head that the faster they went, the better. If they hit a mine, it went off to the rear. It didn't hit in the middle where the men were, or up front where the engine was. If it set off the fuel, it was all over. Rolling coffins, that's what the tracks were, but the LT thought they should drive *safely*, just like they were at home, but they weren't home. Were they home? Were they?

"Enough already, Sal," said Krebbs, and Sal said, "See? See? He sounds more like me every day."

The column was slowing down. "What now?" asked Sal.

"Nothing," said Krebbs. "We're not far from the village. We'll circle around it. We've got our perimeter. We wait for the ARVNs to sweep through, and then we go in, search the place, round up the people for an evacuation, and torch it. The usual."

"I thought the ARVNs were supposed to be here before us," Sal said.

"Look, big guy," Krebbs said, "they found a swimming hole. They went hunting for some black and white porcupine. So they're roasting a monkey. I mean, what the fucking difference does it make, Sal? Go steal some hubcaps."

"I never stole no hubcaps," Sal said.

"No, you were big time," Krebbs said.

"Where'd you get that idea?" Sal asked. "I wasn't a fucking *criminal.*"

"I don't know where I got the idea, Sal," Krebbs said. "It's something about the sweet way you have with people."

"They went into the fucking village and they fucking warned them and when we get there we ain't going to find *nothing,*" Sal said.

"Not this time, Sally," Krebbs said. "This unit's made up of guys who lost close family relatives to Victor Charles. They're the elite. They're out for blood. They didn't warn anybody."

"They're the same guys who think it's fun to shoot at us when we're coming back in to the fire base. They think it's funny to see us dive into a ditch and come out all muddy."

"Sal," said Krebbs.

"Sal," said Sam.

"And every morning at seven thirty, they have to fire off their goddamn weapons for no goddamn reason? Just to tell everyone they're there?"

"So you got even," Sam said. "So you went over and threw in a canister of C.S. gas. So you gassed them and they came out coughing up their lungs and you said next time it would be live grenades. So they stopped firing at seven thirty in the morning. Forget about it."

"I never said I threw in the C.S.," Sal said, and Sam said, "Who else, Sal? Who else?" and Krebbs was saying, "Everyone out and into the village. The ARVNs are in. Maintain your intervals. Two men stay behind with the APC. Who's it going to be?"

"Bravado's staying behind," Sam said. "Just keep your finger on the butterfly of the .50 caliber," he told Pete. "You've got your back to the village, and there'll be nothing going on in there you'll want to look at, so just look at the trees. Just look at the motherfucking trees."

"Who put you in charge, Sam?" Krebbs asked. "Bravado, you want to stay? O.K., let's go. It's starting to rain. Lock and load, ladies and germs. Don't no one drop his rifle today. Last time you lost your sling, Sal, our own tracks nearly blew us away. Let's go."

Left alone, Pete looked out over the fields in front of him, to the crazy quilting of the rice paddies, and beyond them to the tree line, and the hills rising above them, and the hills were dotted with little clouds of smoke that he first mistook for mist, but when the wind blew, he could smell the smoke. Up there the farmers or soldiers were burning something. The sun was up and it was raining lightly. He could see the rain falling in the far distance as it fell right before him. This wasn't like New York City, where the rain fell in narrow places between buildings and where you didn't really see how far it had to fall. You didn't see it coming down from the sky.

The sun rose a notch higher in the wide blue sky and the rain stopped. The line of palm trees bordering the first stripe of rice paddies was struck green and golden, and the wind lifted and dropped their fronds the way seaweed was lifted and dropped by currents of water, or the way ferns waved in the breeze in the woods outside the reform school upstate, and he suddenly remembered he was a kid from Brooklyn, and he'd never expected to see a palm tree unless he went to Florida and he never understood why anyone went there when the place was crawling with alligators, and last night, someone told him to be careful where he put his feet because of snakes, and never to go into a hooch through a door because the VC nailed snakes by their tails to the door frames, and as soon as you went through, they bit you, and you took two and a half steps, sat down under a tree, leaned back against the trunk, and as soon as your head touched the tree bark, you were history. Still, so far it wasn't too bad. So far it was an adventure.

A blast of heat hit him in the back of the head. In back of him, he heard shouting, and out of the corner of his eye, he could see the ARVNs throwing things on an enormous bonfire whose flames were leaping higher and higher. Then they must have found something suspicious. They must have found weapons. He didn't have to turn his head to see that they were throwing low benches and tables, and then he saw two ARVNs carrying a large pig.

It was a brown and white speckled pig and it looked as if it were smiling. One ARVN had its front legs and the other its back legs, and as it got closer, the pig began squealing louder, *Scree! Scree! Scree!* The ARVNs ran over to the fire with it, the pig twisting, trying to get out of their hands, its mouth forming a huge smile, and its voice rose, almost human, completely crazed, and when they reached the bonfire, he saw them counting, one, two, three, and they tossed the pig onto the fire. It flew through the air, its legs working. It was still alive and screaming, and it was still screaming when it began to cook on the fire. Its stomach began to blow up and up until Pete thought it would explode, and then suddenly the pig stopped screaming. One of the ARVNs took his M-16, attached the bayonet, and thrust the knife into the animal's swollen stomach, and its entrails exploded outward. Hot fat spattered and sizzled in the air, and everywhere there was the smell of burning hide and roasting pork, and he couldn't watch it anymore.

He turned his head away, but the sound of the pig screaming was still in his ears. Why did they do that? What had the pig ever done to them? Out of the corner of his eye, he could see them carrying more things to the bonfire, but now he turned his eyes to the palms at the edge of the paddies and watched the wind fan out their leaves so that you could see their spines and each thin blade, and when the wind dropped them, the long blades of the palms dropped down on both sides forming a V, and he saw the palm branches had spines like ostrich feathers.

Their spines were yellow and white, and he was watching them as if they were the last things on earth, when one of the ARVNs thrust his bayoneted rifle up at him, and a piece of half-cooked pig flesh hung from it, and the ARVN grinned at him and said, "Eat. You number one GI," and Pete said, "No, no, I'm number ten. No thanks."

For a minute, the soldier looked puzzled, but not for long. He tore a chunk of meat from the piece of his bayonet and went back into the village. And then everyone was back in the tracks, and before they started up, Sal was saying, "That's it! The next time I shoot one of them! I've had enough of this shit! No more prisoners tied over the track exhausts! No more prisoners dragged by ropes! No more pigs!"

"Forget it, Sal," said Krebbs.

"The animals get the new ones every time," said Sam. "The last one flipped out over a monkey."

"What monkey?" asked Liebowitz, his owl eyes moving from face to face.

"That's enough, Sam," said Krebbs. "I mean it. Enough."

They rode back in silence, and in front of everything Pete looked at, a huge pig, like the Goodyear dirigible, floated, screamed and floated, and he asked himself, If I'm this bothered by a pig, what's going to happen if I have to kill someone? What's going to happen if I see someone get killed?

The tracks stopped, the radio was crackling, Krebbs was saying something, and Sam ducked his head down, got out of his chair, and came over to him. "Forget it, kid," he said. "It's peaceful. Stand on your ammo boxes and take in the scenery." *Scree! Scree!* went the pig.

"Good news, ladies and beetles," said Krebbs. "We get to make another house call. Eighteen klicks down the road, a deserted ville. Check it out. Sam, this time you stay behind. Nothing to worry about. There's a sniper in there but they're calling in artillery and if we get lucky, they'll have it leveled before we roll in. Helmets on. No, Bravado, Liebowitz, Chief, don't fasten the straps. If we hit anything and you're blown out, the strap can take your head off. Ready? Grab the straps. We're going."

The tracks took off in a cloud of red dust, leaving a stripe of black sky farther and farther behind ("That rain's going to catch up with us in a few hours," Sal said. "Now we're eating the dust and everything in it, and by the time we're through with the ville, we'll be ass-deep in mud"), and as he hung on, Pete thought this was no worse than riding the D train during rush hour. You could get used to anything. It wasn't so bad.

"We're almost there," Sam said, and Krebbs said, "Get your heads down. They said snipers," and without warning, everything exploded. The track rocked from side to side on its treads. The flung earth was separating itself from its pebbles and both were hitting the track's armor, and Krebbs was shouting, "Off! Everyone out! Down on the ground! Off! Fast!" and they were out so fast and into the ditch on the side of the road so fast, someone watching might have thought they'd been blown out, and everywhere around them, dust swirled like smoke, and voices were asking, "What did we hit?" "Who got hit?" "Was it a mine or a rocket?" "Were we rocketed?" And then they heard the Lieutenant screaming into the radio, "Cease fire! Cease fire! What idiot called in those coordinates?"

He called in new coordinates, and the red tide behind their eyes began to drop back down, but it took longer for the messages to reach their hearts, pounding as if trying to get out through their rib cages, and then down the road they heard the deafening explosion of more shells falling, and even where they were, they could feel the tremors. "Everyone's all right," the

Lieutenant said. "Three-four just missed taking a round. Friendly fire. There won't be any more of it. Let's go take a look."

In front of track 3-4 was a huge crater in the road, so big and so close to the track that the track seemed about to fall into it.

"That was close," Liebowitz said. "If that had been an air burst, we'd be history."

"And if it got three-four, it would have gotten us, because they were in front of us and if they went up, we'd have gone up with them. *Who* called in the coordinates?"

"Can we forget about that and get moving?" asked the Lieutenant. "Pull up three-eight and let's get the bridge over that hole in the road. Bravado, Liebowitz, Sal, pick up the pieces of shrapnel. What for? What *for?* Because if we leave it behind, the gooks will find a use for it. *Don't* pick it up until it cools off, Bravado. Cochise, get out in the grass and look for smoke and singed grass. That's how you'll know where the shrapnel is."

"The one thing he can do is find shrapnel," said Krebbs. "What are the odds he called in those coordinates?"

Pete poked at the diamond-shaped piece of shrapnel with a bamboo stick. He pressed the hollow stem against the metal and the end of the stem began to blacken. "That's *hot,*" he said, and Krebbs said, "Don't pick it up with your bare hands. Cover your hands with a towel," and Sam said it was hot enough to cauterize a wound, if there was enough of anyone to cauterize after a hit like that, and the Chief said it was bad enough being called Chief, but he didn't want to be called Cochise. Sal asked, "Who was Cochise?" and the Chief said how the hell did he know. His real name was Ten White Feathers, and someone else, bent over in the bushes, asked if a white feather wasn't what people got for cowardice, and said *he* thought Cochise was a good name, and when he straightened up, he held a long, jagged piece of shrapnel, and said, "Look what missed us. Man, I've had enough adventure for one day."

"So what's it going to be, Cochise or Chief?" asked Sal, and the Indian didn't answer him, and Krebbs said, "Enough."

When they reached the village, artillery hadn't destroyed much. Most of the huts were still standing and most of the village looked peaceful. They went from hut to hut, or hooch to hooch, that was the word, and they saw the dirt floors and the woven bamboo sleeping mats, and the roofs thatched with dried banana leaves blackening and rotting in the sun, and the tables still set with stew and dishes of fish sauce.

The men picked up and ate whatever they wanted, and if they saw a wooden ladle hanging from a roof and they wanted it, they took it, and through it all, the people, either very old men and women or young children, kept smiling at them: Yes, yes, take whatever you want. You see how friendly we are. They turned the large cooking pots upside down, looking beneath them for entrances to tunnels, or caches of weapons. They thrust bayonets into the mud and thatched walls.

"What's this stuff made of?" Liebowitz asked.

"Buffalo dung and mud," said Sal. "That's life here. Houses made of crap." They climbed up on the roofs and looked there for arms, and down at the other end of the village, the rest of the platoon was digging up graves, looking for buried weapons, finding nothing.

"We're wasting time," said Krebbs. They began milling around in the center of the village, scooping up handfuls of roasting nuts from the communal roasting pan, cracking the shells open and popping the nuts in their mouths. One of the soldiers lit a cigarette, got tired of it after one puff, and near him was a bamboo pole that seemed to have pulled away from the thatched roof of what looked like a sun shelter. He started to flick his ashes into the hollow bamboo pole, and as he did so, one of the old women jumped back and began muttering something to the old man next to her.

"Did you see that?" asked Sal.

"I saw that," said Krebbs. "Everyone out of the area. Get the people out of the area. We're blowing the hole under that shelter."

"What hole?" asked the Lieutenant, coming from the opposite end of the village.

"Just get back, Lieutenant," Krebbs said. "Liebowitz, let's go."

"What, are you crazy? What are you doing with all that stuff?" asked the Lieutenant. "You're not blowing up a mountain here."

"Get back, Lieutenant," said Krebbs again. Liebowitz bent over some C-4 he was wiring into empty C-ration cans. "Just get back." They dropped one bomb after another into the hole beneath the shelter.

"Fire in the hole!" yelled Krebbs, and the Lieutenant was still asking, "What hole, Krebbs? What hole?" when the explosives detonated, and were followed by one explosion after another, and the whole village levitated. It lifted into the air. For an instant, it hung there, hutches, shelters, trees, betel plants, tea plants, huge ceramic vats full of water, a small brown dog, his thin tail hairless, his expression surprised and panicked, two chickens flapping their wings as if trying to outfly the event, a monkey, as if there were no such thing as gravity, walls, roofs, doorways, openings for windows, everything hung brown and dusty in the air. A cloud of red dust began to rise up beneath the village, as if, below it, huge cauldrons were boiling. And then there was another tremendous explosion. Red flames licked through black smoke and leaped into the air, and the smoke began rolling toward them, blown by the wind, and the village sank down, quickly, like a stone falling, and it kept sinking until it was below the level of the earth. The smoke rolled, thick and black, hiding the flame, and then the smoke parted, and the flames leaped wildly at the sky as if wanting to pull it down.

"Christ!" said Krebbs, his mustache twitching, the muscles in his face jumping. "There must have been tunnels underneath the whole place. Lieutenant, they better B-52 this valley."

"Yeah," said the Lieutenant. "Yeah."

The old people were crying and holding on to one another. The women's teeth were black and when their mouths opened in sorrow, they formed perfect black circles. The children clung to them, weeping, and there was one old woman whom Pete watched, so wrinkled she didn't seem real, toothless, a few strands of hair left on her head, and she looked at the place where the village had been and kept shaking her head from side to side as if she couldn't believe what she'd seen. Well, neither could he.

"Get up on the frequencies and advise the Colonel," said the Lieutenant. "He'll want to get helicopters to take these people out. Find out if we can call it a day."

After the helicopters came for the prisoners, said the radio, they could call it a day.

"I wonder," said Krebbs, "if there'll be any mail."

"He's always wondering about the fucking mail," said Sal. "The world could come to an end, and he'd be wondering about those big red sacks of mail."

"That's not the point, Sal," said Krebbs. "If there's mail, the world's not coming to an end. It's still out there. Sometimes you forget. When I get back, I'm getting my job back with the U.S. Post Office. I am going to be a barefoot postman."

"That's an ambition?" asked Sam.

"So?" asked Krebbs. "You want to be a gym teacher. That's an ambition?"

"I don't forget," said Sal.

"Yeah?" asked Krebbs. "Just when did you last think about the world, Sal?" but Sal didn't answer him.

18 **A**FTER I LAY with a boy in the sun, I knew what would happen, and the day after, I felt like a ghost who had come back to haunt the site of its previous life. Already I watched my mother with sad eyes, knowing how she would miss me, and how she would be disgraced when she understood what had happened. Because she was from Siam, and because her children were only half Vietnamese, she believed the other villagers looked down upon her, and she believed that since we were already unlike the others, we had to be better than the other villagers or they would not accept us. Carrying water and pounding rice are the duties of the daughters, as is helping with the other children, cooking rice, spinning cotton, and weaving cloth. I looked at my mother and foresaw that all these tasks would fall to her, and she would have no one to help her, because my aunts all had children of their own. They had their own rice to pound and their own fields to till. Now, as the nights grew cooler, I would ask my mother all the questions I had ever wanted answered, because I foresaw that I would not soon have another chance.

As I ground maize, and as she sewed, I asked her how we came to Vietnam from Siam, and she became uncomfortable and said her father had been a great smoker of opium, and in Siam his ways were not approved of, and so he and her mother had left his country and gone to live in Laos, and while he was there, he met a white man from Hanoi who wanted to learn how to grow opium, or to buy it, and so he came to live in Hanoi. But after some time, the foreigner, the *farang*, went away, and her father knew nothing but farming, and after many conversations and much planning, he decided South Vietnam had better farmlands, and so he came south and eventually settled in our village. Was there more to the story? She supposed there was more; there is always more to a story that begins with two people leaving one country and going to another, but that was the story they told her whenever she asked to hear it. Never did they add or subtract one word. While she talked, she did not suspect me. Not once did she suspect me. When an anniversary of one of our ancestors came to pass, she gave me paper clothes and paper money to burn. I was sent to the river for lotus blossoms to place on the family altar. In her eyes, I was as I had always been.

But I saw my breasts were growing fatter, and I feared the other women in the village might soon notice. Now when I pounded rice and a young man came to help me, or to tell me stories as I pounded the rice, I would turn my face from him, and soon he would leave, discouraged by such shyness. As every other girl in the village carried water, so did I, once in the morning when I brought the water for the betel and the tea plants, and once in the evening. Before my breasts began to fatten, I, like the other girls, would return more slowly in the evening, because the young men would wait for us at the landing or the well or the pool. I often went for water to the crater left by the bomb, and while I was there, two young men would appear also, and they would talk beside me as I made my way home. I did not often carry water myself. My water pots rode the shoulders and heads of the young men. The young man who had always sung to me in the fields when we harvested the rice now wore the saffron robe of the monk, and in the days before I had lain in the sun with another, I would ask him how long he was to be a monk? Would he ever leave holy orders, or would he become the most spiritual monk in the monastery? But now I dared not look at him.

When he came to my mother's house and sat across the room, because he dared not touch the garment of a woman, I saw I must say something to him, and so I began to ask questions about our religion. We would reach nirvana, I said, if we gave up passions and material things. Wasn't that true? He seemed puzzled, for I had never spoken of religious things before, and he said yes, it was. But, I said, we care for material things. The farmers care for the small frogs they catch and eat in the rice paddies. They are proud of their water buffaloes and the graceful curve of the wooden plows they make for them, and the young girls are proud of their bamboo poles and vie with one another to see who has the strongest pole and the most lovely.

My mother, who was in the room, mending, asked if I would forever be talking of religious things, for already she could hear the frogs croaking loudly in the fields, and soon it would be night and their voices would be deafening. And the young man (his name was Trong, even now I dislike saying it) told me that we were meant to love the things that served us and let us live, the frogs we ate that kept us alive, the bamboo sticks on which we carried our reaped bundles of rice, whereupon my mother broke her silence again, saying that if one became entirely pure one would not care for food or bamboo poles but would exist in contemplation until the small hands of the world let go of one's ankles.

Then Trong looked at me and said that a transplanter of rice always works with his back to the sun so that his face will not be burned, and was I now working with my back to him so that he would not see my face? Did I fear to look at him as the women feared looking into the sun? I was speechless, for I felt the sharp lash of the truth in his words and yet I could not speak to him. There was no one in the village, no one, perhaps on earth, to whom I could speak. I, like the harvested rice, bore the ghost's streak, the streak of bran ashes smeared on a heap of rice to protect it against spirits, the streak that shows the rice is defective. Yet in my case, the ghost streak was not evidence of deception but of truth.

After that night, I began to wander the fields, learning the look of the country over again, as if I had never seen it before. I saw how comfortably our small village nestled in the fields between the encircling mountains. I would walk far from the village and climb up into the hills and look back at the houses of my village, their thatched roofs, the smallness of them, brownish-grey against the deep, brilliant greens of the leaves. I saw the small ponds behind each house, and the women washing their clothes in the ponds, their pots in the ponds, and bathing themselves and their infants in the same muddy brown water. I saw the little ornamental bridges some families built out over the ponds and the dogs swimming in the water on hot days, or lying as if dead in the shade once the sun had climbed the sky. I watched the children mixing manure and clay and fashioning toys from it, then baking the clay and manure in the fire until the mixture grew hard. I saw the men of the village carving large tops for themselves or their children, and the children spinning their tops as the day cooled, and when the rice was in and the day was done, the men would take their tops and compete as the children did. The oxen came slowly down the road, pulling the large-wheeled wagons piled with mahogany logs. The white Brahman cows grazed in the fields with the water buffaloes and the children chased them and played. I thought of how the people said, "There is rice to spare and salt is cheap," or again, "The fields are full of rice, the water full of fish," and I saw my village was a heaven of its own, perhaps even nirvana. Who was to say that everyone who reached nirvana recognized it at once?

And then I heard a woman come into our house and say to my mother, "Watch your daughter well. Her breasts grow large. Has she washed any bloody clothes in the pond?" and my mother grew angry with her and said, "They say to have a drunken husband is like reaping rice beaten down by pigs. Then it is also true that to have such a neighbor is to live in a thatched hut next to a raging fire," and she chased the woman away. But I, who did not stir on my mat, knew it was I who must go away. I had listened to the elders when they gathered at the temple or in the village square. Now when the women whispered to one another and guessed at what was to come, many young girls were no longer what they were. Some had gone to the large cities and sold their bodies to the white men. Others had found these men and lived with them. Some ran away and hid their shame and then came back, and if they brought enough money with them, their families welcomed them. Such families were worse than the girls!

When I packed my few things, wrapping them in a piece of black cloth, I knew I could not come back. I knew if anyone learned the truth, there would be no forgiveness. I believed my mother and father, and the village itself, would think I had become lost in my wanderings and fallen prey to a snake or a tiger, or worse yet, had been kidnapped. They would mourn me and their lives would continue. But they would not be shamed by me.

I had been the first to see the white men, the first to see what their guns did. I felt now as I had felt then, as if my *kwan* had gone and not returned. I wanted to find the white men and I could not say why. Did I foresee the end to our world? Did I believe that only the white men understood what was happening, and only they could explain this new world to me? Did I know they were powerful and hope that their power would protect me? Was I angry at my village and my people because I saw how defenseless they were against the men who had the planes and the weapons? To this day I do not know why I wanted to find them. Perhaps I was doing what an exile must do. If one leaves one world, one must find another. One cannot remain forever poised between two spheres. I had been the first to see the white men and I belonged with them, or so I believed. And when I left in the middle of the night, stepping over the sleeping body of my mother, unheard by anyone, as if I had already died, the voices of the frogs loud in my ears, don't you see: I was going to those who had placed the mark of the ghost on me. I was already a ghost.

 **19** IRE BASE Pluto was on top of a flat, gently sloping hill, and from the air, its appearance was unusual, not the customary lozenge shape surrounded by rows of concertina wire. No, from the air, it resembled a distorted sunflower, a sunflower that someone had taken hold of at either end and then pulled. The Colonel in charge of the battalion was known for two things: his promise never to leave anyone behind and his knowledge of tactics, and, whenever his troops dug in, they formed an oval perimeter and then, all along the perimeter, they dug out triangular bunkers so that, from above, the fire base appeared to be surrounded by sharp petals or thorns. This gave the fire base's perimeter a far greater area of defense, and since the men could fire from either side of the triangle, or from its tip, they could create many tight, overlapping fields of fire.

Once they dug in, he assigned the best men to booby-trap the wires and to lay mines beyond them. He did this in full daylight, and then at night, on the assumption that enemy troops had watched during the day, squads were sent out to move some of the mines and booby traps, and day and night, dummy traps were set up. On some nights, when enemy activity was known to be unusually great, illumination rounds were set off at random, and it was not unheard of for them to silhouette a sniper exactly where the Colonel had anticipated he would be.

After they finished complaining about the extra work, the men felt safer in their thorn-surrounded fire base. On the other hand, they were nervous about going out on night listening posts because no matter how many maps and charts and instructions were given them, they were never quite sure they knew where their own mines were. Nevertheless, none of them had yet been blown up by one of their own land mines.

The fire base was nothing more than a cleared area of land, surprisingly raw and naked in the green jungle surrounding it. The earth was soft and red, and crisscrossed with lumber planking that no one bothered walking on during dry weather, but that became sidewalks when it rained, and under heavy rains, the planks became muddy and then slick as ice until they finally disappeared under the thick tide of mud.

The color scheme here was olive drab and red earth. There were olive drab tents and men in olive drab fatigues. The Enlisted Men's Club, made of C-ration crates, drew the eye with its strange, red-lettered wall paper. COMBAT MEALS, COMBAT MEALS, COMBAT MEALS, said each plank of each wall. The eye, seeking some variety, automatically sought the razor-thin purple mountain ranges, darkening as they faded into the distance, or the wide sky, sometimes a thick green, signaling a coming storm, or a black sky over the mountains, moving toward them fast, presaging the rains of the monsoon, or an iron grey sky that could mean anything, or no sky at all, but thick, enshrouding mists that meant they were on their own. No helicopters could get through.

When they came back to the fire base, some of the men slept in the tents. A few had mattresses, although those were rare, and many of the men took pictures of these mattresses when they came in from the field and mailed the pictures of these curiosities home to the puzzlement of their families, who looked at the pictures and asked, "Why's he sending me a picture of a mattress?" Others found it a luxury to spread their poncho out on the springs and sleep, and still others, who were out in the field for months, slept on the naked springs as if they were feather beds.

When the cavalry returned to the fire base, their welcome was ambiguous. Everyone—the artillery crews, the cooks, the mechanics—was always happy to have the extra tracks just inside or just outside the perimeter. They constituted another powerful layer of defense around the base. Extra tracks meant extra .50 calibers and M-60s and men who were used to getting down on the ground and going out beyond the wire. But the cavalry were also regarded as wild and dangerous. Once, when they were refused warm food, a track opened fire on the mess tent and leveled it, and when the Colonel was not present, the fire base, which was responsible for feeding the tankers, would bring heated C-rations out beyond the wire. Then the cavalry would swing the barrels of the .50 calibers toward the personnel bringing out the meals and the complaining and threatening would begin: "You're in there eating hot food every day and you bring this crap out to us?"

The Lieutenant reminded them that the last time they were back at base, someone lost at cards and turned his .50 caliber on an empty tent and blew it away. Who was going to forget that after the mess tent? Or the way they ate when they came back in from the field, as if they'd never seen a knife and fork, or how if they ever saw toilets, they flushed them and flushed them, kneeling down and watching the water swirl and disappear, as if they'd never seen toilets before. Well, given all that and the way they'd arrive when the infantry got into trouble, charging straight ahead and blasting away as if they weren't afraid of anything, going in anywhere, because there was nothing human they feared, not when they had the firepower (what they were afraid of were the land mines and the booby traps, and in a firefight, no one was going to stop and start examining the ground or the trees. If their number was up, it was up, and they were going to get it, so they might as well go ahead, and they did, straight ahead, shooting from the hip), so was it any wonder they had reputations as crazy men?

"Which we deserve," said Krebbs. "Which we deserve even when we're motherfucking naked and nowhere near a track. Point to one man in this outfit who's not crazy," and someone would always say, "You, Krebbs, you. You're not crazy," and Krebbs would say, "Oh, yeah," and he would take a pineapple grenade fastened to his web gear and pull the pin and hold the spoon while the others hit the ground, eating the dirt and the bugs, and at the last instant, an instant past the last instant, he'd replace the pin. "Straighten the pins and tape them, my men," he'd say. "It saves you time."

The big topics now, a day after coming back in, were boredom and Christmas. "They're not going to do it to us again," Sal said. "Thanksgiving was the *last* time." Krebbs said Thanksgiving worked out just fine. The whole goddamned unit was medevaced out with food poisoning. "See," said Krebbs, pulling on a corner of his mustache, "there's justice in this world."

"Yeah," Sal said, "but before they were medevaced, they had shrimp cocktail, and turkey with stuffing, and choice of potatoes, choice of ice cream, fresh fruit, choice of pies. They had corn and asparagus and corn bread and mixed nuts and hard candy! I *saw* the menu. If I'd eaten that first, you could have medevaced *me* out. I'd die happy."

"You want to die happy," said Sam. "You'll die as sour as you are today."

"I'm not sour. Am I sour?" asked Sal. "I wasn't sour when I got here. Was I sour when I got here, Krebbs?" and Krebbs said, "Knock it off."

"Hey, man, we need food for Sam," Paganini said. "Look at his hair. It's white! He looks like a stalk of corn, green body and white hair."

"That's from the sun, you jackass," said Krebbs.

"It's the food," Paganini said. "Isn't it the food?"

"It's the food," Sam said. "You going scouting, Krebbs?"

"Nah," said Krebbs. "Send one of the new guys. Liebowitz, you going scouting?"

"Scouting for what?" Liebowitz asked, polishing his glasses with the flap of his shirt, and Krebbs said, "Scuttlebutt. There's always something going on around a base. Sal's already complaining about the food. By tomorrow everyone's going to be bored and dangerous. Go out and find what's going on. Chief, go. Everyone wants to talk to an Indian," and when the Chief and Liebowitz got up to go, Krebbs said, "Oh, what the hell. I might as well go," and as soon as he was out of the tent, Sam said, "Bravado, come over here. Why are you staring into space like that? We're going to shoot at each other. Go get the 3-0s," and the crew of 3-0s came over with rounds from their M-60s and Sam took out the tracer rounds, opened their caps, took out most of the powder, put a little back into the bottom of the shell, clamped the top, but not too tightly, and said, "All right, gentlemen, let's go to *war*," and when Krebbs came back, the two crews were divided up into two teams and were firing tracer rounds at one another. The rounds would pinwheel through the air, turning over and over, and if they hit, they'd burn through their T-shirts. You could get hit by them. It was live ammunition, after all, and Krebbs said, "Goddamn it, Sam," and Sam shook his mane of white hair and said, "It's all in the compression. Come on, Krebbs, you know you love it," and they had their own firefight until they ran out of ammunition, and when they went back into the tent, Krebbs lay back on the springs of his cot and folded his hands over his breast and said, "Aren't I the best scout in the world or aren't I?" and Sam said, "Tell us, Krebbs, tell us, Krebbs, or I'll play mumblety peg with your toes," but Krebbs just wiggled his mustache, smiled, and said, "Wait until morning. This takes some *thought.*"

After dinner, they cleaned their weapons and played cards, listened to the radio if they could pick up the signal, played tapes if they had them, read letters if mail waited for them, and wrote to their families. "Bravado, is that the same letter or are you writing a new one?" asked Sam, and Pete looked up at him. He thought if he could write it down, he could sort it out, make sense of it, the screaming pig, the floating village, the diamond-shaped shrapnel. He already knew that he'd never look at a queen of diamonds without seeing that piece of shrapnel, but when he tried to write, he'd end up saying how green it was here, and where the guys came from, and not to worry. Where he was it was safe. No one fired a shot. And even if he could write it down, who would he write to? Who would understand? Who could understand what *he* didn't understand? So there'd been a few close calls. A bomb had almost gone off. It was a war. What did he expect?

"Give it time, man, give it time," Sam was saying, but he thought about time, and how it would bring more of the same, and worse. The only good days were the ones already dead, because you'd gotten them. They hadn't gotten you. The new days were faceless and full of bullets. They said the first one to come close had your name on it, and the next ones said, To Whom It May Concern. But as far as he knew, they *all* had his name on them. "Give it time, man," Sam said again. But he didn't want to give it time. He wanted to talk to Sal, who looked and sounded like Eddie Lugano, but Sal didn't want to talk to him.

It was Sal's opinion that all anyone needed to know about him was that he was Italian and came from the Bronx. But in the first few weeks the new guys joined the track, they tended to pair off. Liebowitz and the Chief stuck together. If one went out on LP, the other asked to go also. If one pulled guard duty, the other stayed awake and the two talked. "What, are those two joined at the hip?" Sal asked, and Krebbs asked, "What's the matter, Big? You jealous?"

"Out here," Sal said, "you're better off alone."

"Yeah, and who's going to cover your ass, man?" Krebbs asked him.

"You're alone and you're together," Sal said. "You know what I'm talking about. It don't pay to get too close."

"So keep your distance," Krebbs said.

"Tell them," Sal said, pointing to Liebowitz and the Chief. "Tell them that."

"Yeah, the day my grandfather died," the Chief was saying to Liebowitz, "I went out to the grave, and a big hawk hung in the air the whole time I was there. It was so beautiful and you wouldn't believe how big its wing span was. So whenever I see a hawk, I know he's there. The first animal you see after someone's death, that animal stands for the person."

"All Indians think that way?" asked Liebowitz.

"The ones brought up with the old beliefs," said the Chief.

"And the center-of-the-earth pole?"

"Same thing, different tribe," said the Chief.

"See?" said Sal.

"See what?" asked Krebbs. "Every time you turn around, you trip over Bravado."

"Yeah, I know," Sal said. "But I don't encourage it."

"Hey," Pete said, coming up to him. "You busy?"

"Nah," Sal said, looking at Krebbs's retreating back.

"I heard you're going for a second tour," Pete said.

"Yeah, that's right," Sal said.

"How come?" Pete asked.

"Why not?"

"How'd you get here anyway?" Pete asked.

"By plane."

"I mean, why'd you enlist?"

"Did I say I enlisted?"

"Did you?"

"Yeah."

"Why?"

"Why? You're from the Criminal Investigation Division?"

"I just asked," Pete said, but he looked so miserable, Sal relented.

"Look," Sal said, "you're Italian, you're from Brooklyn. I'm Italian. I'm from the Bronx. What's the big deal here? You had such a good time at home?"

Pete started to tell him about his father, and his brother, in a home since he was three, and Sal stopped him. "I don't want to know all that shit, man," he said. "You got your problems. I got mine." Why didn't the kid slink off somewhere?

"I don't even know what I want to do when I get out of here," Pete said.

"No? I know what I want to do," Sal said. "I also know I can't do it."

"What do you want to do?"

"Be a doctor," Sal said, taking his yo-yo out of his pocket and starting to bounce it up and down.

"You're joking, right?" Pete asked.

"See what I mean?" Sal said. "I hang around the medic. I borrow his books. I ask questions. But studying? Who had time to study? My father died, my mother went to work, and I baby-sat my younger brothers. I got more black eyes fighting on the streets. I'd go out and everyone called me Big Momma. 'Stand here until I knock his teeth out.' Those kids stood there until I was through. They're tough kids. They are."

"Big Momma," Pete said.

"You tell anyone that and I'll knock your teeth so far down your throat they'll come out your toes," Sal said. "Yeah, I could be a doctor. You know why I could be a doctor? Because I can turn it all off. Like *that.* The shit hits the fan and my mind's out of here, man. The body works, but the mind's gone. I'm on automatic. Out in the field, they need somebody to dig up a fresh grave, they call me. Everyone else loses their stomach. Not me. I want to see what the body's like, how it rots. I'm a ghoul, right?"

"I don't know," Pete said.

"Yeah, I'm a ghoul. So when I get back, what'll I do? I'll go to work in the business. Another *tu tu ru.* They told me before I left, you're tough, you're cool, when you come back, you'll know how to use a gun. So I'll come back a killer. In the Bronx, you don't need the want ads. *Position Available: Killer.* I'll be available."

"You think that's what'll happen?"

"Yeah. Why not?"

"You gotta have hope," Pete said.

"Yeah? So someone can hit me on the nose? Forget the hope. What am I now? What's an animal once it's tasted blood? What do you do with it? You tell me that."

"Don't talk to him," Sam said to Pete. "He has moods. What he needs is a good set of Lionel trains. A little set of trains running around a banana tree out here in the middle of the jungle."

"You really want to know why I'm here?" Sal asked Pete, ignoring Sam. "I'm here because of a goddamn English teacher. A fucking English teacher. My English teacher and President Kennedy, between them, they bought my ticket. 'Ask not what your country can do for you,' and all that shit. And my English teacher, he was one crazy bastard. He comes in one day in the sixth grade and closes the door. And he says, It just came over the radio. Russia's launched its missiles and there's nothing we can do about it and we've just got to sit here and wait. In an hour we'll all be dead. Man, I still remember the chalk lying in the chalk rack and the air was dusty. It was hot. We just sat there in our chairs, waiting. We sat there and looked at the pink and blue maps on the wall. And then he told us it was all a fucking joke and we should write about how we felt. So I liked Kennedy and I hated the Communists and I wrote about how I wanted to kill them and here I am. Now I hate Kennedy and Johnson and the American government and the gooks and the ARVNs, but here I am. It doesn't fucking matter why we're here. Getting out, that matters." He sent the yo-yo flying: around the world.

"Yeah," said Pete.

"Yeah," said Sam, who'd been listening.

"Liebowitz, Chief, where are you going?" asked Krebbs. "We put out all the claymores. We put out the booby traps."

"Yeah, but you don't have enough dummies," Liebowitz said. "You didn't change the pattern. Anyone watching knows where everything is. Just a *few* little changes."

"So long as you're happy," said Krebbs. "Keep your eyes open."

"Just dig a fucking trench around the AO, fill it with C-4, and get it over with," Sal said.

"Don't knock a little initiative, Sal," Krebbs said. "Don't knock it."

"He's going to blow us all up, his fucking traps are so complicated," Sal said.

"No he's not, big guy," said Krebbs.

This is no kind of war, Sal thought. He saw the village rising up in the air and remembered his great-grandfather's stories about the First World War and how he'd gone over before the U.S. even came in. He was in the battle of Ypres. He used to tell him about sleeping in cellars. They were cold and damp and smelly and overrun with big black rats. Some of the guys slept with their coats over their faces, and after his great-grandfather felt cold, clammy feet on his cheeks, he did, too. They went across no-man's-land and got trapped in a German trench full of bodies, German and English. The bodies were torn apart by the shelling. Some of them were buried in the mud when the shells caved in the trenches. There was a dead German lying on his back, and his rifle stuck up in the air, and a bayonet was plunged all the way into his chest. A dead English soldier was lying over his feet, so his great-grandfather thought the English soldier had shot him before he got it.

Someone propped a machine gun up on a dead body, and when it fired, the tripod resting on the body made the body shake so that it looked alive. There was a German foot in its boot just sticking out of the earth and they hung extra bandoliers of ammunition on it. His great-grandfather said the foot got on his nerves. At night, he thought it moved around and he'd get up and grab it to feel if it was shaking, and when he told someone about it, he took a saw and cut it off and plastered over the stump with mud, but then his great-grandfather missed it. He missed the foot.

There was another dead German he and a friend used to argue with, telling him why Germany was wrong. They never said anything that would hurt the man's feelings. Sometimes they'd even negotiate with the Germans in the trenches opposite from them and they'd call their own cease-fire. And if they got wounded, they took you back to Blighty. That's what they called England: Blighty. When his great-grandfather was wounded, they brought him through the streets on a stretcher and he was almost buried in roses and chocolates. His great-grandfather never thought he'd die, either. "Going west," that's what they said when someone died. Or "clicked it." Not "bought the farm," or "bought the ranch," or was "sniped" or "zapped" or "wasted." You were brought up on war stories and you ended up in a war.

"You want a beer?" Pete asked him.

"Yeah, I want a beer," Sal said. What he wanted was to get dead drunk, blind drunk, wasted.

"GOOD MORNING, ladies and buzzards," said Krebbs in the morning.

"Good morning, you old bum," said Sam. "You know you can't wait to tell us what you found out. You're choking on it. Let's hear it."

"Food," said Krebbs, chewing on a John Wayne Bar, coconut candy covered with chocolate, a wrong bite could take your front teeth out. "Only food."

"What *kind* of food, Krebbs?" asked Sam.

"I'll never tell," said Krebbs.

"Put him in the fucking poncho," Sal said, his mouth full.

"Put Sal in the poncho and I'll reconsider," said Krebbs.

"What *kind* of food?" asked Liebowitz.

"Steaks," said Krebbs.

"There's a good part and there's a bad part, right, Krebbs?" asked Sal. "What's the bad part?"

"The good part is they're filet mignons. The bad part is they were flown in this morning for a major who's retiring and there's a case of them sitting in the mess hall freezer right now. The good part is, if we get them, we'll get to eat them. The bad part is I don't know how to get them."

"Where are they?" asked Liebowitz.

"In the mess hall freezer. In a crate right under the lid of the freezer next to the back door. That's where they are, safe as in Fort Knox."

"They're not safe," said Liebowitz. "What we need is a diversion. It's still dark. Look at that. It's still dark. We're going to *liberate* those steaks."

"What are you thinking?" asked Sam.

"You guys get some ice for the poor Chief here who's got a fever. I've got some of the flares and grenades command detonated. I can trip them from here."

"Say no more," said Sal. "Let's go. Sam, Bravado, you coming?" But

Krebbs said he and Bravado would stay behind, and when the grenades blew, they'd go outside the wire and check, you know, make it look right, and Sal said if they wanted it to look right, four of them better go out beyond the wire, and Krebbs said then everyone had to wait until they got back with the steaks because they all had to be outside the wire *with* the steaks. If they weren't, they'd be caught with them when the major searched the tents, and Sal wanted to know what good it would do them to leave the steaks outside the wire.

"Just get them and get back here," Krebbs said. "I've got it all worked out."

It was still dark, before reveille, and when they opened the flaps of the mess tent and went through the mosquito netting, another PFC asked them what they wanted and they said they wanted ice for one of the guys. He was so hot you couldn't touch him, and the PFC said, Sure, help yourselves, and they went over to the freezer, and sure enough, there was a carton stamped STEAK in red letters, and they picked it up, each carrying a handle, and they went out the back flap with it, and then ran back to the tent, and just as they got inside their own tent, a flare lit up the sky. All over the base, men were grabbing weapons and helmets and diving into bunkers. Illumination rounds went off, the tanks opened up, but nothing was there.

"If it's another groundhog," said the Lieutenant, coming into the tent, "I'll have *all* your asses," and Liebowitz said he and Krebbs had taken care of that sector, and Krebbs said, "Yeah, I'll take Liebowitz, Bravado, and the Chief, and we'll go out and check. Probably it was just another little creature. Probably the U.S. government just spent another ten thousand dollars sending a groundhog to heaven," and the LT said, Fine, but wait until he called this in. They didn't want the tracks opening up on them.

"Tell them all to go back to sleep," Sam said magnanimously.

"Shut up, Sam," the Lieutenant said automatically.

When everything quieted down, they went toward the perimeter, the frozen steaks unpacked and buttoned under their fatigue jackets, the wooden sides of the steak box dismantled, one side under each of the men's jackets. There must have been twenty-four steaks. Liebowitz said the cold meat *felt* better than anything could ever taste, and then they were outside the wire, Liebowitz and Krebbs making a show of checking the flares, while Bravado and Sal got busy with entrenching tools and dug a deep pit for the steaks and buried them in their reassembled box. "Outstanding!" said Krebbs, standing back and surveying the burial place. "They'll keep until tonight." They went back and reported that they hadn't blown up a little creature. They didn't know what set off the flare. Maybe it was one of those big blood-sucking bats the Chief was always talking about.

Geronimo Davis stopped in, and Krebbs decided to tell him what they'd done. After all, they'd just buried twenty-four steaks and there were only five of them in on it. He liked Davis and Paganini, and if they wanted to come along tonight to dig up the steaks, they were welcome. Hell, all five of their crew were welcome. The Lieutenant, of course, wasn't. Ten into twenty-four still left a lot of steaks per person. "You *went outside the wire?*" asked Geronimo, and Krebbs said, "For steaks, man, for steaks," and Davis thought it over and said nothing had been going down for weeks, and hell, with almost all the battalion pulled back in to base, the gooks wouldn't attack unless they had a human wave, and if they had a human wave, he'd just as soon be outside the wire with some steaks. Yeah, he and his crew would come along. "Set the table," he said. "We is polishing our silverware," and he held up his ten fingers. "See them *shine!*"

Three hours later, the crew of Big Annie Fannie were sitting in their tent, playing cards, when the Platoon Sergeant from Bravo troop came in with the First Sergeant from the artillery battery, and the First Sergeant looked around and asked if anyone knew anything about a crate of missing steaks. "No, sir," said Sal, "but we'd sure like some," and the First Sergeant said they were going to search every track and every tent and every bunker and every ruck and every crib and anyone caught with those steaks was going to be court-martialed, not Article 15'd, but court-martialed, and Krebbs said if he saw the steaks, he'd turn the men in himself, and the Platoon Sergeant said, "You know, Krebbs, if you've got them, you better give them back. The Major's a friend of the Colonel's and the Colonel's real serious about stealing," and Krebbs said he knew the Ten Commandments as well as anyone else.

"Hey, Liebowitz," Sam said. "They can court-martial us for stealing *steaks?* You're always reading *The Uniform Code of Military Justice.* They can do it? What are the grounds?"

"Maybe for being in an off-limits area," Liebowitz said. "If you're in an off-limits area, they can say you deserted."

"Deserted in the middle of a fire base?" Sal said. "You better read that code again."

"Never mind the code," Krebbs said. "Don't eat much at dinner."

Two hours after dinner, the five of them met Geronimo Davis's crew at the wire, and then the ten of them were out beyond it, taking a radio with them, digging up the buried steaks, which had now defrosted, cooking them in their steel pots with C-4, and they heard chatter over the radio. Someone was wondering what was going on beyond the wire, and Krebbs told Davis to fire off a few rounds, and he called in, saying they were taking some fire from sappers and they'd gone outside the wire to chase them. "You think they'll find us?" Sal asked, his mouth full, and Krebbs said, "You know what artillery's like. Nothing's going to get them out beyond the wire," and Sal said, "Look at Bravado. For a skinny guy, he's not doing bad. He's on his third steak."

"Well, chew," said Krebbs. "Eat them or bury them."

"They'll know who did it," Sal said, and Krebbs said, Sure they will, but they won't be able to prove it, and Sam said this was the first intelligent thing Krebbs had done since he'd enlisted, and Krebbs said now he knew all you had to do was feed Sam and he was halfway human. He was even *quiet.* He wished he'd found that out before, and Geronimo Davis patted his belly and said thank you for the invitation.

"Like the steaks?" the LT asked them the next morning, and Sal said, "What steaks, Lieutenant?" and the Lieutenant told them to smile now, while they had the chance, and they looked at one another and wondered what was coming next.

For days, nothing came at all and they pulled KP. They were sent out on listening posts at night, and observation posts during the day, and the Lieutenant, who was still mad about the steaks, used his influence and they found themselves cleaning out the grease pit, or they were on shit-burning details, and still they had time to sit in the tent and play cards and talk, and Sam said the army was made up of people dumb enough to run away from home. Liebowitz objected, saying he loved his home. He couldn't wait to get back to Brooklyn. When he got back, his mother could stop pretending he was going to school in North Carolina and he'd spend his first few weeks with a glass of chocolate milk in one hand and a glass of white milk in the other and his head in a bowl of Oreo cookies. But the others didn't say anything. They sat still, staring down at their jungle boots, like people blown farther and farther from shore, only beginning to realize, as they lost sight of land, that land was what they wanted.

"The world, the big PX," said Sam. "Don't go crying for the dog that bit you. Here if you want to take someone out, you do it, no ifs, ands, or buts. There ain't no one more powerful than a man with a loaded gun. It's not a bad life for a nineteen-year-old. You're king of the hill here, man."

Pete, Liebowitz, and the Chief stared at him with blank eyes. He'd made it worse. He should have known better. They were new. They still worried about what they'd do if they had to kill someone. For them, the game wasn't serious, not yet. They'd come in together and they were all still here. If they were lucky, they'd be out of it before it got serious, out of it, one way or another, for good.

"Don't talk so much, Sam," said Krebbs. He thought about the monkey one of the men had tied to the back of the track, and they were rocketed, and the track took off, and everyone forgot the monkey. When the track stopped, there were bits of blood and fur stuck to his collar, blood and fur and a string of muscle, and the guy whose monkey it was freaked out, lost it completely, wouldn't get back in the track even when the sniper started up, and a bullet took his head right off. It seemed to Krebbs, it seemed to everyone on the track, that the next day Sam's hair had turned white overnight. That's when Sam started raving, about the monkey, about the guy who lost his head (Krebbs couldn't remember his name, but the monkey, he was called OhJoe), about the war, about halos around the heads of certain new arrivals, until he had them all spooked. For weeks now, he'd been quiet and Krebbs wanted to keep him that way.

"We're going out tomorrow?" Sal asked. "That track can *book*. Ever since we took out the baffles in the muffler and straightened out the pipe, that thing does forty miles an hour. That thing can fucking *book*, man."

"Just keep steady with the others," said Krebbs. "You hear that, Sam? Stay in the tracks of the track in front of you. If they don't hit anything, we don't either. That's what it's all about."

"Nah," said Sal. "It's about steaks. That's what it's about, man."

20

THEY'D NEVER seen a sunrise like that. The sky was an unearthly blue, but here and there it was flame red, not red all over, but flame red in patches, as if fires were starting up all over the sky. Whoever looked at it couldn't take his eyes from it, and soon the whole troop was staring up at the sky.

"The good news," said the Lieutenant, "is that we're making a run into the city riding shotgun for the convoy. The bad news is that when we come back, we're going out for two months, maybe three. There's a lot of activity in our sector. We're familiar with the terrain and they want us out there and available. Write your letters now. Mail your letters now, and pick up what you need at the PX in the city."

"Two months," someone said.

"Maybe three," said the Lieutenant. "Let's go."

They were assembled and moving out through the gate, under a sky that seemed as if fire after fire had started up behind it, and Pete asked Sam what was so bad about going out for three months, and the Chief said it sounded good to him, like cowboys and Indians, only this time he'd get to be the cowboy, and Sam looked at them and said, "When it's three months, it's only you out there. Every day or two, they radio in orders or you call in your coordinates, but it's you out there. You do what you want."

"Sounds good to me," said Liebowitz. "I'm taking plenty of circulars. I told my aunt, every time you go shopping, send me all you can get. All those ads about food: cheesecake, baked beans, corn beef and cabbage, smoked breast of turkey. This was a good month for circulars."

"Other people get pinups," Krebbs said. "This jerk looks at food."

"He's Jewish. Jews love food, right?" Sal asked.

"Food and topless go-go dancers," said Liebowitz, "and *The Uniform Code of Military Justice.*"

"Why read that thing?" Sal asked. "First Davis, now you."

"Because it annoys the LT every time he sees me reading it," Liebowitz said. "That's why."

"That's a reason?" Krebbs asked.

"It's one fucking good reason," Sal said.

"You guys are nuts," the Chief said.

"All bets are off. The rules are out the window. It's survival time, man," Sam said. He was nervous and pushed his white hair back from his forehead. When he lifted his arm the bones of his rib cage showed through his T-shirt.

"That's war," said Liebowitz.

"Yeah, and what do you know about it?" asked Sam.

"No, man," Sal said, "that's you. *You* decide to hunt, you live with the heads on your wall. It's *you.*"

"What's he talking about?" asked Liebowitz.

T H E Y knew they were near the city when the traffic on the road began thickening. A stream of Lambrettas, some resembling small trucks, a frame built over the rear wheels and covered with canvas, packed with stems of green bananas, old tires, pieces of sheet metal the sun struck viciously, carrying live chickens, pigs, and even small calves, began passing on both sides of the convoy, one leaving the city, one entering it.

Little carts shaded by striped fabric awnings went by pedaled by children, or men who looked like children. There were ox carts pulling loads of long teak logs, ox carts carrying families, all heading to the city. The slower the convoy went, the more nervous the soldiers became. By now they had heard the stories of the smiling people who came up to you, offering to shine your shoes, dropped their shoeshine box at your feet and blew you and everything within two hundred feet to hell. They'd heard about the little children who came up smiling and blew up like bombs, taking everyone near them with them, wired, walking bombs, wired by their own people. Little children, wired to explode. They'd been warned to be careful when they bought bottled Coca-Cola, to hold it up to the light and inspect it for pieces of slivered glass, to turn the bottles upside down for a few minutes to see if any acid ate through the cap, and if they found any ice in this godforsaken place, to be careful because the natives laced it with sharp bits of transparent plastic that could and would tear up your stomach. Bravado and Liebowitz and the Chief had been in country three weeks and already heard the story about the soldier who'd finished out his 365 days, and as he was about to get on the freedom bird taking him home, a rocket took him out and he was all over the airfield. He was history, *sin loi,* man. It didn't make any difference whether the story was true.

When the convoy reached the city, the streets were a mass of people, pulsing and moving like a living wall, and the convoy crept forward to the base, a perfect target for anyone in the crowd or on a rooftop. Neon signs shaped like shocking-pink martini glasses blinked on shanties that passed for buildings. On the other buildings, neon girls ground their hips and gyrated while pink flamingos lowered and raised their heads. Some buildings were three stories tall and covered with so many signs it was impossible to read them all. It was Broadway and 42nd Street.

Flocks of blue and white taxis drove this way and that through the carts and the people. Whatever space there was between the cars was immediately filled with doll-like people wearing bamboo hats shaped like peaked flying saucers. Children and young men were catching on to the track handholds, trying to sell whatever they had to the GIs, and in the track up ahead, the gunners had their M-16s out and were threatening to hit in the head with their rifle butts anyone who refused to get off.

The sun was shining, but in the narrow streets, it seemed dark. To Bravado, Liebowitz, and Sal, who came from New York, the city didn't resemble a city at all, but a huge slum. They would pass one decent building with good solid walls, and next to it were slatted wooden walls letting the light and the weather through, roofed with sheet metal, leaning to the left or to the right, drunken soldiers of buildings, and in front of the buildings were even more flimsy stands that seemed made of balsa wood, and endless varieties of unidentifiable foods were skewered and roasting on their charcoal fires, and all these were thrust at you, waved in your face, and the odors of the foods, the charcoal smoke, the smoke from burning garbage in black, rusted trash barrels that had once been oil barrels, the carbon monoxide from the exhausts of the cars, it was all mixed together into a blue smoke. It was unbearable, pure pollution.

"Let's get out of here," said Pete, watching a girl in a tight blue satin dress try to climb the side of the track, and the others had their eyes open, searching the crowd. Was anyone getting ready to throw anything? Was anyone carrying anything looking suspicious? Hell, *everything* they carried looked suspicious. *They* looked suspicious. Sam pointed and they saw a Buddhist temple, except that it didn't look like a temple. It looked like a storefront with a giant carnival Buddha, fat and ugly, cheap and gold, in the middle of the huge plate-glass window, and in front of them was a crash, and the track came to a stop, and before they had a chance to ask him what he was doing, Bravado was out of the track and on the ground, shouting at the drivers of the taxi and the car that had collided right in front of them and were now blocking the road.

"Go away!" Bravado was shouting. "Away! *Di di mao!*" The drivers were pointing at their mangled cars. The fenders were locked together. How were they supposed to move? "*Di di mao!*" Bravado shouted again, and the drivers began jabbering in their own language, and the crowd began pressing up against them, and Bravado felt the solid wall of bodies against him, the heat of those bodies, the power of their hearts beating. His pulse went crazy; the sweat poured down his forehead and ran, stinging, into his eyes. He could hardly see. He couldn't watch them all, and the fear swept over him like a wave, sucked him under, and he pulled out his pistol and cocked it and pointed it at one of the drivers and said it again: *Di di mao!*

Then everyone moved. Women began screaming and pushing. The wall of people began moving back from the track. People couldn't get out of the way fast enough. An old man fell down and people walked right over his body. Some of the men came up to the cars and began to push them, and when they still wouldn't move, more men came and picked up the vehicles. They picked them up from the ground and carried them. They looked like ants carrying huge crumbs and the cars were on the sidewalk and the men were staring at Bravado angrily, and he got back up on the track and climbed down inside through the cupola and said, "Never! Never again is this track going to stop for anything! I don't care what happens! I don't care who gets killed! We're not stopping!"

Krebbs looked at Bravado and didn't say anything. He motioned to Sam and the track rejoined the rest of the column and moved slowly toward the base.

"I want to go to the car wash," Sal said, and Krebbs reminded him that when they got back to the fire base, they were going out for two, maybe three months. They didn't have long here. They ought to go to the PX first.

"I want to go to the car wash," Sal said again, and Krebbs, who was twenty-one and the old guy of the outfit, and who had a wife and two kids, not that he thought about them here, in fact he tried not to, it was bad luck, and the way he was now, he didn't want even their *memories* close to him, not even in his head, Krebbs shook his head and thought, not for the first time, that this really was a children's war. Listen to Sal, bigger than a linebacker. Next he'd be whining and saying he wanted some ice cream. Half the time, when they were out in the field and Sal started in, he expected him to say, "Are we there yet?"

"You go," Sam said. "We're going to the PX. We need Tabasco sauce, and A.1 and Heinz 57 and chili peppers and Vicks inhalers and cigarettes and matches and new cassettes for the tape decks, none of which we're going to lend you if you don't go."

"Yeah?" said Sal. "Last time we went out, who found the devil's ears? I found the devil's ears and everyone ate them."

"They burned our throats and we threw the fucking things out," Sam said. "Remember? We threw them out."

"All right, all right, I'm coming," Sal said. "But I don't like it."

"Think, Sal," Sam said. "The PX is legal. The car wash is out of bounds. The PX closes early. The car wash is open all night. After the PX, we can walk to the car wash through the black market. The new guys haven't seen it."

"Through the black market?" asked Sal.

"Right, Sally," said Sam.

"So what are we waiting for?" Sal asked.

They went to the PX, bought spices and condiments, Vicks inhalers (the grunts believed they sharpened your sense of smell, although the Colonel was against them, saying if you used a Vicks inhaler, that's what you smelled: Vicks inhaler), cigarettes—Kools, whether they smoked that brand or not, because in the field that's what the Vietnamese wanted. They'd trade their souls for mentholated Kools. Those cigarettes could buy you french bread or fried shrimp or opium joints. Hell, the gooks sell their *daughters* for them, and then they were in front of the black market stalls. There were hubcaps stacked six feet high, fenders, M-16s, every kind of pistol and machine gun, parts for the .50 calibers, uniforms, ponchos, poncho liners, cammies, jungle boots in all sizes ("Get away from those, Krebbs," Sam said. "How many pairs of shoes do you need?"), socks, brand-new helmets and helmet covers, weapons still packed in grease, radios laid out on newspapers, stretching for blocks, the sun hitting their silver trim, sending sharp daggers of light up into the air, blinding you, batteries of all sizes, stereos, ivory fans, propane stoves, gas refrigerators, crates of C-4, blasting caps: if it existed on earth, it was somewhere in these streets.

"I bet you could buy a fucking track here," Sal said, looking around.

"Try it, Sal," Krebbs said. "Go for it," and Sal looked around and settled on a man whose stall was hung with M-60 machine guns and bandoliers of ammunition, marine K-bars, some grenades, and trip flares. They watched Sal talk to the man. He pushed Sal away. Sal kept talking and the man turned back to him, smiling. The two of them shook hands.

"He says he can get it for us, but not today," Sal said, coming back. "He'll have it for us in three days, but he's got to speak to a friend first. If we show him the money, he'll have it. He wants a third down." Sam asked him how much he wanted for the track, and Sal said, "Only five thousand dollars. He says it's cheap."

"Tell him we'll think it over," Sam said, "but ask him to keep his eye out for a chopper. Tell him we need a chopper even more than we need a track." They went over to the stall, and the man began thrusting M-60s into their hands, bandoliers, saying, in good English, that his weapons never jammed. If they bought more than ten bandoliers, they could have a tin can free. If they fed the ammo into the weapon over that tin can, nothing would ever jam on them.

"Let's go to the car wash," said Sal.

The car wash was an unpainted wooden structure, its corrugated tin roof overhanging the sidewalk, creating a thick ribbon of darkness, and from outside, the soldiers peering in could see the glow of peach silk lampshades, and if they pressed their faces even closer, they could see the dark shapes of women lounging in the chairs.

"We're here first," Sal whispered, and Krebbs said they were probably the only ones here. The Captain had been pretty strong about these places being out of bounds. They went in, and inside it was cool. Real air conditioners hummed in the windows and roof fans lazily moved the cool air from room to room. The women began fussing over them, stroking their cheeks, leaning up against them, while the boss of the establishment, an older, stouter woman, said how *clean* the men were, and Sam said yeah, this time they were coming in from the fire base, not the field.

There was some negotiating over the price. They left that up to Sam, who didn't have the experience (Sal did) but who knew how to bargain, whereas Sal didn't. He started shouting and the women sulked. Their prices didn't come down, and when the men went in for their body massages, massages in which the women used every part of their bodies but their hands, they'd come out with one or two black-and-blue spots. Krebbs reminded Sam to set the price for the meal they'd eat afterwards, and Pete looked at the floor, thinking, after all, Krebbs was a married man. If he were married, he didn't think he'd be doing this, but then he wasn't married, so he didn't know. He wasn't comfortable in here. O.K., so they were women, but everyone in here had slanty eyes. And they had air conditioners. What had they done to get them? Maybe they turned soldiers over to the VC.

"You number one GI?" asked a voice near his shoulder. They'd all warned him that the women said that, but he hadn't expected to hear it, and he turned, automatically saying, "Nah, I'm number ten," expecting to look into a wrinkled face, or a toothless face, or a face boredom had made smoother and harder than stone, and he saw a beautiful girl who looked like she'd gotten a good tan at Coney Island.

She had big black eyes that were round and slanted only slightly at the corners, a small mouth with full, red lips, like the mouths of cherubs on greeting cards, and her hair curled. She reminded him of something, some cartoon character his mother used to like. Now he remembered: Betty Boop.

"Instead of massage," she whispered into his ear, "we could go to my room and talk. The price is the same." Blind with relief and gratitude, stunned that she spoke English, he nodded.

Her room was at the rear of the second floor. It was coffinlike, long and narrow, just big enough for her narrow cot. The walls were boards of raw wood, unpainted, stained iodine-dark by the rain, and soft with rot. Her bed was covered by a shiny purple quilt, a large pink heart clumsily stitched in the center. Cotton curtains hung over the room's one window, the pattern almost entirely bleached away by the sun. The floor was rough wood, grey from washing, covered with many small straw mats. When they had squeezed into the room and she had shut the door behind them, she giggled. "Only thin men come in here," she said.

He didn't know which way to look. There was nothing in the room but the narrow bed. The strip of floor between the bed and the wall was too narrow to sit on. But the girl was busy. She was bending forward, picking up shiny purple pillows and propping them against the far wall. When she was finished, she jumped onto the bed, sat with her back against the pillows, and patted the bed next to her. When he sat down, the springs creaked, and he felt his face flush. "The bed sounds like a cat, yes?" asked the girl, smiling. A cat. When had he last seen a cat? People here *ate* dogs and cats. His eyes were filling. He couldn't let her see him cry. What should he do if he started to cry? Should he hit her?

He felt her hand close over his. It was small and warm. The bones in it were tiny, like the baby bird that fell out of the nest built over the side door of his older brother's house. He started to cry, thinking of the bird, his father, standing there watching the bird, watching it for what seemed like hours, the way that man could study something, you never expected it of him; he thought of his brother, his home, and they were imaginary places, just as this place was imaginary, and he felt his anger at her rising. If he hadn't come in here with her, this wouldn't have happened.

The girl was dabbing at his eyes with her handkerchief. She put her fingers over her lips, whispering that the walls were thin and the others would hear. She would take care of him, and she sat up on her knees and put her arms around him. Now he sobbed. "You won't hit me?" the girl whispered in his ear. "Many do. The soldiers come here and hit the women they lie down with. The mistress says it is understandable."

"I never hit a woman in my life," Pete said, feeling, even as he spoke, his muscles tense with the desire to hit her, to let his fingers clench into a fist and smash her nose. "I never did."

"But you want to hit me." The girl sighed, sitting back. "I see it now."

"It's not you," he said.

The girl sighed and said, "I will tell you how I came to this place. First, I lived in a village in the country and it was peaceful until the soldiers came. Then I ran away to the city, and for two weeks, I worked for a Chinese family selling noodles. Then came an American couple needing a caretaker for their child, and in the corner of the shop, they saw me playing with the Chinese baby. The bought me from the Chinese couple and I stayed with them for three months and they spoke English to me and I studied the little girl's books. They thought I was a good person, but there were times at night when I thought of the soldiers and when I had my hands on the child's neck. I thought how easy to choke her it was. At night, I put my hands around her neck and pretended that was what I was about to do. It was our game, but it was not a game. Before they bought me, I had a baby of my own but she was born dead. I was not surprised she was born dead. I knew the baby had no soul. If the mother has no soul, how can the child have one?

"The soldiers should not beat the women who are good to them. They should worry about the women who keep knives in the mattresses of their beds and the thatch of their ceilings." He looked at her, saying nothing. "Do they worry?" she asked. He nodded and said the soldiers worried about everyone over here. "Good," she said. "It is terrible to feel so powerless. Will you hit me?"

"No."

"Then," she said, "I will give you a body massage. Take off your clothes and lie on your stomach." She straddled him. She used her buttocks, the inside of her thighs, her upper arms, her breasts, and somewhere in the middle of it, he felt as if he'd already disappeared inside her, so it was natural to roll over, to roll her against the wall, to climb on top of her, to make love to her, to find that was what he wanted to do. He wanted to love her and he wanted her to love him, and he was surprised to find love and the desire to love in this elevator shaft of a room, in an off-limits car wash. He was surprised to find something human that was all his. He was brushing the damp hair back from her face when he remembered that she wasn't his. If someone had the money, she was his. But now he had done it. Now he had slept with someone. Now he was ready to go back to the base.

"You will come back tomorrow?" asked the girl.

"No," he said. "I can't." He felt the anger rising inside him. He wanted to come back, but he wouldn't be able to. Before, he'd done everything he'd been told because there was no alternative. In the heat, in the dust, there was no place he'd rather be, no one he'd rather be with than the members of his crew. Before he'd met the girl, there was nothing normal beyond the track. Now there was.

"Next week?"

"No, we're going out for two months. Maybe three."

"I can come to the fire base?" she asked.

"I won't be there."

She laughed. "I'll find you," she said. "Operations may be top secret, but the villagers always know where you have gone." He laughed now, too, in astonishment. No one could find him. Not even his mail could find him.

"The villagers do your laundry?" she asked, and when he said yes, they did, she said, "Then they must find you to ask for payment, and they will find you, and through them, I will find you." He looked at her and shook his head. So it was true: if you lived your life in this heat, sooner or later you went off your head.

"What's your name?" he asked her.

"Lotus," she said.

"No, your real name."

"Li."

He looked at her, lying on her back. For an Oriental woman, her breasts were large. He heard her saying, "I'll find you," and he was angry. It was weak to need something here, especially love. You could be killed if you needed something.

"Why do you want to find me?" he asked her. "I'm no different than anyone else. What good would I be to you? You don't want to find me," and he picked up his hand (it felt heavy) and watched it slap her in the face. She looked at him out of narrowed eyes, but she was not surprised.

"If I find you," she said, "it will do me good, not you. I cannot live in the city. I miss the country. The others would be happy to see me. Sam and Sal and Krebbs."

"You know the others?" he asked dully.

"Only a few times," the girl said.

"Why me?" Pete asked. "Why me?"

"You also do not have a *kwan,*" the girl said.

"I don't know what you're talking about," he said. "I'm no different than anyone else."

Would he have hit her again? He always wondered if he would have hit her again. With her, he was once again an individual, not merely one of the members of Krebbs's platoon, a small part with no value separate from the group. He had a personality and it was too much to carry. He couldn't breathe under the weight. But from downstairs came the sound of shouting, a woman's voice raised in a foreign language, and Sal's voice booming, "Raid! Raid! Everyone out the window!" and Pete was jumping into his clothes, and the girl yanked up a shade, and there was a window without glass panes, and she pointed to the slanted tin roof and said, "Slide down! Run! Get your Lieutenant!" and he was out of the house, onto the street, his jungle boots under his arm, running under the tide of laughter rising around him, until he was around the corner, and then he stopped and leaned against a wall and put on his boots.

Out of the corner of his eye, he could see a store window filled with watches. Bulovas and Longines, every kind you could think of, and he was running. He was always fast. He ran all the way back to the base, found the Lieutenant, and told him the others were at the car wash and the MPs had them.

"Come with me, Bravado," said the Lieutenant, and he followed the LT out to the track, and they drove up in front of Geronimo Davis's tent, and the LT jumped out and told Davis to follow him: the guys were at the car wash again, and the two tracks roared out through the gate of the base, Davis following the Lieutenant, while the LT asked Pete, "Which way? Which way? They're *there* again? Don't they ever fucking learn? There's more than one fucking car wash in the city. Goddamn, the MPs go to this one first. *Every single goddamn fucking time.* Are any of them at the bar? Are any of them dressed?"

"I don't know."

"You don't know, Bravado, because you were *upstairs.*" The oily tank exhaust filled the street in back of them. "Book, baby, book," said the Lieutenant. "We're not going out in the field without full crews."

In the car wash, Sal was trying to talk the MPs out of arresting them. "Come on, Sergeant, you know how it is. We've been out in the field a long time. We're going right back to the base. It's our first time."

"You're under arrest," said the Sergeant.

"Come on, come on," said Krebbs, coming down the stairs, fixing his belt. "We're all in the same boat here."

"You're under arrest," said the MP. "Everyone out on the sidewalk."

"Are we going to be Article-Fifteened for this?" Sal was asking. "Because everyone fucking does it. You caught us, you could let us go," and the MPs opened the door, and prodded them out with their rifles. When they looked up, they were looking into the lowered muzzle of Big Annie Fannie's .50 caliber, their own track.

"Well, well, well," said Sal. The two APCs faced the car wash, their .50 calibers trained on them.

"Where are you going with my men, Sergeant?" asked the Lieutenant.

"Sir," said one of the MPs, "these men are under arrest."

"Sergeant," said the Lieutenant, "you better release these men to me."

"Sir," said the MP, "with due respect, these men are under my command and I'm not going to release them to anyone but the Provost Marshal."

The Lieutenant didn't say anything. He cranked the .50 caliber and let his hand hover over the butterfly. "Sergeant, you *will* release those men to me or you will not leave this place."

"Let 'em go," said the second MP.

"Let them go?" said the first.

"It don't pay. These guys are crazy. Don't mess with them."

"Get in the track," the Lieutenant told his men. "Sal, Sam, goddamn it, can't you find a car wash that pays off these goddamned bastards? You never heard of a steam bath or a restaurant? They're *legal.*"

"Where would *you* go, Lieutenant?" asked Krebbs.

"Right here," said the LT. "Right here."

"Davis got his crew with him?" Sam asked.

"No, he's alone," said the Lieutenant.

"I can't take any more of those C-ration tricks, man," Sam said. "I can't take that crew anymore."

"What's he talking about?" Liebowitz asked.

"They have a habit of throwing C-ration cans to hungry kids," Sam said.

"So?" Liebowitz asked.

"So," Sam said, "the way they throw them, the kids end up under the tracks. They *time* the way they throw those fucking cans."

"What are you saying?" Liebowitz asked.

"Nothing, man, nothing," said Sal.

IME, thought Krebbs, was about to do one of its many magic acts; it was about to turn from a segmented worm into a nonsegmented worm because out in the field, you lost track of time. You never knew what day it was or what date it was, not unless you were a short-timer keeping your calendar, but even when he'd kept one on his first tour, it didn't register. He still had no sense of time.

The latest design on the short-timer's calendar was a dancing Snoopy. That seemed to appeal to more of the guys than the one of a soldier who was a pair of eyes sandwiched in between a huge helmet and a gigantic pair of jungle boots. Krebbs would be glad to get out of here, off the base, away from the tents and the spit-and-polish idiots who blew through here wanting to see faces reflected in jungle boots, asking why no one's hair was regulation length.

He liked it out there, on his own. Give him men he was used to and plenty of extra barrels for his M-60s. God, it was a discouraging thing to see a smoking hot muzzle melt and droop even after they'd wasted precious water from their canteens, pouring the water over the barrels trying to cool them down. There weren't roads out in the jungle, just trails. They were usually hit when they came out of the jungle. Inside, the dense foliage protected them. They were fine in there.

He'd miss waking up here and seeing the valleys looking as if they were filled with snow. Then it looked like home, but it wasn't snow: it was only mist. It burned off, leaving the banana trees and the palm trees, those images of distance, like a signature in another alphabet at the bottom of a painting.

He was a little nervous going out this time. He didn't know the new men that well. He liked them enough, especially Bravado, who looked and listened and didn't come to conclusions and everyone always seemed happy around him. Everyone but the LT liked Bravado, but that was because he came from New York and the LT hated New Yorkers. That owl Liebowitz was funny, and he'd bet he was cool in an emergency, and the Chief, he probably was cool, too. He didn't know what to make of all that claptrap about his center-of-the-earth stick ("Pole! Pole!" said the Chief), but it was nice someone thought he knew where he was in this goddamned country. Sometimes, the first day out told the tale.

Three tours of duty. Hell, how long did you have to run from bare feet and police raiding your whiskey stills? He was starting to think like the people here, like the shopkeepers who always said they were giving you the best price because you were the first customer of the day, and they'd keep lowering the price and lowering it, saying it was bad luck if the first customer of the day didn't buy something, until you almost believed they meant it. Some of them seemed downright frantic if you didn't buy what-ever the fuck it was. That's how he wound up with two Longines watches. He took one out on the track and kept the other back at the base. That second one was practically a steal. He felt guilty taking it for two dollars, but he told himself it would stop working a few hours after he got back to the base. It didn't. It worked perfectly. He had it on his arm now. Some store-keepers had five or ten or twenty first customers, he knew that perfectly well. To him, first days out were like first customers. He'd see what kind of day they had today. If it was good, good. If it wasn't, he couldn't do any-thing about it anyway.

It was cool and the mist was still rising like ghosts when the column started out, and it was still cool when they hit the main road and began picking up speed, and everyone was glad to be moving. Everyone felt as if school had let out. The track crews were getting acquainted with the five or six infantrymen they were taking out. Everyone was discussing the weather, how the cloud cover forced this kind of operation. The helicopters couldn't fly often enough to take out the infantry, and if they took them out, half the time they couldn't get back in to pick them up. The men were *tired* of elephant grass soup. They'd gone out too many times with two days' supply and been out four or five. Enough was enough.

Sal was complaining, but then Sal was always complaining. "*Why* do we have to go out with ARVNs? Twenty-five tracks going out and we're so lucky? I mean, it doesn't just rain shit on old Big Annie Fannie," and Sam said, "Man, these are the good ARVNs. A Cobra finished off the bad ones. Didn't you hear about it? A bunch of ARVNs decided to fire at the guys coming in from LP and a Cobra was flying overhead and thought they saw U.S. soldiers taking fire, and then there were a dozen less ARVNs. *These* ARVNs are on their best behavior. *These* are real tough."

"That's too fucking bad," Sal said. "I don't like the tough ones no more."

The column slowed down where the road narrowed and Krebbs said he wanted everyone outside. On this trip, no one rode inside unless he had to. He wasn't worried about snipers. He was worried about mines. They just passed a sign saying AMBUSH ALLEY and that was good enough for him. Everyone but the driver on top. Let the ARVNs ride inside.

They were shouting to one another over the sound of the tracks. The left gunner was complaining that his life was shortened by the exhaust emptying itself directly into his lungs. He didn't even have to breathe it in. Why couldn't he get on a track where he had seniority? The others were pointing out, off to the right, a field of what looked like giant water lilies, and someone else was pointing up at the sky, where what looked like a pre-historic bird was flying in large circles when one of the tracks up ahead hit something. They knew it had hit from the noise, and then from the explosion that sent their own track rocking from side to side, and the track right in front of theirs was going up. Yeah, it had hit something big.

The men were jumping off like swimmers leaping into the water, and then the track blew wide open, the white phosphorus grenades inside went off, burning with a white flame, and Krebbs and his crew were already on the ground as far from the track as they could get before the ammunition caught, and Krebbs didn't have to tell them to get down. Their faces were in the dirt. At least you couldn't fall off the earth.

When Pete looked up, he saw the track burning white, and two black shapes trying to jump from it, and they did jump, but when they hit the ground, they didn't get up and run. Where were they? And then the ammuni-tion in the track went off, the grenades, the mortar rounds, the bandoliers, and the thought crossed his mind like a bird flying through a room, in one window and out the other, *where do the bullets go when they go off?* Explosion followed explosion. The last explosion tipped the track and, like a wounded animal, it fell heavily on its side.

The track quieted down and burned. The top of it had peeled back like a sardine can and the sides caved in, and still it burned, until all the outer skin melted down and nothing was left but the steel plates underneath.

"O.K.," said Krebbs. "Let's go."

They went up to the burning track slowly, their hands in front of their faces, shielding them from the heat. They'd never felt a heat like that before. This wasn't like a flame. This was unnatural, *atomic.* When they got there, Pete saw them first, because he screamed first. He screamed because he wanted to run away, but he had nowhere to run to. The others looked at him, saw he wasn't starting to run and he wasn't shaking, and said nothing. He was all right.

They got on line to look. Two men were pinned under the track, half of their bodies beneath it, half outside. The track covered one of the bodies from the waist down, and the white flame had burned that body from the waist up. The exposed legs and trunks had been burned to bone. The bodies were half-human, half-skeleton. Men from the tracks down the line were coming up and some were crying. Everyone was looking for the rest of the crew of the burned track and finally someone shouted, "Over here!" and everyone followed him. There were two more bodies so badly burned they were cooking. Their flesh was bubbling just like boiling soup bubbled in a pot, but this wasn't soup. It was blood boiling beneath the skin.

"Don't touch them!" the medic said. "They're still burning."

"Wait, Bravado," Krebbs said. "You'll burn your hands."

"Why are they still burning?" someone asked, his voice rising. It sounded like Paganini.

"Damn white phosphorus," said the medic. "It burns forever. It burns underwater."

Now it was quiet except for the sound of the wind, and the cries of birds, and the occasional sound of a toad or a cricket, and, as they watched the two bodies, they blackened. They turned the color of burnt toast. They became ashy and scaly. But still the medic said no one could touch them. They weren't cool enough. He told them not to throw ponchos over them; they would melt and stick to the bodies. Just wait.

When Sal reached the track, he found Bravado trying to pull the hook loose from the VTR in back of them. He wanted to lift the burned track away from the bodies pinned beneath it. He was saying maybe they were still alive, and the driver of the VTR jumped out and knocked him to the ground, shouting, "What are you, fucking crazy? They're dead!" Sal started pulling Bravado away, saying, "The guy's new. It's cool, man," and the driver of the VTR was screaming, "You know what this means? This means they're going to pull back the whole fucking column! That's what this means!" Overhead, they could already hear the steady *whump, whump, whump* of the medevac helicopter coming in for casualties.

"We're going back, folks," said Krebbs, who now had a poor opinion of the coming months, looking carefully at Bravado. The kid didn't look right. He started to put his arm around him, but the kid knocked his arm off, shouting, "Don't you fucking touch me! Don't touch me! That's not going to happen to me! It's not going to happen to me!" Pete turned to look at Krebbs, but really, he didn't see him. There was something, some line inside himself he'd just found, and for an instant, he'd wavered, staying on the same side of the line as everyone else, and then he'd stepped back. He was behind the line, and everyone else was outside, in front. He hadn't known there was such a place inside him, and he didn't know the person he found there, a cold person, hard and angry, who frightened him although it *was* him, and he thought, there will never be words to tell about this.

Then, within a second, not even an entire second, all knowledge he had of that line, of that cold person who was him but not him, was erased. It simply vanished. He didn't know what he'd known for a fraction of an instant ago, and now if anyone asked him what he meant by a line inside, he'd look at them and ask, What are you talking about? I don't know what you're talking about.

That afternoon, thanks to the land mine, they were all back at base, all of them frustrated. They'd finally been sent out and now they were back where they started, and tomorrow they'd have to begin all over again on a venture that was cursed from the beginning.

"You, Bravado," Krebbs said. "Stay here with the body bags until the chopper comes in," and Pete nodded and stood there, wondering how these guys got wasted, when someone came over, pointed at the body bags, and said, "I heard about that track," and Pete realized the bodies in the bag were the two burnt men he had seen that afternoon. The medevac must have landed here and dropped off the ones who hadn't made it. His heart started pounding. He stood stiff, as if he were standing at attention, but he wasn't. He was stiff with fear. The wind blew and brushed his hair back from his forehead. He thought for the first time in years about Judith Mary, who told him what interesting bones he had, and he wanted to bend down and look at the soldiers one more time and tell them something. But what did he want to tell them? That he was sorry it happened to them? That he wished they were still alive?

And now the helicopter was coming in overhead, and he looked up and saw the blades rotating, each one outlined against the sun like a large smoky triangle, letting the chopper down. The men got out, nodded at him, and took the bodies away. That was the end of that. He didn't even know their names. Sal would say he didn't *want* to know their names. He did and he didn't. He wanted to see them once more, just once more. While the tank was burning, he'd never wanted to see them again. Now he wished he'd never seen them at all. He walked back to the tent, wondering how you could feel so many things about one thing, not just two ways, but many ways. And this was only one thing. There would be many more, and the mind was small, at least his was, and he had a sudden image of a lean grey squirrel carrying an acorn in its mouth. The squirrel's teeth were sharp and they were putting pressure on the acorn. They'd soon be piercing it, and he was the acorn: the acorn was his mind or his spirit or his heart (were they separate or were they all parts of the same thing?) and the squirrel was big and powerful. It wasn't an ordinary squirrel. It had muscles like polished steel. The squirrel was grey and the color of the sky was grey and as he thought about it, it grew monstrous. It was the war itself. It was the country. "You're nuts," he told himself. "Seeing squirrels. That's all it means. You're nuts." The pig screamed in his ear. It screamed again.

"SAL," Pete asked. "What about that monkey?"

"What monkey?" asked Sal.

"Someone flipped out over a monkey. You said that."

"Some damn monkey, that's all. It wasn't anything."

"*Who* flipped out?" Pete asked.

"He's long gone, man, and so's the monkey," said Sal.

"Who, Sal?" Pete asked. *Scree!* said the pig. *Scree!*

"Why all this interest in a guy and his monkey? This guy had a monkey. The monkey's name was Jeeves. I don't remember the guy's name. There was some sniper fire and we took off fast, and everyone forgot the monkey was tied to the track so he got chewed up. The guy flipped. Is that the monkey you're talking about? There were two guys who had monkeys."

"How'd you know he flipped? What did he do?"

"He *shook,*" Sal said. "He sat there and *shook.* He couldn't hold a cigarette to light it. You put it in his mouth, it hung from his lip. I mean, he was out of here."

"That's what did it, the monkey?"

"Why are you so interested?"

"I've never seen a monkey. No big deal."

"You're not freaking out," Sal said. "Keep your eye on the road and your finger on the trigger. You'll be fine."

"Yeah, Big Momma, how do you know?"

"I told you," Sal said. "Don't call me that. Call me that again, you'll get something to flip out about."

"How do you *know?*"

"I know," said Sal.

The rain was falling, and Pete lay on his cot, repeating "Monkeys and squirrels and pigs" over and over, until the words mixed with the sound of the rain, lost all sense, became nonsense syllables, mere sounds putting him to sleep.

"Hey, Bravado," Sal said, waking him up. "You want to go into the village for some french bread? I'm borrowing a Honda from the ARVNs."

"Borrowing?" asked Pete.

"Taking," said Sal.

"The village is off limits."

"That's why it's fun," Sal said. "I'm hungry. It's the last good bread we're going to get for months."

"O.K.," Pete said.

"Going for bread?" Sam asked, turning over and looking at them. "Bring me back a loaf. The whole loaf, Sal. Don't eat out the middle."

Sal drove the bike and Pete held on to his waist. The night was rising. The pinks were darkening, turning the color of ink in a school inkwell. The tree line was to their right. Thousands of snipers could be in there loaded down with grenades and mortars but they didn't care. A place where people lived, where stores were open, where you could get a drink in a glass, a real glass, where there was still a thing called normal life.

"I don't like this country no more!" Sal shouted to him.

As they rode along, Pete saw a lone farmer walking along, his arm thrown over the back of his water buffalo, as if the man and the animal had become one. Silhouetted against the tree line was one hooch, and in front of it, even in the dark, he could see figures moving, an animal that must be a dog jumping for a thrown stick. Lives were going on.

They pulled up in front of the bakery. "It's already muddy," Sal said, disgusted. "Man, by the time we start back, it's going to be pouring." They chained the bike to a military jeep. "I see we're not the only ones off limits here," said Sal, and went into the bakery. "Ten loaves," he said, holding up ten fingers, and then the bargaining began. "Not bad," Sal said as they left, his mouth full. "Not bad." They stood outside the restaurant, eating bread. "No weevils, nothing crawling in them, not bad," Sal said again. "Let's get a drink." He stopped next to the military jeep. "Look at that. Wide open. Anyone could steal it. A fucking five-gallon can of gas sitting on the seat. You want to know why we're not winning this war? That *jeep's* why we're not winning this war."

Over the bar was a faded sign, routinely ignored, informing them that no army personnel under twenty-one years of age could be served. "Let's take care of business," Sal said, ordering three Tiger beers, taking them outside, handing one to Pete. He went back in and asked the bartender, "What've you got that's *good?*" and the man scurried into the back and came back with a black glass bottle. "Rice wine!" Sal said. "Rice wine!" He swallowed it and choked. "This ain't rice wine! I don't like this country no more!" But he paid for the bottle and kept drinking. Pete filled his canteen with the wine, drank, and watched him. "I don't like this country no more!" Sal shouted. "And I'm going to do something about it!"

"Your friend drunk," the bartender said nervously.

"I don't like this country no more and I'm going to burn it down!" Sal shouted. "Hell, *tomorrow* I'll be burning it down. Why waste time?" He got up, told Pete to watch the bread, and ran out into the street. When Pete followed him out, he found Sal picking up the five-gallon can of gas, running with it toward the bar. "Don't do it, man, don't do it," Pete said, but Sal was shouting, "I don't like this country no more!" and he ran around the building pouring out the gasoline, and Pete backed away, shouting, "Don't do it, man, don't!" But Sal was holding up a Zippo lighter, saying, "You've seen one of these. You've got to get one. Look!"

He bent down and touched the flame to the gasoline, and there was a sound, WHUMP! and the place was on fire. People were jumping out of windows. The old man was running after Sal, pointing at him, and Sal said, "You got the bread? Let's go," and they were on the motorcycle, the whole town in back of them, shouting, and Sal turned his head and shouted back, "I don't like this country no more!" Pete shouted something about police and stockades and Sal shouted back not to sweat it. They were moving out in the morning, and two hours before, two men were killed on their way to the bakery. No one was going to touch them, and no one did. *I don't like this country no more!* said Sal's voice in Pete's ear as he fell asleep.

It was a bright day. Afterwards, he would always remember how blue the sky was, and how the sun shone, and how clearly the green and gold palms on both sides of the road outlined themselves against the deep purple mountains in the distance and how the rice paddies shone like huge panes of window glass, as if pieces of the sky had fallen to the earth, and clouds swam in them, and the frogs sounded in the fields, and the buzzing of the mosquitoes was dying down as they disappeared with the coming of the sun.

Three companies were going out, and each track was carrying five infantrymen, mostly ARVN soldiers, and he was up on top manning the M-60, on the right side, away from the exhaust. He didn't know how he'd gotten so lucky.

Four of the tracks were ordered to go through a village eighteen klicks outside of town, not to stop, not to search it, but to report anything suspicious, any signs of buildup. No one in the ville would expect them to break rank with the rest of the column. They'd be a surprise. Merry Christmas, folks! Here we are with our fireworks! Don't fire unless you're fired at. Just look.

"Are we burning this village or what?" Sal asked Krebbs. "I don't want to burn no more villages."

"They said to look," Krebbs answered.

"I don't want to burn no villages," Sal said again.

"I heard you," said Krebbs.

"If they fire at us, we'll fucking burn it," Sal said. "I know we will."

"Sal," Krebbs said, "get inside with the ARVNs."

"I don't like this country no more," Sal said.

"We know that, Sal," Krebbs said. "Everyone knows that."

"Well, good," Sal said.

But what was wrong with this country? Pete asked himself as they began driving through the village. Some of the people looked at them and smiled. Some people reached out offering roasted ears of corn. The villages didn't look like any American villages. Here a big house was two big wood-framed rooms whose walls were covered with mud and dung. The roofs were thatched and full of insects. There were wooden water ladles and wooden pestles and wooden pans. It could be pre–Stone Age here, and the people were small, tiny, and the old women had red teeth or black teeth, the blacker they were, the more beautiful, not to the Americans who thought their teeth were black because they were filthy, but the medic told Sal, who told Pete, that he never saw anyone with black teeth lose a tooth or suffer from a toothache, and, as they drove, the water buffaloes in the fields began running. The ARVNs said the tracks' noises frightened them, and also the smell of the white men who manned them. The Vietnamese said the white men smelled like corpses.

Some of the houses, if you could call them houses, were built on stilts, and the little wooden flight of steps going up to the front entrance was picked up and pulled in at night so that snakes couldn't climb up and enter the building while people slept, and under the buildings, smoke pots were set going through the night to keep the mosquitoes away because the mosquitoes caused malaria and fevers that made you bleed beneath the skin, and the people in the houses got used to the smoke. They didn't have mosquito netting, or they couldn't afford it, but they didn't have to take malaria pills the way the GIs did (for the GIs, every Monday in Vietnam was malaria day), and under the first floor, they kept their animals, pigs, geese, chickens, ducks, cows, water buffaloes, but especially geese and chickens, who hated snakes and would cackle loudly at the sight of them, and then the people in the house would come down with a spear made from a bamboo pole, a knife fastened into the hollow end of the tube, and spear the snake and eat it. They said the snake meat was good. It tasted like chicken. And in front of the huts were brilliant bronze and red fighting cocks, strutting about, pecking the earth, and betel plants and tea plants waved in the breeze, and there were mango trees and banana trees and peanut bushes behind the houses, and the sugar palms and the water palms, parts of their trunks hollowed out to collect the water that flowed down from the palm leaves, the palm leaves were like spouts, and as they drove, they saw people eating boiled jackfruit and oily fish, and the ARVNs said that must mean rice wasn't plentiful or maybe it meant that the Viet Cong were coming at night and taking the rice away.

They drove on through the town and out into the open fields and no one fired at them. A pack of beige dogs followed them out, barking, and the last thing they saw when they turned back to look was a young woman standing in the middle of the road, watching them, her arms folded over her breasts, weeping.

"Someone should take a picture of that," Sam said, his mouth full of peanuts.

"Shut up, Sam," said Krebbs.

"Man, I'm getting tired of those three words," Sam said. "I surely am getting tired of them."

The tracks drove on.

The village, the weeping woman, the bronze and red roosters, floated in front of Pete's eyes. It was as if everything else were painted on a thin screen of gauze behind that village, growing paler and more insubstantial as they moved away from it.

THEY HAD eaten their C-rations and dug in for the night, and they could hear the mosquitoes coming in and the sound of animals moving in the forest. In the middle of the circle of tracks, they'd cleared an area of vines and brush. They had their concertina wire out, and their booby traps, and Pete was still out with Geronimo Davis, who everyone said was better at laying booby traps than any man in Vietnam. He lay wire down in patterns. He lay tanglefoot so if it caught someone's ankle and they fell forward, they fell on a mine or a grenade, and when he was through, Pete felt like the worm inside its cocoon. He felt perfectly safe.

"Do you think a butterfly can get through that, Sarge?" he asked.

"Nah," said Geronimo Davis.

Pete said he wouldn't mind riding on Davis's track someday, and Davis asked him what he did, and he said he manned the M-60, and Davis said, "If one of my gunners buys it, I'll ask for you," and they were back in the circle.

"Any gossip?" Krebbs asked Davis.

"Not a thing."

"It was a good day today," Krebbs said.

"Yeah," said Davis. "Nobody died."

ARVNs kept asking the Chief about his center-of-the-earth stick and what it meant, and Sal said what he always said: "It means the fool thinks wherever he is, the center of the world's there, too."

"That's not it, Sal," said Krebbs.

"That's it," said Sal. "Tell me why that's not it."

"I'm going over to Davis's track," said Krebbs. "I don't want to hear this again."

"The center-of-the-earth pole is a sacred thing," said the Chief. "The elders perform ceremonies and the elders bless it and then it's connected to all the spirits and animals of our tribe, and the spirits and animals, they're at the center of the earth, and everyone who's part of the tribe, he's at the center of the earth, and as long as I have this pole, *I'm* at the center of the earth."

"Like I said," Sal told the ARVN, "he believes wherever he is, there's the center of the earth."

"Give it a rest, Sal," Pete said.

"I've been to the center of the earth," Sam said. "You go down into the coal mines and you're at the center of the earth. It's dusty, it's black, it's like a coffin."

"You know who's at the center of the earth?" Liebowitz asked, making clawing motions with both hands. "Bell Telephone's at the center of the earth. Their little black webs reach out all over the earth and hold it together. If it weren't for Bell Telephone wires, the whole goddamn earth would come apart like a fucking crumb cake."

"We don't have phones here, so where are we?" asked Sam.

"I meant to tell you," Liebowitz said. "We fell right off the earth. We're in outer space. You want to see something?" He took a letter out of his shirt pocket. " 'Dear Mr. Liebowitz,' " he read. " 'This is to inform you that your promotion has been approved.' What should I do with that? I'll show you what I should do with that." He picked up the letter, put it on the ground, took off the safety of his M-16, and emptied a full clip of ammunition into the letter. "*That's* what I should do with that letter."

"And Krebbs wants to be a postman," Sam said. "He better watch out. If I were your fucking mailman, you'd pick up the mail at the fucking post office."

"Who the fuck's firing his weapon?" Krebbs shouted from the next track.

"Liebowitz," Sam shouted back.

"Tell Liebowitz to get on the track radio," Krebbs shouted, while the others stared down at the ground and the shredded bits of the letter, lifting from the ground in the breeze like white chicken feathers. "There aren't enough VC for you in this country?" Krebbs was asking. "You want to invite them all over for a cup of coffee? You better have a good reason."

"I don't," said Liebowitz.

"You don't?" asked Krebbs. He was speechless. No one simply told the truth. "I'll talk to you later."

"Feel better?" Sam asked him.

"Yeah," said Liebowitz.

Overhead, the sky darkened and clouds roiled and the rain started to fall, heavily, as if it would never stop, and when everyone was soaked, when the earth had turned to mud, the rain stopped abruptly.

"How are we supposed to keep this fucking track clean?" Sal asked. "I mean, we just fucking got it done and now it's mud all over again. Wipe your feet before you come in."

"Yeah, Ma," said Liebowitz.

"Don't call me Ma!" Sal bellowed. "Don't call me that!"

"It gets a rise out of him every time," Liebowitz said, shaking his head. "Anyone know why?" Sal glared at Pete, who kept quiet.

"What this troop needs is some *mail*," Sam said. "I can see them now, those red sacks stamped u.s. mail. Just up there, coming out of the helicopter's belly, falling right toward us."

"Breaking every goddamn bottle of A.1 sauce I asked my mother to send me," said Pete.

"Just floating down here telling me there's a drought," said Krebbs, coming back, "and nothing's growing in the fields, and the grass is yellow and all burned up, and if there's no rain, there'll be brushfires for miles and miles, or it's been raining every day for days and days, for months maybe, and the grain's rotting on the stalk, or rotting in the silo because they couldn't get it in dry, just floating down here with photographs of fields where all you've got is miles and miles of miles and miles."

"You and the mail," Sal said.

"I don't know what you want mail for if all it brings is bad news," Liebowitz said.

"Miles and miles of nothing but miles and miles," Krebbs said dreamily. He saw himself coming along the dusty road, his feet bare, under the hot sun, round and pale yellow, and from every house he saw faces at windows, smiling, waiting for the mail. There were people down at the post office waiting for the mail to be sorted; there were children following him from house to house to see if he had anything for them. There were sixteen-year-olds waiting for their driver's licenses; there were women standing next to their mailboxes, chrome tunnel-shaped containers mounted on two-by-fours, and they were all happy to see him and he was making all of them happy. He'd see to it that they got everything sent to them, every piece of junk mail, every bill, every birthday card, every letter from every corner of the country. He'd give out letters that would hold families together or drive them apart. He'd be in the middle of every drama, no matter how big or small it was, just the way the men who delivered the mail here were in the center. He'd never again be disconnected from real life. People laughed when they heard he wanted to be a mailman. He'd had ambitions before he came over here, and he had ambitions now, but now they were different. Now he wanted to make people happy. He didn't know how to make people happy in big ways, but he knew how to take care of the small ones. Let people laugh. *He'd* be happy.

"I want a *phone*," Liebowitz said. "There are a lot of people I want to call. My mother. My father. My aunts and uncles. The kids on the block. The man in the candy store."

"If you had mail, you wouldn't need the phone," said Krebbs.

"I don't need mail and I don't need a phone because," said the Chief, putting his pole in the earth next to him, "I am at the center of the earth."

"Hell, man," said Krebbs, "everyone needs the mail. The mail's the only thing that keeps you sane. Them big red bags stamped U.S. MAIL. When I get back, I'm going to get one of those red sacks and I'm going to put the mail in it and walk all over the country."

"So what makes you a warrior anyway?" Sal asked the Chief. "I mean, you don't have any more fucking white men to fight out there."

"I was initiated. I visited other tribes and lived with them. I was left in the sacred places and visited by spirits. I hunted deer and black bear. And here," said the Chief, pointing at his pole, "is where I finish hunting."

"At the center of the earth?" Sal asked sarcastically.

"It's spinning on its axis right here," the Chief said, touching the tips of his fingers to the top of the pole. "And when I get out of here, I'm going to be up there, my hair tangling in the clouds. I'm going to be up there higher than any hawk."

"Where are we?" Pete asked suddenly. "I mean, where are we?"

"We're here, Bravado," Liebowitz said, taking out his map, pointing to one of the squares. "Right here."

"No, I mean *where* are we? What's this place?" His gesture took in the small circle of space around his body. "I want to know where *this* is. It's not on any goddamned map."

"Wherever you want to be," Sam said, looking at him.

"No!" said Pete. "What I want has nothing to do with it! It doesn't! Nothing at all!"

"Calm down, man," said Sal.

"Don't tell me to calm down!" Pete shouted. "You're not my fucking mother!"

"Who's making that noise?" asked the Lieutenant, coming up on them. "You, Bravado? You and Sal, out on LP tonight. It's real quiet out beyond the wire."

"We don't have to go *nowhere*," said Sal. "We're mechanics. "We stay here." He pointed down at the ground.

"Yeah?" said the Lieutenant. "Well, tonight, you're infantry."

"I DON'T like this country no more," Sal said. They were deep in elephant grass, out beyond the wire.

"Oh, man, don't start that again," Pete said.

"Look, Bravado, what did he say? One click or two?"

"One click if they see something, two if they don't."

"They better not see anything," Sal said. "Those bastards can't hit a barn wall. They're firing right over our heads."

"Just where are we?" asked Pete. "I mean, *where* are we?"

"We're out beyond the goddamned wire," Sal said. "You and your questions. We're not supposed to be talking out here."

"So why are we talking?"

"Because you're fucking new and you're fucking nervous."

"They've got starlight scopes," Pete said after a while.

"They can't see anything through them. Everything's green."

"I looked. You can see things moving," Pete said.

"They better not see anything moving."

The radio clicked once. They waited for the second click. When it didn't come, they pushed their faces down into the flattened grass beneath them. The sharp edges of the blades cut into their cheeks but they didn't move. The guns were firing right over their heads and the smoke from the guns stung their eyes and the smell of powder burned in their noses and lungs. The firing went on for what seemed like hours, and then the tracks fired on and off all night, and the two of them lay there, insects crawling over their heads, down their necks and inside their shirts, afraid to lift an arm to scratch, afraid to lift their heads to see what was rustling in front of them, not even turning their heads to look at one another, afraid of the gleam of moonlight on their skin, their skin, that thin substance keeping them from bleeding into the environment, disappearing into it.

In the morning they walked in, greyer than the mists or the sky, their muscles twitching all over, the big muscles in Bravado's belly pulling in and out, the muscles of their upper arms and the long muscles of their thighs twitching, their hearts beating oddly, skipping a beat and then thumping hard, frightening them further, their faces and hands crisscrossed with scratches like paper cuts, swollen with mosquito bites, their ears ringing from the sounds of the .50 calibers, their eyes and noses and the roofs of their mouths stinging from the acrid gunpowder and the grenades and the mortars, their fatigues muddy from sweating in the grass, sweating from fear, not heat, because when the sun set it was cold: they walked in like two dead men.

"Don't *ever*," said Sal, "don't ever talk to me about the First World War. *This* is the worst war."

"Check yourselves for ticks and leeches," Krebbs said, and they found them.

"I thought leeches were in the water," Pete said.

"Yeah, well, here they're everywhere. In the trees, in the grass, everywhere." He picked up his arm and searched his armpit. "Don't ever," said Sal again, "don't ever talk to me about the Big One. Don't talk to me about hanging helmets from dead men's feet. This is the worst war."

Sam looked at him and shook his head.

"Don't tell me the mail will fix it. Don't say a fucking word," Sal said.

Pete stood next to him, bending and unbending his arm. "I put my hand over the helmet when I heard the first click," he said. "I couldn't move it away all night." The elbow joint clicked and crackled as he moved it.

"The ARVNs get a good night's sleep?" Sal asked. "That's what I want to know. They slept well?"

"Look," Sam said, pointing to Krebbs and Davis. "Those two damn Sergeants know what we're doing today, but they're not going to tell us. They don't want us to think."

"Wrong," said Sal. "They know one thing we're going to do today, and the Lieutenant knows two things, but he's not going to tell them because he doesn't want *them* to think."

"And the Captain knows more, but he's not going to tell anyone because he doesn't want the Lieutenant to think," said the Chief.

"And the Colonel's up there in his helicopter and he knows everything but *he* doesn't want nobody to think," said Sal. "And the Generals don't tell the fucking Colonels nothing, and the fucking President doesn't tell the fucking General, so nobody thinks and that's what we're fucking doing here."

"No," Sam said. "I meant they don't want us to think, because if we think, we might not go. Krebbs said that."

"Yeah, Krebbs. Right," said Sal.

"So where are we going today, Sarge?" Sam asked.

"To a monastery," said Krebbs.

"What for?" asked Sal.

"How do I know?" said Krebbs.

"Man, are we going to blow it up?" asked Sal.

"Read my lips, Sal," said Krebbs. "How do I know?" He walked away.

They traded C-rations, they spent more time trading them than eating them, policed the area, and started moving to their track. "The Captain wants to talk to us," Krebbs said, coming up to them. "In the middle of the circle."

"We got word that the Thirty-third NVA division is operating in the area," the Captain said. "This troop's going to be working as a recon unit, covering areas fast. If we find something that looks suspicious, we'll leave four-man teams. Most of the time we'll be operating in units of four or five. On short operations there'll be six or seven tracks waiting at the drop-off point. We're after anything and everything. I've been getting complaints about noise control, unnecessary firing of weapons, shouting inside the perimeter. This kind of thing causes unnecessary death and injury. Anyone caught firing a weapon unnecessarily or giving away their position will be disciplined. Is that clear? If anybody gets hurt, we can get you out by chopper in ten to fifteen minutes provided you put your calls in properly. Any questions?"

"Sir?" someone said. "Isn't this an infantry operation?"

"It's *raining*," the Captain said. "It's foggy. The choppers aren't getting through."

"So much for medevacs," said Liebowitz.

THEY'D BEEN walking for hours. When the patrol began, it was the usual thing, elephant grass, wait-a-minute vines grabbing at them, grabbing the Chief's new Bulova watch and sailing it up into the jungle's canopy. He'd never see that watch again. There were no flowers, but the monkeys chattered, and then a rock came at them through the foliage, but it wasn't a rock. A monkey had thrown a coconut, and they all cursed and put on their helmets. No one wanted to get killed by a goddamned coconut, end up killed in action by a goddamned monkey.

The mosquitoes swarmed all over, and tiny flies that looked like ants, and the sharp edges of the bamboo leaves tore at their faces, necks, and hands, and sweat poured down their faces and ran into their eyes, and it was so dark under the triple canopy that they could barely see, although they were all eyes, looking at everything, every vine that could set something off. Charley was good at using live vines to set off booby traps, and the point man stopped to look at his feet.

Something had been digging there. It could be a pungee pit or an animal might have been going after something. Just then, one of the men let out a yell and disappeared into the earth. He'd stepped into a pungee pit, but the bamboo spikes were rotted. They must have been there from the time of the French. He was lucky, or they'd have gone through the soles of his feet all the way up to his knees.

Soon the trees were gone. They were out in the open, no more slashing their way through the underbrush. They could just *walk.*

"Of course," as one of them said, "we have no cover."

"Neither does the other side," someone said.

It was such a relief, being able to walk, that it took a while before anyone noticed how odd the place was. All the trees were dead. The bark was gone. The branches were bare and the leaves almost entirely gone, the few that were left hanging dead and black from the black branches. The ground beneath their feet was dry. Nothing grew from it. Here and there a horned beetle scurried past, or an ant. The point man stopped and they all looked around them. What happened here?

One of the men was standing next to a tree. It looked ashy. He was tired and put his arm out to brace himself against it, and under his hand, the tree—it must have been twenty feet tall—felt like it was moving. He pushed harder and the tree slanted to one side, away from him, and began to fall, slowly at first and then faster. He moved down the line to the next tree, gave it a good push, and watched it begin falling. The column broke and other men began pushing against the trees which toppled, one after another. Then they stopped and stood looking at one another. There were no bird cries, no animal sounds, not even the buzzing of mosquitoes. The loud sounds were the sounds of their own breathing and their hard-beating hearts.

There was no color. The ground was stained black and the trees were black against the blue sky. No grass grew. It was as if they'd walked out of a highly colored world into a black and white picture.

"What is this place?" someone asked.

No one knew.

Everything was dead. The black beetles scurried back and forth, their horns twitching, like the last survivors on a dead planet. They came to a place where there were upended cones of earth, like so many huge, upended ice cream cones, and Pete was bored and kicked at one. He saw the ants jumping out and jumping up. They caught him at the waist and bit him through his shirt. They were inside his shirt and crawling under his belt, taking bites out of his skin, little chunks, and he began screaming. The other men ran over to him and tore off his shirt and hit him on the chest and back, killing the ants or knocking them off, and then they had his pants off and were doing the same thing, and the sweat ran down his body, and the salt poured into the wounds made by the ants, and stung until the pain became white and hot and he was light-headed and nauseated. They waited until he stood up straight and nodded at them. They helped him button his shirt. They looked back at the ruined anthill and the scurrying, maddened ants and got back in line and walked on.

No one told them to regroup and walk on. No one wanted to stay. Eventually, they came to the green wall of the jungle and disappeared inside it. Anything was better than that dead place. Even when one of the men saw a snake, it was a relief to see it: it was still alive, full of venom, but alive.

They continued walking and the jungle began thinning out. The heat was chewing with rats' teeth through their shirts and their sunburns, looking for more skin to burn. Every half hour, the birds would start up, *karow, karow.* One would start to call, and then the others would join in and the birds would call to one another for fifteen or twenty seconds, and then suddenly fall silent as if something had shut them off. The birds went off like alarm clocks up and down the jungle. They could hear them from far off, their calls faint, in every valley, on every hill. Here and there a deer barked its odd bark, high and yelping like a dog whose foot had been stepped on, and occasionally, owls hooted, a long, sad, mourning sound. When the line paused, there were the sounds of dragonflies swishing through the air, the omnipresent buzz of mosquitoes.

They had been out for five hours and now everyone was beginning to worry about water. The veins in their neck were becoming ropy, standing out, and their eyes burned like lanterns. One of the infantrymen had started to limp because glands had swollen in his groin, and the cav troopers, who were carrying full packs and mortar rounds, were discovering forty pressure points they never knew they had, places that strained and chafed under the loads on their packs. The infantrymen had a flat board fastened to their packs. It kept down the rubbing and chafing, and when they stopped, they propped it against a rock and had an instant back rest.

But now everyone was thinking less about the jungle and the snakes and the booby traps than about water. Their lips were dry and their tongues were dry and felt swollen, like terry cloth in their mouths. When they touched their tongues to the roofs of their mouths, their tongues stuck there as if glued. The men wanted to call in a chopper for a water drop. All the Lieutenant had to do was get on the radio and a chopper would fly over and drop a big plastic bubble of water, but the Lieutenant said no, there was a water hole around here. It was on his map and they were going to find it.

As it happened, they came to the monastery first. The monastery was down in the valley, a tall white pagoda made of bricks and then stuccoed over. It stood there in the middle of the valley as if nothing had ever touched it, not time, not war, not nature. Not a vine grew on it. Its arched doorway was painted red, as were its windows, and its roof was a shiny red tile that glistened and threw back gold glints of sun. The corners of the roof and the corners of the walls were gilded and curved upward sharply, like the tails of birds. It stood in the valley speaking of other worlds, as astonishing as a picture of heaven.

"We blow it," said one of the ARVNs, and the Lieutenant agreed. It was a perfect place for weapons, for people. Half the snipers in the area probably lived in it. Why else would it be in such perfect shape? The Lieutenant squelched the handset three times to say, yes, they'd found the monastery, and the message came through: Pull back.

If they'd been asked to blow it, they'd be angry. Now they were angry to have to leave it standing there. Now that the command came through, they knew it was full of snipers. They could see them as clearly as if the monastery walls were made of glass. There were twenty or thirty gooks in there and all of them were laughing at them, watching which way they went as they left, making plans to get them later. No one said anything because no one had to say anything. Everyone knew how everyone else felt.

The walk back to the rendezvous point began. They used their machetes and cut through the underbrush. *Off the trail. This time we'll shadow the trail,* and within a half hour, everyone was complaining about water. Sal walked up to the Lieutenant and told him to call for water. "We're going to find the water hole," the Lieutenant said. "It's right around here somewhere." But Sal was in a bad way. The veins in his neck stood out. His eyes were popping, his lips were cracked, and he kept licking them with his tongue as if that would do any good, but his tongue was white-coated and dry. Pete moved up and said, "Come on. It's not far," but Sal said every fucking man in the fucking troop knew that the Lieutenant couldn't read a map. Last time they went out on a four-man patrol, he was up a tree. "What are you doing up that tree, Lieutenant?" he asked him, and the LT said he was looking for landmarks. Climbing fucking trees! He was going to find a fucking water hole?

They kept on walking, slashing at the undergrowth with their machetes. The trick was to put one foot in front of the other, watch it touch the ground, and concentrate on picking up the other foot and putting it down, or counting, one, two, three, four, five, six, seven, until you got to twenty and then started all over again. But Sal must have stopped counting, because he broke ranks, pushed through the bamboo and elephant grass, and came up alongside the Lieutenant.

His pistol was out of its holster and it was cocked, and he had it to the

Lieutenant's head. "Call the chopper for water," he said. Krebbs stared through all of them, panting, pulling his wet shirt away from his chest.

Pete's mind was racing. They'd have to say they took some fire in the jungle and fired back and in the confusion the poor Lieutenant got a round in his head. Just then the Lieutenant took the handset away from the radio telephone man and put in a call for water, and they stood there waiting for the chopper, and there it came, and there was the water bubble, plastic and white, dropping out of the sky like the world's biggest pearl.

"You've got your water," the Lieutenant said, but the men weren't listening to him. They were drinking, and when they finished drinking, they were filling their canteens, and then they started walking again, under the sound of monkey chatter, the birds starting up (a half hour must have passed), and they cut their way through some dense growth and came to a clearing, and there was the water hole.

"I told you it was here," said the Lieutenant. "We gave away our position for nothing." But the men weren't listening now either. Their heads were in the water. They were drinking and then splashing one another. They were stripping off their clothes and jumping in and drinking while two men stood guard on the rim of the water hole. The Lieutenant kept saying, "Don't drink the water! Don't drink the water! Use the halzone tablets!" But they didn't care what they were drinking. They didn't care what the oily iridescent substance was that caught and reflected the light on the surface of the water. It was water. That was good enough. Now there were shouts of laughter. There were water fights. One man kept diving down and coming back up, and finally, he surfaced with a huge black thing wriggling in his hand.

"He caught a catfish! Goddamn, he caught a catfish!" the Lieutenant said, but no one answered him. No one looked at him. He might as well have been invisible.

"We are *clean,*" Pete said, coming out of the water.

"Check yourselves for leeches," said the Lieutenant, who was standing far back from the edge of the water hole, and the men began taking off their clothes and checking one another. There were leeches under their armpits and on their chests, on the back of their knees, and they burned them off with lit cigarettes or put a drop of insect repellent on them. Leeches were the only things in the jungle affected by the repellent. They didn't like it and dropped off. Everyone was laughing and pointing. One of the ARVNs was bent over, and another was spreading the cheeks of his ass, and carefully aiming a lit cigarette, and the first one was shouting, "Don't burn my ass! Don't burn it!" and their laughter was so hard and loud it rose up in the trees and even the Lieutenant started smiling.

Sal looked at him and the Lieutenant looked away. He should court-martial Sal but what could he do? If he brought the bastard up on charges, the others would wait for him and one day they'd bring him in from the field on a litter and the men would stand over his body explaining how he took a wrong step or was a little too close to a grenade.

The men stood around the bank of the water hole, every now and then bending over, scooping up some water in their cupped hands, pouring it over their heads, wondering if the water hole was an old B-52 crater, now overgrown, or was it always there, when a man burst through the undergrowth, and the two guards wheeled and pointed their M-16s at him and then slowly lowered their weapons. He was a GI. He wore the uniform, but he stood there and said nothing. His face was the bleached, shiny color of the dead, and from his upper abdomen an enormous and terrible flower bloomed, looping this way and that, hanging below his pelvis. Where flies did not swarm on it, it was shiny, and the man did nothing to brush the flies away.

"Someone go over and see what's the matter," the Lieutenant said.

"Come on, Pete," Sal said, and they walked over. The horrible, looped flower, purple and veined and shiny, was covered with swarming black flies, and it grew right from the man's stomach. It took them an instant or two before they understood: they were looking at the man's intestines.

"You've got to lie down, man," Sal said to the soldier. "We'll lie you down."

By the time they had him flat on his back, one of the ARVNs, a nurse, was bending over the man, whose face was even whiter and shinier than it had been. They searched for the stomach wound, but all they found was a small hole in the abdomen, not more than an inch long.

"How'd this happen, man?" Sal asked.

"I ran," the man whispered. "Four-man patrol. Ambush." He pointed to his stomach. "Bayonet," he said.

"Call medevac," Sal said. "He can't live with those things hanging out. We should push them back." He looked at the hole in the man's stomach, an inch wide. He tried to press the intestines back in, but the hole was too small. He tried to find another hole, one big enough to push the intestines back through, but there was no other hole, and the ARVN was picking up the intestines, examining them inch by inch. Their stomachs turned but they stayed where they were, and the ARVN said the intestines were unharmed, not punctured. They must be put back. As they talked, the wind picked up, the palm trees began lashing back and forth, and the bamboo danced wildly, the sky turned black and the rain came down like a solid thing.

"We've got to push them back in," Sal said, and he put his hands on the intestines and pushed. The man lay there and looked up at him, trying to nod encouragement in spite of the pain. Sal tried for fifteen minutes. It was impossible. He straightened up and said, "It won't work. We need a larger hole."

"I have razor," said the ARVN. "I cut the hole. Perhaps he prefer to die in peace."

"No one prefers to die in peace," Sal said. "Make the cut. You have morphine?" The ARVN had it and injected the soldier. After he made the cut an inch longer, he and Sal took turns brushing off the flies, then pushing the intestines back in through the stomach wall. Pete looked at Sal's hands. He hadn't realized he had such big hands. His own hands were strong. He thrust them deep into his pockets. While the ARVN was threading a needle to sew up the incision, Sal asked again and again, "How did his guts get out through that little hole?"

"If he run," the ARVN said, his fingers on the man's pulse, "the muscles stretch and let them start through. Then the stomach gas comes and it pushes and so we have this."

"He's going to die unless we get a medevac," said the Lieutenant, coming up behind them. "All those flies. The infection will kill him."

"I have penicillin," said the ARVN, filling a hypodermic.

"Use it," Sal said.

They sat and watched. The man's color seemed to come back. The shiny look of white wood was gone from his face, and Sal asked, "What do we do now, Lieutenant?"

"We make a litter from a poncho and we carry him," said the Lieutenant. "The last two in line start first, and we'll pass him up the line and down again."

"He's not going to make it," Sal said.

"Try to find out where he got hit," the Lieutenant said.

"In the *stomach*, sir," Sal said.

"I mean where in the *jungle*," said the LT. "He said a four-man patrol. Three men are still out there."

"The ARVN thinks one klick that way," Pete said, pointing toward the jungle. "He thinks that's how far he ran." The Lieutenant took his map from his pocket and called in a report over the radio. "Possible coordinates, sir," he said. "The man's in bad shape." He turned to Sal. "This troop doesn't leave anyone behind. Remember?"

"You must love that fucking map," Sal said. "You've got it in a nice plastic case and everything."

The Lieutenant looked at him and motioned them forward. Who ever knew what to say to Sal? Sal could make you feel wrong for being alive.

Somewhere in the middle of the dead place where no plants grew, the tortured breathing of the man on the litter stopped, and when they bent over him, he was also dead.

"It don't mean nothing," said someone in the column, and the rest of them repeated it and elaborated on it. "It don't mean nothing. Fuck it and drive on."

After a while, Sam asked when he'd get his laundry, and when Liebowitz reminded him they were out in the field, Sal said, "Man, you're still new."

Krebbs asked how many men had given their laundry to people from the town, and five men raised their hands, and Krebbs considered and said he thought they'd get their laundry in two days, and Pete wanted to know how anyone could find them to bring them their laundry? Weren't they supposed to be on a secret mission? Sam said, "They always know. They know before we do."

At night, they set up camp. Two of the women from the village near the base came up to the perimeter, smiling and nodding, pointing to the baskets of laundry on each end of their bamboo poles. "How'd you get here?" Liebowitz asked them, and they smiled and bobbed their heads, held up fingers for the amount of money they wanted, and when someone again asked how they got there, they said the magic word: *Honda.* They took their money and disappeared into the jungle.

"The night belongs to the Viet Cong," said Sal.

"Man, am I sick of hearing that," said Krebbs.

"But it's true," someone said.

"Bravado, Sal, out on LP," said the Lieutenant.

**22** **T**HEY WERE moving from morning until night, and at night they were so tired they fell asleep immediately, but the days had come to resemble one another, and so, in spite of the danger, monotony set in, and without realizing it, all of them were anxious for something, anything, new to break the routine. The monotony was honing them like knives that were laid to rest every evening still unused, and as each day passed, they became more dangerous. Something new, when it happens, takes up all the space on the screen. Everything else behind it is driven off, out of the line of sight, one enormous event—a pig on a fire, a man blooming from inside his stomach cavity—blotted out everything else, the cracked and sore feet, the fear that every fever is the beginning of malaria.

Now, even the noise of incoming rounds meant nothing, and the men began to sleep through them. During the day, they escorted convoys, or took the infantry to predetermined points, sometimes dismounting with them, usually checking out a ville for signs of enemy activity, and all the villages looked the same. All the people and all the pigs and all the chickens in them looked the same. Sometimes they were ordered to burn down the villages, and sometimes they weren't, and eventually they learned to use their own judgment if they found weapons or if they didn't like the look of the people. Then they'd take a lit cigarette, open a book of matches, put the stem of the cigarette in, filter end first, close the pack and throw it up onto the thatched roof of a hut. It would take the cigarette four or five minutes to burn down, and when it did, it ignited the matches. If the thatch was dry, the roof went up, at first slowly and then with a roar. That happened at roof after roof, and when they looked back, the same red fingers of fire were always clawing at the same sky. No one could blame them. They weren't even there when the fires started. They were already gone. But everyone knew what they'd done.

Now the men were beginning to collect pets. Most of the tracks had at least one dog, and sometimes a chicken, and at night the dogs would be put out beyond the wire, an animal listening post, and in the morning, when they came back in, they ate C-rations. When the troop assembled at night, and all the tracks were together, some of the men set traps for the jungle rats, large, sleek things, not like the rats in the city. Sometimes they'd wake up and see one of them on the trunk of a felled tree, watching them and twitching its nose, and the ARVNs cooked them and ate them, but at the perimeter, some of the GIs poured gasoline on them, and set fire to them, and let them loose, and when someone like Krebbs asked them what was the point, they'd say it was a fire show, something to confuse the gooks.

They'd be sent out on two-day patrols and three-day patrols and they were so used to it, they'd polish their boots and set them in the crook of a tree and look into their boots while they shaved, if they were still shaving, and then they got started, and there was the familiar clammy feel of their sweaty clothes pulling them down as if they'd gone swimming in them. Sweat stung their eyes like saltwater. They inhaled the familiar, thick dusty smell of the jungle, and their feet burned, so they felt as if needles were driven into them, and then the cool, sudden creek water flooding their boots and coming out the grid on either side of the boot like two small streams, the dry paths sending clouds of powder into the air and into their nostrils, sweat clotting the hair on their heads, and the sudden rains with huge drops of water that hit the skin like hailstones, a drop of sweat crawling down their backs like a bug, a bug crawling down their arm like a drop of sweat, and they stopped asking themselves how they got here, what they were doing here. They were *here,* as each day proved, over and over again.

Because of the way they traveled, the mail didn't catch up with them. They didn't get their copies of *Stars and Stripes.* None of them knew how the hometown teams were doing. In the beginning, they'd talked incessantly about sports, but there was a limit to how much you could say when you didn't know what had happened for weeks, and they were tired of talking about girls when they didn't know if their girls were writing them, and they developed their own methods of keeping their minds off snipers.

When Pete walked, he would summon up his grandmother's old room, the walls decorated with wallpaper covered with cabbage roses against a grey background, trying to count how many of them he saw at once, trying to visualize the paper more and more clearly, until he could see where the pattern began to repeat itself. Then he would go on to the cracks in the plaster of his ceiling, trying to remember if the main line forked to the right or the left, or to remember if he slept on his right or his left side when he lay in bed and faced the window. He didn't know what Liebowitz was humming over and over to himself, but it was something in a foreign language, and when he asked him what he was saying, Liebowitz said he wasn't going to tell him because he didn't want to know, and they all went along in that way, anxious for the day to end, but dreading dusk, because at night the enemy was more active, dreading daybreak because Charley liked to make things happen just before dawn. Time is the grunts' enemy, as Krebbs said. No matter what it gives, it takes away.

Sal said there was nothing, absolutely nothing, he hadn't fucking worn out thinking about and now his mind was empty, and perhaps it was, because he was becoming restless. When they were hungry and knew where they were, he'd strip off his shirt, take his shorts from his pack, take off his trousers, and walk into a village carrying his M-16, buy a chicken, and he'd come back with it and cook it. Usually he'd share it with the guys in his track. Sometimes he wouldn't. On the fifth day, they were still stationed in the same place, and Pete decided he'd go into the village and buy his own chicken.

"Buy it?" Krebbs asked in disbelief. "Buy it?"

"Yeah, buy it," Sal said. "It's more interesting that way. Almost human."

Pete walked into a yard where chickens were clucking. A three-year-old boy with a badly swollen stomach was throwing rice for them. The woman came forward. She knew what he wanted, and she picked out a nice chicken for him. He was about to take it when he heard the chickens begin squawking and he turned around and saw the child squatting down, straining to defecate, and his bowels began to move, and even from a distance, Pete could see the worms moving in them, and the chickens were squawking and trying to catch at the worms in the child's rear end.

The child began screaming, the woman dropped the chicken and ran over to the boy, beating back the other birds. Pete retreated behind the hutch and threw up everything he'd eaten for days. He came back without a chicken and when the others asked him about it — Man, how could he do this to them? They were hungry — he said he wasn't. He wanted to quit, but there was no place to quit to. He wanted to tell someone what he saw, but everyone had enough troubles of their own. The rule here was to bite off what you could chew. Don't expect others to chew it for you.

"Come on, cheer up," Sal said. "Our luck's bound to change." But Pete saw the small boy and he thought to himself, There's no luck in this country. And it was raining. It rained so hard and so long it seemed the oceans, not the sky, circled overhead, not inches of rain falling, but acres of rain, and when it stopped, if it stopped, the sun came out, and within hours, the orange mud had turned to orange dust. They were forever trying to keep the inside of the track clean. The inside of the track was home.

They made rules about taking off boots before coming into the track, but of course everyone forgot, especially if they heard the crack of a bullet, exactly like the crack of a ruler on the edge of the teacher's desk, and soon Pete was saying, "Everything in Vietnam's orange. Even black people are orange. The dust turns their hair orange and the mud turns their skin orange and we're orange also. Man, I don't know why they talk about a color problem here."

Sam was asking, "Why do I keep a diary? Why? Every day I write the same thing. Check for snipers. Burn a village. Tomorrow, I'm going to write, Burn a sniper, check a village."

And still it rained. They forgot what the sun looked like. They didn't believe it came up in the morning. In the morning, it got lighter, not much lighter, just not as dark. If they had to cross one more rice paddy in this mud! And then they'd fall silent. If they had to go, they'd go. There was nothing they could do about it, and the next day, they'd be crossing a paddy, and the first man over the dike would make a motion meaning, *It's slippery*, as if everyone didn't know it. It was worse than ice.

Guns were jamming. They spent time covering ammunition to keep it dry. The bulldozer dug out deep holes for the tracks, and they spread ponchos over them and had instant bunkers and were a little drier, but they were never dry, and the Sergeants came by saying, "Take care of your feet, take care of your feet," and sometimes when they took off their boots, their feet looked like swollen marshmallows. Now that Sal had a pet pig his feet were always in fine shape. He'd trained the pig to lick his feet, and he swore the pig's tongue cured the ulcers on the soles of his feet, but no one else was willing to try. In the jungle, they'd found a dead soldier and a wild pig was chewing through the man's skull. The dead man's eyes were wide open. As the wild pig chewed, the man looked as if he were sleeping. And then one day, the rain stopped and the heat and dust were back and of course they missed the rain. That was the way it always was.

The men were getting careless. With boredom, a kind of giddiness was setting in, and now Krebbs encouraged mock firefights with tracer rounds, even suggested games of mumblety peg, the men lying on the ground, their legs spread apart, while those standing threw knives at the toes of the men lying on the ground. One of the men in Geronimo Davis's track almost lost a toe, but the excitement that small wound generated was, according to Krebbs, worth it.

Odd things were beginning to happen. A four-man patrol went out to reconnoiter a mountain and radioed that they were coming in early. Don't shoot. When the Lieutenant asked what happened, they said they'd been turned back, and when they were asked who turned them back, they looked silly.

"All right, Paganini, let's hear it," the Captain said, and Paganini said they'd been crawling up a ridge and everything was fine. They were making the usual amount of noise, each step sending down hailstorms of pebbles, and all of a sudden a hairy arm appeared over the ridge and pulled back, and, like a slingshot, let loose a huge stone. Then another hairy arm appeared, and then another, just like in a cartoon, and they realized they were being attacked by rock apes whose territory they were invading. No one had been there *but* the apes since the beginning of time, and if the VC wanted that hill, they ought to take the beating. Rocks the size of baseballs! Man, those apes should play for the Mets!

Sal seemed uneasy, and said he was used to it, listening for that breath-ing down the road, but now it was fucking apes and fucking mud and fucking rain, and Krebbs asked him what he was bitching about. At least no one was getting killed. The Captain sent out five of the track crews along with the infantry they carried to clear a landing zone in front of the tracks, and the men began buzzing about a big operation coming up. Why else would they be clearing a large LZ? But really, the Captain had orders from the Colonel, who just wanted the men kept busy. They were out in the tall grass in their shirts, some of them in cut-down pants, grabbing hold of a bunch of grass with their left hand, strips of towel wrapped around the palm to keep the grass from cutting into their flesh, slashing at the stems with their machetes, and suddenly the sky darkened. What the hell was it now? More rain? A minute ago the sun had been shining, but the sky was black and it was getting dark, and the sky was buzzing, actually buzzing, and the men farther down the field were shouting, "Bees! Bees!" and that's what they were, thousands and thousands of them.

Everyone panicked. Someone popped a C.S. grenade at the cloud of bees, but as the men said later, the bees must have been wearing gas masks, because they weren't affected, but the wind shifted and blew the cloud of gas into the men, and the bees followed the cloud, and the men were leaping and screaming, calling for help over the radio, and one of the men had hung his poncho as a hammock between two trees, and the bees, probably following their queen, settled on the poncho, and the poncho, under their weight, collapsed to the ground.

The men came back with eyes swollen shut, lips disfigured. Someone was even bitten on the tongue and there were three allergic reactions, one man's throat swelling shut, two shock cases, and a medevac was called in to take them and to bring in cortisone for less severe cases.

No one could talk to Krebbs. He walked around singing to himself, "Birdy, birdy, in the sky, drop some whitewash in my eye." That in itself was a danger sign. From a squad about thirty klicks away came a report of defeat by monkeys, and it came over the radio this way. The Viet Cong had rounded up rabid monkeys and let them loose on the twenty-five men out searching the jungle. Eleven were bitten and medevaced out for antirabies shots, and now everyone was saying the VC didn't *have* to fight. The animals and the disease and the weather were doing it for them. A troop was reporting two cases of malaria, neither of which could be flown out because of the weather. The choppers would try to come in and they'd have to go back. All the others could do was move the sick men into the sun when they were cold and into the shade when they were hot, and the others thought that when help came, it would be too late, because the men had such high fevers, even if they lived, their brains would be burned out. They'd be nothing but vegetables.

Someone said the VC had to put up with the same animals and the same diseases and the same weather, and someone else said, Yes, but they were used to it, and how could you fight people who went underground and stayed there for months at a time? You went down a trail and someone popped up in front of you, *right out of the earth,* took a shot, and then disappeared back into the ground, and you couldn't find him. This wasn't a war. This was a nightmare. And people hid in tree trunks, inside trees, up in the branches, or inside the walls of houses. Paganini, who'd been staring down at his boots, looked up and said, "Maybe the VC already gave up. Maybe we already won the war. How would we know? Nothing's happened for weeks. Maybe we killed enough of them and it's all over."

No one said anything to this. It was preposterous, but it was also true, and it was also time for lunch, so everyone sat down, opened up their C-rations, heated them, and tried to remember what they had come for in the first place: to save the world from communism, to fight and kill Communists who would otherwise come to America and fight and kill them, to help the Vietnamese remain free, to do something for their country because they loved it and it was the best country there was, to do their duty as their fathers and uncles had done theirs, to make their families proud of them, to become men baptized by fire, to prove themselves, to find the gold ribbon of heroism running through them, redeeming even the most prosaic lives, the lives of their uncles sorting mail in the post office, or their fathers washing the mud from their faces and hands after a day down in the sewers, to earn medals and wear them proudly, to discover bravery and put childhood behind them, to start over in the army's green machine, having already, at seventeen, failed in their first world or having been failed by it, to say to themselves, "If the family could see me now," reason upon reason upon reason, but none of them had come to fight (and be defeated by) rock apes and rabid monkeys and ants that jumped three feet and swarming bees and torrential rains that turned streams into raging cataracts, sweeping four men with mortar rounds to their deaths—in the morning, the black men and the white men indistinguishable when people found them, black and white alike both swollen and grey.

At night, when they set up on ambush, a panther would roar and leap over their heads into its tree. It wasn't interested in them. It didn't want to harm them. It was completely indifferent to them. They were in its way. The tree was its home. The men didn't belong there.

Some of the infantrymen spotted tigers from the choppers carrying them into landing zones. There were caravans of elephants and planes fired on them because they carried enemy cargo. What kind of war was this, shooting animals with machine guns, or worse yet, suffering defeat by animals, rabid, insane, but still stronger than they were? Lions and tigers and bears. But there *was* something to fight for. Why couldn't they remember it?

"I don't like it," Krebbs said. The mood of the men was ugly. They had it too good. They'd rigged up showers from spent shell casings, and they sat staring, their eyes angry. And then the choppers began bringing in heavy equipment, tractors, Rome plows, sling loads of logs, and everyone knew something big was coming. Nothing like this had ever happened before. The wind changed. The men were digging bunkers. The Captain made the rounds, checking the overhangs, telling the men to put as much over the bunkers as they could. They were filling sandbags until the palms of their hands blistered and bled. They dug bunkers with their shirts off, and finally picked up enough information from the guys around the command track. No one ever told them what was happening, but they knew it was something big even before they heard the rumors. Usually, they had to fight for equipment, and now every time they looked up at the sky, a chopper was coming in with a sling load. It was something to look up and see a chinook flying in with a plow swaying from its belly.

A battalion of NVA was crossing the border and coming through their valley on its way to the city and they were the only thing in its way. All the other platoons were called back in and were on their way. Two platoons would function as a blocking force, driving the NVA back into the mouth of the valley. The rest of the troop would be waiting farther back. The hammer and anvil routine. There'd be no surprises. But there were more NVA than Americans, and a chaplain flew out with one of the Cobras and offered to administer last rites, and some of the men took him up on it, but most of them didn't. That was asking for it. They dug for two days and the tracks took two platoons to the far end of the valley, and two platoons were dug in near the entrance.

"Well, finally," Sal said. "We get to have something go our way. I'm fucking sick and tired of the gooks starting something and breaking it off at their own convenience. It's about time we took control."

"Yeah, this is more like it," Liebowitz said. "We get to fight them on our own terms. The NVA's regular army. No more of this pooping and snooping in the bush."

The Chief rolled his center-of-the-earth pole between his hands and said that whatever came, they'd handle it.

"Damn right," Sam said. His hair was now white, bleached colorless by the sun. The sun was out, but to him, it seemed dark. "Let's do it." Was his father down in the mines today? Was there mail waiting for him somewhere?

They were geared up. They were ready for a fight. Their weapons were cleaned. Their adrenaline levels were so high they swore they could hear a mosquito at two hundred feet, and then they saw a loach, an observation helicopter, a bubble with a propeller, fly overhead and the radios began squawking and the orders came in: Break down all your shit and get up to the top of the mountain. The tracks could get up there. The incline wasn't sharp, and, since the tracks were already at the base of the mountain, they were starting immediately.

At first, the men cursed and caved in the bunkers. They slashed open the sandbags, emptying them. They'd been cheated again, and the word came round that it wasn't an NVA battalion but a division that was coming through. There was no way they could handle it and the weather had changed. Now it was good and they were going to B-52 the valley. Two tracks and their crews would stay behind to guard the equipment until the choppers came for it.

Everyone started up the mountain. Krebbs and Davis stayed below with their crews and tracks and the rockets began coming in. From the tracks, they began to see pith helmets, and they began firing their .50 calibers, their light antitank weapons, but within minutes, one of the tracks had been hit. Over the radio, the Lieutenant gave orders for everyone but the driver and track commander to abandon the vehicles. Everyone else was to go up the mountain on foot. Bravado and Liebowitz and the Chief hesitated, but Krebbs shouted, "Go! Go!" and Sam was firing the .50 caliber while Krebbs was loading and firing a grenade launcher.

"You're staying?" Pete shouted in disbelief. "You're not staying!" For an instant, they turned to look at him, and in that instant, he felt time stop, saw an emptiness in back of their eyes, a sound like wind, howling, and he had to shout it down. He couldn't hear that sound; he knew what it meant.

"It's a stupid order, man!" Pete shouted. "Think! It's a stupid order! Let's get out of here! A few men! A *division's* coming in. A division! What for? To guard equipment? Sal! Tell them!"

"He's right, man! It's a stupid order. Get out of the track!"

Krebbs and Sam looked at them, dazed, machinelike beings whose power had suddenly been cut off. Krebbs looked at Sam, and Sam nodded.

Over their heads came the familiar crack of AK-47s.

"Get out of the track!" Sal shouted. "Get out and don't look back!"

"Get out and don't look back!" Krebbs shouted to Sam. "Everyone out!" and then they were off the track, off the track and running up the mountain.

"Don't look back! Just don't look back!" Sal kept shouting as they ran. "Don't look back!"

Behind them, they heard the sound of grenades exploding, the sound of rockets piercing the thick skin of the tracks, the unmistakable and familiar sound of the AK-47s, and then the sound they never forgot once they heard it, the sound of the ammo inside the track going off, the track itself beginning to blow, and Krebbs turned around to look, and as he turned, he thought, What are you doing? Sal said, Don't look back, but he had to know: was it Big Annie Fannie? Where the hell were the bombers? And when he turned around to look, something hit him hard in the head, and he touched his forehead, surprised, and fell.

Sam felt, rather than saw, Krebbs fall. He knew he was no longer behind him, and he turned to look for him, and when he turned, he saw a grenade coming toward him and automatically he reached for it and just as automatically caught it and was going to toss it behind him toward the tree where he thought he saw a pith helmet and that was the last thing Krebbs saw, who was lying on the ground, his arms and legs numb, his vision narrowing, so that there seemed to be a black border around everything, the whole world existed in the center of that black border, before the explosion took him out: Sam, who wanted to be a gym teacher, reaching up for the grenade like a baseball player and fielding it, and Krebbs smiled or thought he smiled, because, in fact, the muscles of his face no longer responded to his will, and then they were both gone.

Liebowitz, who was running up the mountain with the others, thought he felt something in his leg, but kept running, and Bravado passed him, and then the Chief, and he speeded up. He was right behind them, and then they were at the top of the mountain. They'd gotten there at the same time as the rest of the platoon who'd begun at the foot of the mountain, not at the mouth, where they'd begun running. Now they could hear explosions from the valley and the radio chatter and the Lieutenant's constant call: "What's happening? What's happening?"

The valley was smoking as if on fire. They could hear some of the tracks coming up the mountain trail, and the Lieutenant was saying, "How many? How many?" He turned back to say both tracks were hit, he didn't know how badly, and the B-52s were shaking the ground, when Liebowitz looked down and saw his leg covered in blood from knee to ankle, went into shock and started screaming, "My leg! I lost my leg!"

The medic ran up to him, looked, slapped him across the face, stuck a huge opium joint in his mouth, and said, "Asshole, there's your leg! You've got three pieces sticking out of your leg. What's the big deal?" He pulled them out, and Liebowitz lay back, watching him bandage the leg, thinking, All right, I'm going to Japan or I'm going home. The medic said, "You're O.K.," and pulled a piece of shrapnel out of his arm. "In an hour you can walk around," he said. "One purple heart, one to go."

"I don't get out of the field?" Liebowitz asked. "Why don't I get out of the field?" But the medic was bending over someone else and had forgotten about him.

Two Cobras were circling the valley and a chopper was coming in. They saw it land. Someone said, "Medevac," and someone else was saying, "It don't mean nothing," when Pete started screaming that Krebbs and Sam were gone, where were Krebbs and Sam? Sal came over to him, his face wet, his eyes streaming, and said, "He looked back. I know it. He looked back," and Pete got up and grabbed the front of his T-shirt and kept shouting, "They ain't dead! We don't know they're dead!" And then the Chief began: "Where are they? Who saw them go down? Who saw them?" and Liebowitz, who was dazed, repeated over and over, "Something happened to Krebbs and Sam? Something happened to them? To Krebbs and Sam?"

and the Lieutenant came by, saying, "Hey, it's not over 'til it's over. Don't go burying them yet," and Pete looked up at the Lieutenant, and asked him, What kind of order was that? To leave two men behind with the track? but the Lieutenant didn't answer him.

Liebowitz and the Chief, Pete and Sal huddled together, crying, and then staring into space, saying nothing, and the radio was chattering, and the Lieutenant listened, looked at the four of them, and moved off like a dog caught stealing a chicken from the barnyard.

But by night, they'd dug in, and LPs were outside their wire, and illumination flares were going up and coming down, *chunka, chunka, chunka,* and the word came back that Krebbs was gone, and Sam, and Davis, not wounded, but dead, and the anger swelled: those men had been thrown to the wolves. It was so important to guard equipment? What was a human life worth? The B-52s were coming in anyway.

In the morning, the two tracks in the valley were towed off by the recovery vehicles. The tracks were damaged, but nothing the maintenance tracks couldn't take care of, and until they repaired Big Annie Fannie and got in a new Sergeant, Sal, Liebowitz, Pete, and the Chief were temporarily assigned elsewhere. But when they reached their new area of operation, the Lieutenant sent them out on ambush with thirteen other men. As usual, Liebowitz paired off with the Chief. Pete paired off with Sal.

It was another ambush, nothing new. The mosquitoes and the sun and the mud, no talking, no smoking, mud on their faces, not to blind the enemy but to cover their smell. They all believed the enemy could smell them, and Sal, who was the point man, made a turn and found himself looking at three Viet Cong sitting next to a charcoal fire, roasting something. They were good. They could cook and no one could smell anything.

Sal said later that the Viet Cong must have been more surprised than he was, because he didn't know what happened next, but when he saw again, one of the bodies was on the ground and he could hear the sound of the other two crashing through the underbrush. Pete, who was three back from the point man, came running forward, asking, "Which way did they go? Which way?" and took after them, thinking: All right, the Lieutenant wants me to be infantry. Now I'm infantry.

He felt something, a quiver in the air, and he slowed down and slid behind the twisted trunk of a tree and waited, trying to gulp air soundlessly. Not far from him the bamboo bushes were moving but there was no wind. His hand was already on the grenade. He pulled its tape and threw it. After the explosion, there was no more movement, no more sound. Later, when he looked for blood trails, he couldn't find them. Neither could Liebowitz or the Chief.

"How stupid can you be?" asked Sal, who had gone farther into the bush. "Look up in the trees."

"I don't see any bodies," Pete said.

"In the *trees,*" said Sal, and when Pete looked up, the trees were hung with human flesh, a torso from one branch, the stump of a leg with its boot still on from another. And then they looked harder and there were white shreds streaked with red. They hung all over the branches.

"Sometimes you don't even find this much," Sal said. "You find a red stain on the ground. They're *vaporized.*"

Pete leaned over and threw up. In the middle of a small, clear space in front of him was an arm, white as stone, its fingers curled up to the sky. Here and there, flies were buzzing thickly through the branches.

"How many bodies?" the Lieutenant asked over the radio.

"We've got one head and three legs and one arm," Sal said. "How many is that?"

"Three," said the Lieutenant.

"I don't know how you count, sir," said Liebowitz.

"Be careful coming back in," the Lieutenant said. "There may be more."

Sal switched off the radio. "I'm taking back the head," Sal said.

"Why?" Pete asked.

"You'll see," he said. "I'll take point going back."

He hadn't gone far when he stopped and called back, "I've got one. A *whole* body." The other men moved up and a VC was lying on his back, half of his head gone, a purplish mass of brain swarming with flies. His eyes were open, staring straight into the sun, through the flies landing on his pupils. "He's not dead," said the Chief. "He's moving."

"Twitching, reflexes," said Sal. "Half his head's gone. He's not here."

"He's *twitching,*" the Chief said. "Make him stop."

"Cut it out," Sal said.

"He's moving," Pete said in a low voice.

Sal turned the VC over. On its belly, the body continued to twitch. Sal emptied a clip up and down the man's spine, then flipped him over. The man sat up, touched his testicles, said something in Vietnamese, and lay back, quiet.

"Satisfied?" Sal asked.

"He's still twitching," said the Chief.

"He's going to stop now," Sal said, and the body did. It lay still. "Liebowitz, booby-trap that body," Sal said. "Sometimes they come back for their own." Liebowitz crept up to the body and put a grenade beneath it. "Let's go," said Sal. "It's getting dark."

That night they heard an explosion, and the next day a patrol was sent back into the jungle where they'd left the dead man. "He has risen up," Sal said, pointing to the trees.

"So someone came for him," Liebowitz said.

"Or he twitched again," said the Chief. "Nothing stopped that twitching."

Krebbs, thought Pete. If Krebbs were here, he'd shout and ask them what they expected. Whole bodies? There were no such things as whole bodies. What did they think they were in, the movies, where people fell over with neat little marks in the middle of their foreheads? He'd rant and rave and run around in circles and pretty soon the noise in Pete's ear would die down. He'd stop hearing the blood pounding against his eardrums. The trees, which seemed to be leaning either right or left, would right themselves and the world would go on. He'd count how many days he had left, and how many days he'd already been there, and he'd look at Krebbs and think he'd gone this far with him. All he had to do was follow him and he'd get him out.

Now there was no such thing as a Krebbs. He didn't believe it. Krebbs was somewhere. He was alive somewhere. They couldn't just *say* Krebbs was dead. They had to prove it. If he didn't feel it in his heart, if his heart wouldn't believe it, how could Krebbs be dead? And Sam, whose hair turned white as if it knew something, as if it knew Sam wasn't going to get any older. This was as old as he was going to get. And Geronimo Davis. Whoever the new Sergeant was, whoever the new track commander was, he was going to hate him. He was going to be loyal to Krebbs, to Krebbs and Davis and Sam.

"You know what a purple heart's called?" Liebowitz asked the day after Krebbs and Davis died. "It's called the idiot award because you were too stupid to duck."

"Yeah, that's what it is," the Chief said.

"What about Krebbs and Sam?" Liebowitz asked. "What do they get?"

"The LT put them in for a bronze star. You know, make the operation look good," Sal said.

"Yeah, it looked real good," Pete said. After that, they didn't mention Krebbs or Davis or Sam again.

The great lull had given way to intense activity. Ambushes ending in firefights were the order of the day, and Pete no longer protested when he and Sal and Liebowitz, the Three Stooges from New York, were sent out, and Pete grinned when Sal stuck his hand up in a firefight. He was bucking, he said, for his second purple heart. That would take him out of the field. Liebowitz and Pete stopped taking their malaria pills, thinking malaria might get them out, but one of the men from Davis's old crew came back from Japan where he'd been sent for malaria and they didn't recognize him. He'd left a big, strapping fellow with shoulders you wouldn't believe, and when he stuck palm leaves on his helmet, everyone laughed and pointed and said he looked like a walking coconut tree, but now he was thin and yellow and muscleless and he tired easily. He looked like an old man, stooped over, hugging himself, even when it was so hot people tried standing in one another's shadow to get away from the sun. They started taking their pills again. And now the Lieutenant was making the rounds Monday mornings, watching everyone swallow their big orange pill.

One night, eight men were out on ambush and the ambush was over-run. In the morning, they went out to look for the wounded and to retrieve the bodies. They were wrapping bodies in ponchos when Pete looked up and saw one of the new guys, he didn't know his name yet, and he didn't want to know it, talking to himself and carrying a leg with an NVA boot over to the body of a GI.

"Well, now," said the new guy whose accent was just like Krebbs's, "this man's missing a leg and here's a leg and now we'll have a whole body." Pete blew up, shouting, "What the fuck do you think you're doing? What are you, some kind of nut?"

The new guy said he just thought the soldier would like to arrive on the other side with both his legs, and Sal came over and got in the middle. "Just wrap what you find of the bodies. This isn't some goddamn mortuary," and the new guy looked at the leg he was carrying. He looked like a dog scolded for picking up a bone, and then he looked up at Pete and asked, "What should I do with this?" and Pete said, "What the hell do I care what you do with that?" so the new guy swung the leg by the boot and threw it up into the air, and it fell, disappearing into the thick, dense green jungle where, by next week, something would have dragged it off and eaten it.

23

H E N I H A D enough money, I was ready to leave the city. I took a taxi to the fields beyond the city and began to walk. It had not taken me long to earn a great deal of money, and I had heard the girls talking, saying these days families were not disgraced when their daughters left the villages to earn money as I had. I heard them planning to return to the villages, but I could not.

At the first village, I stopped and bought a pair of black slacks and a black shirt from a village woman and gave her my red silk dress. She stroked it as if it were a living thing, and I asked her if she would wear it, and she laughed, showing her black teeth, saying such a thing was a marvel and too wonderful to wear. She would hang it from the temple to her ancestors. On its back was the raised design of a golden dragon, and as she talked to me, the old woman's gnarled finger never stopped tracing the design. She begged me to stay and eat boiled jackfruit and small frogs in pepper sauce with her and I did so. The taste of those foods brought tears to my eyes.

A monkey kept swinging into the hut through the window, and I asked her if she had made a pet of the monkey, and the old woman said no, the monkey was wild, but he came and slept in the hut when the sun was high. She said she thought he would be easily tamed, but she could move only very slowly, and he was always out the window by the time she stood up to go to him. I took a piece of jackfruit and held it out for the monkey, who jumped on the little table, leaned forward to take it, lost his balance, and grabbed on to my hand to steady himself. Monkeys can lose their balance too. When the animal righted himself, he studied me and took the jackfruit from me and began nibbling it. Then he climbed on my shoulder. "Ah," said the old woman. "I thought once he had been tame."

I stayed with the woman, doing her chores, crossing the river in a boat, gathering bananas and coconuts for her. I was again pregnant and would have stayed until I had my baby, but I was restless and did not belong here where life still seemed as I once remembered it, and I believed I would bring unhappiness wherever I went.

My first baby, as I had expected, was born dead. How could it be otherwise? It was born of a mother who had no *kwan*. How could it live? I had little hope for the one I now carried, but with every new day, I became more hopeful. It was, after all, a child of the war.

When I was ready to go, I asked the old woman if she would sell me the monkey provided he would come with me. She said she could not sell what she did not own and I was free to take him. I asked her where her children and grandchildren were, and she said her sons had joined the army, but her daughter had been killed crossing the river to bring back bananas for her children, and shortly afterwards her two grandchildren died of cholera. Her husband had been dead long before the war began. I asked her if she would not miss the monkey and she said, as I could see, she could move very little and was content to watch the lizards as they scurried across her ceiling and floor. She warned me to be careful as I traveled because the soldiers on both sides were nervous and shot anyone who appeared suddenly.

I fashioned a collar of string for the monkey and he seemed quite happy to put it on. Then I braided a leash from unwoven cotton threads the old woman kept by her. I took dried fish wrapped in a banana leaf with me and we set out.

The monkey proved a good and affectionate companion. Often, he sat on my head, his legs dangling over my nose, but most frequently, he stood on my shoulder, leaning against my skull. When I stopped to rest, he lay in my lap and I petted him, and when I let him go, he would climb a tree and bring down a banana without first biting into it, so I saw he had once been trained by a farmer. Whether he sensed my nervousness, or whether it was in his nature, I do not know, but whenever he saw someone from afar, or heard someone coming toward us, he would chatter at me and pull my hair so I could easily hide myself.

Once when we were in the jungle near a stream, some swamp fowl suddenly clucked, and the monkey pulled at my hair, jumped from my shoulder to a tree, and began clawing at a huge wooden face someone in years past had carved in the enormous trunk of a banyan tree. I came over to the face in the tree and saw why the monkey was so eagerly tugging at it. The face swung out from the tree like a door, and behind it was just enough room for a person to hide. The monkey and I hid there, pulling the carved face into place after us, and then I saw it was possible to look out through the eyes of the carved face, and in the forest walked two men dressed like farmers but carrying guns. Whose side were they on? It was impossible to tell. Eventually, the monkey pulled my hair and I thought it safe to leave the tree and we went on.

I walked for ten days before I found the base, and even then I did not go up to it, but instead asked the villagers outside the base what had become of the soldiers, and one old man said, "Oh, we will go fetch their laundry any day now. You can come with us," and I saw he was not looking at the monkey. He had seen my swollen breasts and he guessed my situation.

Eventually, the old man's family readied their ox cart and prepared to leave to collect the soldiers' laundry. I asked them if it was not dangerous to make such a trip and they said it was dangerous, but they must eat. They asked me why I was going and what I would do when I arrived.

I said I would stay with the soldiers if they would let me, but really, I could not explain my decision. The soldiers were wandering souls and now so was I. The old man looked at his wife and thought me demented and I thought that was just as well. Now they would ask me no more questions, and so we started out, and when I looked back at the village, I saw a monk in saffron robes pursued across a rice paddy by a water buffalo and I laughed because, after all, some things had not changed. The monk's robes still maddened the animal, and once more a monk was running, for no reason, for his life.

**24** **T**HE BIG NEWS around camp was that a new Sergeant was coming out, a man who'd reupped for a second tour, who had a college education, and was tough, but Krebbs's crew and Davis's crew seemed indifferent. They occupied themselves playing touch football and now they were playing soccer, and the Lieutenant, who was walking by, stopped and watched them, wondering where they'd gotten the ball. He started to walk over to the seven men playing on the field and wondered how the hell Sal was holding the ball like that, holding it out in front of him, and drop-kicking it. He walked closer.

The ball was in play on the muddy field. He couldn't see it, but now someone had it. He was holding it up. It looked like it was floating right beneath his hand, and the Lieutenant got closer and saw it wasn't a ball. It only looked like one. Sal was holding it by its black hair, preparing to kick it. It was a human head.

"Oh, fuck it," said the Lieutenant, turning around and going back to his track. "Fuck it." Things were going from bad to worse here. Where the hell was Krebbs? Isn't that what Krebbs always said? "You're going to miss me when I'm gone." When *Ah'm* gone. He had that accent.

Out on the field, the men finished their game, and Sal picked up the head and threw it to the side of the field, where it landed in the mud with a sucking sound and almost at once it was surrounded by a crown of flies. Now the men were down in the bomb crater, washing and splashing. From here they looked like kids, boy scouts in the water hole, and in the afternoon, it would be search and destroy for all of them. And in the meantime, what was coming down the road? Villagers and a cart full of ice, ice with banana leaves piled on top. How the fuck did these people make ice? "Ice," the Lieutenant called out, and the men came out of the swimming hole stark naked and began grabbing what they wanted. They weren't going to pay for ice, not in this goddamn country.

Pete, Sal, and Liebowitz sat on the edge of the water hole, their legs in the water. "I found something out," Pete said. "The day I chased those gooks in a firefight? Fear is next to God."

"Yeah? What's that supposed to mean?" Sal asked.

"There's only one thing as strong as God," Pete said. "Fear. You're afraid enough, you can do anything. Just like God."

"So what's bravery?" asked Liebowitz, and they all stared down at their toes. They had tried, again and again, to decide what constituted bravery and what looked like bravery but was really fear: for example, running in front of the others and running into enemy fire, maybe that was fear, and you ran because you were tired of everything, and frightened, so frightened, you wanted it to come to a stop. That wasn't bravery then, but what was it? What was the difference between bravery and fear? Nothing, according to Bravado. They were both next to God. They both gave you the strength to do things you otherwise couldn't.

"I could wait awhile before I sat next to God," said Liebowitz. "I'm in no hurry to go up there."

"Don't talk like that," Sal said.

The troop went out in the afternoon, headed toward the village, but halfway there the radio stopped them, and two four-man patrols dismounted, climbed down the riverbank, and prepared for night recon while the rest continued on toward the village. They were traveling quickly when a shot cracked the air and the first track veered wildly to the right and the track commander got on the radio. His driver was hit. The tracks got on line, herringboned, and found themselves facing a nippa palm and some brush. The sniper was in there, and they began opening up at the nippa palm, a single palm outlined against the sky, and for all they knew, a single man in it. They would finish a volley and pause and after ten minutes or twenty, another shot would ring out. This time the bullet shattered the shield of the right gunner's M-60, and the bullet ricocheted and lodged in the flesh of the gunner's neck.

"Everyone in. Everyone down. He's after the first track," came the word over the radio. But the .50 caliber gunners and the M-60 gunners had to stay up on top to fire their weapons, and after two hours, three gunners were wounded.

"We've got to get this guy," said the radio. "We're calling in an air strike. Let's get him and let's kill him."

The tracks watched while the jets came in, dropping bomb after bomb, napalm towers climbing the sky, orange clouds folding in on themselves, black smoke weaving in, turning the sky above them black, concussion after concussion rocking the earth, and this went on for hours, all afternoon, until they were certain nothing was left alive, not one mosquito, not one ant, not one burrowing snake. They were looking at dead earth. And then the bombing halted, and as if on signal, a small boy, about eight or nine, came up from behind the tracks, carrying a basket, pointing at it and waving.

"If he gets any closer, take him out," the track commander told Sal.

"You mean you want me to kill the kid or what?" Sal asked.

"Back off, Sarge!" Pete shouted. "It's a kid! Don't touch him!"

"Di di mao!" Sal shouted, but the boy came closer, this time reaching into his basket as if to show the cavalry what he had there.

"Take him out, Sal!" shouted the TC. "That's an order! Take him out!"

Pete was shouting, Don't do it! Don't touch him! It's a kid! and the TC was shouting *Take him out!* and Sal lifted his rifle and fired one shot. It took the kid's head off. It didn't take much. The child was small. They saw the boy's head roll some distance from the body, and the body fell backwards, propelled by the impact of the round, and the basket hit the ground, and out of it rolled the unmistakable shape of a green Coca-Cola bottle.

Sal looked at the TC, aimed his M-16 at him, his finger on the trigger.

"Don't do it, man," Liebowitz said. "Put the gun down."

Sal, whose face was wet with tears, lowered his rifle, and smiled. "Scared you, didn't I?" he asked cheerfully. He moved closer to the TC. "Don't you *ever* give me an order again."

"You're not too popular around here now," one of the other men said. "Not popular at all."

"I'm not here to be popular," said the TC.

"You're barely here at all," said Liebowitz. "Six feet and you're under, and from where I stand, you're sinking fast."

"Watch it," said the TC.

"Who do you think they'll court-martial?" Liebowitz asked. "You or us?" *This is how you liberate women and children?* thought Liebowitz. *This is how you liberate them?*

"He could've had anything in the basket," said the TC. "What the fuck was he doing out here in the middle of an air strike?"

"Don't give us orders again," said Sal.

They listened while the command track asked what the shooting was about, and heard the TC explain that they'd shot a man with a booby-trapped basket, and the command track said, Fine, two men from each track were to dismount and search the nippa palms for blood trails. See how many bastards we got. Over.

Liebowitz volunteered, and the TC saw Sal staring at him and said he thought he'd go too, and the Chief came from his track along with someone else, and from the fourth and fifth track came two men and one photographer from *Stars and Stripes,* who promptly attached himself to the Chief. "Spread out. Maintain your intervals," said the TC.

"Yes, sir!" shouted Pete, saluting.

"Don't do that!" said the TC. "Don't salute! I'm not an officer! Are you trying to get me killed?"

"No, sir! I won't, sir!" Pete shouted.

The men who were moving toward the nippa palm grinned.

"Anything else, sir!" shouted Pete, saluting.

"I'll have your ass for this!" said the TC.

"Yes, sir! Understood, sir!" Pete said, saluting again.

The TC moved away, but now Sal followed, saluting and asking, "Anything else, sir? Sir, are these the proper intervals, sir?" and so they entered the nippa palms. The bombs had felled entire trees, blown immense craters in the earth, and the men looked round and were about to turn back and return to the tracks when a shot rang out and the TC grabbed his helmet. The bullet had hit its rim and bounced off.

"Goddamn, there's someone in there!" Sal shouted, and they hit the ground and looked around. "Goddamn it, he went underground." Another shot rang out and the TC rolled over, out of harm's way.

"Too bad," said Sal.

"I know where he is," Liebowitz said. "I'm going after him. Cover me."

"Stay where you are," Sal said, but Liebowitz got up, and they all began firing while Liebowitz, crouched over, ran around the edge of a bomb crater, hit the ground, and began crawling forward. A shot cracked the air and Liebowitz sat up as if he'd just noticed something interesting, both hands holding his head as if in true amazement, and then he fell backwards.

"Goddamn it," said the Chief. "Goddamn it," and he let out a blood-curdling scream and took off, running low, straight into the line of fire. Now the others were up on their knees, firing, trying to cover him, and it was machine gun fire, not an AK-47 firing from the brush, but the Chief charged straight ahead, his head lowered as if he were walking through hail or heavy rain, still making that blood-curdling noise, and they saw the Chief disappear into the bush, and suddenly the machine gun stopped. It was absolutely still.

They flattened themselves out and waited. A few instants later, it seemed like hours, the Chief came walking out of the bush, the fragile body of a Viet Cong dressed in black pajamas held up over his head as if the body were a weight he was lifting. "Here," he said, throwing the man down at their feet. "Here's your sniper."

"I just watched the U.S. government spend millions of dollars on ammunition trying to kill one sniper, napalm and five hundred pounders and grenades and mortars, and it took one GI to go in and get him," the photographer said.

"Damn you!" Sal shouted at the Chief. "Damn you! Goddamn heroes!" He picked up his M-16 and hit the Chief on the side of the jaw with the stock of the barrel, knocking him down.

"Cool it off! Cool it off!" Pete shouted, pushing Sal back. The Chief got up, rubbing his chin. "Hey, man, I'm sorry," the Chief said to Sal.

"*He's* sorry?" the photographer said. "What's *he* got to be sorry about?"

"Leave it alone, man," Pete said.

The Chief's jaw was swelling, red and puffy. "I'm sorry," he said again.

"Don't talk to me!" Sal shouted.

The others were beginning to get up and dust themselves off, slap at the ants and mosquitoes that had settled on them while they lay in the dirt. Their eyes searched the bush. If one man had gone underground, there could be more, but after a while, they knew, they didn't know how, but they knew they were alone, and then they went over to Liebowitz. The bullet had penetrated his helmet and blood was flooding out from beneath its rim, covering his face and the back of his head.

"He's dead?" asked the TC.

"No, he's sleeping," said Sal.

The photographer came up, ready to photograph Liebowitz, and the Chief said if he took that picture, they'd break his legs and then they'd start in on his neck, and the photographer lowered his camera and asked, "What did I do?"

"That's just it. You didn't do nothing and you ain't doing nothing," Sal said.

"How about a picture of the Indian?" asked the photographer. "I'm sorry," he said to the Chief. "I don't know your name."

"No pictures," said the Chief. He was kneeling next to Liebowitz, gently rubbing his chest, his hand making steady, circular motions.

"It would be a great shot," the photographer whispered to the TC.

"You can't reason with these men," said the TC.

"You killed Liebowitz and you killed the kid," Sal said to the TC. "Tell the photographer all about it."

"What's he talking about?" asked the photographer. "You killed a kid?"

"He doesn't know what he's talking about," said the TC.

It was getting dark and they had to go back for a poncho, and Bravado, Sal, and the Chief came back, wrapped Liebowitz up, and carried him back to his track.

"I'm at the center of the earth," the Chief said in the darkness. They couldn't see him. "I'm at the center. I am."

"What's the TC going to tell his mother?" Pete asked. "That he was killed at college in North Carolina?"

"He's not going to tell her anything," Sal said. "He's dead."

Pete and Sal, who were next to the Chief, looked at one another, and looked up at the full moon, and their skin prickled, tightened, as if it did not quite fit them, as if their skin were a suit that had grown too small.

25 T HE MUCH-AWAITED Sergeant who was to replace Krebbs as TC in Big Annie Fannie was Douglas Wapniak, whose first name was immediately forgotten, as was usually the custom of the troop. No man was ever known by his full name. He was called by his first name or his last, and more frequently than not, was called by a nickname. To know a man's name was to know the man, and to know another man was to give his ghost terrible power once he was gone.

The men in the troop had power. They were young and carried guns. They could, if they so decided, waste, blow away, or zap anyone not wearing a U.S. uniform (and occasionally someone wearing one), but the power made most of them nervous. It exhilarated them but made them guilty, and so they were careful with it. The power was there, a fact, like a gun in its holster, or a rifle hanging from its sling on their shoulder. They had no theories about it, or opinions. If anyone had asked them about it, they'd have said, "Sure, power is a good thing. It lets you survive. Survival's the name of the game, man."

Wapniak was different. He'd enlisted after getting his master's degree, had refused to take the test for Officer Candidate School, had come to Vietnam as a PFC, and now he was returning as a First Sergeant for his second tour. War, according to Wapniak, was about power and the exercise of power, and he intended to become an expert in it. Power lay on the ground like sunlight. It was in the air like pollen, like lost coins gleaming in the grass. It was there for anyone to pick up, but most people didn't, thinking, Let someone else do it. I'm busy today getting my hunting license or feeding my pig or taking my car in. What does power have to do with me? They had their jobs and their wives, their children and houses and pets, and were, in their own sense of things, complete. And then there were others who, finding no resistance in the people around them, nothing in them that pushed back, reached out into the lives of others. Wapniak thought he was one of these. Everyone said such people were so full of themselves or too taken with themselves, but Wapniak believed that because he saw the emptiness in others, it was up to him to fill that empty place. He intended to begin with the crew of Big Annie Fannie.

He climbed into Big Annie Fannie through the back hatch and looked around him. "Not bad," he said. "We could improve a couple of things, but not bad." When they asked him what he wanted to improve, he waved his hand grandly and said there'd be plenty of time to talk about that later. He wanted to be filled in on what happened to Krebbs and Sam, and they told him, sketchily, quickly, as if they had forgotten the incident, as if it had happened so long ago it was buried under layer after layer of dust and mud.

"I heard about yesterday," he said to the Chief, who braced himself for praise, but Wapniak said, "If I'd gotten the sniper, I wouldn't have brought him back like that, not like a cat bringing a mouse to its owner. I'd have handled it differently," and they stared at him, speechless. "I heard about the head you play soccer with," he said. "Where is it?" Now they looked at one another. This meant trouble. Mutilation of bodies, that was a court-martial offense. They walked over to the muddy field where they'd played yesterday, the Sergeant gesticulating wildly and talking every step of the way, a veritable storm of words, and then he stopped and looked down. "Is this the head?" he asked. They said it was.

"All right," said Wapniak. "You can play one more game with it, and it's mine. I'm going to skin it and put it on a stake and bleach it in the sun, and then we're going to mount it on the track. Let them know who we are and what we did."

Pete, Sal, and the Chief looked at one another. Wapniak picked up the head, covered with black, dried blood, buzzing with flies, swatted the flies, and when they came right back, sprayed the head with insect repellent. He sprayed right into the eyeholes while the other three winced, and then he held the head out in front of him with both hands, stretched his arms out in front of him, and examined the head exactly as Pete had seen his mother examine a watermelon in the supermarket. "We could've put one on each side of the track. It would've looked better. Balanced. No matter which side they'd come from, they'd have to have seen it."

"Nothing to worry about," Sal said wearily. "We'll get another."

"This is serious business," said Wapniak. "This troop's been taking too many losses. We have to make them fear us. Last year, I was out in the field on Wandering Souls' Day, and we made them afraid. They wouldn't come near us. They love to make things happen on holidays, and we were the only troop that didn't hear a shot fired."

"How did you do that, Sarge?" Pete asked. Pete glared at him as if to say, Don't play along with this sucker.

"How did I do it?" asked Wapniak. "Come back to the track." They walked back and Wapniak pulled out a squarish bundle wrapped in a poncho and began unveiling it. It was the largest tape cassette player they'd ever seen. Sal shook his head.

"With this," said Wapniak. "We did it with this," and he pushed the PLAY button on the machine and the track reverberated with high, mourning voices. "Rock and roll!" said Wapniak, smiling broadly. "Played at the wrong speed! Slowed down! We did it with rock and roll!"

Sal looked at Pete. This guy is nuts, his eyes said, but Wapniak was talking. Wapniak had entered talking, and Wapniak, Sal thought, would exit talking. He could see it now, four more months with Wapniak's mouth chewing through their ears right into their skulls like that nightmare hog he saw chewing on a man's head uncountable villages back. "What we did was, I got some guys who CA'd the infantry in to drop leaflets over the neighboring village. You know, the government's always dropping these pamphlets, but they don't do any good. They don't understand the people. I found an ARVN who spoke English and he wrote it out for me in Vietnamese, and then we dropped the leaflets and played those tapes on loudspeakers. Not one shot was fired. Not one."

"I don't understand," said Sal.

"I don't either," said the Chief.

Pete was listening transfixed, like a deer paralyzed in the beams of headlights.

"The leaflets said the voices they'd hear were the voices of wandering souls! Wandering souls!" He looked at the men, waiting for some dawn of understanding, but for them it was still night. "They're *afraid* of wandering souls!" he said. "They *sacrifice* on altars to keep wandering souls away from them! Our leaflets told them the wandering souls were all around our troop! And then we turned on the music. You could hear it for miles! It was terrific!"

"The plan?" asked Sal.

"The music," said Wapniak. "You want to hear the tapes? I'll play them for you."

"Later," said Sal.

"I'd like to hear them," said Pete.

Sal looked at the Chief and the Chief looked at Sal. *Let's go,* their eyes said, but just then the LT climbed into the track. "I see you've met your crew," the LT said to Wapniak.

"Yes, sir!" said Wapniak, and flipped a small notebook out of his pants pocket. "What's your name, sir?"

"Name?" asked the LT, whitening. No one asked him his name. Everyone called him Lieutenant or LT. Except when he talked to the Captain or the Colonel, he forgot he had a name. "What for?" he asked.

"Why do I want to know your name?" asked Wapniak. "Some day this war's going to be important. People are going to study this war. Right now there may be complaints about it, but people are looking at it. This war won't go away. When people come back to look at it, when they see how important it was, what significance it had, they're going to want to know *names.* They're going to want to know who made it possible, because, believe me, Lieutenant, there's meaning in this war. Mankind's never going to be the same after this war. I don't know what it means yet. Nobody does, but it means something. We ought to sit down and talk about this. I've given it a lot of thought."

"Hollingshead," said the Lieutenant.

"What?" asked Wapniak.

"My name's Hollingshead," said the LT.

"What a name!" shouted Wapniak joyously, writing it down. "What's your first name?"

"The name your mother and father argued over," continued Wapniak, as if the Lieutenant actually didn't know what he meant by his first name. "The one they give you that someone had before you. You're named after someone?"

"Howard," said the LT.

"Howard?" mouthed the lips of Bravado, Sal, and the Chief, moving without sound.

"Howard Hollingshead!" shouted Wapniak. "Wonderful! A wonderful name! A name to live up to, right, Lieutenant?" He wrote the name down. "Lieutenant," he said, becoming confidential and serious, "I'd like to talk to you about a certain matter."

"Of course," said the Lieutenant, looking desperately at the others, who avoided his eyes. "What do you want to talk about?"

"Skulls," said Wapniak.

"HE'S NUTS," Sal said.

"As a pecan tree," said the Chief.

"Krebbs used to say that," Pete said. "Nutty as a pecan tree. I don't know."

"You don't know?" Sal asked. "Man, someone left him out too long in the sun. His brain's fried."

"What he said, about it all meaning something," said Pete.

"Bullshit," Sal said. "All bullshit."

"Let him think what he wants," said the Chief.

"Who?" asked Sal. "Pete or that nut?"

"Both," said the Chief.

"This ain't the place to think about the meaning of *nothing,*" Sal said. "You don't think here. You act. Stop and think and you're dead."

"Maybe that's not true," said the Chief, squatting down and thinking it over.

"Aw, shit!" said Sal. "I don't like this! I don't like this fucking troop no more!"

Wapniak popped his head into the track and said, "I'm going to *confer* with the Lieutenant."

"He's going to what?" Sal asked. "Confer? He said confer?"

"Give it a rest, Sal," Pete said.

"Man, Pete, you're already over your head here," Sal said.

The order came over the radio. The tracks were to line up and move out. Eighteen klicks away was a suspected VC village, and Wapniak returned smiling broadly, his eyes darting here and there like gnats at dusk, and Sal thought, Whatever it is, I don't want to hear it. He looked hard at Wapniak, who was tall and skinny. He must have been well over six feet tall, but he was so thin and narrow he gave the impression of being smaller, of taking up less space than a ray of light, and his hair was light red and curly, and even beneath his tan, his skin looked white, and his eyebrows were so bleached out by the sun they looked like pink lines drawn on with ink, but when he talked he had a big voice.

His voice was dark and swelled and filled whatever space there was, and right now it was pushing against Sal and the walls of the track, and he was talking about the war and how every operation was important. Who knew where the effects of one action ended? Something that looked small and insignificant could topple something larger and the effects would be felt down to the last inch of the last corridor of time and what was important was that everything they did be done with honesty and integrity.

Even a skull, if it were skinned and bleached with honesty and integrity, was no longer a skull. It became a symbol, part of the design, and there *was* a design, and they were part of the design, shaped by the design and shaping it, all at the same time. "So today," Wapniak concluded, "we dig up graves. I don't want to hear any complaints about how we're desecrating sacred ground, because in this war, even the dead have a role to play and there are more armed dead men in the villages than there are live ones," and Sal, who had dug up graves before and once found two hundred M-16s packed in grease, the cases stretching from one headstone to another, knew perfectly well what Wapniak was talking about, but he liked to play dumb. You could get away with more that way, and he said to the Chief, "I don't know what the hell he's talking about."

"Let me explain it to you, Sal," said Wapniak, and began a tedious explanation of how graves were often used to conceal weapons, and Sal yawned, sat on an ammo crate, and said, "I still don't get it," and Pete said, "Get off it, Sal," but the Chief sat down next to Sal and smiled. Wapniak was off again. "I do have some rules here. You have to have rules, and one of mine is, no more making sure dead Vietnamese women can't have babies. There's a place to draw limits, and I draw it there."

"I don't understand what the fuck he's talking about," said Sal again, and in frustration Bravado kicked the track wall.

"I've seen men deliberately put knives in dead women's—" Wapniak began, but Sal stopped him and said, "Do you mean to tell me *U.S. soldiers,* men like us, *violated* dead bodies? Is that what you're saying?"

"That's what I'm saying," answered Wapniak, who was beginning to regard Sal with suspicion and even active dislike.

"I don't believe it," Sal said, who, before he was sent to this troop, had to stand by and watch ten ARVNs rape and then shoot a village woman discovered with AK-47s hidden in a hollow wall of her hutch.

Wapniak decided to ignore him. The other men were listening. Sooner or later, everyone listened to him. His mother said he wore people down, but since he'd come over here, he'd found out the truth. He had things to say and people wanted to hear them. His last CO said he had leadership qualities, and this Sal needed leading. Sal was stupid but he was strong, and Wapniak could do something with him.

"One more thing," Wapniak said. "About confiscation of enemy weapons. I think every track should have one AK-47. What about the rest of you?"

"Orders are to turn them in," said Sal, who was one step ahead of Wapniak.

"Sometimes they come through and search the tracks," said Pete.

"No problem," said Wapniak. "If anyone finds it, we just found it, shadowing the trail, or on the last search and destroy. We were turning it in as soon as we got back to base."

"We just do what we're told," Sal said.

"People make mistakes out here," said Wapniak, "and it's a lot easier to bury your mistakes if they're shot with an AK-47. You know what I mean?"

"No," said Sal. "You want to run that by me again?"

Pete sighed and looked at his boots.

"I'll let you *consider* it," said Wapniak. "It's something for you to consider. If you want to use it, take it. It's yours. Maybe it won't come to you today or tomorrow, but it'll come to you. Consider it. Take your time."

"I don't need no time," Sal said.

The radio squawked and they were moving out. Sal was now the driver. Wapniak didn't like that. You had to take good care of your driver. If your driver got hit, you were helpless in the kill zone while you tried to get him out of his seat and get someone else in, but he'd find a way around Sal. The other two were on his side. He could sense it. And if they weren't, he'd find out what they needed and give it to them. He was good at that.

Sal drove, and Wapniak, whose headset was connected to Sal's, kept up a constant stream of words. Sal never knew there were so many words, or that it was possible to fit so many in between the usual orders. "A little more to the left." "A little more to the right." "Watch out for that hole up ahead." "Stay in the tracks of the vehicle in front of you. You get out, that's how you hit mines, my man. You want to be the troop version of a mine detector?" Now he was saying they'd really get a chance to use all their recon skills in the next few months. It was a good thing for them he had special training. Sal said after they'd been out in the bush for a while, they all had special training, and Wapniak said, "Nah. I can smell a gook a mile away. I know from the look of grass if it's been beaten down two weeks ago, or if a human did it or an elephant or just an animal going about its business. I can spot a water tree two hundred yards away. The yellow color of the upper leaves gives the game away. *Right! Right!*" he shouted, and the incessant babble went on.

Hell, Sal thought, they said New Yorkers had big mouths, but this guy wasn't from the east, not with his accent. The steady din of conversation pounded on his skull. The man's mouth was a military hazard. When the road finally straightened out, Sal asked him where he was from, and he said Utah. "You a Mormon?" Sal asked, and Wapniak said with a name like his he was no Mormon. He was a Catholic, just like Sal was. "It's a Roman Catholic army. It's a new crusade," Wapniak exulted over the radio, and Sal shook his head as if to clear it of that voice, but Wapniak's voice continued. It went on and on.

Now the command track was crackling. They were going into the jungle, maybe a klick and a half. Command didn't think anyone had been to this village before. Snipers were a distinct possibility and so were mines. Get ready. They were making good progress when the column came to a halt, but nobody heard a shot or an explosion. Everyone was asking what the hell happened, and the command track said it was stuck. Its rear end was right off the ground, up in the air waiting for vultures to fuck it. They'd gone over two big palms and bent them down, but the palms started to spring back up and the rear of the track was off the ground. Now the VTR had to come around the column and get up in front and tow the command track off the palms, and it took a good two hours before the column was moving again.

While they waited, Wapniak talked. He'd been specially trained in recon. When they got to the village, he'd have a chance to show them what he could do. His voice filled the inside of the track like a gas. Pride made him physically larger.

His face, Sal thought, looks like it's made of candle wax that melted and dripped. His eyebrows dropped. His eyelids drooped, and the skin of his cheeks sagged. The heat of that voice, Sal thought, was melting him down. "Just what do you expect to find there?" Sal asked him. "It's another ville. Another lousy ville. They'll be old ladies walking with fucking canes, and old men walking with fucking canes, and little babies. It's always the same drill."

"Ah!" said Wapniak, throwing his arms wide. "Ah!"

"If there are surprises, spring them now," Sal said. "We don't fucking like surprises."

"A man who doesn't like surprises is already dead," said Wapniak. "That's what Vietnam is about. Surprises."

"Vietnam is about staying alive," said Sal.

"Well, that too," said Wapniak, who was off again, this time talking about his last tour of duty, and hunting in the delta, and all the time they'd eaten black and white porcupine and wild boar and spotted snake. Man, there was nothing like spotted snake. "When you eat enough of the creatures that live on the land, you become part of it," Wapniak said, and Sal said, "Give me a break," but the Chief appeared interested and said that was a very Indian belief. His tribe believed that if you ate an animal, you acquired its qualities.

"Its powers," said Wapniak. "Exactly." Those animals lived on this land since the beginning of time, or since they evolved into what they are, and there was nothing about the land they didn't know. The snakes burrowed into the land making their snake holes, and the monkeys swung through the trees and knew where the birds and the panthers slept, and if you ate those animals, you learned how to hunt them. You knew what they knew.

Sal said any animal that got caught by an American must be a pretty stupid animal. He didn't think you'd learn much from it, except what not to do, but Wapniak ignored him and described catching a monkey and said the meat was awfully strong, almost too strong to eat, unless you boiled it first, and Sal lost all patience and said the montagnards didn't bother boiling monkey meat. If they were going to cook a fucking monkey, they left the monkey out in the fucking sun, and the sun tenderized it, and then they brushed off the flies and singed the meat over a bonfire and ate it. But Wapniak was not one-upped. He said you wouldn't cook filet mignon for two hours over a low flame and you didn't eat monkey meat half raw. Cooked properly, it was something to taste. He wished he had a monkey now. And Pete suddenly said, "He always said monkeys were unlucky," and Wapniak asked, "Who? Why were they unlucky?" and Pete said, "Krebbs," and Wapniak said maybe they were unlucky for Krebbs, but their luck had just changed.

The village was small, huts built in small, separate clearings in dense jungle, the clearings connected by narrow grass paths beaten down and dried out by the sun so that they resembled hay. The women went along the paths, carrying jugs of water on their shoulders, or poles of bamboo with sheaves of rice suspended from either end. As they drove into the village, past the golden thatched huts, small children, naked from the waist down, ran toward the tracks, their eyes and mouths wide, and then stopped at a safe distance. Some of them turned and ran back to the huts screaming for their mothers to come and look.

Sal shook his head and inhaled deeply. He'd said this village would be like the others, some toothless men and women and a few infants, and now look. Somehow the war had swirled around this village without laying a finger on it. Wapniak was looking at him, his look so knowing and full of meaning that, had it been a book, it would have been an encyclopedia. But Wapniak was going on. Things looked normal here, maybe *too* normal.

It was something to consider. Maybe Charley left the village untouched because everyone in it was VC or at least enough of them cooperated. This was, according to him, a more suspicious village than the ones they were accustomed to checking out and he couldn't wait to get down on the ground. There were a couple of things he wanted to look into. Look into *deeply*.

"Can you believe this shit?" Sal asked the others, but the Chief said uneasily that over here nothing was ever what it seemed, although this village *seemed* friendly. No one was giving them strange looks. Their eyes looked fine. Remember how Krebbs used to say you could tell everything from their eyes? Well, these eyes looked clear. They looked *too* clear, said Wapniak. If you were back home, and tracks came rolling down your street, or things equally as preposterous, how would you look? Wouldn't you look frightened? Wouldn't you look suspicious? It was suspicious that they weren't more suspicious, said Wapniak.

"You know," Pete said, "we keep saying we can tell it in their eyes. We know they're not friendly if they run, but if they don't run, it's because something's wrong with them. I mean, how the hell do we really know anything? We want to think we know something, but we don't know *any-thing*. If we shoot someone who runs, we say, O.K., he was VC. I don't got to feel bad. But it doesn't mean he was VC. It means we don't want to feel bad."

"I couldn't agree more," said Wapniak. "That's just what I was saying. We never know. We can't take anything for granted. They're guilty until proven otherwise." That wasn't what Pete meant, but Wapniak confused him, and he'd never said so many sentences together before and he wasn't ready to come up with another paragraph, and even if he came up with one, how was he going to push it down Wapniak's throat, out of which chunks of books kept coming?

"Who wants to get down on the ground with me?" Wapniak asked, and the Chief hesitated. Sal had no intention of going anywhere with Motor Mouth, but Pete volunteered. After months of watching things happen and not knowing what to make of them, Pete was fascinated, if confused, by what Wapniak had to say. The man seemed to understand everything. He could explain everything. All right, he'd been living in a world where there weren't any more rules, where it was all right to kill, where, in fact, killing was a good thing. One day he was at home, and everyone said killing was bad, and the next day, the world was upside down. Eventually, it would all have to add up. It would have to. It couldn't stay this way.

"What are we looking for, Sarge?" he asked (although the last time he'd said that, he'd asked a man named Krebbs, not Wapniak), and Wapniak looked at him. It was a solemn look, a searching, serious look, and he said, "Graves."

"Graves?" Pete echoed.

"*Recent* graves," said Wapniak. "A recon man knows the value of graves. We're not looking for caches in the graves. That's got its use, but we're after something more subtle. We're looking at how these people died. Did they die from gunshots? From shrapnel? From our weapons or Charley's? You can tell a lot about the enemy activity from the bodies."

Two minutes before, Pete thought, he'd been crashing through the jungle, excited and happy. There'd been the excitement of running the road, going over forty miles an hour, trying to stay in the tracks of the vehicle in front of them, looking for any activity on the side of the road. The danger was so close it had its own personality, its own fast breathing, and in the jungle, everything was beautiful. There were drops of water on the foliage, and the sun shot through them, coming at you like rays, and there were purple trees flowering. The beauty made him want to cry. Here you could feel every emotion there was in half an hour, and before he'd come over, he'd thought he didn't have any emotions except anger, but here they were. In Brooklyn, wherever that was, in a past life he barely remembered, he'd forgotten what emotions were, or at least he liked to think he had. But here it was impossible. Ten minutes ago he'd been happy and now he was looking for graves to dig up. Now he was miserable.

A woman was going down the path toward a beehive-shaped haystack, and when she reached it, she began pulling out hay for the water buffalo her daughter was leading down the path toward her, and the water buffalo was grey and shiny. His flat, carved horns curved back, swept back, and his big black protruding eyes examined everything sadly. He must have just come from the water. Around their feet, chickens were clucking, roosters stretched their necks and crowed, and a group of older boys had gathered around them and were evidently discussing which ones were strongest and could best fight each other.

A child ran down the path they walked on, ran past them, and came back carrying a squealing pig, and as they were almost through the village and approaching the woods on the other side, a small boy who was crouching down suddenly jumped and pounced upon something on the ground, and they stopped and watched the child, wondering what he could be doing. They'd never seen that before. And the child crouched and pounced and crouched and pounced and finally let out a shriek of delight, stood up, and examined what he'd caught, and they could see the long legs of the fat brown spotted frog dangling from his hand, and the frog's bulging eyes. A frog, Pete realized, was incapable of looking frightened. A frog always looked one way. It never looked happy or sad.

Nothing here was familiar. Everything was new. It was impossible to let your skin thicken here, and then he thought, no, that was wrong. There were places where his skin was so thick he might never get beneath it again, and there were black things in there, very dark things, like Krebbs and Sam and the burned bodies and the pig crying *Scree!*

"Look, someone's found something," said Wapniak, and they stopped and went over to the Lieutenant, who was watching another soldier digging up a grave, and as they watched, the last spadeful of earth was lifted away, and there was the body, or what was left of it. It had been wrapped in a cloth that had rotted away. The people here were too poor for coffins, and Pete looked into the grave, and didn't know what he was looking at. He saw bones, but they seemed covered with thickly woven fabric. There wasn't much smell. He'd smelled a fresh grave once. You never forgot that smell. It weakened the muscles in your legs. It made you hopeless and crazy with the desire to get away. It was sharp and stung in the nostrils, prickling them, making you want to sneeze, but you couldn't sneeze. You couldn't breathe. The smell stuck to the membranes in your mouth and throat. It stuck to your clothes like a curse. It made you feel as if you were dead also. The thickly woven fabric, that was decayed flesh, and Wapniak was pointing at the flesh, saying that different kinds of tissue decayed at different rates. He could tell from looking at this body that it had been buried over six months, and he told the Lieutenant, "I think, sir, you better turn it over carefully. Sometimes they're booby-trapped," and in a weary voice, the Lieutenant said, "Thank you, Wapniak," and they walked on.

"*That's* what we're looking for!" Wapniak cried suddenly and ran over to a tall, thin white cross tilting crazily in front of the last hut in the village. "See how the mound's still raised? That's a fresh one. That one hasn't been here long. The smell's gonna be terrible. You better tie something around your nose," and Pete said he already knew he couldn't stand the smell. *What am I doing here?* he asked himself, and Wapniak told him to go back and get the Lieutenant's shovel. He should be finished with it by now, and to call the medic and have him take a look at what they found. He knew a lot about bodies, but there was a time when you had to call in experts. A wise man knew the limit of his abilities. "You won't have to dig long," Wapniak said. "The grave's shallow. They're always shallow."

A woman came out of the hut and pointed to the grave and began crying. Her children gathered around her and saw her crying and began to cry with her, and gradually a crowd of villagers was standing in back of them, all crying. "They can't all be related, can they?" Pete asked. "I mean, they can't all be related to whoever's in there," and then he was sorry he put it that way, because now he knew he was digging up someone who had once been a person, not just a dead thing, something to be investigated. He was digging up a person and these people had known that person, and what that person ate and drank and who the person loved, and Pete thought, whoever he was, whoever lay in that grave, he didn't want to see his face.

"It's a woman," said Wapniak. "I'll bet you anything it's a woman. They bury virgins close to the house. People here believe the head of a virgin gives them great powers, so they bury the head right near the house where they can watch it. I bet it's a woman. Young. Thirteen or fourteen."

The medic had arrived, and now Pete dug carefully, because the earth was exposing a body whose head was shrouded in white cloth, and once the earth was removed, and the long thin body lay in the shallow grave, the medic bent forward and carefully began unwrapping the stained yellow and coffee-colored bandages from the head, and Pete leaned forward, watching, and when the bandages were off, he saw the profile of a beautiful young girl. She couldn't have been more than nine or ten. She had olive skin and straight black hair, and even though she'd been lying in the earth, she didn't look dead. She looked as if she were asleep, and he wanted to bend down and touch her cheek, but he knew he couldn't. He didn't know why he wanted to touch her but he did and it took all his self-control not to bend over and reach out his hand, and then the medic lifted and turned her head, and he saw that the other side of her face was missing, gone, as if a giant knife had sheared it off.

"Shrapnel," said the medic.

Pete walked behind a coconut palm and threw up. When he stopped shaking, he walked back.

"No," the medic was saying. "I don't think it means anything. She could have been out in the fields and someone dropped a bomb. We've heard of door gunners bringing down water buffaloes and some pilots drop their loads early and say they flew to the target. I don't know. It could be anything."

"No enemy activity?" asked Wapniak.

"I don't think so. Why, do you think so?"

"I agree entirely," said Wapniak. "Just double-checking. It pays to be sure."

In back of them, cries were climbing the air like vines, intertwining, becoming solid, impossible to walk back through.

"Let's go," Wapniak said, but Pete couldn't move. He was paralyzed by the wailing voices, and the medic was turning to look more closely at him, when someone stepped out of the tree line. For a minute she looked like the girl in the grave, but she had a small grey monkey on her shoulder and she began walking toward them. She was waving, but even if she hadn't waved, they knew she didn't come from the village. She was different. She walked up to Pete and said she'd told him she would find him. She'd come with the people from the base who brought their laundry. Pete stared at her.

Wapniak was talking. His words were a swarm of bees. They were all around Li, turning her dark, and the darkness spread, and the medic was grabbing Pete's arm and saying, "Take deep breaths, *deep* breaths." And Li came clear of the darkness and she was standing there as she'd stood in the car wash in the city. Only her clothes were different, and the monkey. He must be imagining the monkey. He'd have recognized her anywhere, and that surprised him, because he'd forgotten he knew her. What was wrong with him, forgetting so fast, as if he'd prematurely aged, become truly ancient?

"You know her?" Wapniak was asking. "She was looking for you and she found you by coming with the villagers who bring out laundry. This is a *top secret* mission. How do they know where to bring laundry? This requires looking into. People around the base aren't operating with integrity here, or if they've got integrity, they've got poor judgment. Well, that's being charitable. Does she speak English?"

Li said, Yes, she spoke English and she'd come to find Pete, Pete and the others, and now that she had, she wanted to stay. She could help them. She spoke English very well. The monkey, tired from the heat, slept against her shoulder.

"Ask them if the girl in the grave was a virgin," Wapniak asked her, and she did ask, and said, "Yes, she was a virgin, and she was killed when she went out to the river for water. No one knows how it happened, but there was an explosion and they found her," and again she was surrounded by darkness. The medic again told Pete to take deep breaths, and Pete finally said to Li, his voice shaking, "You can't stay here," but Wapniak interrupted, saying, "Let's not be too hasty. We're going to be out in the field a long time now. No one will know if we have a passenger, not unless the Colonel decides to come down in his chopper to talk to the Captain, and even if he does, we could take care of it. She's right. She could be a lot of help to us. If she found us, she could find other people. I bet she knows her way around a jungle."

"I have lived in the countryside almost all my life," Li said. "I know the country as well as anyone in it, and if I stay with you, you will trust me and you will not be sorry."

"Well, as for trusting you, that's something else," said Wapniak, standing up straight and considering her. "Trust is a precious thing, a sacred thing. Trust has to be earned. You're one of them until we know you're one of us. It won't be easy. *If* we let you stay. There are two more men in the track. We have to consult them."

"Sal and the Chief," Pete said, and Li smiled, repeating the words: "Sal and the Chief. Yes, I know them."

"You know them?" asked Wapniak. "How do you know them? Let's go back to the track. I'll take care of the Lieutenant," he said, walking toward the first grave. "He'll give me what I want. The Colonel was saying we needed a scout." Before Pete had a chance to find his voice and say something to Li, Wapniak was back asking what exactly were the powers conferred by the head of a virgin, and why the body had to be buried facing east. He didn't know it had to be buried in any special direction, and Li patiently answered his questions, but her eyes were on Pete, touching his face, and even when she looked at Wapniak, she was really smiling at Pete. He could feel it.

"WHAT do you think?" Wapniak was saying. "A woman as a Kit Carson scout. She speaks the language. She knows the customs of the people. She's invaluable, or she could be." He said something to Li in Vietnamese, and she laughed and shrugged her shoulders. "You don't know what I said?" he asked her. "I said, 'If we don't use mosquito netting, the mosquitoes will bite us.' I went to school for *three months* to learn Vietnamese. You didn't understand me? I thought my pronunciation was good."

"You said," Li told him, "that if we don't use mosquito netting, we will bite the mosquitoes," and she covered her mouth and laughed.

"Yes, well, little mistakes," he said, puffing out. "Explain how it should be said." Li said something in Vietnamese. "Slower," said Wapniak. Li repeated the sentence. "Now I've got it," said Wapniak.

"Congratulations," Sal said.

"Well, do you want her or don't you?" asked Wapniak. "We could keep her here in secret or I could go to the Colonel."

"We like *her* just fine," said Sal. "The Colonel's chopper's on its way in. He wants to speak to the Captain and he doesn't want to use the radio."

"I'll talk to him," said Wapniak.

Beat him down with words, thought Sal. Beat him into a bloody pulp. Leave him a red stain on the ground. He looked at Wapniak and saw a blue-steel gleaming robot, the ball joints of his jaw revolving. Man, thought Sal, I'm fucking out of here, and he lit a joint laced with opium and floated out of the track and looked down on it. The track was surrounded by a cloud of green words: Wapniak. He floated up higher.

He came down to ground when Wapniak, returning from the command track, announced they had the Colonel's approval to try the woman out. It was a risk, a calculated risk, and whoever wanted to take her out on patrol or ambush was risking his life and the lives of the other men. But they needed intelligence. That's what the troop was out here for, trying to gather information. They could take the initiative on this one. He wanted to be notified if she stayed on. He liked to know what was going on in his battalion.

Sal listened to Wapniak but looked at the woman. She was still a girl, almost a child, but there was something about her. He could almost point at it and say, That's it, but just as he thought he had it in his line of sight, it moved to the side. It was like trying to see things at night. If you thought you saw something moving, you didn't look straight at it. You looked off to the side and then you saw it. Whatever it was, it reminded him of home, but he didn't want to be reminded of home. He thought about home, how many days it would take to get back there, but *really* reminded—no, he didn't want that.

"There's a slight change of tactics," Wapniak was saying. "Two-man recon teams are going out and staying out for two or three days. You'll have a radio and rations but you'll have to get water where you find it. You willing to take the girl?"

"Who, me?" asked Sal.

"You and Bravado," said Wapniak, who wanted to stay behind with the track and work on the Chief. There were a lot of things he wanted to talk to him about—like magic. He could learn things from the Indian the man didn't even know he knew.

"Look," Sal said. "You know how long it took us to learn to be quiet out there? If you lie on one side and want to turn over, you take *two* hours doing it. Two hours! You take a half hour raising your hand to your head. If you're lying on leaves, you don't move at all, sometimes all night. She doesn't know what to do. And the goddamned monkey! I'm not going with no goddamned monkey!"

Li said she could sit without moving, not even sitting, but squatting, for four hours watching a waterfowl, waiting for it to move close enough so she could club it and carry it home. The monkey could stay with the track, and when she came back, it would climb trees for her and bring down coconuts or bananas. Sal made a gesture with his hands: do whatever you want. It's all right with me.

"Bravado?" asked Wapniak. "What do you think? We want your input on this."

Input? thought Sal. Input?

Pete stared at Wapniak, and at Li, at Sal and the Chief. What did they want of him? What did the girl want of him? Why had she wanted to find him in the first place?

"What are you doing here?" Pete asked Li.

"I have no good reason," said Li. "Or rather I have so many I believe none of them. It is a mystery to me, too. I saw you were my friend."

"You're going down by the river," Wapniak said. "The Colonel said there's a lot of activity on the river, either civilian or enemy or both. We don't know. If you could get close enough to listen, she'd be a real help. Priceless."

"Close enough to listen!" exclaimed Sal.

"You set up during the day and you don't move until morning," said Wapniak. "If anything happens at night, you'll hear it."

Right by the river. Sal could see the mosquitoes now, not the ones everyone joked about, the ones that read your dog tags and chose their favorite blood type, but the ones the size of helicopters, moving in and injecting you with malaria and then sucking you dry.

"We could do it," said Li. "I can show you. Someone would have to trip

upon us to find us. I have this, too, for mosquitoes. They will not bite." Out
of her pocket, she took a small jar of meat tenderizer, and Sal read the label,
passed it to Pete, and said, "Fine, with our luck, she's a cannibal."

"But," Wapniak was saying, "do we have the honesty and integrity to
live with a woman on our track? Can we do it?" He looked meaningfully
at Li, looked her up and down.

"I am not a nun," said Li.

"And this ain't no car wash," said Wapniak, his gesture taking in the
interior of the tank, as if, thought Sal, it were the Grand Hotel. "We've got
four roosters in here and one hen. Or one hen and four wolves." He looked at
Li. Did she understand what he meant?

"I am not afraid," said Li.

"And the ARVNs? When we go out, we carry ARVNs."

"I will cut my hair and wear a green uniform," said Li, and then Sal
knew what it was. There was something about her breasts and her stomach
when the rest of her was so slender. When his mother was pregnant the last
time, she looked like that.

"I want to talk to you," Sal said to Li, taking her by the arm, and
pointing to the back hatch of the track, and Wapniak was saying, "I'm not
finished," and Sal said, "You're not fucking finished but you're fucking
interrupted. Sorry."

"When are you going to have it?" he asked Li, and the girl reddened. Her
hand automatically went to her stomach.

"Have it?" she repeated.

"Don't fuck with me," Sal said.

"Three months." She watched him warily. The monkey on her shoulder
bared his teeth at Sal, and she reached up to stroke the animal.

"Three months," he repeated, considering. "You don't look it."

"The women in my family do not, not even near the end of their time.
Will you tell the others?"

"I won't have to."

"But for now they do not need to know."

"Babies cry. They make noise. They're dangerous."

"I will leave before the child becomes a danger," said Li.

"You could have it early," Sal said.

"Then I will drug it and keep it quiet until we return to base," said Li.
"You'd do that?"

"Yes," said the girl. "Neither I nor my child will endanger your lives."

"And you? You know what it's like out here?"

"I know," said Li, feeling again the buffalo, who was the world, falling to
its knees beneath her. "Here is where I belong." In the city, her spirit had
haunted the forest places. She heard the sounds of the jungle. She could not
live corpselike, in the city. A corpse could not give life to a child. If the palm

fronds did not rise and fall on the currents of air, if they did not blow in the wind, showing their spines, if she were never again to hear the roar of a panther or the sound of a small animal chewing its way through the underbrush, she could not live. Perhaps, she thought, I have turned on my country and my people because they could not protect me. But surely that could not be it. There was no protection, no safety anywhere.

"I don't know about the others," Sal said. "When they find out."

"But you will help me," said Li.

"Yeah, I'll help you," said Sal, thinking, *Big Mama, Big Mama,* wherever I go, it's the same thing. He put out his hand, and Li, smiling to herself, took it.

"You like children," Li said, and Sal said he didn't fucking like children. But he did. He loved children. He'd raised his own younger brothers. Most of the guys came out here loving children and after a while, after they'd lost enough buddies, after they'd collected pieces of their friends like bits of puzzles blown into the trees, they looked at babies differently. Give them a few years and they wouldn't be babies anymore. They'd be up in trees shooting at them or the ones who came after. Better to get them early. They looked at Vietnamese babies and saw little gooks. *Kill them all and let God sort them out.* One of the ARVNs they had carried said that before he bayoneted a body. Later, the ARVN told them that the VC had come to his village and asked for volunteers, and when there were none, they seized his father because he was the village chief. They cut open his stomach, pulled out his intestines, unwound them and walked away from his father, holding on to the intestines, wrapping them around the bamboo supports of the village's small pagoda. "Who will volunteer?" they asked over and over, and when he volunteered, they asked for more volunteers, and when there were no more, one of the men took a sharp knife and cut through his father's intestines. Another VC held his father upright until he bled to death. Surrounded by the inevitable flies, under a cloudless sky, the palms green and golden and washed in the pure light, it had taken him a long time to die.

Take him out! That's an order! The bullet took the child's head off. One bullet was all it took.

All the ARVNs who rode with them were crazy. Almost all of them had close relatives killed by the VC. They'd been forced to watch while their fathers had been disemboweled or skinned alive. One of the battalion Kit Carsons came over to the Americans after the VC shot his mother and father in front of him. They told the child it was the Americans' fault they had to shoot them and they handcuffed the boy to a machine gun and told him to go out and kill two Americans to avenge his parents. He wandered around in the bush, half-starving, and came into an American camp because he was lonely and needed food. He was loyal to the Americans because they fed him and were not VC. Now he was no longer a child. He was frightening. Even Sal was afraid of him.

"O.K., we're going," Sal said, coming back into the track with Li.

"I'm so relieved," Wapniak said sarcastically. The monkey jumped from Li's shoulder and settled itself on Wapniak's. Wapniak absently began petting it.

"So am I, pal, so am I," said Sal. Even going out to the river, getting close enough to listen to the gooks, even that was nothing compared to two or three more days of listening to Wapniak. He asked how far out the tracks would take them, and Wapniak said they'd be walking from *here*. The Colonel was impressed by the laundry delivery and you could hear a track coming from miles away; he wanted secrecy and surprise, so get going, keep quiet and good luck, said Wapniak.

LI PICKED out a spot near the river. Pete and Sal cleared a space with their machetes just large enough for them to lie down in. Overhead and around them the foliage was so thick that they could smoke because the leaves trapped the smoke and kept it down, slowly mixing it with the humid air, although at night they couldn't take the chance of lighting up. The air was cooler and the smell of smoke traveled farther, but now if someone were three feet away, they couldn't see them through the brush, that's how thick it was.

"We just wait?" Pete asked, and Sal said, "We just wait." They looked around for Li, but she was gone, and they settled back against the trunks of trees. They might as well move around now as much as they wanted to because once it was dark they were going to freeze in position like dead things, like absolutely dead things, like gourds filled with fear.

Fear of getting caught, that was the worst fear.

"We've got that one extra bullet for us," Pete said.

"Yeah, make sure we don't use it," Sal said.

They were filled with helplessness, alone, as if they were the only people left alive, and until morning, they were, and the emptiness wasn't really emptiness, but memories of deaths of buddies, of quick returns to work, of standing over dead bodies, saying, It don't mean nothing, feeling the pocket with the amphetamines the medic routinely gave out as they left through the fire base gate, one medic on each side of the gate handing the pills out. *Here, have a ball.*

They didn't want to take the pills, because when they wore off, you crashed, and if they didn't wear off, they had to take more pills to make them sleep, and they were afraid of those deep, drugged sleeps. They never slept. They closed their eyes and faces drifted in front of them, bits and pieces of the previous day or days at home before they ever knew there was such a place as this, floated by like the rotting coconut husks and leaves that floated by on all the rivers, like the long chains of vegetation tangled with flowers floating downstream. Most people awake weren't as alert as they were asleep and they were alive to prove it.

"Out here, *your skin listens,*" Pete said.

"Your skin?" Sal said.

"Yeah, your skin," Pete said.

Li came back so silently that she startled them, and she said, "This is a good place. They will be back here tonight," and they asked her where they'd be, and she said, ten feet, perhaps twenty down the bank, but first she had something wonderful to show them. Oh, they would enjoy it. Truly, they would appreciate it. They had more than enough time to go and see it and come back before the Viet Cong came back to their camp on the river, and they said, What camp? and she sighed and said she'd found the water tree and look: she opened her hand and in it were four or five grains of cooked rice. "So you see," she said, "they were here."

"Follow me," she said, and she wove through what looked like impenetrable jungle and not once did they have to use their machetes, and then she paused, putting her hand over her mouth. She was laughing and she said, "Just over there," and she crouched down and they looked past her, and there in front of them, on the other side of the bushes, was a large clearing and a huge blue and white Esso sign, a gasoline station right smack in the middle of the jungle, and on the other side of it, a path big enough for trucks.

They stayed there staring at the Esso sign until they lost track of time, and Li tapped them on the shoulder and they followed her back, sat down in their little clearing, and looked at one another. Each knew the other's thoughts. *They* were American soldiers, and they couldn't travel at night, but one night, on ambush, they'd seen a truck with its headlights coming down the road, its lights flickering up and down the trunks of the rubber trees, dancing along the trunks like pale yellow moths, and over the radio came the orders not to stop the truck, just to stay quiet. It was a gasoline truck and if it was free to travel at night with its lights on that meant the VC knew all about it. They'd be getting eighty percent of the gasoline while the United States would get twenty, but would pay for all of it, and that truck could go wherever it wanted at night, but they couldn't move. At night, they had to hole up in fire bases or spend the night rigid and silent in tiny clearings, like terrified animals in their dens. This was some war. And now they'd found an Esso station in the middle of the jungle. Who was that for, exactly? American troops wouldn't come in here at night. Hell, American troops would never find it. The canopy was so dense no one could spot it from the air, and if they found it, they'd never come out alive. This was some fucked-up war.

Li laughed and asked, "Wasn't it funny?" and they looked at her. It wasn't fucking funny. Li asked them if they were sorry they'd seen it. They looked at one another and looked at Li, and said, No, they weren't sorry they'd seen it. It was a little bit of truth, that Esso sign, and here you needed all the truth you could get.

It was getting dark, or darker, and Sal warned Li that she should choose her position carefully because if anyone came, or even if anyone didn't, she wouldn't be able to move or make a sound, not sneeze or cough or clear her throat or even inhale quickly, and she said she knew, and it wasn't long before they heard the sound of voices not far from them, perhaps ten feet, and the gooks had set up their camp. They were talking and laughing and thank God they were upwind from the gooks, Li had seen to that, and they could smell the fish they cooked, and hear the sound of their pots scraping over the little stove they cooked on. They were so close they could almost reach out and touch them. They could stand up, take three steps, and they'd be on them, and they learned again how slowly time could move, and how slowly they could, and how long the night was. It always seemed as if a couple of extra hours were tacked on to every day, and they watched each other, seeing the fear. How would this patrol end? Would they all walk out of it alive? Would one of them walk out and have to bring back news of the others' death? And they were tired beyond description, absolutely collapsed inside, like a building whose outer walls stood, but inside, there was nothing, and for the first time, Sal couldn't stay awake. He was supposed to have the twelve-to-two watch, but his eyes were closing. He took the watch he held in his hand and advanced the hands so that the clock said two o'clock when it was really not even one, and he woke Pete, gave him the watch, and was instantly asleep.

Then Pete woke him and gave him the watch, and the watch said four o'clock, and again he set the hands forward, and in the morning, neither of them said anything, but they knew what had happened, because they'd each had at least six watches. When Li finally said the VC were gone, they made breakfast on their C-ration stoves, shaved, using the water Li brought back in one of their helmets, and asked her what the soldiers on the bank had been talking about and where she thought they should set up tonight.

"They are going downriver to a small village," Li said, "and there they will meet others. We can go to the village and see for ourselves. They say many are soon to come across the border, and one said he hoped his cousin would be with the troops coming down. If we stay tonight in the same place, or almost the same place, perhaps twenty feet away, we may hear more. I think they will come back. Where they sat, there is a notch in the shore large enough for a boat. Weapons are coming down on boats. I am sure they will come back."

"That's good enough for me," Sal said. "Let's go," but Pete looked uneasy, and Li, disappointed. "What now?" Sal asked.

Pete said they were already *here* and there was no point in cutting down a jungle to get *there* when they didn't know if *anyone* would be *there* when they did get there, wherever *there* was, and Li said she agreed.

"They will expect us to come back to the same place or to leave altogether," Li said. "I know."

"Staying here's one thing," Sal said. "Going to a village, count me out. There are only two of us and a lot of them."

"I will go," Li said, jumping up and disappearing into the jungle, and Pete said he supposed now they'd have to follow her, and Sal said they'd do no such thing. They'd wait two hours where they were and then they'd move on. "Bitch! Goddamn bitch!" Sal whispered.

"What'd she do, Sal? What'd she do?" asked Pete, but Sal didn't answer him. What was he going to say? That he didn't want to worry about anyone, especially a woman? A *pregnant* woman. Look what happened to the people he worried about. Krebbs, Liebowitz, Davis. He wanted to forget he knew anyone. He wanted to forget he was alive. He just wanted to *stay* alive until he got out of here.

"That shit about bounties?" Pete asked. "You believe it? You believe they put a price on our heads?"

"She's going to be one rich bitch if it's true," Sal said. "You're carrying a radio. A thousand dollars for the head of a radio operator." They sat in silence. "You been bitten?" Sal asked suddenly. Pete looked down at his arms and reached up, touching the back of his neck. "No," he said.

"You think that meat tenderizer works?" Sal asked, and Pete felt his cheeks and neck and said, Yeah.

"Something new to ask for," Sal said. "Every time I get a package, it's the same thing. Fifty packs of grape Kool-Aid for thirty-five gallons of water."

"I ask for cherry," Pete said.

"I know."

"But last time she sent lemonade and I had to write her and tell her only cherry."

"How's she supposed to know you're the one who asks for cherry?"

"I *asked* for cherry. I didn't *ask* for lemonade."

"So she thought you wanted a change."

"The new guys always ask for cherry?" Pete asked.

"Yeah," said Sal. "I wrote Diana, from the block? I asked her for tropical punch. Hey, if my family sends grape, we'll keep the tropical punch."

"She's always dressed up, that Diana," said Pete. "Like she's going to a wedding."

"Only in the pictures. She's always going someplace in the pictures.

They have sweet sixteen parties. That's all they do for a whole year. Sweet sixteen parties."

"But you like her," Pete said.

"I'm supposed to like her sister. The one who doesn't write. A Dear John letter without the letter."

"Well, if you don't like her, don't sweat it," Pete said.

"You remember how Liebowitz was about mail? He asked for all the junk mail that came to the house? No matter what it was, he wanted it? All those circulars we had from the A&P?"

They missed the circulars. They used to look at the items on sale and imagine what they'd taste like cooked with A.1 sauce or Heinz 57 sauce. They'd say the names out loud, slowly, as if they were exotic words: *rib steak, strip steak, flank steak, Sara Lee frozen cheesecake, Idaho potatoes, Breyer's ice cream, Fudge Ripple, Mandarin oranges, California grapes, collard greens, Bird's Eye frozen peas, Starkist tuna, Skippy peanut butter.*

"It was as good as eating," Pete said.

"Nah."

"Yeah, it was. I miss those damn circulars."

"I still got one," Sal said.

"There was some girl he liked from the neighborhood," Pete said.

"I don't know about that," Sal said, getting up and looking around. "Where the hell is she, anyway, the bitch?"

"How long does it take to get through the jungle, Sal? How long?"

"I said no. When she said 'village,' I said no."

"She'll be back," said Pete. For a minute, he'd forgotten about Li. He missed Liebowitz. "You really got a circular?"

"Yeah. I got it."

"What's on it?"

"Roast loin of pork. Spare ribs. Twinkies. Snow Balls. A *whole* sale on Hostess Cakes."

"Why'd you keep it?"

"I kept it, no big deal," Sal said. It occurred to Sal that every time he saw a Hostess cake or a Sara Lee cheesecake, he was going to think of Liebowitz. Liebowitz loved Sara Lee cheesecake.

"We could hunt," Pete said. "See that bird? It's an elephant bird."

"You shoot the bird, I'll shoot you," Sal said. "Out here in the middle of nowhere waiting for the bounty hunters and you want to shoot off your weapon."

"Forget it," Pete said.

"I got a package coming. My mom said to look out for it," Sal said.

"What's it for? Christmas?"

"It'll never make it."

"Sometimes they do," Pete said.

"Where the fuck is she?" Sal asked.

"Here I am," Li said, stepping out of the brush.

"How'd you get back so fast?" Sal asked suspiciously. Pete looked at him. First he complained about how long she was gone and now he wanted to know why she was back.

"I was gone for two *hours*," said Li. They looked at their watches, startled. Sometimes time crept. Sometimes it flew.

"The whole village is enemy," she said. "They have great amounts of rice. Some of the men have very good guns."

"Have you ever fucking seen a man in a village? A man not all bent double walking with a fucking stick?" Sal asked.

"No," Pete said.

"I want to see this," Sal said.

"No," Pete said, and Sal asked him why not. Pete said if he thought shooting a *bird* was dangerous, going to a ville was fucking suicide.

"Just to look," Li said. "It can easily be done. There are many shortcuts, paths made by water buffaloes."

"Saddle up," Sal told Pete. "Or you can stay here."

"We're a *team*, man," Pete said, getting up.

Following Li through the jungle was not like walking through the jungle at all. She found buffalo paths that cut through dense green walls and once she stopped suddenly, made a severe gesture, and pointed, and when they looked, they found a twisting green vine entwined with a trip wire. "So," said Li, "we must go around," but Sal said no, they had to take apart the booby trap. "No," said Li. "If we take it apart, whoever set it would know someone had been here. It is best to leave it undisturbed."

Pete said, man, he would never have seen that fucking vine and he had the best eyes in the army. Sal kept turning around to look at the vine, the muscles in his arm tightening and relaxing, the muscles in his legs beginning to cramp, as if he wanted to run back and trip the grenade or the claymore, whatever it was, trip it and get it over with.

"Here is a good place," said Li, and she crouched down and began to crawl through a naturally formed tunnel of tree roots and fan-shaped leaves.

"You're going in there?" Pete asked, and Sal said he sure was. The three of them crept inside, beneath the moist brown tree roots. Tiny ants were crawling on the hairlike fibers of the roots, not red ants, but brown, and black ants were everywhere. Two black horned beetles, their armor shiny, were fighting right near his cheek, black male beetles in black armor, their horns locked like two bulls. Not far from his face was a fat, pale pink worm, something brown darkening its center like a ribbon, moving as the worm moved. There was the sound of something slithering but he couldn't see anything, and he wasn't going to move, not when he could see the villagers from here, walking back and forth between the huts, some of the women carrying sheaves of rice ready to be threshed. A woman with her back to them was methodically pounding something over and over. She must be grinding millet. Lately, the peasants were mixing millet with rice because they didn't have enough. What rice they had was taken by VC soldiers.

Some children ran by, tossing a gourd back and forth, and then two men came into view, walking down the central path of the village, its fragile tan huts lined up on both sides of the path, the river, blindingly blue, on one side of the village, the rice fields on the other, an old woman coming out of a hut carrying two coconut husks filled with seeds, another woman coming out after her, carrying a pumpkin. The two men were young. Their black shirts and pants were new, and on their shoulders were the slings of M-16s, not AK-47s, but M-16s, American weapons. The black market couldn't penetrate this deep into the jungle. Somewhere there were two dead Americans. If these two men had their guns, they might have more: ID, dog tags, sometimes entire billfolds full of letters, photos of girlfriends, newborn infants, women smiling so hard into the camera surely their faces must have hurt before the final click of the shutter. *Don't even think about it,* Pete told himself. *Don't think.*

They were staying longer than they should. They'd seen what they came for, but still Pete didn't move. He was watching a group of boys playing a game with sticks. It reminded him of playing stickball on his block. One of the boys would put a stick in a little hole in the ground, and another would hit the stick so it flew out of the hole, and then he would try to hit it as if it were a baseball, and if he missed it, one of the other boys would try to keep it in the air, and Pete began to understand the rules. The longer a team kept the stick in the air, the higher their score, and afterwards, the winning team could hit the stick as many times as they'd hit it while it was in the air, and the losing team had to run after it, barefooted, hopping and hooting with pain as they ran over the twig-covered ground.

A woman came out to the boys with a large fruit, cut it open, and the children gathered around her waiting for a piece. Was it his imagination or did what she carry smell like rotting eggs, and if it did, how could the smell carry so far?

The three of them stayed, close to an enemy village, close enough to study the people's faces and look at the large fruit the woman had brought out, studying its olive green skin and cone-shaped thorns, not because they needed to learn more but because they were close to everyday life.

Here there were the rhythms and routines, men and women, children playing with their parents, dogs barking around the legs of the boys playing with the sticks, a water buffalo cart moving away from the village, down the path through the rice paddies. From here, they could see a small brown pond, and a young mother was bathing her naked baby in the brown water. On the other side of the pond, a man wearing a stained loincloth was brushing his teeth. It wasn't clean, but it was water. Somehow everyone lived. If it was brown water, not red, it was good.

Overhead, clouds like white mountains moved lazily through the sky, and above, birds swept in large arcs. A cuckoo called out and was answered by a crow, and in the fields children chased the birds, clattering dried bamboo sticks hung on strings.

This is life, Pete thought. This is what life's supposed to be. These people wanted to live. That's all they wanted.

Then a procession began approaching the village, and music played, and gaily colored banners flew, and people dressed in white passed by carrying a coffin decorated with flowers and incense sticks and lotus blossoms, and above the coffin was a huge charcoal drawing of the dead man, and some of the villagers joined it and others did not, and soon the procession was out beyond the fields and near the graveyard, and Li shuddered, and they knew it was time to go.

When they were back in the jungle, pushing vines out of their way, wiping the sweat from their faces, trying to avoid the sharp-edged bamboo, following Li, she said the person in the coffin had died a violent death. She knew. She could feel his spirit. It was unquiet. It would perform violence, perhaps assume the shape of a human being and attack a weak animal or a child. It would do terrible things before it found rest and was ready for reincarnation.

"Do you believe all that stuff?" Pete asked her.

"Yes, I do, and what's more, it is true. It is not a matter of belief," Li said. "I am sorry to have seen such a procession and I hope the villagers will perform the necessary rites to pacify the spirit. I am glad to be leaving behind a village possessed by such a spirit," and Sal said, "No talking," and he meant it. They walked silently back in the many, heavy-handed heat, sipping slowly and cautiously at their canteen water, passing the wired vine, and settling in not twenty feet from the spot they had camped in the night before.

"I'm nervous," Pete said.

"Don't sweat it, man," Sal said. "We're all here."

"It's too close. You can reach out and touch them."

"Set out the traps and forget it," said Sal.

They sat still, their muscles tight and on fire, while all night long narrow banana-shaped boats of unpainted wood arrived at the riverbank. Soldiers cooked and ate and talked to one another, and by morning, when Sal had the last watch, they were gone as if they had never been there.

"Oh," Li said, "here is a dreadful thing," and they told her they'd warned her how hard it was, but she said no, what was hard was becoming like the dead. Even for one night it was terrible. She could understand now why spirits were drawn to the living. Their bodies were warm and free while the spirits were cold and had nothing, nothing to eat, no food, no laughter, no feeling. Was it any wonder they were so angry?

26  OW IT SEEMED there were voices everywhere, not just Wapniak's. The Colonel was
talking. He had flown out in his chopper with his executive officer.

The Colonel was so pleased with Pete and Sal that he patted them both
on the shoulder and was about to pat Li on the head when he remembered
that the head was a sacred place. It was a dreadful insult to touch someone
there. "That's a nice monkey you've got there," he said instead, and the girl
smiled at him. He liked her. She reminded him of his daughter, except, of
course, for the eyes. If half of what she said was true, this was a coup. The
girl could be the making of his career.

"Wapniak," the Colonel said, "it was a good idea to use this girl. It was
your idea, wasn't it?" and Pete was about to say it was *her* idea, thinking,
where did the Colonel think they found her, when Wapniak said, "Mine, sir,
with the approval of my crew," and Sal nodded to himself. Sure. Fine. If you
say so.

"Mouths shut on this one," the Colonel told them. "I don't want this
getting out."

"No, *sir!*" said Wapniak. "My men have integrity."

"All the men in this battalion have integrity," said the Colonel, although,
he thought, some had more than others. He didn't like this Wapniak. He'd
seen men like him before. They looked at others, at *him,* as if they were
soon-to-be holes in space, vacuums waiting to be filled. Some of them could
order their men forward into heavy fire and not turn a hair, but he had a
hunch about this Wapniak. He didn't know a fucking thing about the price
of power.

"So," said the Colonel to his XO, as they walked back to the chopper,
"what have we got here? Troops are massing just over the border, and in
five or six days, they're coming across. They've got supplies and they're
bringing more down with them. There's a bunker complex, a way station,
just on this side of the river near this little town," and he pointed at a map.

"If it's true," said his XO.

"This is what the General needs. A big big catch."

"*If* it's true," said his XO again.

"Whether or not it's true, I report it or they court-martial my ass," the
Colonel said. "I want three of the battalion's troops pulled back to base.

Start moving them in today. I'm going to see the General. Get him on the wire."

"Why pull the men in before you see the General?" asked the XO.

"Because he's going to say take the bunker complex," said the Colonel. "That's how we'll find out if it's true."

"Why not send the men out? Why ask?"

"I'm not asking about the bunker complex," said the Colonel. "I'm asking about the city *across* the border. *We* can't order the air force to make mistakes on bombing runs. When something gets this big, you ask. You don't stay alive in this army pretending there's no such thing as a General. If it's something embarrassing, you never heard of him and you swallow it. If it's big, you fly into his nest with it and feed it to him like a goddamn worm."

"I THOUGHT they'd pull us in for this one," Sal said sourly. "I didn't think the Colonel would fucking fly out here."

"Sal's mad about something. Again," said Wapniak.

"So?" said Sal. "So? You want to make something of it?"

And Wapniak was off, saying anger was what made the burning bush. It was the strongest thing there was. You read articles about a man who picked up his car and threw it. Where did he get his strength? He got it from anger. Anger was *pure*. An angry man was strong and pure, and Pete said he didn't want to hear that word, not in this place, and Li said nothing, but the monkey, riding on Wapniak's shoulder, leaned against his ear and fell asleep as he always did when Wapniak started in. His voice hypnotized the animal, absolutely anesthetized him. "There's so much anger in this world and none of it's channeled. None of it's put to use. If it were visible, it would be *lava.* If we could tame it like a wild animal, we'd *be* there. It would be the second coming. That's what this war's about. It's anger trying to find its place. Anger's *sacred,* man."

"Everything's fucking sacred, according to you," said Sal.

"Anger is only good when the head is cool," said the Chief. "It must be kept like a spark in a small box of stone. The warrior knows anger and owns it. It does not own him."

"Don't start," Sal said.

"That's it!" cried Wapniak. "That's it! I've never heard it put better! That's wonderful! Let's consider it!"

"It's not my idea," said the Chief. "It's the medicine man's. It's what he told me. I'm not even sure I believe it."

"Pure, sacred," said Sal contemptuously, and Wapniak looked at him. He saw a beast coming out of its cave, before the invention of the wheel, holding a club. But, thought Wapniak, there was hope, even for him.

"You've got your head so far up your ass it's coming out your neck," Sal said. *Some* hope, thought Wapniak. But not much.

"Outstanding, outstanding, outstanding!" shouted Wapniak.

"It seems to me," said Li, "that what you, Wapniak, say, and what you, the Chief say, are opposites, not the same."

"Outstanding, outstanding, outstanding!" shouted Wapniak. "Everything in life has its opposite. You cannot have good without evil. You cannot have an up without a down. You cannot have peace without anger. What he says is one side of the coin. What I say is the other."

"Of course, I am only an ignorant farm girl," said Li, "but the Buddha did not say that human passions were both good and evil. They are all evil. They keep us from reaching nirvana and we must suppress them and rise above them and so reach nirvana."

"Isn't that what I said?" asked Wapniak.

"*I'm* not listening," said Sal. "Is anyone listening?"

THEY WERE headed back to base, a routine run, traveling the open road only when the jungle thickened malignantly, and through their headsets Wapniak and Sal heard someone in the first track telling the Lieutenant that he saw a man with a rifle down the road.

"It's not a rifle. It's a hoe," said the Lieutenant, and Sal began muttering about how it was a goddamn fucking miracle that that man was still alive, when suddenly someone opened fire with an automatic weapon, and they were firing back.

"He's got a fucking M-60!" Pete said. They turned the .50 caliber on the muzzle flashes in the field and the enemy weapon stopped firing. Paganini got down from the track and walked out into the field as if he were strolling down the avenue at home, not looking to the right or the left, looked around him when he got where he was going, and when he found what he wanted, he picked it up and carried it back. "Here's your fucking hoe, Lieutenant," he said, throwing the M-60 at the officer.

"What's his first name?" Wapniak asked, and Sal, watching intently, answered, "Rosario."

"That's one brave man," said Wapniak, noting the name down in his pocket notebook and taking out his camera and snapping a shot of the empty field, and Pete thought, That's one man who's had enough. Sometimes you'd throw your life away to be right. Just to be right *once.*

"He's not brave, he's stupid," Sal said. "He's got a wife and kid. He wants to get back to break his mother-in-law's balls. Man, at this rate, he's not going to make it. What now?" he asked, noticing Wapniak again. He always had a camera in his hand. Hell, he must have had it grafted to the bone before he came in country. For what seemed like hours, he'd seen nothing but Paganini, advancing toward the track in slow motion, in discontinuous motion, so that now he was putting his hands out to pull himself up by a rung on the track, and now he was halfway up the track. Now he climbed through an enormous, indescribable time and distance, and then he was there, his hand on the butterfly, swinging the .50 caliber around and it was firing, and now everything speeded up. Had Paganini fired one round or a thousand? Sal had no idea. He could have been firing for hours or for one instant before the enemy fire stopped. The scenery had gone. The fields had gone. There were no mountains in the distance, no muddy earth underfoot. There was nothing but the track, the .50 caliber, and Paganini, moving toward it, motion by jerky motion, like a mechanical toy.

"What are you taking pictures of now?" Sal asked Wapniak.

"There's VC out there. I can feel it."

Sal looked at him as if he'd just seen a new and disgusting kind of bug and walked over to the other track. "Hey, Pig," he said.

"I had enough. I fucking had enough," Paganini said.

"Yeah."

"A hoe! Do you fucking believe that! A hoe!"

"I hear you, Pig," Sal said.

"Don't congratulate me," Paganini said. "Don't you congratulate me."

"Congratulations are not in order here," said Sal. Paganini looked at him and started to cry, burst out crying, blubbering, just like a child. Sal locked his arms around him. "Come on, man," he said. "Remember Geronimo Davis? *It be that way, man.*"

"Hell, man," Sal said finally. "You're a hero here. Use it."

"Use it for what, Sal? For what? What's a hero in this war?"

"A man on R and R in Bangkok," said Sal, and Paganini dried his eyes and said Sal was one smart son of a bitch. Sal slapped him on the back and went back to his track, and when Wapniak asked what that was all about, Sal said it wasn't about *nothing.* You couldn't take a picture of it, so it didn't exist.

"You know what I'm going to do?" Wapniak asked. "I'm going to make an audio tape of our next firefight. I'm going to set it all up now and all I'll have to do is push the red button. We'll get it all on tape. Send it home so our families know what we're doing here."

"You do that," Sal said.

T H E Y   W E R E off the road, and two crews were digging up graves outside the village.

"That M-60 came from *somewhere,*" the Lieutenant said, and the men dug wearily in the heat. The graves were shallow and Wapniak muttered that these were stale graves. Look how the fabric covering the bodies had rotted away. Pete, who didn't want to hear another word, plunged his shovel viciously into the soft, wet earth. When he looked down, beginning to bring the shovel up, he saw something round moving with the shovel, slid the shovel beneath it and picked it up. He was looking at a skull. Long black hair still hung from it. He stared at the head and the vacant eyeholes stared back at him.

"What happened?" Sal asked, coming over to him. "What happened?"

"I cut off her head," Pete whispered. "I cut it off."

"Put it back," Sal said.

"Put it back?" Pete echoed.

"Just put it back where you got it."

"Yeah," Pete said. He lowered the head into the hole and began to cry. "Oh, man," said Sal, and Pete turned slowly to look at him, his eyes wide, color draining from his face, his hands and legs weak. Sal sounded just like Liebowitz. For a second, Sal sounded just like him.

THEY WERE back on the road and they passed a sign made from ammo crates, painted with red letters: AMBUSH ALLEY, and below, a smaller piece of wood was nailed on: LAST AMBUSH–3 DAYS, and the column stopped and the men groaned.

"You ever wonder," Pete asked Sal, "why we're always watching? Why we never get hit? People lose their arms, their heads, and we don't get scratched."

"Yeah, I wonder," said Sal, and Wapniak interrupted and said he never wondered. Life was changeable. You'd be sitting here one minute, bored, complaining about how slowly time passed, and someone stepped on the accelerator, and all bets were off and it was rocket and mortar time. Just take what came: don't wonder about it. Wondering was bad luck. Sal and Pete were staring at Wapniak. For an instant, Sal took his eyes from the road, and the column started moving, and as they were picking up speed, something hit. They barely had time to think *Fuck it,* and Pete, who was standing on ammo crates beneath the cupola, felt himself lifting into the air and then he knew nothing.

He was in a quiet place. He'd never known anything could be so peaceful, and he moved through that place as he pleased. There was no danger. There was no such thing as danger, and he had no name, he didn't know what his name was, and the war was gone, he didn't know there was a war. There was only this peace, seamless and silver, drenched in silver light, and the air shone with silver dust like the silver dust on the surface of banana leaves and then it began to lift, like mists in the morning, and Li was bending over him, calling a name. Was it his name? And Sal (now he knew it was Sal), or Sal's hand, was moving his head from side to side, and turning him over, checking for bleeding, and then a little more of the world returned, and he saw Li's face and a monkey's face flicker off and on, and it came back with a rush: tracks, palms, the sky overhead trailing its clouds, and he sat up and looked around, and where was Wapniak?

He got up and ran toward the track, or tried to run. Why was he limping? His hip hurt. He didn't remember hurting it, and he climbed up the track and started banging on the cupola. He was shouting, "Wapniak! Wapniak!" but there was no answer. He kept up the pounding. He didn't want to go down into the track. What if the ammunition ignited and it all went up, and he was getting ready to lower himself into the track when a familiar, deep voice said, "Hel-lo, Bravado," and then Wapniak himself appeared, climbed out through the turret, and asked, "Are you looking for me?" It was funny. Even under the circumstances, it was funny.

"You hurt?" Sal asked him. Pete was beginning to notice his shoulder and how hard it was to move his arm. He sat down and felt himself all over. His right shoulder and his right hip burned. Under his uniform, he could feel them swelling, and now he could remember going up through the air, out through the turret, hitting his right side as he went.

"No," Pete said, but the medic was bending his knee and putting his ear to it, and then moving his arm up and down until Pete screamed out. The medic asked if he wanted to go back for X rays. He didn't think anything was broken, but he wasn't sure. A few days on aspirin and the knee would stop grating. In the meantime, he could bandage it, but Pete could go back to the rear. Why not?

"No," said Pete.

"Go," said Sal. "Put him in for a purple heart," he told the medic.

"I don't need no purple heart," Pete said. "Who else got hurt?"

"No one, turkey," Sal said. "We were all on the outside." He shook his head and helped Pete back to the track. The maintenance crew was already working with it. Not much was wrong. The right tread was loose.

"Hey, Sal," Pete asked. "What do you think happens when someone dies?"

"How should I know?" asked Sal. "Am I dead?"

"Remember how Krebbs used to talk about going to get the mail, how far the mailboxes were from his house? I saw it. When someone dies, all the mail in all the mailboxes in the world rises up and falls back down."

"That's what happens when someone dies?" Sal said.

"Yeah. Everyone feels it. It's a tide. All the mail moves in the mailboxes."

"That's the stupidest thing I ever heard," Sal said.

"I'd like to hear more about that," said Wapniak.

"You guys were lucky," said one of the mechanics, his back to them. "This could've gone right up."

"If we were lucky, we wouldn't be here," Sal said.

• • •

WEEKS WENT BY, and the troop went out on short patrols, dropping infantry and coming back for them, and the complaints began. This wasn't a war. They were a glorified taxi service. Wapniak listened and said, There you heard the voice of inexperience, and someone answered him saying, God, it's fucking *dull* here. Dull! The men on Wapniak's track wondered what the hell happened to the intelligence the Colonel flew his goddamn chopper in for, and everyone said that was the way it was. If you found something, no one knew how to use it, and here they were, sitting around in the mud, while enemy soldiers were staggering across the border, their knees bending under the weight of weapons and food, while GIs held elephant grass aside for them, bent at the waist, and asked how could they help them?

"Sufficient unto the day the evil thereof," said Wapniak, and Li told them her mother always used to tell her that they flew toward the future with small wings and the future flew toward them with great wings and there was no need to hurry it. It would be there soon enough.

Their track had become the most popular on the base. Soldiers from other tracks came by to show Li this or that, ask her what it was, could it be eaten, or, if it was alive, a brown frog or a lizard, what could you feed it? They brought bits of food to her monkey, who now sat fatly on her shoulder, its little paws folded over its swollen belly. They would go off, smiling and foolish. What they wanted was to see a woman, hear her voice, although there were others who came for different reasons and Paganini came by to talk to Sal and said he thought they ought to keep an eye on Li. Some of the men were talking about her. You know, *talking,* and Sal said that was all they fucking needed. He wanted to get out in the fucking field.

At night, Li and Pete talked, and Sal and the others listened, and after a while they had their customary places. Li sat between Pete and Sal, and Wapniak and the Chief sat facing them. If the others slept and Pete was awake, Li talked to him. She described her village to him. She told him about her aunt, golden and glowing behind the mosquito netting, and he listened, his eyes empty. She had no idea what he understood: perhaps nothing. He asked her why she had come to look for him, and she laughed and said she came because he hit her. The blood burned in his cheeks. He looked away from her and said he was sorry about it. If she'd come to get hit again, she'd come to the wrong place. He was tired of the burning and the killing and the smell of blood and the sight of pressure bandages and bodies wrapped in ponchos and slipping in the mud crossing rice paddies. He was tired of the *smell* of rice paddies and what he saw floating in them and there were times he wanted to shoot the farmer he saw walking out to the fields to defecate. Human fertilizer, what a country. He was tired of all of it.

"But still, it is exciting," said Li. He didn't contradict her.

"Why me?" he asked. "Why look for me?"

"Who can explain such things?" she said. "The day I left the city, a girl in the car wash was killed. A soldier killed her because she asked for too much money and it seemed a good time to go."

"Because I hit you? You looked for me?" What did she mean? Did she mean she thought he'd kill her? Is that what she wanted? He didn't want anyone, and he didn't want anyone to want him, no matter what the reason.

"In the city, I thought about the villages, and how much one village resembled another, and I thought, if I could travel through the country, eventually I would find a village to which I could belong. But it is not safe to travel. The roads are mined and the soldiers are suspicious of strangers. People are shot for no reason. They are stopped and searched and what they have is stolen. I asked myself, is it worse for a woman or a man, and I answered it was better for a woman. A woman may be raped or not, but a man who looks suspicious is immediately shot. So I came to look for you because, through you, I could travel safely, I could see what there was to see. I came to you because you hit me and the man who hits his animal does not kill it."

She thought: "I came because I wanted revenge, although even now I do not know who I want to revenge myself against. My own people? The people who bombed my village? I want revenge against the world itself and yet I want to protect everything that walks upon it. My soul is ripped in two."

The ordering principle of the world had been broken. Now all there was was chaos. She was angry at her world for tearing and letting the chaos in through the thin membrane that kept it safe. She wanted revenge for the collapse of order. She wanted order restored. How could she explain why she'd done what she'd done when she could explain nothing to herself?

"I do not know why I came," she said at last. "Not really."

"Sal likes you," Pete said uneasily.

"Ah, Sal," said the girl, her eyes troubled. "Well," she said, laughing, "perhaps I came to find him. We often do not know our true destination."

"Talk to Sal," he said, but she shook her head. There was no need to talk to Sal. They understood one another. They knew enough to keep their distance. One day she'd found his arm around her shoulder, and when she looked up, his face was angry. He withdrew his arm, and said, "Let's keep our intervals." Since then they rarely looked at one another or talked directly, but each of them always knew where the other was.

"It is quiet at the base," Li said at last. "Our posteriors are growing roots."

The next day, two tracks were sent out, carrying two men no one had ever seen before. Both were dressed in brand-new uniforms. It was obvious they hadn't been out in the field. Each arrived carrying a satchel and a miniature machine gun. Near the border, they dropped both men off, watched them disappear into the jungle, and waited for them. At dawn, as the sun was a faint curve on the horizon, the men returned, dressed in black pajamas, their uniforms in their satchels.

"So what do you think they were?" asked Paganini. "I say CIA."

"CIA sounds good," said Pete.

"I think it's got something to do with what we found out," Wapniak said. "With what we told the Colonel. We told him about a place across the border. They sent these men over the border. Something *big* is coming."

"It looks like it," Paganini said. "You hear anything, you tell me, hear?"

"How'd Paganini find out?" Wapniak demanded. "We told the Colonel. We promised him."

"Not from me," said the Chief.

"From who?" asked Wapniak.

"The river speaks with many tongues," said Li.

"Is that a saying?" asked Wapniak, taking out his notebook.

"Yes," said Li.

"You think it's something big?" asked the Chief. Lately, he'd been quiet, sometimes forgetting to set his center-of-the-earth pole in the ground, although he always slept with it, and by now the entire troop had tried sneaking up on him and making off with it, but the last man who tried almost ended up with a broken neck, so that now anyone who wanted to capture the pole tried rolling it away with a long stick.

"I don't think, and you shouldn't either," said Sal.

"They're keeping us together. They're keeping us near the base," Wapniak said. "Whatever it is, it's big."

"What's big?" the Lieutenant asked, coming up to them. "Is escorting a convoy big? Because that's what we're doing next."

"Goddamn it," said Wapniak. "I want something *big.*"

"Wapniak," Paganini said, "you do not have all your ducks in a row. You sure do not have them."

"THIS TRACK can *book,* man," Sal was saying for the hundredth time, when something exploded. The track in front of them began smoking, and from behind them came another explosion.

"Again?" Sal said. "Again?"

"Where's the girl?" Wapniak asked.

"Here," said Li. The monkey clung to her back, its arms tight around her throat.

"Look," said Pete, and they looked up. A booted leg was turning over and over in the air, turning as a football turns, lazily, as if defying gravity, and then it stopped turning and fell like a stone.

"Aw, shit," said Sal.

"This is the pits," said Wapniak.

"You still want something big?" Sal asked.

"Give it a rest, Sal," said Pete.

The Chief thumped the track with his center-of-the-earth pole and said nothing.

"One of these days," Wapniak said, "that thing's going to get you killed." The Chief didn't answer him. Why's he so quiet? thought Wapniak. Why?

"We get four klicks from the base and this happens," Sal said. The chopper came in, *whump, whump, whump.* "Were those bodies coming from Paganini's track?" Sal asked. But when no one answered him, he didn't ask again.

The chopper rose, outlining itself against the clear blue sky. "Hey," the Chief said, "the Lieutenant's going back with the wounded men."

"Yeah, the Lieutenant," Sal said, and Pete said, "Good for the Lieutenant," and they all heard the rocket and hit the ground, and when they heard the explosion, they looked up, and the chopper, blooming with orange and black flame, began wobbling in the air and began falling slowly through the air, disappeared behind a line of rubber trees, and exploded. The explosion rocked the ground.

No one said anything, and in a minute, the word came over the radio. Drive on.

The convoy arrived safely in the city, and on the way back to base, the men were ordered to check out a village. "There's no end to it," Sal said. "There's no end to these damn villages."

"Nothing here," said the Captain after they'd checked the village. "Let's go."

"Well, I don't want to fucking go," Sal said. He walked over to a hut, took out his lighter, and held it beneath the thatch.

"Don't do it," said the Captain, but Sal smiled at him and touched the lighter to the dried banana leaves and within seconds a wall of flame and black smoke was reaching up toward the sky as if trying to pull down clouds.

"Let the rain put it out," Sal said.

"I'll have your ass for this," said the Captain.

"We found a sniper," someone said. "We had to burn it."

"What sniper?" asked the Captain.

"The one pointing a gun at your head," the Chief said.

"You're fucking animals!" shouted the Captain. "Animals! Bravado! Get away from that hooch!" But it was too late. Pete was standing in front of a second wall of fire, staring into it as if hypnotized. The heat, there was nothing like it. It had such power. There was nothing else as powerful. He *was* the heat. He was burning everything. Nothing could touch him. Nothing could come near him. The heat was a wall around him, and inside it, he was invulnerable. If the hut could burn with a white flame the way the track burned!

"Get out of there, Bravado!" the Captain was shouting, and still Pete didn't move.

"Man, he's gonna burn!" Sal shouted. He started to run, and when he reached Pete, he threw himself against him, pushing him back and out of the way.

"Drag him out of there!" called the Captain. "Drag him out!"

"What were you doing?" Wapniak demanded. "Look at your face! It's black! It's singed! Your hair's singed! You nearly went up!"

"Yeah?" said Pete, touching his cheek. "It was nice, the fire."

"Outstanding, Sal," said Wapniak. "You play football?"

"What's wrong with you?" Sal asked Pete, ignoring Wapniak. "What's wrong with you?" But Pete just looked at him, surprised. Was there something wrong with him?

"That was Paganini's leg. Wasn't it Paganini's leg?" the Chief asked, coming up behind them.

"Nah," Sal said. "Someone else's."

"Whose?"

"What difference does it make, whose?" Sal asked. "Someone's!"

"Who's getting the money for the Second Lieutenant?" asked the Chief. "I mean, we all contributed."

"Shut up!" Pete screamed, his voice high and shrill.

"I want him out of the field," Wapniak said. "I'll talk to the Captain."

"He's better off with us," Sal said.

"He just turned himself into a crispy critter and he's better off with us?" Wapniak asked.

"You do what you have to, Sarge," Sal said.

"I'm watching him," Wapniak said. "I've got my eye on him."

"Right," said Sal.

"You *had* to fire that hooch?" Wapniak said. "You *had* to do it?"

"Right," Sal said.

"THAT'S an elephant bird," Li said, and Pete said he was tired of C-rations. He was going to shoot that bird.

"Don't do it," Sal said automatically, and Wapniak nodded, *Don't do it,* but neither of them paid much attention. They'd been set up in a cold area for two days. They had the ARVNs with them, and they'd finished shaving and eating and writing letters and they were bored and sleepy, and for some reason, the Chief was sitting *inside* the track as if it were not hot enough for him outside. "I need the heat," he said as he climbed in.

"I'm going to get that bird," said Pete, and the others shook their heads. He was the best marksman they had. Even Wapniak admitted it. He had the eyes for it. If he shot at the bird, he'd get the bird.

"I got the bird and I'm going for it," Pete said, and they barely looked up.

It was so hot they were loose and sleepy, and it was a cold zone. They were in the middle of the only cold thing in the country and they were roasting to death. The bird had fallen into the dense rain forest, and Pete, who had watched it go down, took his machete and went after it. He was almost there when he realized where he was and that the others were back at the track, half asleep, and anyone could be out here. How stupid could he be? But he wanted the bird and he swallowed his fear and kept cutting, and finally, there it was, hanging from the crotch of a tree limb.

As soon as his hand closed on the dead bird's throat, as soon as he pulled the bird loose from the tree, the fear rose and he looked around him. He saw the thin leaves of new bamboo, unnameable trees choking with thick vines, one tree covered with bright purple blooms, its top branches rustling although there was no wind, not even a breeze, and he felt panic. His skin went cold and he shivered as if he had a fever and couldn't get warm. He retraced his way. This time, every vine, every bamboo leaf that touched him was alive with menace. How could he have done it? And to walk into the jungle in a pair of cut-down pants? The mosquitoes were feasting on him and the bamboo was slashing at him. What made him forget there was no safe place?

And then he was out in the clearing, holding up the bird, and a shot cracked through the air, not near him. He knew the sound of gunfire when it was nearby. The tracks were taking fire. He threw down the bird and ran, climbed up on the track and began firing his M-60 and the hot shell casings began spitting out at him, hitting him on the thighs. While he had been climbing the track, while he had been running, his hands were shaking, his face was shaking. Now that he had something to do, the shaking stopped. He heard the chiming of the casings as the bullets fell apart. He fed the ammo in over the tin can and he saw a purple smoke can go up. One of the tracks had found the sniper's position and was marking it, and a hunter-killer team was flying overhead. The radio crackled. The loach flew backwards, fast, out of sight, and the Cobra dipped its nose down, shredded trees. Tree limbs flew into the air and fell back down to earth. Earth leaped up and fell back toward itself, and the sky was full of smoke, black and purple, and the ground shook and then it was quiet. He'd burned the inside of his thighs.

"The bird," Li said, when he found her (she now fired an M-16) "is too tough for eating," and Wapniak said, "Look at Bravado. He's bowlegged," and Sal said, "See the medic about the burns." Pete asked the medic how long before it got better, and the medic said as long as he kept walking like that, about a month, and Pete said it wasn't funny: how long? "A while," said the medic, "a while," and Pete asked if he didn't have a cream or something, but the medic said in this climate, it would make things worse. Li made a tea out of some leaves she found in the forest, and when it was cold, she told him to dab it on.

She found it very funny. She covered her mouth with her hand, and the others thought it was funny, too, and whenever he went by, his legs bowed as much as possible, everyone said it: Who's the duck?

Then they were distracted by Li, who went into the forest and didn't come back, and they said, not another one. Not the bird all over again, and Sal, the Chief, and Wapniak took their weapons and went to look for her. When they found her, she said she wanted to stay where she was, and Sal told Wapniak she was pregnant. He'd never used that word before. He'd always said knocked up. She didn't show in those loose clothes and her stomach was pretty flat. Wapniak said, "You mean you knew? You knew and you didn't tell me?" and Sal said, "Pick her up and take her back to the track."

They stood around watching until the medic sent most of them out, and then the medic came out and said, "No problem," and some of them came back in and watched. None of them had ever seen a baby born before. Some of them had thought they never would. Some of them would never want to see it again. They'd seen enough blood. They never wanted to see more of it, no matter what the circumstances, and then the girl pushed herself up with her arms. Her face contorted, and the baby rushed into the world, just slid out as if carried out on a wave, and they looked to see what had happened, and some of them flushed when they did. It was a girl.

The medic picked up the baby and washed it off and Wapniak was babbling nervously. This was an opportunity to learn something. They might never see this again; he felt *different,* and then he stopped talking because he was crying, and the medic was wrapping the crying baby in an olive drab T-shirt, and Li was sitting up, smiling, looking at the baby.

The medic asked her if the men could hold the child, and Li smiled, yes, and the baby went from Pete to Sal to Wapniak to the Chief. Sal looked at it, and shook his head, and reached out a huge finger to touch the tip of the baby's nose. Pete took the baby and stared down at it, its cheeks covered with purplish bruises, the baby covered with a white powder, no wrinkles on it. He opened one little hand and looked at the little unlined palm. It was brand-new. Its eyes were squeezed shut as if it weren't ready to look at anything yet, and Pete thought, That's right, keep them closed. Wait as long as you can. They stood there smiling at the baby, concentrating on it, waiting to see what it would do first: would it open its eyes? What would it think of them? And the baby waved its little fists and stopped time for them, and they stood, still and peaceful in the light.

The Chief took the baby from him, and one of the ARVNs, the one whose father had been the village chief disemboweled by VC who came to ask for volunteers, took the baby next, and he looked at it a long time, and later no one knew why they didn't watch him with the child, or even why they'd let him stay there, but all their eyes were on Li, who was smiling and wiping her eyes at the same time, and none of them wanted to say, *I don't like this place no more,* not now. For a while it was washed away. Everything was clean and new as the baby. And then the ARVN who was holding the baby stepped through the back hatch of the track, carrying the child, and Sal went for him, but it was too late.

The ARVN lifted the child in the air and dashed it headfirst against the ground. The fragile skull split open like a melon. It was about the size of a melon, and all the noise in the world came back in a rush, and Pete had the ARVN by the throat. He was lifting him off the ground. He was strong enough to hold him up with one hand and push his face back, push his head back, and his neck snapped. The crack was distinct, and in the new silence, loud, like the crack of a bullet, and he threw the man on the ground like a filthy thing.

The Chief was in back of Pete, his knife out, trembling, and Sal stood in the hatchway, crying, and the medic was sobbing, and then Li stood up and looked outside. For a minute the light blinded her but then she took it in, and when she did, she screamed.

Sal came up behind Pete, looked at the dead ARVN, pulled him up by his collar, and propped him against the treads of the track. Then he took the dead man's head and twisted it as if it were a screw, twisted it until his head was turned around on his neck and the back of his head was above his chest, his face against the track wall. Pete looked at the ARVN, whose head was turned on its neck, looked down at his hands, looked at Sal, and threw up.

People from the other tracks were coming over, and someone from Paganini's track said, "What do we do now? Do we kill the woman?" and Li, who was propped on the ground, said nothing, watched them without fear, and that frightened them. They'd seen that look in men propped against trees and when they went up to them and asked them where they'd been hit, the men didn't answer. They were dead. Pete stood in front of Li. He had the safety off the AK-47 they kept in the track and he didn't say anything. He just pointed the gun. Nobody was coming through him.

"I will not tell anyone," said Li, and the men dispersed, mumbling. How could they believe her? And the seven other ARVNs with them were nervous, and Sal had enough. "Start walking," he told the ARVN Captain.

"Walking?" the Captain said.

"Back to the base," Sal said, "and take that piece of shit with you."

"But we did nothing!" protested the ARVN. "*You* have done something!"

"It's your word against ours," said Wapniak. "Who are they going to believe?"

"Walk, man," said Paganini, and when they saw Paganini and his crew, they saw everyone was against them, and they turned and walked away, waiting for a round in the back. But no shot was fired. They were eighteen klicks from base, the countryside was crawling with snipers, and they had on olive drab uniforms.

Li sat under the banyan tree, its roots curling into the air like hair, and the figure of the ARVN who had killed her child appeared before her. Now that he was dead, the light came through him, and inside his skin, she saw the outline of a black bear. Then the bear disappeared and she saw the outline of a hyena, its mouth still red with scavenged blood. The hyena was replaced by a giant ape whose black leathery hands were cracking the bones of a live monkey and eating it, and the ape was replaced by a wild dog, and the dog by a panther. Animal took the place of animal and still the man stood there, as if he were a man, as if he knew nothing about the creatures inside him.

They came and went faster and faster now until they only flickered inside his skin and finally all that was left was a tiny snake, its forked tongue darting in and out. Then the man's outline changed and a creature that was half-bird, half-woman stared at Li and she knew she was seeing a kinaree, and although she had been taught that these were only creatures of mythology, she was not surprised to see the creature standing in front of her. Her heart leaped like a fish from a pond and her spirit left her body and entered the body of the kinaree where it cried out for vengeance, wailed like a typhoon at the height of its strength, and bade Li remember what she had seen beneath the man's skin.

When Li saw how thinly the skin covered the souls of the animals beneath, she asked herself why she had valued human life when it was no better, no more precious, than the spark of life trapped in a rock or a tree or a spider. She knew that when she died, she would become a kinaree and would exact vengeance.

People in the villages would try to placate her. They would put sacrifices on their altars. They would give gifts to the monks and the monasteries but she would not be appeased. She would wander, a treacherous, vengeful spirit, and they would hear her voice howling at night, and in the morning, they would find the dead child or the dead animal, the woman cooling and cooling as the sun rose, and no one could call her back, not even Sal, who had tried to help her, not even Pete, in whom she saw herself, and who had also tried. Once she became a kinaree, she could not protect them. She would be beyond human feelings, intent on revenge. Between them, the Americans and the Vietnamese had fashioned her destiny, but now she belonged to neither. She was an outcast. Wherever she went, she caused harm. She opened her eyes and looked once more at Pete and Sal and the Chief and felt love for them, knowing it was the last time she would feel such a thing. She asked herself if she was strong enough to leave, and the kinaree, fading in front of her, told her she was.

That night, the crews were nervous. There were several false alarms, unnecessary firing, and illumination rounds lit the sky. The new Lieutenant was furious, getting on the radio and asking, "Who fired that shot! Why was that shot fired?" but it went on all night, and in the morning when they went out to look, there was no trace of the enemy, only many trees and bushes knocked down by the fighting. If you believed trees had spirits, it was a carnage of trees.

Only when they came back from patrol did they notice that the Chief was missing, and the search for him was frantic, but it stopped suddenly when Pete came out of the track holding the center-of-the-earth pole, or what was left of it. It had been broken deliberately into pieces. If you looked at it carefully, you could see where it had been scored by a knife, scored again and again, before it was broken. "I found it in his things," Pete said. "His canteen's gone. *He's* gone."

"What do you mean, he's *gone?*" asked Wapniak.

"Took off, man," Pete said. "Split."

Li came out, looked at the stick, and went back into the track.

"He's *gone?*" Wapniak said again.

They went into the track and looked through the Chief's belongings. Everything was there: the rucksack, the extra change of clothes, several letters from home, a book, *Private Peat*, and a family photograph, his mother, father, and two sisters standing stunned in the white New Mexico sun. "He's gone," Wapniak said. "I'll tell the Lieutenant."

While he was gone, they looked for Li. She must have gone outside the track, nearer the trees, where it was cooler in the shade, but she wasn't there.

"She's gone," said Sal. He snapped his fingers. "Like that. Gone." Pete put his hand on his shoulder. "Don't touch me," Sal said.

Paganini came over and said the medic was out of it, gone, snapped, *nowhere.* The medevac had come in for him. He cried and he shook and he talked about the time they went into a village to inoculate the children, and the next day, when they came back, Charley had cut off all the vaccinated arms. People read about it in the papers but no one believed it. No one knew what they were up against here. There was nothing you could do that was right, nothing.

And everyone went back to his own track and thought. Sal remembered reaching down for a wounded man's hand, and that was what he got: his hand. Wapniak remembered the young girl wounded outside a village and how he'd bandaged her leg, and when he picked her up to put her on the stretcher, her back fell out, the entire back, her spinal cord intact, and the medic who was with him couldn't take it. He turned away and vomited. And now the medic was gone, snapped. When the medic snapped, man, things were bad.

That night, Paganini's track reported a sighting of a white man. The guns opened up. In the morning, there was no trace of blood, no trace of anything but the damage done by the firing, and Keithly, a black soldier who'd reported the white man, was called into the new Lieutenant's track and asked what kind of report was that? A white man? Keithly became nervous and said, "Not a white man like you, sir." The Lieutenant asked what *kind* of a white man? and Keithly said, "Like a mummy, sir." The Lieutenant asked how the man was like a mummy and Keithly said he didn't know exactly, but he looked to be wrapped in white cloth. In movies, don't mummies look like that?

"In movies they do," said the Lieutenant. "You're sure that's what you saw? You weren't sleeping?"

"No, sir," said Keithly. "I saw what I saw. I think he was VC, sir, but he looked friendly."

"What else did you see?" the Lieutenant asked him. "Did you see the ARVN and the baby?"

"I saw that, sir," said Keithly, and the Lieutenant released him.

"He's hallucinating," said the Lieutenant.

"That fucking Colonel," said the Captain. "He O.K.'d that woman. The whole damn troop's coming apart."

"He was dehydrated, that's all," said the Lieutenant. "When they get dehydrated, they see things. It happens to everyone."

"Keithly wasn't dehydrated," the Captain said.

"Then he's seeing things," said the Lieutenant.

27 SIGHTINGS of the White Man became widespread. Men claimed to see him when they were out on LP, and some men on daytime OPs saw the same figure. They always described him in the same way, although occasionally details varied, and some thought he was a friendly VC and others thought he was a deserter from their own side but they all saw a figure wrapped in white. Sometimes he was covered by cloth. At other times, he was wrapped in strips of cloth, as if someone had torn up a white sheet and bandaged him, and still others saw him dressed in something like a white monk's robe, his face covered with white makeup, and a monkey riding on his shoulder. Wapniak had his own theory about the White Man, but then he had his own theory about everything, and for a while, no one wanted to hear it, not until Sal saw the White Man for himself when he and Pete went out on LP.

"Like a fucking ghost," said Sal.

"But he wasn't a ghost," Pete said.

"We heard twigs snapping," Sal said. "Ghosts don't snap twigs." He gave in and asked Wapniak what he thought.

"She used to talk about it," Wapniak said uneasily, "about spirits of people who died violent deaths. And you said" (he pointed to Pete) "you said they wrapped dead people in white. And *I* know people in mourning wear white."

"So who is it?" Sal asked. "Who?"

"Maybe it's her," Wapniak said in a low voice.

"Her? Li?" asked Sal. "She's *tiny*. I rested my elbow on top of her goddamn head. The man I saw was six fucking feet tall."

"*If* you saw him," said Wapniak. "*If* he was a man."

"Spirits don't snap no twigs," Sal said stubbornly.

"She said sometimes spirits took human forms," Wapniak said. "When they wanted to hurt people."

"I'm not talking about no spirits!" Sal exploded. "There's a goddamn maniac out there wrapped up in a fucking sheet!"

"Where's he going to get a white sheet out here, Sal? Tell me that," Pete said.

"All I know," said Wapniak, "is that fucking White Man is a fire control problem. You go out on LP and the cardinal sin is to fire your weapon and give away your position, and every fucking LP is blasting off in the dark. We can see the goddamn muzzle flashes back in the goddamn camp! The LT says he'll court-martial the next man who fires on an LP. We've got to get rid of him."

"How?" Pete asked. "Tell me how?"

Wapniak was thinking of spells, prayers, sacrificing to spirits, making merit with the monks, all things Li had told him about, but Li was gone. The ARVNs kept one eye on them and one on the tree line. They were no help. "Sacrifices," Wapniak said.

"Are you fucking crazy?" Sal shouted. "We need to fucking shoot the fucking bastard!"

"I forgot," said Wapniak. "I forgot what it was like to talk to you. When *she* was here, you spoke English."

GRADUALLY, the Colonel was piecing the story together. The woman scout had had a baby and an ARVN soldier had killed the child and one of the American soldiers had killed him. The woman was gone and so was one of the men from her track. The two of them might be together, or the woman might have killed the missing soldier. It was possible. Mass hysteria, mass shared delusions, that was another possibility. He remembered his grandfather, who'd gone over to France before the United States entered the war, and until the day he died, he swore he'd seen a crucified English soldier held up by the Germans in the trench opposite his. Everyone in his company saw it.

The incident made all the papers, was recorded in books, as was the response of the men, who, in the fog and the mists, at first thought what they saw was an enemy soldier coming over the top and consequently fired on him, only to find they'd killed one of their own men. The newspapers recorded their heroic (and unauthorized) attack on the enemy trench, not endorsed by command, but led by their officers. Later on, a war correspondent interviewed men in the next trench, men who had the same view of the enemy, and none of them had seen anything of the sort. They'd seen crucified kittens, crucified puppies, all booby-trapped, but no crucified Englishmen. The Germans understood the Americans and their passion for small things. The Vietnamese did, too, but they booby-trapped children as well. The Colonel didn't believe in ghosts, but he did believe in history repeating itself. He decided that the White Man was a symptom of mass hysteria.

"What do you think it is, sir?" the Lieutenant was asking.

"I think it's a sign of bad morale," the Colonel said. If he had his way, he'd send half of the men on R and R, but he was waiting for orders to attack the bunker complex near the border and they weren't at full strength now. He couldn't afford to lose more men. "I want better fortifications around the base," he said. "Keep the men digging."

"Excuse me, sir," said the Captain. "You wanted to be kept informed of sightings of the White Man? One of the LPs saw him last night."

"And?" asked the Colonel. "What was the White Man doing?"

"He left them a waterfowl, sir."

"What?"

"They found a waterfowl, sir. Freshly killed. Twenty yards from their post. They ate it today and they're fine. It wasn't poisoned. They didn't use good judgment, but they're fine, sir."

"He can't be an evil spirit," the Lieutenant said to himself.

"What did you say?" asked the Colonel.

"Some of the men think he's an evil spirit," said the Lieutenant.

"Get them digging," said the Colonel. Mass hallucinations didn't leave freshly killed waterfowl. Still, it was possible someone had killed the fowl, meant to eat it, heard the soldiers setting up, and fled. His own explanation didn't appeal to him. He didn't believe it himself. If the men started thinking the VC were friendly, they'd all be in big trouble.

That afternoon, the Colonel got a call saying a helicopter was coming to take him to battalion headquarters for a briefing. Air strikes would be made in the area before the tracks went in and the tracks would carry in three infantry companies. Once they were in, the men would spread out and look for weapons and rice. Two men from each track would stay behind. Because the bunker complex was believed to be extensive, the men on the ground would go out in patrols of eight. How soon could the battalion be ready to move out?

The Colonel was less worried about the enemy than about a battalion sitting around brooding, and said he could be ready at first light. A helicopter took him back to the base. He briefed his officers, and the officers briefed their soldiers, and by the time they had their final briefing, the men were busy loading ammunition onto the tracks. The Sergeants were checking to make sure everyone had powdered his feet and had an extra pair of socks, enough C-rations, enough ammunition for the handguns, enough grenades, enough extra barrels for the M-60s, and of course, enough beer. The base was suddenly a hive of activity, and the Colonel watched with satisfaction. No one was thinking about the White Man and no one reported seeing him.

"This," Wapniak told the crew, "is serious business. The roads around the bunker are thought to be mined and there's a lot of NVA there. The weather's changeable and command doesn't want to bring in choppers because no one knows where the NVA is, so if we get hit out in the field, we're on our own. Air support will be minimal. There's a lot of them out there, maybe a division. And they're well equipped. We're not getting a replacement for the Chief, so when we go out, we leave only one man behind on the track. I want everyone's mind on the job. We forget about Li. We forget about the Chief, and most of all, we forget about the White Man. No one picks up anything that looks suspicious. Even coconuts are booby-trapped. If you see anything, you poke it with a pole. We'll carry poles or we'll cut them as we go. Don't open gates. Don't go down well-marked trails. Tape down your dog tags. No smoking. No talking. Nothing unusual here except there's more of them. We have to be careful. I don't want to hear a helmet strap hitting a helmet."

"We're always fucking careful," Sal said.

"We're going out with the ARVNs," Wapniak said. "We've got to work with them. You can't start seeing targets in the middle of their backs."

AT FIRST light, the Phantom jets began streaking overhead and the tracks began moving out after them. When the tracks reached their destination, smoke was still rising in thick columns from the ground. Trees cut down by the air strike littered the earth and trunks of trees rose like huge sharp nails into the air. The men dismounted and formed into patrols of eight and fanned out, looking for caches and bunkers. Pete and Sal joined Paganini, the Lieutenant, and another man they didn't know. Three ARVNs went out with them. Pete carried the radio and Paganini took point and they started walking toward the jungle. They were to go around a valley and check the hill on the other side where intelligence had reported activity. The ridge was too narrow for tracks, too narrow for helicopters to land on, and the ravine was too steep for anything but men on foot. They looked down the ravine and saw the rocky slopes and the dense foliage and agreed that the ridge was the best approach.

"Who are you?" Pete asked the new guy.

"I'm the cook."

"Oh," said Pete. "I'm the mechanic." He pointed at Sal. "He's a mechanic, too." Pete asked the cook if he'd been out in the field before, and he said, Hell, yes, all he did was hump the boonies. He hadn't been near a real stove since he got here. Pete said he guessed they used everybody. Paganini signaled for silence and they went forward slowly. When they were almost upon the suspected site of the bunker complex, Paganini looked around him as if he wanted to remember the scenery, and signaled them to follow him into the wood line. They took out their machetes and began cutting their way through. No shots were fired. The ground seemed untouched.

It was Paganini who set off the mine and after that the confusion was complete. They were under fire, down on the ground, looking for muzzle flashes, firing through the dense smoke in front of them, the smoke acrid in their nostrils and mouths. Pete was shouting and pointing, and they saw the bunker. The men inside had hand-held mortars and grenade rockets; they fired them, and they were almost on top of the bunker when they heard firing behind them and realized enemy soldiers were coming up out of the ground, out of an undiscovered entrance to the bunker. Three fired straight ahead. Three fired at positions behind them, and the cook was on the radio, requesting air support or artillery support but the answer was negative. All the patrols were meeting resistance.

Sal was covered with grenades. They hung from his uniforms like so many small wasp nests, and he began pulling their pins and throwing them. His aim was perfect, but the soldiers behind them kept on firing. Pete stuck his head up and saw pith helmets to the left of the bunker, to the right of the soldiers Sal was after, got up, and ran backwards, as if he were going after a baseball in the outfield, then stopped, and threw a grenade into the middle of them. They heard screams, saw geysers of blood staining the air, and then there was silence.

Sal, who was lying on the ground, saw a human hand coming out of the earth not ten feet from him, and threw a grenade at it and got up and ran back. When the grenade went off, the hand vanished, and he was about to get up and look at the man he'd killed, when he felt the Lieutenant's hand on his arm. "He may not be dead, man," said the Lieutenant. "Think!"

The hand was coming out of the ground again, wriggling its fingers like snakes, growing out of the ground like a mushroom.

"Wake up!" the Lieutenant said to Sal. "Bravado, get down and stay down!"

The ARVNs were rushing the bunkers and were inside before anyone could call them back, and the Lieutenant said, "Fuck it, we're going in after them. We'll clear the place and blow it."

The bunker opened into a narrow tunnel of damp red earth that grew broader as it sloped down, and the further in they went, the deeper the slope. The walls, covered with a mixture of mud, manure, and straw, were beaded with sweat when they touched them. Exposed roots of trees swelled the tunnel walls like veins, and thin, narrow roots, clammy and cold, brushed their face. The Lieutenant made a motion, *Careful*, turned a corner and disappeared from sight, and when they heard a shot, one of the ARVNs crawled forward, found the new Lieutenant lying on the ground, half of his head gone. His lower jaw had been shot off, and his upper teeth opened onto nothing. His tonsils were clearly visible. The ARVN opened fire, crawling forward until he could throw a grenade around the bend of the tunnel. The six men behind him had crawled after him, their heads as low as possible, and another shot rang out and the ARVN at the head of the line collapsed and didn't move again. Two men were dead in the tunnel.

"Move back!" Sal shouted. "Move back and we blow the tunnel."

"You could collapse it, man!" Pete shouted. "We're under a mountain!"

"Move back!" Sal shouted. They crawled backwards rapidly, bumping into one another as they went, the heels of their boots landing on the chins and foreheads of the men in back of them, and then Sal blew the tunnel. The roof of earth shook over them, and for an instant, they held their breaths waiting for the earth to cave in and bury them. So this is how I'm going to die, suffocated in a tunnel beneath a mountain no one's ever heard of, Pete thought, but the roof and the walls held, and they crawled backwards, bloodying each other's mouths, and the first five came out into the light, and when they did, two NVA regulars stepped out from behind a boulder. They had been there, waiting for them, and they opened up with their AK-47s.

Pete was hit, and the ARVNs were hit with him, but Sal threw a white phosphorus grenade before he came out into the light, and when the smoke cleared, there was blood everywhere. Bits of flesh hung on the bushes like rags, parts of uniforms hung like banners from the trees, and when the roaring in their ears subsided, they heard the silence.

"We made it," Sal said, looking for Pete, but Pete wasn't standing up. He was trying to push himself up with one arm and his other arm hung by his side. The cook was holding his right leg and screaming. One of the ARVNs was bleeding from a head wound and the other was clutching his stomach.

"Give me the radio," Sal told Pete, but as soon as he picked it up, he knew it was gone. The antenna was shot off and when he picked up the handset, it was dead.

"We've got to get out of here," Pete said, looking at the hole in the cook's uniform and the dark rim forming around it.

"The only way to get out is to walk out," Sal said, and none of them could walk, and he was no goddamn medic, but he was bandaging them up. He took his knife and cut the sleeve from Pete's jacket. The sleeve and the front of his shirt were drenched in blood. When he saw Pete's arm, he shook his head with relief. The bullet had gone through the fatty tissue of his upper arm and the pressure bandage stopped the bleeding. "The arm's fine, the arm's fine. Don't worry about it," he said as he bandaged, and then he went over to the cook.

He could see before he bent over him that his leg was broken. The left leg was bent outwards and away from the body at an impossible angle, but when he cut open the pants leg, he didn't find much bleeding. He went on to the ARVN and bandaged the man's head. He was bleeding from behind his left ear, but the wound didn't look deep. The bullet had parted his scalp and a strip of skull was visible, but the bone seemed intact. The fourth man had a stomach wound and said he didn't feel much pain. Sal took the man's pressure bandage and put it on. When he was finished, he looked around him, saw the dead radio and the four wounded men. He was their only chance of getting out. Without a radio, they had nothing. O.K., he said to himself. What are you going to do?

He was standing near a large tree. "O.K., listen," he said. "I'm going to put you guys around the tree so if anyone comes up on you, you'll see them and you can fire. Some of you dropped your weapons when you got hit. I'll give my rifle to Pete here. Now everyone has one. Make sure they're loaded. You've got to stay awake. If you've got bleeding, you're weak. I'm walking. I'll be back for you."

"Sure, Sal," Pete said, and the cook said, Sure, and the ARVNs nodded, and he lit a cigarette for each of them, put it between their lips, thought for an instant about having no weapon but his knife, and began threading his way back, following the trail they'd taken. It wasn't difficult. American soldiers tramped down more brush than a herd of elephants, and with each step he took, he saw the four men sitting around the tree, all pale from loss of blood, in shock from pain, and he walked faster, his head swiveling. He pushed vines out of his way. He cut through vines and grass with his machete, and then he saw the jungle thinning out, and before he came out into the open, he began shouting, "Don't shoot! Don't shoot!" and even so, the tracks swung their .50 calibers toward him, but someone must have recognized him. Someone in one of the tracks must have seen him through binoculars, because he crossed the field and made it to the command track, and the Captain got on the radio and said B troop was going back with him for the men.

"Let's do it fast," Sal said. "Before they have a chance to mine it again."

"They've already had time, so move out," said the Captain. "Take litters and move out."

THE WHITE MAN was in the tree line, looking at the four wounded men at the base of the tree, and Li was with him. "Do you see what I see?" she asked him, and when he looked again, he saw, not four men, but one wounded black bear aiming a rifle, one panther bleeding from the abdomen, holding a rifle, and one huge pig, leg bent backwards from the body, holding an M-16.

"They are not men at all," said the White Man.

"They are and they aren't," said Li.

"Can they see us?" asked the White Man. "They seem to look at us but they don't take aim."

"They see you but they do not believe what they see," said Li. "Each thinks he is about to die and each thinks he sees a ghost." She covered her hand with her mouth, smiling. "They look ridiculous, do they not? Yet you see them now as they are." She turned to leave and the White Man followed her and then stopped. "No," said Li. "You cannot stay to protect them.

Someone will come for them." She disappeared into the forest and the White Man went after her.

Under the tree, Pete thought he saw the White Man and thought he was dying. He remembered his father coming down from the roof where he kept his pigeons, telling his son to come up with him, and when they got up there, he saw the low skyline of three-story buildings covered with TV aerials tilting in all directions like metal skeletons. His father picked up a pigeon and said, "See this one? He lost the race." He picked up the bird and snapped its neck. "You see that?" said his father, holding the bird up in front of the other pigeons. "*You* better win." He thought of Sal as a pigeon flying toward the tracks and he thought, There goes a winner. Sal could snap his father's neck.

The cook thought he saw the White Man and leveled his rifle at him, but remembered the many stories he'd heard about him and decided he was looking at a ghost. He remembered walking home from school one day and seeing a body under a sheet, and a crowd gathering, and when he asked, someone told him an old man had climbed out of his window, intending to jump, had changed his mind and hung on to the ledge for a few seconds before he slipped off. He was under the blanket. He thought about the sod house he passed on his way to school and wondered why anyone would voluntarily live in a house built like a grave into the earth. Some branches of a tree moved in front of him and again he leveled his rifle, but a brilliant blue bird flew out and sat on the ground in front of him, watching him. He thinks he's looking at dinner, thought the cook. That damn bird thinks *he's* the cook. He thinks he's going to eat me.

One of the ARVNs drifted in and out of a light sleep, and when he slept, he saw his brother in the center of the village, his arms and legs staked to the earth, while a VC recruiter threw knives at his ankles, closer and closer, until the knives hit flesh, and then bone. Each time the VC would retrieve the knife and throw it again. His brother lived for hours before the VC opened a large vein and let him bleed to death. He looked up and saw the White Man, said good-bye to his life, and felt a great peace settle down on him like a cool fog coming onto a parched valley.

The other ARVN thought he saw the White Man and thought of his sister, lying in a shallow grave near his house, her head bandaged in strips of unbleached cotton. He saw his mother and father following the priests, who unearthed her coffin, carried it to the pyre, where it was burnt, and they gathered up her ashes, broke the long bones of her arms and legs and put them in a blue and white ceramic urn and placed it on the family altar. His family placed lotus blossoms and paper clothes and money on the altar, and while he watched, the spirit of his sister left her body and traveled upward and he knew she was already reincarnated. When he looked for the White Man again, he thought he saw his sister standing before him.

Then Sal and B troop came through the tree line. The medic bent over each of them in turn, injecting them. They were lifted onto litters and the slow, difficult procession back to the tracks began.

"NOW WE HAVE a situation," said Wapniak. "We've got two dead men still in the tunnel. We've got to go back for them."

"I ain't going back for no dead man," one of the soldiers said, and the others agreed with him.

"It's the Colonel's rule," said the Captain. "We leave no one behind."

"We're not going," someone said.

"No way," someone else said. "No way."

"I say we go back," said the Captain.

"If they're dead, they're dead," said Wapniak. "We know who they are. They're KIA. We did what we had to do. Leave them there. Dead is dead."

The Captain picked twelve men and told them to follow him. All twelve refused. No one was willing to go. What did he do now? He didn't want to go back for dead bodies. Wapniak was right. Dead was dead.

A chopper was lifting off with the four wounded men. A company had found caches of rice so large they didn't know what to do with them, sheds the length of city blocks, ten feet high, solid with sacks of rice. But how do you destroy rice? If you blew it up with C-4, it was still rice. It fell to earth again. If you burned it with napalm, one of the reporters hanging around would get hold of the story, and everyone in the States would cluck their goddamned tongues over the wicked destruction of food when so many people in the country were starving. He radioed in his report and orders came back. Choppers would be sent out and the men would load the sacks onto them. It would be back-breaking work, and the heat and the mosquitoes were evil. By nightfall, half the men would be on the edge of sunstroke.

"And," said the Captain, "we have two dead men in the bunker complex. What are my orders?"

"Your orders are to go back and retrieve those two bodies," the Colonel said. "Let me know what you need."

"All right, sir, we'll be moving out in an hour, sir," said the Captain, but in an hour, he still had no luck with the men, and the Colonel radioed him and asked what the delay was, and he said they'd been taking some fire, but as soon as everything was quiet, they'd be moving out. An hour later, they still hadn't radioed in to say they were moving out, and the Colonel was on the wire again. "It's almost dark, sir," said the Captain. "We'll be moving out at first light."

All the next day and afternoon, it went on. The Colonel would call for a report and the men were always about to move out. Finally, the Captain said he needed to talk to the Colonel in secure voice.

"We can't go back to retrieve those two bodies, sir," he said.

"Why not?"

"The men refuse to go."

"What's your view?"

"I agree with the men."

"Well, that's not your decision to make," said the Colonel. "That's my decision. We *will* retrieve those two dead bodies. That's what *I've* decided. I want you to get on that right away."

"Sir, the men won't go."

"At first light," the Colonel said, "I want you to pop a smoke grenade over your area. I'm coming out there."

"With all due respect, sir," asked the Colonel's XO, "what are you going to do?" The Colonel said he was taking another Captain out into the field with him in case he had to relieve the one already there. The command structure was breaking down in the field. Once he got there, they *would* retrieve those two bodies.

28 A FTER THE SURGEON, after the four stitches in his arm, after the transfusion of a pint of blood, Pete felt fine. It was odd, how he'd never understood the importance of blood before, how he hadn't realized that everything depended on it, what he saw, how he felt, whether he hoped for things or ceased to hope. He sat on the edge of his cot, his arm Saran-wrapped and tightly taped, so that he could take a shower without wetting the incision or the bandage, and looked around him. Everything was new. Everything was haloed, outlined, almost, in gold.

The sheets on the cots shone white like angel wings. The nurses were too beautiful to live. The polished wood floors shone like glass in a wonder world. And the mud that sucked you in like quicksand, making gulping, protesting noises as you pulled one leg loose, then another, the rifle slipping through his muddy hand, his muddy boots slipping as he climbed in through the track's hatch so that he pitched forward and hit his head on a storage compartment, the mud dripping from his helmet into his eyes, the sound of the rain on his helmet like hailstones, the little rivers pouring over the edge of the helmet like a waterfall, the toilet seat they discovered in the city and took back to the track and nailed to an ammo crate and considered a treasure, the showers taken outside, naked, in the rain, first watching the black cloud approaching, standing waiting with a bar of Ivory soap in one hand, lathering as the sky darkened and the rain fell in an iron-grey sheet, stopping suddenly before the soap was rinsed off, taking his upended helmet and splashing its water over him, or using the water from empty shell casings, the C-rations drenched in Tabasco sauce, using both hands to fill his mouth with pineapple crawling with worms, the spotted leopard skinned and roasted and still smelling of live blood, the red-orange flames roiling with black smoke, the green smoke grenades, and the red and the purple, flowering up from the ground, the water running red and the men screaming, the willy peter grenades they carried but that were said to explode for no reason in the heat, the terrible white fire that burned the walls of tracks and ate men's flesh and melted their dog tags—all seemed like a dream in this dream place of whiteness, of cleanliness, of silence, through which nurses moved, bending over beds, bringing little paper cups of pills or shining needles full of sleep.

The trick, he thought, was to stay here as long as possible, but he'd already been transferred from the hospital ward to the barracks.

"A bad flesh wound," said the surgeon, "but only a flesh wound. You bleed easily?" Pete said he didn't think so, no more than anyone else. As far as he could see, everyone bled easily. The surgeon nodded.

In the latrine, the toilets flushed, and he flushed one, watched the water swirl and go down. It was as if he'd never seen it before. He did it again and again, and others went by, smiling or trying not to look. When they'd first come in, they'd all done the same thing. But a shower with hot water! With shiny silver handles! With a silver shower head. He approached this miraculous contraption with the reverence it deserved. He stepped into it fearfully, as if into a confessional, as if into God's very mouth. He turned the handle and the split second of suspense was terrible. Would hot water pour forth from the faucet, or would the water run red like blood, or brown like mud, or cold, smelling of bacteria, like the water in the shell casings, and the water poured down with great force. It stung. He felt it all over his body, not as water, but as hands, charged, electrical, stinging him out of one life into another. He felt his feet. He saw his ten toes. He held his arms out in front of him and saw his ten fingers. He was human.

He took the towel and dried each part of his body carefully, looking carefully at his arm, his leg. He was still as he was. He would fit neatly back into the space he had left in the world. He wrapped the towel around him and entered the ward and was met with a wall of laughter. What were they laughing at? Hadn't he just seen himself? Their laughter grew louder and louder as he stood until one of them took pity on him and said, "Look in a mirror, man," and when he did, he saw a half-human face looking out at him. His eyes were encircled with mud and his cheeks were streaked with it, and although his hair was clean, a line of mud ran like a ribbon at the edge of his scalp.

He opened his mouth. He had plenty to say, but his throat was tightening, and his eyes were stinging, and he couldn't shout, although he wanted to shout, "You're laughing at me? I'm out there risking my ass for you and you're back here taking showers and eating hot meals and you're laughing at me?" He was sorry and he was ashamed. He felt emotions he hadn't felt since going into the field and now he was unfamiliar with them. He didn't know how to handle them. He didn't belong here.

He peeled the Saran wrap from his arm, got dressed, and went to see the surgeon. "Show me how to take the stitches out," he said. "I want to go back."

"No one wants to go back, man," said an orderly.

"I want to go back," Pete said. "Who do I have to talk to?"

"If you want to go back that badly, you can go," the surgeon said. "You think it's a picnic here? The floor of the O.R.'s so slippery with blood you have to stand on straw mats when you operate. They keep bringing in natives with river blindness and we've got one after another staggering around the damn wards crashing into things. We've got to get them out fast before they break everything. They swallow medicine they're supposed to put in their eyes, and there are all these men on breathing tubes and suction tubes, and they carry arms and legs out on gurneys, piled up like meat in a butcher shop. Hell, you can go if you want to."

"How do I take out the stitches?" Pete asked again, and the surgeon shook his head. Some of them were more stubborn than mules, but don't knock it. The stubbornness kept them alive. Even after their hearts stopped, the stubbornness goaded them back. You saw those blips start up on the screen all over again.

"See these?" he said. "These little black V's? Like rabbit ears? You take a tweezer and pull them straight up and with a sharp scissor you cut beneath the knot and pull the ears until you see the string is out. There's nothing to it. Make sure you're after the string, not a blood bead. You wouldn't believe how many guys come back saying I forgot to take out a stitch when all it is is blood."

"Can I have a tweezer?" Pete asked.

"Sure. Have two," the surgeon said. "I'll release you." He turned to the orderly. "Can you believe this idiot is going back the same day he came in? Can you believe it?" But Pete was already gone. He was in the barracks packing up his equipment and out on the airstrip asking a helicopter pilot where he was going, and when the man said he was going back near the base, he asked if he could come along and the pilot said, "Sure, why not?"

"Hey, Bravado's back," Wapniak exulted. "What's the matter? You missed us? You couldn't stay away?" Pete said, Yeah, it was something like that, and Sal said he was a horse's ass. He ought to have played crazy or swallowed five amphetamines and said he was having a heart attack. That's what *he* was going to do if they ever shipped him out. That's why he never went into the field with less than five in his pocket. Did Pete ever see him swallow one? He'd *never* swallow one. He never knew when he'd need them. "What's wrong with you, Bravado?" he asked, and Pete said, "I forgot to wash my face."

"That's a reason!" shouted Sal. "That's a reason? You work with me this long and you still don't know nothing?" Pete said he wanted to come back. "Oh, yeah?" Sal said. "Guess what's coming in this afternoon? The *Colonel's* coming in. He wants us to go back for those two dead bodies. How does that grab you?"

"Dead is dead," said Pete.

"That's what I said, but I respect his opinion," Wapniak said. "When we came in, he told us he didn't want to lose anyone, but he wouldn't leave anyone behind. He said he'd retrieve the bodies so the families could have a proper funeral. He made us a promise and he keeps his word. He's a man of principle. He's got integrity. I respect that."

"Who asked him to promise?" Sal shouted at him. "Who?"

"Your word is your bond," Wapniak said.

"Shit, I'm *Italian* and I don't believe that garbage," Sal roared. "Dead is dead! You heard Bravado. I'm not going!"

"You're going to disobey a direct order? Is that what you're going to do, Sal?"

"I should have fucking gone with the Chief!"

"We don't know the Chief went anywhere, Sal. We don't know that. All we know is he's missing in action. M.I.A. A sniper could have dragged him off. They could be grilling him right now and all he's telling them is his name, rank, and serial number."

"You believe that shit?" Sal asked. "You believe it?"

"I believe he deserted," Wapniak said. "You want the green machine to believe it?"

"Fuck direct orders, man!" Sal shouted. "Alpha troop refused to go out on four-man patrols! They were always getting lost! They were climbing fucking trees! Nothing happened to them! They're fine!"

"They gave them map reading classes at night and sent them back out," Wapniak said. "No one gets away with anything."

"I don't want to die here," Pete said. "There are good deaths and bad deaths. You die here, it's a bad death. It don't mean anything."

"So why'd you come back?" Sal asked, turning on him. "Tell me the name of one person, *one person,* who died of natural causes. One name. That's all I want is one name. No fucking person in this fucking country dies of natural causes! I don't care if you're in a village or on a boat or walking through the woods or swinging through a tree. No fucking thing here dies of natural causes. Name one! Just one! Go ahead! Name one!"

Wapniak was thinking. "I saw a puppy once. He died of worms."

"A fucking dog?" Sal said, slamming his hand into the bulkhead. "Aw, shit!"

"But I think after he died, the ARVNs ate him," Wapniak said.

"A fucking dog? And he died of natural causes and they ate him? That's the best you can do?" Sal said. "Aw, shit!"

AT FIRST LIGHT, the Colonel's chopper came in through the mists, but it didn't land. Still, the Colonel's landing was dramatic. Most of the men had never seen anything like it. He came down on a jungle penetrator, a weighted rope with arm bars to hold on to, and he went straight to the Captain who told him the Sergeants had gotten together and decided that it wasn't worth risking more lives.

"This company's been going downhill for a long time," said the Colonel. "I know about the White Man. I know about the morale here. But I say we retrieve those two dead bodies and my decision's final. The day we start running this war on a committee basis is the day we bury the army."

"The men just won't go," said the Captain.

"We'll see about that," said the Colonel. He radioed the chopper and the new officer lowered himself down on the same jungle penetrator. "You're replaced," the Colonel told the Captain. "I want to talk to the Sergeant Major and the Sergeants." When the NCOs assembled, they said that if the Captain was relieved, they wanted to be relieved also, because they had agreed to that decision, and the Colonel said this was the army, not a goddamn popularity contest.

The Sergeant Major was sent out to evaluate the situation and came back saying, "I think they'll go, sir. They just need someone to lead them. The problem is, no one will walk point."

"If that's the problem, there's no problem. I've walked point more times than anyone in the troop, and I'll do it again," the Colonel said. More time passed. The Sergeant Major returned and said he'd spoken to the men. They didn't think walking point was a position for him. They had a volunteer.

"Fine," the Colonel said. "The Captain and I will be right behind the lead squad. What's your plan of attack?" The Sergeant Major said they'd go along the ridge and back into the bunker complex, but the Colonel said, No, they'd already tried that and they had too many casualties. This time, they'd go down the ravine and climb up the other side. The element of surprise could be a very useful thing.

"Up and down the ravine? Give me a break," said Sal.

"They mined the ridge," Pete reminded him.

"Why are we going?" Sal asked. "Tell me that. Why?"

Wapniak sighed.

THEY CLIMBED down, or crawled down backwards, and when they reached bottom, filled their canteens in a stream and began the slow climb up the other side. They held to tree branches and pulled themselves up the rock face. They lost their footing, slipped, and their boots struck the steel helmets of the men in back of them and they sent showers of pebbles backwards where they hammered on the helmets of those behind them, little rat-a-tat noises like toy bullets from toy guns, but they set off no mines, and when they reached the top of the ridge, they knew they would be taking the bunker by surprise. Not a shot had been fired.

This time they had a use for their gas grenades. Men poured out of the mouth of the bunker and gave up in the face of the leveled guns, and for an instant, it looked easy; it looked like a piece of cake. The firing began without warning, and they were down on the ground, and if there was nowhere for them to hide on the ridge, there was nowhere for the enemy, either, and they aimed carefully at the men they could see and brought them down. They waited. There was silence and the Colonel said, "Let's go," and they went into the bunker.

The two bodies were there, untouched, where they had fallen, and the men who had groped their way in through the clammy tunnels, feeling the roots protruding through the earth floor, inhaling the dank air, seeing the insect holes drilled into the walls, first tied ropes to the dead men's ankles and pulled them backwards, because the bodies might be booby-trapped, and when they discovered they weren't, carried the bodies through the wide tunnels and then, when the tunnels narrowed, again dragged them by their feet.

When they came out into the open air, they were jubilant. One of them began dancing like an Indian, whooping, and the others followed suit, and someone asked the Colonel, "Sir, couldn't a chopper bring in some cold ones?" They were ready to have a party right in the bunker. Now it wasn't as if they'd retrieved two dead bodies. It was as if they'd brought two men back alive. Wapniak stood there crying. Pete put his bandaged arm around Wapniak's shoulder and wept openly and Sal tore his helmet from his head, hurled it to the ground, and shouted, "Goddamn! Goddamn!" until he was hoarse, and now he was doing his version of an Indian war dance, chanting over and over, "I am the White Man! I am the White Man!"

"Victory," said the Colonel to the new Captain, "is sweet."

"Hell, sir," the Captain said, "I don't know *what* this is about."

But it was about getting back to base before anyone else found they were there, carrying the bodies back up and down the ravine, and they saddled up and the veins in their neck swelled. The insects bit them. Leeches stuck to them. The sun came at their eyes like birds of prey, diving. Their arms and legs were scratched by bushes and twigs and thorns. Their feet slipped on the wet ferns and they fell backwards down the hill, pushing others further down with them. They skinned their elbows and knees and blood seeped through their uniforms and stiffened there, and rubbed their flesh raw. Branches snapped back in their faces and scratched their cheeks and at times they had to climb covering their eyes with one hand, and their sweat ran into the scratches and burned there. Leg muscles cramped and hearts beat and bubbled oddly. Pulses fluttered in the heat and eyeglasses misted and still they climbed and this time they didn't mind it.

Under the weight of the daily routine, the euphoria could not hold up. The next day, they were out escorting a convoy of trucks to the city, and for the rest of the week, they were out reconnoitering. They passed paddy after rice paddy and village after village, and Wapniak said he never thought war could get boring, but lately it was. They stopped on the side of the road, and the infantry dismounted, and went into the jungle and some of them sat on a rice paddy dike and looked out over the fields that seemed covered with sheets of glass, improbable mirrors, and they heard the crickets, and felt the peace rising up out of the ground.

"What's that?" asked Wapniak, looking up. "It looks like a white helicopter."

"It's the flying Good Humor truck," Sal said.

"The what?" asked Wapniak, as they watched this unlikely, this unbelievable object, coming down toward them. It glistened and shone in the sun, and as it came closer, its surface began reflecting the green of the grass and the outline of their tracks. The white helicopter landed in the middle of the road.

"What a treat," Sal said.

"Is it really ice cream?" Pete asked. Sometimes they flew in ice cream for the troops. It didn't happen often, but it happened.

"See for yourself," Sal said.

A chaplain got out of the helicopter and walked over to them. "How are you doing, men?" he asked, and the three of them said they were doing fine.

"I know you feel bad about killing," said the chaplain, "but there's something I want you to understand. You boys, you're doing good work for your country, and I want you to know there's a distinction between murder and killing. In the eyes of God, you're not sinners because you're not murderers. You're killing in a good cause. You're doing the right thing. Don't feel bad about it. God understands and forgives you." He made the sign of the cross, looked at his watch, turned, and quickly walked back to the helicopter. The three of them watched it rise up and move to the next rice paddy.

"Very efficient," said Wapniak. "I clock him at eleven seconds."

"A fast talker," said Sal.

"It's all right to kill?" asked Pete. "Wait a minute here. I thought there were ten commandments."

"They're only using nine today," Sal said.

"The Good Humor truck?" Wapniak asked.

"The Good Humor truck," Sal said. "That's what they calls it."

But Pete wanted the chaplain to come back. He wanted to raise his hand as he had in school and say, "Wait a minute. For years they taught us it was wrong to kill and now you come along and tell us it's all right, God doesn't mind? Who are you to tell us?"

How could the chaplain land here, walk over, and say all the rules were broken? Even in heaven, they were broken. What was he supposed to believe in now? When he went back, what would a church be to him? A pile of stones with a man in a woman's dress who said God told him it was all right to kill. It wasn't all right to kill. He wanted to go back and tell that to people. He wanted to go back and find forgiveness. Where was he going to find it now? Not in the church. And if not in the church, nowhere.

Sal had been watching Pete's face. "Look, man, he's an ass," he said. "He's just a man. That collar don't make him special."

"Did he have a collar?" asked Wapniak. "I didn't see a collar."

Pete barely heard them. His heart pounded: the blood roared in his ears. "I want him to come back here and tell me how he knows what God thinks about killing," Pete said. "I want him to explain it to my face."

"He's only doing his job," Sal said. "Forget it."

"Forget it. It's nothing," Wapniak said. "But a *white* helicopter! Only in this war! Only where we're the only ones who have planes. Can you imagine a white helicopter in the Second World War? The Messerschmitts would've had it on the ground in a minute. He'd be down in flames before he could recite the first line of the Lord's Prayer. A white helicopter! That's something! I'm going to write home about that white helicopter."

"I hope he goes down," Pete said. "I hope he goes down in flames like a fucking burning bush."

THE COLUMN moved on. Someone spotted something moving in the grass on the side of the road. The tracks were brought on line and Pete and Sal went out to investigate.

"It's a kid," Pete radioed back. "About three or four."

"Is he booby-trapped?" asked Wapniak from the track.

"He's fucking naked!" Sal shouted. "Tell them he's fucking naked."

"He's naked," Pete said.

"Come on back in," Wapniak said.

"What are we going to do with this kid?" Sal asked. "He's out here in the middle of nowhere. We leveled every village for miles. They went off without him. Wapniak always says it's so confusing he doesn't know why they don't forget a kid. They forgot one."

Pete picked the child up.

"Aw, man," said Sal. "Don't pick him up." He looked at the child, at his face, upturned toward Pete's, the beginning of a smile igniting in his eyes, his hand reaching up in wonder to the dirty white face, until it came to rest on the dark stubble of Pete's chin, and then his hand pulled back as if burned. "Aw, man, he's going to want to come with us."

"Let's go," said Pete. "All clear here," and, carrying the child, he turned back toward the track. He climbed in through the back hatch of the track, carrying the child, set him down on the floor, pulled his olive drab T-shirt over his head, put it on the child, on whom it was like a nightshirt, and put on his flak jacket.

"What now, Bravado? What now? We're fucking baby-sitters?" Wapniak asked. "He's got parents. When you find a nice little bear cub, the bear's got parents. The parents out here happen to live in holes in the ground and have antitank weapons. Put him back, Pete." But Pete was sitting on an ammo crate, the child on his lap, opening a C-ration can of ham and lima beans, and the child looked up at him, down at the can, and began eating ravenously.

"Remember what the ARVN said, Pete?" asked Wapniak. "Remember what he said about little babies growing up to be big motherfuckers who'd come after us? We had enough trouble in the track. Remember the ARVNs? They're still here. Get rid of the kid. He's going to grow up and come after us and our kids. He's nothing. Get rid of him."

"Back off! Don't you fucking tell me how to feel! Don't you fucking tell me how to think!" Pete said. "The *army* says, 'You will take that village.' 'You will shine those shoes.' 'You will shoot that man.' But the fucking army isn't going to tell me how to feel. What I *feel* is *mine*, man! Not yours, but mine."

"He's in the track with all of us," Wapniak said.

"Yeah?" said Pete. "Well, the goddamn troop's moving out. His parents are going to come after an armored cavalry troop? They know where he is? They leave him in an empty field right before curfew and they know where he is? Give me a break, man."

"We're not fucking moving," Sal said. "What the fuck is it now?"

IN THE command track, the third track on line, the medic stood up and looked out over the open fields. The Lieutenant said something to him, and the medic pulled the pin on his grenade and held the spoon down.

"What are you doing, Vinnie?" asked the Sergeant. "Put back the pin." The medic looked at him and began giggling, a high-pitched giggle. "Put back the pin," the Sergeant said. This was a joke. It had to be a joke. The medic giggled, waved the grenade, and with his other hand, began pulling cartons of cigarettes from the storage compartment.

"He's not here. He's *gone*," the driver said.

"Put back the pin or throw the grenade," said the Sergeant. "We don't have time for this shit."

The medic stared at the Sergeant, bewildered, as if wondering who he could be, seeing himself shadowing a trail in the jungle. The foliage was thick. It was dark there. Suddenly he jumped back with a sharp cry. He'd stumbled over something warm and sticky, something that lay still, yet quivered. It must be a wounded soldier, someone missing in action, and as he bent down to look for the body, he heard a yelping. No human made a sound like that.

He forgot about booby traps. He pushed the ferns out of the way and saw a dog, and the dog was bleeding from its ears and mouth, but its body

was still warm, and then he saw that it wasn't the dog yelping. There were
five or six puppies crawling over the dead beast, and as he watched, one
of them tried to lift her belly with his nose to get at the teat she lay on.
Out of the dog's open mouth came emptiness and horror, helplessness and
abandonment and lack of hope. The end of the world poured from the still-
open eyes of the dead bitch. He stood up and the trees blackened, tilted
back and away from him. The noises of the jungle faded and he knew he was
passing out. The next thing he saw was one of the soldiers bending over
him. His face loomed moonlike and huge, enormous and distorted, like a
face in a crazy cartoon, and he started to laugh. "She didn't even have dog
tags," the medic said, and laughed hysterically, and the Sergeant said, "No?
Don't worry about it. We'll find them later." The medic looked into the
huge face and laughed a high-pitched terrible laugh. "I made a funny,"
he said.

"You'll be all right," said the huge face. It was getting bigger, not smaller.
"You'll be all right. Take a sip." The face brought a canteen to his lips. "Take
a sip."

"I'll get the LT," said the Sergeant. "You stay here."

"I'm all right, I'm fine. Forget the LT," said the medic.

"IT'S ALL RIGHT. I'll take care of this," said the Lieutenant. "Vinnie,"
he said, "let's get out of the track. You got your hand on the spoon? Keep
your hand on the spoon. Let's get out of the track."

The medic nodded. Yes, that was a reasonable request, and he and the
Lieutenant climbed out of the hatch and began walking into the field. "Put
back the pin, Vinnie," the Lieutenant said. "Put back the pin or throw the
grenade. You won't hurt anything. There's not a living thing out there."

The medic looked at the Lieutenant. Couldn't he hear the frogs, the
crickets, the sound of birds? There were hundreds, there were millions of
living things out here. Why couldn't he hear them? "Why can't you hear
them, LT?" he asked, and the Lieutenant asked, "What?" The medic looked
at him and wondered why the Lieutenant was yelping instead of talking.
How was he supposed to know what he was saying if he yelped like that?
And the Lieutenant's mouth opened again, and all he heard now was the
yelping. The sound of frogs and birds and crickets was gone and the
Lieutenant's mouth was wide open and black like the mouth of a well,
yelping, and the medic let go of the spoon, and if the crickets continued to
sing, or the bullfrogs to call out, no one knew. An explosion rocked the
ground. Smoke, earth, and stones rose in the air, and the two men, or what
had been two men, fell back with them.

Someone was shouting, *Damn!* and someone was shouting, *I don't
fucking believe this!* and someone in the track was saying, *Go on out there*

and get them, and men were dismounting along the length of the column, and the wind spread word of what had happened and everyone stared down the field, and then down at their boots, and finally everyone climbed back in the tracks, and the column moved on.

The child sat on Pete's lap and Sal wondered aloud what the LT would make of the kid and no one answered him, but that was fine. He was talking to himself. Pete thought about the Colonel and his promise not to leave anyone behind. Wapniak was right. You had to respect a man who kept his word. He ought to have seen it before. Why couldn't he see it before? How important it was not to lie. To always keep your word.

"Again! We're stopping again!" Wapniak shouted. "What is this, a fucking local?"

A new voice from the command track came over the radio. The engineering compound in front of them was taking harassment fire from a sniper in the tree line and the engineers wanted to know if they could help them out.

"What is this?" Wapniak asked. "We're the fucking girl scouts? We're crossing little old ladies over the street? What is this?"

"Three-six, this is three-four," said the radio. "There's a boulder crusher here. Does anyone need gravel?"

"Why the hell would we need gravel?" demanded Wapniak. He was beside himself. He was bouncing up and down. "What are we going to do with gravel, pave the track? If we go over a land mine, we'll get hit with a thousand little stones. What is he talking about, gravel?"

"Take it easy, man," Sal said. "Real easy."

"I mean, where's the war?" Wapniak shouted. "It's an Easter egg hunt! Nothing's ever decided! *What are we doing?*"

"Don't try to make sense out of it, man," Sal said. "When it starts making sense, you're really in trouble."

"Take it easy," Pete said.

"Wapniak's starting to talk like me," Sal said. "You notice that?"

"I don't! I don't talk like you!" Wapniak bellowed, and he stared at Sal, and Sal stared back at him, blank and unreadable, and Wapniak turned toward the bulkhead and burst out crying. "I quit!" Wapniak shouted. "I quit!"

"Fine," said Sal. "Glad to hear it."

"Those rear echelon fuckers," Pete said. "They're so drunk and their eyes are so fat, they're not even going to get the right names on the right bodies."

"Yeah, with luck, the Lieutenant and the medic will be going home together," Sal said, "and the families, if they find out, they'll be on fucking motorcycles roaring from one funeral to another. Those rear echelon fuckers, nothing to do but drink and eat and write down a few names."

"What are you talking about?" Wapniak asked. "They make mistakes?"

"We're *goofing* on the REMFs," Sal said. "It gets your mind off what happened."

"It's not getting my mind off anything," Wapniak said.

"Fine, keep your mind on it and end up like the medic."

The six tracks in the field were blasting away with the .50 calibers, sending in rockets, using their LAWs—their light antitank weapons—for good measure, and tree after tree went down. "Are they going to use the flame thrower? It's new. Are they going to use it?" Pete asked.

"I'd like to see it," Sal said, taking the child and settling him against his chest.

"He'd like to see it," Wapniak said, starting to laugh. "Why not?"

"Three-six, this is three-one," said the radio. "Lock and load. There's more activity in the tree line. We're going out."

Pete climbed up on top. He wasn't strong enough to pull the bolt back with one hand. Only Sal was that strong and Sal was busy with the kid. He put his left hand over the bolt, pulled back on his left hand using his right, and began to feed the first round into the chamber when the gun bolt caught his watchband, pulled it, and smashed it. Now he had to pull the bolt back again because his watch was caught, and he thanked God they weren't under fire. He managed to pull back the bolt, free his arm, free the watch, extract the first round, and begin over again. When he climbed back in, he looked at his watch. It was smashed flat. It didn't tell time. It didn't tell anything. It told how fragile things were and how easily they broke.

"It's only a watch," Sal said.

"A Seiko," Pete said.

"Only a Seiko. The city's full of Seikos."

"I liked this one," Pete said.

"Three-six, this is three-one," said the radio. "The tree line's cleared."

"Hold the kid," Sal told Pete. "I'll take care of the .50."

"Yeah," said Pete, looking at his watch. "Sure." The two hands were loose, floating over the white clock face. If you took the two hands and laid them crosswise, they looked like the propellers of a helicopter. If you laid one at right angles to the other, it looked like a cross. He stared at the hands of the smashed watch until they began lifting into the air, revolving like the blades of a tiny helicopter flying around their heads.

The men from the engineering compound were coming out to the tracks, bringing rum, cold Coke, cold beer, homemade cookies. Hell, they could have whatever they wanted. They'd been down in bunkers for a week, on a first-name basis with the rats. How about some Lurp rations and a bottle of Tabasco sauce? What else did they have? Ice cream and more beer and a lot of canned corn, *a lot* of it. So many cases you wouldn't believe it. They had no idea what it was doing out here. Del Monte corn.

"The medic might still be here if he knew we'd have ice cream," said Pete.

"Yeah, how do you figure that?" asked Sal.

"We're going back to base?" Wapniak said. "Why are we going back to base? There's *activity* out here. That's why they sent us out. Why? Someone tell me why."

"They have intelligence," Pete said.

"Don't even try," Sal said. "He's raving."

"Just once," Wapniak shouted. "Just once I'd like them to tell us why! Is that too much to ask? Just once!"

29 AT TIMES, it was surprising to see lavender mountains rising up behind the green ones, ringing the base, to see the sky rising up over the mountains, still blue, rinsing the flat green fields until they shone, or to see it in the evenings, when the sun set oddly, setting bonfires here and there as if behind the sky someone huge was busy with an immense Zippo lighter and even behind the sky villages were burning. At times, it was hard to believe that the sun rose at all. At times, all the events of past weeks seemed to have taken place in complete darkness—not darkness, but blackness, so dark you couldn't see your hand in front of you. It was a surprise to see the sun-struck palms in the fields beyond the base lit from behind, shining like saints. It was surprising to see the grass still green and growing, and there were times when it was surprising to see that ants still crawled the hot, red baked earth of the base, which now, in the absence of rain, was covered not with mud but with dust.

Everything—the passing of a truck, two men walking together, a dog rolling on his back—drove dust into the air. Ashes to ashes, dust to dust, said Wapniak, but here you didn't go to the dust. The dust came to you. By the time they were ready to bury you, you were already half made of earth. Your lungs were filled with dust, and your gut. There was dust in your ears and your hair. You wore a mask of mud, and dust coated each and every one of the hairs of your chest and your arms.

Once again, there were reports of the White Man, and Wapniak said the White Man was nothing, merely a mirage of dust. And what was he before? A mirage of mud.

It was quiet on the base, and the men played cards and read their mail. They had weeks of it to catch up on. Pete read about his brother Paul, who came home with marks on his body, and about how his aunts and uncles prayed for him, and so did everyone on the block. His mother wrote that she was sending him a special Christmas package and to eat everything in it *himself,* and in the last envelope was a picture of his family, taken around the kitchen table with the two doorways in the background, one opening into his bedroom—in the picture, a square of darkness—the other opening into the living room, and he could remember those doorways and that table, the tile design of the kitchen wallpaper, but who were those people sitting around the table? And there were so many of them, where was he going to fit in? Where would they put him? All the places were taken.

He thought about his father, who was happy to have Paul in the home on Staten Island because it made his life easier, and he knew his father was happy to have him in the army because that also made his father's life easier. He tore the picture up into little pieces, but he needn't have bothered. The new Lieutenant came around and told them the enemy was using the letters they found on the dead and the wounded. Natives on the base were stealing the letters and turning them over to the enemy, who wrote the soldier's family, telling them their son was a prisoner, or dead, or a criminal, a murderer of women and children. They were using their letters to cause pain and suffering back home.

"Burn your letters," said the Lieutenant.

They stood up and set fire to their letters with matches or lighters, one at a time. Some of them stood there crying as their letters burned. Pete watched the flames eat a black border into the pieces of paper. He watched the red-gold border of flame inside the black border, and saw that turn into ash, and he liked it. He liked the fire and how it burned, and when he was finished burning his letters, he felt lost and weak.

The men sat around, playing cards, repeating what they'd read in the letters they'd just burned, going over what they intended to eat when they got out or went on R and R. One was going to fill all the dishes on his tray with ice cream and eat all of it before it melted. Someone else was going to buy fifty Planter's Peanut candy bars and eat them all at once. Another was going to buy a steak and mashed potatoes and cover everything on his tray with gravy. As long as you could eat it, he was covering it with gravy.

They played cards and drank beer. During the day, the Colonel said, they could have as much beer as they wanted, but no beer after dusk. If they sat around all day waiting for a brew, they'd drink as much as they could at dusk and they'd be no good in the dark. At night, he wanted them alert. More LPs than usual were sent out at night, and the wires had never been so thick with flares and grenades or so many claymores, daisy-chained and wired for command detonation, but the men didn't give it much thought. The Colonel had been out here for a while and he was getting spooked like the rest of them, and who could he talk to? You could almost feel sorry for the Colonel, but then he wasn't out in the field when the medic let go of the spoon and he and the Lieutenant became history. He wasn't out there when the boot came down, turning over and over in the air. But still, you could almost feel sorry for him. When it was quiet like this, you remembered he existed.

Pete's kid was gone. It didn't mean nothing. It was just another hole in things for the wind to blow through. The Lieutenant had taken the child to the Colonel and the Colonel arranged to have the child taken to a Catholic orphanage the army was running with the help of the Church.

"He's quiet," Sal said to Wapniak, and Wapniak looked at Pete and said, "He is."

"I'm not quiet," Pete said, and they realized it was the first time they'd heard his voice all day, and Wapniak said he had new tapes, Beatles, Rolling Stones, Country Joe and the Fish, and Pete said right now he didn't want to hear Country Joe and the Fish.

"At least you can sleep at night here," said Wapniak.

WHEN EVERYONE in the tent was asleep, Pete took his M-16 and got up quietly. No one paid any attention. If anyone was awake, they thought he was going to the latrine, but most of them were asleep, dreaming, restless, but asleep, and he turned once to look back at them on their cots, some with mattresses, some without, some sleeping on ponchos stretched tight over the springs, others more comfortable on the floor, and he stepped over a man asleep near the tent flaps and walked out to the track. It waited, iron grey animal, as if it were expecting him. No one stopped him. No one asked him where he was going. Once more the world had emptied out and he was the only person in it. He climbed in through the rear hatch and sat down on his ammo box and looked up through the top hatch to the clear, thick gravel of stars. He put the barrel of the gun in his mouth and grimaced at the taste of the metal and the oil and the gasoline, and his finger was on the trigger for a long time and he stared up at the stars.

He thought of something, or something thought of him—more and more, it seemed to him as if he no longer thought at all, but something would suddenly remember his existence, and he would be switched on by its hand, as a forgotten radio might be switched on—and he took the barrel out of his mouth, climbed up through the cupola and looked out toward the perimeter, and he thought he saw a white figure, waving. It was impossible. The ground was mined for five hundred feet out.

He went back inside, sat down, and put the gun back in his mouth, but now he liked its taste, he was almost used to it, and his finger rested again on the trigger, but when it did, he began weeping. His finger was pulling back on the trigger when a wave of heat swept through him, a blast of fire, and his finger slid slowly from the trigger. The gun came out of his mouth and he looked slowly around him, at the straps hanging from the side walls of the tracks, at the compartments filled with packages of cigarettes and Ivory soap from the Care packages that arrived at the base, at the abandoned flak jackets, at the patch of dried mud not yet washed from the track floor. "Fuck the army," he said, and he put the gun back.

He was filled by anger. The anger pushed out the fear. He was powerful.

He would have gone back to the tent but he'd started crying again. He didn't know what he was crying about, and a single word kept forming over and over in his mind, as if someone were whispering it, *tunnels,* but he had to wait until he stopped crying, and then he felt the anger surge in him, and the anger felt good.

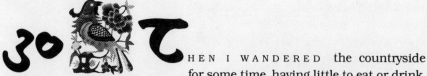

HEN I WANDERED the countryside for some time, having little to eat or drink, unaware of my hunger, aware only of the danger of being seen, but I soon learned to move as if invisible. I made less sound than an animal and often came upon animals drinking at water holes. Water buffaloes did not run from me, but only looked up surprised by my presence, and, as I went deeper and deeper into the jungle, always going uphill because I wanted to reach the mountains and cross them, I came to two deer in a field, and heard them barking as dogs bark when something frightens them. Occasionally, sounds and smells would tell me I was near a village. I would see smoke corkscrewing into the blue sky where the farmers were burning charcoal or clearing a patch of land, and I would change my course accordingly. What I wanted was emptiness, a place with no men, but at the same time I became aware that no matter where I went, how silently, or how far, someone followed me. I kept on for days, sometimes following the track of a river, once seeing an old man chasing a waterfowl, beating at it with a stick, and the fowl, beating its large wings, jumped out of the man's way, but the man pursued it relentlessly, and I saw that eventually the bird would tire and fall prey to the man.

I crossed marshy lands and found deer at a salt lick and hid in the forest and watched and saw children come and gather up the dirt and chew on it to appease their hunger, and I went further into the jungle, always keeping the mountains in sight, always climbing higher. I came to a break in the forest and found myself on top of a mountain and below me stretched field after field of golden flowers, and I entered the jungle again and climbed slowly. Around me were dense green mountains thick with trees, and in back of them, mountain ranges, at dusk almost black, fading into pale shades of grey, each ridge thin and sharp as if cut from a thin sheet of paper.

In the morning, they were blue and shrouded in mists, the last in the chain so pale it was a blue outline of cloud against the shining sky. I found fruits on trees. I found pineapples filled with worms and ate them as they were, and bananas no longer than my finger, but very sweet, and ate them also. When I could find nothing to drink, I climbed coconut trees as the natives do, encircling the trunk with my legs and pulling myself up with my arms. When I had the coconuts, I would cut them open and drink their milk. Then, as I went higher and higher, the jungle seemed to give out, and there were fewer and fewer animals to eat. The birds who lived up here were too high and too fast to hunt, and although I was fast and could catch a pond fish with my hand, I found fewer and fewer ponds. I always carried water with me, but one day I realized I was starving.

Still, I kept going, always upwards. The rains would start up suddenly and then stop, but I no longer noticed the weather. I noticed the ground and how it grew muddy and slippery, or if it grew hard and rocky, and the soles of my sandals began to crack and I looked for something to line their insides. I found smooth wood and polished it as I walked, but walking was what I thought about, always upwards. Sounds were becoming unnaturally clear, my sense of smell sharper. My eyesight, too, was better. I could see the outline of every leaf against every other leaf of every tree against the sky, but I had stopped thinking about what I saw. My mind touched everything, took it in, and put it away somewhere beyond thought.

One day I came to a clearing and saw many men, naked except for loincloths, hunched over, their hands carrying something raw and bloody to their mouths, and my hunger drew me toward them, and, as if in a dream, they made room for me, and I bent forward to take my share, and I saw a dead man stripped of his clothes, his head still untouched. Every feature of his face was finely carved of white and shiny wood, but his rib cage was exposed, and one of the squatting men took a spear and cut a chunk of the dead man's flesh and handed it to me, and I could not take it, but a man dressed in white was stooped over the fire, and he took up a piece of flesh and handed it to me, and when I took it, the man's body changed to the body of a deer, and I ate it, and after the men were finished, and I was finished, one of them took my arm, and another cut a design of a rectangle in my flesh, and another had a leather pouch of red powder and they drew designs on my arms and back and chest, and I saw that the man in white had the same designs on his flesh, and that now we belonged to them.

We began to roam with them and eventually we learned a little of their language, and a little was enough because we had nothing to say. We went with them and saw what they saw, and if we had any memory of what had happened before we ate the dead man's flesh, it did not trouble us and the men did not ask us about it. After some time, we understood the men belonged to a hill tribe that lived in the mountains where three countries met, and few outsiders knew of their existence, and almost no one knew where they lived, because every day they lived somewhere else. They had no camps or sites. They found a place that sheltered them from the sun or the heavy rains and slept on the ground. High in the mountains they lived in a village whose huts were made of sticks and mud and built on stilts and there their women and children lived, but for now, they roamed, and occasionally they traded. All they possessed were the sacks of opium they carried on their backs.

With them we saw many things. From the mountain we saw a plain, and on it we saw a herd of wild elephants running, their skin grey speckled with pink, and a plane came in low and shot four of the elephants and then flew out of sight. We came to a small clearing in the thick jungle and saw a dying man, his eyes already half shut, the ground around him sticky with blackening blood, his hand resting on the head of another man, his eyes filled with love as he looked at the face of that man, and we saw the man on whose head the hand rested was already dead, and the other soon would be, but while he was alive, his hand rested on his head, and was company for him.

Deep in the jungle we heard explosions and saw fire and saw a rock ape with its arm blown off, its stunned look of surprise as it tried to swing down to the ground, saw it lose its hold on the branch and fall, heard the terrified chatter of the other apes, and saw one of the apes come down to try to help, but the wounded ape chattered softly and held his bleeding shoulder with his black, leathery hand. Perhaps his flesh had been cauterized by the heat of the shrapnel because the bleeding was stopping. Later we saw a monkey without a leg, and when we returned, we saw a rock ape climbing awkwardly and slowly through the trees using only one arm.

The Viet Cong were holding guns to the heads of a child's mother and father, telling the child if he did not shoot two Americans, his parents would be shot, and the weeping child took the gun he was given and, followed by his dog, went into the jungle, but the soldiers followed him, and in front of the child, shot the dog because a dog could bark and warn the soldiers of his presence. A GI took his puppy from his flak jacket and put him down on the ground and the puppy scampered into the trees and the GI went after him and a shadow came from behind a palm tree and garroted the man, picked up the puppy, and carried it back to camp, where its throat was slit and the puppy was roasted.

We came to an ancient cemetery whose graves were marked by headstones and footstones resembling old-fashioned headboards on beds, decorated with pieces of blue and white crockery, and in the moonlight, we saw soldiers asleep on each raised grave, the rain running from their bodies, asleep as if on so many beds, their flesh white and ghostly even under the mud they had smeared on their faces, their hands curled around their weapons, soundly sleeping on the dead as if on soft beds. We saw tanks with flamethrowers lined up facing a village, firing in sequence, and saw the plows come in later to level the scorched, dead earth. We saw the dead places where nothing grew, and the farmers returning to what had once been their homes, carrying baskets of worms, leaving the worms there, and then returning to see if the worms could live in the soil, and when they found the worms had died, they wept because even the earth was dead. No life could spring from it.

On rivers, we saw huge barges carrying herds of water buffalo, their eyes in their broad skulls puzzled and wild, and the boys who tended them pushing the boats from the shore with their poles and traveling down the river to some unknown place. We saw trucks full of villagers, chickens, ducks, geese, and pigs, all traveling to some unknown place. In the middle of the jungle, we saw a Viet Cong soldier drag two wounded off, seizing each by one leg, bumping their heads and backs over the rocky, sharp, twig-strewn ground. We saw a man take aim at a huge white bird and the bird fell to the ground in the thick jungle where the man could not find him, and the bird hopped from foot to foot, one wing useless, wondering what to do next. We saw tanks rolling through villages with skulls mounted on either side of their cupolas. We passed trees to which soldiers in olive drab uniforms were nailed by their palms and ankles, their heads drooping on their breasts. We saw decapitated bodies of Viet Cong, their heads set beneath their knees, an ace of spades in their mouths. We passed villages whose walls were hollow and filled with machine guns and grease guns and we watched Viet Cong fire on American soldiers with their own weapons. We saw the Viet Cong line up everyone in a village and bury them in mass graves outside the city. We saw a panther patting at C-ration cans while three terrified soldiers hid in the hollow trunk of a tree until the panther tired of the game and moved off.

In rivers we saw the living standing amidst bodies of the drowned, grey and swollen with water, unable to make a sound while the enemy waited on the bank. We saw a peaceful valley become an inferno, leaping with rivers of flame. We saw a soldier throw a white phosphorus grenade into a river and it kept on burning even beneath the water. It burned a fish to death deep in the water. Beneath the ground, we saw miles and miles of tunnels, and pale people with brittle bones in underground factories were cutting up discarded C-ration cans and making spearheads. They took abandoned mess kits and unexploded grenades, fixed them, and assembled booby traps. In large cities, we saw people's heads rising out of the cement sidewalks as if they'd been buried standing up. They were standing in cement canisters, bomb shelters sunk in the sidewalk, ten feet apart. When the all clear sounded, they came out. They thought nothing of it.

We saw villagers digging bunkers for water buffaloes and huddling beside them when bombs dropped. We saw native women with long black hair entering American bases with razor blades hidden in the buns pinned to the back of their head. We saw wells into which Viet Cong threw living bodies or animals so that the water would be poisoned, and the faces of the soldiers who lifted the lids and looked in. We saw rats, sleek, fat, and clean, on fire and screaming while the soldiers laughed. On trails from the north, soldiers coughed, spit blood, and died and the others left them and moved on. Mothers ran back into walls of flame looking for their children. Children ran blindly across fields of fire looking for their mothers. Soldiers threw C-ration cans at the heads of people begging for food and one split a skull and shattered it. In the forest, the Viet Cong took human excrement and smeared it on sharpened bamboo poles and dug pits in the road and covered them well. Soldiers came down a narrow path and in front of them a man jumped out of the earth like a jack-in-the-box, fired, and disappeared into the ground as if the earth had swallowed him. The earth was filled with deadly jack-in-the-boxes, who buried themselves standing up and kept a small roof of dirt and grass over their heads until they had what they were waiting for. Soldiers went down trails past trees whose twisted roots were part human and fired at them and three men fell dead and still the column didn't know what had fired at them. The trees themselves appeared to be firing. Down other trails, men stepped on booby traps that sprang up into the air and began revolving, cutting the men off at the knees.

We saw three men in a platoon raping a young woman, and two men up on a track watched and found it amusing, and after a while, they began to notice the noise of it, the struggle of it, and although they were still smiling, they got down and stopped the raping. On the other side of the village, no one stopped the raping, and two young girls were left, their blood running slowly and steadily into the darkening ground.

We saw helicopters fly in for their cargo of casualties, the living piled in with the dead, the floor slippery with blood and mud, and the soldiers, living and dead, sliding from one side of the helicopter floor to the other. We saw the living pushing away the dead who were sliding toward them in body bags or in uniforms, threatening to roll on top of them, and when they landed, a man would call out in terror, "I'm not dead! I'm not dead!" but he didn't sound sure. He sounded uncertain. We saw the men on mountain fire bases, shaving and looking down into the valleys that seemed filled with snow, looking around them, their eyes blank or puzzled or angry.

We saw colonels and generals bargaining with grunts for enemy weapons, offering them money for rolls of film taken in the field. We saw village chiefs accept money during the day from Americans and during the night from Viet Cong. We saw natives selling the men french bread and at night throwing homemade bombs. In villages, we saw go-betweens arranging marriages, and women who had given birth recede behind mosquito netting, rubbed with turmeric until their flesh glowed golden. We saw a wedding procession in which the participants carried pink umbrellas they were proud of. We heard the young boys singing to the girls in the field as they reaped the rice. We saw a young boy coming home to his village and asking to see his father, and a woman took him to a casket in the temple, and the young man opened it and looked into the eye sockets and cried and reached out to touch the body. We saw the villagers pick up the body of a young girl and wrap her head in white bandages, and then wrap the rest of her in white sheeting, and afterwards, her family dressed in thin white clothing to show they mourned her, and the white clothing was thin and spidery so that the mourners themselves looked like ghosts who, unlike the girl, remained above the surface of the earth. We felt in ourselves the spirit of the man whose flesh we had eaten. Sometimes it stirred and was restless. Other times, it was hungry and chewed at his own bones, and when that happened, the men with whom we traveled said that was the way with spirits. What you ate, ate you.

We saw a tiger on fire, running across a plain. We saw elephants on fire, trumpeting. We saw a pig thrown on top of a blazing bonfire, screaming. We saw fish explode out of a pond into which a grenade had been thrown, the water steaming. We saw a rock ape sitting up high in a tree playing with a set of dog tags, putting them in his mouth, tasting them, clicking them together. We watched a platoon leave the village and set up for the night and wake to find themselves surrounded by fires set by the villagers who had followed them. We saw one man reach for another's hand and the hand was not fastened to the body. We heard the men joking about a man who lost his head, and saw their eyes as they joked. We saw a man disappear and leave no trace behind, not even his dog tags, only a red stain on the ground. We saw a track go up in a burst of white flame, pinning two bodies, burning them down to their skeletons. We saw men left behind to guard ammunition overrun by the enemy. We saw a badly burned man blown from a track saying to his buddy, "Take care of my stuff," and the helicopter carried him away forever.

We saw sleeping men wake to find the enemy had crawled through the wire and their shadows were the last things they saw. Like children caught in a nightmare, they never knew what came for them in the middle of the night. We saw a man escape from an ambush on a motorcycle, the only one of his outfit left alive. We saw a company begin to cross a rice paddy and saw them fall, one after another, muzzle flashes thick in the tree lines. We saw men on one hill watching their sister company get hit on the next hill, and when they were taken to that hill by helicopter, they were so hungry they had to stop and eat before they could help them carry off their dead. We saw their wolfish, guilty faces as they ate.

We saw goodness turning to evil, and evil turning to good, and from the fire shone the mystery of human character. And when the spirit of the man we had eaten gnawed at our bones, we came to see the war as an animal with a life of its own, whose breath was fire, whose eyes saw no difference between the living and the dead, because to stay alive a man had to let much of him die, and those who lived had seen so much death, had lived so surrounded by the dead, they felt closer to the dead than to the living. We saw the vast army of the dead in silver cases, waiting to go home. We saw there were many truths, or there was no such thing as truth. There were the truths of the armies fighting one another, the truths of the animals and the truths of the trees and even the truth of the dead, scorched earth. And none of these truths stood against the will of nature, its insistence on dailiness, on weddings in the midst of fire, of burials in the midst of rejoicing, on vines growing up over dead trees, changing them from barren, dead things to green beings waving with arms, assuming the shapes of birds and animals, and men moved ignorantly among these truths, surrounded by spirits, by animals, by trees, putting their feet upon the ground as if they had created themselves and owed the earth nothing. And one day I looked up and saw someone who was half-woman and half-bird.

"I have seen everything you have seen," said the kinaree, and I could not take another step. I knew she was what I would become.

31 AT NIGHT, the silence had a feel, was threaded with owl cries, wind in the palms, random crickets, studded with stars, felt cool to the touch, often so cold the soldiers slept wrapped in their ponchos and poncho liners, and the soldiers had been back long enough to sleep soundly, or at least to sleep, and the Colonel liked walking through the base, passing the tents, looking in at the sleeping men, and at that moment, life was comprehensible, this making rounds, looking in on the sleeping men as he looked in on his children when he was back home. It couldn't last. Of course it couldn't last, but he'd lived long enough to know it didn't matter. You had to save these things, remember them because the time would come when the scales tipped and you needed everything you had, every good thing to right the balance. The Colonel was careful to treasure the good things when he found them. No matter how small they were, he hoarded them. He passed the last tent, looked in, and pitied the sleeping men who, when the scales were tipped, had little to right them. They would have enough: if they lived long enough. But this train of thought was unfriendly. It didn't have a place in a night like this.

He was back in his own tent, sound asleep, when one of the LPs squelched once, and the track behind them roared, and illumination flares went up, and the men in the tracks on the perimeter saw an amazing sight. The fire zone in front of them, as far back as they could see, was thick with men dressed in loincloths, holding weapons, crawling across the ground like enormous bugs, advancing steadily like a wave. Every few seconds, a mine would go off and the naked bodies would be blown skyward; blood tinted the smoke, turning it pinkish-red, but the explosions did not slow down the men coming toward them. No matter how many of them were blown up or shot down, more replaced them, and now that the white light lit the night sky, some of them were running toward the perimeter, and where the first flare had gone off, some of them had gotten through, reached one of the bunkers, thrown in a grenade, and they were inside.

The base was roiling in smoke. Everyone was running to the bunkers and firing and a thick wall of smoke punctuated by muzzle flashes grew up around the thorn-edged perimeter. The men in the bunkers threw ammunition to one another and kept firing. They seemed to be firing into a solid wall, and no matter how many they brought down, there were more. They fired automatically, sweeping from right to left. The Colonel was putting together a counterattacking force of cooks and bakers, sending them out to recapture the bunker taken by the sappers. Everyone was running in the dense fog, trying to see before they shot. The searchlights on the base went on and dark figures emerged silhouetted against white and silver fogs. The cooks and the bakers were after them, firing. One man who was shot staggered backwards and was impaled on a cook's carving knife.

When they recaptured the bunker and secured the perimeter, they began firing into the wave of men still coming, some of them with tourniqueted arms and legs, so that, if they were shot, they could keep on going. The loss of blood wouldn't stop them. Some of them came on through a hail of bullets, shot so many times it seemed the light should have shone through them to the men behind, with glazed wide eyes and blank faces, and the men in the bunkers thought they must be on something. No one could keep on coming in the face of so much firepower. Dead men could do it. Men who were already dead could keep coming like that. Grenades exploded. LAWs went off. Bodies flew apart, flew up, and rained back down. A soldier started screaming uncontrollably and when the medic reached him, he was trying to pull a human bone from his shoulder. It was sticking out of his flesh, a deep wound made by another man's bone.

The men firing from the points of the triangular bunkers were splattered with the blood of the men trying to come over the top at them. The enemy came at the tracks as if they could take them with their bare hands and the tracks gunned them down, but still they came on, trying to throw grenades through the cupolas into the tracks. "Stop firing! Stop firing! Fire in bursts!" Pete shouted at Wapniak, who had the butterfly depressed, and as he watched, the muzzle of the .50 caliber began drooping, melted, and stopped firing. And the fog was still thick and swirling.

It took some time before they realized there were fewer and fewer people to fire at, and finally, there were none at all. The men began sitting back against the bunker wall, checking themselves and each other. There were their arms. There were their legs. Was the blood on the uniforms their own blood or someone else's? Shirts were yanked up, pants were pulled down, while everyone checked his chest and belly, and then everyone began checking one another. Ponchos became litters carried by four men, and the wounded were carried off.

"Medic! Medic!" came cries from all over the base. The dead bodies of the sappers who had entered the perimeter were picked up, carried, and then thrown out into the free fire zone. One of them landed on a live mine, and the explosion lit the foggy sky and the blood once again tinted the fog.

"Leave him alone! He's already dead!" a man was shouting from another bunker. "How many times do you want to kill him?" The answer was the high-pitched sound of laughter. No one went over to that bunker to investigate. They knew what was going on there. All of them had enough to handle, coming down from the high, coming back into their own skins, when a few minutes before, they had been enormous, limitless, like the fog itself, like God, omnipotent and omnipresent. Now they shrank. The fire base, the size of a football field, shrank to the size of a lozenge. They waited for the fire base to expand, for themselves once again to take up a space that mattered. Their eyes strained through the fog. They wanted to see the men they'd killed, but the illumination flares were no longer going up, and the fog was thickening. They would have to wait until morning.

In the morning, the fog lifted and they saw how close to destruction they had come. If it hadn't been for the LP, the sappers would have been in. They would have died in their sleep, their throats cut, never knowing what happened to them. Then they began to hear rumors of bases that had been overrun, some of them not more than three or four klicks from theirs. The count from the night before was circulating rapidly: nineteen wounded and none killed. They could not believe their luck.

The ground they looked over was thick with bodies, one twisted over another. Men lay on their backs, staring up at the sky, a leg resting in the crook of their arm. Others lay facedown against the swelling bodies of the men beneath them, moving when the gas in the stomachs of the dead men expanded or shifted, and the dead belched, farted, their stomachs moved, swelled, and sank back, the smell was terrible, and Pete saw one dead arm move. It moved slightly in its stiff sleeve, and he stared at it, unable to take his eyes from it. A huge black bug crawled from beneath the sleeve and out, down the man's middle finger. Everywhere flies were swarming over the bodies, settling first on their eyes and in their open mouths, then flying in wild circles, beginning to buzz around the base. Insect repellent was useless against them.

As the day wore on, the smell became worsened. Faces greyed, losing color, and swelled. Stomachs ballooned. Bodies began moving, loudly belching gas. Rats were coming in from the woods and feasting until their own bellies were swollen. Some of the men couldn't stand to watch, and began shooting the rats, and more rats came in and gnawed at the bodies of the dead rats, and the smell of blood and human excrement mixed with mud and decay. Men began throwing up and that added to the stench.

The Colonel got on the radio, asking for a bulldozer. A helicopter was bringing it in. When it came, it brought sacks of lime and some of the men went out, stepping on the dead and over them, sometimes slipping in their blood, scattering the lime, but no one had the stomach for the job. The men would stay out for five minutes and then begin retching and would turn back, and the next men would take their place.

Now they saw what people could do to one another. There were at least six hundred dead bodies lying on the field, almost none of them whole. It was a warehouse of body parts, and they saw what the inside of the head looked like, the stomach, the arm, and the leg. No one who saw it would ever see flesh as permanent again. Pete had already concluded that the most ridiculous phrase in the language was thick-skinned.

The bulldozer dug a huge trench, a deep red scar in the earth, and pushed the bodies in and they saw them fall over the edge and vanish, and then they were sent out to police the battlefield. They found fingers and toes, parts of scalps. Sal saw something odd on the ground, bent over to look at it, and saw with horror that he was looking at a man's penis. Embarrassed, as if it were his fault, he kicked some loose dirt over it, burying it, and in his hurry to get away before someone saw what he'd seen, he tripped over half of a rib cage, exactly half of a rib cage, the ribs neatly exposed as if by a surgeon. Even as the men fanned out over the blood-laced mud, they knew no human being ought to see such things. They looked at the ground and avoided looking at one another. The few who thought to look up at the mountains were horrified. The sun shone and the mountains shimmered. The universe had its own concerns. What had happened here was of no interest. Nature had no opinions.

Even after the bodies went under, the smell was impossible. They couldn't wait to get back out in the field, away from this. If they went far enough, they would forget it.

"No one forgets," Sal said.

"Sure you forget," Pete said. Wapniak said nothing.

"There's only one way to cool off in this damn country," Sal said, and Wapniak looked at him, questioning. "You fucking die. That's how you fucking cool off."

"The believers are real cool," said one of the others.

"Believers?" repeated Wapniak.

"Yeah, believers. The dead men. They're believers."

"In what?" asked Wapniak. "In what does anyone here believe?"

"In coolness," said Sal. "In coolness and fucking flies."

DAYS WENT BY, turned into weeks, and weeks turned into months, and the men knew this by marking off the days on their short-timer's calendar. The current favorite was a dancing Snoopy whose body was divided into three hundred and sixty-five amoeba shapes, all numbered, and some of the men had asked for and been sent Crayola boxes by their family members and were slowly coloring in a Snoopy who, after a while, looked as if he were wearing odd-colored cammies.

The troop was split up into platoons and sent out on patrols. They covered an area of eighty square miles. They escorted truck convoys. They searched and destroyed. More and more, they used their own judgment. If they found a few weapons, or many weapons, and were told to pull back, half a dozen of them flipped matchbooks with lit cigarettes inside them up onto the thatched roofs and five or six minutes after they left, hut after hut went up in smoke. "We didn't do it. We don't know nothing. We weren't there."

Command heard it over and over, but there was nothing they could do. The men believed they were right and who was to say they weren't? No one who had seen the dead bodies ringing the fire base believed the population was friendly. Men riding shotgun or going into villages were picked off by snipers. Women walked up to them, smiling, holding out their hands, and the children on their backs threw grenades. After that, the men who fired on those women and children were good for nothing. One had been medevaced out in a straitjacket.

Time ticked on, and the short-timers began going by the rules. Pete insisted that Wapniak take the skulls off the track. They made too good a target in the dark. Men who had never worn flak jackets wore them now, whereas before they had sat on them. The men in the company began wearing their pistols over their groins, telling one another the guns were another layer of protection. They drank less beer and some of them began to take the amphetamines the medics handed out at the gate. Pete began to worry about the new Lieutenant, who was, if possible, even more prejudiced against New Yorkers than the first one had been.

When Pete was sent out on ambush, he talked back to the Lieutenant. Whenever he had a chance, he began saluting him in the field, as he had done with the first Lieutenant. He began saying that the war was no good. They were out here like sitting ducks. The army was experimenting on them. They wanted them to try out weapons, to find out what was wrong with the M-16 so they could fix it for their next war. They wanted them to find out how to fight a guerrilla war because they hadn't fought one since the Revolution and they'd forgotten.

"You're becoming a radical," Wapniak said.

"And don't tell me all this means something," Pete said. "The whole damn thing doesn't mean anything. It doesn't add up to one life lost out here."

"Fucking right," said Sal.

"It means something," Wapniak said. "It may take years to find out what it is, but it means something."

"Sure," Sal said. "It means Li was right. Remember? She used to say, 'Don't bring meat to the tiger's mouth': We're the meat. They brought us to the tiger." But Li was off limits and their eyes skittered from one another's faces and the three of them fell silent.

"He's not going to let me leave the field," Pete said. "When my time's up, he's not going to let me out. He's going to keep me here until I get killed."

"Don't go paranoid on me, man," Sal said.

"I'm short now," Pete said.

"He'll let you out," Wapniak said.

"They kept Paganini's radio operator here. They said his MOS was critical."

"A mechanic doesn't have a critical MOS," Sal said.

"Some people think they do," Wapniak said. "You don't even work as a mechanic."

"He could use it," Pete said. "As an excuse."

"He'll let you out," Sal said again. "By the time I'm back from R and R, they'll be processing you out."

"No, they won't," said Pete.

"Maybe the rear echelon fuckers ate so much last week they're still sleeping on your papers," Sal said.

"You can't argue with him," Wapniak said.

"R and R?" Pete asked. "You've got R and R?"

"Don't worry about it. I'll be back," Sal said. "Meantime, if you're real lucky, you'll pull guard duty with Wapniak. Then all you've got to worry about is when Motor Mouth's going to forget where you are and start talking."

Pete didn't answer him. He thought: I've seen hundreds of people die. I've seen millions of people die. People are busy. Mice are busy, too. People worry about their children. Monkeys worry about their children. What's so special about a human? Why did God make a heaven for humans? Why bother? They're just animals. When they blow up, their guts are like the guts of any animal. When they bleed, they die. Mice don't chew holes and say it's for God and country.

Seeing things the way he did now, how was he ever going to take anything seriously again?

"Lighten up," said Sal, who left on R and R and was back before they turned around, and Pete said, "You're back," and Sal said, "Yeah, I'm going out on ambush with you tonight."

The talk around the base wasn't good. Forces were massing on the border, and they knew how close to the border they were. "Last time I was on an ambush?" Pete said. "I was on watch and I fell asleep and someone shook me and told me to wake up. There was trouble in the field, and I woke up and the other three guys were dead to the world, and there was this, this White Man fading into the tree line."

"You didn't fall asleep and you didn't see nothing," Sal said, and Pete asked if he'd seen him, too, and Sal said, "Sure, I've seen him. I just keep it quiet. Once, I was sleeping in the track and he looked in through the cupola and said, 'Read maps. Learn to read maps.' "

"Oh, man, you were dreaming."

"And you weren't?"

"I never fell asleep on watch. You never heard me say that," Pete said.

"I never heard nothing," Sal said.

They waited for him to tell them about the girls in Bangkok, the massage parlors, but he didn't say anything, and because he was quiet, because he had a new, closed look, they assumed he'd done well with the ladies, and he didn't tell them he'd taken a room in a fancy hotel with its own pier on the river and its own boats and spent his first few days going up and down the canals in long-tailed boats, looking at the women bathing their children in the muddy brown water, washing their clothes by hand in the river, going by canoe or motorboat or public ferry to stores farther down the canals, watching the men brush their teeth in the water, the banana trees blooming on the side of the canals, the flame trees blazing orange under the blue sky, and old teak buildings on stilts collapsing into the water, and no one repaired them. The families left them to the river and moved on to another nest, and then he took a trip up north and saw the rice paddies, the children riding the omnipresent water buffaloes.

The farmers and the faces of the people were different. The people here were a little taller, but he was seeing Vietnam as it would be if there were no war, if he weren't there, and the peace of the country was painful, the beauty of it was painful, and he came back to Bangkok, went to the floating market, saw vegetables and fruits he never knew existed and didn't dare to eat. One of them was red and covered with bright green tentacles, and it was too much to bear. He slept and walked and spent his last night drunk in a massage parlor. This was like the city in Vietnam. It was all he could take.

"R and R?" he said to Pete. "It's great, but it ain't home. What the hell? You just gotta come back."

"I wouldn't turn it down," Wapniak said. "I wouldn't throw it out of bed."

"Wapniak, Sal, Bravado, ambush," said the Lieutenant. Pete started shouting this was the *fourth* time in ten days. He was keeping track.

"Yeah, and what do you want to do about it?" asked the Lieutenant.

"How far out?" Sal asked.

"Eight klicks," said the Lieutenant.

"Eight klicks! You're joking," Wapniak said.

"These goddamn map soldiers!" Pete said. "They sit around looking at their maps and someone says, 'Look at this. This is a good place. Let's send them there.'"

"They know what they're doing," said the Lieutenant.

"Yeah, sure," Pete said. "Fucking map soldiers!"

"And go *all* the way out," said the LT. "The last four-man patrol thought it was too far to go and set up near the base. They called in a position, but it wasn't their position, and they got hit by harassment fire. The artillery thought they were six klicks away. They were *supposed* to be six klicks away. There's nothing left of them but the fucking dog tags. They're going back empty caskets, man."

"We're going all the way out?" Pete asked Sal, and Wapniak said no, they were going *farther* out: 3-6 had an arrangement in one of the villages and all they had to do was get there and they'd find 3-6 parked inside the hooch and they'd have the whole second floor. No problem. They'd radio in their positions from there.

"You're not worried about harassment fire?" Pete asked, and Wapniak asked, "How stupid do you think we are? We're *out of range* of artillery fire," and they spent the night inside the house, playing cards, listening to the beetles and rats moving in the thatched roof, and every two hours, calling in their positions.

"Have a good time last night?" the Lieutenant asked them, and Sal said, "Sure, it was a picnic, a piece of cake. Isn't that why you sent us?" The Lieutenant had his suspicions. He had his suspicions about the whole platoon. He'd never seen morale so low.

"Good, you liked it so much you can go out on ambush tonight," he said. "All the way to the border. A chopper's taking you in."

"Hell, we don't have to do that!" Sal shouted. "That's the infantry! The *infantry's* supposed to be CA'd in. We're supposed to *ride!*"

"You're going," said the Lieutenant. "And you're taking Filipini with you."

Filipini was the cook. Pete asked how Filipini got so lucky and Sal looked at him and said, "You have to ask? He's from the Bronx. That's what he did."

They found themselves on the side of a hill, and they dug in, and set out their traps. By now, each of them had his own routine. Wapniak dug a little trench around the ground he slept on, convinced insects and snakes were less likely to crawl across it and get to him. He placed an open bottle of insect repellent near his head, believing the odor from the bottle kept the bugs away, whereas if he put it on his body, the enemy could smell him for days.

Sal used his Vicks inhaler and under his eyes smeared drops of green fluid laced with opium, convinced the opium sharpened his vision, although all the others could see was that it turned his eyes red and made them stream with tears.

Pete took the devil's ears, the green peppers, out of his ruck and said he'd do the cooking, and they went a hundred yards from their camping place, pretended to set up there, asking one another, "What do you think? You think anything's going down here?" and Sal said, "They sent us out in a fucking *helicopter,*" and Wapniak asked, "What difference does it make?

If Charley's starting something, he doesn't send out engraved invitations," and Sal said, "Yeah, but we've got to RSVP anyway," and as soon as it was dark, they went back to the first place. Anything to confuse the enemy. They were in no hurry to begin a night of absolute silence.

"Who goes first?" Wapniak asked, taking out the watch, and Sal said he was wide awake, and so the night began.

At five o'clock, someone shook Pete awake. He reached blindly for his watch, shook his head, and looked around him. He saw a familiar white shape disappearing into the trees and he broke through the thin surface of sleep. He paid no attention to it. Then he looked toward the mountain and shook his head once more.

Torch after torch was winding down from the top of the mountain, and he began counting, and the longer he counted, the more torches began coming over the hill, flaring out just behind the ridge, then weaving their way down the mountain. It was a procession. He woke up the others and they began counting, and Sal whispered, "Nine hundred! At least nine hundred!" and Wapniak got on the radio and tried to call in artillery, and the report came back: Sorry, we can't raise the air force and you're out of range. Stay there until morning. Then go out and reconnoiter. Over.

"How the hell do you like that?" Wapniak asked. "They're not even afraid of us. They know we're out here watching and they don't even bother to hide! They're taunting us!"

"Maybe it's only four hundred and fifty," Pete said. "Maybe each man carries two torches."

"And elephants fly," said Sal.

In the morning, they went out and Wapniak got on the radio and said they had trails here God hadn't seen. It made the Indiana Freeway look like a one-way street. There were on ramps, off ramps, cloverleafs. They called in the information and the order came back: Stay there. A chopper was coming in for them, and Wapniak asked, "How? There's no LZ here."

"Hey," Filipini said. "I'm going to look around." He was a short man, heavily muscled, his nose flat as if he'd spent a lifetime in a boxing ring, and his hair grew from his head in black corkscrews.

"Be careful," Wapniak said.

"I don't hear the helicopter," Sal said a few minutes later.

"No," said Wapniak.

"I hear something," Pete said. "Hear it? The popcorn?"

"Everyone down," Wapniak said. "Where's Filipini?"

In back of them came the sound of rustling grass, and Filipini, like an enormous, speedy baby, crawled in toward them on his hands and knees. "That's gunfire," he said.

"Yeah, man, it's O.K. We've got the claymores out," Pete said, and then they heard the sound of rockets.

"Aw, shit, RPGs!" Sal shouted.

Filipini sat up on his knees and shouted, "Are they crazy? There are human beings here!"

"Knock him down," Pete said, but he didn't have to tell Sal, who threw himself on Filipini's back, and the two of them fell against the earth while Wapniak set off the claymores and around them the noise became deafening, the smoke sealed them off from one another, they fired straight ahead and prayed the nine hundred men they'd seen the night before were miles away. In the smoke, Pete thought he saw something, a man, maybe it was a man, drawing back his arm as if to throw a grenade, and he fired a clip at him, and the man, if it was a man, vanished.

When the smoke cleared, when everything was again quiet, he and Filipini crept over to where he thought he saw the man go down. "We find him, I'm bringing this one back," Pete said. "I'm taking him back on the chopper and I'm sitting there while they pull off his fingernails."

"Hey, come on," Filipini said.

"Every single nail. If they miss one, I'll take over myself."

The dead soldier had his back to them. "Damn it, he's dead!" Pete said. "I'm taking him back. This one's mine." He started to pick the man up, lifting him by the shoulders, and was surprised at how light the dead man was, when he heard Filipini shouting in front of him. "No, I'm taking him back," Pete said, still pulling, starting to drag him back toward the listening post, when Filipini flung himself on Pete, babbling incoherently, and Pete stopped to look at him, and Filipini was pointing at the dead man, babbling, and when Pete finally dropped the dead soldier, letting his head bang against the ground, and took a few steps forward, he saw the body had been cut in half. He was dragging half a body back toward the base.

"Oh, shit," Pete said. He backed away from the body, slowly, taking small steps, then turned and ran. Filipini ran after him.

"You get him?" Sal asked.

"Later, Sal," Pete said.

Sal looked at Filipini. "Why's he looking like that?" he asked Pete.

"We found the gook," Pete said. "The top half."

"Oh," said Sal.

"Yeah," said Wapniak.

Then the chopper was overhead and they were lifted out by the jungle penetrator.

"YOU SEE!" Pete said when they got back to the base. "He wants to kill us!"

"No seat belts! One thousand feet up in the air and no seat belts!" said Wapniak.

"He hates us and he wants to kill us. He's not going to let me out of the field."

"Again?" said Wapniak. "Again?"

"I've got my calendar. I know how many days I have left. I've got thirteen more days and then I'm going."

"Sure," said Sal.

"How many days?" asked Wapniak. "Thirteen?"

"Today's almost over," Pete said.

"Out here," said Wapniak, "there's no such thing as *almost over.*"

"Thirteen days," Pete said again. "*How* could you extend?" he asked Sal. "You're almost out of here. You *were* out of here."

"Just one more month," said Sal, who thought if he knew seven months ago what he knew now, he'd be out of here too.

"Are you crazy? There are human beings here!" Wapniak said, imitating Filipini, and they started to laugh. Filipini turned red and glared at them. Maybe when they'd first come in country, they'd been that naive. Maybe, but they didn't think so.

"Hey, what do you want from me?" Filipini asked. "I'm only the cook!"

THE NEXT morning the mail arrived, and the Lieutenant went around handing out a stack of Christmas cards made and signed by girl scouts in Nebraska. Then came the letters and the packages. Sal saw his and said, "It's from my father." Whatever his mother wrapped arrived half-unraveled, but his father took his packages to work and someone there wrapped them for him. It took a machete to get them open.

"What the hell is this?" he said, and when the others came and looked, they saw row after row, blue plastic baby bottle after blue plastic baby bottle.

"Baby bottles," Wapniak said, disappointed.

"They are. They're baby bottles," Pete said, picking them up, looking at them as if at relics of a lost civilization. Look how the ounces were marked on the bottles. Look how the numbers were raised: 1 oz., 2 oz. He saw his mother standing over the stove stirring glass baby bottles in the huge pot she now used for cooking lobsters, the steam coming up and erasing her face. How old could he have been? Two?

"There's gotta be a reason," Sal was saying as he unscrewed the cap of the first bottle. "Whoa! This ain't no milk!" He tipped the baby bottle and drank a third of its contents, and Pete was saying, "What is it, Sal? What is it?" and Sal handed him a bottle. It was one-hundred-proof Smirnoff vodka.

By now Sal had found the note and read it and the card was addressed "To My Little Boy."

"Sixteen bottles!" Pete said. "Holy shit!" And Sal said, "Let's do *serious* drinking," and they started in, but a package arrived for Pete, huge and clumsy, addressed in his mother's awkward, childlike printed letters, and when he opened it, he sat down on the floor of the tent and said, "Close the bottles. I've got some *heavy* cooking," and food was always a priority, so they closed the bottles, set them back in the box, and looked into Pete's carton: spaghetti and sweet sausage, and hot sausage, and a big plastic jar of tomato sauce, Italian bread with garlic butter, round licorice-flavored cookies coated with white powder, and a bottle of Sambuca. "And today they're flying in turkey with dressing," Wapniak said.

"They can keep their turkey," Pete said. "I don't need it," and he had his C-4 stove going and looked up from the floor and said, "What's the matter with you guys? There's enough for all of us," and they all hunkered down around the little stove, and Sal thought it would go faster if he lit his, and Wapniak thought it would go even faster if he lit his, and they were so busy they didn't hear the cries of, "He's here!" "Who?" "The White Man!" "Where?" "Here!" or the Lieutenant threatening the men, saying, "I told you, the next one who started that was going before the Colonel! It's Article Fifteen time, guys," and then the Lieutenant calmed down and said, "Think about it. Who could get in and out of here? The place is mined. The wire's *sagging* with frags. How's he going to get in? A goddamn fly can't get in without a password," and the others mumbled and shook their heads. There must be a way. They knew what they saw.

When they finished the spaghetti, saving some for later—there was so much of it they *had* to save some for later—their faces were smeared with tomato sauce, shiny with its olive oil and the oil from the sausages, and they began on the blue plastic baby bottles, and then they were ripped, four sails to the wind, and they curled up on the floor, around their stoves, and they were on the best R and R there was. There was no such thing as war.

They spent the next two days vomiting and doing the green apple quickstep, but it was worth it. They'd do it again. The only thing they regretted was that they couldn't do it again, and the Lieutenant took one look at them, and for once sent someone else out on LP and then on ambush, but he had his eye on them. Pete knew he had his eye on them, and it was only a matter of days before they were out there in the middle of nowhere, out of insect repellent, even out of meat tenderizer. They'd written for it, but no one remembered to send it. Adhesive tape was holding their clothes together. Their shoulders were rubbed raw by the straps of their rucks, the weight pulling them down until they bent forward to make the carrying easier. Water squished through their boots and came out the sides through the little metal grilles, and Pete said, "I was five foot eight when I started this damn war. I'm going to be five-five when I get out," and Sal said, "Don't complain. A short man's harder to hit," and Pete said, "Yeah, but now I'll never be a cop. You have to be five foot eight to be a cop."

"When I get home," Sal said, "I'm never going to walk again. Even if I go around the corner for a carton of milk, I'm gonna take the car. I'm never gonna get in a car either. It's not safe in a car," and Pete asked him, "So what are you gonna do, fly?" and Sal said, "Yeah, fly. That's what I'm going to do. Fly. I'm going to be a fucking angel."

The column moved on for days and nothing happened. No one fired a shot at them, and the muttering began. It was *too* quiet. Something was going on they didn't know about, and the men sat around when the column stopped because maintenance was working on the head track's treads, and the rumor spread about the nine hundred torches coming down the mountain, and the men stared out at the fields, studied them with binoculars, and someone said, "They're out here somewhere," and someone said, "Why look for trouble?" and the column started up and one of the men said, "It's like a goddamn boy scout trip. When nothing's happening, that's what it's like, only more boring," and then they took fire from a clump of nippa palms, and the tracks were on line, firing, and the air force came in for a strike, and they sat there watching the bombs fall, the beautiful white fireworks alternating with the hellish red flames unrolling their red smokes and everyone said, "Here we go again," and "Isn't this where we came in?" and "Drop the big one. I wish they'd drop the big one. I'm tired of this shit," and in the middle of it, Sal discovered they'd run out of beer. They had had five bottles of Tiger beer and one bottle of Ba Mui Ba, but it was gone.

"The first priority in the armored cavalry," said Sal, "is never run out of cold ones. Give me the radio." He raised Paganini's tank and got Rufus, Paganini's track commander, another New Yorker. "Three-six, this is three-four. What's the problem there, Sal? Over," Rufus said, and Sal said, "Three-six, this is three-four. We have a critical situation here. We just ran out of cold ones. How are you fixed? Over."

"Three-four, this is three-six. We're fixed pretty good. Why don't you come on down and have one? Over."

"Hey, Wapniak," Sal said. "Get up there and give me covering fire."

"Hey, Sal," Wapniak said. "You going to bring me back one?"

"I don't know," Sal said. "But you know something? Lately, you're almost human. I'll think about it." Wapniak said he better think fast, and Sal asked why, and Wapniak said, "Because otherwise I ain't gonna give you no covering fire."

"Three-four, this is three-six. How come you ain't here yet, Sal? Over."

"Three-six, this is three-four. I'm having a problem with my TC. He won't give me covering fire unless I bring him back one. Over."

"Three-four, this is three-six. That's a major problem. I don't know if we have a cold one for your TC. Over."

Wapniak grabbed Sal's helmet and said, "Uh, three-six, this is three-four. You don't have a cold one for me, I'll give you covering fire, but I can't guarantee the direction. Over."

"This is three-six. I roger you, three-four. We'll return a cold one for you. Over."

Wapniak said, "O.K., Sal, go and get it," and Sal, naked from the waist up, naked and with a beer belly, wearing Ho Chi Minh sandals, climbed out of the track, and because the tracks were still receiving fire, tried to run. The tracks were firing from dried-up rice paddies, and he ran through the paddies and their dried-up chunks of mud, running like a duck, his feet turned out, bullets occasionally kicking up the dust around him, 3-6 and 3-4 giving him covering fire, and then he was in 3-6, two tracks away. A half hour went by and still he wasn't back with the cold ones.

"Three-four, this is three-four delta. I'm coming back," Sal said. "Over."

"Three-four delta, this is three-six," said Wapniak. "You got my cold ones, Sal? Hold them up where I can see them. O.K., come on back. You've got your covering fire. Over." Wapniak opened up, Rufus opened up, and Sal was on his way back, bullets still coming in, running with his feet splayed, almost hopping from foot to foot, coming back with two beers in each hand.

"O.K.!" said Wapniak. "All right!"

"You know, you're fucking crazy?" Pete said, and Sal asked him if that meant he didn't want one, and Pete said, "Just give me the beer," and they sat in the track and sipped their beer. It was better than champagne, or their idea of champagne, and when they went into the nippa palms to look for blood trails or bodies, they found them, the leaves streaked with blood, the grass beaten down and covered with blood, but the soldiers were gone. No one fired at them and the only problem they had now was how to quiet the wild beating of their hearts, and their maddening, unfulfillable desire to close their hands around someone's throat, to drive their fingers into someone's eyes, to snap someone's neck, to see them twitch and lie still, dead, not wounded. They saw what looked like tire tracks in the mud, prints from sandals cut from old rubber tires, and they wanted to find those men. If someone was dead, he could never hurt them again.

"Hey, over here!" Filipini called. "I've got one! Over here!"

A dead Viet Cong soldier dressed in the familiar black pajamas lay on his back, one knee pulled up, on arm up in the air, stiff, its palm facing up to the sky, its fingers curled, as if, when the man had been hit, he had been holding something, whatever it was, and his fingers had frozen around it. "I've got something for you," Filipini said, addressing the dead man, pulling a green glass Coke bottle from his pocket. "Here," he said, putting the bottle in the dead man's hand. He looked at the dead soldier holding the Coke bottle and started to laugh. Then the others began laughing. It was the funniest thing they'd ever seen.

"O.K.," Wapniak said. "The natives aren't friendly. That's it, turkeys," and they turned around and began walking back to the tracks, every few feet stopping to turn and look back at the dead soldier grasping his empty

Coke bottle, and each time they turned around, they were overcome by laughter.

At night, they pulled security at a fire base, and when the artillery's eight-inch guns fired, their tracks lifted right off the ground, and red dust thickened the air. They couldn't see through it. They couldn't breathe in it, and they ate the dust and everything in it, and Wapniak said those guns made him feel safe, and Pete had only three days in the field. He was supposed to be back at division headquarters, processing out, and here he was. He had to get out. Look at the side of his face. It was swollen. His feet were white and cracked. They looked like wet marshmallows and what did the LT always tell them? Take care of your feet. Your feet are your most important organ. And he had a fever. What did he have to do to get out of here? Wapniak and Sal looked at him and didn't answer because there was no answer, and Pete slammed the wall with his fist and then yelped with pain, and Wapniak said, "Don't complain when you do it yourself," and Pete yelled, "You sound like my fucking mother!"

THEY CAME in to their own fire base, and choppers were flying in and out. One of the troops had been hit hard in Ambush Alley, and medevacs were coming in, and people were flying in to see the Colonel. Pete packed his things into his ruck, set them on his cot, and went out to the helicopter pad. A chopper was there, revving up. "Where are you going, man?" Pete asked him, and the pilot said, "Near the city."

"I'm going back to base camp. Can you give me a lift?" Pete asked, and the pilot said, "Sure. We need a door gunner."

He went back to the tent and said, "Sal, I'm getting out. I'm leaving."

"What are you talking about?"

"I'm leaving. I should be back in base camp, turning in my equipment, taking a shower and shave, eating three hot meals a day. I should've been there thirty days at least and I ain't doing it yet. They're gonna keep me here and I'm gonna get killed, and I'm not gonna die here, so I gotta go."

"All right, Pete," Sal said. He didn't believe him. He'd heard it so many times before, he didn't even look up. He was cleaning his M-16. Pete looked around the tent for Wapniak, but he wasn't there, and he picked up his ruck and went back to the chopper.

"I'm ready," he said, climbing in.

"You're short?" asked the pilot. "You're the shortest of the short? You're getting out?"

"Yeah," Pete said. "I just want out. That's all I want."

"Hey," said the pilot. "Look down there. It's a hot LZ down there."

To their right, helicopter after helicopter landed a battalion of ARVNs. They sat on the skids and jumped out into the slime of the rice paddies and crossed them slowly, holding their rifles out before them, or above their heads, advancing on a company of Viet Cong hidden in the tree line. Rifle fire began to light up the night and men began to fall into the paddy while the others moved closer and closer to the tree line. Then the chopper flew off.

"Who won that one?" Pete asked wearily.

The pilot looked over at him. "They're already flying out the dead and wounded," said the pilot. "The first of the wounded are landing now. They fight two hours but they're back in ten minutes. As if it never happened."

The helicopter veered right. Below them, a loach was marking a target with white phosphorus, and, as they watched, the jets came in and began their bomb run, releasing their bombs one at a time, and then, ten at a time, the helicopters came in, the grunts sitting with their legs on the runners, the noses of the choppers tilted downwards, their little tails in the air, like so many fish feeding on the bottom of an aquarium. They landed, or hovered, right over the fields, inserting eight men at a time until an entire battalion had landed, and then they rose in the air, veered left, and headed back to base. "Aren't they fucking outrageous beautiful?" asked the pilot. "The largest, the most deadly mosquitoes in the world. You know there's a tribe that worships God in the form of an eye. You ever hear anything like that?"

"This is some war," Pete said.

"Pave the entire country. Kill everyone over five years old. Hell, kill everyone over *two* years old. At five, a kid's a person. He thinks."

Beneath them, the white phosphorus flares lit the air and artillery flares bloomed like so many fiery flowers. "It's never quiet. It's never just dark," said the pilot.

Pete's tooth throbbed—it had been throbbing for days, but he paid no attention to it, any more than he paid attention to his throat when it was sore, or his forehead when he felt feverish, and he was forgetting everything, his name, his rank, his serial number, what he was supposed to be doing: *going home.* What did that mean?

"Why fly so low, man?" Pete asked. "It's safer higher up."

"Yeah, but higher up, the lower the air pressure, and the bodies start burping and farting and I can't stand the smell," the pilot said. "You had enough sightseeing? We're almost back," and all the way in, the crew was goofing on him. "We're going down for a firefight," the pilot said over the radio, and Pete screamed back, "No, no, I've got to get out of here! Just pull out!"

The chopper flew on. He saw its shadow black against the dark green foliage, the round, fluttering circle that was the shadow of the chopper blades, and a call came in. They needed a medevac on the ground, and they went down, and he was on the M-60. Two grunts carried on a man wounded in the leg and arm, and they were in the air, and the pilot started in on him again. "I see muzzle flashes on the ground. We're going in."

From the air base, he hitched a ride with a truck to the city. They drove through thickening traffic, and when the truck slowed down, Pete saw a child stroking a GI's arm, apparently asking for money, and then the child suddenly grabbed the GI's watch and began running. The soldier pulled out his gun, locked and loaded, and began chasing the child down the street. The child suddenly veered into an alley and the soldier stopped, looked around him, and saw he was surrounded by natives. To find the child he would have to go into that alley. But if he did he wouldn't come back again. "He was going to shoot him," Pete said aloud, and the driver said, "Yeah, it happens all the time."

They drove down the streets, past the houses with their red-tiled roofs and their gardens of banana trees and palms. In front of them, the road was blocked, and the driver turned into a narrow lane and Pete looked nervously at the brown wooden houses, their rusted, sheet-metal roofs, the chickens running under the house, the pigs poking their heads out of windows, geese honking, ducks following their mother, dogs, all with their ribs visible, barking at cats whose backs were up, brown faces staring at them in the truck through narrowed eyes. Inside the truck, the heat was gaining strength, pressing down on their chests.

He had to get out or the heat would kill him before the people would, and Pete had his hand on the door handle, when the driver saw what he was doing, and said, "Cool it, man. We're almost there." The truck was making its way out of the city, toward the base on the other side, down the wide, palm-lined avenues, past the large houses with their porches and red-tiled roofs, and then the city suddenly stopped and gave way to the country, its endless rice paddies stretching into the distance, dotted with little black figures bending over the water with bundles of rice, water buffaloes grey with mud, groups of people dressed in black, dipping triangular fishnets into the water between the rows of rice, and trucks went by carrying entire families and their animals, crates of live chickens tied to the roof.

He knew all this better than he knew the street on which he had lived for seventeen years. The red dust of the road looked like rouge. He remembered that color from his grandmother's pocketbook. She'd had a tiny, round compact filled with rouge exactly that color. What had she called it? Carmine. Red dust rose and swirled round them, and when it cleared, he saw the brilliant green palms and the chartreuse banana trees heavy with thick bunches of green bananas, and behind them, the air base.

"You know what?" Pete said. "I never want to fucking see any of this again. Never. I've had it, man."

"Right on," said the driver.

. . .

• • •

A T T H E air base, he reported to the medic, who took one look at Pete's jaw and sent him to the company dentist. "Do I have to go back?" he asked the medic, and the medic said, "Hell, no, you're not going anywhere. You've got a hundred and three and your tooth's abscessed and I don't like the look of that arm. That looks infected, too. I might have to lance it. You've got an enlarged liver. I'm going to run some tests on you. You're out of the field. You've got two more days? Three? Hell, I don't want *anyone* in the field."

"Three days left," Pete said. "Three days."

"You're spending them here," the medic said. "Go find the dentist."

He asked someone for directions, was pointed to a building on the right, and walked over. "That big building," the man said. Pete was in a daze and the man's words came to him as if he were underwater. He must mean this hangar, Pete thought. He opened the huge, sliding door. Inside the dome-shaped hangar, he saw row after row of shiny aluminum containers rising to the ceiling. They were long and lozenge-shaped, and men with gurneys were going by, carrying two or three aluminum containers at a time to the end of the aisles, where a machine like a forklift carried them through the air and slid them into place on the top of the pile. Even while he was asking himself what this huge place was, an airplane hangar big enough for ten planes, he recognized it. He knew what was in those shiny silver boxes, and he began backing out, and then he stopped himself from running, and when he got outside, he leaned against the wall of the building, trying to breathe.

"Something wrong, soldier?" someone asked. He looked up and saw a full bird Colonel, his wings painted black (no one in country wanted to stand out in the field), and he said he was looking for the dentist. The Colonel took him by the arm and steered him around the corner and he let himself be led. They stopped in front of a large cinder-block building painted olive drab. He didn't know when he'd seen anything with walls that thick. You could survive an atom bomb attack in there. He went in and asked for the dentist.

"It's abscessed," the dentist said, and the nurse bent over him with a needle. The dentist put his hand on her arm and asked Pete if he was allergic to penicillin, and he said he didn't know. He'd never had it before. "We better try it," the dentist said, and the nurse gave him a shot. He didn't know what it was that made him lose his balance, the sight of the nurse, the familiar feel of a dentist's chair dropped down from another world, thinking, *I never had a chance to say good-bye,* but when he came to, the nurse was applying a cold compress to his cheek and the dentist was victoriously holding up a bloody tooth. "You're going to be fine," he said. "Chew on the other side."

"Are you hungry?" the nurse asked, and the sound of a woman's voice asking that made him shake. His throat tightened and he couldn't answer.

"Take him over," said the dentist. "He's not too steady."

"I saw it," Pete said.

"Yeah? What?" asked the dentist.

"I was in a chopper and I saw all of it. I know what it means."

"Sure," the dentist said. "What does it mean?"

"Chaos," Pete said. "Is that a word?"

"That's a word," said the nurse.

"Yeah, and it's beautiful," Pete said. "If it wasn't made of men dying, it would be beautiful."

"You better go back with him," the medic told the nurse. "He's not too steady."

"It's the same as a sparkler. You push the handle and the wheel turns and sparks come out. I love those sparklers. But it could be horrible. If the sparks were living things. If they were, I couldn't do it. I couldn't push the handle. But some people could. Some people *know*. They do it anyway. But it's beautiful."

"Yeah, gorgeous," said the dentist.

"And the pilot who flew me back was the White Man," Pete said. "Even if he didn't look like him."

"I don't think he's out from under," the dentist said. "Look, sit here and she'll take you back in a half hour."

Pete nodded, Yeah, sure, that was fine with him, sat down on a chair on the side of the room, closed his eyes, and saw the lights twinkling on the coast line. It was so beautiful. By the time the nurse came for him, he was wide awake.

"You still know what it means?" asked the nurse.

"What are you talking about?" he asked her.

"I thought so," she said. "It was the gas talking."

IN THE mess hall, they gave him a clean stainless steel tray and shining silverware. He got on line. Every time the man behind the counter put something on his plate, mashed potatoes, roast beef, carrots, he said, More. Put on more. He took the tray and looked at the food heaped six inches high on his plate. He sat alone and looked right and left and wrapped his arms around the tray as if someone were going to take it from him. Finally, he picked up a fork, swallowed one mouthful of mashed potatoes, then another, took one bite of roast beef, and started to cry. He couldn't eat it. His stomach had shrunk. His jaw throbbed where his tooth had been pulled, and he looked at the tray and knew he'd have to bring it to the trash can and empty it out, and that hurt, because what he wanted to do was take the food and bring it back out there, to Sal and to Wapniak and to Paganini, who would kill for real food, for a hot meal. He scraped the mashed potatoes from his plate and watched them fall, and the roast beef followed, and he'd never felt so guilty. He felt guilty because he had the food and guilty because he couldn't eat it and Sal and Wapniak and Paganini were still there while he was out of it. He thought of the silver cylinders and felt guilty for being alive.

But when he got to the showers and felt the water on his body and saw the streams of dirt running from him and swirling around the floor toward the drain and then disappearing, he began to believe he was alive, part of this world of knives and forks and mashed potatoes. Sal and Wapniak, Paganini and the LT, moved away from him, grew smaller, moving like tiny figures in a scale model of the war. He went into the barracks, was given a cot, and fell asleep. Later, the nurse woke him and gave him another shot, and still later, the medic came by and lanced his arm where the stitches had been, but although he sat up and asked questions, he wasn't awake, and as soon as they left, he was sound asleep.

In the morning, he woke up and found his Lieutenant bending over him. His face wasn't friendly. As soon as Pete saw him, he was wide awake. The Lieutenant was grinning at him and reading him Article 15.

"Article Fifteen? What for?" Pete asked him.

"For running from the field in the face of the enemy," said the Lieutenant. "It's court-martial time."

"Oh, yeah? Well, the medic signed my papers. What are you gonna do about that?" Pete asked. The Lieutenant's face fell. The medic's word was final.

"We'll see about that," said the Lieutenant.

"You flew all the way in here to court-martial my ass?" Pete asked. "Where are my papers? I should have been here a long time ago."

"Here are your papers," the Lieutenant said, and he threw a manila envelope onto the bed. "I just got them from the Captain."

"You had them all the time."

"*Now* you can turn in your equipment," said the Lieutenant. "You know what they think back there? They think you ran."

"No, they don't, man. They know I did what I had to do. My time was up. I'm taking care of business and they're going to do it, too."

They kept him at base camp for three days. He turned in his equipment, went to the medic for a final checkup, got his papers, and was told to be ready for an evening flight out. He hitched a ride into the city, bought a bottle of Johnny Walker Black Label, a new Seiko watch, came back and lay on his cot, his mind blank. He tried to summon up something familiar, like Sal's face or Wapniak's face, but he couldn't do it. He drew them on the canvas of the air, but as soon as he thought he had the mouth right and tried to start on the eyes, the whole face would vanish. He tried to picture the track, the red words BIG ANNIE FANNIE painted on its side, the two skulls mounted on either side of the cupola, but he couldn't remember what it looked like.

He felt the sudden suck of mud as his boot sank into a wet rice paddy and he sat up suddenly, wiped his forehead, and stopped trying to remember. The hours went by in silence, in blankness. Now, when he went into the mess hall, he had no trouble eating. He was going to get on a plane and it was going to take him to a home he couldn't picture either. He could remember the sound of the plane as it flew. It sounded like a car going through the Brooklyn Battery Tunnel, but when he tried again to picture his house, it jumped up in front of him like a cardboard house in a book and everyone in it moved around jerkily, like puppets. It was a small house, too small for people. Where had he seen such small houses? His grandmother used to visit such small houses. He'd seen them in graveyards. He didn't believe anyone back there was left alive. They weren't alive for him, but they would be. They would be when he got there. All he thought about now was how tired he was. He couldn't remember a time when he hadn't been tired.

HE WALKED up the gangplank to the civilian jet, the same airline he'd flown out on. He recognized the peach and grey interior and took a seat in the back. Sal used to say that was the safest place. Survivors of plane crashes always came from a plane's tail. It wasn't near the engines, and sometimes when the plane crashed, the tail fell free. Down the runway was a Flying Tiger Airline jet, the letters FTA painted on its side: FTA. Fuck The Army. He fastened his seat belt and cracked open the bottle of Johnny Walker. The stewardess bent over and said, "I'm sorry, but you can't drink that here," and he said, "No problem," and pushed the bottle down among the magazines in the pouch in front of him.

The plane rose steeply and he leaned out, looked out the window and saw the yellow crater holes arid amidst the greenery, brighter yellow halos around their edges. Now they were passing over the green coastline, the beige line of its beaches, and he thought, Take a good look. That's the last you're going to see of Vietnam. He covered himself with a grey airline blanket, put the bottle under it, and began to drink.

He took out his wallet and from it took two cards. One had been issued to him before he left the United States, and on it was printed the day his tour of duty in Vietnam would end. The other card had the *Nine Rules*. The first rule told him to "Remember we are guests here: we make no demands and seek no special treatment." He skipped to Rule Number Five. "Always give the Vietnamese the right of way." *We are guests here.* The helicopters he'd seen last night, noses down, fish feeding on the very air, huge mosquitoes taking big chunks out of the landscape. The land below him was a body and the steel helicopters fed on it.

He looked at his watch and saw they'd been flying for half an hour, and after that, he didn't know anything, didn't notice the stopovers in Hawaii and Alaska, until the stewardess picked up a corner of his blanket to make sure his seat belt was fastened and they were landing at Travis Air Force Base. Three hundred and sixty-five days later, and he was coming home.

THREE
Parades

HE WIND BLEW in from the Atlantic Ocean and swept the smell of salt down the streets of Brooklyn, and ruffled the curtains and the window shades of Mrs. Bravado's bedroom, and she saw the window shade beginning to poke into the ballooning curtains and went over and shut the window, and as she did it, she thought, It's windy on the block today.

As she grew older, her world shrunk down to her street and the block on which she lived, and she found it more and more difficult to imagine the world beyond. When she thought of her son Paul, who was in the home, she thought of him existing at the end of her street, which had, as if in a dream, grown longer and longer until everything she cared for existed on one side or another of it. When she thought of Pete, she grew puzzled, thinking of him as floating somewhere so high above the house she could not see him.

She sat down on the edge of her bed and took out his last letter, which said no, what she read in the papers had nothing to do with him. Where he was, up north, nothing was happening. It was so quiet it was boring. Would she send more packages of cherry Kool-Aid and Tabasco sauce? Everyone said her spaghetti and sausages were the best in the world, even Sal, who ought to know, because he was also Italian. He might be home before she received this letter, but if he wasn't, and if her letters were returned, she shouldn't worry because he was probably back in base camp processing out. "Don't worry. I'm fine." He ended every letter that way.

In the boys' room, she heard the venetian blinds hitting against the windowsill and she thought about the wind and her son flying home across the Pacific Ocean. She imagined the wind pushing the plane faster and faster, and in her imagination, the plane grew larger and larger until she expected to hear it outside the house, landing in the middle of the street. She went into the boys' room and stood there, puzzled. She hadn't thought in this way, seen things as she now saw the plane, since her son left. If she only knew when Pete was coming home, she'd have Paul at home. Whenever he came home, he looked at the framed picture of Pete she kept on the mantel and he studied the uniform his brother wore and said, "I want to be a soldier, too."

But he would never be a soldier. His slowness would keep him with her forever. Every day, she watched the news, looking for her other son, but she never saw him, although when pictures of the wounded flashed on the scene, she sometimes thought she did. Daily, there were tallies of men killed in action, wounded in action, missing in action. How was he supposed to get back? Even if he got on a plane and flew out of the country, the plane could crash in the ocean. Until he was safe in his own bed, she would not know he was safe.

She went into the kitchen and found her husband standing near the stove. "Make me a cup of tea," he said. She sighed and turned on the burner and the little blue flames leaped like blue flowers under the teapot. She liked to look at the flames while something cooked on the stove. Sometimes she imagined the flames as tame blue animals helping her feed her family. Who could she tell such silly thoughts? When Pete was a small boy, she used to tell him these things and he would regard her seriously, inspect the flames, and nod agreement.

The teapot whistled and she got up and poured hot water into her indigo blue teapot with the gold flowers that had once belonged to old Mrs. Bravado. She missed her. As she sat, watching her husband silently drinking his tea, she missed her more, and she looked out the window and through the snow. She saw old Mrs. Bravado looking up at the grapevines hanging from the white-latticed trellises, pointing: here and here and here they need fastening, and then she would place her lawn chair under the vines and close her eyes, sleeping in the sun. She had no fear of the bees and yellow jackets buzzing in the leaves over her head. Her son would see her there, asleep in her housedress, her knees apart, her mouth open and think, She looks like an old dog. When he looked down at the top of her head, he saw her pink scalp beneath her thinning white hair and it made him uncomfortable, how old she had become. Her pink scalp seemed almost indecent. In the sun, it turned red, sunburnt. "Wake her up," he'd tell his wife. "She's got no sense," but his wife said the old lady was used to the sun. She never complained about it. She only complained of the cold.

"I got thin blood," old Mrs. Bravado used to say. "You'll see. When you get old, you get thin blood." In the winter she walked around wearing a flannel undershirt, a blouse, a skirt, thick black stockings, and three sweaters. On very cold days, when the wind blew and shook the windows, she wore her winter coat.

"Dress right!" her son shouted at her. "The neighbors, what are they gonna think? I got no money for heat? Look at the thermostat! A man could die in here!" He walked around in his T-shirt, fanning himself.

"You're telling me how to dress?" his mother shouted back. "You shout at your mother?" and her son would back down, mumble, and go out into the shed and work. "What's he building now?" asked old Mrs. Bravado. "Tell me! What is it now? When he's wrong, he builds. We don't need another bench! Where's he going to put a gazebo? Not near my grapes!" But she had been dead a long time, and the beautiful gazebo, too big for the yard, stood in front of the grape arbor, so that to prune the vines one had to stand on its porch, or climb up on its back railing to pick the grapes when they ripened.

Angelina talked often to her sister-in-law Theresa about old Mrs. Bravado, and occasionally, her husband, hearing them, would say, "You live in the past. The past is such a great place? What's so great about it? Tell me that. She was so wonderful when she was alive?"

But Angelina didn't believe she lived in the past. What was part of her once was part of her now. If anyone had thought to ask her if she believed in the death of people she knew, things she knew, she would have said no: what's alive once is alive forever. You put some things away, like a favorite pair of tan silk gloves, and one day you clean out a drawer and there they are, with all the years and all the memories clinging to them, the way vines cling to a wall. You pick up the gloves and out fall little pieces of your life as it was when you put the gloves in the drawer. The past was like Thanksgivings she remembered from childhood, so full of relatives they had to pull up additional chairs, folding metal chairs, living room chairs, the folding stool from the kitchen, and the future was the same table, but there were fewer and fewer of the old faces at the table, fewer places to set. Still, past, present, or future, it all took place in the same kitchen, the same dining room, the same apartment, the same building on the same street. She looked for a word to describe the blessing and curse of her life but she didn't know it. The word for the way one link of a chink fit into the next link and the next, that was the word she was looking for. The way her husband sat at the table, drinking his tea, saying nothing: the word for that was the word she was looking for.

IT WAS drizzling. Rain beaded the plane windows. The air, when Pete stepped through the plane's doorway onto the metal platform with its metal-studded surface, was cold. At the bottom of the steps, one tiny, thin old lady waved a toy flag and said, again and again, her voice quavering, "Welcome home. Welcome home."

"That's it?" one of the soldiers said. "That's all there is?" and the Sergeant at the gate said they should be grateful it was night. During the day, the protesters would spit at them.

They went through processing, shivering constantly. The California temperature was too cold for them. Three hours later, Pete and two others were on a United Airlines flight heading for Kennedy Airport. "I'm out," one of the men said. "I'm out of this green machine." Pete, who had six months to finish up, had a thirty-day leave and orders to report to a base in Colorado. "It's all parkas there," said the soldier. "Parkas and snow. I reupped over there to get out of this spit-and-shine shit here. Now all I gotta do is go home."

The other soldier asked him where home was, and he said North Carolina, but he was going to New York because everyone should see New York once in a lifetime and he wanted to see if it was really like Saigon. "Is it like Saigon?" he asked Pete, and Pete shook himself and said there were streets in New York he wouldn't go down. "Is it like Saigon?" the soldier asked again, and Pete said, No, in New York the buildings were higher. "Why do you call it New York?" the soldier asked. "New York's the name of the state."

"The city's so nice they named it twice," Pete said. "You never heard that?"

"I'm from Queens," the third soldier said.

"Brooklyn," said Pete.

"Brooklyn, Queens, where are they?" asked the soldier from North Carolina.

"They're boroughs outside the city, like suburbs," said the second soldier. Pete was relieved. Now he didn't have to answer. He leaned back in his seat and pretended to sleep. Sal had three more months and two days. Wapniak had eight more months. He'd see Sal soon. Give him time to get processed, get home, look around him. Then he'd find him.

"You going home?" asked the soldier from North Carolina.

"Yeah," said Pete. "Home." It occurred to him: *he didn't know Sal's last name.* He had to know it. Someone must have said it, the Captain, the Lieutenant, *someone.*

"Hey, what's the matter, man?" asked the soldier from Queens. "You're shaking the plane apart."

"I don't know his last name. Everyone called him Sal. It was on his dog tags. It was on his *mail.* I can't *remember.*" They were saying, *Take it easy. It don't mean nothing. It'll come back. Give it time,* and he looked up at them and said, "I don't know Wapniak's *first* name."

"Oh, man," said the soldier from North Carolina.

"What's his last name?" asked the soldier from Queens. "You can find a man with a last name."

"You'll find him. Won't he find him? You'll find him," said the soldier from North Carolina.

"Yeah," said Pete. "I'll find him."

"*I* don't know his last name," said the soldier from Queens. "I don't know his *first* name. We called him Pokey. Goddamn nicknames! We all had nicknames!"

"Oh, man," said the soldier from North Carolina. "You're going home and you're flipping out over names?"

He was answered by silence. "I don't know their *names,*" the soldier from North Carolina said at last. "I want to find people with *no names. It can't be done.*"

"Forget it," Pete said.

"Forget it? You started it."

"Don't cry, man," said the soldier from Queens. "You cried enough over there."

"People with no names," the soldier from North Carolina said again. "I can't believe I left without their names. I left without getting their last names."

"Sal's Italian," Pete said, thinking out loud.

"That really narrows it down," said the soldier from Queens.

"Drop it!" Pete said, and he stared out the window and the other two stared straight ahead, and when they landed, they had nothing to say until they were on line, waiting for cabs. The soldier from Queens and the soldier from North Carolina got in one cab, but Pete said he'd go alone. He was going the other way. The soldier from North Carolina tried to talk him into coming with them, but the soldier from Queens said, "Let him go, man. This isn't the army anymore," and their cab drove off. Pete got in the next cab, gave his address, and leaned back against the cushions.

They were driving through the salt marshes. Occasionally he saw a cattail outlined against the grey black sky. The salt smell of the air was familiar, and the smell of the garbage dump, that was familiar, too, and the tiny, ink-black skyline of Manhattan, that was also familiar, but these things were familiar as if they had first been glimpsed in a dream.

"Where you coming from?" asked the taxi driver, and he said Vietnam, and the driver said, "Vietnam, what's that? Yeah, I guess I heard about it."

Pete stared out the window, beading with rain turned quicksilver by the oncoming headlights, and tried to remember Sal's last name, Sal's face, or Wapniak's face, or what the tracks looked like in the jungle or at the edge of the rice paddies, and everything he saw was tiny, like scale models, cunningly shrunken, as they said heads could be shrunken. A Captain from his company had been arrested for trying to shrink heads. Now he remembered being told that. While he was there, he heard it and then forgot it. There was too much else going on.

"Turn here," Pete said. "Straight down." They were driving under the elevated tracks. He'd forgotten how colorless everything was here, black steel and cement, although rain made the streets shine, reflecting the red and green streetlights, the headlights, and the neon signs, flickering. "Right and right again," Pete said, and there it was, the house on the corner with its huge yard, but it had grown smaller since he'd left it. It looked like a house on a postage stamp. What happened to it?

"They expect you?" the taxi driver asked.

"No."

"Oh," said the driver.

He opened the white wrought-iron gate to the garden and walked up the steps to the front door. Everything was off-scale. He was ten feet tall and the house was small. The door was small and the roof was low enough to touch. He rang the bell and when the door opened, he saw his father, but his father was tiny. He stared at his father, and his father stared at him, and while he watched, his father grew to his normal size.

"Oh," said his father. "You're home."

In back of his father, a woman was screaming his name over and over. He saw two white puffy hands reach around his father and push him out of the way and a short, stocky woman with white hair was clinging to him and crying, repeating his name, stroking his face, pressing her head into his chest, and his father was saying, "Angelina! Angelina! It's raining! Let him in the house!"

"So you're home," said his father. "For how long?"

"Give your Aunt Theresa a hug!" someone said, coming up in back of him and putting her arms around his waist. "Give me a big hug!"

"Don't sneak up on me, please," he was saying, but his aunt had turned him around, and hugged him, squealing and crying, and his mother stood back, watching him, her hands clasped tightly over her breast, crying, and then someone said, "Let me look at you," and he stood alone, looking at his mother, father, and aunt, and none of them looked familiar. He'd come to the right house and the people in it seemed to know him, but to him they were strangers. Give it time, he told himself. You know them. You know who they are.

"Where's Paul?" he asked.

"Devil! You devil!" his mother cried. "He's in the home! Tomorrow we get him, you and me! Oh, he's been waiting! Every day he asks for you. 'I wanna be a soldier like Pete.' All the time. 'I wanna be a soldier like Pete.'"

"He ain't going nowhere," said his father. "There's plenty of time to get him."

"Tomorrow," Pete said.

"I'll make eggs and spaghetti and sausage and garlic bread, cheesecake, all your favorite things. We'll have a picnic! Oh! Tomorrow!" said his mother, drawing out the last word as if it were the secret name for heaven.

"It's too cold for a picnic," said his father.

"It's not cold," said Angelina.

"You turn up the thermostat to seventy and it's not cold?" said his father.

"I don't want to hear about cold. I don't know what it means, cold. Look how tired he is. Look how black under the eyes. Look how *thin.*"

"Look how big," said his father sourly.

They were in the kitchen and his mother started up a big pot of coffee, and while it percolated, he looked around. "I remember the wallpaper," he said finally.

"Of course you remember it!" Angelina cried. "It's only a year!"

"It's not even dirty," Pete said.

"Every two months we wash it, Theresa and me," Angelina said proudly.

"Every week you ask for new wallpaper," his father said.

The smell of coffee filled the kitchen. "Sit down, sit down," said his mother, pressing him down by the shoulders, and there it was, the fake pink marble tabletop scored by years of knives and forks, and there they were, his family, and he stared at them, trying to make them come alive. They weren't real, not for him, and none of them were covered with mud. He'd never seen such clean people. "It's so clean here," he said aloud, and his mother and aunt exchanged looks, and his father said if anyone wanted him, he'd be out in the shed.

"No more gazebos!" shouted his mother. "No more gazebos."

"Gazebo?" Pete said. "What's a gazebo?"

"You want milk or cream?" asked his aunt.

"Samey same," he said, and both women stared at him. He was talking baby talk! "Oh," he said, seeing their expressions. "Everyone said that. Samey same. Nicey nice. We talked that way."

"Baby talk?" his aunt asked. "In the army?"

"They understood," he said, seeing the medic bathe one baby and then point to another and say, "Samey same," and the woman holding the unwashed child smiled and understood. "Washy wash," said the medic.

"Who?" said his mother. "Tell me who?" and she sat down, ready to listen, but he said, "I'm tired, Ma." His mother jumped up, ran down the hall to his room, switched on the light, began pulling down blankets from the closet's top shelf and then stood in the doorway watching her son put his things away. "I'm going to bed, Ma," he said, turning his back on her, but when he looked again, she looked so small and lost he turned around and hugged her and the pain stabbed him so hard it took his breath away so he let her go and pushed her away. "In the morning, Ma," he said and she said, "In the morning, sure."

SAL AND Wapniak and three new guys were looking at a bridge made of thin branches, so thin the bridge looked like a web built by a giant spider, and Sal was saying, "*Again?* We have to take the bridge *again?* We've taken that goddamn bridge *five* times, and you know what? *It's not worth taking.* It's bamboo poles, sticks, and straw mats. We ought to torch it."

"The Captain says take it, we take it," Wapniak said. "It's a job. We're not paid to think."

"We're not paid enough *not* to think," Sal said, but Wapniak was dismounting, ready to go out with the infantry. "What do you want to do that for, man?" Sal asked. "Someone's always killed taking that damn bridge."

"Not me," said Wapniak, and from the track, Sal watched through binoculars. The Sergeant from 3-3 was on the bridge. He advanced six, maybe ten feet, and fire from the tree line brought him down. Wapniak was on the bridge, and was almost to him when a shot rang out and Wapniak fell. The tanks opened up on the tree line. Sal called in artillery. He did it nervously because, although he knew by now what he was doing, how did he know if the goddamn artillery knew what *they* were doing? And for once the rounds hit right and the tree line was quiet.

"I'm going out there," Sal said, and two of the ARVNs went with him. Wapniak was hit in the leg and Sal carried Wapniak on his back and the two ARVNs carried the Sergeant from 3-3. "I knew it would happen," Wapniak was saying. "I *knew.* To be wounded on a bridge, over water, that means something. It's all about connection, man. It's all connected. It doesn't hurt that much. I thought when you got hit, it hurt more. You think I'm in shock?"

"I think you should shut up," Sal said. "Save your strength."

"You know what Search and Destroy really means?" Wapniak babbled on. "You know what word the initials form? Think about it? S.A.D. Sad. Don't tell me that doesn't mean something."

"It means something. Now shut up," Sal said.

Men from the other tracks came over and the medevac was on its way in. "When I get back," Wapniak was saying as they lifted him on the chopper, "I'll tell you about the symbolism of water and bridges. It's very important how and where you get wounded. It's—"

"Go on," said Sal, and the helicopter carrying Wapniak and the cloud of words flew out of sight.

"Now," said Sal, "we take the bridge and we give it to the ARVNs and Charley takes it back. I say blow the bridge." A small man from 3-2, the demolitions expert, nodded his head and said, "Let's blow it. It won't take much."

Four of them went down to the water and watched the demo expert set the explosives in place. They moved back. "You want to detonate?" the man asked Sal, and Sal said it was his pleasure. He pressed down the lever and the bridge went up in a cloud of smoke and came down in a rain of sticks and splinters. "Now," Sal said, "anyone wants to cross that river, they can swim." He called in a report to the fire base. "Artillery blew the bridge, sir," he said, and over the radio the Captain said, "Fine, go on to the next village."

"That's it?" said the demo expert. "No arguments?"

"He's gonna come out here and look? Out here it doesn't pay to explain,"

Sal said. "The river's still blue, the field's still green, and we're still here. That's all I care about." He looked around him.

WHEN PETE awakened, it was raining, and he lay on the ground and listened to the sound of the rain, and watched a heart-shaped leaf from the lilac bush bend under the weight of the water, and the stream of water, tinted silver by the streetlight, fell and hit the side of his head and trickled down his cheek and lost itself in the back of his T-shirt. He turned on his side to look for Sal or Wapniak, expecting to turn silently and quickly, his body lubricated by the mud, but when he pushed down with his left hand, he felt cold, stiff grass beneath it, and he turned quickly, looking for them, but no one was there. Out of the corner of his eye, he saw an odd structure, an octagonal porch attached to nothing, its roof a fat, truncated steeple. Its columns were painted white and shimmered through the rain, slanting silver behind it and in front of it. He looked down and saw his T-shirt and shorts were white and reflected the light. Automatically, he slid backwards until he was behind the tree he had curled himself around while sleeping.

Now he could look around safely. Where was he? He heard the sound of chickens and ducks from the shed, and when he looked at the shed, it was familiar. Old habit made him turn his head from the shed to the house, and there it was, most of the windows shut against the rain, beading with water, and then the beads swelled into streams and ran wavering down the black windowpanes. He was home and he was out in the yard, under the willow tree, near the lilac bushes, listening to his grandmother's chickens and ducks, although now they were no longer hers. They belonged to his father, who paid no attention to them, and his mother and his aunt fed them before and after school. It didn't frighten him to be out in the rain. He liked the rain and the soothing, running sounds it made on its way from the heavens into the earth, cleaning and feeding everything in its path, but he didn't know how he'd gotten out here. That frightened him. He couldn't remember. Had he gotten up to get something to drink, a glass of milk, and walked out the back door? Even if he went back in and found a glass of milk in the sink and knew he'd gotten up and opened the refrigerator and taken the bottle and poured out the milk, he still wouldn't remember. What if one of the neighbors awoke, came to her window, and saw him? If she called the police and they came, expecting a burglar? If he was shot here in his own backyard?

Or worse, they might see him and recognize him and in the morning, around the kitchen table, opening their boxes of dried cereal, Mrs. Lugano would say, "The Bravado boy? He's back. He's *sleeping under a tree.* All night, out in the rain." And she would tell someone else and someone else would tell his mother and his mother would be frightened. He couldn't tell her the truth. He couldn't say, I was sleepwalking. Only crazy people walked in their sleep. He hugged himself in his wet clothes and shivered. The rain was turning solid, beginning to fall like snow. To survive the war, to come home and die of pneumonia, that would be ridiculous. But how was he going to get back in the house? He didn't have a key. And then he noticed the open kitchen window. Had he climbed out of it? He would have had to climb up on the sink and step into it to get onto the sill. He must have let himself out the front door.

He slipped around the side of the house, staying in back of the shrubs, pressing against the wall. He looked up and down the street, and when he saw and heard no one, he ran up the wet brick steps, ice-cold against his feet, and turned the knob. It opened. He must have left it unlocked when he came out. He turned the little knob, locking it, and made his way silently to his bedroom, where he changed his underwear and got under the covers, shaking from the cold. He was asleep almost instantly, dreaming about Sal and Wapniak. Even before he fell asleep, he knew he was beginning to dream, and he told himself to remember Sal's last name in the dream, and Wapniak's first name, and in the dream, he did remember, but when he awoke in the morning, he'd forgotten them again and he turned on his side, punched the pillow, and cried, holding the pillow tight against his face, because he could not remember.

Angelina, who was always the first up in the house, saw the muddy footprints leading to her son's bedroom, and followed them backwards along the polished oak parquet floor her husband installed last year after he finished laying linoleum in the kitchen and the bathrooms and went on to tile the bathroom walls which now looked as if they'd been wallpapered. Even the bathroom ceilings were tiled, and every morning, she looked up at the tiles as she sat on the toilet seat, expecting them to fall on her head, but they never did. Her husband was good at his work. He talked with his hands, but she didn't understand a word his hands said.

She found her first muddy footprint inside the front door, went into the kitchen and got a damp rag and a dry one, and quickly wiped all traces of mud from the floor. She was going back into the kitchen when her husband came out of their bedroom. Automatically, she hid the rags behind her back. "What you got there?" her husband asked her as if she were a child, and she thrust the rags forward, saying, "Tiles! Mold! Always mold!" He turned away in disgust. Did she ever appreciate anything? Wallpaper dirtied and turned dingy, but the tiles would shine forever, just as they did the day he put them up. All she had to do was wipe them down. People in the city paid him a fortune to put up tiles like that, and she complained about mold. At two dollars a tile!

She was making oatmeal and pancakes and an omelette with mush-rooms and tomato sauce and grinding pepper and as she finished each thing, she put it in the oven to warm. "Who's that for?" he asked his wife, and she turned on him and said, "Don't say nothing. Not one word," and he kept quiet. After a while she asked him if he'd like a little oatmeal. He nodded and that was what he got: a little oatmeal in the center of a bowl. "You can afford it?" he said, picking up the bowl and looking at it. "You're sure?" But the look she gave him, he'd never seen anything like it, and under her eye, he swallowed the oatmeal quickly and went out, banging the front door. That's right, thought his wife. Wake the dead.

The door opened and closed again, this time quietly, and her husband was back. "Don't let him wear his uniform," he said.

"Why?" said Angelina.

"You want trouble on the subway, let him wear it," her husband said.

"There won't be any trouble," said his wife. But later on, when they were on the subway, a woman was staring at Pete, and Angelina stared at her and when she wouldn't look away, Angelina said, "Whatsa matter? There's something to stare at?" and the woman looked away, her face red and swelling.

"I can fight my own battles," Pete said.

"Yeah," said his mother. "I know that."

THEY WERE back on the ferry and the wet mists swirled around them, moistening their faces, and his mother was pressed up against his side, as if they were sweethearts, her arm tucked through his, saying, "Your old parka still fits you. It's too short, but it fits," and the wind rose and the ferry rose and fell and he could see the beginnings of the Manhattan skyline and its three bridges and the loop of the Brooklyn Bridge cables. They still looked like necklaces around the neck of the sky, and his mother said no, she hadn't told Paul they were coming. It was a surprise. No, he couldn't carry the picnic basket. This was the best day of her life. She had her young sons together again. But she'd have a better day, the day she had them both at home again. How long would he be gone this time? Sixty days? In Colorado? She took a deep breath and exhaled fully. Who died in Colorado? No one. Every day she watched the news and no one ever died in Colorado.

He looked down at his mother and awkwardly patted the top of her head, and she turned her face up to him, and that pure, silly, uncritical look of adoration took his breath away. For an instant he forgot the war. He forgot how easily people took a step forward and vanished. He wanted her to last forever. He never wanted to lose anyone again.

On the island, they walked through the crooked streets slanting steeply uphill and he noticed how his mother panted slightly as she climbed and he began pausing to wait for her, and she smiled at him as she came up to him, remembering how she used to wait for him when he was a child, climbing after her on his fat legs: this was the way it should be. Old Mrs. Bravado used to say that: *the old geese watch the young geese fly.* They turned down the cobblestone road, shiny with rain, and past the houses, splotched with rain, and the trees, the bark patterned dark and light green by the water, camouflaged trees, and then they came to the gate of the home, freshly painted black, its surface uneven from many paintings, a relief map. There was no telling how many coats of paint had been applied to it. They went in through the basement, through the rec room with its pool tables, Ping-Pong tables and televisions, and came to the elevator, and his mother pressed 2 and when they got to the lounge, she said, "Wait here," and he said he was old enough to go up now, but his mother shook her head and said it again: wait here.

He looked around the lounge, at its grey walls, its tired couches and chairs covered in cracked orange and blue-green plastic, its pictures of a tree in the middle of a field, or a daffodil, blown up to monstrous size, the long neon lights in the ceiling turning everyone the color of corpses. Nothing had changed. He sat down on an orange couch and it was cold against his hands and neck: cold in the winter, hot in the summer. In the summer, you stuck to it and when you got up, your shirt peeled from it as if the couch back had been covered with glue, and he bent forward, experimenting, but no, it was too cold, nothing stuck, and when he looked up, his brother Paul was standing in front of him, saluting, but his idea of a salute was to raise his hand to his forehead and press it there, palm out, as if he had a headache.

"Not like that," Pete said, getting up. "Like this," and his brother imitated him correctly, but with his left hand, and by now his mother was grinning and so was he.

"I want to be a soldier like Pete," Paul said, and Pete said, "Sure. When you get home, you can wear my uniform." Paul's face darkened.

"I'm too fat," he said. "Where's Daddy?"

"Working," said his mother. "Always working. You know that."

"I know that," Paul said.

"You checked him for marks?" Pete asked her.

"I'll do it at home," his mother said. She was backing away from them to see them better. Her two sons.

"Who could resist him?" Pete asked. "His heart's bigger than he is," and Angelina looked at him and smiled. If he were only her husband and not her son. Was it sinful to think that, that you raised the man you wanted to marry? Other women on the block said as much. *If I were a girl, I'd marry him. I'd jump at the chance.* That's what they meant. They weren't thinking about young girls ready to marry their young sons. They were remembering themselves, young women looking for husbands, wishing they'd met their sons, not the fathers of those sons. Why not think it? It was Saturday. Tomorrow she could confess it all to the priest.

"Tomorrow," she said, "we go to church."

"No," said Pete.

"No?"

"The only church I know is here," he said, thumping his breastbone. His mother looked at him, worried, but said nothing. It was his first day home.

THE FOG had lifted and the skyline was magical and many-spired against a greenish sky. "Storm," said his mother, looking up at the sky, and Pete nodded. The sky looked that way, greenish-yellow, all the time in Vietnam. Paul was looking at the pictures in *Sports Illustrated* his mother brought him. "Every week I bring the same one," she whispered in Pete's ear. "He doesn't remember," and Pete said, "It's not right. He should get new ones. If he got new ones, he might try harder," and Angelina felt old and shabby. He was right. Next week, she'd buy a new issue. "I'll pay for it," Pete said, but his mother said he didn't have to pay for it. She'd do it. "I'll get him a *subscription,*" Pete said. "It'll come with his name on it. He can show it around."

"They'll steal it anyway," said Angelina. "All they'll do is rip off the cover."

"He'll know it's his," Pete said. "While he has it, he'll know."

Inside, she bustled around, taking Paul's jacket and hanging it in the closet, trying to take Pete's, but he'd already taken his off and hung it over the back of a kitchen chair, and Theresa came in and said, "Remember Mrs. Lugano?"

"I remember," he said uneasily. He knew what was coming next, something about Eddie, who'd enlisted because he was tired of sitting in his red convertible listening to the radio.

"She said Eddie's home," Theresa told him.

"That's good," Pete said.

"He'd like to see you. She said to call when you got in. Look, I got the number."

"Maybe later," Pete said. It was hard enough remembering who he was, remembering to use his knife and fork when something was put on the plate in front of him.

"She said he's changed," Theresa began, but Pete interrupted her, saying, "Sure he's changed. He's almost three years older. I am too. What's the big deal?"

His aunt looked at him, startled.

"Hey, Pete," his brother said. "Like this?" and he saluted again, the back of his hand to his forehead, his hand facing out.

"No, like this," Pete said, showing him. "You'll be my soldier." His brother grinned and stood closer to him. "Hey, Aunt Theresa, what about a uniform for Paul? You could make it?"

"Sure, I could make it."

"What does he need with a uniform?" asked Angelina. "All week he wears uniforms."

"I want a *soldier's* uniform," Paul said. "I wanna be a soldier, too."

"Why not, Ma?" Pete asked. Theresa looked at his jacket and said it was a big job, so many darts and a lining, and all those buttonholes, and Pete said it didn't have to be exact, and his aunt told him to take off his jacket and she'd make a pattern and cut it larger and the pants shorter. Sure she could do it.

"There's no harm in it, Ma," Pete said, but his mother was regarding his jacket as if it were something evil, worse than a snake.

"Don't forget Mrs. Lugano," his aunt said. "Last week she called three times."

"Y O U   W A N N A do something?" Eddie asked him.

"Yeah," Pete said. "Why not?"

"I'll pick you up."

Outside, a car horn honked three times. "Go," said his aunt, looking out the window. "Still the red car." She watched Pete and Eddie greet one another with the oddest, longest handshake she'd ever seen, and then the car pulled away. "He's back," she said to Angelina.

"Yeah," Angelina said. "Twenty-nine more days."

"Don't count. It'll last longer," Theresa said.

"No," Angelina answered. "You're wrong."

"S O   W H A T ' S it like being back?" Pete asked.

"Who's back?" asked Eddie. They pulled into Riis Park and walked through the empty parking lot toward the water. "You know why I like it here? It reminds me of the bay. After I got wounded, they sent me out to the bay. Every night we watched the gooks blow up the fuel line. Every night we went out and fixed it. Every night there were traps because they knew we were coming. Now I miss it."

"The traps?"

"The water. Sometimes I come out here and sleep. In the car."

"It's not safe," Pete said.

"Nowhere is."

"So what do you do? You work?"

"Yeah, I work," Eddie said. "For the phone company. I tried an office but I can't take the bullshit. And shut up all day, who needs it? I work and I run around." He looked over at Pete. "When I came back, the girls from the neighborhood were all over me. I didn't know what to do. Was I supposed to put my arms around them or what? I was used to the Oriental girls. That's what I wanted. Sex. There we were, in a drive-in, and I was asking myself, Should I put my arm around her? Should I kiss her? How much of this goes on before I do what I want? Over there you were honest. Your feelings were your feelings. Here no one wants to hear about them. Feelings? What are they? Over there, you wore olive drab, the guy next to you wore olive drab, you ate the same C-rations. The same lead flew over your heads. Over there it was a *democracy*. Here it's bullshit."

"I can't remember their names," Pete said. "The best friends I ever had and I can't remember their names."

"Remember Basic? Remember what they taught you in Basic? Don't get too close? It don't pay to get too close? That's why you don't remember their names."

Pete remembered Liebowitz getting up and running forward and the bullet bringing him down and how, after that, the Chief was never the same again, and then the Chief, too, was gone. "Yeah, that must be it," Pete said.

"So what do you want to do?" Eddie asked. "Tie one on?"

"Yeah, let's get ripped," Pete said.

They drove back to the neighborhood. Eddie went into a candy store for a pack of cigarettes and Pete waited outside on the sidewalk, looking up and down the street, looking for someone, he didn't know who, maybe a face he recognized from public school, maybe Dolores, the prettiest girl in his class. He'd thought of her over there, even clipped a picture out of a magazine because it looked like her, pasted it to the side of his compartment, and he'd tell the others, "You want to know what my girlfriend looks like? Like that."

The pizza parlors were open and people were coming out with slices wrapped in wax paper, the paper turning translucent as the olive oil saturated it. A beautiful girl with long black hair, very straight hair, stopped and tilted the pizza upwards so that the point of it hovered above her mouth. She bit off the point and licked off the tomato sauce and the oil and began chewing the pizza along one edge of the slice, wanting it to last longer. The sight of her made him uneasy, he didn't know why.

Men coming home from work on the subway stopped in front of the outdoor telephone booths and called their wives, and afterwards some of them went into the pizza parlor and came out with large white boxes, a smiling pizza man drawn in red ink on the box lid. Young men and women coming home from work came out carrying cans of soda and calzone, eating as they walked. Two blocks away, a fat woman hesitated in front of a candy store, then moved on quickly, and went into a door, walking beneath a sign marked WEIGHT WATCHERS. People were stopping at the newsstand up the street and buying copies of the *Post*, tucking it under their arms and walking home. Men in overcoats carrying attaché cases walked quickly, their heads bare and bent slightly against the wind. From the back, you could tell who the older men were by their hats. The felt hats were gone, replaced by a knobby black fur. Once, his mother had a coat like that: Persian lamb.

He had been gone almost three years and the people he watched hadn't left the neighborhood. Oh, some of them had gone into Manhattan and gotten jobs, but at the end of the day, they got right back into the subway— if they were very hungry, buying a pretzel first, but eating it on the train, not on the street—and before they knew it, they saw the lights of the Manhattan Bridge and they were back in Brooklyn. Most of them never left the neighborhood. Some of the girls he'd known in grade school were probably already married, living in an apartment upstairs from their mother or their mother-in-law, and to them what was important was who the child looked like, the mother or the father. Endless hours could be spent on this question, and out would come the black, pebbled photograph albums with their black cardboard pages, the old photographs held in place by little black triangles in each corner, and the older members of the family would bend over, saying, "See? He has Salvatore's nose. See? She looks just like Romina."

He stood on the sidewalk, turning his collar up against the weather, wondering what was taking Eddie so long, and he tried to fit himself into one of those living rooms, tried to imagine himself as the father of one of those children, and when he couldn't do that, tried to imagine himself as the brother-in-law or the uncle of one of those babies, but he couldn't see himself in the room. He was there, but a ghost, and when he forced himself to imagine the family turning to look at him, he saw the heads swivel, and the stares, and finally someone said, "Who are you?" Then he imagined himself in a hooch in one of the villes, looking down at a baby in a hand-made crib, and he was *there*. He shivered and looked around him. He was back.

Already he had a sense he didn't belong, a premonition of how hard it would be to come back, and he remembered someone saying that when he did come back, he'd fit right in, just like a piece of a jigsaw puzzle, right back into his slot. Wouldn't *that* be boring? But the edges of the puzzle piece could be broken off, or worn, and then it wouldn't fit back in.

Still, why shouldn't he fit? He'd gone with his mother to see Paul in the home. Nothing had changed there. Tomorrow morning, when they ate breakfast, his father would shout at Paul for eating too much and being too fat. Nothing had changed. His mother was the same, or almost the same, smaller and older, but as he watched the people coming and going on the avenue, rarely looking up at the sky or looking up or down the street, putting one foot in front of the other until they got to their front door, he wanted to say something. *What about that life I led over there? I led a whole life over there.* He saw it floating high above him in a bubble, attached to the top of his head by a kind of string, looking for a place to come down, but the places down here were already filled.

"We're living whole lives here," Wapniak was saying. "Whole lives. We're seeing things and feeling things other people won't see in a lifetime. We're in a parallel world. We stepped across a line to get here. Look at this skull. Look how white it is. A few more weeks in the sun should do it. When I was in college, if anyone had asked me, did I expect to find myself skinning and bleaching a skull, I would have said, Man, are you crazy? But I'm doing it. It's perfectly natural here. When we go back, we have to tell them. We have to tell them everything we know."

Tell everything he knew to these women in short skirts walking down the avenue, eating pizza, steam rising from the slices into the air? Stop the men coming home from work carrying white cartons to waiting families? Tell them what? I saw a newborn baby with its head smashed against the ground? It was easier than smashing a cantaloupe. There are ways of going into villages and setting fire to them so no one can say you did it. See this grenade? If you throw it into the water, it will keep on burning and it will burn to death an enemy soldier hiding under the water. Even in the water, it keeps on burning.

They wanted to get home. They wanted to eat and sleep and go back to work and argue over whom the baby looked like. They didn't want to come back knowing about the smashed heads of infants, or how white phosphorus kept on burning. *Why are you telling me this? Ma, why is he telling me this? Make him stop.* He could hear them already. He could see his father running in from the shed, taking the wooden back steps two at a time. *Are you crazy? What do you think you're talking about?* He was stuck with an extra world. He looked at the people going by on the avenue and he envied them their lives. He envied them and he hated them. They didn't know anything about his extra life and they didn't want to know, and even if he found someone who did know, he didn't want to talk to him.

It was an extra world, but it was his. In that world, he knew the rules. The people who died there were real to him. What was he going to do, tell someone about the two bodies burned to skeletons under the tanks and see him smile and say, "Oh, sorry"? If he could write it all down, save it, so that later he'd remember it, show it to people later, when it cooled off, when enough had happened to them so they knew things *could* happen, when they had scars of their own and became interested in how other people got theirs—but he couldn't write. He'd never tried, except in reform school. Maybe he should go back to school. He could learn to write there. Put the extra world in a book and put the book in a box. He could learn enough to join the people on the avenue, going back and forth to work, empty, because what did they know? That's what he wanted to be, like them, empty but full of purpose.

A girl his age passed in front of him. He hadn't realized he was staring, but of course he was. Her skirt was so short it didn't even look like a skirt, and he'd never seen stockings like that. They went right up under the skirt. Where did they hook onto garter belts? And they looked like black lace. When he left, skirts were skirts, long, and stockings were coffee-colored. "What are you staring at?" the girl asked him and walked past him quickly. Her lips were almost blue. Wasn't she cold? Why did she talk to him that way, as if she hated him?

"Let's go," Eddie said, coming out with a large brown paper bag, and Pete asked, "Where? You know a good bar?" Eddie said that's what took him so long; he asked the man in there where to go with someone who was too young to drink, and there was a bar a few blocks away they could go to, but first they better get four sheets to the wind sitting in a car, because no one would let him drink on the premises. "Don't forget, man," Eddie said. "You're back in the U.S. of A. You're underage."

"No, man," Pete said, "I'm not underage."

"No?" said Eddie.

"No," Pete said.

They sat in Eddie's red convertible and talked and drank vodka ("You don't get so sick on vodka," Eddie said). "You remember Vince? You don't remember Vince?" Eddie asked. "He lives in the projects. He came home last month. His mother fixed him all his favorite foods and it got quiet, they were all staring at him. So he thought, If they want a show, I'll give them a show, and he picked up the mashed potatoes with both hands and shoveled them into his mouth. He fell off the chair, laughing."

"What did they think?" Pete asked.

"They thought it was funny," Eddie said. "When they were sure he was joking. But they didn't think it was funny when they found him hanging from the bedroom windowsill shouting, 'Airborne! Airborne!' They live ten stories up. He just left last week. Four months in Fort Knox, Kentucky, and then he's out. He was *wild.* He couldn't sleep. He'd drink all night and when the guys got off the night shift, he'd be waiting for them. He wore everyone out. He said his parents couldn't wait for him to go. And on the way to the airport, you know what happened? A car backfired and he jumped out in the middle of traffic and tried to *walk* to the goddamn plane. He missed it and had to come home. He said you should have seen their faces when he walked back in the door. They thought he was finally out of their hair. Your parents glad to see you?"

"My mother, she is."

"Oh, yeah, your father," Eddie said. "My father, he's a joke. I stay away from him. I'm working for my uncle. He's in the business. 'You're the kind of person we need.' That's what he said."

"Hey, man, you want to shoot more people? Why shoot more people?"

"Because I don't like school," Eddie said, taking another drink. "I do not like school."

"I'm going to school," said Pete.

"Good for you."

"Let's go to the bar," Pete said.

"O'Halloran's Bar and Grill," Eddie said. "Nice place. Hardly any lights and he likes Vietnam vets. O'Halloran, hard-boiled eggs in jars, and a wall of whiskey bottles. Is there any sight in the world more beautiful than a wall of bottles filled with booze? What else is there? Leave the bottles in the car."

They wove down the street toward the bar, their arms around one another, their voices loud although they didn't know it.

They stood leaning against the bar until O'Halloran saw them, and he slapped two mugs down in front of them. "You know what?" Eddie said to O'Halloran. "I'm already sober. I can't drink enough."

They stood at the bar, looking at nothing, catching glimpses of themselves in the mirror between the bottles. Someone tapped Eddie on the shoulder, and when he turned around, a young policeman was grinning at him. "I wanna buy you guys a beer," he said, and Eddie said O.K. O'Halloran hesitated and brought over two mugs.

"You guys really had it hard over there," the policeman said.

"Yeah," said Eddie.

"You had it rough, not knowing who the enemy was."

"Yeah," said Eddie.

"You guys were fucking heroes," said the cop. "I couldn't have done it."

"No?" said Eddie.

"No. You guys are the best."

"He's drunk," Pete said.

"But you know what?" said the cop. "I asked my father. He said during the war the enemy had planes and tanks and all that shit. You didn't have to worry about none of that. You had planes and tanks but they didn't have nothing."

"That's it," Eddie said.

"You're heroes, you are," the cop said.

"You know what you're doing?" Eddie asked the cop. "You're *apologizing* to me for being a Vietnam vet. I don't need you to *apologize* to me. Who are you to *apologize* to me?"

"'Apologize' isn't the right word," Pete said.

"He's telling us it's all right to be Vietnam vets," Eddie shouted. "He stayed here sucking his mommy's tits and he's telling us it's all right to be Vietnam vets?"

"Not in here," said O'Halloran. "You want to fight, take it outside."

"You want to fight?" Eddie asked the cop.

"Yeah, I wanna fight," said the cop.

"You got a gun?"

"I gotta gun. I'll leave it in the bar."

"Outside," Eddie said.

Pete followed them past the bathrooms, the black silhouette of a woman's head on one door, a man's on the other, out into the alley.

"What are we fighting for?" Pete asked, his head clear. "Why are we fighting?"

"*We're* not fighting. I'm fighting," Eddie said, unbuttoning his jacket, his face joyous. Then they saw the cop reach under his coat.

"You got a gun?" Eddie asked. The cop smiled. Yeah, he had a gun. "O.K.," Eddie said, putting his hands up and backing off, "I'm stupid, but I'm not crazy. I'll see you later, man." He began walking backwards toward the back door of the bar when he heard O'Halloran's voice behind him. "You put that gun away, John-O," O'Halloran said. "You know better than that. No guns in here. Get inside," he said to Eddie, "you and your friend. John-O, go home. Your wife's on the phone."

"He wanted to shoot us," Pete said, amazed. "Why'd he want to shoot us?"

"*Because we're Vietnam vets,*" said Eddie.

"Why? What'd we do?"

"Our country said they needed us and we went. They said, We need your help, and we said, O.K., you've got it. What do you want? Maybe your lives. We said, O.K., take them. We'll keep the world safe from communism. Now they say they shouldn't have asked us and it's our fault for being alive. The enemy didn't have tanks. They didn't have planes. We should've died there. You know what you do? You go to Colorado or wherever you're fucking going, and you come back and hang up that uniform. You fucking bury it in a box and forget you were there. If anyone asks, for the last two years you were driving a truck. You want to survive? Just move on, man. Find yourself a woman, buy a house, and go to work. I'm getting out of the neighborhood. Everyone here knows where I was."

"Out of the neighborhood?" Pete asked.

"You think I want to be in alleys fighting dumb cops for the rest of my life? I pick my own fights. I can't do that here."

"Out of the neighborhood?" Pete said again.

"Yeah. Me and Margaret. Out. You got a good mother and father, you got your family behind you, you got a job waiting for you, that's something else. I don't got those things. You got them, you stay."

"Margaret?"

"An Irish secretary from Manhattan. Nothing from the neighborhood, man, not even the girls. I don't want *nothing* from here."

"Your family's your family," Pete said.

"Yeah, and rat poison is poison, but you don't have to eat it."

"You ever see Dolores?" Pete asked. "I always thought about Dolores. In school I never talked to her."

"Who am I talking to? The wall? Dolores is from the neighborhood. You wanna go to school, go to school. Take your benefits and split. Girls are all over. You gotta look here?"

Pete looked through the bar window, out onto the street, where men and women were passing—infrequently now, only those who had worked late or were meeting friends or were bored and waiting as if they needed something, a bottle of milk, a loaf of bread. He knew every store on the block. He knew the man behind the counter in the candy store and what his egg creams tasted like, where he kept his chocolate-covered halvah, where to turn the corner and find the Jewish deli and its hot knishes, the dress store where his mother sometimes worked after her husband had left for the day, coming back in time to make dinner, using the extra money to buy them clothes or a special cut of meat when company was coming, his father puffing out his chest because he made enough money to keep the family so well, not suspecting his wife of working in the corner store, although sometimes he especially liked a new housedress she wore and looked at its big red roses and wondered how she managed money so well, but he forgot about it and congratulated himself on having married a woman who knew how to handle money. Pete knew the building two blocks down with fancy metal grillwork in the shape of spiderwebs over the doors where the doorman let you ride up and down in the elevator until you were tired of it. He could find his way back to his school with his eyes closed, or to the playground where they played handball, to the stoops of the houses where he'd played stoopball, to the house three blocks away with the brown granite lions roaring on both sides of the front door, and the house further down the block whose lions were painted enamel red. He knew every stick and stone in the area, and while he'd been gone, he'd thought about every brick in every building, about the snow slanting in front of the streetlights drooping their long birds' necks, and the neighborhood was the one solid place. It was where he'd come back to. It was where he'd live out his life, knowing exactly what to do because everyone in the neighborhood knew exactly what to do, and outside of the neighborhood it was all confusion, unknowable, anything could happen. He'd had enough of that.

"You think this is home?" Eddie said. "I'll drive you home."

PAUL WAS trying on the uniform his aunt had made for him. It was finished sloppily and the pants were baggy and its chest was covered with decorations made from her daughter's hair ribbons, but that didn't matter. Paul was happy in it, and when Pete came into the kitchen, he saluted. "Not like that," Pete said automatically. "Like this."

"He's gonna go out on the street like that?" his father asked. "He don't call enough attention to himself? What is this, Halloween?"

"I'll go with him," Pete said.

"You think you're invisible?" asked his father. "We got two of them parading up and down. You see that, Angelina?"

"I see it," said his mother.

Paul was saying he'd go by himself. Soldiers could go by themselves to the store.

"They'll beat him up," his father said.

"A loaf with sesame seeds on it," his mother said, and Paul repeated it solemnly: sesame seeds.

"Back at the home he could be learning something," his father was saying as they went down the front hall, and he heard his mother yelling back, "Yeah? What'll he learn? How to take a beating? Another beating? You wanna see the marks?" and his father was saying, "Calm down, calm down. No one beats him. He fights. He's strong and he fights."

Paul picked out the bread and gave the baker a dollar. Mr. Fumifreddo: he'd known them since childhood. He used to say he'd known them before they were born, when they were still in their mother's stomach and she came in for bread. The baker nodded confidentially at Pete: *come over here.* "You're going into the city to pick up girls?" the baker asked him. "Don't wear the uniform. Mrs. Lugano's boy, he came back bloody. I never saw such a shiner."

"Eddie?" asked Pete.

"Yeah, Eddie," said the baker. "Don't wear the uniform. This ain't the Second World War. There ain't no parades."

"I wanna be a soldier," Paul said again.

"Him," said Mr. Fumifreddo. "He don't know any better."

"You get the change?" his mother asked Paul. "You get the right change?" His brother stretched out his hand. She counted the money, beamed, and hugged him. "He's getting big. Isn't he getting big?" she asked Pete, and later that day, they took him back to the home.

"You sleep all right?" she asked Pete on the way back. "You got enough blankets?" and he said, sure, he was fine. "My brother, God rest his soul, when he came back from the war, he used to walk in his sleep," his mother said.

"Well, I don't walk in my sleep," Pete said.

Angelina looked at him, stared into the mists toward the skyline, and said nothing.

· · ·

"FOUR WEEKS he lays around the house?" his father shouted at his mother. "He couldn't line up a job? In six months, he's out on the streets."

"He needs his rest," Angelina said.

"He doesn't need rest, he drinks!" his father shouted.

"Who's gonna give him a job now?" Angelina asked. "Who's gonna give him a job and wait six months for him to take it? Someone needs someone, they need them now, not six months from now."

"You know everything?" her husband shouted. "You don't know *nothing* about jobs. He could work with me, but he doesn't want to. He'd rather clean sewers. Ask him. He said that."

Angelina pointed out that none of the other boys wanted to work with him. They were living far away out on the island. She never saw her grand-children. Whose fault was that? Why did he think they didn't want to come to the house? Why did he think they came when he wasn't home?

"They come when I'm not home?" bellowed her husband. "You tell me my children come when I'm not home?"

"That's what I tell you," his wife shouted. "Now you start on him. Soon he won't come home anymore."

Her husband hit her and she fell back against the sink, her elbow sinking into the grey, sudsy dishwater.

"You," Angelina said, straightening up, her hand over her eye. "You get out of my kitchen."

Pete walked in and saw his mother, a white dish towel filled with ice pressed to her eye. "What happened?" he asked her.

"Nothing," she said.

"What happened?" he asked again.

"Nothing. I fell."

"You fall again and I'll beat the living shit out of him," Pete said. "I don't care who he is. I'll kill him."

"He didn't do nothing," said his mother.

"I'm going out, Ma," he said, his voice disgusted, and when Angelina heard the back door slam, she remembered the sound of his voice and she sat down at the table, the ice pressed to her eye, the melting water staining the dishcloth grey, the cloth dripping cold tears, and wept.

"He said he'd beat me up? His father?" her husband asked, coming out of the bedroom.

"Don't think he can't do it," his mother said. "Don't think he can't."

HE WAS walking down the avenue when a girl's voice called his name and when he looked up, there was Dolores, standing on the other side of the street, waving. She looked quickly both ways and ran through the traffic toward him. "You're back," she said, and he said, Yeah, he was back.

"I'll buy you a cup of coffee," she said, and he said, "No, I'll buy you a cup of coffee," and he noticed her teeth were chattering. He asked her what she wanted and she said coffee and a cannoli and he ordered a coffee and looked at her. "So," she said. "You're back," and he said, Yeah, he was, and how did she walk around in those short skirts, and she said, "Oh, you get used to it," and they sat there staring at one another, senselessly smiling, and finally he asked her if she'd like to go to a movie over the weekend. "On Sunday," she said. "I'm busy on Saturday."

He watched her sip her little cup of coffee. He liked the way she picked up her cup and the way she curled her fingers around it to warm them, how clean her fingers were, the glimmering pink paint on her nails, the way she kept her head lowered and looked up at him. He liked her short blond hair, cut in layers, teased, and sprayed almost stiff. She wore dark mascara that made her eyes hugely round and her eyelashes were thick with black mascara. Red rouge lit her cheeks. She wore two gold chains around her neck and a gold bracelet encircled her arm. Her face was a perfect oval and her chin was slightly pointed. Her eyebrows had been tweezed and darkened with eyebrow pencil. He looked at her and thought she was perfect. She was small, almost tiny. She was what all the other girls in the neighborhood were trying to look like. She was perfectly typical and because of that, absolutely beautiful. She looked just as he'd remembered her, only smarter, more sophisticated, and he could imagine a life with her. He could imagine going to work and bringing home a paycheck and looking at the baby safe in its crib. It was what he'd always wanted. He'd be like everyone else: normal.

"So," she said, "you came back safe and sound." She smiled at him, stirred her espresso with her small coffee spoon, and thought about her father, sitting in their living room at home, felled by a stroke, who, when he thought he heard suspicious noises, rang a gold bell to summon her mother. She sat across from Pete and felt protected.

He took her out Sunday night and they went to dinner and talked so long they missed the movie. She told him about everyone he knew from grade school, who they were dating or who they married, who'd gone to Vietnam and who was back and who wasn't. Billy Frescica wasn't back and his mother was worried, and by the end of the evening, he was holding her hand, thinking how hard it would be to leave for Colorado, and when he took her home, he stood in the doorway to her house, and said, "Wait for me," and she smiled oddly, looked at him as if he were joking, and said, Sure.

When he got home, Eddie's red convertible was parked outside, the motor running. "Get in," Eddie said, and he slid in onto the red leather seat.

"So where are we going?" he asked.

"Your last night home, we're tying one on," he said. "I know a bar on the island. Good beer, good conversation."

"Good conversation?" Pete echoed.

"Yeah, you'll see," Eddie said.

They drove to Long Beach, down to the edge of town, and found a bar on the edge of the salt marshes. Inside, the walls were decorated with old rifles, some of them dating back to the Civil War, and old newspapers proclaiming victories in previous wars. D-DAY! screamed the headline over the bar. Young men their age sat in the back around a round table, drinking and talking. "Hey, Eddie!" one of them called out. "Bring the cherry over!"

"I don't know about this," Pete said uneasily.

"Come on, man. They're just like us," Eddie said. "It took me a while to find them."

"Yeah. We don't talk to just anyone," said the guy nearest him. He had curly red hair and a curly red beard and his blue eyes were watery. "Hey, I'm Mike," he said. "You glad to be back?"

"Hey, he's still counting his arms and his legs, right, fella?" said the man sitting next to him. He was immensely overweight. His shirt gaped over his stomach and strained against the buttons, and where it gapped, the hairs of his stomach curled upwards, catching the light of the neon sign flickering in the window. "My name's Joe," he said, patting his stomach.

The men moved over and made room for them. The waitress brought them their beers, and while Pete watched his fingers form circles in the frost on his mug, they went on with what they'd been talking about.

"Hey, when I flew back into Oakland," Mike said, "I called up relatives. You know what I did? I sat in their living room with a jug of vodka in one hand and a bottle of red wine in the other, and I took a swig of the vodka and a swig of the red wine, and I didn't say one word. But I can describe everything in the room. I could hear the dust fall." He pulled a red curl, stretching it out, and let it snap back.

"Oh, yeah?" the heavy man said. "Describe it. I was back three weeks before I stopped seeing palm trees."

"You dare me?" asked Mike, running his fingers through his red hair, pulling a curl straight, letting it go.

"*I* dare you," Eddie said, rubbing his belly.

"There was a white, gold-specked couch and there were matching chairs and they were covered with plastic, and you stuck to the plastic. When you tried to get up, the cushions came up with you, and they had chandeliers and one hung over a coffee table with a mirror on top of it, and the coffee table had gold legs, and all over the walls were paintings of horses. *Walls* full of horses, and there was a box full of cigars that played the song from *Gone With the Wind.* So, is that enough?"

"No," Eddie said.

"No," said Joe, rubbing his enormous belly.

"They had pink wall-to-wall carpeting, and the bathroom had a green sink and bathtub, and there was a finished basement with paneled walls, and four tennis rackets hung on the walls, and guys, that's it," Mike said.

"You remember anything else?" Joe asked him.

"You know something?" Mike said. "Before Vietnam, if someone said, 'Tell me what the house looked like,' I couldn't do it. It's a house. It's got a roof and walls. Now I see everything. I'm a goddamn *woman!*"

"So what are you saying?" Joe asked, flushing red. "The war made you a sissy?"

"Yeah, well, you know," Mike said.

"Don't worry about it, man," Eddie said. "We changed but we're not sissies."

"Yeah, but *wallpaper,*" Mike said. "Who remembers wallpaper?"

"You still know the difference between boys and girls, don't worry, man," Joe said. "Me, I got into Oakland, and I go over to Avis to rent a car so I could visit a friend who got out before, and the man in the office, he asks for a credit card, and I say, Well, I don't have one. I just got back from Vietnam. And he says he's sorry, but no credit card, no car. I offer him a *six hundred dollar* deposit, and he says he's sorry, rules are rules. That's when *I* realized I was back in the fucking States.

"I go and get a cab to the bus station and buy a ticket, and I call my friend, and he tells me to turn in the ticket and wait in the bar in the bus station, and he'd come for me. But I kept the ticket and waited in the bar, you know, just in case he didn't show. So my friend showed up and we stood in line to return the ticket, and a girl was waiting in front of me, and I said, 'Don't buy a ticket. Don't give the bus company your money. *We'll* give you a ride.' So she smiled the way girls do when they pretend they don't hear you but they're listening? And the woman behind the counter starts shouting, 'Lousy soldiers! Lousy soldiers! Leave the girl alone! I'll have you arrested!'

"I said, 'You'll have me arrested? You'll have me arrested for offering a girl a ride?' I was ready to take the place apart. I had my hands around the bars. My friend pulled me off. I would've ripped out the bars and gone over the counter after that fucking bitch. I'm home twelve hours and she's threatening to have me arrested?

"Then I go back to New York and I go down to Wall Street to look for a job and what's going on? Guys with long hair and beaded headbands are running around on the streets, and girls are hanging on to them, and guys in hard hats come along with baseball bats and they lay into them. They were cracking heads open, man, and I don't agree with those peaceniks. I don't think they know what the fuck they're talking about, but they're saying stop the war and bring the guys back, and I believe that, so I'm on their side, and I wade in there to put my big body between the police and the rest of those jokers and one of the policemen cracks *me* over the head and starts dragging me off, and he calls me a no good Commie free-love hippie. And the next thing I know, I'm yelling, 'I was *there,* man! You want to see my silver star?' And he *arrests* me. He fucking *arrests* me. My wife had to come down and get me out. For disorderly conduct and assaulting an officer. I didn't assault him. If I'd wanted to assault him, he wouldn't have lived long enough to arrest me. I mean, fighting in the streets! They're fighting each other in the streets! What's the flag *for,* man? What does it *mean?*"

"It don't mean nothing," someone said.

"It does," said Mike. "This is the States, man. This is what we fought for. It does mean something."

"Yeah?" Joe said. "Well, they stopped the bombing. The big bombing halt. Cause for celebration, right? Well, when I was out there, those B-52s were like hummingbirds in the morning. You heard them coming over and you knew whatever was out there was going to stay out there, and now, what is it? It's an open door. Come and get them. They're fucking *targets,* man, that's all they are. The government went out and pinned big red targets in the middle of their backs. That's when I lost faith in this country. The flag didn't mean shit. I mean they're *out there.* My friends are out there and they halt the bombing. Come and get them. They're not worth anything."

"Oh, man, don't start that," said Eddie. "Don't even think about it."

"That house in San Diego?" someone asked. "Did it have a garden?" and Mike said, "Yeah, it had a garden, and there were orange trees in it and palms and they had a great zoo. I saw a puma there."

"Yeah, a puma, what else?" Joe asked.

Eddie looked over at Pete. "Let's get outta here, man," his eyes said.

They drove back to Brooklyn in silence.

"We had to go there?" Pete asked. "We had to go?"

"Listen, man," Eddie said, "you don't know what you got there. They don't look at you and ask you how many women and children you killed."

"Colorado," Pete said.

"Yeah. It's gonna pass like a dream," Eddie said. "Snow and parkas and watching your breath in the air and before you get used to it, you'll be back here," he said, and that was what happened.

34 E STILL DOESN'T have a job?" his father asked, walking through the house in his underwear.

"Quiet," Angelina said. "The news is on."

"He's back, why does he have to watch the news? If he gets a job, he can watch the eleven o'clock news."

The camera was coming in closer and Pete recognized the insignia of his outfit, a white horse rearing, filling the television screen, replaced instantly by the face of a newscaster standing in a field, his hair ruffled by the wash from a helicopter lifting off behind him. "Whether it's a case of mass hysteria is not open to argument. Some of the men here swear they've seen the White Man. Sightings are reported daily from men in different sectors who have no way of communicating with one another. Some see a bandaged figure. Others report seeing a man dressed in white monk's robes with flesh painted or powdered white. Typically, the White Man is sighted on a battlefield once the battle itself is over. Wounded soldiers claim to have been given first aid and even water by the White Man. Commanders here refuse to comment, although all seem agreed that there is a real connection between appearances of the White Man and low morale."

Hello, said the White Man to Pete through the television screen.

Hello, said the kinaree to Pete. *Remember, I promised to find you.*

Pete heard them and didn't hear them.

"You ever see that White Man?" asked his mother.

"No."

"What's he supposed to be, a ghost?"

"I don't know, Ma."

"He *could* be a ghost," said his mother. "He brings water to the wounded. Or God could have sent him. On Sundays on the block you can hear the mothers praying. From our mouths to God's ear. Maybe it happens."

"God must have sent him, Ma."

"You didn't see him? Never?"

"I never saw him, Ma."

· · ·

"I'VE GOT benefits," Pete told his father, "and I'm going to night school."

"Yeah, and during the day?"

"I've got my job in the butcher shop."

"What does he pay you? You could make ten, twenty times more working for me."

"Forget it," Pete said. He looked at the Day-Glo crucifix fastened above the stove. It was the ugliest thing he'd ever seen. "Where'd that come from?" he asked.

"Your mother painted it, Sunday afternoon at the church. She won a kit at bingo."

"I'm going out," Pete said.

"With Eddie?"

"With Dolores."

"Look, big man," his father said. "Now you pay sixty dollars a month rent. No more free rides."

THE COURSES were given at night in a large red bright high school across the street from the college. The rooms were large, square boxes once painted bright yellow. Now the paint had chipped and faded. The huge windows were dust-flecked, and, because they were on the first floor, were fitted out with metal grilles. The rooms were overheated. The students came in, looked nervously at one another, and took seats as far as possible from the front desk, a huge wooden affair whose veneer had chipped off in various places. In back of it was the expected bluish-grey chalkboard. Most of the students settled shopping bags and briefcases they'd brought from the work they did during the day. It was eight thirty and dark, and the students who were accustomed to night courses set brown paper bags on their desks, from which they extracted large Styrofoam cups of coffee. Some of the women looked around as they sipped, and nodded shyly. No one spoke. Many could barely speak English. Everyone waited for the teacher.

The day before, Pete had seen the guidance counselor, a young man wearing blue jeans and a red flannel shirt, only a few years older than he was, who told him, "These are the basic courses. When you pass them, you can take the exam for the G.E.D. and move into the regular program. What do you want to take first?"

Pete said he wanted to take an English course, and the guidance counselor said that the best teacher taught the section beginning at eight thirty.

"I'll be there," he said.

The teacher, Andrew Verner, was tall, white, and blond. The instant he walked into the room, the desks seemed too small and the room appeared even shabbier than before. Mr. Verner wore blue jeans, a blue and white striped shirt with a red tie, and a blue flannel sport jacket. His hair was perfectly trimmed and he had a nervous habit, almost womanly, of pushing a shock of it back from his eyes. Everyone fell in love with him.

In back of him, or through him, they could see refrigerators, polished cars, immaculately trimmed green lawns, lovely blond children at play with spotted dogs. When he spoke of summer, they saw open windows, white curtains stirring in the hot breeze, and sprinklers arching back and forth. His transatlantic accent was the sound of money and security and faith. In his accent, in his person, he embodied the American dream. They would have done anything he asked them. *Follow me,* his manner said, and you too can become what I am. It was his great gift to make the students who sat in his classrooms want to be like him, and as a consequence, he was known as an excellent teacher.

If he spoke with a certain touching ruefulness about unfulfilled ambitions and frustrated hopes, his students, to whom he was utterly unfamiliar and immeasurably wonderful, thought no less of him for it. They were naive and they were hopeful. They assumed he sensed their own frustrations and was, out of generosity, giving them voice. They looked up at him, spellbound, and knew why they had come to this country.

For six weeks, Pete, who spent the first few weeks taking notes on subject-verb agreement, run-on sentences, and sentence fragments, knew why he had so desperately wanted to come back from Vietnam. He came to class early and a Cuban woman stood with him in the hall and looked at his homework and explained the mysteries of run-on sentences to him. "Of course it's easier for me," she said. "I studied grammar in my own language."

He remembered diagramming sentences in public school, the dismembered sentences like giant insects sketched on the board, and his utter failure to understand a word the teacher said. But now he was learning. The teacher seemed patient and kind and corrected their pronunciation automatically and without condescension. Everyone's pronunciation needed correction and everything was fine. He began to think he could do it. He got good grades on the daily quizzes and began to read ahead in the anthology assigned for the class, and then one night the teacher distributed cards, asking them to fill in their previous educational background and what they'd been doing for the last two years. *Last two years.* Without thinking, he wrote, "Served in U.S. Army, Vietnam."

Two nights later, when the class met again, the teacher sat on the edge of Pete's desk. He was a young man, twenty-five or twenty-six, and he said, "Tonight we're not going to talk about English. We're going to talk about history." Fine, thought Pete. History's interesting. "Tonight," said Mr. Verner, taking out a copy of *Life* magazine, "we're going to talk about Vietnam," and Pete saw that he had the issue whose cover story was about Mylai. Oh, he thought. No.

"Would you like to tell us your thoughts about Vietnam?" the teacher asked, coming over to his desk, sitting down on the edge of it, holding the magazine in his lap.

He didn't know which way to look. His face was burning; he was afraid of bursting into tears. Maybe the teacher wasn't picking on him. It might be his imagination, but he couldn't look up, and the silence in the room grew. Mr. Verner picked up the magazine and returned to the front of the room and sat on the edge of his own desk.

"Let me tell you about Vietnam," he said, holding up the magazine. "This is what happens when our country enters a civil war. We send good men over there and they end up mass murderers. Look at these pictures," he said, opening the magazine. "Never again will we be able to think of our-selves as the best country on earth. Never again are we going to look at the Nazis and call them war criminals. Now we're all war criminals. By proxy. These soldiers have made us war criminals *by proxy*. The people over there don't have automatic weapons. They don't have planes. They're help-less and because they're helpless, our men can do this to them. These people are dying over there for no reason. They're dying because this coun-try believes it's the policeman of the world. How are we going to live with this evil?"

He talked and talked, but Pete didn't hear a word he said. The other students in the room had receded and grown smaller. In back of Mr. Verner, every house, every car, every lawn, every sprinkler, moved away from him in distaste. The blood pounded in his ears and a large hand pressed down on his chest. When the bell rang at the end of the hour, he got up and went into the hall and knew he would never come back. The Cuban woman came up to him and tried to say something, but he couldn't understand her. He made a motion with his hand, *Stay away,* and walked down the empty hall, down the metal steps, and out into the darkness. *Let me tell you about Vietnam.*

"IT'S NOT for me. I'm not a student," he told his mother the next day. "I want to drive a truck."

"You could be a student," his mother said. "Your grandfather always said you could."

"Try once more," said his aunt. "Just one more class."

"Nah," said Pete. "I already tried. To tell you the truth, I didn't under-stand a word he said."

"You want to drive a truck? Why do you want to drive a truck?"

"Drive a truck and see the world," he said.

. . .

H E   O F T E N   watched television, looking for his unit in the newsreel footage, and whenever he watched television, he thought he saw them. Now they were heading toward a village further south than usual. The village had been sealed off by the Viet Cong, who for two years had taken all the food the villagers had, but now the VC had been driven out of the area and the American forces were helping the villagers. The tracks moved along the roads, carrying sacks of salt. There was no salt in the village and all the people were sickening. The villagers chewed mouthfuls of dirt, trying to suck the salt from the earth. Children could barely stand and old people were dying. Everyone chewed on leaves, hoping to find traces of salt, and as a result, everyone suffered from stomach disorders, walked about, if they could walk, with distended stomachs and constant diarrhea. "This is some war," Sal said. "Some fucking war."

"But it means something," said Wapniak, who was back. "Look at it this way. If someone's murdered, and they report it in the papers, everyone's horrified. But even a murder is meant to happen. There's something to learn from it you wouldn't learn if it didn't happen. Good comes out of it."

"Not to the corpse," Sal said.

"Of course not to the corpse," Wapniak said, aggravated. "To the people. These people don't have *salt*. How many times do you hear the expression, 'The salt of the earth'? You ever think about it? You don't think about it. *Now* you'll know what it means. There's a message here, man, and the message is, Get back to basics. Salt, bread, those are basics. You need refrigerators? You need color TV sets? You need 'Star Trek'? You need *salt*."

"You need a fucking picture in a fucking book," said Sal. "That's all you fucking need, man. You don't fucking need to fucking kill people and then kill more fucking people bringing them fucking salt."

"You'll understand later," Wapniak said. "You're part of the *plan*, man. Maybe pieces of the plan don't need to understand the plan."

"Don't give me that shit," Sal said.

When they got to the river across the village, the rains had swelled it and it was too deep for the tracks to cross. "Ford the river," came the order over the radio.

"And the fucking leeches?" asked Sal. "Where do they fucking fit in?"

"They fit in," said Wapniak. "Maybe after the next war, leeches will be the only things left. And *your* blood will be running in *their* veins."

"You're fucking nuts, man," Sal said.

They started fording the river, some of them holding the sacks of salt on their heads, some of them holding their rifles up in front of their faces, their arms raised in what looked like a sign of victory. Halfway across the river, the flash flood hit, and two of the men carrying mortar rounds on their backs couldn't get loose from their packs and were swept downstream. At the same time, there was fire from the tree line and three of the men were hit. But the flood had divided the troop. Half was on one side of the river, half on the other.

Sal and Wapniak were on the far side, helping the medic drag the wounded men into the jungle and bandage them. One of the men unrolled the medic's stretcher, and they carried the soldier who'd been shot in the stomach until they found a place where they seemed secure. "I want to go home," said the soldier. "Take me home."

"Don't sweat it, man," Sal said. "You're going home."

"I want to go home," the man said again, crying.

"Sure, you're going home. You hear the chopper? That's your taxi, man."

"Let me have a look at him," the medic said, coming over to the stretcher, but the man was dead.

"How is he?" Wapniak asked.

"He bought the farm," the medic said. "Wrap him up." As if, thought Sal, he were a fucking package from Macy's.

It was night and it was cold and the men were wet and had nothing to eat. The First Sergeant, who sometimes carried extra food for emergencies, said no, he didn't have a fucking thing, and the men sat down and shivered, trying to sleep. After a while, the Sergeant got up, came over to Sal and Wapniak, and said, "Here. Wrap up in this." He gave them the bloodstained stretcher and they wrapped themselves in it just as it was. Sal noticed that the Sergeant kept fooling with his helmet as if it were suddenly too small for him, but he didn't think anything of it.

In the morning, the Sergeant came over, took off his helmet, and in it were two packs of cigarettes and two cans of fruitcake.

"Now you see why he's the First Sergeant," Wapniak said. Sal didn't answer. He was too busy chewing. Out here, you learned to chew and chew and delay swallowing as long as possible.

"Let's go, we've got salt to deliver," the First Sergeant said.

When they got to the village, two women were clawing at the dirt, stuffing it into their mouths. When they saw the salt, when they realized what it was, they tried to eat it as if it were sugar and the medic shouted and waved his hands and the men tried to restrain the villagers, but it was hopeless. Finally, they locked and loaded, trained their guns on the people, and slowly began handing out cups of Kool-Aid laced with salt. Some of the people were too weak to come for the salted Kool-Aid and the soldiers brought it to them.

"You ever see anything like this?" Sal asked. "You ever fucking see anything like this?" He was crying. Wapniak wanted to say how important it was that they see this, but he looked down at an emaciated child whose stomach was so swollen you could see every vein in it, and his throat tightened and he could say nothing.

PETE SWITCHED off the TV, went out to buy a paper, and began reading the want ads.

N BROOKLYN the winter was beginning to crack. The brownish red leaves covering the hard ground were softening into powder, and through them came the sharp green knives of crocuses, hyacinths, and daffodils. Raking began in the backyards and men holding pruning shears appeared on ladders, clipping back the bushes in front of their houses, because when the bushes leafed out they provided excellent hiding places for muggers. Children began walking home from school with their jackets over their arms, and men got off the train with their ties loosened and the top button of their shirts undone.

On warmer days, windows were flung open and curtains began billowing outwards. Housewives carried loads of damp laundry up from the basement and hung them up to dry on outside lines that hadn't been used all winter. Occasionally, the weather changed and clothes froze on the line, their arms stiff in absurd, awkward postures. The old people began taking their folding beach chairs out onto the porches of the adjoining row houses and from porch to porch, the gossip traveled.

Along Ocean Parkway, old ladies sat with their dogs, their stockings rolled into fat brown sausages around their knees. Strollers were dusted off and children were taken for walks, nervously parked in front of supermarkets, the family dog tied to the handlebars, the mothers on line peering at the children through the windows. In supermarkets, women who had spent the winter glumly picking out groceries and thrusting them into shopping carts began enthusiastically clipping coupons and advising younger women on which brands were the best bargains. People came home, paused on their stoops and talked to neighbors. Here, thought Pete, nothing changed. How could anyone leave the neighborhood when the neighborhood was almost eternal, almost immortal, with a character of its own, purposes of its own? Daily life at its dailiest, that was what he wanted. That surfaces were like thin ice, a lesson he thought he'd learned in Vietnam, was something he was now anxious to forget.

If he made his family uneasy, he tried not to notice, although one morning he woke up early, and heard his mother shouting to his aunt, "There's something wrong with him! He's not the same! There's something wrong!" and he heard his aunt's low voice, answering, and then his mother, shouting again, "I don't know what's wrong with him! He's not the same!" He listened intently, but lately it seemed he didn't hear well with his right ear. That was the ear he held the gun to when he fired, that was the ear the radio squawked in when orders came in, but he heard his mother saying, "He sleeps on the ground! Outside! In all weather! Sometimes I come in and he's sleeping on the floor! Right next to the bed! Under the window where the draft is! Mrs. Lugano, you know what she said? She said the first morning she woke Eddie up he jumped out of bed and had his hands around her throat! His own mother! I saw the purple marks! Five on each side of her throat! Now you know what she does? She leaves a tray outside his door, knocks a few times, and runs down the hall until he opens the door and then she says good morning. She says he doesn't like it, but what's she supposed to do? She's afraid of him."

"She shouldn't be afraid of her own son," said his aunt. "That's not right. She has an umbrella. She could stand in the doorway and poke him. She doesn't have to treat him like an animal."

"Poke him with an umbrella?" asked his mother. "You poke an animal with an umbrella! You don't poke a person with an umbrella!"

"I mean," said his aunt, "she should find a way to wake him up."

"She knocks on the door," his mother said.

"Never mind, Angelina," said his aunt.

"So when he went to Chicago, she wasn't so sorry," Angelina said, "but *I'd* be sorry. I would."

"You should talk to him," said his aunt. "Maybe he doesn't know."

"Doesn't know he's sleeping outside?" asked his mother. "Who doesn't know he's sleeping outside? Only a crazy person doesn't know."

"He's not crazy, Angelina."

"Did I say he was crazy? Did I say that?"

He listened and thought, Am I crazy? Am I? No, he wasn't crazy. If he were leading a normal life, he'd be normal. It wasn't normal for a man his age to live at home with his mother. In a few months, he'd be twenty-one.

His uniform now rested peacefully in a straw-colored suitcase at the bottom of his closet, and when he opened the closet door, he no longer saw it. Eventually, his mother would want to wash the closet door, see the suitcase, and move it up to the attic. It would disappear, as if it had never existed. He was putting it all behind him. He was going to forget he was ever there. He was going to forget everyone who was there with him. It wasn't hard. Wherever he went in the city, he saw people doing it. Eddie was out of the state, somewhere in Chicago, sending postcards saying, "I wish you were here." He no longer wanted to find Sal or Wapniak or to know what happened to the Chief. All that had taken place in another life. He came in one day and told his mother he was moving out.

"I'm getting married," Pete said.

"To who?" shouted his mother. "Who are you marrying?"

"Dolores."

"You know Dolores? You know enough to marry her?"

Pete said Dolores didn't even know she was marrying him yet. He'd asked her and she'd said no. "Remember when I answered that ad for a mechanic upstate?" he asked her. "I filled out the application? I've got the job. I asked her to go with me and she said no, she doesn't want to leave her mother. She wants to stay in the neighborhood. But she'll change her mind. All I have to do is wait. She loves me, Ma. Don't go beating on the tom-toms about her."

"My son comes home and tells me he's getting married and I'm not supposed to ask questions?" shouted his mother. "You're not ready! What's her last name?"

"Pescatto."

"You need our consent!" said his mother. "Until you're twenty-one you need our consent! Tell that to Miss Pescatto when she changes her mind and says yes!"

"Ma," he said, "I'm going to work."

His mother and aunt sat at the kitchen table and glumly stirred rock sugar into their thick coffee. "So," said his aunt. "Dolores Pescatto. She's short, she's blond, she was no student, she likes a good time, and she runs around."

"Runs around?"

"Pete's not the only one she sees. She sees someone else who's older and who's in the business. Mrs. Lugano says she's no good. Eddie went out with her and dropped her. They go out with her and they drop her like a hot potato, or she drops them, but every week it's someone else."

"Maybe," said Angelina, "she's a nice girl looking for a nice boy."

"A good long look."

"He says she loves him."

"Angelina, you better talk to him," Theresa said.

ANGELINA sat her son down, set out two plates, piled them high with anisette cookies, and poured them each a cup of coffee. "Let's have a heart-to-heart talk," she said.

"A what?"

"A talk," said his mother, flushing. "About Dolores."

"What about Dolores?"

"If she loves you, she loves you. If you love her, you love her. Fine. Good. When I got married, I loved your father. He loved me. You get married, it goes on forever. It's—" She hesitated. "It's a death sentence. You divorce, it goes on forever. You have children, they tie you together. She understands you? You understand her?"

"What's there to understand? I'm a simple guy. I like staying home. I'm going to like being married."

"And she will too? She's going to like staying home running after babies? Up and down the block I hear the same thing. The girls don't want to stay home. They want fancy clothes and cars and jobs. They leave the babies with their mother and the husband works late and they go out on the town."

"She's going to like being married to me."

"Who told you? You know what it's like if she doesn't like it? I know what it's like!"

"You want fancy clothes and cars and going out on the town?"

"Don't be fresh!" his mother shouted, jumping up. "What did you tell her? You told her you sleep on the floor? You told her you sleep in the garden? You told her that?"

His blood thudded. He didn't answer.

"You didn't tell her? Why didn't you tell her? Because you don't want to scare her off. She doesn't know *anything* about you."

"I don't want to talk about it, Ma."

"Talk about it!" his mother shouted.

"Why? *We're* not married."

"It's funny?" asked his mother. "A funeral is funny?"

Pete said they weren't talking about funerals and his mother said if they were talking about his wedding, that's what they were talking about.

"If you keep it up, Ma, I'll have to move out."

"She told you to say that! Didn't she tell you to say that?" his mother demanded, and he didn't answer, because it was true.

Six months later, Dolores walked up his red-brick front steps, paused and looked at the handmade Christmas wreath on the door, sighed, and rang the bell. Mrs. Bravado wouldn't be happy to see her. The rest of the family would look at her as if she were a scarlet woman, and to tell the truth, she didn't lead the purest life, but she wasn't a nun and the times were changing. She wasn't happy to come here either. The Bravados were an old-fashioned family and people always asked, "Pete Bravado? Doesn't he have that brother in a home?" and her mother asked her, "So, Dolores, why do you waste your time? You want children like that brother? It could happen. You want to be the next Mrs. Bravado? The first one isn't so happy. You should hear what her neighbor says about the fighting and the hitting, all because of the brother."

If the truth was told, she didn't want to marry at all, at least not yet. She liked being single, picking and choosing the men she wanted. She thought of it as her way of seeing the world, and she told her girlfriends that, and one of the girls repeated what she said to her brother, and he said, "Yeah, join the army and see the world." In the neighborhood, the word got out: "Yeah, Dolores joined the army. She's seeing the world. You want to know how she's seeing the world?"

She wanted to get out of the neighborhood. She'd taken typing courses at a business college in Manhattan, and now she could type and take shorthand, but it didn't interest her, sitting in an office day after day, taking orders when what she wanted was to give them, and one of her friends, a legal secretary, asked her what she'd like to do most and she said she wanted a job where she had to wear fancy clothes and sit behind a desk and sign papers. "Sure," said her friend. "Run for president."

"What you want," said her mother, "is a rich man. Then you can wear fancy clothes and come kiss the children at night. You marry a rich man, you don't even have to change your own kid's diapers." She knew her daughter. Regardless of what her daughter thought, she'd been brought up to be a wife and mother, and one day, she'd wake up and see that's what she wanted. So she wanted money. Let her marry a rich man.

When Dolores stood naked in front of the bathroom mirror, admiring her body, she had vague dreams that included the words "jet set" and "famous" and "wealthy," but as she stood there waiting for one of the Bravados to answer the doorbell, she knew they were dreams, and if she were lucky, someone would marry her. Pete wasn't what she had in mind. She'd liked Eddie. He'd had a future. He was already making money. Even before he went into the service, he had that fast red car, and now he had a long black Cadillac and his mother bragged about the big house he had on the lake in Chicago and how beautiful his wife was, and she pulled out pictures of Eddie and his wife and child, and his wife was wearing a fur coat and the open collar showed the sparkle of diamonds. Her mother said money like that was dirty money, the devil's money, but she didn't care where money came from. Money was money. The stores were full of things, and things were *life:* if you could buy enough, you could buy yourself a new life. Who cared where the money came from?

"You know him?" her mother asked her. "You know this Pete? You know what the neighbors say? He sleeps on the ground outside." Dolores said he'd get over it. Judith Mary married the guy who used to hang from the tenth-floor project window, and now he had a good job and a child on the way.

"Judith Mary," said her mother, "is a good girl who likes to stay home."

"When I get married, I'll like to stay home, too," said Dolores, and her mother shook her head because she knew it didn't happen that way. Even women who grew up wanting nothing but a husband and children felt the ropes round their ankles, pulling them down, and the kitchen sink, such an innocent thing: who would think you could come to regard it as something evil, something alive, something from "The Shadow" on the radio. It filled itself with dishes even when you weren't cooking, and one day, you had everything in the house clean, everything, even the baby's diaper was clean and changed and the baby was asleep, and someone came in, sat down, and there were newspapers all over the floor and someone else spilled coffee with milk on the new rug in the bedroom and when you got up off your knees and looked at the window the sun was gone. It was dark.

And if you liked babies, you took good care of them, even when they cried so steadily you found yourself, not often, but it happened, standing in front of a stove, holding them, wondering how long it would take a fifteen-pound infant to cook in a 375-degree oven. These were the kinds of problems women had once they were married. If the turkey weighed eighteen pounds, how many hours did you cook it at 375 degrees, or was it better to wrap it in an aluminum tent and cook it at 450, in which case it would be done faster, but when you took it out it wouldn't be brown, and it would taste a little bit different, not exactly traditional, so was it any wonder you stood there with the baby, wondering how long it would take him to cook?

Before she had Dolores, she was leaning out the window, hanging the laundry on the line that went from her house to the big telephone pole in the yard, and her first child was sitting up in a small yellow plastic chair with big red plastic wheels, and she heard Mrs. Lugano, who used to live next door, saying to Eddie, he couldn't have been more than four, "You see that shirt hanging there? You don't shut your mouth and I'm going to hang *you* out on the line. With clothespins, right through your shirt. Until you learn to keep quiet, you'll hang there." The child screamed his head off, terrified, and she watched, fascinated to see if Mrs. Lugano *would* do it. Maybe it could be done. Maybe clothespins were strong enough to hold up a four-year-old child. But was the line strong enough? Maybe strong enough for *her* child. He was a lot smaller than Eddie. "Are you crazy?" she said to herself. "Get away from the window."

Then the children grew up and went to school and they talked back to the teacher, and you had to go to the school, find something to wear so the other children wouldn't see you and laugh at you and say, "I saw your mother. Boy, she's a dog," and listen to the nun or the priest saying if he kept this up, she'd be visiting him in jail, and you came home, and the bright one, the one you liked having on your lap, or taking with you to the supermarket, that one said in a snotty voice, "Let me tell *you* something about your husband," and went through a list of all his faults, faults you didn't want to think about, because if you did, how could you live with him, and if you were poor, like her, and ignorant, you couldn't live without him because he earned the money that filled the refrigerator.

Right now, a green scum was forming on the bottom of the vegetable tray because she'd left a lettuce in there too long and it started to rot and turn slimy. To this day, she hated the feel of it, and while she cleaned, her husband complained, saying it was his good money that paid for the lettuce and she let it rot right in his own refrigerator. And even if you had a job, you were damned to the worst circle of hell if you divorced. None of the women in the neighborhood would talk to you. When they saw you coming, they'd clutch their own husbands as if you had a hook and were coming to drag them off, as if you wanted any of their husbands. They were no better than yours. It would only be more of the same thing.

And then the children were older and talked back and broke your heart. Hadn't her own mother said it? Hadn't she heard it before she married? Not one word had she understood, and Dolores wouldn't either, and Dolores wasn't like her. *She* would have swallowed Clorox, drunk the whole bottle, if someone could have proven to her that no one would marry her, that she'd never get to live in a mother-daughter house, that she'd never have children. Now *her* mother said, "It gets better when they're forty." Who lived so long?

Maybe the Bravado boy brought excitement into her daughter's life. Dolores had already bailed him out of jail after the two of them went to Chinatown for dinner in the Bravado family car, and on the way back one of the men in the car in front of him started honking, and motioning for Pete to back up his car. There was no room behind him, and Pete honked back, shaking his head. The car in front of him backed up and hit his front fender. Then the driver got out and began banging on Pete's door. "Stay inside," Pete told Dolores. "Don't get out. I can handle it."

He got out of the car. "What's your problem, man?" he asked, and the other man took a swing at him, and as he did, two men got out of the other car and came toward him. Dolores, who was in the car, thought Pete was in trouble and started to climb out, and Pete saw one of the men going toward her. Now it wasn't just him. Now they were threatening someone near him. He picked up the first man, threw him over the roof of his car, and when the police came, Dolores was crying and he was pounding someone's head against the curb.

"What happened?" he asked Dolores.

"Don't you know?" she asked him.

"All I remember is his throwing a punch," Pete said.

"You practically killed them!" Dolores said. But she was impressed. She didn't mind bailing Pete out, and after all, the charges had been dropped. She wanted someone to protect her. *He* could protect her. He wasn't like her father, a good man whom her mother could beat up. She looked at him differently now. He wasn't a kid from the neighborhood. He'd learned *things*. He'd been places she'd never been. He had secrets. There was something mysterious about him. She didn't know how it happened, but it had. His face changed, became something she had to look at. Something inside her softened, a small place filled with light. She'd fallen in love.

. . .

PETE OPENED the door. "Oh, thank God," Dolores said, her teeth chattering, and he said, "What's the matter? You're cold. You're white," and he took her into his bedroom and they sat on the edge of his bed facing the white wall and its low chest of drawers and its large carved wooden crucifix, the one his grandfather brought with him from Italy.

"We're getting married," Dolores said.

"We are?"

"I'm pregnant."

She's going to get pregnant, said his mother's voice. *She's going to get pregnant and then what choice will you have?* But his mother didn't understand. He didn't want a choice.

"Yeah," he said after a minute. "I'll do the right thing."

She looked at him. Shouldn't he say he loved her? *I'll do the right thing.* That made her feel cheap.

"When are we getting married?" he asked her, and she said, "Next month. I want to make a dress and buy a few things and have a bridal shower. Yeah, at least a month."

Pete said he'd better tell his mother. She'd want to do something.

"No," said Dolores. "Wait. She doesn't like me. She'll start trouble. Let's start it off good."

"Fine," said Pete. He didn't ask any questions. Almost a year ago when she thought she was pregnant, she'd tried this with Eddie and he said, "Yeah? You're pregnant? Go tell Bobby to marry you." But it was a false alarm. She wasn't pregnant. This time she was. The doctor said there was no question. *Get married fast or they'll crucify you.* But to tell the truth, Pete was too soft. She respected Eddie for what he said. He didn't let women push him around. He made his own choices. "What's the matter, Dolores?" she asked herself. "He's too good for you?" That was the trouble. He was. And he didn't make much money. She wanted a big ring to show her girlfriends. She wanted a big house. But she didn't care as much as she thought she would. Something inside her had softened. Even in the cold, she felt like a cat in the sun.

"What about the job?" he asked her. "I'm taking the job upstate."

He loved the little towns that came up suddenly around the curve in the road, dug in at the foot of the green mountains. On weekends, he took his motorbike, bought with his army savings, and got up early Sunday morning, and by six o'clock, he was upstate and people were just beginning to turn on their lights and everything was shut up tight, and the sun began coming up, reflected itself in all the windows, was displayed in the plate-glass windows of the few storefronts, and the only thing open was the truck-stop coffee shops and he'd stop in one of them and order eggs and bacon and fried bread and then he'd be on his way again, not stopping until lunchtime. He liked the feel of the wind, and the rain when it didn't come down so hard it blinded him so that he had to stop, and he kept going from town to town, looking at the different plants in the yards of different houses, purple lilacs here, white lilacs there, asking the man behind the coffee counter, "What do you call a plant that looks like this?" and then he'd describe it.

He stopped at lumber yards and watched men sawing lumber and piling it and inhaling the smell of fresh-cut wood and sawdust. He liked looking at the wrecked cars and trucks in the yards, imagining what they needed to fix them and get them running again. He liked the way people said hello and good morning even though they didn't know who he was. He noticed the way no one used their front doors, but only the doors to their sheds or garages. He liked to see the women come out of the house in their robes, their hair still in pink curlers, carrying out the trash. Here and there a raccoon crossed an empty field followed by its cubs, and cats curled up on porches in front of the mice or moles they'd caught during the evening, waiting to be let in.

All the little differences fascinated him, the stone fences some people built to enclose their meadows, the horse grazing in a yard right in the middle of town in back of a white house with green shutters, a sign in its front window saying, in hand-painted letters, TVS REPAIRED HERE. There was peace and quiet out there. He was starved for it. He didn't know how, but his love of the neighborhood had been replaced by his need for the silence of the country.

"I don't want to go upstate," Dolores said. "My mother's here. Everyone's here. I'll need help with the baby."

"What for?" he asked. "I've got two legs."

She looked at him and saw the way he'd clenched his jaw. Now his face looked hard. "What do I know about the country?" she asked. "It has bees and a lot of grass."

"I'm going," he said. "I need it."

She was almost three months pregnant and she loved him. "Sure, I'll go," she said. "You can get used to anything, right?"

"You're going to love it up there," he said.

"I love *you,*" she said.

"I love you, too."

"Do you?"

"Yeah," he said, surprised at the question.

Why doesn't he kiss me? thought Dolores.

His mother heard the news and didn't say a word. It was no use. "If I say something and it works out, he'll tell her, and she'll never forgive me. If, God forbid, it doesn't work out, in every word out of my mouth he'll hear 'I told you so.' You can't win. With daughters-in-law you can't win."

"Bite the bullet," said Theresa. "That's what my mother used to say."

"God rest her soul," said Angelina.

"Maybe they'll be happy," Theresa said, but Angelina said no, it wasn't possible. A car backfired and Pete was on the floor. When it rained, he slept outside. What did he know about women? What did he know about marriage? He's taking a loose girl up there to live in the woods and it *snows* up there. She remembered the drifts from when she worked in the Catskills and how high they got from the time she used to work up in the mountains.

"I remember what it's like. She's going to wait all winter for the bingo games to start? You can't even listen to the radio. The mountains get in the way. She'll go crazy and she'll drive *him* crazy."

"No," Theresa said, "when you first get married, everything is wonderful. Even washing dishes. You remember."

"We fell in love. That's why *we* got married," Angelina said.

"Why shouldn't she love him?"

"She should, but she doesn't."

"So maybe after a while she will. Sometimes it happens. In the old country, that's how it happened."

Angelina lost patience. "Who does she love?" she shouted. "She loves herself, that's who she loves!"

"Pete knows what he's doing," Theresa said.

"Yeah?" said Angelina. "When did he learn? Tell me that. He *wants* to be married. They think women want to get married, but men want it too. 'When you grow up and get married and have your own house, then you can talk.' How many times's George said that to him? Two thousand times? Three thousand times? So after a while, he thinks, Oh, I get married. I get my own house. I say what's what and I'm like my father. He thinks he gets married, it's all settled, nothing more to think about. Don't tell me we were that way! Men are worse than women! You see the way he picks a woman? She's little, she's pretty, he thinks she'll turn into his mother. What does he know about her? What does he want to know? Nothing! He knows nothing!"

"So, if he makes a mistake?" Theresa asked. "A lot of people make mistakes."

"He makes big mistakes. Remember juvenile court? Remember the school windows? She's not what he wants, he's going to take it quietly?"

"He doesn't like disappointment, it's true," Theresa said.

"Doesn't like it! He can't stand it!" Angelina shouted. "What can he stand? He's a good boy, but he wants things so hard, he sees what he wants."

"So," said Theresa, alarmed by her sister-in-law's breathing, "even if she isn't what he wants, he'll see what he wants. A fool's happy in a fool's paradise. Ma used to say that."

"Yeah?" said Angelina. "And your father? What did he say? He said nothing's worse than being married to a fool. I remember. He meant George, his own son."

"Angelina," she said, "what can you do about it? Nothing, right? Make the best of it. The others are buying them a used Studebaker Lark for a wedding present. Up there he'll need a car."

"She can't drive!" Angelina said. "I forgot she can't drive!"

36 I T W A S the fourth day of a four-man ambush. Sal and Wapniak were sitting with their backs against a banyan tree, watching the two new guys, one white and one black, trying to clean their mess kits. They polished them with rags. They wasted water from their canteens. They sprinkled salt on the pans, hoping that would prove abrasive enough to help in the scouring, and still they were caked with old C-rations. They looked up at Sal and Wapniak, whose mess kits rested on their laps, shining—from a distance, where you could not see the many scratches patterning their surfaces—looking new. Sal and Wapniak grinned at them. They continued scouring until Topper, a short fat black soldier, threw his pot on the ground and said, "Fuck it. All right, what's the secret?"

"Maybe Mr. Right doesn't want to know," Wapniak said. Whenever they did something, the white guy (the splib, as white guys were now called, while black guys were called chucks) always told them what the *right way* was. The right way consisted of what he'd read in various manuals or been taught in basic training.

"Fuck him," said Topper. "I want to know."

"Yeah, I want to know," said Mr. Right. "You know what's wrong here? These kits weren't intended for cooking with C-4. They can't take such high heat. They bond with the food. It's useless. No one can get them clean."

"But theirs are clean," Topper pointed out.

"Ah, who cares?" said Mr. Right.

"He doesn't want to know," Wapniak said.

"You want to know, don't you?" Topper asked Mr. Right, who looked at his face and said, Yeah, he wanted to know.

"Should we show him?" asked Wapniak.

"No," said Sal.

"Maybe they'll do us a favor if we show them," Wapniak said.

"Like what?"

"Like go look for Paganani's AO."

"You'd do that?" Sal asked.

"I'll do anyfuckingthing," Topper said. "I can't *look* at this pot no more."

"O.K.?" asked Wapniak.

"Yeah," Sal said. "Show them. Topper, toss him your pot."

"So this is how you do it," Wapniak said, taking out his entrenching tool and digging up a chunk of dirt. "The best dirt comes in a clump with grass growing out of the top. It's easier to hold on to. You hold the dirt by its hair, and you rub dirt all over your pot like this, and you rub it back and forth, like this, and maybe you add some more dirt, like this, and *voilà!* It's clean."

"You used *dirt!*" Topper said.

"So? It works, doesn't it?" Sal asked.

"You used fucking dirt!" Topper said again.

"You got something against dirt?" Sal asked him. "You sleep in the mud, it gets all over your face. It gets in your eyes, it gets in your mouth. You walk in the dust, you breathe in dirt. There's ten pounds of dirt ground into your uniform. You're gonna get fussy?"

"I don't have to *eat* dirt, man," Topper said.

"You don't clean pots with dirt," said Mr. Right.

"I just did," Sal said. "Now I'm going to wash it off with unpurified water. You know why? Because when we run out of water, we drink whatever we find, scum and frogs and all. So what difference does it make? We eat dirt and we drink dirt and we're still alive but they medevac people out of here with food poisoning, so I clean my mess kit with dirt and I don't lose no fucking sleep over it. You want to eat out of those caked pots, you go right ahead."

"Sure," said Mr. Right. "You rinse the dirt off, Topper. That's what you do."

"No," Sal said. "What you do is you go find Paganini."

Birds called. Frogs croaked. Insects hummed. Somewhere an animal was moving through the brush. Then all sounds stopped. It was too quiet, and the quiet was suddenly replaced by a muffled explosion.

"What's that?" Mr. Right asked, but Sal and Wapniak were already on their feet.

"A booby trap," Sal said. "Stay here. Don't move."

By now Sal and Wapniak each knew what the other would do before he did it, and they took off, each shadowing a side of the trail between them and Paganini's area of operation. When they got there, they found three soldiers bending over Paganini, who was shouting, again and again, "Where's my leg? Where's my leg?"

"Whatsa matter, Pig? You misplaced your leg?" Sal asked, pushing through the others, bending over Paganini, cutting open the leg of his pants with his knife, making a tourniquet and tying it above the knee. "Where'd you put it?"

"Where's my leg?" Paganani repeated again and again.

"We're looking for it. It can't be far," Sal said. "Go get the leg, Wapniak. Pig, will you shut up? We're looking for the leg."

Wapniak came up in back of him, carrying the bloody leg and the foot, still in its jungle boot. He tapped Sal on the shoulder. *You really want this leg or what?* asked his eyes. Sal took the leg from him.

"Here it is, Pig," Sal said. "Here's the leg." He handed it to Paganini, who smiled up at him and tucked the leg under his arm, against his chest, as if it were a toy. "Happy now?" Sal asked, checking to see if the bleeding had stopped. It had. He looked at his watch. A few more minutes and he'd have to loosen the tourniquet. "Anyone call for a medevac?" he asked casually.

"We weren't too sure of the coordinates," one of the new guys said.

"Call for a medevac," Sal told Wapniak. "So what happened, Pig? You're too old for this. How'd you make a mistake like this?"

"Man, I got tired of looking where I put my damn foot," Pig said. He looked down at the leg clutched to his chest, up at Sal, and started laughing. "You know?" Pig asked.

"Yeah, I know," Sal said. "What are you gonna do with that leg?"

"I'm going to fucking stuff it," Pig said. "When I get home, I'm gonna stuff it and take it to my shit-faced mother-in-law, and say, 'See? Fuck you, bitch, I told you I'd be back,' and I'm going to beat her over the head with it."

"You're going to show it to your kid?" Sal asked.

"Why's he talking to him?" one of the new guys whispered to another. "He's gonna wear him out. The guy fucking lost a *leg.*"

"Yeah, but he's not in shock," Wapniak said, coming up on them. "He's not screaming."

"I'm going to build my kid a shelf and put the fucking stuffed leg over his bed," Pig said. "When someone says, 'Join the army and see the world,' he'll look at that leg."

"That's a good idea, man," said Sal, who heard the helicopter coming in. "If I ever have a kid, I'm gonna write you and ask if I can borrow that stuffed leg."

"No one's getting this stuffed leg," Pig said, patting the boot as if he were patting a dog. "No one's taking this leg away from me."

The sky had darkened rapidly and the air was misty. Rain would be here within a half hour. Wapniak was on the radio, talking to the pilot. "I can't see too well down there. Can you give me some directions? Over."

"There's a tree on your right and a palm on your left. It's a tight fit," Wapniak said. "You see our strobe? Over."

"I see it," said the pilot.

"Very tight fit," said Wapniak.

"Just keep the strobe on," said the pilot. "I'm coming in."

"So," Wapniak said, when the helicopter lifted off, Pig still clutching his leg like a trophy to his chest, "you three guys come back with us."

"Why?" asked one of the new guys. "Now Pig's gone, I'm in charge."

"You come back with us because you don't know where you are and you can't find your way back without us. Is that a good enough reason?" Wapniak asked.

"Look, don't get macho out here," Sal said. "Macho guys go home in body bags."

"What about Pig?" one of the new guys asked.

"Ah, Pig's gonna be fine," Sal said. "They'll fix him up with a nice wooden leg. He's still got his knee and all, and he has trouble at home, he unscrews that leg and clubs someone to death."

"Yeah," said one of the new guys. "Sure."

"Hey, Sal," Wapniak asked, taking him aside. "He's gonna make it?"

"He's gonna be as fine as any one-legged rooster in the barnyard," Sal said. "Just as good as that."

"You think those two morons got their mess kits cleaned yet?" Wapniak asked.

"No," Sal said.

"They're worrying about a little dirt and Pig's going home without a leg."

"But he's got his *knee,*" Sal said.

"You know what?" Wapniak said. "You're starting to think like a doctor. So he lost his leg? He's got his knee."

"Well, he does, doesn't he?" Sal asked. A mosquito stung his cheek and he slapped himself in the face and saw blood on his hand. "Man, am I fucking sick of the sight of my own blood," he said. "So what about mosquitoes? Do they mean something, or are they too small?"

"Nothing's too small not to mean anything," Wapniak said.

"Yeah?" said Sal. "When you figure out what it means, you be sure to tell me. I wouldn't want to miss it."

"You know what?" Wapniak said. "You're a real asshole."

"That's why you love me," Sal said.

"Nobody loves you, not even your mother," Wapniak said.

"*Uncle Sam* loves me," said Sal. "He do love us all."

 **37** **T**HE SNOW FELL and fell outside the windows of the great stone building where they took their vows in City Hall, and outside, during the brief ceremony, cars and buses honked, punctuating their vows, and so did the rumble of the underground trains. Dolores' sister was her maid of honor, and Paul, dressed in his homemade soldier's uniform, was the best man. There was nothing Pete wouldn't do to please him, and Mrs. Bravado didn't know which way to look, because although Dolores looked up at Pete with adoring eyes, it was plain to her that Dolores was furious at having a retarded boy for her best man, turning her wedding into a Halloween party, and George was equally furious Paul was there. Every time she looked at Dolores, who wore a white minidress and a short veil, she thought, How could this happen? They'd all come back to the house for champagne punch and cake and coffee and then they'd be gone.

When Dolores was finally sitting in the car, her fingers thrumming impatiently on the misting windows of the egg-blue Studebaker Lark, Angelina hugged her son and said, "Call me every day."

"As long as the calls are on his bill," said her husband. Then the car pulled away, and her husband said, "Well, he's gone. When's Paul going back?" She sat down at the kitchen table and cried and Theresa chased him out. "You don't have any feelings?" she asked her brother. "She waits all this time for him to come back, and now he gets married and leaves?"

"No one told her to wait so hard," George said. "She overdoes everything."

"IT'S A NICE house, isn't it?" Pete said, and Dolores saw a small, square white house with green shutters, a square shoe box with a green roof, and outside the front windows, empty window boxes filling with snow, and said, "It's nice. Where are the other houses?"

"The closest one's half a mile away," Pete said. "We've got plenty of land. We can raise chickens and geese and plant a big garden, and in back, there's a grape arbor, better than the one we have at home."

"I don't want to raise chickens and geese," Dolores said, her eyes filling. "I don't know anyone here."

"You know me," he said, smiling broadly. She looked at him, frightened.

Couldn't he hear what she was trying to tell him? *There were no houses.* It was lonely here.

"Don't worry," he said. "You'll make friends."

In the city, thought Dolores, I had friends.

But when the house was warm, and they heated up a casserole some-one had given them and two loaves of bread wrapped in aluminum foil and opened a bottle of red wine they drank from plastic glasses, Dolores felt surprisingly happy. It was lonely here, but she had Pete, and soon she'd have a baby. It came to her with a shock: this was what she'd wanted all her life. She wanted excitement and money and clothes, but she didn't want them as much as she wanted this. By chance, pure luck, she'd gotten what she wanted most without trying.

The winter wore on, and Pete bought Dolores a sewing machine and drove her to the stores after work, and she bought yards of material, and in the mornings after he left she sewed curtains, and when he came home at night he hung them. He took her to bingo games on Monday nights and she began to meet people, women who told her horror stories about giving birth, offering advice about what diaper service to use or what kind of disposable diapers were best, and she listened, fascinated. She met a short, chubby woman named Marge who wore her hair in ringlets dyed straw-berry blond and who knew what everyone in town was up to, and at night, when Pete came home, she'd repeat everything she heard: who was sleeping with whom, why Fred's wife ran away and why she came back, how Alice's husband beat her, and who were the town alcoholics.

Pete felt uncomfortable listening, as if he'd been caught peeping in at someone's bedroom windows, and because she saw he wasn't interested, she stopped telling him what she knew, although every now and then she'd look up at him as he ate his dinner, shake her head, and say, "It's a regular Peyton Place."

"Life's too short for this garbage," Pete said one night. "People don't understand. They don't understand how short life is. Their priorities are all screwed up."

"Like how?" Dolores asked. She was swollen and when she ate, she had trouble breathing.

"Like Al's wife, still going on about her weeping willow. So it died? It's a tree. That's all it is, a tree. Why can't she see it's just a tree? Or Marge? What's the big tragedy now? Her son's suspended from school for two days? He's not *dead.*"

"But to them, it's important," Dolores said.

"A tree is a tree. It's not a person. A few days are nothing."

"Well," said Dolores, thinking, "in a war, it's different. But this is real life. If your son gets suspended, you worry. You worry about what will hap-pen next. It starts with a few days, it ends in jail. Al's wife wants her house to look nice. She loves that tree. Maybe if she had a kid, she wouldn't care so much about a tree."

"They don't know a fucking thing about living," Pete said. He looked at Dolores, thinking, You don't know anything about living either. Who have you seen die? You know how a man looks when he's a piece of raw meat?

"They're alive," Dolores said. "They know about living."

"They don't have their priorities straight. *I've* got my priorities straight. I go to work and come home and eat dinner and make love and go to sleep and get up in the morning and one morning, I'll get up and have a wife *and* a kid."

"That's all you want?" Dolores asked, frowning. "You don't want to better yourself?"

"What's bettering yourself, Dolores?" he asked her. "Getting another TV? A bigger house? You know how fragile life is? You snap your fingers, three people died while you were doing it. You can be happy with nothing." He saw the villes rise up in front of him, the old people going from house to house, visiting, the young children riding the water buffaloes in from the fields. Who did he know in the United States who was as happy as they were? No one.

"Everyone wants to better himself," Dolores said. "Everyone."

"You know how to better yourself?" Pete asked. "Be happy. If you're happy, you don't have to better yourself."

"I'm happy," Dolores said.

"So?" Pete said. "So what more do you want? Who gets even that much? We're lucky."

"But I wouldn't mind having more things," Dolores said thoughtfully. "I wouldn't mind another car or picking up the phone more and not worrying about the bill."

"Forget things," said Pete. He saw the boys in the village square spinning their handmade tops, made from mud and dung and baked in a fire until they were hard. "Earth, air, fire, and water, that's all you need. That's what Wapniak always said."

"Who's Wapniak?"

"Oh," said Pete, flushing. "Someone I used to know."

"Marge is coming over tonight to do my hair," she said. "You don't mind?"

"Why should I mind? I'll work on my models."

Usually, Dolores liked sitting quietly, watching Pete work on his model ships and planes, but now when he began work, she thought, What if he means it? What if he doesn't care about bettering himself? I don't want to spend my life in a house like this. I want a better life for my child. But a happy life was a better life, wasn't it? When he forgot about the war, she concluded, he'd become like everyone else. He'd want more money. He'd want a bigger house. He'd want to see his wife parade up and down the avenue in a fur coat. All she had to do was wait.

He got up in the mornings before Dolores was awake and set a pot of coffee on the stove and cooked his own breakfast, made a large pot of spaghetti sauce and set it simmering while he showered, and when he was ready to leave, he turned the fire off and covered the top of the pot with a plate. When he came home, he'd cook the spaghetti and ladle the sauce over it and she'd make the salad, or if she was too tired, he'd do that also. There wasn't anything he wouldn't do for her. When he got up, he liked to watch her sleeping. He liked looking at the walls of the rooms, knowing his money had paid the rent, and no matter what the weather, he kept them warm and dry inside. He wouldn't have believed he could miss the neighborhood so little or that he'd think so often of the villes, changed somehow by his imagination, purified of sorrow or suffering, visions, really, of heaven.

He liked going down to the lumberyard, standing around talking to the men who came in, stocking up on lumber to build new porches, or buying Sheetrock to replace the old plaster they'd knocked down from the rooms. One morning, one of the men came in with a chunk of plaster in his hand and showed it to him. "Look, horsehair. That's how old the plaster is," and sure enough, there were long strands of hair woven in with the plaster. He liked parking the car on Saturdays and walking to the general store to get the paper, and the way people said, "Good morning, Mr. Bravado."

In the mornings, the sun lit up the sky behind the mountains and the clouds poured over the mountaintops and the outline of the mountains was so clear and so sharp you could almost see through them to the towns and the horizon beyond. Now in the mornings there was a steel frost on the grass, and above the metal grass the melting water glittered on the dry, shaking leaves like mirrors. During the days, the sun grew smaller, but the moon, when it bloomed at night, was huge and round and the stars were clear and the sky was the color of ink. In Brooklyn, the stars were hidden by the streetlights, the headlights, the pollution. Now when he walked, the soles of his boots rang out like metal on the frozen ground and on the pavements. Only in town were there sidewalks. The outside world faded, wavered, and ceased to exist.

For a while, he'd watched the nightly news, still looking for his troop in Vietnam, but he never saw it, and the reports were worse than ever. There were fewer accounts of the war and more of the protesters at home, and he knew what was happening there. Men were dying every day. They'd never have a chance to come home and get married and have children. He turned off the television set when the news came on, or changed the channel. He bought the newspapers on Sundays for Dolores, who liked to clip coupons for the supermarket, but he never looked at them. He'd never been there. He hadn't done anything. He didn't know anything about it.

Vietnam, what was that? Just like the cabdriver who'd brought him home from the airport.

Other things were more important. Would the baby be a boy or a girl? He was praying for a girl. He never wanted a child of his to see what he'd seen. Standing over the body of the dead girl they dug up in Vietnam, he knew he never wanted to have a boy. His wife, of course, was praying for a boy, but then she was Italian. She'd never been out of the country. The war couldn't get at her from the television, which trapped it and tamed it like an animal, almost a pet, annoying, but a pet. "It's on again," she'd say, making a face, switching the channel before he could.

He never asked himself why he loved her because he thought he knew. All men his age found a woman, loved her, married her, and had children, and if anyone had said he loved her because she knew nothing of the war, he would have said, "Are you crazy? She's my wife!" He loved the word "wife." He knew women loved saying "my husband." They said, "My husband said," or "My husband did," and you could touch the satisfaction in their voices, but he thought he loved the words "my wife" even more. He had hundreds of pictures of Dolores, who liked the attention at first, but was now so tired of posing she didn't look up from the table when she heard the shutter click. "I'm going to buy a movie camera when the baby's born," he said, and Dolores ate her oatmeal and said, "That's good." When he was out of the house, she studied the pictures and tore the unflattering ones to shreds. At work, as he unpacked the lunch pail he'd filled himself, he said my wife this and my wife that, and he was so happy he assumed Dolores was happy.

More and more Dolores was tormented by a suspicion that her husband didn't know her. This feeling frightened her, as if she'd looked into a mirror and no one looked back. When she talked to Pete about things that happened in the town and he said, "It don't mean shit," she felt slapped, bruised and sad. At night in bed, she heard him moaning and sometimes he'd sit bolt upright, covered in sweat, the sheets wet beneath him and they'd get up until he changed the sheets, but when she asked him what he dreamed about, what was bothering him, he wouldn't tell her. She was shut out. And when she tried to tell him her father was sick again, having fits, and her mother was worried, he'd say, "He's *alive.* How old is he? Sixty-three? That's *old.* He's had his chance." She could understand that the war had changed him, that he'd seen friends die who were only seventeen and eighteen, but why did that misery erase the rest of the world's suffering? How was she supposed to make herself count? How was she supposed to make room for what was important to *her?* She was a person. Even if what she cared about was stupid and idiotic, shouldn't someone care about it? Her husband?

"Sometimes," she told Marge, who was putting her hair up in pin curls, "I think he could come home and get in bed, and the woman in the bed would have long black hair, and he wouldn't notice anything. Do you ever feel like that?"

"No. My husband notices every little thing about me and he doesn't like a single thing he sees."

"But he *knows* it's you he doesn't like," Dolores said. "Pete comes home and he likes everything he sees, but he doesn't see me. I could be a talking doll."

"He treats you like a doll," Marge said, taking a bobby pin from her mouth.

"You know what I think? I think he loves me because I knew him before he went over there. He'd never marry anyone who didn't know him before."

"What are you talking about?" Marge asked.

"He changed over there and he doesn't want to see it, and he thinks I don't see it. He thinks I see him the way he was before he left. He sees *me* the way I was before he left."

"So he sees you," Marge said comfortably.

"He didn't *know* me before he left," Dolores said desperately.

"Look," Marge said. "You live together long enough, he's going to see you and then you'll think of this as the good old days. It could be worse. He could be running around."

Dolores' hands turned to ice. When someone said, "It could be worse. He could be running around," then you knew you were in trouble. After Marge left, she went to bed and wept. Somehow, although nothing she could point to had happened, she had become unhappy.

**38** **W**HO'S GOING to be the last man to die in Vietnam?" asked Wapniak. "He's going to be famous, man. He's going to be the biggest piece of the puzzle."

"I'm not going to be the last man to die in Vietnam," Sal said, "but I'm going to be the first to get plastered tonight. Look." He held up the carton full of blue plastic baby bottles.

"Man, I haven't gotten over the last hangover yet," Wapniak said.

"All the more for me," Sal said, unscrewing a cap and drinking a third of the bottle.

"Yeah, well, it's been quiet on the fire base lately," Wapniak said, unscrewing a cap from another bottle. "Ready for some serious drinking?" he asked Topper and Mr. Right. Topper said, "*All right,*" and turned up the volume on his tape deck. "Hey, Tina, baby!" he shouted. "I see you!" Mr. Right was drinking quietly. "See?" Sal said. "He's a midwesterner. They drink like they're doing homework. You're not laughing now? You only laugh when we're in a firefight? Man, when you're in a firefight, you sound like a hyena."

"So, he's nervous, man, big deal," Topper said. "Drink, man. Don't find fault."

They drank until they were laughing senselessly and staggered to their cots and kept on drinking.

"Incoming!" someone shouted, and they lurched up from their cots and staggered off to the bunkers. Sal and Wapniak's bunker had such a well-fortified overhang that the Captain brought other soldiers by to look at it. "That's an example of serious shelter," the Captain said, and then he took Wapniak aside and asked him if he was sure there was enough support under all that stuff because if the bunker overhang ever caved in on them, they'd be smothered by their own protection.

"It is a work of *architecture,* Captain," Wapniak said. Now, when he heard the explosion, he headed directly for the bunker. He thought he saw the bunker next to him take a direct hit, and if it had, those guys were gone. They didn't bother with overhangs. He looked for Sal, but he wasn't in the bunker. Sal knew what he was doing, Wapniak thought, and he settled himself against the bunker wall and fell asleep. The incoming roared in; the explosions deafened, but he slept. After a while, you didn't hear it. But in the beginning, that was the unbelievable thing about war: the noise of it.

Sal made his way across the fire base watching the incoming land. Illumination flares were going up and falling back to earth, *chooka, chooka, chooka.* Man, he was sick of this. He looked down at his feet, saw smooth earth, and thought, This is a good place to sleep. He curled up on the ground.

In the morning, someone was shaking his shoulder.

"Goddamn you!" Wapniak shouted. "Goddamn your fucking skull! You scared the fucking shit out of me! You do it again, I'll chew you a new asshole!"

"What are you talking about, man?" Sal said, sitting up and looking around. "What am I doing out here on the LZ?"

"You *slept* here, you fucking idiot!" Wapniak shouted. "They mortared the hell out of us and you slept through it out here on the LZ. Why are you alive? Give me one good reason you're alive!"

"God loves a drunk," Sal said.

"Get up!" Wapniak shouted. "Get up!"

"So what went down?" Sal asked. His head hurt and his stomach was clenching.

"Mr. Right went down and he's not getting up," Wapniak said.

"Topper? What about Topper?"

"He's drunk as a skunk but he's fine," Wapniak said. "You fucking do that again and I'll fucking kill you."

"You better get out of here soon, man," Sal said. "The only word you know anymore is the *f* word. We got any more baby bottles left?"

"No, we don't," Wapniak said. "You know why? I *poured* them out."

"You did what?" Sal said. "You did what? Say that again!"

"You fucking heard me," Wapniak said. "You wanna do something about it?"

"Yeah," Sal said. "Yeah. I want to take an aspirin."

"Goddamn it!" Wapniak said, kicking a stick into the air. "Goddamn it!"

"Look at it this way," Sal said, holding his head. "You got another piece for your puzzle."

"You're lucky you're not in *pieces!*" Wapniak screamed.

"Hey, man," Sal said, worried, "you better cool down quick."

"Yeah," Wapniak muttered. "Thanks a lot."

"Don't mention it," Sal said.

ETE CAME home one afternoon, knocked, called out, "I'm home," and no one answered. He started running through the rooms. What if something had happened to her? Maybe she was already in the hospital. But there she was, lying on their bed, stretched out across it on her back, her arms flung out, her stomach bubbled up toward the ceiling, weeping, big, gulping sobs, her face shiny and streaked with mucus, rubbing her eyes like a child with her fists, smearing her eyelids with the tears and the mucus, a picture of the end of the world.

He had to make her stop crying. How did you make a woman stop crying?

"You'll hurt the baby," he said. The writhing mass of sorrow, his wife, awkwardly sat up, moving unusually fast, and hurled a pillow at him. "All you care about is the baby!" she shrieked in a voice that tore at his ears. "The baby, the baby, the baby! Not me! You don't talk to me! You don't care about me!" The other pillow flew through the air toward him.

"Don't throw things at me!" he said, his temper rising, but his wife had collapsed again, forgetting him entirely, sobbing until the bedsprings shook. He wanted to sit down on the edge of the bed, but somehow the bed had become her territory, some private place for grieving. "What happened?" he asked finally.

She lay on her side and with her head still buried in the pillow, lifted one arm and pointed at something. His eyes followed her finger. The phone? The phone was out of order? He went over to the telephone table and saw a large piece of notebook paper and a note written in black crayon. MY FATHER DIED! In capital letters. Her father died? That was what this was about? This was nothing. Didn't she know that? People died. It was natural. A natural death wasn't terrible.

There were good deaths and bad deaths. He'd figured that out a long time ago. If you died for a good reason, that was a good death. If you died when you were happy, that was a good death. If you died of natural causes, that was a good death. If you died in a car accident coming home from a party and you were happy, that was a good death for two reasons: you were happy when you died and to die in a car in America, that was a natural death. To die in Vietnam because the artillery got the coordinates wrong or because you had to take a bridge that no one wanted, or because you had malaria and the command chopper wouldn't fly you out because it was the *Colonel's* chopper, that was a bad death. To die alone in the mud, that was a bad death. To die before you had a chance to live, that was a bad death. Whatever her father died of, he'd lived a long time, he'd seen a lot, he'd raised a family, he'd had a life. He had a good death. All he had to do was explain it to Dolores. She didn't know.

"Of what, Dolores?" he asked. "What did he die of?"

"This morning," she said. "At nine o'clock. I was sleeping!"

"No," he said. "What did he die of?"

She stopped choking great, gasping breaths, shuddered, and pushed herself up on one elbow, looking at him, her eyes swollen, her cheeks blotched and shiny, her blond hair sticking up in stiff spikes. "Cancer!" she cried. "Cancer! They opened him up for a hernia and it was all over him! Everywhere! He died under the knife! Before they even closed him up!"

"I'm sorry," he said.

"You're sorry?" she shouted. "*He* was sorry! Where was I? I was up here! What am I doing here? Why did I come here?" She got up heavily, waddled to the closet, and began pulling dresses from the wire hangers. "I come up here and leave them alone and look what happens! If I'd been there, he wouldn't be dead. He wouldn't! He'd wait for his grandchild!" She started pulling a sweater on over her nightgown. She didn't know what she was doing.

A wind roared in his ears and the rooms of the walls wavered. Liebowitz was lying out in the field and they were holding the Chief down bodily, and he kept crying, and then he started talking. "I could've stopped him. When he got up, I could've knocked him down," and Sal said, he said it over and over, "Man, there was nothing you could do. Nothing. It had his name on it."

"I don't believe that crap. Nothing has your name on it," the Chief said, and Krebbs said, "Nothing brings back the dead, man. The dead have their own place. You want to survive, leave them in it." But was Krebbs alive when Liebowitz died? He couldn't remember. Where was Sal? Sal would remember. What was Sal's *last* name?

He struggled to focus on the room where his wife was flailing about, tangled in her clothes, trying to pull a pair of maternity slacks on over her nightgown, staring puzzled at the zipper that wouldn't close over the white fabric with its blue flowers. He heard his words coming from far away, not from behind the mountain, but farther. By the time they reached this room, the life would be out of them. They would be cold. "He would have died anyway, Dolores. Cancer all over him. It's better he died now. All that pain, all that time in the hospitals." He thought of his brother Paul locked up in the home, beaten, taken to the hospital for a broken arm, left there swimming in his own urine, his black eye turning purple and then yellow and then green.

"It's better?" his wife was shrieking. "It's better?"

He tried to tell her to calm down. She'd do herself harm. But she was taking off the sweater, pulling the nightgown over her head and yanking the sweater back down over her swollen breasts.

"He died a good death," he said, but he already knew she wouldn't understand. The words fell to the ground like dead things. He felt like a cat, its mouth bloody, delivering bloody mice to its owner and the owner couldn't appreciate the gift. She screamed and kept on screaming.

"A good death!" his wife was shouting. "A good death alone in the hospital asking for me? What am I going to do now? I have *no father.*"

"You have me," he said, but that only infuriated her more.

"You? You and your models! You brought me here. You know what we have here? Nothing! Six rooms and windows full of curtains! A television that doesn't get CBS! I watch soap operas on CBS! All my life I watched soap operas on CBS and I can't anymore! My mother calls me and tells me what happened. Lisa, Kim, and Bob, they were like friends to me! People I lived with! Funerals! Weddings! Every day, I could turn them on! No matter what else, they were there! This afternoon, after she called, I turn on the television and what do I see? NBC! On those soap operas I don't know anyone! We have nothing here! You know what we have here? We have *time.* Every day we have twenty-four hours of time!"

The wind roared again in his ears. Why was she talking about soap operas? The worst tragedy for her was soap operas? She didn't know anything. She didn't stand by while the medic dug up bodies; she didn't smell that odor. She didn't know what it was like to shake in a bunker waiting for the next shell to hit, and you knew where your skin was, every inch of it. There was a line of light around it separating you from the air around you. You saw that long enough and you wanted the next shell to hit. You'd never know you were gone and the line of light around your skin would be gone and the fear with it. All this over soap operas and one old man?

"I'm not enough for you?" he asked. "You don't care you have me?"

"No," she screamed. "You can bring him back? Can you bring him back?"

Inside him, something turned over and stalled. He might as well be back there, he was so cold. He knew he should do something about her. She was hysterical. But he couldn't call "Medic!" because there was no medic. He couldn't slap her or knock her down. She was a woman and she was pregnant. He didn't have a big opium joint to stuff in her mouth. He didn't have a hypodermic full of morphine. What was he supposed to do with her?

"I'll drive you home," he said. "Stay until after the funeral."

"I'll stay as long as I want!" she shouted, and then she sat back down on the bed, collapsed on her side, sobbing violently. What's this all about? he asked himself. What's all this fuss over one dead person? Sooner or later, he

3 8 0 BUFFALO AFTERNOON

had to die of something. Why was it so hard to tell someone something you learned over there? It wasn't a secret. Everyone ought to know. Sooner or later, everyone died of something.

"You have no heart!" his wife screamed at him.

"YOU'VE GOT to go back to him," said her mother. "You're married and you're pregnant. A baby needs a father. He cooks for you. He brings home a paycheck. He doesn't drink it away at the bar. He's buying you a house. He lets your girlfriends come. You sit in the beauty parlor when you want. Not everyone has it so good."

"He plays with models and he doesn't talk to me and he has no heart!" said Dolores.

"What does that mean, he has no heart?"

"He said Daddy died a good death!"

"Yeah? *My* mother said the same thing. You die in your sleep, it's a good death. The old people say that."

"He's not old!" shouted Dolores.

"So what?" said her mother. "So maybe what he said was true."

"I hate him," Dolores said.

"Don't say that! Don't let him know!" In her mind, all the old stories she'd been told as a girl rose up, of women who scorned their husbands and were murdered by them, buried under the piazza or in the garden, or beneath the stone wall of the olive orchard, or hung on hooks in the attic. But that didn't really happen: the hooks. That was a story. Surely that was a story. She thought of all the times she'd felt hatred rise like bitter bile in her throat, and her husband wasn't a man anymore. He was a monkey, an ape, something terrible. *If I were strong enough, I'd kill him.* With this knife. With my bare hands. How many times had she thought that? And now he was gone and she walked up and down in a stony place she called her kitchen, smashing glass and walking on it, feeling nothing. It was normal to hate your husband, but you couldn't let him know. "Whatever you do," she told her daughter, "don't let him see it. You can't let him see it."

"And why not?" asked Dolores.

Her mother thought. "Men are killers," she said.

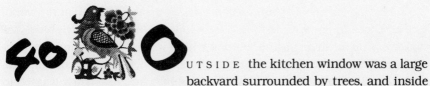 **4O** UTSIDE the kitchen window was a large backyard surrounded by trees, and inside the tree line it was always dark, and so Dolores usually avoided looking out as she did the dishes. This morning the baby was asleep in his bassinet. The wives of the men who worked with Pete had given it to her, along with a surprise shower, although she barely knew them. She knew she was the outsider. She wasn't interested in hearing about impetigo and who had the chicken pox and how long immunities lasted in the child.

She was already calculating how many bottles and how many diapers she would have to change before the child was old enough to talk to, before the child was company. At the last minute, she'd decided she wanted a girl, not a boy, but she had a boy, and she remembered what her mother said. When a girl marries, you get another son for the family, but when a son marries, you lose a child. She knew her husband wasn't too happy about having a boy, either. He was the only Italian male she'd ever heard of who prayed for a daughter, and occasionally he stood over the crib or held the baby and said things like, "I'd shoot his foot off first," and she thought she ought to ask him what he was talking about, but even if she did, he wouldn't answer her. In any event, she knew. It had to do with the war.

For her, the war didn't exist. It was something that interrupted her soap operas, or used to interrupt them while she still lived in Brooklyn, but now the war was something inside Pete, waking him in the middle of the night, sometimes moaning so loudly he woke the baby, keeping him asleep in one position from night until morning. "How do you sleep all night without moving?" she'd ask him. "How?" The war was what caused her such embarrassment when a car backfired and she found her husband crouched behind garbage cans. Other wives here had the same trouble, but they didn't seem to mind. After the shower, one of the children had shaken a can of Coke, and when he popped the tab, it exploded, and there was Pete, as usual, flat on his stomach. "Last time my husband did that, he pulled down the whole tablecloth," said one of the wives, but Dolores was so mortified she wouldn't look at her. "It's not normal," she mumbled, and the other woman stared at her, said nothing, and she went back to her seat on the couch.

She often thought of Pete as he'd been in the city, before they came up here. She remembered bailing him out of jail. That wildness in him, that violence, she'd liked it. She knew that now, because she missed it. It called to something deep in her, her own love of excitement, her own desire to shatter anyone who got in her way. And it must still be inside him, because there were days when she felt her own anger rising up as if to meet his, her own blood heating up, her own hands tight with the desire to hit out at the world. She had been happy with her husband's violence but she was frightened of her own. And out here, in the country, with nothing to stop one's imagination, no walls of other houses hemming her mind in, she was becoming wild. Something in her was growing long, sharp nails and teeth. She wanted to explain it to Pete, but if he couldn't understand why she cried when her father died, how would he understand this? She didn't understand it herself.

She left the dishes in the sink, and because the house was so quiet, she turned on the television and sat down before the picture lit up the screen, and when it did, she saw a tall, heavyset man with black hair, and she didn't know what it was: did he remind her of her father? Was the accent familiar? She didn't change the channel.

An older man was asking him how he came to testify at the winter soldier investigations, and he said, Well, like most things, it was a long story, and there were a lot of ways of coming home, and his way had been lucky. He was wounded, but not badly, and after he came back to Travis Air Force Base, he visited a friend at Berkeley, and got into an argument with a girl in the hallway about Vietnam, one of those chicks with long blond hair. She'd said they were taking part in a civil war, and he said, No, she didn't understand; they were building hospitals and treating children, and if they didn't stop communism in Vietnam, one country after another would fall until all of Southeast Asia went under, and in the middle of it, he began hearing what he was saying, and realized he didn't believe a word of it. It was all rhetoric, rot, lies. "You want someone to sign your petition?" he'd asked her, and he'd signed it.

After that, it all happened fast; he'd started dating the girl, and she encouraged him to start school, and to take the courses he needed to matriculate, and that's what he was doing and now he was on his way to becoming a doctor, not far on his way, but on it.

"So all you needed was the love of a good woman?" the interviewer asked him, and he shifted in his seat, and said, "Come off it, man."

Dolores sat up straight and stared at the TV screen. Was it her fault? Maybe she should encourage her husband to go to school.

Now the interviewer was asking him why it was that he'd come through the war but was ready to turn against it, and the black-haired man looked at the interviewer as if he were seeing an insect, and said, one day he was in a restaurant and the woman he was with started to look like an animal, and so did everyone else in the place, odd animals who walked upright, their faces on the ends of long stalks called necks, small, flat faces, just animals, ugly animals if you compared them to panthers or tigers, not even cute, like kittens. And these ugly animals believed all the other species on earth existed only to serve them. They say, "The whole world's my territory, man." They were pale and ugly. They resembled bamboo shoots and they were weak, but they were more dangerous than anything on earth because they thought the entire world and everything on it belonged to them. Hey, man, the *world's* my area of operation. "You understand?" he asked the interviewer, and the man said he did.

"He doesn't," Dolores said aloud. "I see it in his face. I don't and he doesn't."

"And the decision to testify?" asked the interviewer. "Was that difficult?"

"What do you think?" the ex-soldier asked. He'd thought about his friends, whom he intended to find, Wapniak, who might be back in the field, and another one from Brooklyn, who was home; maybe he'd see this program and contact him, and the Chief, who was lost, and Liebowitz, who was gone, and the other men he'd seen die, and he said, "I thought, What are they asking me to do here? Turn against my friends? Turn against everything they stood for? But some of them don't stand for anything anymore and they never will again. And why'd they die? I couldn't think of one good reason for any one death. That's what one of the guys always said. And I was back here, and it was still going on, and when I read the papers, or watched TV, I knew exactly what was happening. I was there. Somewhere, some guys were taking a bridge for the fifth, maybe the sixth time, a pile of bamboo poles and sticks, and each time a man was killed. Then the VC took the bridge back, and the ARVNs called in the U.S. Army for help. In the end, who needed the bridge? The VC ferried things across the river where the water was shallow. They didn't need boats. They lashed bamboo poles together into rafts strong enough to carry jeeps. It was hopeless. It was evil. I know how fragile human life is. I know how much of it there is, but is that a reason to waste it? I thought about all the things I burned, the villages, a bar I set on fire. Man, it was too much. I asked what I had to do."

"You have no regrets?" the interviewer asked.

The ex-soldier fidgeted in his chair. "Over there," he said after a pause, "I had a friend, a Lurp, and everywhere he went, he took his dog, a big shepherd, a black dog, and he went through everything, human waves, everything. He went through the worst stuff. *But I've always got my dog.* He always said that. They cut his orders to come home and they took away his dog. *You can't bring an animal like that home. They're dangerous.* He said he'd take the responsibility, but they said the dog was army property. He said if they took the dog, they'd have to take him first, but they knocked him down and they shot the dog. Right in front of him. So you know what he did? He took out his .38 and put it in his mouth and pulled the trigger. He couldn't live without that dog."

"That was smart?" Dolores said aloud. "To kill yourself over a dog?"

"If a dog's all you've got," said the ex-soldier, "you don't throw it away."

"I don't understand," the interviewer said. "What does this have to do with testifying?"

"In the old days, somewhere," the ex-soldier said, "they used to kill the returning soldiers. Shoot them, poison them, set fire to their camps, sink their ships. They were going to let trained killers come back in? Let them mix with civilians who didn't know their rear ends from their elbow? After they taught them how to gouge out eyes with two fingers or crush a windpipe with one hand? You're going to let them come back? They're not the same. They're different. They know things. They can blow up houses. They can bring down a man a block away. Conserve your ammunition. Fire discipline. Noise control. They should've shot us like the dogs, but they didn't shoot us, and now they should hear what happens when you send men over. We're not dogs, but we're not the same. They've got to bring the others back and they've got to help the ones who *are* back. That's why I'm testifying."

"Are you happy testifying?" asked the interviewer.

"Do I feel good about it?" the black-haired man said. "I don't feel good about it. I go testify today, and others go testify, and what's going to happen? They'll fear us. They'll wish they shot us like the dogs. 'You a Vietnam vet? How many women and children did you kill?' You know how many times I hear that? You know who I'm doing this for? I'm doing this for the dead."

They're all crazy, Dolores thought, but she didn't change the channel.

Now the television showed a small town in Oregon, and then the camera moved inside a large room where a senator, a priest, a doctor, and several army officers sat at a long table. An American flag hung from the wall behind them. The testimony had been going on for three days, the announcer said, and everyone was weary. The men in front of the room looked haunted, as did the man who testified. Someone's voice was saying, "None of it was new to me, but hearing it like this is new. Now there's a new frame around the old pictures. Now I'm not trying to stay alive. I'm not nineteen anymore. I'm someone else, someone older, and I sit here, I'm two people, the younger one who did the things I just described, and the older one who's sitting in judgment."

The ex-soldier who'd been interviewed before went up to the front of the room, gave his name, the name of his outfit and the areas he worked in, and the dates he was there.

"I saw an ARVN soldier take a newborn child and dash its head against the ground. I saw soldiers throw C-ration cans between the trucks of a convoy so the children would dive for them and be hit by the next truck. I participated in setting fire to villages. Usually we warned villagers before we came in to burn or bomb them, but sometimes we didn't. Sometimes we didn't want them to know.

"I took part in mutilating bodies. I cut off ears and tongues. When the enemy cut off men's private parts and stuffed them in their mouths, we cut off enemy heads and set them between their knees because we knew the Vietnamese believed the soul resided in the head. Sometimes we took off the head with a machete and hid it, because they were frightened by the sight of a body without a head. Sometimes we threw heads into the middle of villages when we swept through.

"I fired at a child and took off his head when I was ordered to do so. It bothered me then and it bothers me now. Once I set fire to a bar in a village for no reason at all. I was tired of being there and seeing so many people burned and killed. I didn't know what else to do. I watched my TC, my track commander, skin and bleach two skulls and our track drove through the countryside with those two skulls mounted like trophies. We burned villages we were ordered to leave alone because we found weapons there and knew they were enemy villages and we'd been taking casualties there. I personally never saw any raping of women, but a woman who worked with us told us a soldier murdered a prostitute who asked for too much money. I'm sure there's more, but there's a lot I can't remember.

"I remember seeing a priest standing on some ammo cartons preaching a funeral service. I remember the pile of bodies under ponchos and who those people were a few minutes before. An hour before, they were alive. I remember eating a piece of someone's birthday cake, and an hour later, he was under one of those ponchos. I remember being medevaced out with a lot of dead bodies and wounded men were sliding from one end of the helicopter to the other because the blood made the floor of the chopper so slippery, and the door gunner kept pushing one of the bodies away from the hatch with his foot so the body wouldn't slide out. I remember seeing one man go up in front of me and nothing was left of him but a reddish stain in the dust. I remember a lot of things like that. When you think about what we're telling you here, you should remember these things, too. We didn't choose to go over there. Most of us didn't want to go and some of us wouldn't be here now if we'd played the game. None of us rowed over in our own boat. So," he said lamely, looking around, "that's it."

At the end of the day, the camera followed the ex-soldier out the door. He walked out into the cold light and someone put a hand on his shoulder. The ex-soldier turned around and found himself looking at a marine gunner, a lifer.

"You're Italian, I'm Italian," the man said. "War's the *soldier's* secret. Sometimes it's all he's got. How could you do it? You're *Italian.*"

"Let me tell you about Italian," the ex-soldier said. "Italian is my Uncle

Giuseppe who locks my aunt Gina in the closet whenever he goes out. *That's* Italian."

"Michelangelo, Da Vinci, Cellini, Vivaldi, Dante, Machiavelli!" shouted the gunner.

"Uncle Giuseppe!" the ex-soldier shouted back.

Both men faced each other, their faces sheets of water. The camera took their pictures.

DOLORES got up and turned off the television. "Terrible things," she said, hugging herself. "Terrible things." She went to the kitchen window and looked out.

She saw a brown animal come from between the trees and begin moving slowly toward the house, every two or three steps turning his triangular black and white muzzle up to look at the window as if he knew she was there and might mean him harm. Occasionally he stood up on his hind legs and looked around him, his front paws dangling like tiny seal flippers. When he moved along the ground, he looked like an enormous loaf of brown bread, and his paws seemed too small to hold him up. As he moved along, he stopped, nuzzled the grass, burrowed with his front paws, found something to eat, ate it, and moved on. He was completely wild.

The baby was sleeping. The house was warm and there was something comforting, almost familiar, about this brown animal, so industriously inspecting the grass. Dolores pulled a kitchen chair over to the window, picked up her bowl of oatmeal, grown cold while she'd watched television, and her cup of coffee, and sat down to watch it. After a while, she could perfectly predict when the animal would look toward the house. Sometimes the animal seemed to stare directly at her and she stared back at it. It occurred to her that the animal might be a female, not a male, or it might be very old, the way it waddled on its tiny black paws. Somewhere in the woods, it might have its cubs. She wondered what it was. It wasn't a raccoon. Raccoons had striped tails and masks. She knew that much. In high school, she'd had a coat with a raccoon collar. Maybe it was a groundhog or a badger.

She sat there for hours, watching the animal move slowly through the grass, burrowing here, nuzzling there, chewing, standing up on its hind legs, showing its beige-white underfur, and miraculously, the baby slept on. It didn't cry. She was sitting at the window, motionless as a statue, when Pete walked in, and she motioned to him with her hand: stay back. She turned to him and put a finger to her lips: keep quiet. He moved silently to the window and saw the animal, then looked from the lawn to his wife. He saw she was still in her robe. Nothing in the kitchen had been touched. She must have been sitting here since breakfast, watching the animal eat.

Pete put his arm around her shoulders, but her body didn't yield against him. She sat upright, her muscles tight, watching the animal move back and forth along its zigzag path. Finally, the animal must have had enough, because it stood up on its hind legs, looked around, and headed back toward the woods, stopping every two or three feet to be sure it was safe.

"I want to go home," Dolores said. "I want my mother." *I want to go with the animal into the woods,* she thought. *I want to know what it's like there.* Pete didn't answer. He didn't protest. The sight of his wife sitting in the kitchen watching an animal from the woods with such concentration, that was so unnatural, even he knew what was coming next. She'd stop eating. She'd stop bathing. She'd forget about the baby. Soon there'd be nothing left of her. Then he'd have two people to visit in homes, his wife and his brother.

"All right," he said. "We'll go back."

"It's good here," one of the men had said at work. "You can forget here." He was a veteran, too, Korean, or possibly Vietnam. Pete didn't know and he didn't want to know. *It never happened. I wasn't there.* The magic sentences that closed the doors whenever he thought back, and they worked, too, except when he dreamed, although since coming here, he'd dreamed less and less frequently. *She's catching it from me,* he thought suddenly. *She's catching it from my dreams.* But that was crazy. He couldn't think like that.

"We will?" she said, turning her face up toward him, her features softening slowly, the blood returning to her cheeks. His heart twisted. He was looking at someone coming back from the dead.

Dolores was hugging him and kissing him and saying, "Oh, thank you, thank you, thank you, thank you," and he couldn't bring himself to say more than, "Yeah, I'll give two weeks' notice. You better start packing."

THE OLD neighborhood was the old neighborhood. There was nothing to say about it, only now he had no job, and until he found one, he lived with Dolores in her mother's house and was lonely. His wife had her friends over all the time, and during the afternoons, she and her mother passed the baby back and forth as they watched the soap operas on CBS. He found a few guys hanging around O'Halloran's, and when he asked them if they knew of any jobs, they laughed and asked him what he thought they were doing there. He looked at want ads, but he wasn't qualified to do anything except drive or repair cars and the city produced more car mechanics than it needed.

His father had an old car that needed a new engine, and during the afternoon, he worked on it, suspending the new engine from a thick oak limb, lowering it into the car and beginning to fasten it in. Up and down the block, in garages, boys worked on stolen cars, dismembering them for spare parts, leaving the wrecked hulks on the curbs for the city to haul away in the morning. On Sundays, he went with his mother and his wife to visit his brother in the home on Staten Island, and although Dolores went sulkily, she went.

"I don't think it's a good idea," she said, looking at the baby.

"Why not? It's not catching," he said.

"I don't want to go," said his wife.

"You came back here for your mother. I came back for my brother. We're going."

When he sounded like that, she listened to him as he knew she would. He knew, too, that if he hit her she'd listen more often, make love more often, look at him with more respect, but he was never going to hit anyone again. He never wanted to hurt anyone again. He wanted to be good.

At night, he'd wake up from a dream: a dog was chewing at his face, a small dog, powerful and ugly, and he'd try to push it away from him, but he couldn't do it, and when he awakened, he'd sit and think, I don't want to do that no more. I don't want to hurt no one no more. I've seen the evil and I've seen the good and I didn't like the evil. I'm going to try the good. He'd repeat this over and over until he was again sleepy and then he'd return to bed. If Dolores knew he'd gotten up, she gave no sign. In fact, she did know, but she didn't want to know what had awakened him. She knew the war was there, as the animal had been behind the tree line in the country, but now she was afraid of the war. The war had nothing to do with her.

"You know," Pete told his mother, sitting in her kitchen while the sauce bubbled in its huge pot, occasionally spattering the white stove with drops of its blood, "Daddy used to say I was an evil kid. I'm not evil. Over there, I looked around me and I said, 'Hey, I'm a good kid. I'm a cupcake.'" His mother turned toward him, her wooden spoon shiny and red in the morning light. Over there? He'd never said anything about life over there. She waited, but he'd changed the subject. When had her husband said he was an evil kid? She didn't remember him saying that. He *thought* it. She knew that. Pete was saying he couldn't find a job, and he'd been driving two weeks for a car service, but that wasn't much. He didn't bring home enough to move them out of Dolores' house, but he could drive a truck. He thought he'd answer an ad for a moving company.

"She'll be home all alone," said his mother, who rarely used his wife's name.

"She's got plenty to do," he said.

"She'll have even more," said his mother.

He continued to drive for the car service, and then one day an old man yelled at him for taking the bridge instead of the tunnel, and kept it up: he should have come across town on 60th, not on 59th, and he held to the wheel harder and harder until his knuckles showed white. He wanted to stop the car and go over the backseat after him, not to kill him, not to hurt him, just to shut him up. The constant noise in his ears, the sound of whining, he couldn't stand it.

The next day a blue car made a right turn and cut him off and almost ran him into a fire hydrant. He had no passengers and took off after the blue car, pulling it over to the sidewalk, jumping out, yanking open the other man's door, and pulling him out. He was shaking him with one hand before he knew what he was doing, and when he saw what was happening, he dropped him.

"Man," said the driver of the blue Chevy, "you've got a problem. I should call the police."

"Yeah?" said Pete. "*You've* got a problem. *Me.*"

This couldn't go on. He had to chill out or someday he was going to pull someone over and that guy wouldn't just have a tire iron or a baseball bat. He'd have a gun. He went down to the offices of the moving company and asked for a job.

"You're sure you can keep awake?" the owner asked him, looking at the sheet he'd filled out. "Oh, a veteran. You can keep awake." They shook hands. "Just one thing," the man said. "No drugs. They find you with drugs, I throw you to the dogs."

"I never took drugs," Pete said, reddening. "Even over there, I never took them."

"You Spanish?" the man asked him. "You look Spanish."

"With a name like Bravado?" Pete asked. "No, Italian. You don't like Italians?"

"My name's Funicello, like the actress. Sure, I like Italians. Almost all my drivers are Italians. Except for the Chinese. They're the best. They never fall asleep. Work, work, work is all they know."

"Yeah, they're vicious little fighters," Pete said. "They don't need sleep." He saw one of them, arms and legs tourniqueted, coming across the fire base before a bullet from a cook or a baker finally stopped him. How long did you have to live before you forgot?

"You weren't fighting the Chinese," said the man. "A good thing you weren't."

"We confiscated plenty of Chinese rockets. We took Chinese advisers prisoners."

"So if you captured so many, how come you didn't win? Just kidding," the man said, but of course he wasn't. He'd won *his* war.

On the way home, he stopped for a drink, and then two drinks, and then O'Halloran said, "Go home. She's waiting for you. Buy her some flowers." Pete asked him if he had a deal with Mrs. Lupone, the florist, and

he came home with a bunch of daisies. Dolores was sprawled across the
bed, crying.

"What happened?" he asked. "Somebody died?"

"Worse!"

"Worse?"

"I'm pregnant again!"

"So?" he said. "I'll support you. I'm a driver with Acme moving. The
pay's good. You're home. You've got your mother. You've got your soap
operas. So we'll have another. They'll have each other to play with."

"*I don't want to be pregnant!*"

Where did women get these voices? These high-pitched squeals, they
drove you crazy. They were part of their defenses, like their long nails and
their high heels and the keys they carried between their fingers like brass
knuckles. What did she want? If she'd stop that shrieking, he'd do it.

"I don't want the baby!" his wife shrieked.

"Stop screaming!"

"I don't want it! I don't want to be a mother! I don't want to be married!"

"It's just the shock. That's all it is."

"Yeah? Then *you* have it! You know how long nine months is when
you're pregnant! I'm too young! It's your fault!" She went on and on, the
shrieks becoming shriller and more high-pitched. *Scree!* said the pig. *Scree!*

"I'll be back later," he said, putting the daisies down on the bedside
table. She saw them, sat up, picked up the flowers in their white wrapping,
and threw them at him.

"That's right! Walk away! You don't care about me! All you care about is
yourself! Why'd we come back here? Not because of *me!* Because you
wanted to see that crazy brother!" But now she saw the look on his face and
was frightened. She thought: He could *kill* me. He stopped near the bed,
picked up the flowers, and cracked their stems through the paper. "Here,"
he said, throwing them at the bed, "are your flowers."

He went out and walked on the avenue and a turning car brushed
against his thigh. Without thinking, he brought his fist down on the man's
hood and then hit the man's windshield. The glass windshield starred,
broken, as if it had been in an accident. He walked on, unaware of his hand,
swelling in his pocket. After a while, he became aware of someone following
him. "Hey, did you see that?" someone was whispering.

He turned around and saw two teenagers staring at him. Their hair was
black and slicked back, two toughs from the neighborhood. "You want
something?" he asked them. "Hey, it's cool, man," they said, crossing the
street.

When he came back, his wife was all apologies. Her mother hovered in
the background, an eye on her daughter.

"You tell him you don't want his baby! You don't want to be a mother!

You crazy? Why should he feed you? Your father, God rest his soul, he'd beat me black and blue. You make it up with him, you hear me? You want to stay here, make it up with him. I don't want to hear no more about how he doesn't understand you! Who understands you? I don't! Get him into the bedroom. He can only make you pregnant once."

He let himself be led into the bedroom and watched his wife close the door behind her. The baby's crib had been moved out of the room.

"My mother thought, you're going to be on the road, we need the time," his wife said, and he thought no more of it. He had a wife and a child and now he had a job. He looked out the window and for an instant saw the clouds boiling up behind the dark mountain behind the house in the country, but his wife's body was on his, and he forgot where he was.

ETE LIKED driving. He liked seeing the country, stopping at truck stops at odd hours, if he was awake enough, and if anyone else was there, talking and joking with the other drivers or making conversation with the waitresses. The farther west he went, the pinker their uniforms became, the longer and more frosted their nails, the blonder and more teased their hair.

Out west, when the scenery thinned out, he studied the sandstone cliffs and their red shadows on the desert. He began to pick up small books about the local Indian tribes, and eventually he bought longer ones, with fewer pictures and more print, and he'd read in bed beneath a stuffed moose head or a pair of crossed swords. In one midwestern state, he was frightened by the flatness of the landscape. It reminded him of something, but in the morning, he had breakfast with the man and the woman who rented rooms overnight.

"Don't miss the stuffed animal museum," they told him. "The town's real proud of it."

Before he left, he stopped to look at it. In it was a stuffed black bear, a stuffed giraffe, a stuffed elephant, and a carved wooden Indian.

At night, in the empty states, beneath the big skies, you could see the weather approaching, the future coming closer, rainstorms at the edge of the horizon clearly visible, but taking a day to arrive. In those places, he began to dream. In one of the souvenir shops on the highway, he bought a pad of paper and a package of ballpoint pens, and at night, before he dreamed again, he began to write his dreams down.

If, after a day and night's driving, he was still awake, still saw the white line running down the middle of the road when he closed his eyes, he would turn on the light and begin to write on his pad, a thick notebook with a metal spiral instead of a binding, the holes punched for a looseleaf, a red cover saying in large black letters, *Notebook*. Occasionally, he would find himself writing about digging up a grave, taking aim at a child with a shotgun, and he'd ask himself, Who wrote that? He'd tear the pages up.

When he came home, his son was beginning to teeter around the house, and his wife lay on the sofa with her feet propped up, her mother waiting on her. "Toxemia," said his mother-in-law in hushed tones, and Pete asked her what that meant. Would Dolores be all right? When she said she would, he forgot about it. While he was home, he brought her meals to her. He laid his head against her stomach and she put her hand on top of his head. He didn't see the way she glared into space.

After a year, the driving began to lose its novelty. He wanted to be home. He missed the routine, knowing what to expect when he awakened and when he went to sleep. Out on the road, anything could happen. You could see anything. You tried to keep your schedule, and you wound up waiting for a herd of cattle to cross the road. Or you were on schedule, even ahead of it, driving through New Mexico, and down a red clay cliff came two boys, naked from the waist up, on shining brown horses and you stopped to look at them, watched them out of sight, and when you got back in the cab, it had heated up like an oven and you had an hour to make up.

There was too much to see, too much to take in. His head felt swollen with what he saw, his eyes dry. He was crushed between what he'd already seen and forgotten and what he was seeing now. The eyes were supposed to be the only two doors to the mind, but all the doors of his body opened. Things rushed in through his ears, his mouth, his nose, even through the pores of his skin. He began to dread getting up in the morning and driving on, the hawks circling in the desert, the dead bodies of animals at the side of the road, a sharp curve that brought him alongside a hawk tearing at the bloody insides of a still-living rabbit.

Wherever he went, the afternoons brought schoolchildren coming home, on foot or in school buses that stopped in front of swinging wooden gates. He saw them disappearing down the path leading from the gates to the houses, so far back from the road that you took their existence on faith. In southern towns, the children walked home from school under thick leaves and sat on porches of houses like gingerbread cakes and did their homework together, right outside, and occasionally a black woman brought them glasses of lemonade and plates of cookies. When they saw his truck parked on the street, they looked at him suspiciously, and he moved on. He began thinking about school, wondering what was in their books, envying the children from families who thought books were important.

Once he picked up a boy on the road in Wyoming, fifteen miles out of town, in the middle of nowhere. The boy said he was running away. He didn't like home. He didn't like going to school, and Pete was shocked. He found himself shouting at him. "You don't like school? You know what happens to kids who don't go to school? They go into the army and people shoot at them and they watch their friends die! That's what happens!" His throat swelled because he wanted to cry, but instead he hit the horn and the loud blast terrified the night, bouncing back and forth between the stone bluffs. He got on the CB and called the state troopers and pulled in to the barracks with the boy. "Some day you'll thank me for this," he said, but the boy wouldn't look at him.

"They don't know what's out there," the state trooper said. "Last week, we picked up a man with a woman's head in the trunk. They asked him if he did anything wrong. You know what he said? He said, Yeah, he should have hidden the head somewhere else."

"I don't need this shit," Pete said.

"Yeah?" said the state trooper, bristling. Then he subsided. "Thanks for the boy," he said.

More and more he felt he was driving through other people's nightmares. One afternoon, he drove through Lubbock, Texas, and as the sun was setting, he saw a tract of suburban houses. On the side of the corner house, the large yard was fenced in to form a corral and in it was a lone buffalo. He stopped the truck. Was it still alive? The buffalo sensed him watching and moved farther down the yard. There it was, the only one of its kind. He got out of the cab and walked toward the yard and looked into the buffalo's terrified eyes. He rang the bell to the house. A woman came to the door. "Excuse me," he said. "I'm driving through and I saw the buffalo. He's yours?"

"He's ours," said the woman, the door open a crack. Maybe he was trying to sell her something. He could be a murderer. He could be anyone.

"What do you want with him?" Pete asked.

The woman looked at him, and beyond him, to the truck, and into his eyes. She considered the question carefully. "I always wanted a buffalo," she said. "He was in a zoo. When he got sick, I took him."

"He's miserable," Pete said.

"He's alive," the woman said. "The zoo wanted to kill him."

"Mind if I look at the buffalo?"

"Sure, go ahead," she said, closing the door.

He looked at the animal for a long time. He'd never seen a more unhappy-looking beast. After a while, the buffalo got tired of watching him, and lay down on its side, his back to him, his head twisted around toward him. "The land belongs to you," Pete told the animal. "You and the Indians." The buffalo's tail whipped back and forth. Flies were thick on its nose. What a life, Pete thought as he got back into his cab. The vinyl seats were so hot they burned the back of his thighs, and now he had an hour to make up if he was to keep to his schedule.

He was having more and more trouble staying awake. In Nevada, he passed a weighing station and didn't see it because he'd fallen asleep behind the wheel. A state trooper pulled him over.

"Didn't you see the sign?" the man asked him.

"I thought it was closed," Pete said. "They're always closed."

"This time it was open," said the trooper and took him into town to see the judge, who slapped him with a forty-dollar fine. He couldn't say he'd fallen asleep for a few seconds and passed the station. He hadn't known it was there.

But it happened more and more often. He'd awaken with a jerk and know he'd been driving in his sleep.

In Arizona, he stopped in a little town whose only buildings were aluminum trailers shimmering and wavering in the sun. At the coffee shop, also in a trailer, he asked the owner where he could find a doctor. "You sick?" asked the owner, and he said, No, he couldn't stay awake. "You want some pills for that?" the owner asked. "I've got pills. A lot of the men need them. You won't sleep if you take these pills. How many you want?" Pete asked for twenty. "Take fifty," said the man. He gave him a brown glass bottle filled with red and white capsules. "And take these." He gave him a bottle of yellow pills. "The reds keep you awake but afterwards you're left staring at the ceiling, you know what I mean? The yellows, they'll put you to sleep."

"How much do you want for them?"

"Ten. It's what I paid. I used to drive a truck. That's how I found this place."

"How much for a room?"

"Two dollars."

He slept in a room in the rear of the trailer and shared a bathroom with the man and his wife. Before he went to bed, he filled a glass of water and took two of the yellow pills. He got out of bed in the morning wide awake and happy, sure he'd had no dreams. The day was clear, the breezes that blew through the cab were almost cool, although in an hour, the sun would be up and soon he'd have to drink every ten minutes from a plastic gallon milk container he filled with water every morning. It was dry out here. He'd never imagined anything so dry. He stopped for lunch in restaurants decorated with sun-bleached cow skulls and signs on the bathroom door: twenty-five cents for use of the bathroom unless you're a customer. There was no water anywhere. Windmills revolved hundreds of miles apart, and in the middle was nothing. He dreaded a flat tire, or worse, engine failure. Now it was a high-wire act, getting from one destination to another. When he pulled in, he couldn't believe he'd made it.

Home, when he thought of it, was always small, a country on a postage stamp. At odd hours of the night, he began to call Dolores, but she asked him to call early. She was up all night with the children. Sometimes he'd wake up, have no idea where he was or why he was there and call her anyway. "Don't waste your money on the phone company," his wife said. "You're working too hard."

He came home to their new apartment after three weeks and saw his second son, small, still bruised purple here and there, still slightly yellow from a case of jaundice, and thought, What about girls? What about answering prayers? He was angry at God. There were times when he wanted Him to come down and explain His ways, get out of the sky altogether and come down and fight it out in an alley. Instead, He hid up in heaven like a gangster in Glencoe. Come out into the open and fight, thought Pete.

Dolores was arguing with their first boy, Petey, persuading him to eat a cookie. "Why are you arguing with a one-and-a-half-year-old?" he asked her. "Tell him what to do." But she continued arguing, and he watched the two of them, and then swung around and punched the wall. Immediately, his hand began swelling.

"Oh, fine," said Dolores. "Let me see the hand." He said there was nothing wrong with his hand and said he was going for a walk, but the hand continued swelling, and by the time he was in front of his mother's house, the pain was unbearable and the pinky was discolored.

"Eat," said his mother. "You're too thin. You sleep when you drive?"

"Yeah," said Pete, smiling. "I sleep when I drive."

"I mean at night!" shouted his mother.

"I sleep at night."

"Good. Eat."

"Ma," he said. "I don't want to drive anymore. I came home and I don't know the kids. Dolores doesn't know who I am. She has her ways, and if I don't like them, so what? I'm not there. They're not used to me. I'm a stranger. In my own house, I'm a stranger."

"Hmmm," said Angelina.

"On the road, I dream. I saw the moon last night. There was some kind of battle up there in the sky and the moon was covered with bodies. They were all grey and dusty from moon dust. All of them lying on their back looking up at the stars and the earth. It could happen, Ma."

"So why did you come back here? Tell me that."

"The woods were pulling her in. A few more months and her mind would've gone into the woods. Just like an animal. I saw it coming. When I don't dream, I think she dreams my dreams. It's a look in her eye, the way she holds herself."

"Oh," said Angelina. "Then you had to come back."

He sat back, sighed, and relaxed. He could talk to his mother. She always knew what he meant. Someone else would hear him say that the woods were pulling his wife in after them, or that the moon was covered with bodies, and they'd say, "He's crazy. He's crazy."

"You know what?" Angelina said. "I think she's a good girl. Some girls, they're wild before they get married, and then they settle down, they get fat, they wait for their husbands. So if she's afraid of the woods, don't take her out of the neighborhood. The mother of your children, that's what counts."

"Yeah, but if she's afraid of the woods, she's afraid of me," he said. He reached out for a piece of anisette toast and his mother saw his hand.

"What's that?" she asked.

"I closed a door on it."

"Yeah? I've seen a lot of hands like that and you don't get them from closing doors. You get them from punching someone."

"I didn't punch anyone, Ma."

"No son of mine hits a woman."

"I hit a *wall.*"

"Put on your coat," his mother said. "We're going to the hospital."

42 A NGELINA was thinking, and as she thought, she stirred sugar from the pink, diamond-faceted sugar bowl into her coffee. She thought and whirled the sugar into the coffee with the spoon, until the spoon moved slowly through the coffee, which was, by now, coffee-colored sludge. She didn't notice what she was doing. She watched the liquid whirl in the cup and thought how water always emptied out of the kitchen sink so slowly, but the last drops whirled quickly away. When she was a child, she'd watched for the exact moment when the water began to whirl faster, but something always happened: someone shouted for her from the yard, one of the ducks gave an alarmed quack or a chicken squawked and flew into the air, or she lifted her eyes to look at the kitchen clock, something that simple, and when she looked down, the water was whirling itself away. Trouble was like that. It moved slowly and then when you lifted your eyes or blinked them, it was all around you, moving fast, like a tornado. She'd seen tornadoes in the movies.

There was trouble in Pete's family and every day it got worse. Now her son said things like, "I didn't come back to make everyone miserable," and "Who'd miss me? Tell me that?" and she shouted, "Who'd miss you? What am I, wood? What are your children, wood? You sick? Tell me the truth. You sick?" He'd look at her and say, "No, Ma, I'm not sick."

"Besides, you have to visit Paul! He knows how many days in a week because of you! I tear up a paper into seven pieces and every day he throws one away. When he's got no more, he knows you're coming."

"She doesn't like me. My wife doesn't like me."

"How do you know? Tell me. How?"

He couldn't tell her. It was in the expression on Dolores' face when he came back from a long trip across country. It was in the excited gestures with which she filled his lunch pail on the days he left. It was in her exasperated looks when he gave advice on how to discipline the children, in the way he saw her roll her eyes upward to heaven when she thought he wasn't looking, in the secret, satisfied half-smile he saw on her lips when he came in and saw her watching the evening news and what she said and didn't say. "Xuan Loc fell," she said, her voice bored. "They took Hue."

To protect himself, he'd go into the bathroom and close the door, but from the living room, she'd keep up her commentary. "You should see this one! He looks like a bear! These protesters! He's pretending to shoot an old woman! He's burning a bag with a picture of a town on it. Why does he do it? Look how angry the crowd is. There's a woman holding up a sign: GOLD STAR MOTHER. What's a gold star mother? Listen to that chanting! Oh, they're saying *U.S.A., U.S.A., how many kids you kill today?* See, that's how they think of you. That's why you can't get a good job. *U.S.A. U.S.A., how many civilians you kill today?* You think I like it? You think I don't hear about it? 'You married a *Vietnam vet?* They're all nuts. They killed women and babies.' "

Now she was thinking out loud, because the bathroom door was closed, and she knew her husband didn't hear well, and besides, why should she be the only one to suffer? He'd enlisted and now she suffered for it. She was cooped up in the house while he got to drive around the country, a woman in every state.

"He's handsome, your husband," said her girlfriend. "A regular James Dean. Even if he is a Vietnam vet. I wouldn't mind a vet who looked like that. But aren't you scared? Aren't you afraid he'll wake up some night and cut your throat? Kill you in your sleep? I read about it in the papers. They say all you have to do is touch them to wake them up and they go for you. You sleep in the same bed? He tells you about it? I wonder what he did there. Don't you wonder?"

She did wonder, but he never said anything to her. He didn't trust her. He didn't even see her, she'd figured that out a long time ago. If she had the news on TV, he left and didn't come back until it was over. Sometimes she thought he'd really forgotten the war was still going on or that it ever happened. And in the meantime, she had to put up with it: the sympathetic looks from the butcher. The lowered voices asking, "How's your husband?" as if he were some kind of lunatic. And how was she supposed to know when he didn't trust her enough to talk to her? Maybe if he'd talked to her in the beginning, it would have been different, but now it was too late.

Pete was in the bathroom so long she'd forgotten he was there.

"You think I'm crazy?" he asked her, his face white.

"What?"

"Your friends think I'm crazy. You think I'm crazy?"

"No. I don't think you're crazy."

"You think I don't know what people say? You think I don't know? It didn't happen to *you.* It happened to *me.* "

"Well, it's over," Dolores said comfortably. He didn't know if she was talking about the war or the news broadcast.

"It's *never* going to be over," he said. "No one should have seen what I saw there."

"Yeah? What did you see? They show it every night on television. Everyone sees it."

"No! They don't see it! They're going to show you a body hanging from the trees like crepe paper? They're going to show you that? They're going to show you the feelings? They're going to put the feelings on television? No one sees it!"

"All right," Dolores said. "Don't get excited. You'll have a stroke. You notice every little thing, like a little old lady."

His hands went up, palms facing her, fingers spread. "Back off," he said.

"Back off?" she repeated. "That's a way to talk to your wife? The boy doesn't behave and you put your hand through a window and he's watching you bleed all the way to the hospital? You throw his toys against the wall. You say you're sorry? He doesn't even hear it anymore. So you go out and buy him a big present. How many presents are you going to buy him? It doesn't change what he saw. The baby's afraid of you, too. They're both afraid of you!"

"I'm going out," he said.

"Yeah, sure. Get drunk! You think I'm not afraid of you? Sometimes I think, He's going to kill me. "

"You think I'm going to kill you?" he asked, his hand on the door. His eyes were stinging. "That's what you think?"

"Yeah, that's what I think."

"O.K., Dolores," he said and went out. He walked rapidly, crossing one street after another, heading in no particular direction, relieved when he found himself in a different neighborhood where no one knew him, no one knew he was a veteran. He kept on walking. If he walked far enough, he'd get to Sheepshead Bay. He had the weekend off. He'd get on a boat and go out fishing. He wouldn't come back until a few hours before he had to start driving.

There was a crowd on the block ahead of him, looking at something, probably an accident. The crowd looked like a bunch of brown and black ants around a sugar cube, but no one was walking away, bending over the curb, retching. He remembered when he couldn't look at an accident without losing his stomach. He could look at anything now. He joined the crowd and edged his way forward.

There were five soldiers, their faces smeared with black and green camouflage paint, wearing cammies, and five Vietnamese, or five people dressed like Vietnamese, in black silk pajamas and those broad straw hats that came to a point, and the soldiers were beating the Vietnamese with their rifles, hitting them in the face with their rifle butts, shouting, "Talk! Where are the VC! You VC?" On the other side of the street, a Vietnamese woman wailed, her voice high and shrill, winding itself through the air and around his throat.

What was happening? The newspapers said this happened. You walked along, minding your own business, and you were back there. But he wasn't really back there, and the soldiers didn't look right. Their uniforms were too clean, too new. No one's pants were held together with tape. The smell of unwashed bodies and rotting fabric wasn't coming to him on the currents of air, and the Vietnamese were too tall, and what was that sign doing here? He'd just noticed it. Some middle-aged women wearing large gold stars were holding it up: A SEARCH AND DESTROY MISSION. This was the guerrilla theater his wife had watched on TV.

Now the soldiers were burning a cutout hut, and suddenly, he could smell it, the smell of burning thatch, the odors of fish sauce and roasted peanuts and animals mixing with the smoke.

The performers were finishing up. They were passing a shoe box around, collecting for something, and he began backing away. If they saw him, they'd recognize him. They'd know he'd been there. They'd know he was a veteran. He kept moving back slowly, away from the performers who were starting to move through the crowd, and then he was on the periphery and the performers were gathering up their equipment. His feet were made of stone.

The performers were getting into a broken-down van, and as they got in, the man who had been stooping over the van's ramp straightened up, looked around, climbed up on the ramp, and disappeared inside.

"Sal!" Pete shouted. "Sal!" But the van was disappearing down the street. Its muffler was gone and Sal couldn't hear his voice over the racket. Pete turned and kept walking. Lately, he thought he saw things. One night, he was driving and he looked across at oncoming traffic and thought he saw a track coming down the road. It wasn't Sal. It couldn't have been. He walked until he came to the boardwalk, sat beneath it, and hugged himself, wanting to weep but unable to do anything but shake until the sound of the waves crashing on the sand calmed him.

He thought about last week, driving through Pennsylvania before dawn, through the high, black mountains, slopes diving down into steep ravines and deeper darkness, outlined against sky the color of indigo ink, and stopping for coffee in a tiny coffee shop. There were two, maybe three stools in the whole place, and a pot of coffee on the stove put there in the morning and kept there, getting stronger and stronger until it was used up, a plastic dome over some white-powdered doughnuts the owner had baked. You could tell he had, they were so misshapen. On the walls were faded, framed newspaper clippings. D DAY! Two strips of yellow flypaper hung in front of the grill, speckled with dark flies.

He came in and rang the bell on the counter, and the woman came out from the room behind the shop, rubbing her eyes. He asked for some ham and eggs and she said, "Sure, but you have to wait 'til I go for the eggs," and he said, "Yeah? Where are you going to go for them?"

"Out to the hen house," she said. "Where else?"

"I'll just take a walk in the meantime," he said. He went outside and crossed the highway. There were no lights on the road, only the moonlight soaking into the ravine at whose bottom the mountains met. After a while, his eyes became accustomed to the half light, and deep in the ravine he saw a dark figure moving, a man with a rifle, climbing up toward him. Over his shoulder was a string of rabbits, freshly killed. Look at that, Pete thought. You can get so far away, you have to go out and hunt for your breakfast. You can get too far away.

He went back in and told the woman what he'd seen. "Oh, everyone here hunts," she said. "During deer season, you don't walk out without a red scarf around your neck. If you've got a big dog, you keep him in. Back up in the woods there's a farmer who puts up a sign. 'My children are *dear* to me. Make sure they are not *deer* to you.' Every year some kid gets shot. Hunters are something terrible. They shoot anything that moves."

"Yeah," said Pete. "They do what they have to do. They take care of business."

You shoot Commies, man. If it's a Communist duck, you shoot the duck. If it's a Commie rat, you shoot the rat. Hell, if it's Commie grass, you shoot the fucking grass! The day he hesitated before firing on a farmer in a field, Sal said that to him. "You act first and think later. A man out here's got a hoe. He's a farmer. He puts down the hoe and picks up a rifle. Now he's a soldier. In a second. Like *that,*" and he snapped his fingers.

"Yeah," Pete said. "Deer season's a problem."

"But they've got to eat. Here if they can't bring down a deer, they starve. The game warden looks the other way. You know, salting the garden, turning on a spotlight, shooting the deer down in the garden, then saying you shot it because it was eating your vegetables. Some say it's not sporting, but if it's that or starving? So the warden looks the other way. Here a quota doesn't mean anything. You ever tasted venison? You want to taste it?"

"No, thanks," Pete said. "I don't like guns."

"No?" the woman said. "Everyone here's got a gun. I've got a gun. Most truckers have a gun under the front seat."

"Not me," said Pete.

"Brave man," said the woman.

"I just don't like guns."

Even in the backwoods, even in the mountains where people hunted to eat, there were things to remind you. Even there.

"I DON'T KNOW, Ma," he said. "At night, I close my eyes and the road's still running. I take pills to stay up and pills to go to sleep."

"A doctor gave you them?"

"Yeah, a doctor."

"What doctor?"

"A doctor at the VA."

"What doctor at the VA? What's his name?"

"What difference does it make?"

"Wake-up pills are no good for you! Sleeping pills are no good! When you're home, you don't take pills!"

"Yeah, but Ma, what's there at home for me? I got married. I have kids, live happily ever after. That's what I thought. So it didn't work out that way."

"Give it time."

"How much time? I've given it three years. Three *years*. Three summers, three winters, three springs. You know how many days there are in three years?"

"Things can change," said his mother. "Go to church. Pray."

"Whose side is God on, Ma? You still believe He's on our side?"

She stood up, stood behind her son's chair and put her arm around him. "Don't, Ma," he said. His skin was tight, sensitive. Under her hand, it burned. Once someone touched you, what then? You wanted them so much you wanted them inside you. You wanted to open your mouth and swallow them down, inside you, so you could never lose them again. But no one wanted to be swallowed so you kept them away and after a while they kept away too.

"What's wrong with him?" Theresa asked after he left.

"I don't know. He's different. He's changed."

"That's what all the mothers say. You should hear Mrs. Lugano."

"I don't want to hear it. There's enough trouble here," Angelina said.

"I'm not driving anymore," Pete told Dolores, who sighed and nodded. *You be good to him. He makes the money.* She could hear her mother now. "I'm going into business for myself. Why not? My father taught me a trade."

"You don't have any customers!" said Dolores.

"I'll get them. Don't worry. Let's watch some TV. Relax."

This time when the news came on, he didn't get up to change the channel. There was more and more talk of pulling out: more protesting, more veterans testifying to war crimes, and then a map appeared on the screen and the newscaster began pointing to places and reading their names: Parrot's Beak, Xuan Loc. "I was there!" Pete said. "I was in all of those places." He got up and began pacing up and down, three steps in each direction, then turning. Each time he took another step, he saw something else. He saw Liebowitz falling to the ground, on his knees, then falling forward. He saw Li's face in the track, shiny with sweat. But in a few minutes, it would be over. It would be gone.

"What's for dinner?" he asked Dolores, following her into the kitchen.

On the stove, she was cooking something, hamburger patties bubbling in brown gravy. He backed away from the stove. "What is it?" he asked her.

"Salisbury steak."

On the stove, the bubbles rose through the thick brown gravy. The brown bubbles moved to the surface, formed domes, then burst and sank back into the surface as bodies burned when tracks were hit by rocket-propelled grenades and the ammunition inside went off and no one could get closer. It was all bubbling in the frying pan on the stove.

"What's wrong with you?"

"Nothing. I'm not hungry."

"You like Salisbury steak," Dolores said. She'd gone to the store specially to buy the can she needed to make the gravy. Her husband stood, his back to the frame of the kitchen doorway, saying nothing. "You like the steak!" she said again, and without warning, he began to cry. He was crying for all the men he'd seen burned, for all the times he'd imagined his own body burning, for the men he'd seen die, for the times he'd almost died, for everyone who was still there and for everyone he couldn't find.

How do you live where people die? How do you live where people die?

"What's wrong with you? Why are you crying?" she asked.

"I shouldn't be alive," he said.

"That's why you're crying?" Dolores asked, all the bitterness she'd felt welling up suddenly in her. "That's ridiculous." She began laughing.

Stop laughing, he said to her silently, but she kept on. It was the most ridiculous thing she'd ever heard, feeling bad because you were alive. He felt his hands swell. They were around her throat and he lifted her from the floor as if she were a doll, a rag, his hands tightening around her neck, and her face was turning purple. If he didn't let go of her, he'd kill her. He let go and she crumpled on the floor, half-conscious, her hand moving vaguely to her throat. "I don't want to hurt anyone anymore," he told himself. He put on his jacket, went out, and took the bus to the VA hospital.

"You did what?" asked the doctor in the emergency room.

"I tried to kill her. I didn't *try* to kill her, but I almost killed her. You gonna lock me up?"

"Well," said the doctor, "I think we ought to keep you here for observation. Just for a while. You'll feel safer."

"Yeah," he said. "Safer." He wanted to tell the doctor: That reality over there should *never* have existed. But you want to know something really crazy? I felt safer over there. Over there, I knew the rules. They were simple. There were no bills, no rent, no family to worry about. Everyone was in the same boat. Everyone felt the same things. That was democracy. Here there was no democracy. There, there was no need to talk. Everyone knew. Here you had all the same feelings you had over there—helplessness, hopelessness —no one cared about you, no one told you the truth, but here you didn't know what to do about it. Here, there was no one you could explain it to, no one you wanted to explain it to. They were civilians. You had to protect civilians.

"Am I crazy?" he asked the doctor. "You think I'm crazy?"

"You're angry," the doctor said.

"That's all?" Pete asked. "That's it?" The doctor heard Pete's voice rising, and nodded at the orderlies behind him and the doctor bent over him and said, "I'm going to give you a shot," and his head swiveled, he saw the orderlies, and he collapsed in the chair. "Don't worry," he said. "I'm not struggling. Make it good. Knock me out. I don't want to know *nothing.*"

"When this starts to work, you won't," said the doctor.

He awakened in a large room full of tall, dusty fly-specked windows covered with heavy iron grilles, looked down and saw row after row of narrow beds, and men moving slowly through the room, shuffling through the aisles, their eyes unfocused, some twisting their hands, others holding one hand with the other, some hugging their chests, others sitting on the edge of their beds, shivering. On the edge of the bed next to him, an extremely tall, thin black man sat staring at the grillwork over the windows.

"What's this?" Pete asked him.

"The locked ward. The violent ward. The crazies. The heavy stuff. The take-your-medicine-and-keep-quiet place. The place-where-the-brothers-go-when-they-come-back place."

"What are you in for?" Pete asked.

"I see things."

"Oh, yeah?" Pete said. "Me, too."

"Yeah? You know what I seen? Last week I was out on the street and I went up top the Empire State Building and you know what I seen? I seen all the brothers lit up like Christmas lights walking all up and down the streets. They were all yellow, you know? Like yellow glass with lights on inside. And man, there were so many of them! They thought they them-selves were invisible, but I saw them. I know where they all are. You can't be a brother without me seeing you, man. I just go up there and look down and you're all lit up and you is yellow. You know that? You glow in the dark. You do. At night here? Everyone lights up. Man, the light, it hurts your eyes."

"You see that?" Pete asked. "You see a lot of them?"

"I see them and they is all alone. Two of them run together and them too is all alone. They don't know they're there, but I see them. What kinds of things you see?"

"Bodies, things like that."

"You *remember.* That ain't seeing. That's why you're here?"

"No. I'm here because I tried to kill my wife. I almost killed her."

"How you do it? Gun? Knife?"

"My hands."

"They're strong hands."

"Yeah, they got strong over there, pulling back the bolt on the .50 caliber, fixing the treads on the tracks, but who was a mechanic over there? I didn't spend my time over there fixing things. Over there, I used to see things. Yeah, now and then I did."

"Over there's when I first seen things," the man said. "I'm lying there, out under the moon, and all around me, there's the little cries the men make when they're tired but their eyes still open so they's still hurting, and out comes this man and he's all dressed in white? Not in clothes, but in bandages. And he got a canteen and he comes around and gives it to everyone. Not me. I didn't get none. He says no water for stomach wounds, but I seen him. I heard him. We all seen him. Like a walking mummy."

"The White Man!" Pete said. "We saw him! I saw him!"

"They believe you?"

"They said they'd court-martial the ass of the next man to mention him."

"They didn't believe me. I says, Ask the others, but guess what? All the others, they dead. When they find me, the others gone and left me. You know how they figured me for alive? I was warm. That's how they knew I was alive. Under two cold dead men. A bunker made from bodies. You ever hear tell of that?"

"Yeah, I heard."

"You want to tell them? Tell them you seen the White Man? Nurse," he called out. "This man, he seen the White Man."

"Oh, yes?" said the nurse, coming over to their beds. "You've seen the White Man?"

"When I was over there, I saw him," Pete said, flushing.

"I'll just tell the doctor," the nurse said.

"IT HAPPENS," the doctor said. "A contagion of the mind. Sedate Bravado. Start him on Thorazine and we'll switch him to Valium when he calms down."

"He seems calm," the nurse said.

"He's awake one hour and he thinks he's seeing the White Man?" the doctor said. "He should be sedated."

"You don't want to talk to him?"

The doctor looked at his watch and down at his schedule. "All right," he said. "Bring him down. I'll take a history."

He went through it all: how Pete got along with his parents now. How he'd gotten along with them when he was a child. Where he'd been in country. What memories came back. What he did when they came back. Did he fight them off, or let them finish, or did he take a drink? How many times had he seen friends die? How many times had he seen enemy dead? Had he ever dug up graves or worked burying his own dead? Had he ever attacked anyone before? How often was he troubled by violent impulses? Had he ever been violent before he went over? Had he ever been arrested?

"Oh?" said the doctor, sitting back. "You've been in reform school?"

"Yeah, what's that got to do with it? I attacked some desks. They sent me to the school. I did my time. I came out knowing the difference between right and wrong." But the doctor's attention was wandering. He could see it. He thought he understood. Pete was violent before. He was violent now. The war was irrelevant.

"You don't understand!" he said. "I was a good soldier! I was! I did a good job over there! I never hurt anybody! Nobody got hurt because of me. You know how many lives I saved? By saying, 'Don't touch that gate. Don't go down that trail'? By asking, 'You got enough C's? You got an extra pair of socks?' By saying, 'Take care of your feet'? By staying awake for an extra watch? I got blown out of a track and I woke up and the medic was talking to me and I wanted to know where the driver was. I didn't care if I was hurt! I was a good soldier! I was a good person! I didn't want to hurt anyone there! I did what they asked me! I did more! I was a good soldier!"

"Well," said the doctor. "Well, we'll get your records and then we'll see."

"*Then* you'll see?" Pete shouted. "Here I am! This is me! You don't need no records! No one should see the things I saw! And then she laughs at me? She's fucking lucky she's not dead! Put yourself in my place, man!"

"We'll talk again soon," the doctor said, pressing the button for the orderlies. "Right now, you'll go up, have some lunch, and after you have a rest, we'll talk again."

"Take him up," the doctor said.

He saw the orderlies coming toward him, looked back at the doctor and saw the fear in his eyes, and the next thing he knew, he had one of the orderlies on the floor, and the other was on his back, trying to pull him off. His elbow jammed back into the man's stomach. He heard him groan and let go. When he looked up, four men were coming toward him, and the first orderly was standing up, and then they had him down. The nurse was giving him a shot, and although he struggled, they had the straitjacket on him and were tightening its straps. They brought him back through the heavy door of the locked ward.

"Oh, man," said the brother on the bed next to him, "you are glowing in the bright light of day. You is something else!" But the man on the next bed was drifting further and further away, as if his bed were on a raft. The walls were ballooning out in the middle and the floor was rising up like a huge bubble, and he said, "The walls are swollen," and the man next to him said, "Don't sweat it. It's the meds. That's all it is. Next thing is lights out, man." And the lights went out.

For a long time after that, he fought the medication. He stayed awake, talking to the man in the next bed. "As soon as you stop the shots, I'll show you how to get off the meds," he said. "You watch when I get my next pill." He watched him swallow the next capsule, and so did the nurse, and Pete was handed a little waxed paper cup with a capsule in it, and, under the nurse's eye, he swallowed it. "So?" said Pete. "I thought you weren't taking it."

"Here it is, man," his neighbor said, laughing. He put his finger under his tongue and plucked out the capsule.

"How'd you do that?"

"You put it in your mouth like this," he said, his hand covering his mouth, "and you put it under your tongue and you take a big swallow."

"What are you going to do with the pills? They'll find them. They'll know what you're doing."

"I am the princess and the pea," the man said. "My insides is my mattress. They are all there. I'm going around the ward, man. Going to get myself some more. Going to trade for some capsules. You never know when you needs one."

"What are you going to trade with? You don't have nothing."

"I've got *light*," said his next-door neighbor. "I've got the air on the other side of the bars. You understand me, man?"

"No. What's your name?"

"Leroy."

He watched Leroy walk up and down the aisles, stopping at certain cots where the men propped themselves up, looked around the room for the nurse, and if no one was watching, they handed something to Leroy.

"I got me a whole bouquet," Leroy said. "When I get out, I'm going to buy me some sweetness and light. Ain't it just like Vietnam? You see something, you trade for it. Don't worry yourself none. She'll visit. They tell them to visit. My wife, she visits once a week. I know her since we was two years old. She knows me better than I know myself."

"I can hear her laughing all the way from our house," said Pete. "All the way from the house."

"Yeah?" said Leroy. "Ain't that something? She run around?"

"I don't know."

"Mine, she runs all around."

"This baby-killer shit. You fight over there and you come back here and it's worse."

"You talk to them? What they know? I never planned on seeing friends blown up in little pieces. That is one thing I never planned on. Man, we saved lives. We lived in a village and we gave medication and we built buildings and we helped whosoever came through. You know what I can't forget? The sounds of illumination rounds coming down. *Chuka chuka chuka.* The wind through the canister and the parachute. *Chuka chuka chuka.*

Twenty seconds of light. They were all over the place in that light, just all around us."

"Yeah," said Pete, "and the lines of the tracers, those white lines like dashes in Morse code? I close my eyes and I see those lines. I look at the dotted white line down the middle of the road and I see those tracer rounds."

"Yeah, I see it too."

"Hell, I see it better than I see my own kids," Pete said. "I can't see my own kids through all that smoke."

"The willy peter, man," Leroy said. "I smell it now."

"And the smell of the jungle. The smell of the country."

"We is never going to smell that smell again," Leroy said.

"And the heat. When we Zippo'd a village, just a solid wall of heat. And when a track went up. The heat's like God, man. There's nothing stronger than the heat."

"The amtracks. You remember the amtracks? The army didn't use amtracks? Whole villages fit into the insides of those amtracks. They carried in everything they owned in those big baskets at the end of them poles, even pigs and chickens. Man, they *love* those pigs and chickens. And the hatch when it closes? Like the door to the biggest furnace? That sound? I never forget that sound. And they're sealed up in there like Jonahs in the whale. And trucks take away the animals but they're inside. They can't see nothing. And they're standing there crying. They're always crying. You ever seen anyone happy when we come to the ville? You ever see anyone wave?"

"And the rain," Pete said. "The way it cooled you off. The waterfall coming off the helmet. And then you were so clean. If you weren't up to your chest in mud, you were so clean."

"Fire and water, fire and water, my man," said Leroy.

"Sometimes I sit and I see things burning. I see the living room on fire. It would be so easy, just hold a match to the curtains. It would all go up. Or this room. I look around and see it burning. It makes me feel better."

"You're still scared, man," Leroy said. "You still fear the fire."

"I don't fear it. I like it."

"You *fears* it," Leroy said. "I know. Fire and hell fire."

"Yeah, and how could hell be so beautiful?"

"Who had time to look? You had time to look?"

"I wanted to look. Everything was new. Animals I never saw. Plants I never saw. People I never saw. Why don't the doctors ask you about that? How you wanted to love over there? How you wanted to love when you came back here, to feel human again, not to see them blown up before your eyes? Why don't they ask about the pain? You can't feel through the pain. They have to ask about reform school? They have to go back to when you were twelve?"

"They blame it on you, man. They don't blame it on the army. They blame it on the army, they have to pay you."

"What?"

"Compensate, man. The name of the game."

"I don't want money. It's funny. You have to laugh. I went over there for God and country and the American way. A dishwasher for everyone. A color TV. That's happiness, right? And then there are these people living in houses made of mud and shit, and *they're* happy. So who's right, them or us? I went over an American and I came back a Communist."

"We all came back that kind of Communist," Leroy said. "We sure did."

"I never wanted to hurt anyone. I want to be good," he said and started to cry.

"Me, I sing in the church choir. I have a wonderful voice. So they all say."

"So what was it for?"

"You are asking me?"

"Eight years later, and look where I am."

"You is back in the green machine," said Leroy. "White is olive drab in here. One way or another, they get you back in. I got three wounds and I stayed in, but when I left, I thought I was gone. I was out. And here I am. I got me a silver star. My wife, she doesn't know what it's for."

"What is it for?"

"For nothing, man. I led a squad up a hill. I was advancing under fire. I got three wounds and I stayed with the company. They sent the letter to my mother. 'For valor under fire. For refusing evacuation,' all that stuff. They scared her to death. She thought I was driving a truck in the rear. Every week, I write and tell her I am driving a truck and I am in the rear. After the medal came, she don't sleep at all. It was a big operation. They gave medals to make it look good. You know the story."

"Yeah," said Pete. "I know."

D O L O R E S came to see him. They sat awkwardly in the visiting room, looking at one another. He asked how the boys were. She said they were fine and asked if he was sure he didn't want his mother to know he was here. He said he didn't. The marks on her throat were still livid. Her blond hair looked as if it had been sprayed stiff. "When you come out, I'll have more patience," she said.

"Yeah, thanks."

"You blame me. You blame me because you're in here."

"Yeah," he said. "I do."

" H O W ' D   I T   G O ? " Leroy asked, and Pete said the doctors told her to be nice. "She told you that?" Leroy asked, but he said no, he figured it out for himself. "My old lady, she's moving out," Leroy said, and Pete tapped him on the shoulder and said, "Yeah, that's how it goes."

"Yeah, well," Leroy said, "it's like the puppy in Vietnam. I had this puppy? The heat, the humidity, it got sick. My CO he said he'd shoot it. I said he shot it, I'd shoot him. So he said, *You* shoot it. I took it behind the tracks and man, I shot it. You love something in the middle of a war and you shoot it yourself so someone else don't get it first. A little puppy, brown with a black patch over its tail. Who cares about a puppy? Fuck the army, man!" he said, and hit the bed with his fist. "Fuck the army!"

"Yeah, fuck the army," said Pete, watching the nurse out of the corner of his eye.

When he awakened again, he turned toward Leroy's bed, but Leroy was still asleep. The nurse came around with medication, saw Leroy still sleeping, and gave Pete his pill and watched him while he swallowed it. When he was awake again, Leroy was still asleep on his side, facing away from him. Pete got up and walked over to his bed and called his name softly but Leroy didn't move. He reached out to touch his cheek, but even before his hand touched his skin, he knew he would feel the cold. He knew what he'd see. Under the sheet, the skin was fading, going grey. So that was how Leroy bought sweetness and light, the air behind the grillwork on the windows. There was no point in saying anything to the nurse. After they found Leroy and took him away, they'd find the hole in the mattress. They'd figure it out. He looked at Leroy and thought, I don't want to end up like that. I didn't go through all that to die here.

Leroy lay stiff under his sheet and there was no line of light around his body.

FOR TWO WEEKS, he took each capsule the nurse brought him. He spent his time walking up and down the length of the ward, starting at the locked door with its little window through which he could see the nurses' station, where, behind glass, the nurses laughed in their own world, and then he would walk to the opposite, blank wall, its paint grey and chipping. When he reached it, he'd stand staring at it, sticking his tongue in and out. Then he'd walk back and begin again. After two weeks, he noticed how many patients shuffled. "Why do they walk like that?" he asked the nurse, and she said, "Oh, it's temporary, an effect of the meds. It wears off." He began hiding the capsules under his tongue. He didn't feel better or worse without them. He felt like the grey painted wall.

At the end of the second week, the orderlies took him down to the doctor's office and he waited outside the door for him. "I have your records," the doctor said.

"I want to get out. I'm not angry anymore."

"You feel better because of the medication," the doctor said.

"Can you keep me here?"

"Not against your will. You committed yourself. But if you leave, we want you to stay on the medication. It helps you."

"For how long?"

"If you need it, for the rest of your life."

"Sure, I'll take my medicine," Pete said.

"We'd like to keep you under observation for another week. Then you can go. Once a month, you'll come back in for a checkup and to renew your medication."

"Did you tell my wife to come?"

"No," said the doctor. "Why do you ask that?"

"Something Leroy said."

"Leroy was a very disturbed young man."

"Yeah," said Pete. He wanted to say, Leroy told me the truth, man! Leroy didn't lie! But he wanted to get out. All those men screaming at night in fear, shuffling down the hall, getting thinner or fatter, and his mother with two sons locked up. He kept quiet.

"You going to tell my wife when I'm getting out?"

"Of course."

"I thought I'd surprise her. It'd be nice."

"I think she could do without surprises," said the doctor.

43 T HE TREES on the street outside took him by surprise, leaning black and solid against the brilliant blue sky, their trunks brown and mottled, their sharp black branches bare and so sharp against the glassy sky they seemed to scratch it. The street itself was a surprise, longer than he remembered any of the streets in the neighborhood, tapering to a sharp point, and the buildings were cleaner and fancier. He stopped to look up at the line of their roofs and saw the ornamental borders over the curved bay windows. Some were urns. Some were faces. As he walked, he saw more and more of the buildings decorated in the same way. Some of the borders must be made of bronze. They turned green. He was surprised to see it was late winter, not because he'd lost track of time while he was in the hospital, but because it was so long since he'd noticed the weather.

What he wanted was simple. When it was summer, he wanted to feel the summer. When it was spring, he wanted to know it was spring. He wanted to feel the seasons. His jacket was light, and he shivered inside it. How had he gone through winters without feeling the cold? In the summer, he drove with the windows up and the heater on until he noticed the windows of other cars, and then he opened his and turned off the heater, but he didn't notice the heat. You don't know if you're alive, he thought. The living feel the heat and the cold.

He went into his apartment building and rang the bell and let himself in with his key. His furniture, the couch and its matching chairs, the curtains his wife had made, all leaped at him. Dolores came out of the kitchen wearing an apron, walked up to him and embraced him awkwardly. "I made your favorite things," she said. "I made Salisbury steak."

"I ate at the hospital," he said.

"Oh," said Dolores.

"You got some coffee? I'd like some coffee."

She had coffee and coffee cake, and they sat there, picking at the cake, sipping the coffee, staring at one another.

"Where are the kids?" he asked.

"They're still at my mother's."

"What did you tell them?"

"Well, Petey saw it," Dolores said. "I told him we were playing."

"He was scared?"

"Sure he was scared. Just tell him what I told him. Say we were playing."

"We'll start over," Pete said. "When I got out today, the world looked new. Brand-new, like a baby."

"That's good," Dolores said, but now when she looked at him, he saw fear in her eyes. "You love me?" she asked. "I mean, if you're not happy, we could call it quits."

His throat tightened. His hand tightened on the cup until it felt fragile as an egg. "No," he said. "I don't want to call it quits. I want a wife. I want my children."

"Why did you marry me?" she asked. "I mean, I'm nothing much. I try to understand what you want, but I can't. I'm not smart enough. I'm not brave enough. Whatever it is, I can't do it. You don't want me. You think you want me, but you don't." She was staring down at the table, moving some crumbs with her index finger. Her blond hair was parted in the middle and pulled back, fastened at the nape of her neck. The white line through her hair reminded him of the white line on the highway. *No passing on a solid white line.*

"Why did I marry you?" he asked. "You know why. I knew you in high school. You knew me from before."

"That's a reason?" she asked. "I don't think that's a reason."

"Because you knew me before. You remember the person I was. If I was that way once, I could be that way again. I could."

"I don't know what you're talking about," Dolores said, starting to cry. "I tried. I thought I understood, but I don't. Maybe I can't pay attention. Maybe you're too different. I don't know what you mean. I'm never going to know."

"I just told you!"

"I don't understand," she said, shaking her head.

"Try!" he said. "Try!"

"I don't know what you're talking about! I never know what you're talking about. You say such things. *'Fear is next to God.'* I don't know what that means. I asked my mother. I asked my girlfriends. I asked the doctor at the hospital. No one knows what it means! You talk to me, I don't understand you. You shouldn't live like that. A wife should understand. I don't want to understand! You frighten me!"

"So what are you saying? You want a divorce? That's what you're saying?"

"You could visit the children. You're out on the road all of the time, you don't see them so much anyway. It's better."

"I don't want a divorce."

"When you think about it. When you have a chance to get used to the idea."

"No divorce."

"Look," she said. "I'll spend a few days at my mother's and you think it over."

"No," he said, but that afternoon, Dolores went to her mother's house and stayed there and he found himself alone in the apartment. What do I have left? he asked himself. I have a couch, two chairs, some curtains, and a kitchen table. He wasn't in this world to cause people trouble. There weren't many doors into life but there were a lot out. He'd have to think about which one he wanted to go through. He didn't want the family to know what he'd done.

He went into the bathroom and saw his wife's blow dryer on the shelf under the mirror, filled up the bathtub, checking the temperature carefully. He might as well be warm and comfortable and clean. He took off his clothes, folding them carefully and putting them in a neat pile on the blue plush lid of the toilet seat. He tested the water with his toe. It was just right. In a few minutes, it would be too cold. That's how things were. They were just right, but they were just right for a few seconds, and then they were cold.

He got into the tub and sank down until the water came up to his lower lip and he looked at his toes, sticking naked out of the water. He held his arm out before him and saw the red welts on it. They first showed up in Vietnam but now they were always there, and during the summer, they were more plentiful and swollen. He stared at the water, lapping gently at the walls of the tub, and he was walking through a field, cutting down what was left of the shrubbery with a machete, and he saw the trees. They didn't have a leaf on them. Even the bark was gone. O.K., he'd thought, so they burned. But he didn't see any ashes. The dead grass he moved through pierced his shirt and stung his skin which rose up in tiny pimples around the scratch marks. He turned around and saw the Chief place his hand against the trunk of a large tree, and the tree began to tilt and fall. How many times was he going to remember these things?

Each time he remembered, the memories were absolutely new, as if they were still happening, as if they'd been frozen and then dug up, still the same, like that mastodon they found that he'd read about somewhere. If the mastodon had anything to say about it, he'd want to stay frozen. The mastodon stayed frozen and he lasted for thousands of years, eons, while he was warming up little pieces at a time. He was a walking corpse. The weather was bad for him. The heat of his blood was bad for him. The sun was bad for him. He ought to be dead, not decaying a little bit at a time, disgusting everyone.

He turned around, picked up the pink enameled hair dryer, inspected it carefully, its round little mouth with metal netting over it. This was the key to the door. This was the thing that would save him. He pushed the switch. Immediately it began whirring, blowing a stream of warm air at him. The water in the tub was cooler. This is the end of my story, he said to the air, and he dropped the hair dryer into the water.

Nothing happened. The water stung him. The water was filled with uncountable sharp needles, but nothing happened. The hair dryer was working, stirring the water up from the bottom of the tub, sending a stream of bubbles up toward the surface of the water. He picked it up to see if it had a higher setting, but it didn't. He lowered it back into the water. The needles stung and the water in the tub was cold. He got out, picked up a towel, and dried himself off. He unplugged the hair dryer and put it back on the bathroom shelf. It gushed water. The puddle around the dryer grew larger, spread out, folding over the edge of the shelf, dripping onto the blue-tiled floor. He let the water drain from the tub and put his clothing on. Then he got into bed and went to sleep.

He slept for a long time. He remembered getting up for a glass of water and going back to sleep, and when he awakened, Dolores was there. He asked her why she'd come back, and she said, Oh, she didn't know. He was her husband. She'd married him, and the two kids, well, she was back. That was all there was to it.

HE WENT back to driving a truck, but he lasted two months and then he couldn't tolerate it. When he got more than four or five miles from home, he'd see Dolores packing her bags, leaving, the two children holding on to her hands. He quit and tried going into business on his own, but even when he was working, he had to run around, lining up new jobs, so when he finished one he'd still have money coming in. He'd take a job fixing a tiled wall, give the people an estimate, and when he took down the tiles, the wall behind it would be rotten, the pipes rusty, and it was a nightmare, just like when he worked for his father. He had to do it all, and he was late getting to the next house.

He was entering a long, dark place, a cave in which there were no other people, only their shadows moving on the walls filled with rusted pipes, and old bathtubs, and mold-encrusted caulking, and when he was lucky, he got a job fixing a porch or laying a foundation for a patio or a gazebo, but when he lay awake at night and thought about the day, everything he'd done took place in the dark. He walked from day to day as he'd walked in country, putting one foot in front of the other, too tired to do anything else, not asking when the trail would end or when they could stop, or where the days, which lay like flagstones in the mud, were leading. In the darkness, his wife flickered like a light, and his children, more brightly. He knew he was a trial to his wife and that she barely put up with him, but she did put up with him and he didn't believe anyone else would.

One night as he lay in bed, the wind blew the blinds in. They knocked off an ashtray. It hit the floor and when his wife came in, she found him crouched on the far side of the bed. "Get down!" he said.

"Why? What's the matter?"

"A sniper."

"You're crazy."

He wanted to shout at her "Don't say that!" but he couldn't afford to lose his temper. He didn't want to go back to the hospital.

Now his worst fear was of losing his temper, losing control, of once more becoming the killer he'd been before. He'd have to learn to be passive. He'd have to become like a woman. He'd have to swallow whatever came at him. Every day he heard it on television. He saw it in the papers. He was the lowest of the low, the most minor of the minorities. The government sent him over, asked him to kill, and then took him and blamed him for what he could do. He'd been stupid. He'd been naive, but his motives were good. His heart was good.

Late at night, when everyone was asleep, he could hear Leroy's voice. "Man, you are *naive*. You are one *naive* son of a bitch. They see this stuff on the bitch box. They see murder and mayhem, and you think you're going to tell them you was doing good? They're going to call you Hitler. They're going to say, How you better than a Nazi? They're going to ask, Why you so stupid to go in the first place? They're going to say, There's Canada. Why didn't you go there? You going to tell them how a black man's skin looks after a night in the water? You going to tell them how willy peter burns black and white the same color? You going to take their hands and make them touch the cold skin? You can't tell them *nothing*. There be wars before. Anyone tell you anything? You know better before you went? Now you want them to know what you never knew? This is how it is. War is the best kept secret, man. It goes wrong, it's the soldier's fault.

"We're already dead, man. I got me medals, and you know what I did after I came out of the field? I was on graves registration duty. The Captain, he says I'm lucky. I push the gurneys and see what could have come to me. I see it all. I see all the dead and I count them. Suddenly, I am the recording angel. I see what goes in them shiny coffins. I see how many souls it takes to send one VC to his maker. I try to tell this to anyone and you know what they hear? 'I didn't do it! I is innocent!' You think you can go back outside? Forget trip wires. The earth here is mined, man. They are all walking mines. Man, you is one *naive* son of a bitch."

Late at night, Pete heard Leroy's voice, the voice of exhaustion, the voice of entropy, the voice of a soul left to bleed on a kitchen counter. If he could, would he let anyone hear that voice? No. He still wanted to protect them from it.

Now his wife's friends looked at him oddly. He saw the way they grinned at each other or raised their eyebrows when he came into a room. His wife must have told them. He could hear her saying it. "He's a wacko, a psycho." Some nights, he woke in his sleep, took off his watch, handed it to her, and said, "It's your watch." In the morning when she got up, she'd hand him the watch and say, "It's your turn," but her face was cold, and her eye, stony. One day she asked him if they should be sleeping in the same bed. She showed him the bruises on her shoulder. The night before he'd grabbed her in his sleep.

She was unpredictable. First she wanted to buy a house and complained because they lived in four rooms. Now she wanted to move into a one-bedroom apartment. It would be easier to clean, cheaper. He wouldn't have to work so hard. He said, Sure, he'd help her move, but was it a good idea? They'd be crowded. The kids would be sleeping in the living room. Oh, she said, she didn't mind. What about twin beds?

Twin beds? He didn't like the idea of twin beds. Married people slept in one bed.

They put an ad in the local paper and when the double bed was sold and moved out, he went down to O'Halloran's and got so drunk he came home and slept until the next morning.

On weekends, he drove his bike upstate and watched the towns wake up and didn't come back until the lights began winking out in the houses. When he got home, his wife would watch him wheel the bike into the hall, throw the sheet over it, and say, "What do you need it for? Get rid of it! Get rid of it!" She hated the machine, but what else did he have? He and his wife barely talked unless they had the children with them. When they visited Paul at the home, she was pleasant. She threw balls for the children to catch. She fastened paper towels around Paul's neck to keep his shirt clean, but if no one spoke to her, she stared into the distance. Three years went by, putting one foot in front of the other, and he would have put up with it forever. Then she asked for a divorce.

"Because I'm not happy," she said. He asked her to name one person who was happy and she said, "You think it's normal to be miserable? It isn't normal." She'd made up her mind, gone to a lawyer who suggested a legal separation, and then, if they couldn't work things out, they'd get a divorce.

"Why now?" he asked. "It's seven years. Things get better."

"They don't and they won't," said Dolores.

"Where will you live?"

"Here. It's the right size."

"And me?"

She shook her head.

"No divorce," he said. "I told you. I'll kill myself."

"That's disgusting," she said. "To threaten me that way."

"I will, and they'll all know it's you."

"I can't stop you," she said. There it was, the hatred in her eyes, naked and terrifying.

He had two bottles of sleeping pills he'd collected from the hospital dispensary, and he took them all, washing them down with the red wine he'd bought to bring to his mother's for Sunday dinner. On television, he was losing the war. At home, he was losing his family. Now he had nothing. He sat down on the couch and drank the last of the wine. In the hospital, one of the vets said if you took too many pills and drank too much, you threw up, and you were back where you started, only sicker, but he didn't feel nauseated, just tired. He started to lie against the armrest, and the war, his wife, the children, his brother in the home, all of it flew up like so many pigeons disturbed by the honking of a car horn.

Dolores came in and saw her husband lying on the floor. "What are you doing there?" she asked him, but he didn't move. She walked over to him and kicked him with her shoe, and when he still didn't move, she kicked him again. "Pete!" she said. "Pete!" Damn it, couldn't he move? He must be drunk out of his mind. She bent over and saw a plastic pill bottle under the couch, pulled it out, and saw its lid was off and the bottle was empty. "Oh, for God's sake!" she said. Then she saw the top of the second bottle between the couch cushions. "Oh, Christ!" she said. She sat down on the couch, thought, and went to the phone and dialed the police. "Yeah," she said. "He tried to kill himself and now he's unconscious. They put him away once before. He's not all there."

He awakened in the lobby of a hospital and found two policeman standing over him, and when both of them couldn't restrain him, the orderlies joined in. Here we go again, he thought, but they had him, and they were taking him up to a locked ward. The two orderlies pushed him through the door, slammed it shut, and one of them said, "Good night. Take any empty cot."

He awakened in the morning, his head clear, wearing the same clothes he'd been wearing the night before, wondering why he was still alive. He'd taken enough pills to kill a horse. In movies, they pumped your stomach, gave you coffee, and made you walk, and here he was, wide awake. Everyone else on the ward was wearing blue and white striped hospital pajamas. A janitor opened the door, locked it again, set down his pail, looked around, saw he'd forgotten his mop and went back to the door, opened it again and went out. Pete waited at the door for him, and when the janitor came back, Pete said, "Here. I'll hold the door for you." The janitor said thanks. Pete held the door open until the janitor took in his mop. After he went through the door, Pete smiled at him and went out. Behind him, he heard the janitor locking the door. He went down the stairs, came out onto the floor below, and went down the elevator. In the lobby, he looked like everyone else. He smiled at people who looked at him and they smiled back, and the heavy glass doors of the hospital swung open easily and he was outside. A cab was waiting at the curb and he gave the address of his apartment. He went in, opened the refrigerator, found it empty, and went to the grocery store.

When he got back, a Western Union messenger got in the elevator with him. When Pete got off on the third floor, so did the messenger. He heard the messenger coming down the hall behind him, and when he paused at the door and turned around, the messenger was right behind him. "Can I help you?" he asked him. "I live here."

"I have a message for Mrs. Bravado."

"I'm Mr. Bravado," he said. "I'll take it."

"Fine. Sign here," the messenger said.

He went inside and read the telegram. "Your husband has escaped from the hospital. In his best interests if you persuade him to return."

"You know," he said aloud, "that's funny." He looked at the telegram and laughed. He thought of the janitor thanking him for holding open the door and laughed.

When she came in later, Dolores said, "I'm still getting divorced. Crying won't do any good. Killing yourself won't do any good."

"I can't even kill myself," he said.

"Guess not," said Dolores. She didn't care. He'd made her miserable and he'd tried to kill her. He asked her if she ever loved him. She must have once, she said, but she couldn't remember.

"It's not fair," he said. "It's not right. It's because I know things."

"What do you know?" she asked him. "You never even finished high school!"

"Everything else!" he said. "I know everything else!"

"Yeah? What do you know? How to use a gun? How to kill people? How to strangle them? What do you know?"

"I don't know nothing," he said. He couldn't get angry. "I'm supposed to get out? I pay for all this for seven years, and I'm supposed to get out?"

"In two weeks."

He went to his mother's house. "It's because of what I know, Ma," he said, and she sat down at the table, poured some salt from the saltshaker, and stirred it into patterns with her finger. Swirl, swirl. Another nervous habit, like rubbing her forehead, but she'd always had this one, as long as he could remember.

"So what do you know?" Angelina asked him. Her voice was so full of sympathy, of love, it was the only voice in the world. The affection in it came at him like a physical blow. It took his breath away.

"I know about the dead bodies. I know how fast the soul goes. I know how easy it is to kill. That's the worst thing I know. Everyone's a killer. There's a line inside you can cross. The first time you cross it, it's hard. The second time it's not so hard. The third time it's easy. I go down to the bar and what's the first question? How does it feel to kill someone? *Give me a .38 and I'll show you.* You have that much feeling? You want to feel that much? That's what I want to say. *I'll show you.* They smile when they ask.

You're an *animal* again. You thought you were human but you're not. *I'll show you.* They want to know, let them find out.

"I came home, I couldn't even kill a fly. A fly was in the kitchen and I'd watch it fly around and I couldn't snatch it and knock it against my leg. It was a fly. It wanted to live like anything else. *Now* I see the fly and I catch it. You see signs on people's cars? I brake for animals? I brake for goddamned *frogs.* I'm driving in the country and it rains and the frogs start jumping across the road, and I brake for frogs. I ran off the road one night braking for a frog. And they come to me and say, 'What does it feel like to kill?' You can't tell them. They're never going to know."

"They don't mean nothing by it," said his mother.

"They mean something by it. They *want* you to show them. They're daring me. Go ahead, be a killer. Tell us what a killer does. You cut off the ears? What'd you do to the body? Is it true they were so small they looked like kids? Big, brave man. Tell me a story. To them it's a story."

"You didn't do nothing wrong," said his mother.

"I did, Ma! I killed people! There's nothing worse!"

"Not because you wanted to. Because they told you to," she said.

"Ma, no one who was over there says that. No one who went over there says it was just the war. I wanted to. I wanted to kill as many as I could. A good soldier kills as many as he can."

"So," said his mother. "It was your job."

"I liked it, Ma."

"You did?"

"Yeah. I liked it."

"I don't know," said his mother. "I never liked wringing the necks of chickens, but I got used to it. Maybe it's natural. Animals hunt. The chickens, they peck each other to death."

"After a while, I didn't like it," Pete said. "I knew it was wrong. But then they'd mortar us or they'd rocket us, and the fear, you'd do anything to stop the fear. You kill them, they can't hurt you again. You want to kill them and you don't want to kill them. No matter what you do, it's wrong. You die, it's wrong. You live, it's wrong."

"Dolores frightens you? That's why you hurt her?"

"Yeah, she frightens me. I'm the crazy Vietnam vet and *she* frightens *me.* It's funny. She laughs at me. She says she'll take the children." He started to laugh and his mother watched him, stirring the salt on the table into figure eights, counting to ten. By ten, he'd start to cry. "So now I'm nobody and nothing again. What do I do now?"

"You put one foot in front of the other," said his mother. "You tear the days off the calendar one day at a time. You know what I used to do when Paul was five, in the home on the island? The day was bad, I took the page and burned it. The week was bad, I took the pages and burned them. One year I burned a whole calendar one day at a time. Your father, he'd come home and say, 'What's that smell? What's burning here?' He'd say, 'You burn dinner again? Every night I come home and smell smoke.' "

"Yeah, I know about smoke," Pete said.

"So long as I'm here, you come and talk to your mother."

"As long as you're here," Pete said, wiping his eyes. "Yeah."

HE RENTED a one-room apartment. The kitchen had a sink and a stove fitted into the wall, closed off by folding wooden doors, their panels slatted. He lived alone and learned to like the silence. On TV, he watched special programs about animals. He stopped by the library after work and read articles about polar bears in the Antarctic, alligators in the Congo, the migrating habits of birds.

Day followed day. This was bathtub day, that was toilet day. Today was tile day. Yesterday was a foundation day. On weekends, he bought presents for the children and went over to his ex-wife's house and took them to the Kiddie Park, sat in the miniature trains and the swinging seats of the small Ferris wheel. He played with them in the park and brought them back sticky and happy. Two days out of seven. That wasn't bad, and sometimes, when he stopped at his mother's, it was three days out of seven. It could be worse. He could be dead. He could be burning all the days. Then, after work, he stopped at his mother's house, completely muddy, comfortable because he was covered with mud, and his mother was standing in the kitchen, crying.

"What happened?" he asked her.

"Nothing's the matter," she said, but she kept her eye covered with her hand and stood half-turned from him. He went up to her and took her hand from her forehead and saw the swelling around the eye. The eye itself was swollen to three times its normal size. He noticed her housedress was white, and printed with bright red strawberries and brilliant green leaves. "He did it, didn't he?" Pete asked. Angelina didn't answer. "Where is he?" Pete asked.

"Who wants me?" asked his father.

"You hit her?"

"It's your business? She's your wife?" his father asked.

His first punch knocked his father down. All sound disappeared. The kitchen became completely silent, and then he was on top of him, pummeling him. He felt something beating him over the back, but he kept on, methodically punching the body beneath him. The blows on his back began to hurt, and he looked up and saw his mother beating him across the back with the red painted wooden handle of the broom.

"You're killing him! You're killing him!" Angelina shouted. "Stop! Stop!"

I'm killing him, he thought. I'm killing someone. He pushed himself up with both arms and looked down at his father. His face was a mass of purple bruises and blood trickled from his mouth. "You touch her again and I'll fucking kill you," he said. He looked at his mother. She was standing in front of the calendar the oil company sent, its picture of autumn trees on top of the little pages.

"Why'd he hit you?" he asked. "I'm not leaving until you tell me."

"I want to bring Paul home. There's room. Everyone's out of the house. I have time. I have too much time."

"And he says no?"

"He says no. So now you know what it's about, go home."

He went home, soaked his hand in cold salt water, watched television, and went to bed. Two weeks later, the phone rang.

"Your brother's very sick," his mother said. "I want you to come to the home with me."

"What's wrong with him?"

"I don't know."

"Stay here," his mother said when they got to the home. "Don't come up. You'll get sick," but he said, "No, I won't, Ma," and followed her through the basement rec rooms, into the elevator and through the familiar rooms with their beds like traps, the rooms with children lying in their own waste, and into his brother's ward. They sat on either side of his brother's bed. Paul's eyes were closed and above his right eye was an egg-shaped swelling. After a while, Paul opened his eyes, saw his mother and turned, saw his brother and smiled. "Where's Daddy?" he asked.

"He's working," said his mother.

"I wanna be a soldier," Paul said.

"Sure, when you're better, I'll bring your uniform," Pete said. After a while, Paul fell asleep, a deep sleep that frightened both of them.

"What's wrong with him?" Angelina asked the doctor.

"A subdural hematoma, a blood clot."

"He's got a bump on his head," Pete said, pointing it out.

"Whatever it is, it's got nothing to do with it," the doctor said. "We think he had a stroke. We're moving him to the hospital. We'll take care of him, but we want you to prepare yourselves."

"I don't know," Angelina said uneasily.

"Mrs. Bravado, he has to go to the hospital. We don't have the diagnostic equipment here. You have to prepare yourself. He could be dying."

"Dying!" she shouted. "Someone hurt him! He was fine yesterday. Now he's dying? He's fine one day and next he's dying? Someone did something!"

"No one did anything, Mrs. Bravado."

"Ma?" said Pete.

"Nah," she said, looking at her son. "No one did anything."

. . .

THE DAY of the funeral, he was at the funeral parlor before the rest of his family. The casket was open. He looked down at his brother. From the time he was three, his brother was a prisoner of war in that home. His own father turned him over, turned the key in the lock. What kind of a country was this? People talked about democracy here. Where was the democracy? Everyone could suffer. That was the democracy. You came home from the war and the government put you in a cage. You were a murderer, an outcast. You were in a concentration camp with invisible wire, but you couldn't say that. You said that and people looked at you and said, "You crazy? This is Brooklyn. What are you talking about, a concentration camp? This is America, man."

All they'd done was taken his brother out of a big box, the home, and put him in this smaller one. He knew his mother thought they'd killed Paul in the home. He was getting big and strong and hard to handle. When Pete was still married, his brother went on picnics with them. He knew Paul could do more. He was starting to take pride in himself. He could see it. One day they told him to do something and he said no, and when they tried to make him do it, he fought back and someone came and hit him with something and knocked him down. They knocked him down and cracked his skull and he bled until he died. This was some kind of country, some kind of war.

He saw the makeup the mortician had applied to his brother's face, and beneath it, he saw his brother's face bluing. He knew how cold he was. If you touched their flesh after they were in the earth, if you dug them up, for a moment your fingers stuck to them like ice. Nothing could warm them. What fire could warm them?

"You're my soldier," he said to his brother. He took his medals and his ribbons and pinned them onto the blue suit jacket his brother wore. "Yeah, you're my soldier." He saluted and turned away from the casket, weeping.

"He asked for you!" he shouted at his father when he came in. "He wasn't so retarded! Not if he asked for you! And you wouldn't come! You made Ma say you were working!"

His father backed away from him, frightened. His mother thrust her body between them. "Not at the funeral!" hissed his aunt Theresa. "Not in front of the dead boy!"

In front of the room, the priest shook his head. He remembered the funeral of old Mrs. Bravado. The Bravados couldn't bury anyone peacefully.

SIX MONTHS later, Father D'Angelo was standing in front of the funeral parlor again. This time it was Angelina lying in the coffin. "You killed her!"

Pete shouted at his father. "She died of a broken heart! She was a young woman!"

"She died of cancer!" said his father.

"No! Of a broken heart!"

"Stop it, stop it, stop it!" shouted the weeping Theresa. "This is a funeral! This is no time to fight!"

"He's not my father!" Pete shouted. "He's not a man!"

Again? thought the priest. Again? *His* mother said the family was cursed.

"They're not cursed," he said. "I don't believe in curses."

"It started with old Mrs. Bravado," his mother said.

"No," he said. "It *stopped* with old Mr. Bravado. After old Mr. Bravado and old Mrs. Bravado, they got lost." His mother watched him as he ate. She wanted to believe in a heavenly lost and found for souls, but she didn't believe. She confessed her doubts to her own priest. Her son heard enough confessions. He didn't need hers.

44  OW THINGS were beginning to happen to him. On television, the commentators talked incessantly. Colonels and Generals speculated as to whether or not the caliber of the soldiers in this war had affected its outcome. "We took too many category four soldiers," one Colonel said.

"See?" said the men in O'Halloran's. "You lost your war."

He thought about the jungles and the men lost there. He thought about going in, supporting an air drop, and the wind shifted, the men's parachutes drifted into the trees, and his troop was sent out to climb the trees, to cut the chutes loose, to bring the men down. There were branches through some of their arms, and they had to climb back down and go up again with a machete. They lowered them down by ropes and passed them down from one person to another. From below, the men and their chutes looked like newspapers blown up into the branches.

They'd seen choppers and Phantoms going down in smoke over the thick green blanket of jungle, and they thought, That was all right. In a war, you took your chances. When the war was over, they'd go all the way in. They'd get back the prisoners. It happened in Germany. When they swept through, they got their men back. But now they were leaving the men there. They weren't going after them. He'd been home ten years and men could still be there, ten years later, still thinking they were fighting for America, still giving only name, rank, and serial number, still believing they were doing the right thing. They didn't know and no one would tell them.

He'd read about a Japanese soldier they found on an island in the Philippines thirty years later. He thought the war was still going on. When they tried to come near him, he fought.

All over the jungle, there were dog tags blown loose from the bodies that wore them. Up in the trees, rock apes played with them, bit them, used them to scrape at tree bark. Up in the trees, in birds' nests, were parts of bodies, chewed on by birds and insects, parts of bones carried off to their holes by pack rats. They were fat and healthy animals who'd eaten human flesh. No one was going back in for them. The Viet Cong found them in their shallow graves and dug them up. Who would ever go back there? Who'd be crazy enough to walk through that jungle? It was full of land mines, trip flares, booby-trapped C-ration cans. Tigers would walk through and blow themselves to hell and never know what hit them. A monkey would pick something shiny from a tree and it would explode in his hand and the animal's blood would be all over the leaves. A family would visit their relatives in the next town and the first person on the trail would detonate a mine. It would go on forever.

Now his wife was living with someone named Junior, and when he came for the children, she came to the door wearing a robe, her hair uncombed, wearing no makeup. She didn't want to get married. She never wanted to get married again. "So what do you expect?" his aunt asked. "You hurt her." He didn't want to think things could have been different. It was all he could do to accept things as they were. He was beginning to like the silence and isolation. He came home when he finished work and cracked open a bottle of Johnny Walker Black and drank until his head was between his knees and he didn't know anything about the world and the world didn't know anything about him. There was no way it could touch him.

The phone rang and Dolores said she and Junior were moving to St. Louis. "You can't go," he said. "You can't take the children," and she said she didn't want to fight with him, but she was going, and in six months, she'd take them, not forever, just for a year, maybe two. He could come up on weekends.

"Where am I going to get the money, Dolores? Where am I going to get the time?"

"Don't worry about it," she said. "It's not for six months. You know who's home? Vinnie's home."

"Yeah, Vinnie."

A month after he'd come back, he'd gone with Vinnie, another kid from the neighborhood, to see Mrs. Pellegro, whose son John had gone to school with them. "Yeah," said Mrs. Pellegro. "I just got a letter from him. He says he's fine and you know what he did? He went to Bangkok! I never even heard of Bangkok and he went there."

"My friend went there," Pete said.

"Me, too," Vinnie said.

"Yeah?" said Mrs. Pellegro. "What's it like? You have a good time there?" The doorbell rang and Pete said, "I'll get it, Mrs. Pellegro." He opened the door. Three marines stood there in dress greens. He stared at them, speechless. It seemed to him they'd just been fixing their bikes in his shed, playing Ping-Pong in the community centers. "Who is it, Pete?" Mrs. Pellegro called again. In back of him, he could hear her footsteps coming.

"Uh, Mrs. Pellegro," he said. She was coming closer. Any second she was going to see them.

When she saw them, she began to scream, and when she was calmer, they were telling her about how brave her son had been and how his medals would be coming home soon, and his coffin. If the family wanted a military burial, they could have it. "No, no," she said. "In the church." She wanted them out of the house. While they were there, she had to pretend she believed her son was dead. They went out through the door and shut it with a final sound. It echoed through the apartment as if the rooms were empty, as if the furniture had yet to be moved in, as if her son were not yet born. "Oh, Mrs. Pellegro," Pete said again and again, and she grabbed him. She took him into her bosom and kissed him. "I'm glad you're alive," she said.

At John's funeral, he and Vinnie sat in the back. "I'm going over there," Vinnie said. "I'm going to kill some of those bastards for John."

"Don't do it, man," Pete said. He was staring at the closed coffin in front of the room. Their friend wasn't in there. There was no whole body. Maybe nothing was inside. He knew they sent back empty caskets and he knew why.

"I'm going," Vinnie said as they walked toward the bus.

"No, you're not going," Pete said. "You're *not* going. I know what it's like there. You don't know anything."

"I'm going," Vinnie said again, and Pete jumped on him, knocked him down, and began beating him.

"You're not going," he said with each blow. "You're not going."

But Vinnie went and he never thanked Pete for trying to stop him. Now Vinnie was back and the gossip in the neighborhood was that he'd come home with the top of his thumb shot off, and now Vinnie knew everything he'd known and he still wouldn't thank him. The word was that Vinnie was going back to school. He'd always wanted to be a lawyer. "Italians are always mixed up with the law," he used to say, "so you're a lawyer or you're in the business."

Some people didn't get derailed. He didn't know why. No matter what happened to them, they got what they wanted. They didn't go to school and have the teacher hold up an edition of *Life* with Mylai on the cover, and even if they did, they'd keep going. Why couldn't he do it? Why couldn't he want things enough? Why did everything look silly to him but his picture of the people in No-name Village, happy with nothing but the food they grew and one another? There was no ambition in him unless it was a hope for happiness.

Since his wife said she was moving, he couldn't even read a page. He didn't want to see Vinnie. He didn't want to be a veteran. He didn't want to be himself. When his wife moved away with the kids, there'd be no more Pete Bravado.

45 ATER, he would say his cork was coming unglued, although at the time he didn't know it. When his wife said she was taking the boys, he hid in the bushes outside her house and watched them through the windows. They had lacy curtains and he could see right in. He could see them moving cartons back and forth. Every night when he came back, there was less and less on the walls. One night, when the walls were almost bare, he took some lighter fluid and his lighter (he still had the lighter he was issued over there) and poured gasoline into the backseat of the car and dropped a match into it. It burned hot. It was *hot.* He was excited, powerful, humongous, unkillable. The heat felt so good he wanted to go over and shake its hand and stood there and watched, only wanting to feel the heat. The frustrations were gone. The anger was gone. He was burning something and no one was in it. He felt good and stood there. Then he heard Dolores screaming from the window and he took off. He didn't want to get arrested.

For a few weeks, he hid out. He slept in the churchyard under the bushes, or in the park where the trees were thick. They would never have caught him, but he wanted to see his children. He knew they went to the park on Saturdays, and Saturday he hid in the bushes until he saw them, and then he came out. They were all over him. They didn't know why he wasn't coming to see them, and he kept telling them, I'm your father. I'll always be your father. You're not going to forget me?

But his wife knew he'd try seeing them in the park and that's where the police caught up with him. They arrested him right in front of his children. He saw his wife watching him from across the park. She was pointing and shouting, "That's him! That's him!" The police had their hands on their guns and they came after him, and the boys were there, so he went quietly. He didn't give them any trouble. His wife said she'd drop the charges if he'd go into the hospital, and he spent four or five weeks there. When he got out, he went around looking for odd jobs and found out what her number was in St. Louis. He'd call at all hours of the day and night and hang up. He threatened her, and one day the police came to the door and he answered it and saw them and said, "What can I do for you, officers?" and they said they had a warrant for his arrest, and he thought, Shit, they can't arrest me. My wife doesn't live in the state, but when he told them that, they said, Yes, she does, buddy, and you're coming with us, so that was how he knew she was back. He must have been bothering someone else, someone he didn't know, calling and hanging up, for weeks.

Every time he got out of the hospital, he came out with two bottles of pills and two prescriptions. They knew he'd tried to check out before. They didn't care. *Give him more pills. If he takes all of them, he's one less headache.*

After the first time, he left her car alone, although every time he went by her house, he looked at it and thought about burning it. He'd think, They want me to be a crazy Vietnam veteran, I'll be a crazy Vietnam veteran, but then he'd think, Why should I hurt myself when everyone's ready to do it for me, and he'd stop himself. He forgot about love. He forgot about wanting to be good. He forgot he didn't want to hurt people. He forgot himself.

Later, trying to describe that time, he'd think, You know what it's like when you're drunk and you park your car and you come back and walk around the block and twenty minutes later you find it? Well, he hadn't lost a car; he'd lost years — eleven.

And there was something new. He couldn't stay in the house. He had to be outside where there were no walls. When he came in, he'd get drunk and drink until he passed out, but there were nights when it rained, and he had to go out. He'd walk down to the churchyard, climb the fence, and hide under the bushes and watch the people go by. He knew they were there but they didn't know where he was. He liked the feeling of the rain on his skin; he liked watching the weight of the water bend down the leaves. When he was outside, he was calm. Sometimes, when he'd been in the villages and dropped the matchbooks in the thatched roofs, the sky would open up and the water came down and put the fire out. He wanted the village to burn but then again, he didn't want it to. The villes would burn unless it rained. And you were warm when it rained so he hated the rain to stop because then he got cold. He could get clean when it rained even if he didn't have soap: he just scrubbed himself with a handful of grass or some crushed banana leaves, or even a few twigs he rolled up and down his arms and legs, so between the rain and the heat, he was busy.

Years went by. He stayed by himself, drinking; he was one mean son of a bitch. He didn't want to know anyone and no one wanted to know him and that was how he liked it. If he didn't see his children, he gave his ex-wife a hard time. What was he supposed to say to his family? His mother was gone. His brother was gone. His older brothers didn't know anything about the war, but one of them knew enough to tell him off every time he saw him. His father remarried, lived on in the old house, and in the back he built himself a stone shed, a stone room with a big window and a fireplace, and he closed the door and no one else had the key. "You like this?" he asked his father.

His father shrugged. "It's a tomb," he said. His father didn't answer.

"You killed her," Pete said. "You killed both of them. You happy?" To him, his father looked like one miserable son of a bitch and his brother told him his father's new wife, his *stepmother*, was busting his father's ass. "She need any help?" he asked him.

Later on, Pete calmed down. His wife wasn't a used car dealer. How many cars was he going to burn? How many times were they going to arrest him, take him to the station, ask him questions: What's your name, what's your address? What were you doing there? How many times was he going to wait and see if his ex-wife would press charges? Because after he did it, he was sorry. He wasn't sorry when the car was burning, but afterwards, he was. Afterwards, he knew his children must have been looking out the window. How many times was he going to have to meet them in the park? How many times was he going to have to win them back? When he calmed down, she didn't cause any trouble. If he had money, he gave it to her for the boys.

The welts on his back were as big as his thumb. He finally went to a private doctor who said he didn't know: he'd never seen anything like that.

Much later, he collapsed and his brother's wife took him to the hospital. He walked around the hallways for days with an IV and a bottle on a stand. He asked the nurse, "What's going on? What's wrong with me?" He was yellow, like a dandelion. He asked the doctor, "What's in this bottle anyway?" "Don't worry about it," the doctor said, and Pete said, "I am worried about it," but the doctor wouldn't tell him anything. His father came in and said, "It's the beer, the beer," but Pete had seen drinkers. They didn't collapse and turn yellow. He asked the doctors why he suddenly lost twenty-five pounds and couldn't gain them back, and they said probably he was more active. If they had the answers, they weren't going to give them to him.

The longer he spent alone, the more he thought, and soon, he didn't know how it happened, the civilian world vanished, like a ship into fog. There was Vietnam and what happened to veterans after they came home. The rest of the world was gone, sunken, irretrievable. There were days when it tried to get his attention, when he wanted the world to get his attention, but it was impossible. He thought about the same things again and again; again and again, he tried to puzzle out what had happened to him in the war, what had caused the war, and he did it alone, as if he were the only person alive on earth.

He would sit on the couch, drinking, and think: They sent an army over there and now they're waiting for us to die. A roomful of people sat down around a table. They didn't argue about the shape of the table. They sat down at that same table every day. They're a group of people like you and me. They looked at each other and said, "Let's experiment with this generation. Let's spray them with this stuff and let's experiment with this weapon. Let's see if the spray makes them sick. Let's see if the gun jams on them. Then we'll know better what to do next time. If they come back sick or in boxes, we'll get the data. We'll study the ones who come home alive."

After he burned the car a second time, he went to a VA therapist. He wanted to talk to her about the war, about the things he remembered, and why there were other things he couldn't recall, and she wanted to know about his parents. Did he love his mother? Did he get along with his father? and he'd say, "We'll get to that later," and she'd say, "No, no, no, we have to do this first." *No, no, no, no.* Just like one of the nuns talking to a child. He would sit in the hall outside her office, waiting for her, sometimes an hour, sometimes two, and sometimes he'd get up and ask the secretary, "Where's Dr. Blue?" and she'd say, "Oh, she's not coming in today."

He'd think, You drive by on the highway. You see those VA hospitals and they keep the grounds looking good. They hire a man who has nothing to do but walk around with a big nail on a stick and stab up pieces of paper and pick up twigs. They police the area. There's a man dangling from a fifty-story window who just stuck his hand in a gutter to clean out leaves and he stirred up a nest of yellow jackets, but he'll clean that gutter. He'll go down for a can of spray, kill the yellow jackets, and the gutter's clean. The rain comes down where it should come down. Someone else scrapes the wood and paints it white. You come over from Russia, you see the building, and you think, This government really cares about its soldiers.

That's outside. Inside on the thirteenth floor, they've got the locked ward.

On the fifth floor, the psychiatrists have their offices. There's one armed guard outside each door and an extra one at each end of the hall. They trust you? They want the best for you? The doctor sits on the other side of a big desk. Her chair's pushed so far back she's falling out the window.

The first one talked to him for twenty minutes, looked up, and said, "Oh, I've never seen you before, have I? I better read your file," and for the rest of the hour, she sat there and read it. She'd talked to him for twenty minutes before she realized she didn't know him? And outside the door were two armed guards. And she finished reading his file and she said, "Oh, I see you were in reform school. You want to tell me about that?" And he didn't, so he said he'd talk about it next time. When was his next appointment? And the therapist asked him how about the same time next month? Next month! He thought, Here they don't exactly knock you down with their concern.

He asked himself, How long can you feel hopelessness? How long can you feel fear? How many times can you feel abandoned? He remembered patrols where men were climbing the fucking *trees* trying to figure out where they were, and over the radio, they heard, "We're pulling out." They were pulling out and he and three other men were eight klicks away in the middle of triple canopy jungle. They were leaving them there. Where were they going? Wait for us! He was eighteen years old and the night before a panther was knocking his C-ration tins all over the place and they were terrified. He's a *panther*. And they were scared of Charley. The VC had guns. So they kept quiet and hoped it was true: panthers don't attack unless they're provoked. But he was a kid from Brooklyn. Did he know what provoked them? Maybe finding him lying in their territory provoked them.

Meantime, a big tree had fallen down in his area, and he and two other guys were lying on the ground under the tree trunk. They were lying on their back farther in, but he was lying on his stomach looking out, and he felt hot breath on his neck and he didn't know what it was. He couldn't fire because Charley was all over the place. He twisted around and looked at Davis, and he saw his eyes in the dark. They were big white circles, and he twisted his head around again, and there were two big green lights looking at him. It was the panther.

He panicked and Davis panicked and Pete fired off a shot, and then because he fired, he had to break radio silence and call in his position and tell them what happened, and then he had to get out of there, and it was pitch dark, and somewhere there was the panther, and somewhere there was Charley, and they couldn't see a fucking thing, and their pants were all wet, the VC could smell them a mile off, and they were crashing into trees and they were trying to be quiet and move in the right direction, and now they'd listen for rustling in the grass and the trees, because they were afraid it was the panther and there was no way in hell they were going to get out of there. And in the morning, they called in and the CO said, "Oh, you should have brought him back for breakfast. We could've eaten him," and in the background, they heard guys laughing, and *it wasn't funny.*

And the stories he heard out there, like the one about the rabid monkeys who routed A Troop. They used M-79 grenade launchers on the monkeys, but before they got the monkeys, the monkeys got them. Eleven men were medevaced out with bites. The whole troop came back with dented helmets, the monkeys threw so many rocks, and the way they heard the story, the VC caught one monkey with rabies, put him in a cage with other monkeys, waited until they all had rabies, took them out in the jungle, and let them loose on A Troop. Of course they knew when A Troop was coming through. They followed the laundry. They were supposed to fight a country that wins battles with rabid monkeys and snakes nailed by their tails to the doorways of hooches? After a while they didn't trust anything. They were angry at Mother Nature.

He thought, I set fire to villages. All right, it was a matter of survival. But the people there had to live too. Everyone loves. No one had a right to end those lives. It wasn't a matter of good guys and bad guys.

He saw the way they cried over there when someone got killed. They suffered less than he did? They had children, their homes, their water buffaloes. He felt bad when he was over there because he already knew how it was, but he was eighteen. What was he going to do about it? He didn't want to come home in a box.

He thought, There was so much to love over there, so much beauty, so much to feel, but you couldn't feel it. "I'm not going to let them fucking kill me." That's all he could feel. But he also loved those little buildings made of sticks. He loved the walls made of manure and straw. He loved the way they lived on nothing. They shouldn't send Americans over there to see things like that. You come back asking what's important. All of a sudden America doesn't have all the answers.

He thought, You see them there in the halls, the veterans of all the wars and you know: it wasn't just this war. All the wars did this to people. The consequences go on for generations. You know why a new war comes along every twenty years? Because that's how long it takes the country to forget what the last one was like. Twenty years later, you've got a new generation. The new ones don't listen to their fathers. What teenager listens to his father? What father tells his son or daughter what it's like to see a friend vaporized? In pieces? That's what you want to protect them from. So every twenty years, you can count on it. There's a new crop ready to go. And who sends them? The civilians send them.

When other men were home finding first love, what did they love? Their buddies and their M-16s and a high body count and the high they couldn't come down from afterwards. So when other men got jobs and got into bed with their women and found out what they could feel, he and the others got into a bunker and found out what they could feel. So when they came back and someone told them so-and-so died, and to him it's a tragedy, so what? Someone died? It happened to someone he knew! And he and others like him would say, "Yeah? That's too bad," because they *knew*.

So people fussed about this and that. The car wouldn't start, the car was too small, the kid wouldn't do his homework, and if they'd been over there, they'd look at these people, so busy complaining, and think, You're alive, man. Don't you know what's important? You could be dead. Get your priorities straight, man. Life's too short for this shit. And the others would look at them: they were hard; they were insensitive. So they tried to worry about why the car wouldn't start, or why it was too small, or why the kid wouldn't do his homework, and they couldn't last it out. The next thing they know, they'd put their hand through the wall. Then what did they have? They had a swollen hand and a hole in the wall and a wife looking at them, their kid looking at them. And then they'd hear: You're crazy. That's it. You're crazy.

He thought, You tell your wife to pick up the laundry and she forgets and you go crazy because, over there, someone did something right away or they were dead. They didn't have the time to learn from mistakes. You saw the men who made mistakes. They were the believers. They got on helicopters wrapped in ponchos. So here the laundry's not a matter of life and death. If it's not picked up, no one's dead. If the rug's not vacuumed, no one's dead. But when it's happening, you don't remember. Either everything's a matter of life and death or nothing is. *Can't you care about anyone but yourself? Do you have to live in the sixties? You're still over there! Can't you forget it!* They're crying because of the way you behave. Your father, who was in the Big One, says, "Why don't you forget it and go on?" Good idea! I wish I'd thought of it! I'll do that! Why didn't you tell me before!

He had a dream over and over. He dreamed a fat, ugly dog was biting his face and he was biting him back, trying to get him in the belly. He was trying to get to his neck, but he couldn't reach it. He was biting the dog and the dog was biting him. What was the difference between them? None. They were the same. He wanted to know who the dog was, but the doctor couldn't tell him; he was busy with why he went to reform school. So he began to work it out himself.

He was the person the dog was biting and he was the dog doing the biting. The dog was the war and the dog was the way he was in the war. He worked it out himself because he knew no one was going to do it for him. If he couldn't work it out, he'd have to live with it, and sometimes he couldn't live with it, so out of desperation, he grew smarter. He started to read. He started to write things down. He wrote down his dreams; he wrote down things he remembered. He didn't show these pages to anyone else. They were his. He started to think. He was alone and he had no one to talk to but he was beginning to think.

The more he thought, the more he learned, the more the dog kept biting him, and the dog was getting weaker, and one day one of his boys said, "You know, Dad, you've changed for the better." But he was still alone in his room with his head between his legs and he asked himself, What keeps you going? What keeps you from checking out?

He knew there was a better place; he'd found it when the mine blew and he didn't know he was Pete, didn't know he carried a gun, didn't know there was a war or what war was. He knew his mother was there, and his brother. That's when he'd heard God and he was saying, "Don't worry. I've got your ass covered." He didn't need the church, he had a direct line, and when he wanted to check out, he thought about that place.

Now when he saw a girl with olive skin and long black hair walking down the street, he thought about the girl in the grave, but he also thought, I'm glad you're alive. I'm glad to see you alive.

But the dog: he was biting the dog back. He was the ugliest, hairiest, meanest dog in the world. He was small and fat and when Pete dreamed about him, he felt as if his hand were tied behind his back, but he was biting him back, right in the belly. The dog wasn't getting his face, but those teeth, the way he foamed at the mouth. The dog scared him to death.

One day the VC were shooting at them from across the rice paddy and considering the direction the bullets were coming from, he should have gotten hit, but instead, the bullet made a right turn, *a right turn*, and it hit the man behind him and to his left. He didn't remember his name, but Pete remembered thinking, He wasn't mad enough; *he* was so mad the *bullet* didn't want to come near him.

Every six or eight months, he came across something new to grieve about because he just remembered it. People wanted to know how much fear they could live with, but he knew. When it rained, he would go out and buy takeout Chinese food and hide in a bush in the churchyard and watch people passing. He was silent and deadly, as he was over there, having the same emotions he had over there, silent and deadly and terrified, living it over and over, hoping it would wear off, lose its edge. It didn't. Now he had a new fear: that he was always going to be this angry, that he would die this angry and violent. *Now* he had limits. Now he didn't trust anyone. Now it was terribly difficult to get close to people. Now he didn't, he couldn't give one hundred percent of himself anymore. He couldn't give his whole heart. He thought: I gave it to the country and I gave it to my wife and I saw what happened. It's very important not to do that again.

Now he thought about the POWs endlessly, he didn't know why. The government said they were all back, but he didn't believe it, and one day, he thought, one of them would come out. He wouldn't care if it was someone he knew; he wouldn't care who it was. Then he'd be happy.

If he had it in his power, he'd take the POW to his apartment and feed him a bowl of soup a day. He'd feed him a spoon at a time. Little by little, he'd bring him back. He would think about feeding the POW, watching him sleep, first on the floor, then on the couch, and often he'd fall asleep and sleep quietly.

Once, his aunt asked him what he had to do to be happy. Forget the anger. Forget he was once a whole person. Forget that there was this crack in the pane of glass. Forget that he could still smell the dead girl in her grave. They can't figure out what makes the brain able to pick up a smell. And certain humid days bring it back, the smell after the rain. It follows you. You walk out the door, you don't have to worry about losing the war. You're not going to lose it. You're always going to have it. The war's the one thing you can trust. It's always going to be there.

"God's always going to be there," said his aunt. "Go talk to Father D'Angelo." As soon as she said it, he wanted to confess. Over there, he thought about confession when the mail came. When the mail came, the world he'd known sprang back into place and he felt bad about what was happening, but when he sat down to write someone at home about it, he had to move out, and so there was no time. But he thought, When I get back, there'll be some kind of pardon. Where would it come from? He didn't know. From society. But it didn't come from society. From the Church? But he turned away from the Church when the chaplain came down in the Good Humor truck.

But after he talked to his aunt, he dreamed he was an American Indian and he was with another Indian and they were on the bank of a river fixing their canoe and a white man came and looked over the bank and he shot both of them in the chest and killed them. He knew he wasn't supposed to die in a dream, but he did. So he thought, This country doesn't belong to anybody. This country belongs to the Indians. This country is only a baby. He thought, Once I was an Indian and I came back as an Italian in America. I came back because my soul was good and I'll come back again.

He wanted absolution. He wanted forgiveness. He wanted it all washed away. His aunt said the priest could do that. "Try it," his aunt said. "What can you lose?"

He thought often about unborn souls, and he thought of them up in heaven, floating around. They were on some kind of recon mission. They would pick their parents but God wouldn't send them out until He had a use for them. Sometimes He kept them up there for centuries before He sent them back out again. God waited until he had a use for them. God, he thought, must love time, He made so much of it. And since he was thinking about heaven, sitting out in the rain under a bush, eating Chinese food with chopsticks, he thought he'd talk to Father D'Angelo. Hell, he couldn't be worse than the VA.

**46** HEN FATHER D'ANGELO was a child, he had dreams of the heroic life. He read stories of the great popes who lived in times of war and of the priests who gave up their lives for their beliefs. As he grew older, he came to see there were great wars and great suffering taking place on his own streets, great passions acted out in kitchens and bedrooms and backyards. But from time to time, he would open his book of Hieronymus Bosch and look at his pictures of hell and study the tortures depicted there, and in spite of himself, in spite of what he knew about the enormity of suffering in even the smallest space, he wished to see these great canvases for himself.

He believed that, in normal times, in times of peace, a priest is a bystander, listening to the hum of human sorrow and the great hymns of God swelling the earth which brings them forth. Priests do not marry, although their parents married. They do not have children, although their parents had them. Their great challenge is to understand things second-hand, to enter into human hearts as if they were doorways into their own, to make themselves at home there, no matter how uncomfortable they feel, or sometimes, how tortured.

To them, the man who separates his wife's head from her body comes and confesses. To them, the wife who has locked her children in the house, first setting fire to the living room curtains, confesses. They are not there for the event. They are there for the autopsy. It is their privilege to give up the wound in their own flesh for the ability to pour balm on the wounds of others. Father D'Angelo thought that the tears they cry are different, compounded of others' sorrows. He liked to think he heard the grand sound of sorrow, the symphony, and the coda, which is God's, resolving everything into harmony. The smaller arrows, a child's disobedience, a son's disrespect, a husband's drunkenness, a wife's spendthriftiness, these were not his and were not meant to be. Usually he did not regret it. Today he did.

Today, Pete Bravado came in to see him. He said he wanted to confess, but he didn't want to sit in the confessional, so Father D'Angelo said fine, he could use his office. Pete said he didn't know where to start, so the priest said, Start anywhere. Pete said he didn't know where anywhere was, so he'd start at the beginning. After a while, Father D'Angelo asked him if he was confessing or telling him what happened, and Pete said if he was telling him what happened there, he was confessing. Father D'Angelo asked him what he meant. He said everything he did once he set foot on that soil was sinful because everything he did was aimed at killing other human beings. He said he wasn't big on the Ten Commandments. He broke some of the more trivial ones all of the time. *Thou shalt not steal. Thou shalt not covet thy neighbor's wife nor anything that is thy neighbor's.* These were trivial commandments. But *Thou shalt not kill,* that was the big time, and he'd broken that one, or tried to break it, every day he was there.

He said he didn't want to hurt people then and he didn't want to hurt people now. But he was afraid of losing control. He lived with that fear and that anger all the time. Father D'Angelo listened and asked him if he was ready to confess. Pete asked him what good that would do. Father D'Angelo told him that God forgave him, and once he had confessed and received absolution, his sin would be washed away as if it had never existed. God's forgiveness and God's pardon are absolute.

No, Pete said, he didn't agree. There were some sins that shouldn't be forgiven. If he could come in here and tell a priest what he did and God would forgive him and pardon him, that made the sin smaller, and the sin wasn't small; it was huge. Taking a life was the biggest sin there was. Father D'Angelo tried to explain that God's forgiveness was infinite, as it had to be to pardon and absolve him of such an enormous crime, but he objected and said that he couldn't be absolved in this lifetime. Nothing could change what he'd done. He asked Father D'Angelo if anything could change what he'd done.

He said no, nothing could change the consequence of events. What was done was done and there was no undoing the toll in human misery, but Catholics believed in a world after this one, and in that world, all could be done and made right.

If that was true, Pete said, he would wait to receive forgiveness in the next world because in this world he had murdered. He had blood on his hands. He didn't want to kill. He didn't want the blood on his hands, but it was there.

The priest tried to tell him that even in law there was a distinction between murder and killing. If you were culpable, you had committed murder. If you were nonculpable, you had killed. People who went to war in a just war were nonculpable and guilty of killing. The guilt was not theirs alone, but shared by the people who sent them. In a just war, no one was guilty. Pete interrupted Father D'Angelo and said there was no such thing as a just war. He didn't know anything about the teachings of the Church, but he knew his Ten Commandments, and one of them said, Thou shalt not kill. He said he was sitting here talking because he was alive at other people's expense.

Father D'Angelo had just come from a symposium on survivor guilt in which he heard Holocaust survivors bewail the fact of being alive at the expense of other people's lives, and the rabbi on the panel, himself a survivor, pointed out that some survivors *were* alive at other people's expense. One man in the audience survived because he stole another man's shirt before the lineup, so that when the shirtless man appeared, he was instantly shot. But most of them were not alive because they had stepped over the bodies of others. They might feel guilty because they were alive, but in fact they were not guilty.

He repeated some of this to Pete, who said that was all well and good, but he was alive because he *had* stepped over the bodies of others. Literally, he had stepped over them. The people he knew who came back alive, or who were alive when he left, were alive because when they turned a corner and saw a gook, they didn't freeze. They fired. He told Father D'Angelo about a man who kept twitching after twenty-five rounds of ammunition were shot up and down his spine, and how later that night, the man set off five grenades they'd placed beneath his body. Pete said he was right to feel alive because others were dead. He took no particular pride in it. It was the simple truth.

The priest asked him if he believed God should forgive him. Pete said God could forgive him but He shouldn't. Father D'Angelo told him that was presumptuous of him to say. It was not for him, any more than it was for the priest, to say what God could and should not do. The priest asked again. Did he believe God *could* forgive him? Pete said he remembered what he'd been taught, and there wasn't anything God couldn't do. Father D'Angelo asked him if he intended to kill again, and he said he'd never kill again as long as he lived. He would rather be killed. Then, the priest said, God forgives you and absolves you of all sin. If you take communion, and are determined to go and sin no more, you are absolved, forgiven, absolutely and unconditionally.

Fine, he said, but I don't feel forgiven.

Father D'Angelo heard that week after week: I know God's forgiven me, but I don't feel forgiven, whereupon the sinner confessed again, received absolution, went and tried to sin no more, and returned the next week. He still didn't feel forgiven. Then the priest would tell him, God has forgiven you. Now go and forgive yourself. So he told that to Pete Bravado, who looked at him and shook his head.

After a while Father D'Angelo forgot to whom he was speaking. He forgot this was Pete Bravado, the little skinny kid he took upstate to reform school after the family court sentenced him. He said, "I understand your reluctance to accept pardon. If you accept the pardon immediately, you devalue the enormity of what happened, the enormity of what happens when moral controls are loosened. For you, the *sin* is absolute, not the pardon."

He smiled at Father D'Angelo and said, "Exactly."

"But to God it is the other way around."

"No, to the Church it's the other way around. God isn't the same as the Church any more than the government's the same as the Constitution. I'll take the Constitution over the government. I'll take God over the Church and the Bible. Who wrote the Bible? Men like you and me wrote the Bible. Who's to say what God really meant? I have to believe what I know in my heart."

"God," said the priest, "never mitigates the enormity of the sin. But He said you should forgive, not seven times, but seventy times seven."

"I couldn't do that," he said. "I'm not *that* good. I've forgiven myself seventy times seven. What is that? Four hundred and ninety? And I still feel guilty. You know what that means to me? It means I'm supposed to feel guilty because what I did was wrong."

"How was what you did different from what any other soldier did?"

"It wasn't."

"You," said Father D'Angelo, "are a moral absolutist."

"I believe in God and I believe in evil," he said. "I don't know why God allows so much evil. I try to work it out, but I can't work it out. That's the big fear, that God's evil too."

"That's heresy," the priest said. Pete made him shiver. "I believe in evil. I believe in a personal evil, a devil, a Satan. Every believer must sooner or later confront the issue of evil. Perhaps evil exists so one can choose goodness over it. God wants love to be freely given. He wants, He needs, He demands a free response. Whether or not we do evil is our choice. Evil is the result of human decisions."

"Where does that idea come from?" Pete asked. "How do you know that God wants love to be freely given?"

"From the notion that He created man in His own image. Once He created them in His own image, He could not and would not change them. Christ would not intervene in a war if that meant killing people, even as He did not intervene in His own historical life. He always remains apart. His way was not the way of the world. He set the example. He showed the way. Now He tests people to see if they can follow the example that's been set."

Pete nodded. The priest waited to see what he thought.

"Your God wants power. He's no better than a politician. My God wouldn't let children walk around wired to live grenades. He wouldn't send boys out into the jungle to look for arms and legs. He wouldn't do it. The evil's got to be turned into good."

"You're intent on turning evil into good," the priest said. "That's God's way, too. God writes straight with the crooked. Moses and Jeremiah and David were great sinners. Paul, the leader of the apostles, denied Christ three times. God used weaknesses, evil events, as occasions to reveal great things. An evil occurrence became an occasion for great revelation. The

Bible's full of such stories. Mary Magdalene, to whom some people pray. Your war may be such an occurrence."

"It has to be," he said.

"It is," said the priest. "Most of the time the reality and seriousness of evil is not apparent. It became apparent to you. It gives you the choice to decide whether or not to continue along an evil path or to choose another path. You have a real choice. Maybe it's better than living as if you're not living at all. Maybe God's given you a special gift. You have no choice. You *have* to live your life. You cannot be one of the living dead."

"I believe that," he said. "I believe if it weren't for the war, I'd be in jail. I was headed that way." The priest said he remembered. Father D'Angelo said, "Things like the Second World War, the Holocaust, your war, perhaps humanity as a whole, came into contact with certain very basic questions and realities it would not have come into contact with otherwise."

"Not humanity as a whole," Pete said. "Only those who were there. And most of them don't want to remember. Ask them. 'I can't think about it. The memories are too painful.' It's understandable. So who learns anything? The ones who were there learned, but most of them don't want to think about it. You think about it and they say you're living in the past. What's history for? It's supposed to let you teach the ones who come after. The ones coming after *don't want to know.*"

"Basically and fundamentally," Father D'Angelo said, "war and Christianity cannot mix."

"See!" Pete said.

"The most pure expression of love is to allow one's life to be taken."

"I'm not that pure," he said. "I had to survive."

"Perhaps only God is that pure."

"No, there were men there who were that pure. Most of them didn't come back. The animals were more pure than the men, but the Church says animals have no souls. But I say they have souls."

"They have animal souls."

Pete wanted to know what that meant. The priest said animals aren't created in God's image, and so their souls are not immortal. How did the priest know that? From reading the Bible. But maybe everything was created in God's image and whoever wrote the Bible forgot to put that down. The pig he saw tossed onto the fire had a soul and it tore out of the pig's mouth, screaming.

"You want to reinvent religion," Father D'Angelo told him, and he said, "Yeah, well, you can't have a chaplain jumping out of a chopper saying, 'Don't feel bad about killing. God understands.' He understands, but He doesn't approve. Yeah, I want to reinvent religion."

Outside, the rain fell and fell, visible now through the leaded casement windows as slush.

"How do you live where people die?" he asked. At first, Father D'Angelo didn't think Pete was talking to him. His voice had softened. He seemed to be thinking aloud.

"How do you get used to it?" Father D'Angelo asked him. Now his own voice sounded unfamiliar to him, unreal, as if they were talking in another place altogether.

"If I told you that tomorrow someone was going to drop the atomic bomb on Brooklyn, and you looked around, and everyone was going about their business as if nothing were going to change, you'd forget about the atom bomb and go about your business too. That's how you live your life. If you asked a few people, 'Is it true? Are they going to drop the atom bomb tomorrow?' and they said, 'Yes, so what?' and went on doing what they were doing, loading a truck, unloading a truck, changing a tire, plucking a chicken, sewing a button on their son's coat before school, you'd say, 'O.K., so I'm frightened, but so are they and they're not stopping. They're going about the way they always do, so what's the matter with you?' That's what you do. You look at other people, and O.K., you know the world's coming to an end, but no one's acting any differently, so you don't either. You think, O.K., so this is how it is.

"So if everyone around you says, 'O.K., in this place, someone dies every day,' you ask why and you don't get an answer. They just say the same thing. 'In this place, someone dies every day.' You don't want it to be you. You don't want it to be your buddy, so you make sure it's someone else, someone else who could kill you or your buddy. You've never killed before, so you look around you and see how it's done. You learn by watching, and after you've watched for a while, what everyone's doing, that's normal. Cut off an ear? O.K., that's how we live here. We cut off an ear. They say, 'Cut off both ears so we have proof you killed one person, otherwise someone's going to take the other ear and the army ends up counting one dead body twice.' O.K., we'll cut off both ears. Put a death card in a dead man's mouth because that scares the VC away and saves lives and makes you feel better. O.K., everyone's doing it, so you do it, too. Shoot a kid because last week two kids went into a mess hall and blew everyone up? O.K., you've got your orders. That's what you do here. That's how you live where people die."

They sat there saying nothing. Outside the rain was falling. Father D'Angelo was aware of how thick were the grey, enclosing walls, how the grey stones had become a kind of skin in which he lived. Inside, it was cold. He hadn't expected to be in the office and the fire was unlit. Without a fire, the inside of a stone church was always damp. What would he have done in Pete's place? He asked himself that and then he asked Pete if he would like to take confession.

"Sometimes I sit in the bushes outside this church and take off all my clothes and let the rain wash me clean. Other times, I take out Chinese food and sit in the bush watching the people go by, and they don't know I'm there. Is that a sin?"

"Why do you sit there?"

"Because I feel safe."

"It's not a sin to feel safe."

"But I could be arrested," he said.

"Yes, you could be, but you are not sinning against God."

"Even if I'm sitting there naked?"

"There are laws about nakedness. Man's laws, not God's. The policeman arrests you in man's name, not God's."

"But should I stop?"

"Do you want to get arrested?"

"No."

"Then you should stop."

"And if I can't?"

"What you can't do today, you may do tomorrow."

"I'd like you to hear my confession," he said.

So, Father D'Angelo thought, he believes I can absolve him of the sin of sitting naked in the churchyard because I am like the proprietor of the church, and now he wants to make his confession because he believes he may feel better, although he does not believe he will. Suppose in the end he is right, and I am a useless old man, a therapist in long robes, a quack, a profferer of sugar pills to the mortally ill? These were night thoughts, and he pushed them aside to consider later.

And he said the words, the *Confiteor.* "God the father of mercies, through the death and resurrection of His son has reconciled the world to Himself and sent the holy spirit among us for the forgiveness of sins. Through the ministry of the Church may God give you pardon and peace and I absolve you of your sins in the name of the father and the son and the holy spirit," and the penitent would answer, "Amen."

And Pete did answer, "Amen," but when he left, he did not feel forgiven, and Father D'Angelo, who had listened to his story, did not feel forgiven, but felt guilty by proxy, and doubted his Lord in Heaven and asked himself if his faith had ever been truly tested, and if it had, would he now believe in God's infinite mercy or would he turn his face from Him? Would he have concluded that there were some acts so morally atrocious they ought never to be forgiven? If he had been tested, would he have been as good a man as the one who confessed to him today? Pete did not believe, and so according to doctrine, he ought to be damned, but Father D'Angelo could not bring himself to believe he was damned. Instead, he thought of him as a crooked man with whom God writes straight. But Father D'Angelo was not so tested. When the day was over, he said his prayers and he went to sleep a peaceful man. To sleep, a priest must put aside what he hears, and for the night, he did so and he prayed for Pete Bravado and hoped he too would sleep peacefully, but he did not believe he would. Perhaps Pete never would. His soul had been touched by fire and now it was burning, and there were others like him, an army of men on the streets he thought he knew, all burning.

47 TIME PASSED as he once wished it would, quickly, the seasons succeeding one another so quickly, he barely noticed what they were and some days he would look up in surprise, surprised it was snowing, or surprised the leaves on the elm had turned golden, or unprepared for the humidity and the heat. He came home from work, watched television, drank any brand of beer until he found a brand called White Horse, and then drank that until he fell asleep. When he couldn't sleep, he took a job driving nights for a car service, and during the day he repaired bathrooms and back porches, replastered ceilings through which water from broken pipes had leaked. No matter what he did, he felt a sense of loss, and there were days when, alone in the apartment, his heart beat so loudly he could *see* the beats hanging in the air, then swirling up like a swarm of gnats, disappearing.

Days passed and there seemed less and less of him. He filled less and less space, and when he stared at the television screen, he thought, This happened in the war. In the war, I got old fast and I'm getting old now. Time was passing and he had nothing to show for it except the lines in his face, the creases in his hands, the sense that he looked back at what had already happened to him as if from a great distance.

Because he had no one to talk to, he sometimes went to see Father D'Angelo, who always seemed happy to let him in. He told him more and more, his hospitalizations, how he had burned his wife's car, his dream about the dog biting his face, and, because of the way the priest's attention warmed him when he talked about the war, he told him about the bodies burnt to skeletons, Wapniak's skulls, fastened on each side of the cupola, Li and her baby, whatever he remembered.

"What do you think?" he asked the priest.

"Think?" asked Father D'Angelo.

"Am I bad or good?"

"I don't judge."

"That means I'm bad, right?"

"No, no. Once before, I told you you were intent on turning evil into good. When you talk to me, I see good men caught up in evil events. Not all of them end up as you have, wanting good to come from evil. Will you succeed? I don't know. God doesn't give us troubles greater than we can bear. I believe that. But sometimes I wonder. Do you have to break your damned back? Oh, sorry. No one's perfect."

"See what happens when you hang around Vietnam vets?" Pete asked.

"I'll take my chances," said the father. He thought about Angelina, whose confessions he had heard, and how she had feared for her son. He thought of old Mr. and Mrs. Bravado, who had confessed their hopes for Pete, the special one, and prayed to be absolved for their partiality. He thought about George Bravado, who rarely came to confession, and who, when he came, rattled off a year's worth of sins as if he were reading from a grocery list. He thought about Dolores Bravado, whose confession he had also heard. He remembered her crying, saying when she married, she'd hoped to be a good wife, but there was something wrong in her or in the marriage. She didn't know which. One night, her husband grabbed her by the ankle and said, "Don't move! There's a snake in the bed!" and she was tired.

Every day she spent with him, she became more sour and more bitter. What did they expect of her? How long could you be married to a man who didn't see you? He saw someone, but it wasn't you. If you cried, he said you had nothing to cry about.

Her friends were sorry for her, but one of them said she had no sympathy because she had no soul. If she had no soul now, what would she have in one year? In two years? If she kept trying, for her sake, for his, for the sake of the children, and woke up one morning with no soul at all?

No, no, no, he said. That won't happen. The soul is immortal. God sees how you try. His ways are mysterious, but in the end, it will be clear. She was still waiting for the clear light of heaven. So was he.

Lately, Pete had not been coming. When it rained, Father D'Angelo would go to the window of his study and look out at the bushes, trying to see an outline of a figure, but no matter how hard he looked, how bright the moonlight, he could see nothing.

When it rained heavily, he would open his casement window and lean as far out as possible, watching the water, lit by the streetlights, turn silver as it hit the leaves, and imagine the water falling from the leaves and finding Pete Bravado, beneath their canopy, bringing him both peace and fear. Once, when he was leaning out the window, the janitress came in and scolded him. What was he thinking of, a man his age, hanging out of a window, soaking wet, and in such weather? Now, when it rained, he turned the key in his office door before looking out, but he never saw him, yet he knew he was there. One day he would see him. In the meantime, he leaned out the window, studying the bushes, sometimes for hours, until the poetry he wrote as a young man began to come back to him:

And now the rain's silver streams
Depress the leaves like piano keys
Until the sounding (was it brass? what was it?)
Dilutes the palette of the hills.

What would he have been like had he not gone into the Church? He remembered how often the nuns once summoned his mother to the school. He remembered the monk who told her he couldn't look at her son without seeing him in invisible stripes with a number across his back. When he was younger and there was nothing he wanted to do, when he believed his life had no significance, that had been a terrible time. If he hadn't looked up and seen the water flowing in the sky, the pure water, washing everything clean, the people rising up from the sidewalks, rinsed and shining, ascending, complete with rain boots and pocketbooks and umbrellas and briefcases and transparent plastic rain hats beaded with raindrops, if he hadn't seen their belongings raining back down on the earth, growing insubstantial as they fell, if he hadn't seen their souls circling the church steeple before taking off for the last, long flight, what would have become of him?

He'd come into the Church, taken his vows, and then came the study and the hearing of confessions, a life given over to others, *their* marriages, *their* baptisms, *their* confirmations, *their* funerals. But if he had to live his own life? If he hadn't had so many constraints upon him? If, instead, he'd been plunged into a vacuum where the rules were suspended, where the passions of heart and soul met no pressure from outside and so dug themselves up from where they were buried, then what?

Now, even when there was no rain, he thought about Pete Bravado, sitting out in the churchyard beneath the bushes, sometimes eating Chinese food with chopsticks, invisible to everyone who passed by, thinking, *I am silent, but deadly,* thinking, *I am safe here,* thinking, *When will they see me and come for me?*

He knew Pete didn't come in through the gate. In his imagination, he saw him swinging over the church fence, landing on the other side like a cat, moving like a dark shadow from tree to tree. On Sundays, his mind wandered while giving his sermons, and he saw the dark figure in the bushes, and at times he saw him crouched beneath the shrubbery, dark wings sprouting from his sharp shoulder blades. At other times, he saw him spreading his wings, and his arm raised in defiance, in his hand a pitchfork. The image of Pete in the old churchyard began to obsess him. In back of him were the flat stones, their names covered with black mold and moss, and behind the stones, the walls of the church, and behind the walls, the priest, the father, watching, able to do nothing. This image, or sequence of images, haunted his days.

One day, the janitress came in and put a piece of paper on his desk. It was a flyer announcing a veterans' homecoming parade. "May seventh," he said aloud. "Thanks."

"Where were those people fifteen years ago? Where were they when the three marines knocked on my door? I spit on them!"

"Mrs. Flannery!"

"I spit on them the way they spat on me!" She was sobbing and sobbed against the priest's chest. He looked down at her iron-grey head. When had people started growing taller? She was under five feet. His mother had been under five feet. Now most of the boys in the church choir were already six feet tall. In the war, too, they were six feet tall, taller than the last generation, better targets.

Mrs. Flannery's voice emerged from the fabric of his robe. "I have this paper in my purse. A person always remembers God saying He'll work with her forever, and when bad things happen, she looks back and sees two sets of footprints, His and hers. But one day, something happens and she sees only one set of footprints. So she complains to God and reminds Him He said no matter what happened, He'd always walk with her, and you know what He says? He says, 'When you see one set of footprints, that's when I carried you.' Isn't that beautiful?"

"Yes. It is."

"I still spit on them," said the woman, wiping her eyes. "How many times can you turn the other cheek?"

"Oh, you know the answer to that," said Father D'Angelo. He was studying the pamphlet, wondering if Pete Bravado knew of the parade.

"It's on the radio, it's on TV. It's all they're talking about," Mrs. Flannery said.

But Pete told him there were days when he did nothing but work and stare at the walls, when he never turned on a radio or television or heard the phone ring. *Let him that has ears to hear, let him hear.* He switched on his answering machine, looked at it, thought about how odd it was to have a machine taking messages meant for a priest, and went out.

Pete lived in a four-family house, his apartment a small room on the third floor, and the priest rang the bell and waited. Eventually, he heard the sound of feet stumbling down the steps. "Yeah?" asked a voice behind the door. He said his name and the door opened. "No one died, no one died," Father D'Angelo said quickly. "I've got something to show you."

"Come up. Have some coffee," Pete said awkwardly. "You make house calls? I didn't know."

"You don't remember, that's all," said the priest.

The couch was covered with newspapers, the coffee table with empty beer bottles, bottle caps, and overflowing ashtrays. Crushed cigarette packs littered the floor and tucked themselves between the sofa cushions.

"No way to live, right?" Pete asked, sweeping the newspapers to the floor, clearing a space for the two of them. "Underneath, it's clean. One thing I know how to do is clean. We used to scrub floors with a toothbrush. Who has the whitest grout in the neighborhood? I do." He disappeared into the kitchen and returned with two cups of coffee and a plate of anisette toast. "So," said Pete. "I'm listening."

"Read it," said Father D'Angelo, handing him the paper.

"A parade? For us?"

"Will you go?"

"I don't want no part of no parades."

"You deserve it."

"They'll frag us."

"Who?"

"The people." The priest said nothing. Pete put the paper down, then picked it up. He couldn't leave it alone. "Even if they fragged us, I'd be with my buddies," he said. He put the paper back down, picked it up again. "What are they going to say? 'Welcome home'? 'Thanks'? It's a little late, isn't it? Just when you forget, they want to open it all up? Thanks, but no thanks."

"You haven't forgotten," the priest said.

"No." said Pete. "I haven't forgotten."

"Can it hurt?" asked the priest. "Can it do any harm?"

"I'll think about it," Pete said.

"At least call the number. They can't force you." He watched Pete turn it over. "When it rains, do you still come to the churchyard?"

"Yeah," said Pete. "I do. You come here to talk about that?"

"No, we talked about that already."

"Yeah," said Pete, reading the paper over again.

"Well, I have to get back," the priest said, pushing himself up from the couch, grimacing. "These old bones. God doesn't make exceptions for His old dogs."

HE READ the paper so many times he memorized it. Still, it didn't seem real. Finally, he took a match, held it to the edge of the paper, and burned it. When it burned down and burned against his fingers, he dropped the remaining corner of the paper into the ashtray and watched the orange border eat up the rest of it. He picked up the phone and dialed the number. The voice at the other end of the phone patiently answered questions. Yes, there was going to be a parade. No, they were asking people not to wear uniforms, but you could do what you wanted. They'd meet in Cadman Plaza and find their units and march with them over the Brooklyn Bridge and go on down Broadway. Did he know where Cadman Plaza was? Was he coming in from out of town?

"I have to go, man," Pete said, hanging up, cracking the cap on a bottle of scotch. The phone was ringing and wouldn't stop. "Yeah?" he said.

"It's me, Petey," said his son. "You read about the parade?"

"Yeah, I read about it."

"You gonna go?"

"I don't know."

"*I* want to go with you," his son said. "So does Joey."

"I don't know yet," Pete said. "I'll call you." If it was a dream, it was a better dream than he'd been having, but when he decided to go, he was so frightened and cold he got under the blankets and pulled them over his head. It took him several hours to warm up. He called his ex-wife's apartment and told his children to meet him where the parade ended. When they asked where that was, he told them to look at the newspaper. If he had to think about one more thing, if he had to think about it in advance, he wouldn't go. Until the instant before the parade began, he'd pretend it wasn't happening. Why was he going? He was marching for the men who couldn't march. He was marching for Liebowitz and the Chief and everyone else who died there. He'd say he was marching for himself, but he didn't believe he deserved a parade. No, by now he believed what everyone had told him. He used to ask, "What, did I do something wrong in Vietnam?" Now he didn't ask. He took it for granted.

The morning of the parade, he left the house wearing his dress green jacket. At the station, the warm breeze lifted his hair. He felt every eye on him. In the train, he stared down at his feet. Out of the corner of his eye, he saw two or three other men dressed in green but he didn't look up. On the platform, he saw more and more men wearing dress greens and he didn't like it, the excitement, the old feeling of belonging to something, of somehow knowing more about these men than he knew about his own family, of having a purpose.

At Cadman Plaza, men in dress greens or suit jackets had megaphones and were calling out, "First Marines, over here! 101st Airborne, over here! Sanitation Department, over here!" He turned and saw a big Italian, six feet four, holding up a sign: SANITATION DEPARTMENT. They were marching together. He looked for his own outfit, for familiar faces, and finally he saw his friend Vinnie who'd gone off after Johnny Pellegro's funeral. *"I'm going to kill the Viet Cong! They killed Johnny!"* He turned away from him and someone said, "Hey, man, you can't find your own outfit? Come march with the real men. We're the Big Red One, man," and he said, "No, no, I'll keep looking." Two scruffy characters wearing cammies were standing together, each one with a bottle in a bag.

"Man," one of them said to him, "we do not belong here. We just privates. Everyone here is an officer, man."

"You belong here," he said. "Everyone belongs here," and one of them said, "You an officer?" and he said, "Do I look like an officer?" and they looked him over and said, "Yeah, man, you look like an officer." "Well, I'm not," he said, and kept on walking. He found two men from his outfit and the three of them got behind the men from the Sanitation Department.

"I don't see anyone I know," Pete said.

"No, we don't either," the others said.

They went over the Brooklyn Bridge into Manhattan and in the windows of office buildings women were dancing and clapping and blowing kisses. Confetti was everywhere, and streamers, white, purple, red, blue, and the streets were lined with people, clapping and cheering, shouting, "We love you!" "Thanks!" "You're great guys!" and one woman was holding up a poster with a gold star and her son's name on it, and farther down the street, a young girl, she couldn't have been more than thirteen, was crying, saying again and again, louder and louder, "My brother died in Vietnam! My brother died in Vietnam!" He wanted to stop and talk to her, but he couldn't stop, and that too was familiar. It was too familiar. He began crying and couldn't stop. His face flushed with shame. His eyes felt swollen, so did his cheeks, and when he finally looked around, the men from his outfit were crying, and he turned to look back, and the men behind him were crying.

The enormous green worm made its way down Broadway. People standing on the side grabbed and hugged the soldiers near them. Women kissed them. Mothers held up their children, took confetti from their children's carriages, but beneath it Pete still heard: how many women and children did he kill? Murderers. Baby killers. Were they still thinking it? If they weren't, what made them stop? They didn't trust him before and now they did. Why? He didn't trust himself.

"You know how I feel?" he said to the man next to him. "I feel human again. I really do! I feel human!"

"You feel human? I don't want to feel human!" the man next to him said. "I don't want it coming back!"

"Nothing you can do about it now, man," said the man marching on the other side of him.

And then the parade was over. Pete looked around for his children, found them, and walked aimlessly back and forth, his arms around Petey and Joey, their faces radiant with pride, and he thought, This is a good day to die. If I died now, I'd die happy. Look how proud of me they are, and Joey said, "You're not crazy!" and he bent over and kissed him. Then he and the children were back on the train, Petey carrying the sticker he'd been given: *I'm a Vietnam vet and I'm proud of it.* They stopped on the avenue and he ordered everything they asked for, sausage rolls, calzone, a pizza pie, ices, and they ate until their stomachs hurt, and he looked from one to the other, thinking, I don't want this day to *ever* end, but outside it was already getting dark, and now he could see himself and his children reflected in the plate-glass window, and there he was, wearing his class A uniform and people were smiling at him. Even in the window he could see that. "Let's go home," he said finally. Before he got in his van, he put the sticker on its bumper.

"O.K., let's go," he said.

"When's the next parade?" Joey asked, and the coldness came back, and along with it, fear. He didn't want it to start all over. He didn't want to bring it back. "It took them seventeen years," he said to his son. "Maybe they'll have another in seventeen years."

"I'll be *old,*" cried Joey.

"We don't need parades," he said. "Do we need parades?"

There are events with long legs. You leave them behind and they follow you. You get in a car and step on the accelerator, and they run so fast, they blur, but they keep on coming. He was working on the weekend when someone from the telephone company found him in the bathroom where he was working with a crumbling pipe and asked him, "That your van out there?" and he looked up and saw someone wearing a bush hat covered with buttons, *P.O.W. M.I.A. Third Marines, I attended the University of South Vietnam,* and under the hat band were four grenade pins. "Yeah," he said. "That's my van."

"Here's my card," the man said. "Robert Scanlon, Secretary. Vietnam Veterans of America." He said they had their own charter. They did good work. They didn't sit around telling war stories. They conducted business. They were raising money to bring back POWs. Why didn't he give it a shot? He asked when the next meeting was.

"Tomorrow night," said Robert Scanlon.

"Tomorrow?" Pete asked.

"Yeah," the man said, pointing at him. "And you're going to be there, right?"

"We'll see," Pete said.

He went. He was introduced to some of the others and said, yes, he'd like to come to Bobby Scanlon's house for a barbecue, and the next thing he knew, he was watching tapes of *Apocalypse Now* and *The Deer Hunter.*

"I don't know," Pete said. "I've got to take it slower than this, man."

"So take it slow," Bobby said. He was tall and thin and his features drooped as if his face had been carved from wax that had been left too long in the heat. His eyes were green, like a cat's, and when he smiled, he looked as if he were fifteen years old. "What about the parade in Chicago? You want to go? A lot of guys from the chapter are going. The plane leaves from Newark." Pete said he'd see.

At the airport, he was confused. He didn't know where to go and then he saw the green uniforms, and Bobby's shaggy head towering above everyone. Oh, he thought. So that's where I go, and he got on the plane and settled back. "I'm nervous," he said to Bobby.

"Relax," Bob said. "We'll do it together."

"What outfit you with?" Pete asked.

"Third marines."

"Oh, yeah. You said that."

"You won't have no trouble," Bobby said. "I'll find third marines. I won't find people I knew. Not too many came back. What about you? What's your outfit?"

"White Horse."

"You'll find them."

"I didn't last time."

"It's bigger this time. They're expecting sixty-five thousand. You'll find them."

In Chicago, he checked into his hotel and wandered around the city alone for a few hours, walking out to the lake that had no horizon, walking on the beach, picking up the tiny shells exactly like the shells on the ocean beach in Brooklyn, but these were tiny, smaller than the size of a fingernail. He bent down, picked up an assortment of them, sorted out the best ones and wrapped them in a paper napkin and put them away for his sons.

He climbed the cement blocks shoring up the lakefront and looked down at the waves, crashing and foaming against them. The skyline reminded him of home, but everything here was cleaner, shined, as if someone had just polished it. He picked out a block of concrete and sat on it, looking out over the aqua and green water. There were other places. Brooklyn wasn't the whole world.

He took the little shells out of his pocket, touched each of them, and began to push himself up with his left hand, when he saw a familiar figure begin to appear over the topmost block of white concrete. It was the man who dressed in bandages or a white monk's robe. Funny, he'd always assumed the person beneath the bandages was a man. Today he wasn't sure. The figure was climbing up over the topmost concrete block, seeming to grow out of the earth, and because of where he was, taking his place as part of the skyline.

"Hey!" Pete called out. "Hey! I know you!" The White Man hesitated, looked at him, waved, and began sinking back into the concrete block. "Hey!" Pete shouted. "Come back!" He clambered up the cement blocks but when he got to the top and was in sight of the Outer Drive, the White Man wasn't there. No one was there.

He left the lake shore, left the black granite skyline, found the assembling parade and began looking for his troop, for familiar faces, but he didn't see anyone. Then a voice called out, "Hey, White Horse," and he turned around and there they were, hundreds upon hundreds of them, and he went over and lined up with his troop and marched. This, he thought, was a *parade*, and at the end of it, at Soldier's Field, there were tents set up. There was food served and he bought something at each tent, and someone from the White Horse said, "Come with me, man. There's a newsletter to sign up for," and he followed him to a table surrounded by people five and six deep and he waited on line, his stomach full, his eyes full of White Horses.

He bent down to sign his name at the end of the column and as he was signing, someone tapped him on the shoulder, and he picked up his head and there was Sal.

"Bravado!" Sal was shouting. "Bravado, you animal!"

"Sal?" Pete said. "Sal?"

"The one and only," Sal said.

"What's your *last name?*" Pete asked. "What's your *last name?*"

"Castiglione, stupid! Castiglione! You heard it every day!"

"No! Everyone called you Sal!"

"You going to stand there and argue about it?" the man in back of them asked, and they started to laugh, and it was as if no time had passed, and they were hugging one another, pounding one another on the back, crying.

"You're coming back to Brooklyn with me!" Pete said again and again. "You've got to come back with me! Where do you live, man? What do you do?"

"Hey, I'm a *doctor,* man," Sal said. "Can you believe it? Me? A doctor? Yeah," he said, looking at Pete. "I'll give my wife a call. I'm coming back with you!"

"Your wife?"

"Allison. I'll give her a call."

THEY SAT on the floor in front of Pete's couch, and Sal asked what Pete had been doing for the last seventeen years.

"Oh, I don't know," Pete said. "I got stuck. After I got divorced, I couldn't find my way. I was lost. Remember that time we got lost in the jungle? We came to a fork in the road and one track went one way and we went another? Where the fuck were we? You found a compound and pulled in so fast we almost turned over. Remember? The next day we got on the frequencies and joined up with the rest of the troop? I got divorced and I couldn't join up again. That was the end of the road. And then my brother died, and my mother, and the dreams. I'm still lost."

"Yeah. You're the only combat vet who came back alive."

"There it is."

"Except there are a lot of us. Half an army's worth."

"You know what?" Pete asked. "I look around me, and all the protesters, they're all doing so much better? What did I do wrong? Should I have been out there, protesting?"

"Yeah, you should've. The anger's like a cancer, man. It eats you up alive. It just gets worse. Yeah, some of us did better. We got it off our chests. We had people around us. We didn't go it alone. The war over there was nothing compared to what happened when we came back. So what now? What are you going to do now?"

"I drink pretty good."

"You need a *therapist,* man."

"At the VA? You ever been to the VA?"

"Don't go to the VA. I'll get you a name. You say you'll go and I'll get it for you."

"You know what? You stay here and I won't *need* a therapist."

"I can't stay here forever, man. You know that."

"Yeah," Pete said. "You live alone and you die alone."

"No, you *die* alone. You *live* with other people."

"A *doctor.* How'd you do it?"

"It wasn't easy," Sal said. "But I did it."

"So why can't I do anything?" Pete said. "Why? What's wrong with me?"

"Don't make comparisons, man," Sal said. "I'm a meaner, tougher son of a bitch. I always was. I was never as good as you. I wanted to blow heads off. Hell, if it weren't for you, I *would've* blown heads off. Remember Davis? This is the *world,* man. Goodness doesn't always pay."

"I'm not good. Don't tell me I'm good, because I'm not."

"You're good, man. We all knew that. You're good. You're stubborn and you've got the self-control of a flea, but you're good."

"So that's why I'm sitting here in one room drinking myself under the bed?"

"Yeah," Sal said. "That's one reason. Go see a therapist."

"I remember what you said about shrinks. Sissy motherfuckers treating sissy motherfuckers."

"Did I say that? I don't remember saying that," Sal said.

"You said it," Pete said.

"So I was wrong," Sal said.

"You went to one?"

"I *still* go to one."

"Write the name on a piece of paper," Pete said. "You're not embarrassed? Sitting there watching me cry?"

"Cry on," Sal said. "It's only water. It's good for you."

"What?"

"Crying."

"Where's Wapniak? What happened to him?"

"When I left, he was in one piece."

"I'd like to find him," Pete said.

"Yeah? You got plenty of cotton for your ears?"

"After I left, anyone see the White Man?"

"Yeah," Sal said. "You know, that's the one thing I don't like talking about? At the parade, someone asked me about the White Man. Did I believe he was real? Did I ever see him? When I left, the word was that the White Man was a deserter from our side and was coming back after the war. He could be you. He could be me. I don't want to hear that shit. They called us enough names. Now a fucking journalist's going to go out looking for the White Man, and he doesn't find him and says everyone in the troop went crazy. Give me a break."

"But we *saw* him."

"So? It's our business, no one else's business. You want to explain to some civilian what we saw? A man wrapped in bandages?"

"Maybe we knew him."

"Maybe. It don't mean nothing."

He wrote Sal's number on the kitchen wall, wrote it down on the back of his license, wrote it on his DD2-14, and then memorized it. He saw Sal off at the airport. "Call the *number,* man," Sal said. "Call me anytime."

"YOU CAME here because Sal Castiglione told you to?" the therapist asked him. She was a short, thin woman, tiny, really, flat-chested, bird-necked, a distracted air, as if she'd just misplaced something she badly needed, but her face was pretty, her black hair layered and fitting her head closely, like a cap. She wore no makeup except lipstick and stared straight at him while he stared at the walls of her office, one completely covered with diplomas, the others covered, floor to ceiling, by bookcases. A patterned red rug of a kind he'd never seen before covered the parquet floor, and the furniture looked as if someone had made it from old aluminum pipes, and there were no ashtrays. How was he supposed to sit in a room with no ashtrays?

"Well, yeah," he said. "I trust Sal."

"Sal's a good man," she said.

"Yeah, well, they were all good men."

She said nothing, but watched him. What huge black eyes she had, like the animals that used to swing through the branches in the jungle. Lepers. No, *lemurs.*

"So," she said. "What do you think of the office? Do you like it?"

"So many books. I never saw so many books."

"Not even in a library?"

"Well, people don't live in libraries."

"Anything else?"

"Yeah," he said. "There are no ashtrays and there are no guards outside the door."

"I can supply an ashtray," she said, swiveling around in her chair and taking something from her desk, "but I'm afraid I can't do anything about the guards."

"I told someone I was coming to see a shrink, a woman, and you know what they said? They said, 'Is she crazy? She wants to talk to Vietnam vets?' "

"I want to talk to *you*," the doctor said. "Not Vietnam vets."

"They asked me, 'She's going to treat you over the phone? Because they all think we're crazy.' "

"Oh?" said the doctor.

"Well, Sal said you're smart. So you know."

"Know what?"

"How crazy we are."

"And the rest of the population is normal? You've met a great many sane, sensible people who aren't veterans?"

Was she laughing at him? "Look," he said, "you know what you're in for? You want to be dragged down every jungle trail? Into every ambush? Into every track before it blows? Outside every track *as* it blows? You want to know what it's like to see your best friend pull a trigger and blow a kid's head off? You ready for that? You want to walk down a trail and see the buzzards diving at the branches, eating what used to be your buddy? I mean, you were talking to him an hour ago. You weren't there. You're going to understand it?"

"Do you understand it?" the doctor asked.

"What?"

"Do you understand it?"

"No, I don't understand it!" Pete shouted. "I didn't then! I don't know! I spent so much time asking myself, 'What am I doing here?' I never even tried to find an answer. I forgot about an answer. No, I don't understand it!" He stopped shouting and found he was crying.

"Here," said the doctor, handing him a tissue. "I think you'll do fine."

"I yell and scream and you think I'll do fine?"

"Why not? You want to change. I'm here to help you."

"What's your name?" Pete asked.

"I'm Dr. Sit."

"What kind of name is Sit?"

"I'm half-Japanese, half-Chinese," she said.

"A gook," he said. "Just my luck."

"This time tomorrow?" Now she was smiling.

"*Tomorrow?* I was just here!"

"Four times a week every week, a dollar a session. I'll mail you an application for the clinic, but it's a formality. You're already accepted and you come here. Well," she said, standing up, brushing imaginary crumbs from her lap, "it's been nice meeting you. I'm looking forward to this."

"Well, I'm not," he said.

"You shouldn't be," she said.

"But it works?"

"It works. You go out through that door," she said and went back into her office.

He stood in the waiting room and looked at the paintings and the small clay statues. She was leaving him alone with these valuable, fragile things. He looked back at the closed office door, shook his head, saw a small piece of paper on the floor, picked it up, and when he couldn't find a wastepaper basket, put it in his pocket.

48 H E OFTEN dreamed himself deep in the defoliated wood, walking among the trees without leaves or bark, looking at the bomb craters, looking for ashes, leaning against a tree trunk, forgetting the tree had no roots and would fall to the ground, knocking down smaller trees as it fell. In the dream, he was thirsty and wanted to fill his canteen with the oily water from the streams, but he knew better, and would move on to the next water hole until he was so thirsty he plunged his head into the water and then lapped the water up out of his cupped hands. In the dream, everything was in black and white and he was always alone there and there was always the smell of smoke and gunpowder and the knowledge that if he turned the corner, he'd be walking in a full-color film and something was there that he didn't want to see. But that was when he slept.

On weekends, he joined up with a group of men he met at the chapter. Within a few weeks, he believed he'd known them forever, especially Bobby Scanlon, who knew every joke in the world. Bobby's wife refused to hear the word *Vietnam*. She didn't want any chapter members at the house, and when her husband watched a movie about the war on the VCR, she left the room, slamming the door, and often left the house.

"I've never met his wife," Pete said to Mickey, a short, thin man with wire-rimmed glasses, and Mickey said, "Man, you don't want to. You have one nice conversation with her, she finds out all about you, and after that, you call the house and she gives you an argument. 'There's no one else you can call but my husband?' She'll tell you straight out you're the lowest of the low. She's something. We hang out together, but we don't hang out at Bobby's."

"Hey," Bobby said. "You hear this one? Some soldiers are dressed up, camouflaged like trees. The Colonel comes out to inspect them, and he doesn't see them right away. He thinks they're trees. All of a sudden a tree streaks past him. He calls out, 'Halt!' The tree stops in its tracks, and the Colonel walks over to him. 'Why are you running, soldier?' he asks him. And the soldier says, 'When a bird flew over, and dropped whitewash on me, I said it was for God and country. When birds landed on my head, I said it was for God and country. When it thundered and lightninged, I said it was for God and country. But when two squirrels ran up inside my pants and

I heard one say to the other one, Let's eat one and save one for later, *that* was too much!' "

"That's very funny," said Mickey, polishing his glasses, "and you know why? Because that's how it was."

Every night, they met at someone else's apartment, and they talked. You could close your eyes and you were on stand-down, pulled back into the rear, and everyone was wearing olive drab. No one was firing at you. There was no incoming, no outgoing, no land mines, no trip wires, no spider holes, no snipers popping out of the ground, no sappers, no claymores, no willy peter, no pungee sticks, no patrols, no ambushes, no *Fire in the hole!* The talk went on. It went on.

"It was so dark, and we were out on patrol," Mickey said, "and every star in the sky was out, and the moon was full, and it was so bright you could see them. You could *see* the men on the moon. We lay there all night, watching them jump around in the moon dust. We *saw* them. Yeah, we saw them better than you guys back home saw it on television. We just lay there and smoked our O.J.'s and looked at the man in the moon."

"You guys lay out in the middle of a jungle and smoked?" Bobby asked. "Hell, you were lucky. We never smoked *anything* out in the field. We never talked. We never took fucking baths or showers. The gooks could smell a clean body a mile away. You wanted to smoke, you waited until it rained and then you smoked under your poncho and let the smoke out every minute or so."

"If we smoked in the bush, we were going down, man," said someone else. "That's the only way a door gunner spent time in the bush."

"Yeah, you guys took us out there and *left us,* man. You *left us* and took off. You *pushed* us out. I used to jump fifteen feet to the ground. I was the last out. You didn't even touch down. You guys!" Mickey said.

"We're taking fire from the tree line and you want us to stay there? You gotta be kidding, man. You know the life expectancy of a door gunner in a firefight? It's forty seconds, man. Forty seconds! You expect us to hang around? We're making eleven trips in and out of a hot LZ. Let's go, man. Move it. Push 'em out. Most of the MIAs came from fucking choppers, man."

"So why'd you go airborne?" Bobby asked. "You went over a grunt."

"They *asked* me. They said, Hey, you want to walk around the jungle carrying sixty, eighty pounds? They've got snakes down there. They've got panthers, lions and tigers and bears. They've got bugs *National Geographic* never heard of. You want to be a door gunner? You go in a taxi. You don't carry nothing. You fly in and out. You're one of the glamour guys. So I says, Sure, why not? I *volunteered.* That's how stupid I was. Later, I found out. They lost twenty door gunners the month before I came over. Twenty."

"You left us there, man," Mickey said.

"Yeah, but we came back for you."

"What about the jungle rot?" Bobby asked. "Everyone said, 'Watch out for it. You've got that pale skin.' So we cleared a bamboo patch and I didn't want to get it and I went to see the medic and I said, 'What do I do? I don't want jungle rot.' And he said, 'You've already got it.' There were these two pimples on my arm. He put Mycogel on it and sent me back, and two hours later, I couldn't believe it, there were four more. He said come back in two hours, but I was back in half an hour. They were popping out like in a cartoon. Pop, pop, pop! My arms swelled up to my elbows and the medic sent me in, and I took off, and when I came out, you know what happened?"

"Yeah," said Pete. "I know what happened. They laughed at you."

"They did! They laughed at me! Like I wasn't out there covering their asses! I went in to the doctor and said, 'Clean them. I'm going back.' He scraped them. I bit through twenty tongue depressors and I was back out there. They still swell up. Here. There's a couple on my arm. It's worse in the summer. And the welts all over? For years I wouldn't go to the beach."

"Yeah," said Pete. "I know."

"You got welts?"

"I got welts."

"I *had* welts. They went away after fifteen years. You should've humped mortar rounds."

"I should've stayed home listening to John Lennon," Mickey said.

"Yeah," Pete said. "We all should have stayed home."

"What are you talking about, man?" Bobby asked. "It was the best time of our lives! It's going to be that exciting again? When's it been that exciting? There's nothing like it, man, not even sex. A firefight, it was a total mental orgasm, that's what it was."

"You tell that to your wife?"

"She doesn't want to know about it," Bobby said. "She says when we got married, I never talked about it. Now all I do is talk. She says, 'Why do you have to live in the sixties?' I'm not living in the sixties. But I was *alive* in the sixties and now I'm supposed to pretend I slept through ten years? I never went over there? I never did anything? I never saw anything? I'm *proud* of what I did over there. I was *good.* They wouldn't let me out of the field. They kept me there for sixteen months. You're going to tell someone you did good work over there? They say it was a stupid war. That doesn't mean what you did was stupid. You didn't do your job right, people died. *You* weren't stupid."

"Let's not get serious," Mickey said, taking off his eyeglasses and polishing them. He looked exactly like John Lennon. "Nothing heavy. That's what we agreed. We have a good time. We do it over, and this time we do it right! A great fucking stand-down! Don't start no chain reaction, man. We're not up for it. Tomorrow's Monday, man. Over there, there were no Mondays."

"Over there, every day was Monday."

"Don't start, man."

"You know something?" Pete said. "I don't remember anyone talking over there. I don't remember anyone saying anything. I remember doing things, but it was always quiet. And dark. And there was something thick about it. I never heard so many words in my life as I heard here tonight."

"We're telling too many war stories for you?"

"No, man. But you didn't talk about it. After it was over, you didn't talk about it."

"All we do is talk," someone said, holding up a beer bottle, shaking the last drops onto his tongue. "Talk, talk, talk."

"I don't know where I am," Pete said. "I'm here and I'm there. You stand on a dock with one foot in a boat and the boat moves away? That's how I feel."

"No problems. That's the rule."

It was a good rule.

"HOW IS IT disloyal to the others to come here?" asked Dr. Sit.

"I didn't say that. Did I say that?"

"But you think they should be enough? You shouldn't need anyone else?"

"I don't. I need someone. I call one of the guys, they come right over. They leave their dinners, they leave their families, they come get me. We're closer than family."

"So tell me something," said the doctor.

"Yeah?"

"Where does a woman fit into this?"

"This isn't about women. I'm not ready for a woman. I just got a regular job."

"Did you tell the others? About the job?"

"Not yet."

"What else don't you tell them?"

He said, all right, all right, he didn't tell them he hated it there. He hated everything. He hated the country. He hated the track. He hated the gun he carried. He hated the bullets in the gun. He hated the men who got shot because they were shot. He hated the men who shot the gooks because the gooks were people, too. He hated everything! He hated the sun. He hated the stars. He hated the sky.

"I sat on the track and I got a haircut from a bullet. I was insulted! I was sitting there minding my own business and someone shot at me! Even though there was a war I was insulted! I wasn't doing anything! I was eating a can of C-rations!"

"It wasn't real," said the doctor.

"If it wasn't real, what am I doing here?"

"Was it real?"

He said no, it got real when he saw the burned bodies. It got real when he saw them drag the pig to the fire. Now, when he remembered, everything was new. "Why was everything so new?"

"Because it *is* new. Because when it happened, you didn't take it in. Now you're taking it in."

"I wrote down this dream. I'll leave it for you to read. It took me two days to write it down. I mean, it didn't take me two days to write it. It took me two days before I wrote it."

"Why don't you want to read it to me?"

"I'll read it to you," he said. His voice was sullen.

"I'm not daring you," said the doctor.

"I'll *read* it." He looked at her. She was sitting quietly in her chair, her eyes focused somewhere above the top of his head. He began to read. "I had this dream. I was in a hospital or bunker. Suddenly, I was escorted to the basement and it was filthy with dust. I had to walk with my head down under the pipes and beams. I walked past a doctor and he told me to follow him. He told me he would show me the way out and told me not to look.

"We walked past a woman, a nurse. She had a body on a table. Its legs were twisted and bent up into the air. I couldn't tell if I was looking at its back or its front. It was black from charcoal and stiff. Now the man had hold of my neck and head, as if he were pointing it in a certain direction. I stood next to another woman and this man had my head, making me look at a meat slicer and I saw the parts of bodies in wooden trays and I recognized what looked like the inside of a stomach of a human being.

"Now the man handed me to another woman and told her to get me out of there. We walked for a while. I was still ducking my head so I wouldn't hit the pipes or beams. They were pipes and beams at the same time. And it was dark. Then the woman told me that I needed this to get out of there. We walked up to a pile of burnt tree limbs. She handed me a boot and it was stiff and crumbly. The boot was the key and I was supposed to use it to get out. Then I realized that what I thought was a pile of burnt wood was a pile of bodies, just parts of bodies, all different parts, like a chicken's legs and thighs, but not parts of a chicken's body, a human body. I looked into this boot and I got scared and I ran, and the walls were getting thick with crust and scaly, and I came to a dark corridor and I felt this was the way out and I came to a door and cried after I opened it to find myself lost.

"I woke up. I remembered part of it. I wanted to remember it all. Here it is, Saturday, and I remember it, not all of it, but enough. This was the most frightful dream I ever had."

He looked at the doctor. She hadn't moved. She still stared at the same spot above his head. He turned to see what she was looking at, but there was nothing on the wall, only a spot of light. He started reading it again, slowly. When he finished, he said, "It's about all the things I didn't want to see. All the things I didn't want to happen. The bodies and parts of bodies. The walls were black and scaly like toast. That's what the bodies looked like when they burned. Ashy and scaly like burned toast. Burned stiff. You could crack them. Like potato chips."

"In Japan," said the doctor, "after they dropped the bomb, people saw terrible things, but what my mother said was the most terrible were the shadows left on the ground. You know why the shadows were terrible? They were all that was left of a human being. The person was gone, vaporized by the heat, but before he was vaporized, in that instant, his body cast a shadow, and that shadow stayed on the ground. People came to look for family members and they saw those shadows but no one could tell them who those people were."

"A red stain on the ground," Pete said. "Something so white you knew it was bone. There was nothing else so white in the jungle. One time it was an elephant bone. They were a means of transport. There was always the smell of smoke. You popped smoke flares, red, yellow, green, purple. Green usually meant a cold LZ. You saw green smoke, everything was fine. Red meant hot. The rest you decided on beforehand. Once we had to go back into a bunker to get two dead men, but we didn't think they were dead. We picked them up. They were cold. But we didn't think they were dead."

"You were too young," said the doctor. "What nineteen-year-old believes he's going to die?"

"We slept on mounds in graveyards. We walked into towns built over tunnels. You could be walking right over people's heads and not know they were under there. Right under your feet. *Dig a tunnel to China.* My mother used to say that at the beach. You know, to keep us busy. You dig and you think you see the tops of their heads at the bottom of the hole. Over there, it was real. You turned a corner and someone popped out of the ground. In basic, it was mechanical pop-up nonliving targets. Over there it was living pop-up targets with guns that shot back."

"After the revolution, my father was rusticated," the doctor said. "He was sent to the north. He had no place to live, so he lived in a hole in the ground. When it snowed, he dug the hole deeper. Now his bones break easily because he didn't have proper food then. My father says, 'We did it to ourselves.' Why are you crying?" She took a tissue from the box near her chair and handed it to him. He leaned forward, took a tissue from the box, and handed it to her. "Thank you," she said.

"Who's the woman in the dream who makes me look? Who's the man who says he'll show me the way out but doesn't do it? Who are they?"

"It's your dream," said the doctor.

"Even in the dream," he said, "I couldn't trust anyone. The doctor and the nurse, they were working together. They wanted to keep me in the tunnel."

"Because there was something they wanted you to see."

"I didn't want to see it."

"But you'd already seen it."

"I didn't want to see it *again.*"

"Who were they?" the doctor asked. "The man and the woman? The nurse and the doctor?"

"Everyone I couldn't trust. Everyone I could trust. They weren't lying to me. They were asking me to look. I trusted them and I didn't. They were bad and good. They were split down the middle. I don't understand."

"As many devils as the war produced, it produced angels," said the doctor.

"And sometimes both in the same person," said Pete.

"s o ? " Sal asked over the telephone. "How's it going?"

"I got a steady job. I started going with a woman. I met her at work. I burned my tongue drinking coffee in the cafeteria and she got me a glass of water."

"She's good for you?"

"Yeah, she's a good woman."

"Take it slow," Sal said. "You still talk to Father D'Angelo?"

"Yeah, the man must be nuts. He likes talking to me."

"Talking's what you've got to do, man," Sal said. "You need the words. There's a lot inside. You can't act it out. All the world's a stage, you end up in prison."

"I'll be careful," Pete said.

"How's Dr. Sit?"

"She's O.K., but sometimes I miss a few sessions. What does she expect? I'm a *veteran.*"

"Don't go getting cocky, man."

"Four times a week's a lot of time."

"Yeah? Remember what you used to say? God must love time, he made so much of it? What else are you doing?"

"I'm *dreaming.* All I do is dream. I dream with my eyes open. I write down my dreams and bring them in there. I dream on the train going there and I dream on the way back. I get together with the guys and we talk about the war. It's payback time. We're playing catch-up here."

"It's never too late."

"It's not over till it's over," Pete said.

"Remember that," Sal said. "You're from Brooklyn. Remember the Dodgers. There's always next year."

"*This* year's not bad," Pete said.

"Life's made up of waves, man. Where there's an up there's a down. Be prepared."

"I'm *tired* of being prepared. Remember those animals that sat in the trees with their arms open to the sun? That's *me*. Hey, you want to hear a joke?"

"It's your nickel."

W H O M I N D E D the passing of time now? If he was confused by the difference between what he said at the doctor's office and what he said or heard when he was with the others, he didn't mind. He couldn't remember a time when he hadn't been confused, but at least now he was enjoying it. He began to hang around with Bobby Scanlon and Mickey, and the three of them fit so well together the others began calling them a clique.

"What's a clique?" he asked Bobby, and Bobby said, "Like those little groups that always stuck together in high school," and Pete said he didn't finish high school, and in reform school, there weren't any cliques. It was just like the army, short-timers and long-timers, and Bobby said, "Hey, in this country you need a high school diploma," and the next thing he knew, he was studying for his G.E.D., and the third time he took the test, he passed it.

"Now what?" Bobby asked. "You going to college?" but Pete said no, he thought he'd rest on his laurels. He had his kids and his job and his friends and he had this new woman named Joanne and this was his time. He wasn't ambitious anymore. He didn't think he would be again. Give him a grass hut somewhere, and some rice, and he'd be happy. The war had to mean something. He knew it did. Something happened over there that was important to the human race. He didn't know what it was yet, but sooner or later, he would. They all would.

"I had this weird experience after I came back," Bobby said. "I was sitting in my room and all these thoughts started coming and I started writing it down, but I couldn't write it down fast enough. You know what I saw? I saw I was alone in the middle of my house, even when my wife was there, so I said, All right, *be* alone, and I began by eliminating the furniture and the chairs and the other people in the building, until there was nothing left but me. Everything else was gone. And then, when everything else was gone, when there was nothing left but me and this space, I tried to make these two things into one thing, and when I tried to reduce the two things into one thing, everything started rushing back in. My family rushed in, and the animals in the jungle did, and I was up high where I could see everything, the animals and myself. I could see every soldier in the jungle, the ones on our side and the ones on the other side, and the Colonel in his command post and the Generals back in Saigon, and I saw Saigon and the rickshas and the *tuk tuks* in Bangkok and things that happened to me before I went over and things that would happen to me after, and I thought, this is what it's like to be God. We're all part of God. The whole world's part of God. Everything's part of Him, every twig, every bird, every thing.

"When you get up that high, you see it. Nothing happens without a reason. I looked down at the war from up there and it was sacred because God made it for a purpose and what we did was sacred for the same reason. When my friend died, that was sacred. His last words were sacred. 'Take care of my things.' I didn't like it when he said it, but when I was having this experience, I saw he had to say those things and I had to hear them. It was *all* sacred. You know what it was about? *No one died.* No one who went over there died. We think they died, but they're back with God, watching us, waiting to see if we'll figure it out. It meant something. I don't know what it is yet. No one does. But it's coming."

"I'm starting with my kids," Pete said. "I'm telling them all about it. I can't tell the whole world so I'm starting with them."

"Yeah, well, I don't have kids," said Mickey, taking off his eyeglasses.

"So you do things your own way," Bobby said. "No big deal. What we did was sacred, but what's not sacred? What's sinful? Forgetting it happened. Not passing it on. But who do you pass it on to? I have a few brews, and my wife and my ex-wife talk. Now they *both* say I live in the sixties."

"S O I F she doesn't return your calls?" Bobby asked Pete. "That's something to come unglued about?" Silence. "So where were you last night?"

"Out walking," Pete said.

"Yeah? So why's Joanne calling your ex-wife?"

"Who told you that?"

"Last night she called me. She said she was afraid of you. She looks out the window and sees you standing there. Or you're sitting on the hood of her car. Or hiding behind a tree across the street. She's *frightened,* man."

"What's she got to be frightened about?"

"You tell me, man. What's your major malfunction?"

"She went upstate with me," Pete said. "She said she didn't want any more kids. She was finished with that, and now she won't return my phone calls. What am I, wood?"

"There's more to it," Bobby said. "There always is."

"Yeah, she says she's too old for me. I told her I didn't care and she says she does. She says she wants *things.* What *things?* I told her up front. I don't have money. I just got a steady job. I've got two kids and myself. That's all I've got. She said that was fine, and now she wants out. She wants *things.* "

"So let it go. So it didn't work out. You could've gotten married and *then* it went sour and you'll be paying alimony. Like me."

"She gave me back my ring."

"You had no business giving her a ring. You knew her eight weeks."

"It wasn't that kind of ring."

"So what else did you do? You stood across the street and looked at her window. What else?"

"I called her a few times. I lost my temper. I left the ring in a box on the hood of her car. I don't know why she's frightened."

"How? How'd you leave the ring?"

"In a box."

"In a box *covered with grass* with a threatening letter. She said she thought you'd mined her car."

"If you know so much, why are you asking?"

"She wants to call the cops. She thinks your elevator doesn't go all the way to the top. If you keep it up, she's getting some guys to smash you up. You know what that means? You'll pull in all the chapter. No one's going to let them touch a hair on your head."

Pete said it wasn't their business. He didn't want to involve anyone.

"Yeah, well, I've got news for you," Bobby said. "We're already involved. Joanne shows up on Mickey's doorstep, crying. Everyone knows. Chill out, man."

"Sure."

"You promise?"

"Sure."

"There are lots of women out there."

"Sure."

49 OU THINK you're on solid ground," he told the doctor. "You think you're getting somewhere, and you go to sleep and it rains and you slide all the way downhill in the mud and when you wake up, you're looking up at where you were when you went to sleep. When I fell in love with Joanne, I thought, O.K., this is what I waited for. This is the cream on the cake. She was a little woman, older than I was, short, very short, even shorter than my mother, dark-haired, happy all the time. She had a lot of friends. She kept her body in good shape and she loved me because I was me. What else was there?

"So I let her meet my kids. She met my friends. She looked around. She seemed happy enough. She took my ring, and then we go away one weekend. We're happy. On Sunday, we come back, and on Monday she says she can't go out with me. She promised an old friend she'd go out with him. So what happened? I thought this was different. This time we *talked*. We knew each other.

"She told me when she was a girl, after her mother died, she was playing with the perfume bottles on her mother's vanity, and when her father came home and saw it, he swept all the bottles to the floor and broke most of them. He couldn't stand looking at her because she looked so much like her mother. I thought we were close. I had it all planned. We'd get married. We'd live happily ever after. Then it's *so long, kid?*

"Who says only women feel used? *I* felt used. So I called her up and told her off. I lost control. I said some bad things. I hung around her house. People noticed. She lived on the same block for thirty years. People knew her. They didn't know me. Yeah, I put the ring in a box with a note and left it under a heap of grass on the hood of her car. And she talked to my ex-wife and my ex-wife told her how I burned her car and she thought I was going to do that to her. Her car broke down coming home from work and she thought I did it. A car breaks down and you blame me? My car breaks down, who do I blame? She sends two *tu tu rus* to my house, and after that, I carried a gun for two weeks.

"In the meantime, what's Joanne doing? She's talking to my wife and my kids. Now I have to win the kids back all over again. For years, my wife told them, Stay away from him. He's a psycho. He's crazy, and they come to the parade, and they say, 'You're not crazy, Dad,' and she comes along and says she loves me and then she says she doesn't want to see me, and she talks to them, and I'm right back where I started from. I'm going to lose everything. Why should I have to feel like that? Why should she do that to me? And for two weeks I've got a gun. I wouldn't go hunting with my brother because I'd have to carry a gun.

"Bobby says, 'Look at your hands. You ever see hands like that? You don't need a gun. You've got those *hands.*' And I say, 'Yeah, Bobby? How long does it take to kill someone, Bobby?' So I kept the gun for two weeks.

"Mickey took me to his house upstate for a weekend. He said it would blow over. They were punks. They didn't want trouble. They wanted to scare me. They won't come back. They know what'll happen if they touch you. We *let* them know. By the time you go home, it'll be over. He was right. It was.

"But I could've done it. I could've set fire to her car. I stood next to the car and for me it was on fire. I felt the heat. I wanted to do it. I wanted to flip a lit match into the backseat. I had a can of lighter fluid in my pocket. I wanted to see it go up. I wanted to say, 'See, bitch? See?' When I put the box there under the grass, I said, Well, it's camouflage. I don't want anyone to see the jewelry box and take it. But I could have flicked a match into that dry grass and it would have gone up. I wanted it to go up. I wanted to feel the heat and the power. And then I thought, I don't have to do this anymore. I walked away. And it started to rain, and I thought, even if I'd set it on fire, maybe the rain would have put it out, and I jumped the churchyard fence and spent the rest of the night under the bushes looking out. And then I was frightened. I'm getting older. It's cold out there at night. Why am I doing this? So I thought I should come back and see you, but then two weeks went by, and I thought, she won't let me in. But you called *me.* And I said, 'What, are you crazy? You miss me?' and when you said, 'Every day at five thirty, I sit here looking at an empty chair,' and I looked at my watch and it was four forty-five and I thought, I'll take a cab and I'll be right over. So here I am."

"What about the fire and the water?" she asked, and Pete said, "When we burned things, I didn't feel the fear. I *became* the fear."

"During the Second World War," she said, "in the concentration camps, people who were afraid began to identify with the people who tortured them. The Gestapo tortured them but they identified with the Gestapo."

"I identified with the fire," Pete said. "It was the most powerful thing there was. We threw a willy peter grenade into a stream and it was so hot the fish came up to the surface half-cooked. It went on burning right through the water."

"So you loved the fire?" she asked.

"Yeah," Pete said. "I loved it. I loved setting fire to the villages. We'd throw lit cigarettes up in the thatch and five, six, seven minutes later, they'd go up. I did that. They'll never hurt us again. Unless it rained."

"Unless it rained," she repeated.

"So?" Pete said. "Why so quiet all of a sudden?"

"Why are we picking it up so fast all of a sudden?" she asked. *Unless it rained.*"

"Rain puts out fires. Everyone knows that."

"Yes, but you love to sit in the rain. You love to eat in the rain and take showers in the rain and watch people go by in the rain. You like the way your shoes squelch in the rain. You like it when you're covered with mud. You like the fire and you like the rain."

"That's what I said."

"And you love the fire, but sometimes the rain puts out the fire."

"So?"

"So you tell me."

"I walked away from the war and I went and sat in the rain," he said. "That means something?" Everything meant something to her.

"You tell me," she said again.

"I was frightened by the fire. Those tracks were rolling tombs. When they went up, man, you couldn't get near them. Bullets were flying all over. People were burned like *cookies*, crispy critters. I *became* the fire. I hated the fire."

"And rain puts the fire out," the doctor said. "So now when you feel the fire and you hate yourself, you sit out in the rain. Is that it?"

"I don't know."

"If the fire frightened you, and you became the fire, you weren't frightened anymore. You *were* the thing you were frightened of."

"Like the people in the camps," he said.

"Like them."

"So that's why I sit out in the rain? Because when I get angry, I feel on fire and I'm afraid of the fire and the rain puts the fire out?"

"Maybe," she said. "We'll see."

He said if he wasn't frightened, he wouldn't need to be the fire, and if he didn't need to be the fire, he wouldn't need to sit in the rain. Was that it?

"We'll see," she said. "Only time will tell."

"But if the fire's me, and I love the fire and I hate the fire, then if I put the fire out, I'm going to die, and if I don't put it out, I'm going to hurt other people."

"Yes," she said. "That's true. That's why it's so hard to stop setting fires or sitting in the rain."

"Because some of the time I hate myself and some of the time I don't?"

"I think so," she said.

"I can imagine a time when I'll sit in my room, and outside it will be raining, and I'll hear the rain and I'll know it's outside, splashing on everything, cleaning everything, and I'll think, once I used to have to go out in the rain and sit in it, but now I don't have to anymore. It's something I used to do but I don't do it anymore."

"It's raining outside now," she said. "Look."

Outside it was pouring and the streetlights were on. "You mind if I get up?" he asked her.

"Walk around," she said. "Don't fall out the window."

Outside, people were crossing the street, some running across, some walking through the green and red splashes of light on the shining black streets, fighting with their umbrellas. Women stood under the awning of the building across the street, trying to hail cabs. They were all trying to stay dry, and he was inside, dry and warm.

"I don't want to be out there," he said. "I don't want to get wet."

"But you will want to," she said. "You'll always want to."

"Will I always have to?"

"If we unfrighten you enough, you won't have to. If we unfrighten you enough, you won't get so angry you need to go out in the rain. It starts with the fear and the fear turns to anger, and then you become afraid of the anger, and the fear of the anger makes you more angry. It goes on. It's a circle."

"A spiral," he said.

"You're reading more, aren't you?" she asked, and he said he was, when he could concentrate. He asked her: *unfrighten.* Was that a word? And she said, no, it wasn't, but there were times when you needed a new word and so you made it up. Words saved a lot of time. If he'd known what to say to Joanne, he wouldn't have to make up symbols and leave them on her car.

"Symbols?"

"The box with the grass. Don't play dumb. Don't hide behind the stupidness. You're not stupid. We're past that."

"Yeah," he said, "but when I'm upset, I need the right words. People have to say the right words."

"They can't say the wrong ones. They can't say, 'Calm down.' "

"No," he said. "Calm down's bad."

"When *you* have more words, the other people can have more words, too," she said. "They won't have to be so smart before you understand them."

"Look," he said. "I'm used to being stupid. That's me."

"Get used to something new," she said, getting up. The hour was over.

"You really missed me?" he asked her. She looked at him and grinned.

"Would I lie?" she asked.

It was still pouring when he went out. He put up the collar on his jacket and ran to the van and when he got home, he put his feet up in front of the television and thought, I like thinking and I like being dry.

Now when the rain fell, it fell outside his window where it belonged, but each time he looked at it falling, in silver streams, or dotting the windows with the periods to hundreds and hundreds of sentences, he was trying to say to himself, or hear himself say, he wanted to go outside.

Watching it made him so thirsty it was as if his skin were thirsty, not made up of cells, but little mouths, wanting to drink the rain in, and when he thought of himself that way, he didn't like it, because he thought that's how corpses must be, all the mouths of the skin open to the rain, to whatever else was opening them up so they could bloom again.

WHEN HE went back to see Dr. Sit, he wanted to know how she was going to unfrighten him. She said it wasn't easy. It took a long time. First you dug up what was hidden and then you looked at it and looked at it until it became commonplace, until, really, they wore it out by looking at it. "Like sanding off varnish," he said, and she said, "Yes, we sand off the fear. It takes a long time." She asked him if he wanted to try, and he said, "Hell, yes, anything's better than being frightened for the rest of my life and not knowing what it is I'm frightened of." So she said, "Let's begin with the fire and the water. Let's go over everything you can think of that has to do with fire and water," and the next thing he knew, he was talking about Salisbury steak bubbling on the stove and bodies too hot to touch and villages rising up in the air and falling back down and a live pig roasting to death in his own fat, and after a while, he got used to talking and crying, talking and crying, and when he got home, he'd talk to himself and cry, and he'd say to himself, You're not getting better. You're getting worse. But at night, he'd sleep, sometimes for four hours at a time.

NOW HIS life was so full he had to write down what he was doing every night or he'd end up with two things to do and one person mad at him in the morning. He told the doctor about the brothers, and how they were living the war over, but doing it right this time, and how you never needed to worry when you were together. If there was something you needed, there were thirty guys you could give a bang on the pipes and most of them would be right there.

Over the weekends, the guys would get together and have a few brews and they'd be back there, traveling on Vietnam, and then one day, he went to the doctor's office and he said, "When we were there, all we wanted to do was get back to the world. Now we're back here, and all we do is go back there. The music, the films, everything. Look at me, the way I dress. I don't *have* a shirt that doesn't say Vietnam on it. Bobby's wife tells him, 'Anyone who looks at you and doesn't know you're a veteran has got to be blind.' Last week, they arrested a guy named Steve out in the bushes in Sheepshead

Bay. He didn't know where he was. He was pooping and snooping out there, his face all painted up." And he asked Dr. Sit, "Why? What's so frightening about coming back?" She said, "You tell me."

It drove him crazy when he asked the doctor something and the *doctor* said, "You tell me." He didn't give her much of a break, though. When she tried to tell him something, she got halfway through a sentence and he stopped her. He said it was too frightening to come back. "You have the same feelings you had over there, but here you're not safe. You don't have a weapon. You don't have your brothers around you to watch your back."

She said most people don't have weapons. Most people don't have anyone to watch their back. Pete lost his temper. He shouted at her. He banged on the arm of her chair. "Twenty years and you know what's different? I have two kids! Otherwise, nothing's different. The anger's the same! You know what I used to say over there? 'Mommy, take me home.' I meant it. 'Mommy, take me home.' That's how much a kid I was. You tell me why I had to see it! I used to run down the trail and I was foaming at the mouth! I mean *foaming,* like a *wolf* or a *dog.*

"I sit there on the bus with my head down like a sissy, like a *woman,* because I know if I look up and see something, I'll kill them. Yeah, I'm afraid of the anger. Because I know what it does. I was sitting on a track, eating my C-rations, and a kid came up to me with a basket and he wouldn't stop and I had my finger on the trigger. I had my goddamn finger on the trigger. *Squeeze and please.* You know how that frightened me?

"I want to get these goddamn kids out of my dreams. Last night, I dreamed about the dead girl again. Always the same thing, that smell, her face. She was perfect. Like what they used to tell us when we were kids: she's not dead, but sleeping? In this dream, I'm bending over and she's reaching up. She wants to touch my face."

"When it happened," the doctor asked him, "did you want to touch her?"

"I did. I wanted to touch her face. I wanted to say things. I wanted to say I wish you were alive. I wish this didn't happen to you. I didn't say anything. I went behind a tree and lost my lunch."

"You know, most of your dreams are about not hurting other people. You dream you're in your van with the other guys and someone throws in a grenade and you open the door and get them out and you can't get out. Or you're in a track and there's a child on the road and you pick him up and put him inside and he's safe."

"I don't want to hurt anyone again," he said. "I never did. Even when I was a kid. I broke *things.* I never hurt a cat or a kitten. My father, he did things like that. But once I did, too. My mother closed the refrigerator door on a little kitten. She didn't do it on purpose. She didn't see it there. It was bleeding from its ears and she was crying. She said she didn't know what to do with it, and I said, 'Don't worry about it, Ma. I'll take care of it,' and I took it out to the shed and I didn't know what to do with it, so I filled up an old fish tank and I held the kitten underwater and I saw the bubbles coming up out of its nose, two little streams of bubbles. They came right up to the surface of the water and then they stopped. That was the first thing I killed. I had to. My mother was in the kitchen, crying, so I said, 'I'll take care of it, Ma.' I took care of it.

"I went over there, I thought, I'll take care of it. My mother, she tried to stop me but she didn't know enough. My friend's mother, she tried to stop him after I beat him up. He brought the papers home for her to sign and she said no. No, no, no, no. She was sitting at the kitchen table eating Chinese fried rice, and he picked up the rice and threw it up in the air.

"When I took the kitten out to the shed, I cried. I went into the kitchen and my mother was *still* crying. She thanked me. She made some cookies for me. When you're seventeen, your country's your mother. It's got this big meat grinder, this propaganda machine, and it grinds you up. You know what I call the meat grinder? It's war. I was so happy to help this country. During the Bay of Pigs when I was afraid everyone would be killed, I thought, at least I'm an American. At least I lived my life in America. That's how stupid I was. There's love in the world, man. Why do people have to mess with it?"

Dr. Sit asked, "Why is there evil in the world? That's what you're asking."

"Why?" he said. "Why?"

"I don't know."

"No," he said. "You don't know. You don't know what you are. You don't know what you're capable of. You don't know what's inside. You don't have to know."

"No one should have to know."

"No, people *should* know. But they don't have to find it out, not by going to *war.* Not at seventeen or eighteen. We were babies. When we were over there, I felt *old.* We all did. I was eighteen. I felt like thirty-five. And in the middle of a firefight, it was, 'Mommy, take me home.' I went to a party three years ago and someone there was taking pictures. The girl I was with showed me one and I said, 'Who's that with you?' She hit me on the side of the head. 'Dummy! It's you!' I didn't know myself in the picture. I looked happy in the picture. Sometimes I call Mickey and go over to his house because I feel like crying, but I don't want to cry alone. I can't cry there either. I want the time back. I wasn't young. I didn't get the chance. You want to knock your head against a wall? Wish for the time back. What's it like to be young? I don't know."

"I understand."

"I want to believe people are good," he said.

"And when they're not, you're angry," she said. He said he was angry all the time. She said that he might be angry the rest of his life. He'd have to live with what he saw for the rest of his life. He said it was so confusing. You tried to do good and you ended up suffering for twenty years because you'd been lied to and you believed the lies and you'd ended up doing bad things. "You're still confused," said Dr. Sit. "You still refuse to accept people as both good and bad at the same time." He asked her why. He said everyone knew no one was perfect. Why *couldn't* he accept it? Why did anything anyone did wrong become such a big deal to him?

"Because," she said. "Because you want it so badly. You so badly want everyone to be good."

He laughed at her. "You think that's funny?" she asked him. "Why is it funny?"

"You know who you're talking to? You're talking to a kid they sent to reform school twice. You're talking to a man who beat his father up. Last week, one of the brothers stole twenty dollars from me and I caught up with him in the neighborhood and had him up against a brick wall and broke his nose and everyone was yelling at me, 'Leave him alone! He's a veteran! He's sick!' and I yelled back, 'I'm sick too! I'm a veteran too!' I want so badly to be good? It's funny. It is."

"If you're laughing now, you'll be crying in a minute," she said, and he was.

"Why are you crying?" she asked.

"About the kitten," he said, looking at his hands. "Look at these hands."

"About the kitten?" she repeated.

"Yeah, well, like Li," he said.

"Li?" she asked.

"Well, not Li," he said. "Like the ARVN."

"The ARVN?"

"The one I strangled." Now he was sobbing.

"Oh," said Dr. Sit. "You left something out. Maybe the most important thing."

"What now?" Pete asked.

"We go on," said Dr. Sit. "And someday, we finish."

"When?" he asked. Like a child, he rubbed his fists into his eyes.

"We'll see," she said.

**50** T HE CHRISTMAS dance was on everyone's mind. The chapter began planning for it eleven months in advance.

"Is this a dance, or what?" Bobby Scanlon asked.

"This one," Mickey said, "is going to be *perfect.* We're going to invite *everybody. Everybody's* going to be there. The guys from my troop? They're going to come."

"Another reunion," Bobby said.

"Yeah," Mickey said. "Why not?"

And Pete said: Why not? He called Sal and told him to set the time aside.

"A year in advance? You want me to mark it down a year in advance?" Sal asked, and he said, yes, that was what he wanted. "You got it, man," Sal said.

"And if you find anyone else from the troop, he's invited."

"This is going to be some dance," Sal said.

"It's got to be some dance," Pete said.

"Don't keep your eggs in one basket, man," Sal said, but this time Pete knew. They'd had dances before, but this was going to be special. No one could miss it.

"You know the name of this dance?" Pete asked Sal. "It's called the three hundred and sixty-sixth day."

"The three hundred and sixty-sixth day?" Sal asked. "You mean January 1?"

"No, I mean the three hundred and sixty-sixth day, an extra day in the year. *I* thought it up."

"Yeah, well, it's a terrific idea, whatever it means," Sal said. "How's life with Dorothy?"

"She's good," Pete says. "I like her, the guys like her, and she doesn't have a problem with the war. She's taller than me, she's got dark skin, her hair's long and straight, and the guys say if you saw her from a distance, you'd level your rifle. From a distance, she looks like a gook, but she's Italian. She reads a lot and she found out I listened to classical music on the radio, and she started lending me her tapes."

"You're listening to classical music?" Sal asked.

"Yeah. You know how I started? I watched *Apocalypse Now* and I liked

478

the music when the helicopters flew in, so I watched the credits and found it was Wagner. When I met Dorothy, that's all I had, that one cassette. Everyone started asking when was I getting married. So I was wondering too. Everyone's getting picked off here. Last month it was Justin. His bachelor party was a disaster, man. One of the guys said he knew where to hire strippers and we all chipped in and the night of the party, no strippers showed up so we sat there all playing cards. It was some night."

"Take it slow, man," Sal said.

P E T E B E G A N to watch Dorothy speculatively, wondering what it would be like to be married to her, and as soon as he did, he began to have trouble with her and he didn't know why. He could talk to her about anything, even Vietnam. It was too good to be true. He called his brother in New Jersey and told him he wanted to bring Dorothy to meet him. The morning they were to leave, he called her and asked her if she'd be ready in half an hour and she said she'd been trying to get him on the phone. Her sister had a ruptured appendix and she was getting on a plane to New Mexico to help take care of her sister's children.

"It just happened now?" Pete asked her. "She just called you this minute?" She said her sister called an hour ago and it was a good thing she'd packed to go with him, because she was all ready and now all she had to do was go to the airport.

"I don't believe it," Pete said. "I don't believe it about your sister." Dorothy said she couldn't *prove* anything to him right then and there, but she could later. Right now she had to get to the airport. Would he take her? No, he said, he wouldn't take her. "You're frightened of going away with me," he said. "*That's* what's wrong with your sister." Dorothy said no, he was wrong. They would talk about it when she got back.

"Why?" he asked. "We're not married."

Dorothy called Pete selfish, self-centered, and self-absorbed. She said she'd call him when she got back, and he told her not to bother.

When she got back from New Mexico, she called Pete, but he didn't want to listen. "We can talk about anything else," he said, "but I'm not going to listen to you lie to me." She hung up on him. When Pete called her back, he got her machine, and each time he did, he hung up. Finally, Dorothy called him and said they had to talk. "Why do we have to talk?" he asked her. "I know what I know."

"You're a self-absorbed jerk," she said.

"I know when you're lying," Pete said. "I can spot a liar a mile away. I can spot a liar in my sleep."

"It wouldn't be the first time you saw something in your sleep," she said, and Pete asked her if she was accusing him of something, and if so, what was it? Dorothy hung up. After that he didn't call her. He walked past her house. He saw the light in her window. He thought about the books on her shelves, the ones he wanted to borrow, and the ones in his house that he had borrowed from her, but he wasn't going to give her the satisfaction of calling her. She'd lied to him, all that crap about her sister.

"s o, " said Dr. Sit, "let's talk about abandonment."

"All right," Pete said. "I admit I feel abandoned."

"You feel abandoned even when no one's abandoning you," she said.

"She *was* abandoning me. I know when I'm being abandoned," he said.

"Oh?"

He knew what that "Oh" meant. "Let's hear it," he said, and she said, "This happened while I was on vacation," and when Pete asked her, "So what?" she said, "You tell me," and he said he didn't have anything to say. She asked if he didn't mind her going on vacation and he said he didn't. She was entitled to a vacation.

"Oh?" she said. He said he was busy while she was gone. He was busy with the chapter and he was busy writing down dreams. He wrote down so many dreams he'd never have time to read all of them to her. He had a drawer full of dreams, and when he was finished, she said he was angry. He said he wasn't. She said he was angry because he wouldn't have time to read all his dreams, and he said the world wouldn't come to an end because he'd had so many dreams.

"You're sure?" she asked. He told her he'd survived his brother's death and his mother's death and he'd survive hers.

"My death?"

"Your going on vacation."

"But that's not what you said. You said my *death.* "

He said, "So what? What's the big deal? I made a mistake. I knew you weren't dying. I knew you didn't spend your vacation in a hospital," and Dr. Sit said, "Oh?" And then he asked her, "Did you spend your vacation in a hospital?" She asked him what he thought. "How the hell should I know?" he asked her. "You *look* healthy as a horse to me."

"But in an instant, I could be dead. I could be gone. You could be looking at me in my chair and I could slump over and be gone."

"You're not going anywhere," he said, but he was getting hot. His hands were swollen. His chest was tight. He was having trouble breathing.

"Get up," she said. "Walk around."

He got up and walked up and down the office. The blood pounded at the back of his head and the pain in his chest grew sharper. He grabbed the headrest of her high-backed leather chair. "What's wrong with you!" he shouted. "Tell me what's wrong with you!" She said someday she was going to die. Someday we were all going to die. "I know that!" he said. He was still holding to the back of her chair. "You don't have to do it now!"

"To you, any vacation is a death. Any separation is a death. Any separation is an abandonment. Next comes reform school or a home on the island or the jungle and a voice over the radio saying we're pulling out."

"Garbage!" he said. "Shit!"

"I thought you weren't angry."

"You're *making* me angry."

"Garbage," she said. "Shit." It made him laugh, hearing her say that in her little, proper voice. He sat down in his chair.

"I have this pain in my chest," he said.

"When two people are so attached, if one dies, the other one dies, too. That's why attachment is so dangerous. That's why you were so unfair to Dorothy. *She* can't have problems. If she has problems, they could get worse. Finally there'll be nothing left of her at all. You can't bear that."

He was furious. He said he could be having a heart attack.

"Should I call an ambulance?" she asked.

"That's not necessary," Pete said.

"If you're having a heart attack," she said, "it's my responsibility. I'm a doctor."

"I'm not having a heart attack!"

"You just said you were."

"I was wrong!"

"Should I take your pulse?"

"There's nothing wrong with me!"

"Maybe," she said, "it's just a broken heart."

"Give me a break, man," he said. "I don't need this shit. You're trying to make me cry. You want me to set a record here. The doctor who made her patient cry the most times in a year! Another plaque for the wall. No, not me. I'm not crying and tomorrow I'm not coming."

"You're taking a vacation?"

"No, I'm not taking a vacation!" he said.

"If you're taking a vacation, I'd like to know."

"I'm not taking a vacation! If I took one, I wouldn't tell you! I'd let you figure it out!"

"You'd abandon me? Tit for tat? You want to make me suffer? When you're angry, you want revenge."

"Yeah, I want revenge! This is fair? You have all the power here! You set the times! You say when the hour's up! You say when you're going on vacation! I'm not a man here! I'm a child!"

"Completely helpless?"

"Completely helpless!"

"Like you were over there?"

She'd won. Now he was crying. "You see?" she said. "Dorothy said she was going away and she frightened you. You were afraid she was leaving you alone. I'd already gone away and frightened you in the same way. When you're frightened, you become angry. We know that. Now we know this: when you're frightened, you can't afford to see that anyone else has his own fears, his own problems. They might shrivel up and blow away. They won't be able to take care of you. That's why you can't sympathize with others. The fear gets in the way, and then the fear turns to anger. It always comes back to that, the fear and then the anger."

He took a tissue from her box.

"Don't worry," she said. "I know you're a grown man."

"Oh?" he said.

"Yes," she said. "The grown man came all the way home. The nineteen-year-old kid is still rowing back."

"How close is he?" he asked.

She sat still. In the silence, he could hear the clock ticking. "Are you listening to me?" she asked finally.

"Of course I'm listening," he said, but he knew why she'd asked. There were times when anyone could say anything to him and he understood them, no matter how complicated what they said was. At other times, they would ask something simple, a question like, "Where did you put your car?" and he had no idea of what they were talking about. So this time she wanted to know: could he understand what she was going to say or did he have his paws over his ears? That's what she used to say when he couldn't understand her. He was a porcupine with his hands over his ears. He'd listen to her say things like that, and think, Who was she talking to? She's forgotten I'm a Vietnam vet? She's forgotten it's dangerous to make us angry? Outside this office, I'm mad at the world because they look at me and see a killer. Inside, I'm mad because she looks at me and sees a little animal. He said he was listening.

"All right," she said. "All life is one lesson in loss. You lose favorite things. You send away for a sundial with a luminescent dial that's supposed to let you tell time by moonlight, and you turn the house upside down looking for it, but it's gone. A pet rabbit you stroke at night lies on its side in the morning. It's stiff and it won't move. An Easter chickadee dies in your sink and your mother buries it in the backyard. Then a brother leaves. Then a sister. A friend is hit by a car crossing the street. Your grandparents leave one at a time. Your father leaves, or your mother, and no one comes back, and the last thing you have to do, the task your life prepares you for, is leaving yourself. Your life makes you ready to part with it. Usually it happens slowly, but however it happens, it scars you. When it happens too fast, the scar is the most important thing there is. It holds you together. The last thing you have to do is greet your own death. Most of us learn to do that, if we do it at all, slowly. We learn there's loss, there's separation, there's death. We learn to tell them apart because we have the time. To you, they're all the same, so they're equally frightening. To you, there's no such thing as a peaceful death. Any weakness frightens you. It can lead to death. You understand?"

"The nineteen-year-old kid who's rowing back?" he asked. "How close is he?"

"Pretty close," she said.

51 HE OFTEN THOUGHT of himself as a pane of glass, still whole, but with a crack down the middle, a crack like lightning, and now cracks were appearing in the brotherhood. They got together, and the guys went on and on about what they did over there, how good they were, and he thought, I don't want to hear this shit. It's not glamorous. It's not good. We were taken for a ride. We should be telling people about it so it won't happen again. It's happening now, in the Gulf, in Nicaragua, everywhere. We should be telling people what it's like, not competing over who had the worst time over there, who saw the most action, who was best at his job. More and more of the time, he was impatient and went home early. He needed time to talk to himself. He was tired. He came home from the doctor's office and fell asleep on the couch, woke up, turned off the television, and went back to sleep.

He went to the church and talked to Father D'Angelo, who said he was like one of the first prophets. He wanted to go forth and bear witness but he didn't know how. These days, the old priest said, the world was larger and harder to bring to attention, or so it seemed. He didn't know why he was so tired, and Father D'Angelo said the struggling soul grew tired, too.

He awakened one morning feverish and tired, barely able to walk, and was admitted to the VA hospital.

"What's wrong with me?" he asked the doctor, who said it was nothing. The nurse who came in to take his pulse smiled at him and when she came again later, it seemed to him that she held on to his wrist longer than was necessary. She looked at his chart and said his name. "I'm Madeleine," she said, and the next thing he knew, he was discharged, and in his wallet, he had two prescriptions and written on the back of one of them, Madeleine's phone number. "I don't know," he told the doctor. "Women are trouble. I'm better off without them. I can handle things without them."

"Oh?" said the doctor.

He asked Bobby Scanlon where he should take her. He asked Mickey. He asked Davies at work and then he had a list of restaurants, but he still hadn't called Madeleine. "You called her yet?" Bobby asked. "What are we waiting for?"

It was what he wasn't waiting for. How was he supposed to explain that? The sulking when he picked a restaurant that wasn't good enough, the way someone he'd taken out a few times asked, "You ever bring anyone here before?" as if she couldn't believe she alone had such bad luck or was being treated so badly. The raised eyebrows if he ordered beer, not wine, if he ordered a glass, not a bottle. You asked a woman out to dinner. You thought you'd talk and eat but that wasn't it. They opened the door to their apartment and they were giving you a test. How much trouble did he take getting dressed? Why isn't he wearing a suit? Even if you're going bowling, who wears a T-shirt? Oh, so we're going here! He doesn't think I'm worth the money. You looked in their eyes and you saw disappointment. *I want things.* What was he, a store? What was he, a stone? How many times was he supposed to go through this?

He called Madeleine and asked her out for dinner Friday night. On Friday, he came home from work, showered, dressed, and sat on the couch, the television on, but watching the phone. Should he take it off the hook so she couldn't call to say she wasn't coming? She was sick. Her aunt had broken an ankle. She'd been attacked by killer bees. Termites ate through the ceiling and now she was trapped beneath the rubble. She had to take her puppy to the vet. Bobby, who had a girlfriend on the side, got calls all the time. "My puppy's sick."

"Bobby," he said, "don't you think that's getting a little old?"

"No, man," Bobby said. "I know the dog. It's not a healthy animal."

The phone rang. He stared at it, picked it up, saying, I knew it, saying, I should have taken it off the hook, saying, Goddamn them, they're all bitches.

"Listen," Madeleine said, talking fast, "I'm a little late getting off work. We had three Dr. Frosts. It's been crazy here. Would you pick me up at the hospital?"

"Where?" he said. His throat had tightened so his voice was hoarse.

"At the entrance to the Emergency Room. I'll be standing outside. I won't be dressed up. You mind?" Hell, no, he didn't mind. Now she wouldn't climb into his old blue van looking at her skirt as if it were her favorite relative, soon to be dead, drowned in a bath of oil and filth and torn cushions.

Outside, the wind was blowing, and it was beginning to snow, fat, slushy flakes that floated lazily down until the wind caught them up and then hurled them at whatever moved below. He turned on the windshield wipers. The front window was already steaming up. He couldn't see out the back, so he rolled down his window and the cold wind began blowing his hair straight up from his head, blowing into his left ear, which was always infected and stung now with the cold. Oh, shit, what if he couldn't shut the window when he picked her up? She'd freeze to death in the next seat. He could try driving peering through the fog on the windshield, but he'd drive right into a truck.

He pulled into the curved drive of the Emergency Room entrance and saw a tall woman in a quilted red coat standing near the sliding doors, her head down, her arms wrapped across her breast. Was that her? She heard the van and raised her head, began waving wildly, running around to the passenger's side. The wind picked her hair up and blew it.

"Oh," she said as she climbed in. "My hair! Don't look at me!" She was running her gloved fingers through it, trying to comb it down. She pulled down the windshield visor to look for a mirror, found it (he'd pasted one on it with a glue gun when he dated Dolores), laughed, and pushed it back up.

"Your hair looks fine," he said.

"You're a gentleman," she said. "I'll comb it when we get to the restaurant."

"Don't worry," he said. *This* was confusing. She was apologizing to *him.*

"I told you I was in the air force? On Guam? Did I?" He said no, she hadn't. "You don't mind?" she asked. "A lot of the guys mind. They think all the women in the armed forces were whores or lesbians, *especially* the nurses."

"Hell, no," he said. "I don't think that."

"Oh, good," she said. "Did I tell you I go to college at night? I'm almost finished. A lot of the vets don't like that either. They think I'm too high and mighty, whatever. But I like to read. I like to write. What am I supposed to do, stay home and watch 'Sunrise Semester'?" He said it was always his ambition to go back to school. "True?" she asked. "True," he said.

"Look," he said, "we're driving around and around the block. Where do you want to eat?" and then he bit his tongue because he'd had a whole speech prepared. We could eat at this place or that place. This place has atmosphere but the food isn't as good, things like that, and instead he was talking to her as if he'd known her for years. She'd think he was a jerk. "You turkey." That's what the last one said to him. "You turkey." He wasn't a turkey.

She looked over at him and her gloved hand touched his arm lightly. "You live on the Avenue, don't you? You know what I'd really like? I'd like to go to Giuseppe's and have a calzone and a cup of coffee."

The pizza parlor? She wanted to go the the neighborhood pizza parlor? Didn't she think he had any money?

"We can go someplace better," he said, flushing.

"I know, I know," she said, "but we had these three Dr. Frosts, and I'd feel better in a familiar place, but I don't care. Anywhere's fine."

"Why shouldn't you go where you want to go?" he said, but who ever heard of a woman asking to be taken to Giuseppe's on her first date? "So who's this Dr. Frost?" he asked. "On the ward, I used to hear them calling for him."

"He used to be Code 100," she said, "but the word got around what that was. A heart stops, a patient stops breathing, that's Code 100. So now we get on the intercom and we call Dr. Frost. *'Paging Dr. Frost, Dr. Jack Frost,*

Dr. Frost.' That's Code 100 all over again, but no one else knows. The patients think he's a doctor. You thought so, didn't you?"

"So three people died today?"

"Two died, one came back," she said. "I was on emergency call. I was there for all three. That's why I want to go to Giuseppe's."

He looked over at her. She'd rolled her window partway down. "Oh," she said. "Should I roll it up? I thought the windshield would clear off faster."

"It's fine that way," he said. "If you're not cold."

She said if she got cold, she'd put on her hat. Now where was he going to park? On Friday night, it was impossible to park on the Avenue. "Um," he said. "I'm going to park in my driveway. It's just around the corner."

"Fine," she said. Fine? She wasn't afraid he was going to try dragging her upstairs to his apartment?

The plate-glass windows of Giuseppe's were steamed up when they pushed the door open. "You got a booth?" Pete asked, turning red, as if Giuseppe knew he was here on a date, a first date. When he was in high school, he used to bring girls here.

"Sure, I gotta booth. In the back?"

"I love these places," Madeleine said, sinking into the red, cracked vinyl booth. "They never change. The color of the electric tape on the rips never changes. It's always silver. Where else are you going to come and find an Italian restaurant with pictures of Greece all over the walls?"

"These are pictures of Greece?"

"Sure. There's the Acropolis. He must have bought them at a sale. I love it. These red glasses covered with netting and candles inside? Either they made three million of them and put them in a warehouse somewhere or they're made out of steel. They never break." She looked at Pete and smiled. He'd never seen anyone look so happy.

"You really like it here?"

"Yes," she said. "I really like it here."

"You're laughing at me."

"No," she said. "I'm happy. I laugh when I'm happy."

"What are you so happy about?"

"Being *here!*" she said.

"Oh, yeah?" he said, flushing. "So what do you want to eat?"

"A calzone and coffee," she said. "Is that O.K.? My mother says, 'Don't be such a cheap date. They don't appreciate it.' You don't mind? How late does he stay open?"

"Late."

"Good," she said, folding her coat neatly on the bench seat. "You get the calzone and I'll comb my hair."

When she came back, he asked her about Guam. "The people there," she said, "they were called Guamanians. You know, when I was over there

we were still paying them for damage to their banana and coconut plantations from World War Two? They didn't *have* plantations. They had a
banana and a coconut tree there in the front yard. If they had that many
plantations the island would have sunk. And the Japanese were coming
there for their honeymoons, and you know where they'd go? To a cave where
Japanese soldiers were sealed up alive. We were close enough to Vietnam.
The planes came in to refuel. You know how they looked, painted black as if
they were covered in black bunting? They'd refuel and take off right away.
We knew what was inside. We called them the black drops. I remember one
medevac nurse telling me how they cheered the soldiers up. You know they
didn't come in on beds? They were on stretchers hanging from the walls,
swaying back and forth, full of morphine and Dramamine because if the
bleeding didn't kill them, the airsickness would. 'For you air force and
army personnel, it's 2200 hours, and for you navy guys, it's eight bells,
and for you marines, the big hand's on the twelve and the little hand's on
the ten and it's dark.' You know, it's nice to talk about it. People outside
don't understand. They don't want to hear about it."

"I never thought about it," he said. "I never thought about the people on
Guam or the people back home or the people in Thailand driving bombs
through the streets."

"You can't think it all," Madeleine said. Her hand was resting on his, hot
and dry, and then it fluttered away. He said she had warm hands, and she
said, Oh, her body temperature was higher than normal. It always was. She
didn't mind the cold, but it made life hard when she was on Guam.

"You're not on Guam anymore," he said, and she smiled and said, no,
she wasn't. He looked at her. She was really very pretty, too thin, too pretty.
Her face was long and her chin pointed, her cheekbones were high and
flushed, and faint freckles covered her cheeks evenly, like sand. Even her
eyelids, when she lowered them, were freckled, but her blond hair curled up
in a cloud around her face and he'd never seen eyes that color blue,
aquamarine, the color of the water in the bay on certain days before winter.

"You're pretty," he said.

"No, I'm not." She said it flatly, as a statement of fact, no cause for
regret. "But you. You're handsome."

"I'm not."

"Like the hero of an old silent movie," she said. "All the nurses used to
stop by your room and look at you. Didn't you notice?"

"I noticed how no one came in when I rang the bell," he said. "Except
you. You came in."

"Can I help it?" she asked. "I have a weakness for Rudolph Valentino
look-alikes with high temperatures."

"You're laughing at me," he said again, but this time she shook her
head slowly and asked him why he thought so, and he began to tell her. He

told her about his first wife who'd laughed at him, and why he'd committed himself to the mental hospital. He told her about burning his wife's car, sitting out in the bushes outside the church, visiting Father D'Angelo, and going into the city four times a week to see Dr. Sit. He didn't leave out anything he could think of. When he was finished, she'd be finished with him.

"That's a terrible story," she said.

"I never said I was good."

"It's terrible those things happened to you. You could have turned into a monster. You could have *died.*"

"I'm a survivor, that's all."

"No, you're good," she said.

"I'm not good."

"Yes," she said. "You are."

He was confused and frightened. Now he dragged out everything he'd ever done wrong, the desks he'd smashed as a child, the fighting in the school yard, beating his father, the time he drowned a kitten in the shed, even the medals he put on his brother's chest when he saw him sleeping in the coffin. That wasn't right. You weren't supposed to bury medals. "And once," he said, "I went down to the beach and took off all my clothes and took a shower in the rain. Naked. And once," he said slowly, "once I killed someone. With these. My bare hands. An ARVN on our side."

"Well," she said, stirring some salt on the table with her forefinger (his mother used to do that), "I don't know why you did it, but you must have had a reason. Anyway, I admire you. I do. There's nothing you can do about it."

"You shouldn't admire me," he said.

"Why?"

"Because I'm not admirable."

"so," said Dr. Sit, "you told her everything you could think of and she still thought you were admirable. Were you disappointed?" He said he was. "You wanted her to get up and walk out?" she asked, and he said, No, he didn't. She asked him if he was testing Madeleine, and he said maybe he was, and the doctor asked if she'd passed. "No," Pete said. "She expects me to be perfect."

"You realize, don't you, that you set up tests for women that no one can pass? If they criticize you, they don't like you. If they can't meet you, they're abandoning you. If they admire you, they're asking too much of you. They're asking you to be perfect. There's no woman alive who can pass your tests."

"You can," he said. "You're always here."

"Oh?" she said.

"Yeah, whenever I come, you're here."

"Are you looking for a woman or a mother? A woman or a baby-sitter?"

"I'm a grown man! No one sees that! I'm thirty-eight years old! I'm a grown man!"

"Oh?" said Dr. Sit. "And did you forget about my vacation?"

Who was he to test people? Who was Dr. Sit to tell him he acted like a child? He'd take Madeleine out again. *Don't do it as a favor to me.* He could hear the doctor saying that.

At home, the phone rang. "Hi, guy, you want to come over for some chili?" and he'd say, "No, thanks, Mickey, I'm busy." The guys were buzzing, he knew that. "Her name's Madeleine. I don't know what she's like. He's keeping her under wraps."

Now he had a key to her apartment. It was a spring night and he let himself in. She was sitting on the floor in front of a tall wooden bookcase he'd built for her, pulling books out, one after another, flinging them in back of her. " 'Something something contracts, and death is expected,' " she said, " 'as in a season of autumn.' I'm sure it's Wallace Stevens! I can't find the damn book!"

He stood where he was and looked up and down the bookshelves. "Here," he said, pulling out the book and handing it to her. "Is this it?"

"That's it!" she said, jumping up.

"Where do you want to eat? I have an executive committee meeting tonight."

"We're eating here," she said. He said she couldn't work all day at the hospital and then come home and cook, and she said, Why not? She had a microwave and a freezer compartment and she defrosted the sauce he'd made over the weekend. "You don't think the house is *too* clean?" she asked him. "I mean, I'm a nurse and I scrub things and you were in the army, and you scrub things, and people come over here and I think they're afraid to put their feet on the floor."

"I'm comfortable here," he said. He was. Everything was in its proper place. It was nice. You knew a woman lived here. He could live here. She couldn't pass behind his chair without hugging him and this time when she did it, he said he didn't deserve it. He didn't know why she'd picked him.

"Same old song," she said. "If I'd wanted a kitten, and went out and found twelve kittens, and said, 'I want this one,' how do you explain it?"

"I'm not a kitten," he said.

"How do you explain why you like one person more than another?"

"Love," he said. She was bending over, ladling out the sauce. Steam rose from the spaghetti, losing itself in her hair, which would curl more tightly. "You don't ask me if I love you."

"No. I don't."

"Because you don't think I can love anyone?"

"Because," she said, sitting down, not looking at him, "I don't want to be disappointed."

"Well, I do love you," he said.

"Don't sound so mad about it," she said. "I'm not forcing you."

"I don't *want* to love anyone. You know that."

"I know that."

"My kids think you're all right. They say, 'Marry her, Dad.' "

"They have big mouths," Madeleine said.

"You don't want to marry me?"

"I didn't say that."

THE BUZZING among the guys got louder. "It's six months. If he didn't come to meetings, we wouldn't see him," Mickey said.

"That's not true," Bobby said. "When you need him, he's there."

"He doesn't carry on anymore," Mickey said. "I miss it."

"He's never going to be calm and quiet. He's always going to be wired about something."

"Yeah, but when was he last smashed out of his mind?"

"Maybe she doesn't let him," Mickey said. "Plenty of guys don't bend an elbow when their wives say no."

"Maybe he'll bring her to the dance," Bob said.

But he brought her over the next weekend. She told her stories of Guamanians and they told their stories and she fit right in. "You're lucky, man," said Bobby, and Pete said, "You get out of that marriage and you could be lucky, too."

"You know what he said to me?" Bobby asked. "You know what he said?" But no one was listening and he didn't really want to repeat it, and when he went home, he looked at his sleeping wife ("You're the lowest of the low") and thought things over.

"You're going to marry her?" Mickey asked when they were standing outside and Madeleine was already in the car.

"If I ever get married," Pete said, "I'm keeping my apartment."

"Yeah," Mickey said. "That way you can just move back in."

"I won't have to move back in. I'll just open the door," Pete said.

SUMMER PASSED, and autumn. The dance was drawing closer. Sal would come back, and the plans were getting more and more elaborate. They were renting a huge hall and some of the wives were involved, and there would be booths set up as surprises, rooms filled with surprises, but you couldn't get a word out of the women. Dr. Sit sat in her chair. Madeleine cooked or was cooked for and rifled through her books and stayed up late reading or writing papers, and one day Pete realized he didn't have to get married. He was already married.

"I don't deserve this happiness, man," he said to Dr. Sit.

"Oh?" she said. "What are you going to do to spoil it?"

"I can't spoil it. She won't let me."

"You know, when you say that, you sound disappointed."

"It's a feeling I have, that it can't last."

"Remember what I told you about self-fulfilling prophecies?" asked the doctor.

"Madeleine says she doesn't have any bad self-fulfilling prophecies."

"Then you're caught," the doctor said. "She's not going to punish you and you're going to have to feel the guilt."

"Why should I feel guilty? Still?"

"You tell me," said the doctor.

"You know," he said, "this is like the war. It never ends."

"Oh?" said the doctor.

"Except," he conceded, "there's a purpose to this."

"Well, that's a difference," said the doctor.

"SO I DON'T feel well. It's nothing," Pete said.

"No," Madeleine said. "You never complain. Let's go."

"Where?"

"To the hospital."

He asked her if she couldn't take his temperature, and she said she'd take it in the car. She'd drive. At the first red light, she took the thermometer out of his mouth. One hundred and three. "You've got a fever," she said, and he said, "Let me see that." He looked at the line of mercury. His eyes were hot and the inside of his lids felt dry. He asked her what she thought it was and she said she was a nurse, not a doctor. He'd been in last for an abscessed liver. She'd seen his chart. He'd had repeated abnormal liver readings over the last ten years, but the liver biopsies showed nothing. "If you've got a fever, you've got an infection, and they'll put you on intravenous antibiotics for a few days and we'll go home."

We.

"I've got to give Mickey a call and tell him I'm missing the meeting," Pete said, and Madeleine said she'd tell him.

"Maybe they'll visit me," he said.

"Of course they'll visit you. You, Mickey, and Bobby, the three-headed monster. The Iron Triangle."

"I feel spacey," he said.

"You'll feel better in bed on antibiotics," she said.

. . .

"HE'S NOT responding *at all?*" she asked the doctor.

"His fever's climbing. His white count's out of sight. His liver enzymes are crazy and his color is terrible," the doctor said. "You tell me. You can't live without a liver."

"You're running sensitivities? You're doing blood cultures?"

"I've ordered every test in the book. Every one. It doesn't look good. Does he have a family?"

"I don't want to hear that!" Madeleine cried.

"They won't thank you for it later."

"I'll call his aunt. She'll call everyone else."

"Good," said the doctor.

"What next?"

"An ice blanket to bring down the temperature. A respirator if his breathing fails."

"It's not going to come to that," she said.

"Look, Kathy's covering for you. You can stay in there but you ought to get a rest."

"I'm not leaving the room. It's not hepatitis?"

"We should be so lucky."

"What about the experimental antibiotics? I read the report on them."

"Only a last ditch thing, if everything else fails. I've got to get permission."

"Get it," Madeleine said.

"*You* said it wouldn't come to that."

"*If* it does, it'll be too late to get permission."

"I'll get it," he said.

She went back into the room and pulled the chair up to the edge of the bed. He was sound asleep, way beyond her, dreaming. She'd known he was handsome before, but she hadn't realized how handsome. Lying there, he looked like one of those Spanish noblemen El Greco painted, those fine features, that sharp nose: he was beautiful. But he'd been painted with a yellow brush and she knew if she touched the pillow near his head, it would be hot. She took the sheet and pulled it from his body. He was hot enough. He didn't stir. He didn't look at her. She got up and looked in the metal closet. His jacket hung there like a coat in a gym locker. She went through the pockets and found a piece of paper rolled like a cigarette. She flattened it out and read it.

"With their eyes, they would touch wood, trees, rocks, earth, the sky, the water in their canteens. They would see themselves in each other's eyes, look back again, until finally, like fish in the same school, they would move off together through the thick currents of air, saying, We are still young, we are still here, the world is still here. They had no doubts while looking in one another's eyes."

Who wrote that? What books should she look through to find out who wrote that? Why had he copied it out? She sat down at the side of the bed and listened to his breathing, regular but hard, and lowered her head onto his chest and heard his heart beat, pounding, and still he didn't wake up, see she was there, call her name. The heat coming up from his body, the smell of his body, made her sleepy, and when she woke, it was as if she'd heard an alarm go off, and then she knew what it was. His heart had stopped. She hit the red button on his headboard and the speaker came alive: Dr. Frost, Dr. Jack Frost, Dr. Frost, Room 408. They pulled her mouth from his mouth and then he was on a respirator. He was in an ice blanket. He was on life support, and they were changing the IV bottle. The experimental drug was beginning to move through his veins, slowly, up through his arm, and the doctor held her back, her arms locked behind her. She couldn't move. She raved. Why hadn't he been on a cardiac monitor? What were they waiting for? What if she hadn't been there? What if she'd kept on sleeping? Why hadn't she insisted? Why hadn't she seen it coming?

"It's not over yet, it's not over yet," the doctor was saying. "The heart stops when the fever's that high. It's not over yet. Madeleine, it's not over," and he looked at her. She was nodding agreement, yes, yes, he was still here, but she was crying as if she were throwing the first handful of dirt onto the coffin and he said, "Stop it, Madeleine. Sometimes they can hear you."

And Pete heard him say, "Stop it, Madeleine. Sometimes they can hear you," and he wanted to say, "It's all right, it's a good day to die, but I don't want to die. Why don't I want to die? I thought I did," and he saw Madeleine float down toward him from the ceiling of the room, her hand touching his arm, the only part of him not entubated, not controlled by machines, and then she faded, and in her place appeared a huge golden chicken wearing a brass breastplate made of brass feathers, and layer after layer of the feathers opened up, and as they did, they turned into soldiers, and the soldiers flew up in the air like so many feathers lifted by the wind, and Li was there, and she said, "Now you must look for me in the pig," and he found the pig, a huge sow with suckling piglets, and the piglets turned to soldiers and flew up into the air like gold drops of fat burning over a flame, and Li returned and said, "Next you must look for me in the shells," and he went to the beach, but Li said, "No, you must look for me in the shells of the guns," and when he looked at the rows and rows of ammunition, they would not become soldiers. The bullets would not move or fire, and Li said, "Not even in the fire will you find them, not even in the fire," and then she was gone, and he saw the top of Madeleine's curly head and heard her sobbing and he struggled to say something, but the tube was down his throat. He couldn't talk. He concentrated on moving his arm. He did move it. Madeleine looked up and a nurse was saying, "Doctor! Doctor!" and then he was going under, but he heard the doctor's voice. "It looks good, Madeleine. This time it looks good."

When he awakened next, it was dark in the room. His throat was sore but the tube was out. The cold blanket was gone. He could feel the soft weave of the white blanket over him and so he turned his head and saw the moon through the window. He felt something pressing on his chest and put out his hand, the needle still in the vein on the back of his hand, taped to it, and he touched the top of Madeleine's head.

She was sitting in the chair at the side of his bed, leaning forward, sleeping. When she felt his hand on her hair, she awakened suddenly, looked at him, and smiled. He'd never seen a smile like that. "I was dead, wasn't I?" and she began crying and couldn't stop. He pressed the button for the nurse. The doctor came in, took a look at Madeleine, and said, "What do we have here? Another patient? I'm giving you a shot."

Madeleine asked, "Is the cardiac monitor on? Does he have the cardiac monitor on?" The doctor said, "It's on, it's on. You're getting some sleep." She said she wasn't leaving the room and he said she didn't have to. The other bed was empty and he was putting her in it.

"There are only two beds in here?" Pete asked. The doctor said, "Don't worry about it. You don't have to pay for it," and Pete turned slightly to watch Madeleine climbing into the bed near the window, and the doctor said, "Now don't stay up worrying about her. She's just tired."

"You know what I *saw*?" he asked Madeleine in the morning, and she said, "No, tell me." He started to tell her about Li and the chicken with the brass breastplate, but as soon as he began to speak, the vision disappeared. He began to cry because it was fading, and she stroked his chest and said, "Don't worry. It's the fever."

"I heard you," he said. "I knew you were there. I heard you and I heard the doctor saying, 'Stop it. It's not over yet.' What happened?"

"Your heart stopped."

"You know why I don't go to church on Easter?" he asked. "I've been resurrected enough."

"Stop crying, Madeleine," said the doctor, looking in the door.

"I want to get married," Pete said.

"When?"

"After the dance."

"O.K.," Madeleine said.

"O.K.? That's all?"

"Look," Madeleine said. "See this roll of quarters? I'm going out in the hall and calling your aunt and Dr. Sit and at least one of the guys."

In the hall, she saw the doctor. "What is it? What is it really?" she asked him.

"Come on, Madeleine," he said. "He's alive. What more do you want? He's good as new."

"Is he?"

"I really don't know," he said.

"Because I'm going to marry him," she said.

"I knew that a long time ago," he said. "A long time ago."

52

IFE SPEEDED UP; life thickened. Why hadn't he seen how funny life was before? He took Madeleine to a meeting and she sat next to Bobby's wife, June, who was making one of her rare appearances, trying to find out how long meetings lasted, how often meetings were called. In short, she wanted to know where her husband was when he wasn't home. She cornered Madeleine. How long did these meetings last? "Sometimes," Madeleine said, "they go on for days. They talk all night and all morning, and the next night, and they wind up in front of the Wall on Water Street, still discussing POWs."

"You think it's funny?" June asked her. "You're still new to this. They disappear. They lie. They don't have any sympathy and when you confront them, they say they're Vietnam vets. That's an answer for everything? They suffered more than you suffered. You're not worth anything. You wait."

"They went through a lot," Madeleine said.

"And we didn't? We don't? All suffering took place between the dates they enlisted and the dates they were discharged? They don't care about anyone but themselves. They're selfish. You'll find out."

Sessions with Dr. Sit had become more frightening, but after them, Pete found himself less frightened, and then one day he took out the switchblade he carried on the train and showed it to her.

"Is it legal?" asked the doctor, and when he said no, she asked him why he carried it. "Because," he said, "when I have to go home late at night, I'm the only one on the train."

Dr. Sit, who had been playing with the knife, pushed the button, and the switchblade jumped out of its sheath. She dropped it with a little shriek and he saw the man coming over the top of the bunker in back of the fire base, his arms tourniqueted above the elbow, a knife in one hand and a pistol in the other, and he pushed the butt of his M-16 into his own stomach and plunged forward, driving the bayonet into the man's body. He tried to pull the bayonet out, but it was stuck, and he remembered someone telling him, "Don't waste time trying to pull out the bayonet. Just fire the weapon." He fired and the discharge and the recoil freed the bayonet in time for him to fire at another man coming over the top. He was looking at Dr. Sit and the switchblade and this was happening in front of her, as if it were a film playing on a transparent screen.

"What are you seeing?" she asked him. He told her. "You never remembered this before?" she asked. No, he hadn't. "You see?" she said after a
while. "We unfrighten you. As we unfrighten you, you remember more, and
then we unfrighten you of those things. Eventually, it will stop."

"Eventually," he said.

"Are you still writing things down?" she asked him. He said he was, but
he wasn't showing them to anyone. "Well," said Dr. Sit, "tell me about the
bayonet again. Start from the beginning, just one more time."

"Just one more time *today*," he said.

"You know how much strength it takes to remember that?" she asked.

"It took more to go through it," he said.

"No," she said. "It takes more to remember."

O N E   N I G H T ,   Madeleine came in late from work and found Pete and Bobby
sitting on the floor, their backs against the couch, their arms around one
another's shoulders. The couch snored, and she saw Mickey rolled against
the couch's back. Pete and Bobby were throwing bits of popcorn at the TV
set. "Got 'em," Bobby said. "Score one for the polar bears."

"Hi, guys," Madeleine said.

"You wanna know what we're doing here, right?" Bobby asked.

"I'm a curious person," said Madeleine.

"First, we're here because of the polar bears. You hear about the polar
bears? We're having a polar bear vigil. Second, we're here because Pete put
his hand through the bathroom window. Don't worry. He didn't cut himself,
but he broke his pinky finger when his hand hit the wall."

"What about the polar bears?" Madeleine asked, sitting down.

"It's in the papers, Madeleine," Pete said.

"I don't read the papers."

"Let me tell you about the polar bears," Bobby said. "You know the big
polar bears in the Brooklyn zoo? Yeah, you know them. We went to see them
on field trips when I was in public school. Those great big white bears?
Three kids, three fucking kids, climbed the zoo fence, climbed another
fence, got to their moat, swam their moat, and got in the bear caves. I mean,
Madeleine, the bears *live there*. It's their territory for *thirty-five years*."

"Twenty-five years," said Pete.

"So they threw stones at the bears and one of the bears got a kid and
tore him apart. So what do you say? Good for the bears? I say good for the
bears. Someone breaks into your house and you tear them apart. They
deserve it. The bears are in there. They're not hurting anybody."

"Didn't hurt anyone," Pete said. His speech was slurred.

"And the other kid goes and tells someone, a cop or someone, that his
friend is being eaten by a bear, and you know what the cop does? He goes

down to the cave. He turns on a searchlight. He sees a pair of shoes and a shirt or some fucking thing, and he empties twenty-five rounds into the bears. That's how many rounds it took to kill them. You know why he killed them? He thought the bears ate the fucking kids. But they're *bears*, man. The kids are in their caves, throwing things at them. What does he expect from bears?"

"Can you imagine it?" Pete asked her. "A more miserable destiny? You live in Antarctica or wherever you live and some little animals come after you. You think, look at those pathetic things. They're going to die in the cold out here, but they have tranquilizer guns, and the next thing you know, you're in *their* cage, and the next thing after that, you're in a zoo in Brooklyn, and it's hot, and all day long people throw things at you, just to see what you'll do, if you'll eat it. They throw knives in, they throw aluminum foil in, they throw plastic. You know how much they hate those people? For twenty-five years they hate those people every single day, and the children are the worst, *they are the worst,* and then three of them climb in there and you've got your chance, now you can get even and you tear them apart, you rip their fucking heads off, you start eating them, this is what you waited for for twenty-five years, and someone comes along and shoots you down with twenty-five rounds from a *gun?* They didn't even realize they were being shot for a while, that's how big they were. They turned around to see the noise and the muzzle flash. They didn't even know they were being fucking shot."

"Oh," said Madeleine.

"Oh?" said Pete. "All you have to say is 'Oh'?"

"If I had my way, you know what I'd do?" Bobby said. "I'd tell those fucking parents, wait until the fucking bear *shits,* man. Then you can have your kid back. They don't know if they ate one kid or three kids. They're doing autopsies on the fucking bears. They're cutting up the fucking bears. You know what's gonna happen? Let me tell you what's gonna happen. The parents of those kids are gonna sue the city. The goddamn parents are gonna fucking sue the city. They're gonna say there shouldn't have been a hole in the fence. There should have been guards around the bears. Their kids killed two fucking polar bears who never did a goddamn thing to anybody and they're going to fucking sue the city?"

"They should take those parents," Pete said, "they should take those parents and put them up against a tree in Central Park and they should shoot them. Your kid's out at eleven o'clock at night swimming a bear moat and you don't know where he is? They should shoot the parents and they should shoot the other kids if they're still alive."

"Ah, don't talk to her," Mickey said. "Women always go for the kids."

"A bear's a creature of the earth," Pete said. "He has as much right to walk on the earth as we do. You're going to kill a bear for protecting his home? A tree's a creature of this earth. It grows out of the earth and up to the sun. You're going to bomb it for casting a shadow? Man's the worst animal, the worst. The whole *world's* his fucking territory. Who told him? The Bible told him. God told him. The Church told him. The Church's the worst fucking thing there is. People believe that shit. They believe they were created in God's image. They weren't created in *any* image. You ever look at a salamander standing up on its hind legs? Man was created in the salamander's image. Yeah, the whole world's his territory. Kill anything that crosses his line of sight. Blow it away. Waste it. Zip it. Zap it. Oh, so today two bears bought the farm. What the hell? They're only fucking bears."

"The news is coming on," Madeleine said.

"Late breaking news on the tragedy in the Brooklyn zoo," said the newscaster, his voice awash in false pity, swollen with the attention the event brought him. "Autopsy reports show only one child, not three, as was feared earlier, was eaten by the polar bears. The other two children escaped, but the police, seeing their clothes, fearful that the bears might still have them trapped in the caves, shot the bears to protect the lives of the remaining two children."

"Turn it off," Bobby said. "It's disgusting. I wish they'd eaten them. I wish they'd fucking chewed them up in little bitty pieces."

"Madeleine doesn't," said Mickey from the dusty depths of the couch.

"If they were your kids?" Madeleine asked Pete.

"If my kids climbed in there, swam a moat, and threw stones at the bears, then let the bears eat them!" Pete shouted. "Let the bears eat my kids!"

"It don't mean nothing, fucking drive on," said Bobby.

Madeleine looked at them in the blue light of the TV screen. They were both crying. The phone rang.

"Madeleine, it's June. I can't find Bobby."

"If I see him, I'll tell him to call you," Madeleine said.

"Is he there? I know he's there."

"I'll tell him to call you if he calls here," Madeleine said again.

"Who was that?" Bobby asked. "My loving wife? She wants me to come home and hold her hand about the kid who was eaten by the bear? I want the name of the cop who shot the bear. I want an explanation of where the tranquilizer guns were. It's a zoo. Where were the tranquilizer guns? I should be home, right, Madeleine? You're pissed at me."

She looked around the living room. Beer bottles and beer cans everywhere, a thick snow of popcorn in front of the television set, and she had to get up early in the morning. "Sleep on the floor," she said to Bobby. "You can't fall off the floor."

"She's all right," Bobby said, "but she doesn't understand about the bears."

"Who would?" Mickey asked.

The alarm woke her in the morning. The harsh light fell in and lit up the empty half of the double bed. She went into the kitchen and started to pour a cold cup of coffee from last night's pot. She was late for work. Pete came in rubbing his eyes like a child, and that brought it all back, the bears, the beers, the popcorn, how she didn't understand. She was cranky.

"So?" she asked. "Did they have a military funeral for the bears?"

He saw his raised fist moving toward her face in slow motion, and regarded it with a kind of detached curiosity, as if it were someone else's fist, not his, but before he had a chance to say to himself, That's my hand, put it down, Madeleine had picked up the knife from the kitchen counter and was screaming, "Don't hit me! Don't you ever hit me!" and he was so amazed at the sight before him, her face wild, her eyes white, her pupils shrunk to black dots, he forgot what he was angry about and said, "Madeleine, put the knife down."

"Don't you hit me!" she screamed again.

"I'm not going to hit you," he said, and she looked at him, she looked at the knife, and she stood in front of the kitchen counter shaking.

"Give me the knife," he said, and she dropped it on the floor and stood with her back to him, shaking and crying.

"You're afraid of me," he said.

"No, I'm not afraid of you!" she said. "When I was fifteen, I went after my father with a knife and I got him. Eighteen stitches. That's when I decided to be a nurse, when I saw how neatly they stitched him up and how they stopped the bleeding. He'd never tell anyone where he got that scar, that's how ashamed he was. In five years, all it was was a thin white line. But he never hit me. I almost killed him."

"Stop crying," he said.

"Why should I stop? Why?"

"I thought I knew you," he said. "The way you know me."

"Well, think again! Think again! I wasn't born in a nurse's uniform! I was born in the hills of Arkansas, and when I went away to nursing school, my father said, 'Don't come home. You're a scarlet woman. Don't go near your mother's grave.' The nuns bought me a dress and a pair of shoes or I'd have gotten on the plane barefoot in a flour-sack dress. But I'd have gotten on! You guys and your P.T.S.D.! You think the only casualties take place in wars?" Now that she'd begun, he couldn't stop her. He didn't want to stop her. "I don't ever want to say what June says! I don't ever want to say you only care about yourself! That's the worst thing!"

"That's not the worst thing."

"To me it's the worst thing! To me it's worse than being dead! All right? Do I have to agree with you about everything? Do I have to live in a cage like the bears?"

"No," he said. "You don't have to live in a cage."

"If you want out," she said, "just say so."

"I don't," he said. "I don't even have to think about it."

"s o, " said Dr. Sit, "the kitten has claws."

"I almost hit her! I almost hit her and I don't know why."

"Yes, you do," said the doctor. "Think about it. You almost hit her because she understood what the bears meant to you."

"But that's what I want! I want people to understand me!"

"Oh?" said Dr. Sit. "But some things are private. Some things aren't for civilians. Some things are yours, certain sufferings, certain slants on things. Like spoils of war."

"It's not true. I want to let people in."

"Oh?" said Dr. Sit again. He stopped pacing up and down.

"I don't understand it," he said finally. I have what I want. I have a job I like. I like the construction company. I've got a woman who likes me." ("Loves," corrected the doctor.) "It's still not enough. When I came here, I said I'd be happy if I had a good job. I have it. I have a good woman. What am I looking for now?"

"You know," said Dr. Sit, "if you don't know what you're looking for right now, it's not such a tragedy. Your life's moving forward. Once progress starts, it's hard to stop it. You've got problems, but so does everyone else. If there's something you want and you don't know what it is, perhaps you can trust the world to bring it to your attention. You're not exactly helpless. You seem to find what you need."

Was she trying to tell him he no longer needed her? Was she telling him that she had someone new to sit in his seat at five forty-five Mondays through Thursdays?

"Lately," he said, "I've been thinking if I found what I wanted to do, I wouldn't have time to keep coming here."

"You could come here and work all night," said the doctor. She was laughing at him. He didn't mind.

"You don't think I'm well enough to make it on my own?"

"I didn't say that."

"What did you say?"

"Nothing."

He looked at her. She watched him with her wide eyes. She'd never looked more like a bird in a nest. "What's your first name?" he asked.

"I beg your pardon?" said the doctor.

"What's your first name?"

"It's on the little black plaque over the doorbell. You see it four times a week."

"I don't remember it," he said, rubbing his forehead. "I don't remember a plaque."

"It's there. Take my word for it."

"Well, what is it?" he asked. "Your first name. Do I have to wait until the end of the session?"

"It's Mai," she said. "A very common Chinese name."

"Like the month?"

"M-a-i," she said. "As it's spelled on the little black plaque."

"I don't like black plaques," he said.

"You know," said the doctor, "it's odd we've never talked about the Wall, the memorial in Washington."

"The Wall," he said, thinking. "I went down to the Wall after the second parade. I drove all night and I got there at five thirty in the morning. It took me two hours, maybe more, to go up to the Wall. I kept moving through the trees and moving back. And when I got there, you know what happened? I forgot the names I was looking for. I forgot my own name. I thought I was looking for my own name on the Wall. I saw my face in the Wall, looking back at me. Someone asked me what name I was looking for and I said my own name. He said it wasn't there. That's when I believed it. Then I looked for Liebowitz's name and it was there. I went over and touched it and said 'Hello.' I said hello. He heard me. There was my face over his name. Then I looked for Krebbs and Davis, all of them. I didn't feel like I deserved to go. I didn't think I deserved to be there. I wasn't good enough."

"So," said the doctor, "there's a real confusion between the living and the dead. There's real guilt over not paying enough of a price for what you did to stay alive."

"I'm alive. I bleed," he said. He looked at his hand as if it frightened him. "Am I alive?"

"You tell me."

"If I didn't feel so guilty, I'd know I'm alive," he said.

"That's right," said the doctor.

"But in the hospital, I almost died. I had to be alive to do that, right?"

"Right," said the doctor. "And I'm sorry about the polar bears."

"No one's going to build a wall for the polar bears."

"And they should?"

"Yeah. They should." He sighed. "You want to come to our Christmas dance?"

"I can't. Professional principles forbid. We'll talk about it. You know, you also feel alive when you're angry, don't you?" He nodded. "That's another reason to feel angry, then. When you're afraid you're not alive, you provoke a fight, feel angry, and then you feel alive. As you did with the polar bears. Is that true?"

"It's true," he said, "but why do you always hit me with these things at the end of the hour?"

"I'm a slow thinker," she said. She walked him to the door as she walked patients to the door on their last sessions. Six months to a year and then he'd be gone. *Flown the coop, gone home.* She had her own set of expressions. For her, every closing of a door was a death. How strange when death is only the closing of a door.

53 N BROOKLYN, early in the mornings, newspaper boys would fling their newspapers onto stoops, doors would open, and housewives still in their robes, their hair in curlers, would bend down, pick them up, and take them back inside. In the winter, they were cold to the touch, in the summer, warm.

Pete, who had once had a newspaper route, remembered coming home from delivering his papers, his hands black from the newsprint, and by the time he got his hands clean, in would walk his mother with a fish wrapped in newspaper, a dead fish. To this day, he didn't like the smell of fresh fish and he didn't like the smell of newsprint, nor did he like the stories of disaster the paper invariably contained, disasters his father would threaten him with: "See? They locked this one up for ten years? You know what's going to happen to you? They're going to lock you up for fifteen. Just keep it up." He preferred not to read them at all.

One night, coming home from work, up and down the train everyone was reading the same newspaper with the same picture of a Vietnamese soldier holding a gun to the head of a man in a plaid shirt. After that, he decided he could do without newspapers. His mother, however, subscribed as long as she'd lived, saying, Your grandfather said you paid a price for citizenship. You had to be informed. But in Vietnam every hour was a Sunday paper full of confusion, the illustrated edition, and he thought he'd read his lifetime quota of papers, and when he passed a newspaper stand, he'd think, Now leave me alone.

Life, however, would not leave him alone. He thought, Does a mouse leave a cat alone? Life's the cat. You're the mouse. You bust your ass trying to keep your tail out of the cat's mouth, but it's impossible.

He didn't read newspapers, but on TV there were living, moving newspapers. He turned on the radio, and it ambushed him. If he walked the streets of Manhattan and looked up, there it was, running around the border of a skyscraper in electric lights. U.S. BOMBS SHIP IN LIBYAN WATERS. If he didn't want to know the confusion of the day, too bad: they interrupted his favorite TV show. He thought he was safe with Archie Bunker reruns. Think again. It was a TV program that brought the polar bears into his house and nearly drove Madeleine out. He didn't want to know. He still didn't want to know. But, he thought, this is a democracy. He didn't have the right not to know. He *had* to know.

He began ranting to Dr. Sit about newspapers, and she said, "You wanted to live, so find out what life's about. Will that kill you?" And he thought, Yes. It's going to kill me. It could kill me. Does she know how much I can stand?

One morning, he picked up the paper left outside Madeleine's door and read the headline. MISSING CHILD THOUGHT BURIED IN GROUNDS NEAR HOME, the same home where they put his brother when he was a child, the same home Paul was in when his mother thought they killed him. They'd closed the home down almost ten years before. He thought, Fine. Good. Now forget it. Get on with things.

Two weeks later, he went to the chapter meeting, and found them passing a resolution to search the grounds and help the father of the missing child. The father was a Vietnam vet. It would make the chapter look good. "Well, fuck that, man," he said, "we're not doing this to make the chapter look good. We're going out there to find a missing kid."

"That's all you've got to say, Bravado?" someone asked. "Sit down."

He sat down and thought: How am I going to explain this to Madeleine? He was supposed to meet her sister's family the same weekend they were supposed to search for the little girl, eleven or twelve. Were they going to find her? He didn't think they would find her, but she was a human being. She deserved to be looked for. They didn't need him to find her. They had plenty of volunteers, but he needed to be there. How was he supposed to be in two places at once? He'd promised Madeleine he'd meet her family and he'd stood up in the chapter meeting and said, "She's a human being. She deserves to be looked for."

He knew Madeleine was tired of Bobby sleeping on the couch or the floor every night. She'd get out of bed and go into the living room without turning on the lights and automatically step over his body, even when he wasn't there. She'd think, We're going to get married and how many of us are taking the vows? Two of us or the whole group? Me and Pete, or me and Pete and Bobby and Mickey? She said she didn't mind, as long as he didn't hit her. She laughed a lot, Madeleine, and she made him laugh. And now he had to tell her he wanted to go out on Staten Island to look for a little girl?

"O.K.," she said. "We'll go another weekend. You have to go."

"I do?" Pete asked her. "Why?"

"You know why," she said. She sounded like Dr. Sit.

"I know why?" he said. "I don't know anything."

"You're going with Mickey and Bobby and the boys," she said. "You'll be all right."

And now there he was, out on the island, only this time there was a bridge to drive across, no more having to take the ferry, getting ready to search the grounds, and it was hot. It was hotter than it was in the Nam, and they were dividing up into groups and they had on their jungle boots and their cammies and their P.O.W./M.I.A. T-shirts, their canteens and their machetes, and he was getting nervous, and he told Bobby, "I'm nervous," and Bobby said, "Don't sweat it, man. We're in this together," and he took deep breaths and they moved out toward the buildings.

The minute he got to building eleven, he knew where he was. The place was overgrown. There were vines everywhere, bushes everywhere, animals burrowing in the lawns where the croquet hoops used to be, where the badminton nets once were. The windows were cracked or broken from the weather or the kids, big holes in them with spiderweb cracks radiating out, and what was left of the glass looked poisonous, the color of mercury in thermometers. The rain gutters were full of birds and birds' nests and birds were flying in and out of the windows and even though the kid was missing for weeks, they were hacking their way through the underbrush, looking for signs of a trail. By now the trail would be cold or not a trail at all, and Pete thought, What if I find her? I want to be the one to find her, and he kept slashing at the underbrush, looking down in the grass for yellow jackets, and then he was in front of building eleven. "I'm going in there, man," he said to Bobby, and Bobby said, "Fine. You know where to meet up?" He knew. He could find the place in his sleep.

He went in through the basement door. Nothing had changed. The same furniture was in the basement. There were the same salmon plastic chairs, the hard plastic aquamarine chairs, hard plastic. You could kill someone with one of those chairs. Why did they have them in a place where they had crazy kids, violent kids, not screwed down, just loose, like weapons waiting to be used?

He went upstairs. He knew the way. There was grass on the steps, dirt, dust, rat droppings. Insects scurried away from him when he walked, and he ducked down beneath a spiderweb in the doorway, and there were the cribs with the metal bars that closed down over the bodies of the violent kids, or the kids they said were violent, the trap beds they put Paul in.

It was all there, but now it was empty. The people were gone. No one came here but crazies and animals. There were piles of animal shit in the middle of the beds, and he went up to the top floor. He went up and down the corridors, into every room, every toilet. If he was going to find anyone, he was going to find him here. No one. He walked into a bathroom and a flapping frightened him, a darkening, the sight of wings retreating. He'd found his way into the home of some huge bird and he got out of there quickly. They could be vicious. They went for your eyes. Why shouldn't they? He didn't belong here. They did.

He went back to the room with the beds and the steel straps and stood there and looked. There was no one else in the building. He could have broken windows. He could have picked up the beds and thrown them against the walls, but he didn't have to do anything. The place was empty, shut down. The animals had it, the animals and the birds and the snakes. It was never going to hurt anyone again. No one else was ever going to be hurt here. No one was going to be tortured here. He leaned with his back against the wall. The wall felt cold. He said, "Hey, Paul? This is it, man. You're out, man. You're free and clear."

The ghosts were all over the place. He could feel them on his skin. He could see them in the doorways. He could see them sitting on the edges of the beds, that's how strong their feelings were when they were alive. His mother was here, too. *Don't come in here. You'll get sick. No, I won't, Ma.* So it was over.

He had a sudden vision of shelf after shelf in a store, each shelf lined with bottles of black milk, and people coming to pick up their bottles of milk and filling their shopping carts with bottles of black milk, old-fashioned glass bottles, not like the paper cartons they had today, and for an instant, he was back in Catholic school, studying the Baltimore catechism, and the three milk bottles, one pure white (that was the pure soul, cleansed of sin), one filled with grey dots (that was venial sin), and the bottle filled with black liquid (mortal sin), and those were the bottles everyone was buying, and then the bottles vanished, and he was in Detroit looking for Davis, and three black men were sitting near an oil barrel, keeping warm. Orange sparks leaped in the air, zigzagged like gnats. In back of them, the buildings were dark, like black teeth against the night sky. "Hey, what do you want here, man?" one of the men asked him. When he talked, his gold tooth glinted. Pete was afraid and backed away, and said, "I'm looking for Geronimo Davis."

"Oh, you're looking for Geronimo Davis," the black man said, and got up. "We'll help you find him." They got up and started searching the Detroit streets. Through the windows of the buildings he could see the jungle on the other side. When they found Davis, his track was burning and he was trapped inside.

So it was all coming back; it would all come back. Nothing would be lost forever.

Then he told himself, Come on, man, you're not here for this. You're here to look for a little girl, and he went back outside and it was hot, it was scorching, and he drank a little water and he was sweating and his clothes were wet and stuck to his skin and he kept going through the underbrush until his water was almost gone and the sun was going down. It was almost four o'clock. He knew the time without looking at his watch. He met up with Mickey and Bobby. Everyone was standing there, scratching.

"It's the bugs," Mickey said.

"No, it's the poison sumac," Bobby said.

"Anyone find the girl?"

No, no one found her. Pete hadn't expected to find her.

He went back to his place and had a few beers. Madeleine was working, and when she came back, Pete was alone, and they went to bed. They lay in bed and talked.

"Your brother wasn't there?" she asked him.

"Yeah, he was when I came, but when I left, he was gone."

"Good," she said.

He fell asleep and in the middle of the night, he awakened. He couldn't breathe. He had a pain in his chest and Madeleine said, "You know, I think it's nothing, but let's check," and they went to the E.R. and the doctor said he thought it was nothing, just a pulled muscle. While he waited for the doctor to come back and finish taking tests, the nurse took away the book he'd brought along to read, and he complained, and Madeleine said, "You've got to relax," and he said reading relaxed him. Madeleine lost her temper and said, "For once, follow orders!" He did. He lay there.

And while he lay there, he thought that he wanted to wake people up. The daily grind was a daily grind, and sometimes the sleepers liked the cries and the blood and the pain because it awakened them and it was exciting. People shouldn't sleep through life waiting for a war to wake them. He thought, You want something to make a man out of you, you don't need a whole army. *You* make a man out of you. I've got to tell them. This is what it's like. Don't send your sons and daughters. Don't say it can't happen to you. It can happen to you. Don't say war's inevitable. It's people who say that who make it inevitable. Once you say something, you're halfway to creation.

Tell the whole truth. Tell them about the love between the men over there. Tell them that's not the only way to find love.

He knew what he wanted to do. He wanted to go out and tell people: this is what war is. Don't do it anymore.

And he knew what people would say. "He's stupid and he's an idealist. He doesn't understand how complicated it is. Don't listen to him." But he'd already started writing things down. He'd write them on little pieces of paper and roll them up and keep them in his coat pockets. But, hey, you've got to start somewhere and he got up off the table and said, "O.K., my heart's fine. There's something else I'm worried about," and he saw Madeleine's face, and he said, "Don't worry. Doing this is going to make me happy," and she said, "You said that about going to the home today," and he said, "I was right. Even though I ended up here, even though I'm covered with a poison sumac rash, I was right."

"So what do you want to do now?" she asked him, and he told her, and she said, "Father D'Angelo was right. You're one of the prophets. Get ready, kiddo. You know what they say about a prophet in his own land?" He said, "I don't care what they say," and she said, "If you're ready, get started." So he began. After a few months, he picked up a paper, found a picture of himself in it, and brought it home to Madeleine. "My mug's all over the papers," he said. "Read all about it. Ask me."

FOUR

Bravado's Dance

# 54

SIGNS WERE UP on the Avenue. Eleven more shopping days until Christmas. Storefronts were decorated with green and red lights. The windows were sprayed thick with white snow. In the windows of clothing stores, gift-wrapped, beribboned boxes lay in cotton drifts strewn with red felt poinsettias. The florists displayed their dahlias and their lilies and their gladiolas amidst the rented reindeer and fat white Styrofoam snowmen. Inside their windows, and over the counters of Giuseppe's and all the other pizza parlors, O'Halloran's and the other bars, the owners strung red and green foil letters spelling out *Merry Christmas.* From streetlight to streetlight, from one side of the street to the other, green and red Christmas lights hung from wire arcs, and at night the bare trees glowed yellow with light bulbs strung along their branches and trunks.

In the yards of the houses, the pink flamingos were eclipsed by huge plastic Santa Clauses and Rudolph the Red-Nosed Reindeers, their red noses tinting the shadows on the snow rose red, and on the roof ridges of every other house, Santa Claus and his sleigh had landed weeks earlier. When the sun set, the houses themselves became outlines of light, green and red, and the pine trees glowed blue and mysterious. The blue lights were a new fashion and when there was snow on the ground, the intense blueness of the drifts made people stop and look. What kind of light was that? It looked like the broad light of day.

At night, some of the houses stepped back behind their decorations and became entirely something else, something new, creatures of light, outlined in Christmas lights, sketched against the inky sky, a child's drawing of a house, the windows glowing with lights, in each window an electric candle with a red bulb, on the front lawn, the electrified crèche, and on the roof, Santa's sleigh.

That Christmas, the houses in the neighborhood seemed to be competing, and it wasn't unusual for cars to pull over and stop in front of a corner house that had moving statues of the Three Wise Men, each reaching out toward the Christ child, holding his spectacularly colored and gilded gift in his hand. Further down the block, people parked and got out of their cars to watch three Victorian ladies in hoop skirts and feathered hats bend over a carriage, straighten themselves, and wave at the passersby.

The neighborhood had never seemed happier or shinier, and the mer-chants threw out their chests and said business had never been better. They'd been out of stock a month before Christmas, and they were almost out of what they'd reordered. The local Woolworth's filled its stacks of outdoor trash cans with giant rolls of Christmas wrappings, and people bought three and four rolls at a time. Eleven days before Christmas, and people were still buying outdoor electric lights as if this year Christmas couldn't be bright enough, and inside, the trees were so heavy with ornaments—little Humpty Dumpties, small plastic angels, their wings painted gold, Styrofoam bells—the decorations were constantly falling to the floor and replaced on the branches or chased about the living room by the family cat until they were rescued by a member of the family.

There was no need to wonder whether this would or wouldn't be a white Christmas. It had been snowing for four days, and at night, the weather-man stood in front of his map and pointed to the thick white cloud traveling down from Canada. Real snowmen were growing up in backyards and front yards. Shopkeepers were taping cardboard over jagged holes in their windows and calling twenty-four-hour glaziers. The children came home with ridges of ice lining the inside of their gloves and their snowy hats and coats melted onto linoleum kitchen floors.

"Come around the back! Come around the back!" the mothers called when school let out, and in through the storm doors walked children in mufflers, hats, gloves, and boots. People thought twice before going out, but at the last minute, they had to get dressed up and go out to buy the additional gold foil garland for an empty place on the tree, the Timex watch they'd told their daughter was too expensive, but now wanted to see lying beneath the tree with the other presents.

For the chapter, whose dance was three days away, the worry was whether or not the airport would stay open. Since the parades, many of the members had attended reunions. Many had found buddies they'd served with and some of them had placed finder ads in the Locator. *If anyone knows the Chief, White Horse, 1965–6, call Pete, 718-KL5-6565.* These were placed without much hope, but at chapter meetings, the Sergeant at Arms came up to Mickey and said, "You know a Fats? He's looking for you," and handed him the little ad he'd clipped out of the newsletter. Little by little, they were finding one another.

"Hey, look at that," Bobby said. "We're not all on the Wall."

The lost members were flying in from all over the country. Fats was coming in from Indiana, Sal from California. Only the tickets committee knew how many were coming, and at the last minute, they took a count, discovered they'd already sold five hundred tickets and their usual hall was too small. They went to the neighborhood church and talked to Father D'Angelo, who said that, yes, miraculously, the church hall was empty that night, and the price was right. They rented it. The members were busy selling tickets to friends at work and friends on the block, to family members and storekeepers, to high school teachers they remembered and met on the street. "Ten dollars a ticket!" someone said. "How come? It's always six!" and they said, this time it was ten. This time it was something special. This time everyone was cooking for days in advance, but it wasn't just the buffet. There were special booths, special rooms, special events. Everything was special. It was *the three hundred and sixty-sixth day of the year!*

"For ten dollars a ticket," Giuseppe said, "it better be special. It's not Leap Year. What's it mean, the three hundred and sixty-sixth day of the year?" but no one told him. They smiled mysteriously.

"So how many pizzas do you want to contribute?" Mickey asked him.

"Aw!" said Giuseppe. "I'm a guest!"

"Eight? Nine?"

"Ten! Let me get to work!"

It snowed constantly, but the planes came in. The airports remained open, and the night before the dance, Pete left Madeleine at home watching a pot of spaghetti sauce and went to pick up Sal at the terminal. "So," Sal said, when they were in the van and the heater was turned up and the windows rolled down to get rid of the steam, "this must be some dance."

"Yeah," Pete said. "I didn't think the guys could get so excited. *Months* of planning. And the women got in on it. They've got their own booths, their own surprises. No one knows what's going on. This time we're really organized."

"Yeah?" Sal said. "Usually it doesn't take organization to make sure no one knows what's going on. You've got a group of veterans, no one knows what's going on."

"This time it's different."

"How's this Madeleine?"

"You're going to like Madeleine," Pete said.

"Any other changes?"

"Yeah, I'm not confused anymore. Remember how confusing everything was in the Nam? That doctor, she said she would unfrighten me and she did. I have dreams now, they're things that happened over there, but they take place in Brooklyn. It's coming home, and I'm getting hold of it, man."

"Yeah," said Sal. "I know. You still want to write about it?"

"I'm going to talk to people. I'm going to the schools. I'll write for myself."

"You know how to do it?"

"Yeah, I know where to begin. Don't worry about me! I survived all this time, almost twenty years. I'll survive another twenty. Dr. Sit? She thinks it's a good idea. I may stop seeing her. There aren't enough days in the year anymore."

Sal looked at him.

"This is where we live," Pete said, pulling up in front of a small brick apartment house. "In Madeleine's apartment."

"You still keep yours?"

"I still keep mine."

"Once burned, twice shy," Sal said, and then Madeleine opened the door. "Hey, Madeleine, what do you like about this turkey?" he asked her, but she was taking his coat and Pete was pouring a beer into a glass, and he said, "A glass? A glass? Since when do we drink out of glasses?" and Pete said, "Once you live with women, you drink beer out of glasses."

"She likes me," Pete said, "because of the way I look at birds. I look at birds for hours. She says I'm like my father. We took him up to see Madeleine's family and he stood on their porch and looked at a spider making a web. He said he never saw anything like it before."

"*You* saw a hummingbird," Madeleine said.

"Yeah, a hummingbird. I read about them, I saw them on TV, but I never saw a real one. They never land."

"He doesn't miss anything," Sal said to Madeleine. "He never did."

"Show him your dress," Pete said, and Madeleine said, Oh, no, it could wait until the dance. "No, show it to him," Pete said, and she brought out a gold-sequined dress.

"It's nice," said Sal, who now tended to like black jersey, what Allison perpetually wore. "Look," he said, "I'll take the car and go back for Allison at ten o'clock. She had to come on a later flight. She won't miss a class unless she's dying."

"We'll go with you," Pete said.

"You go," said Madeleine. "I'll stay here."

LATER, Allison and Madeleine stayed in the kitchen and talked while Madeleine rolled dough. "Just anisette cookies," she said. "I'll make some without the anisette. Only Italians like anisette so much."

"Whenever two women get together, I think they're talking about us," Pete said.

"They are," Sal said. "They are. Misery likes company."

"He's a changed person," Allison said, and Madeleine said Pete was, too. Allison said she meant Pete. She'd heard about him for years and now he was different. Even over the phone he sounded different, not so nervous.

"He's still nervous," Madeleine said.

"They're all a little nervous."

"And they have tempers."

"Sal broke his hand so many times I told the doctor to put on a permanent cast."

"See that white plaster on the wall?" Madeleine asked, pointing with the wooden spoon. "And there, over by the doorway?"

"You frightened of him?"

"No, I never was."

"I was frightened of Sal. Once, he made dinner. Well, he usually makes dinner, and I came home late, and we got into an argument, and the next thing I knew, the roast chicken and the pot and the carving knife were flying out the screen door. I said something else and he ran into the yard and picked up the chicken and the knife and the pot and threw it all in the trash can and picked up the trash can and threw it against the fence. I told that story to a friend when she came over and Sal asked her to stay for dinner, and she said, 'What's for dinner?' and he said, 'Chicken,' and she wanted to know if it was the same chicken. *Now* I laugh about it."

"Pete cooks most of the time. A lot of the guys do the cooking. I said if I cooked, he should wash the dishes, but he says he likes washing the dishes. After being out in the mud and the dirt, who can't like washing dishes in hot water with soap?"

"Women are lucky," Allison said.

"Yup."

"Over there," Allison said, "Sal prayed for girls. 'If I ever have children, I don't want them to go through this.' We've got two girls."

"Pete said the same thing," Madeleine said, surprised. "But he has two boys."

"Come out of the kitchen," Pete said to them. "See those little pads under her eyes? They get red when she stays in there too long. I think she's allergic to something."

"These fatty pads under my eyes?" Madeleine said. "I've had them since I was born. Unless I wear makeup, they're always red."

"They're not," Pete said. "You know Dr. Sit? She has pads under her eyes like that."

"All Orientals do," said Sal.

"Are we going to walk to the dance or take the car?" Pete asked.

"Do we have to decide now?" asked Allison.

"It's around the corner," Madeleine said.

"Let's walk," said Sal. Pete noticed the silver peppering his black hair.

"What's so special about this dance?" he asked Pete.

"He's determined it's going to be special," Madeleine said. "He's going to find everything he ever wanted there."

"Yeah?" asked Sal, looking at Pete.

"Yeah," said Pete.

"Well," said Sal, "you want something enough, you find it."

"You think so?" Pete asked him.

"Sure," Sal said. "All you have to do is dream with your eyes open. You can do that. You can have your *own* dance."

THEY WENT through the church gate and in through the side door and down the steps to the church hall. Mickey stood at the doorway, taking tickets, bowing from the waist, sweeping people in with a grand gesture of his hand. The ceiling was a solid mass of streamers and accordion-pleated Santa Clauses and bells and even one Thanksgiving turkey.

"Tickets for the booths," Bobby said, coming up to them.

"What are these for?" Sal asked, and looked at the various tickets: Reincarnation Room, Payback Room, Parade Room, Your Show of Shows, This Is Your Life, The Good Humor Truck. "What is this all about?" he asked.

"Buy a ticket or you won't find out," Bobby said.

"Do you know?" Sal asked Pete.

"No, I don't. It's just like over there. I'm following orders. Buy a ticket. You'll find out."

"How much are they?"

"They're free, man," Mickey said. "Everything's free once you're inside."

"They learned something from the army. They learned how to complicate things," Sal said.

Allison was smiling and following Madeleine toward a group of women behind the punch bowl. They were all wearing gold-sequined dresses and they were all grinning and waving. "Oh," Allison said, looking down at her black wool jersey dress, "you should have told me."

"It was a last-minute thing," Madeleine said. "We didn't buy the dresses. They bought them for us."

"This punch is delicious," Allison said. "What's in the punch?" The women laughed but didn't answer her. "Where's Sal?" she asked, but the women started talking, and she forgot to look for him. He was in a church. He could take care of himself.

Father D'Angelo tapped Pete's arm. "It's nice to see you inside," he said. "I'll see you later. In the Payback Room."

"The Payback Room. The Reincarnation Room. It makes me nervous," Pete said.

"Nothing to be nervous about," said the old priest. "Excuse me. I'm looking for someone. Someone over there's looking for you. He's got a cane."

"Hey, Bravado!" someone yelled out. Pete turned and there was the Chief, walking toward him carrying his center-of-the-earth pole.

"Is that you?" Pete asked, holding on to him by both shoulders.

"It's me, man! I came home."

"You saw my ad?"

"Yeah, I saw it."

"You were missing over there."

"For a long time. Man, I've *seen* things."

"You back to stay?"

"For a while. I've got an apartment in the city. You know where it is? Opposite the goddamn United Nations building. They're always demonstrating outside the fucking place. I can't get a good night's sleep. I'm going to move. I walk the high beams, just like I said I would."

"You've got your pole," Pete said.

"But now I know what it is. It's a center-of-the-earth pole because I've been to the center of the earth, where it all boils up, rocks and mountains all boil up in orange flame. *That's* the center of the earth."

"Sal's here. We've got to find Sal," Pete said.

"Hey, Sally!" the Chief yelled, raising his pole above everyone's head, and Sal came over, grabbed him, stepped back, looked again, and hugged him.

"Where's Li? What happened to Li?" Sal asked.

"Oh, we roamed around together for a while and she got thinner and thinner, not like a normal person, but like something the light was coming through, and then one day she was just drawn there on the light and when the sun came up, she was gone."

"She's dead?" Sal asked.

"I didn't say that," the Chief answered. "She's gone."

"Is she dead or isn't she?" Sal asked. He was getting angry.

"Leave him alone, Sal," Pete said.

"You have to decide for yourself," the Chief said.

"Yeah, and how am I supposed to do that?" Sal demanded.

"May I cut in?" said a voice at Pete's elbow, and someone's hand grabbed his upper arm. Even through his shirt he could feel the plump fingers. He could smell the perfume. Lily of the valley. It had been years.

"Ma!" he said.

"That's what they used to say at the resort in the Catskills. May I cut in? You know, she's a nice girl, Madeleine. I've been watching you. You'll be happy!"

"Ma!" he said again.

"So what are you crying about, idiot?" she asked. "The priest said you were here. That's why I'm crying. You going to stand there and cry and leave your grandmother in that cold room?"

"Grandma?" he said.

"Yeah, in that cold room in the back. Come on. He's thirty-eight years old, going on thirty-nine, and he still doesn't have any sense."

"Where is she?"

"Back here. You got a ticket?"

"Yeah, I've got a ticket. Which one?"

"For the Resurrection Room."

"I don't have it," he said, starting to cry. "I've got a ticket for the Reincarnation Room, that's all I've got."

"Let me see those tickets," said his mother. "Here! It's the yellow one."

"I've only got one ticket," he said, still crying.

"I don't need a ticket, you devil," she said. "Go on. Let's go."

Old Mrs. Bravado sat in the corner, rocking in her old blue wooden chair, the paint chipped on the armrests where it had always been chipped. "So," she said, looking at Pete, "in the hereafter they can't afford paint. You know why? They spent so much money on the war."

"She gets confused," Angelina said apologetically.

"I'm not confused. You're confused. You still won't read the papers," said old Mrs. Bravado. "Where's Pietro?"

"He's coming," said Father D'Angelo. "He stopped to tell someone why he came to this country. It was so big, it had so much money, no one ever starved in America. There were no wars. You've heard it before."

"The same old song," said old Mrs. Bravado.

"He thought there were no wars here?" said Pete. "Why'd he think that?"

"That's how it all started," old Mrs. Bravado said. "We all thought that. Such a big country, so far away, what did it have to do with Europe? He still blames England for pulling us into the First World War. You think politics ends with death? It doesn't. Neither do overdue fines at the library."

"She gets confused," Angelina said again.

"So," said old Mrs. Bravado, pointing at the floor next to her. "Sit down by me. See, Angelina? He turned out special."

"He turned *out,*" Angelina said.

"No, he's special. Can't you see he's special?"

"I'm embarrassed," Pete said.

"Embarrassment never hurt anyone," old Mrs. Bravado said.

"If he'd read, then he'd be special," said old Mr. Bravado, coming up and hugging him. *I forgot you were so short,* Pete thought. *I forgot that.* Old Mr. Bravado still smelled of green cigars and wet wool jackets. Was he going to cry all night? "I've got something for you," old Mr. Bravado said. He took a long, thin white box from his pocket. "Nothing fancy," he said. "It doesn't tick. Open it."

"What is it?" Pete asked.

"Open it," said his grandfather.

Inside were hundreds, thousands, ten thousands of tiny pieces of paper, each with a tiny black mark on them.

"Words," said his grandfather. "From now on you have words. I'm giving you back the words you had as a child. Now you won't have to play things out. If you're angry, you don't have to hit the wall. You have the words. If you love something, you don't have to touch it or see it. You have the words. You can't lose anything anymore. You have the words. Remember we walked on the beach?"

"I remember a silvery light, widening," said Pete. "That's all I remember. The light was you?"

"The light was me," said his grandfather. "I should have known. You were too young. And then you hit your head on the curb. And your father? My son? I used to see him erasing the words like the world was a blackboard. Every day he erased the words, but now you have them back. You always had them."

"No," Pete said. "I didn't."

"You forgot you had them," said the old man.

"I didn't have them at all."

"You're going to stand there and argue?" asked his mother, hanging from his arm. "You haven't seen everyone yet. Look how crowded it is here." She fanned herself with her hand.

"Where are we going, Ma? Madeleine's out there alone."

"Madeleine's a big girl," said his mother, elbowing her way through women her own age, dressed in rusty black dresses, wearing black velvet hats with nets lowered over their eyes. "If they think they're going to make me feel bad for not dressing up, they have another thought coming," she said. "Here's Pete!" she called out to someone, and a short, fat soldier turned around and saluted with his left hand, the back of his hand pressed against his forehead.

"I got 'em!" Paul shouted. "No one took them away! I still got 'em." He tapped the medals on his homemade uniform with the palm of his hand.

"Oh, no!" Pete said. "Paul!"

"Don't worry," said Angelina. "Daddy's not coming."

"Let me look at you," Pete said, crying. "You know I saw you? I went to the home looking for a little girl and I saw you. You were leaving. You never have to go back there."

"Well," said Paul, "they shouldn'a killed me, but they killed me and that let me out. With one of those blue plastic chairs, right here," and he tapped the side of his head.

"I knew it! When I saw the chair, I knew it!" Pete said.

"Water under the bridge," said his mother. "But you know," she said to Pete confidentially, "there are others buried out there. *In shallow graves.* The little girl, she wasn't the only one."

"Not tonight," said Father D'Angelo. "Not tonight."

"I want to go to the Reincarnation Room," said Paul. "I heard people talking about it. I want to go there."

"Sure, we'll go there," said Angelina, hanging on his arm. "Take his arm, Pete. These people won't move. The old neighborhood never changes. Someone stands on a piece of ground for five minutes, they think they own it. Their feet grow roots. Push! Oh, it's nice, like a sale at Gimbels!"

"Where's the Reincarnation Room?" Pete asked someone who looked like Mickey, but wasn't Mickey. Maybe it was Mickey's brother or cousin. "You go into the bathroom and out the back door in the back wall and in through the door under the blue wreath," the man said.

"Through the *men's room?*" Angelina asked.

"I want to go," said Paul.

"Come on, Ma," Pete said. They went through the men's room and found the door in its back wall. "I don't remember this door," Pete said uneasily, but Paul said, "I want to go," and he turned the door's handle and they were out in the churchyard in the snow, and Pete said he didn't see a blue wreath, and Paul said he saw it. It was there, over the door in the church-yard wall.

"You got your ticket?" his mother asked Pete. "The yellow one?"

"I got it," he said. "But I've only got one."

"*We* don't need tickets," said his mother.

Bobby Scanlon took the ticket and they went inside. The room was crowded. Everyone was quiet, watching the front of the room roped off by a thick gold braid. The people inside watched the door on the left.

"Push, push!" said his mother. "We have to watch everything from the back?"

They pushed their way up front. "I never saw so many old people!" his mother said, annoyed. "Look at those thick shoulder pads! The women look like football players."

The door on the left opened and a deer poked out its nose. Then came its head and its antlers. It stood for an instant as if paralyzed by the lights, and then bounded across the room and left by the door on the right-hand side. When it exited through the right-hand door, people began clapping loudly and chanting, *Next! Next!*

"Do you want to go next?" Li asked Pete. "I can arrange it."

Li!

"I want to get out of here," Pete said.

"I wanna stay!" Paul said.

"I just saw the Chief," Pete said. "He said you were dead."

"He said I turned into light," Li said. "It's not the same thing."

"You understand what she's talking about?" asked his mother, whose eyes were riveted on the door.

"You knew where he was the whole time?" Pete asked. "After he was gone, you knew where he was?"

"We traveled together. After a few days, I found him in the forest. Sometimes he traveled with the hill tribes, sometimes with me."

The crowd was clapping and watching the left-hand door, chanting,

Bobby! Bobby! and the door banged open and a tiger stuck out its head, picked up a paw as if to claw something, looked at the people in the room, and bounded across and out the right-hand door.

"You should try it," Li said. "You have nothing to lose."

"I'm not ready to be reincarnated," Pete said. "I just got here."

"But don't you want to know what you'd be?" asked his mother, her eyes on the door. They were chanting again, *Mickey! Mickey!*, and the door on the left opened and out came the head and neck of a camel, its lips drawn back in a snarl over its teeth, and the camel stooped down, squeezed itself through the doorway and crossed the room, out through the right-hand door.

"Go!" said Paul. "Go! I want to see."

"Come," Li said, her hand on his. "I'll take you."

They went outside through another door in the wall behind them, and stood in the blue light outside the left-hand door. "Go through," Li said.

He stepped through and he was in the room, but everyone was laughing and pointing. Even his mother and Paul were laughing. His mother had her hand over her mouth and Paul's mouth was wide open. He was roaring with laughter.

What had he become? He looked down at his body and saw he hadn't changed. He was just as he was before he'd gone through the door. He went back out into the night. "Go through again," said Li, but he shook his head. "Yes, go again," she said, and the same thing happened. "Try one more time," said Li, and he stepped through the door once more, and this time, there was silence and he saw the faces tilted up at him like flowers looking at the sun and on the ground he saw his shadow.

He could see the tiniest speck of dust moving through the air and falling to the wooden floor and he beat his wings and he felt himself rising on a current of warm air and he flew to the door on the right and flew out of the door, up and out, over the neighborhood, up until he saw the Bay and the Verrazano Bridge and the Brooklyn Bridge and the Manhattan Bridge and the ships making their way in and out of the harbor and the cars crossing the bridges and threading the streets with lights, and the children in the yards smaller than mice, and a mouse crossing the street near the pier, and a rat running behind a crate on the dock, and there he saw his shadow. He was a hawk. He saw the mouse and wanted to dive at it, tear it apart, but he pulled himself back, higher up in the sky. Let the mouse live. "I want to go back," he called out in a voice that wasn't his, and beneath him appeared the church steeple and the Avenue and the stores and houses of the neighborhood and he landed outside the church door and felt his feet in his shoes. They were tight against his skin and bones.

"You can go back in now," said Li. "The Chief is going through next. He wants you to watch him."

"A hawk!" said his mother, grabbing his arm.

"An eagle!" Paul said.

"What difference does it make?" Angelina asked.

"It makes a difference," Pete said, but everyone was chanting, *Chief, Chief!* and the door was slowly opening, and through the doorway came the head of a strange animal, an ugly animal with a terrible, high laugh, and then the rest of the creature followed, bounded across the stage, laughing and showing its teeth.

"A hyena," said Li.

"That's what he'll be?" asked Pete.

"That's what he chose," Li said. "As you chose."

"I didn't choose."

"You did," said Li.

"You know," he said, "Madeleine has little pads of fat under her eyes like yours."

"What Sal told you is true," said Dr. Sit, coming up to him. "All Orientals do. I have them, too."

"You weren't coming!" Pete said.

"A last-minute change of plans," said Dr. Sit.

"Let's go to Payback," said Paul.

"Yes, let's go," said the doctor.

"I came to a dance, I want to dance," said Pete.

"We can dance in Payback," said Dr. Sit. "Follow me."

PAYBACK was filled with dancing couples and Father D'Angelo swirled by, his arm around old Mrs. Bravado. "I gave her an aspirin. Nothing hurts her!" he called out to them as he crossed the room, and Angelina shook her head and said, "You see how red her cheeks are? She'll pay for this in the morning. And him, too. There's no fool like an old fool."

"Dance with me," said Dr. Sit. "I have something to tell you."

"You go," said Angelina. "I'll dance with Paul."

He put his arm around the doctor and the music changed to a waltz. "Where's the music coming from?" he asked, but she didn't seem to hear him or it wasn't important. He forgot he asked. "What?" he said. "What'd you want to tell me?" She was so thin, all bones. A man on top of her could break her in pieces. Why hadn't he noticed how thin she was before? Or the perfume? But he must have noticed that. It was so familiar now.

"I want to tell you something," she said. "During the Second World War, I was in an internment camp in San Francisco. My mother died of tuberculosis there. She's still ashamed of it."

"Of what?"

"Of being in the camp. Of being in a camp in this country."

"*She* was ashamed because *she* was put in a camp? She didn't put herself in."

"The victim is always ashamed," said Dr. Sit.

The music was dying down and a crowd was gathering in the corner of the room.

"You had better check on that first," said Li, touching Pete's elbow. "Some things in here aren't for everyone." He followed her into the thick, dark clump of men in the corner, and saw an ARVN, his hands and legs tied, crouched against the wall. He looks familiar, Pete thought, and then Li stood over the ARVN, raised a huge stone, and brought it down on his head. No, thought Pete. I don't want to see this. He turned back and stood looking down at his feet. He was shaking. "It was not for everyone," said Li. Her cheeks were flushed. Her eyes sparkled with triumph.

"Now I must go," she said, and she went over to a window, opened it, and before his eyes, she turned into a kinaree. Wings sprouted from her back, and below her waist she was feathered. Her naked breasts quivered as she began to move her arms, and her wings began to beat, and she was rising up in the air. "You must watch the Chief for me," she said. "He watched you. All these years we watched you." And then she had risen to the height of the church steeple, and then she was a small, dark shape against a white cloud, an outline against the full moon, and then she was gone.

He found Paul, who wanted to return to the Reincarnation Room, but Bobby Scanlon said, "Sorry, they're closing it down," and Paul said, "One last look," so they went back, through the door in the men's room, out into the churchyard, and through the door in the churchyard wall, but now the room was empty. Everyone was gone. Paper cups and plates littered the floor and bits of tinsel the animals and birds had pulled from the walls in their flight across the front of the room. The room looked grey and cheap, the light fluorescent. It reminded Pete of waiting rooms in bus stations and railway terminals. "Let's go," he said to Paul. "Let's go back to the dance."

"No," Mickey said, coming up in back of him. "Let's go to Your Show of Shows. It's great. Just down the hall. This way."

"Isn't this the same room? Isn't this the Reincarnation Room?" Pete asked. "Weren't we just here?"

"No, this is something else," Mickey said. "Look what it says under the big sign: YOUR FAVORITE AMBUSH, PATROL, OR SNIPER."

"I don't know," Sal said. Where had he come from? "I don't know about going in there. What's in there, anyway?"

"You get to go back and do it again," Mickey said. "Only this time you get to do it right. You pick the thing you want to do and you do it."

"It's not real, is it?" Pete asked. "I mean, if you go back, you can't get killed?"

"You don't get killed, but it's real," Mickey said.

"Maybe it's too real," Sal said. "You could go in there and not come out."

"I told you. You don't get killed!" Mickey said.

"But you might not want to come back. You might like it in there," Sal said.

"I *do* like it in there," Mickey said. "I've been in there three times. I go back to the same ambush again and again. This time I get them. Man, it was the most exciting day of my life. Nothing ever came up to it again. Nothing's *ever* going to come up to it again."

"Don't go in there," Sal said to Pete. "Don't take a chance."

"You can feel the heat, you can smell the country. You can hear the mosquitoes. You hear the choppers. You hear the birds calling from tree to tree. The foliage's so thick in there you can hardly see your hand in front of you. Nothing's changed, man."

"That's it," Sal said. "I'm not going in."

"Red ants! Black ants! Rock apes! The black cloud moving toward you! The heavy-duty raindrops! All the guys you knew! There are *tracks* in there! Land mines! Two-steps! You take two steps and you die! Elephant grass, bamboo, mangoes, pineapples, bananas, lions and tigers and bears. It's all there!"

"How do you know you'll come back?" Sal asked Mickey. "How do you know that?"

"I don't care if I come back, O.K.?" Mickey said. "You don't know how I missed it! No one knows."

"Don't go down that trail again," Sal said.

"Take me! Take me!" Paul pleaded, hanging on to Sal's arm. "I want to go! I want to be a soldier!"

"Not you," said Pete. "No."

"Let's get out of here," Sal said.

"I'm going back in," Mickey said.

"He's gone," Sal said. "He's really gone."

"HEY, BRAVADO!" someone called out. It was Liebowitz.

"What are you doing here?" Sal asked.

"I came to tell you why you're a doctor. You owe it all to me," Liebowitz said. "You could've hung around me and ended up with a go-go dancer. Hey, let's go back to the dance. I love to dance."

"He's flickering," Pete whispered to Sal.

"Don't say anything," Sal said.

IN THE main hall, the six hundred guests swirled from side to side, dancing in the middle of the room, filling plates from the table on the side, and then he saw Madeleine and Allison slicing lasagna and heaping it on people's plates. "Madeleine?" he said, coming up. "I want you to meet my mother and brother. My grandmother and grandfather are somewhere here, too."

"So happy to meet you," said his mother, not looking up, and Paul muttered, "So happy to meet you," but he didn't look up either, and when Pete turned around to pull them closer, they were gone. "They'll be back soon," said Father D'Angelo. "Dance, my man, dance."

The band was in full view. It played "Paint It Black," "Imagine," "Great Balls of Fire." Out of the corner of his eye, he could see Sal dancing with Allison, the Chief dancing with Bobby's wife, June, and June was smiling. June never smiled. "I didn't know you could dance," he told Madeleine, and she said, "You never took me dancing." The music stopped and the Chief went on dancing with June, who smiled and smiled, and Bobby came up to them and said, "You see that? You see that? She's smiling! What's his secret?"

"You know something?" Pete said. "I still don't remember his real name. We called him the Chief."

"Yeah, but what's his secret, man? That bitch never smiles!"

The music was faster. It caught the dancers up. Their feet flew across the polished boards. They swirled like snowflakes outside the windows, and while he danced, Pete saw his mother and brother waving in the doorway and he wanted to stop and say, "Wait for me!" but the music got ahold of him, and then he saw his grandfather and grandmother in the doorway, and again he wanted to say, "Wait for me!" but the music was irresistible, and as he danced, he could feel the long, narrow white box in his jacket pocket.

"This is some dance!" Madeleine said.

"The best!" Pete said. "The best!"

"We did a good job?"

"You did a good job." He cried and danced and cried and danced, and from the doorway, Dr. Sit waved, but he didn't see her, and the room was hotter. The dancing went on. A new guy he didn't like came up to him when he was standing in front of a punch bowl and pushed his head down into the icy liquid. "You hang around with marines?" he asked Pete. "I don't like your hanging around with marines. You armored cavalry guys let one thousand marines die."

"Yeah?" Pete said. "I wasn't there at the time. What am I supposed to do about it? Just walk away from me, man."

"Outstanding," Bobby said. "Outfuckingstanding. I'd have taken his head off."

"This is a *dance*," Pete said. "No stupid buzzard on a ball's going to spoil this for me!"

"Outfuckingstanding!" said Bobby again.

"Hey, we're proud of you, man," someone said.

"You know what?" Pete said. "I'm proud of myself."

"Where's Mickey?" asked Bobby. "Anyone seen Mickey?"

Sal and Pete looked at one another. "Who saw him last?" Sal asked. "I saw him going into Your Show of Shows. That's the last time I saw him."

"Did you go?" Pete asked. "You went in?"

"Naw, man. It's a long time ago. That's the saddest thing, when people can't realize it happened a long time ago."

"I gotta find him," Pete said.

"Forget it," Sal said. "He's MIA. He's gotta find you."

"What about Wapniak?" Pete asked. "Where's Wapniak?"

"Wherever he is, he's still talking," Sal said.

"Where's the Chief?" Pete asked.

"I guess he left," Sal said.

"Let's go home," Madeleine said. "Allison, you and I can take the bed. Give them the living room floor."

At home, on the floor, Pete and Sal looked at one another. All that was missing was the jungle, the heat, and the track. As they talked, the window outside brightened. When Sal and Pete fell asleep, their backs to the couch, the Chief, who had been watching through the window, saw his face reflected in the glass, pulled on the skin of his cheek, and lifted his skin. Beneath was the face of the hyena. "Time to go home," he told himself, and he left without making a sound.

FIVE

Buffalo Afternoon

55 N THE MORNING, the White Man awakened, went to his dresser carrying a pillowcase, and looked in the drawers. They were filled with roll after roll of white bandages. He put the rolls in the pillowcase and went down the hall to the incinerator, emptied the pillowcase, and went back and repeated the process until all evidence of the bandages was gone. When he was finished, he sat down on his bed and looked out the window. "I've seen too much," he said. "I've seen enough."

Anyone watching him would have thought he was talking to the empty air, but in fact he was talking to the kinaree who hovered outside his window, twenty-two stories up. He thought of the ARVN soldier. He remembered the feel of the new baby, more slippery than ice. He saw it hurled to the ground. His mouth still held the taste of the deer he'd eaten with the hill tribesmen and, as he watched, the deer became human flesh.

Outside, in front of the UN, a demonstration against abortion was in progress. He'd read an article saying a Vietnam vet had blown up several abortion clinics. He was tired of newspapers. He was tired of the UN. The noise of the demonstrators was endless and accomplished nothing. The building stood there, a slab reflecting the sun, casting a shadow over his building so that his apartment was dark most of the day.

"You left me and turned into light," he said to Li. His tone was hurt and reproachful.

"But I came back. You were the one to leave. You wanted to come home," she said. Her wings floated her in the air. She hovered outside his window, noiseless. Once, helicopters hovered above them every day, as she hovered now.

"I was wrong," he said, but that wasn't what he meant. He meant he was right to have come home, but now he was tired. He didn't want to stay. He was too tired to explain what he intended to say. "Can I come with you?" he asked her.

"You always came with me," she said. "Why not now?"

"Then I'm coming," he said.

"As the White Man?" she asked.

"As myself," he said. And he got up from the bed, walked over to the window, threw it open, climbed up on the sill, crouched there for an instant, and then stepped off into Li's outstretched arms.

A GREY light fell in through the kitchen windows and woke them. They heard the women in the kitchen, their voices low. As they looked around, the day brightened, turned blue. The sun was out. It had stopped snowing.

"We forgot eggs," Madeleine said, coming out of the kitchen. "We'll go get some." They put on their coats and went out.

"Hey," Pete said, "life's a bitch and then you fucking die." He laughed. "I never understood why that upset Madeleine. It's the truth."

"They put that truth on bumper stickers," Sal said.

"You know what Bobby says? He says, 'Life's a bitch and then you fucking die, and if you don't die, you fucking marry her.' He's a funny guy."

"It's a beautiful day," Sal said.

"A beautiful day to die."

"What's wrong with a beautiful day to live?"

"You like that better? O.K., it's a beautiful day to live." He stretched, rubbed both sides of his head with his palms and got up and looked inside his suit jacket. He pulled out a thin, narrow white paper box.

"What's that?" Sal asked.

"I don't know," he said. "It's full of paper." He showed it to Sal. "Little tiny confetti."

"Yeah," said Sal. He looked uncomfortable.

"You see anything odd at that dance?" Pete asked him.

"What do you mean, odd?" Sal asked. His face was flushed. He wouldn't look Pete in the eye.

"Never mind," Pete said.

"Yeah," Sal said. "It don't mean nothing. Fucking drive on."

The sun had gone behind a cloud. The women came back. "You mind if we go out for a walk?" Pete asked.

"Sure, go ahead," said Allison.

Pete stepped through the front door after Sal. The sky was the color of leaded glass, a thick sky filled with snow that had yet to fall.

"It's a good day," Pete said.

"Yeah," said Sal.

"But you know what?" Pete said. "It never ends. It never will end."

"We know that."

"Don't die with it. Pass it on."

"I know," Sal said.

"It's supposed to be in the past, but sometimes I'm afraid. You know, that it won't stay there."

"I know," Sal said.

"Last night, I don't know if it was a dream or what," Pete said, "I thought I walked into a room with a sign over it. YOUR SHOW OF SHOWS.

And they had a television there and it showed what your life could have been like, and I was going to one doctor after another, and one didn't recognize me when I came in, and she talked to me for twenty minutes before she realized she'd seen me before, and then I was burning a car, and then a house, and then I was killing someone. It could've happened like that."

"But it didn't," Sal said.

"But it could've," Pete said. "Maybe it still could. Sometimes the past's a volcano and I'm standing on it and holding a lid down on it and if I move off, it'll blow up in my face."

"Like a mine," Sal said.

"Yeah, like a mine."

"The past casts long shadows," Sal said.

"Yeah, well," Pete said, "we all know the past's right here in the present, but it's worse than that, man. The past just sits there waiting for the future so it can ruin that, too."

"What do you mean?" Sal asked. He stopped walking and looked at Pete.

"I think about it a lot," Pete said. "Things happened a long time ago. Some of them hurt. Some of them didn't. I used to think, Why do some things bother me and other things don't? Man, I was one naive son of a bitch."

"I don't understand," Sal said.

"Yeah, well, I didn't either. I thought, O.K., so the burned bodies in the track, they were going to haunt me forever. But the body we dug up, the little girl. That never bothered me. It didn't bother me until my son was almost the same age as the girl. All of a sudden, the dead girl was back. All of a sudden, she was all over me. You know what it was? All of a sudden, I *knew* what it meant for a child to die like that, a child that age. Because I had one. When my son was twelve, I went through one mattress after another. The sweat, the smell, I couldn't stand it.

"The past, man. They don't tell you it's like a minefield. You think you forgot something. You think something didn't bother you. You didn't forget. You just didn't know how to understand it when it happened. The past's a minefield, man. You learn more about life, you walk on new ground, you set something off. It turns out you didn't forget after all. So who wants to go forward? Who wants to learn something new? You move forward, you set off things you don't want going off. Memory's so great? I hate memory. I hate change, man. They don't tell you. They say you'll get better. They don't tell you what happens when you get better. You get better and you haunt yourself. I mean, how safe should I feel? How do I know I won't start any more fires? How do I know I won't sit out in the rain?"

"You don't know," Sal said. "None of us know."

"So what do you do?" Pete asked.

"You try," Sal said. "What else can you do?"

"Sometimes I think we should be locked up," Pete said. "Just for safe-keeping."

"You want to be locked up?" Sal asked.

"No, man," Pete said.

"So keep standing on the mine," Sal said. "Don't let it go off."

"Other people don't have to live this way," Pete said.

"They don't," Sal said. "But we know things they don't."

"I could do without it," Pete said.

"We all could."

"Nothing's safe from it. Not even the *future's* safe from it. It makes me bitter."

"It makes me bitter *and* angry," Sal said.

"Angry too," Pete agreed.

"Yeah," said Sal. "And then one day, you say, 'So what?' I said, I've got to trust someone and I'm going to trust myself. It took me twenty years but I trust myself. Who else am I going to trust? So these things happened. So what? I want to keep going. I like it here. One foot in front of the other and here I am. I'm where I want to be."

"I'm where I want to be, but I don't know if I can stay there," Pete said.

"Who knows that?" Sal asked him. "Who knows that?"

"That's true," Pete said.

"Don't forget it," Sal said. "You're almost forty. By now, we're all in the same boat. No one's safe."

"But we're less safe."

"You want to drive yourself crazy, keep thinking that way," Sal said. "O.K., so you know it's a high-wire act. So you know that. You want to get to the other side, you go."

"I don't know," Pete said. "Sometimes it's too hard."

"What's the choice?" Sal asked. "You're going to let go and go burn a car? You're going to say good-bye to Madeleine and go kill someone who annoys you? What's so funny?" he asked Pete, who started to laugh.

"Whenever anyone bugs me, I think, over there it would have been simple. Over there I could have taken him out."

"Right," Sal said.

"Yeah, one day I had a fight with Madeleine and I was over in the corner of the room and she asked me what I was doing, and I said, 'Oh, I'm just rigging up a claymore,' and I wish I had been. I can think of a lot of people I'd like to claymore off the face of this earth."

"So can the civilians," Sal said, "but they don't know they can do it. They never did it, so they sleep well at night."

"Every step I take forward, I worry about turning a corner and finding something from the past staring me in the face," Pete said.

"You think you can make it?" Sal asked.

"I'm going to try. That's all I can do, right?"

"Right." They didn't look at one another. Both of them were crying.

"You know what's so ridiculous?" Pete said after a while. "They sent us over there for God and country and the American way and half of us came back different. Everything for each other. Everything for the brothers, everything for the group. We don't have the same kind of ambition we're supposed to have. You know the story. Give us a grass hut and a bowl of rice. And over there? Over there, they want to be like us. They want to get rid of the grass hut and get a television set. It's fucking ridiculous, man."

"It is," Sal said.

"You ambitious?" Pete asked him.

"Sure. I want to be happy."

"You care about big cars? Big TVs?"

"I can afford them," Sal said. "I don't care about them."

"See?" said Pete. "I can't afford them and I don't care about them. We're not Americans."

"Maybe we're new Americans," Sal said.

"I like the sound of that," Pete said. "Yeah. I do."

They walked past the church. "I used to hide in the bushes there," Pete said, pointing. "When it rained, I came out here and scrubbed myself down. Naked."

"I know," Sal said.

"It's a good day. It's even a good life. I'm gonna make it," Pete said.

"Yeah," Sal said, smiling. "Now you think so?"

"It's *afternoon*," Pete said. "It's buffalo afternoon for us, man. We're going to make it. It's the peaceful time. It's time to wander the fields and bring it all back home."

"A little late, but better than never, just like the parade," Sal said. "Yeah, it's buffalo afternoon for me. Hey, the sun's out."

"A little late, but not too shabby," Pete said. His eyes were moist but he was smiling.

A NOTE ON THE TYPE

The text of this book was composed in a film version of a typeface
called Bookman. The original cutting of Bookman was made in
the 1850s by Messrs. Miller and Richard of Edinburgh.
Essentially the face was a weighted version of the popular
Miller and Richard old-style roman, and it was probably at first
intended to serve for display headings only. Because of its
exceptional legibility, however, it quickly won wide acceptance
for use as a text type.

Composed by Superior Type, Champaign, Illinois
Printed and bound by The Haddon Craftsmen, Inc., Scranton, Pennsylvania
Designed by Iris Weinstein